HAWTHORN

Book 2 of the Sin & Salvation Series

Jayne Anderson

RLJ & Associates, LLC

Published by RLJ & Associates, LLC

Pittsburgh, Pennsylvania

ISBNs:

Paperpack: 979-8-9922744-3-1

Hardcover: 979-8-9922744-4-8

E-book: 979-8-9922744-5-5

Edited by Rebecca L. Jayne

First Edition: May 2025

Printed in the United States of America.

For Mike

Thanks for being there through every chapter, every rewrite, and every boss battle—in game and in life—even when I talk about plot twists at 1 a.m.

You're Player 2 in this whole journey.

J.A.

Contents

The Fallen'
Riichi 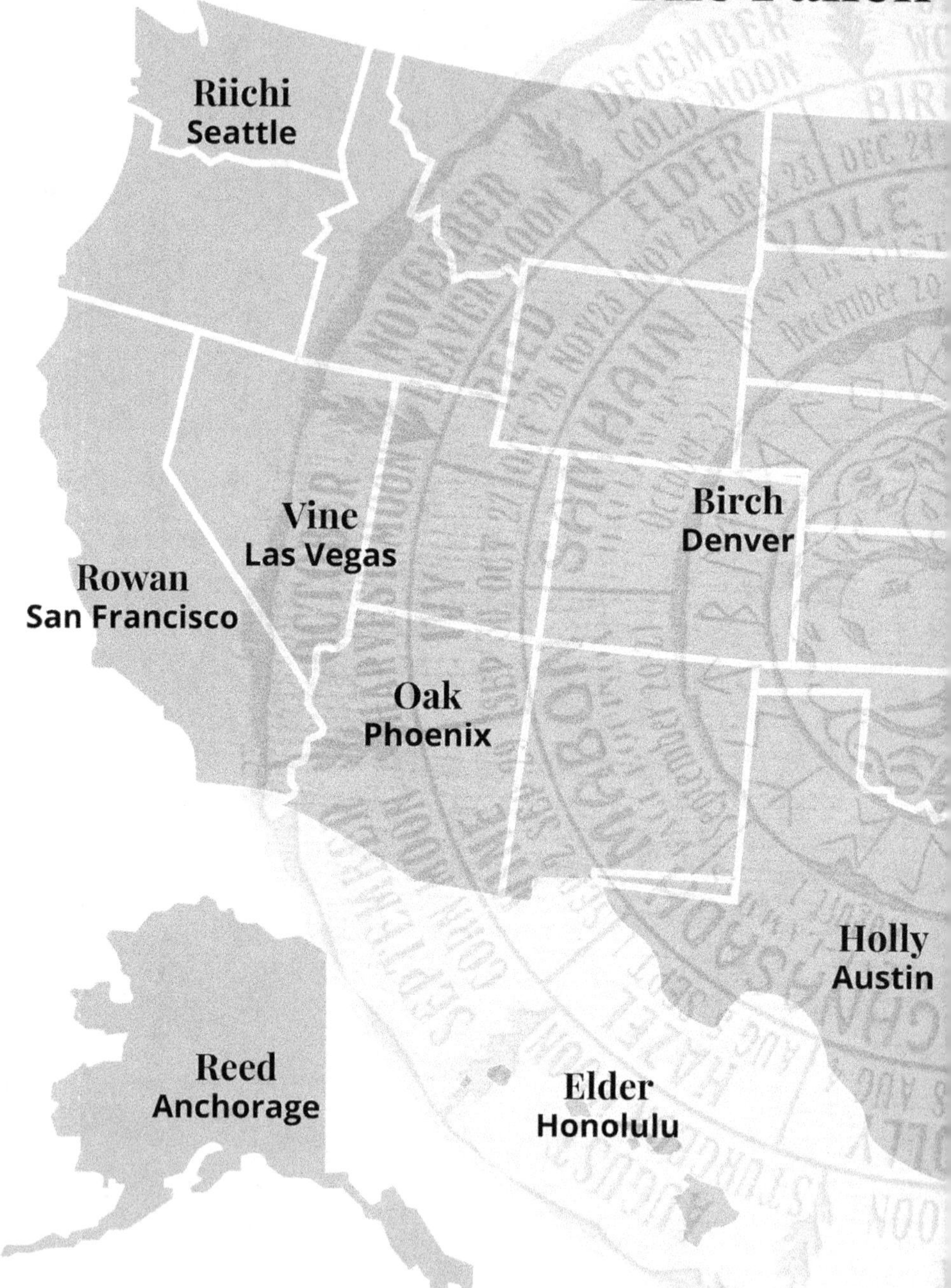
Seattle
Rowan
San Francisco
Vine
Las Vegas
Oak
Phoenix
Birch
Denver
Holly
Austin
Reed
Anchorage
Elder
Honolulu

Branches

From their humble origins to their present-day roles as guardians, the Fallen have established themselves across the United States. This map showcases where the Fallen now reside, each location serving as a cornerstone for their mission to protect humanity and preserve hope, much like the branches of a tree extending toward the sky.

Who Are the Fallen?

They are the men and women tucked into the pages of this series.

Dear Reader,

The Fallen are not born as heroes. They are ordinary people from different times and places, plucked from extraordinary circumstances, each carrying the weight of their final moments. *Born under the light of a full moon,* they live lives marked by *kindness, strength, and virtue*—until a single act of *sin* in their last breath seals their fate.

Caught between life and death, they are offered a choice: to let go and embrace the unknown or to *rise again with purpose.* Those who choose to rise are reborn as a Fallen, *tied to a Celtic tree* that mirrors their essence. The tree becomes part of who they are, grounding them in the supernatural world while reflecting their truest selves.

At their turning, each Fallen meets their *potential soulmate.* Though this meeting is fleeting and fades from memory, *the bond is set.* A connection as powerful as it is elusive, it ties them to the natural world and waits patiently for the right moment to bloom. Only when the Fallen are ready—when they *face their deepest fears* and *overcome the shadow of their sin*—does the bond awaken, unlocking *a power that reshapes their destiny.*

The Fallen live to *fight for humanity,* standing as a barrier between darkness and the fragile light of hope. They are guardians, protecting against evils that seek to corrupt and destroy, even as they carry the shadows of their own sins. United by a shared purpose, they prove that even those who fall can rise again, stronger than before.

So, get ready to join them on their journey from *sin to salvation*.

Turn the page, and let the story begin.

Yours truly,
Jayne Anderson

Hakata Bay, Japan, November 1274

S ome nights fade with time. This one carved itself into his soul.

Candlelight flickered across the modest room, casting warmth over a moment that would soon be shattered. Riichi sat cross-legged on the woven tatami mat, his posture straight, his expression composed as he shared the evening meal with his family. The room was quiet but comfortable, the soft clink of chopsticks against lacquered bowls filling the space. Across from him, his father—a man of few words but unyielding determination—chewed slowly, his gaze lifting just enough to meet Riichi's with a glint of pride. That look spoke volumes. His father never needed to say much; his silence carried approval more powerful than words.

Next to his father, Riichi's mother moved with graceful precision, serving the last of the rice with hands that bore the evidence of a life spent in labor. Her fingers, both callous and tender, brushed the bowl's rim as she set it before her son, offering a small, reserved smile. She had always been the unshakeable pillar of their family, guiding them with a soft-spoken strength that held them all together. Her face, lined with years of work, radiated a quiet resilience that Riichi had admired since childhood.

Across the mat from him, his younger sister, Aya, was a burst of youthful energy, contrasting with the calm of the room. She giggled as Riichi made a teasing face, her bright eyes dancing as she looked up at him with admiration. At ten, Aya was at that age where everything her older brother did seemed extraordinary. To her, he was invincible—a warrior and protector, a figure from her stories come to life.

A rare smile tugged at the corner of Riichi's mouth as he returned Aya's playful look, a brief warmth piercing his typically composed exterior. Moments like this—simple, unpretentious, filled with laughter and quiet affection—were the heart of his life. And yet, beneath the tranquility, a familiar sense of duty stirred, reminding him of the responsibilities he carried as both a son and a samurai.

He allowed himself a brief glance around the room, letting his eyes rest on each family member. His heart swelled with the knowledge that it was his duty to safeguard this life, this small, fragile world that meant everything to him. Stories had circulated lately—whispers of a looming threat from the mainland, an invasion that could strike their shores at any moment. The possibility stayed in his thoughts, deepening his resolve. If the rumors held any truth, he would be ready.

As the meal continued, Riichi's mind drifted, thoughts turning to his training, to the techniques and principles that had been drilled into him since he was old enough to lift a wooden sword. The way of the samurai was a life of honor and sacrifice, a path he had chosen not only for himself but for them. Protecting his family, his village—that was his purpose. And for that, he would fight with every ounce of strength he possessed.

The peaceful quiet of the evening shattered in an instant.

A low rumbling, like distant thunder, echoed through the village, followed by the harsh, guttural cries of foreign voices. Riichi's head jerked up, his hand freezing midway to his teacup. His body tensed instinctively, his senses on high alert as he registered the unmistakable sounds of hooves pounding closer, the commotion escalating rapidly.

Without a word, he rose from the table, moving with deliberate skill to the corner of the room where his katana and armor rested. His fingers wrapped around the hilt, the familiar weight centering him as his mind shifted fully to the warrior's discipline he had honed over years of training. He looked back at his family, his face resolute, his intent clear.

"Chichiue, hide!" he ordered, his tone brooking no room for hesitation.

His father's eyes locked with his for a brief moment, a silent understanding passing between them. Bowing his head, his father quickly moved to guide Riichi's mother and sister away from the open room while Riichi quickly dawned his armor. Aya's wide eyes met Riichi's, a hint of fear crossing her face. But before she could say anything, their father's arm wrapped around her shoulders, leading her toward the concealed cellar that lay beneath the floorboards.

Riichi waited just long enough to see them disappear into the shadows of their hiding place, feeling a slight, calming rhythm in his heart at the thought of their safety, even if only for a little while longer. With one last look at the floorboards they vanished under, he stepped outside, his katana securely at his side.

The scene that lay before him was one of turmoil and devastation. Mongol soldiers flooded into the village, their torches illuminating the familiar streets and homes with a menacing light. Roofs were already engulfed in flames, sending thick, black smoke billowing into the night sky. The piercing sound of clashing metal, combined with the anguished cries of neighbors, filled the air, creating a cacophony that grated against his sense of peace.

There was no time for doubt, no space for fear. He was a samurai, bound by duty and honor, and his village depended on him. With steely determination, he clenched the hilt of his katana tighter and advanced, joining his fellow warriors as they surged into battle, a thin but steadfast line standing against the invading enemy forces.

Each movement was precise, calculated. His katana became an extension of his arm, slicing through the air with lethal accuracy. He sidestepped an enemy's blow, countering with a swift strike to the side, his blade cutting cleanly through armor and flesh. Another soldier lunged at him, but he pivoted, using the momentum to strike the man down with a powerful, controlled swing.

The chaos around him was immense, but Riichi's mind remained clear, his focus sharp. Every strike was a defense of his home, every enemy he felled an act of preservation for the life he cherished. He moved with purpose, each step bringing him closer to the heart of the conflict, where the fight was thickest, the stakes highest.

For the people he loved, he would face this darkness. For his family, hidden and waiting, he would not falter.

In the midst of the battle's uproar, a sudden movement caught his attention, drawing his eyes to his family's home. A wave of panic disrupted his composure. He had told them to take refuge in the small cellar beneath the floorboards, a secret spot known only to them. Trusting his instincts, he fought his way through the mayhem, his katana rising and falling with meticulous strikes as he carved a path toward the one place he couldn't afford to lose.

He reached the house, his heart pounding with desperation. The familiar sight, once a safe haven, now felt foreign and vulnerable. He dared to hope for a fleeting moment, whispering a silent prayer as he rushed to the cellar entrance beneath the floor. But the sight that met him brought his world crashing down.

The opening to the hiding place lay exposed, the floorboards splintered and askew, as if they had been ripped apart by ruthless hands. His breath caught in his throat as he dropped to his knees, calling out, "Chichiue! Hahaue! Aya!" But only silence answered him, thick and stifling, wrapping around him with a cruel finality.

Frantically, he searched, his hands trembling as he uncovered their hiding place. There they lay—his father, his mother, his sister—motionless, their faces drained of color, their eyes shut in eternal rest. The sight hit him with the force of a thousand daggers, each one tearing through him, leaving raw, open wounds. They had been his reason to fight, his reason to hold onto honor, and now they were gone. Everything he had fought for had been stripped away in a single, brutal instant.

Riichi's chest heaved as he took in the sight of his family's lifeless forms, hidden away in what should have been their safe haven. The grief tore through him, sharp and unrelenting, but it was the rage—the blistering, all-consuming fury—that gripped him, twisting the pain into something more sinister, something primal.

A roar erupted from him, raw and unrestrained, echoing over the sounds of battle. His grip on his katana was so fierce that his knuckles blanched, and he could feel the fury pulsing through his veins, unstoppable and overpowering. The training, the discipline—crumbled, crushed by the intensity of his wrath. His vision tunneled, blurring the lines between enemy and friend, between honor and vengeance.

He charged back into the fray, his movements erratic and unplanned, each strike of his katana fueled not by the principles he had adhered to, but by the single, all-encompassing desire to destroy. Every Mongol soldier in his path symbolized his grief, every face a haunting reminder of the family taken from him. He cut through them with merciless accuracy, driven by a need for retribution that blinded him to everything else.

There were no allies, no strategy—only the need to punish, to make them suffer as he was suffering. He fought with a ferocity that bordered on madness, his formerly controlled actions now chaotic and unrestrained. The katana he wielded was no longer a weapon of honor; it was an instrument of wrath, an extension of the storm raging within him. He barely noticed as his own blood mixed with the sweat and grime of battle, the sting of wounds dulled by the fire that burned in his soul.

But even the fiercest anger could not sustain him forever. As the battle raged on, the strength in his arms began to falter, his swings losing their power, though the rage remained, unquenched. He stumbled, his vision growing hazy, but he forced himself to press forward, striking down another enemy with sheer force of will.

Finally, as a fresh wave of invaders surged toward him, he felt his legs give out beneath him. His katana slipped from his grasp, clattering to the ground as he collapsed in the village square, surrounded by the wreckage of his wrath—a mix of fallen foes and villagers alike, the remnants of his home reduced to ashes and blood.

The world around him faded in and out of focus, his breath coming in shallow gasps as he lay on the cold, unforgiving ground. The smoke stung his eyes, filling the air with the acrid scent of burnt wood and charred lives. His vision blurred, and he struggled to make sense of the scene before him.

Bodies lay scattered across the square, faces he recognized, friends and neighbors now lying lifeless beside the very enemies they had tried to fend off. The buildings he had known since childhood, homes that had once pulsed with laughter and life, were now crumbling, reduced to smoldering husks. The village he had sworn to protect was gone, lost to his failure, his fury.

And it was then, as he lay there, battered and broken, that the weight of his actions began to settle over him, oppressive and inescapable. He had let wrath consume him, had allowed his grief and anger to blind him to the very principles he had vowed to uphold. In his desire for vengeance, he had become the very thing he despised—a force of destruction, unrestrained and without honor.

A pang of regret twisted through him, sharper than any sword. His father's teachings, his duty as a samurai—all of it had been cast aside in a single moment of rage, leaving him hollow, a mere shadow of the man he once aspired to be. He had failed them all—his family, his village, and himself.

His strength waned, each breath more labored than the last. He closed his eyes, feeling the cold seep into his bones, wondering if there could be any redemption for a man who had strayed so far from his path. Or was this his end—a warrior stripped of his dignity, left to die amidst the ruins of his own wrath?

As the shadows engulfed him, he found himself hoping, perhaps foolishly, that there might still be a chance, somewhere beyond this existence, to atone for the wrath that had claimed him.

Through the haze of smoke and the shroud of encroaching darkness, a subtle glow emerged, delicate and constant, piercing through the ruinous night. The light expanded, casting a soft, otherworldly radiance across the scorched earth and broken bodies, as if an untouched fragment of another world had slipped into this place of despair.

Emerging from the glow was a figure, tall and graceful, exuding an unearthly serenity. Light clung to her like a blessing, a quiet radiance that was both calming and constant. Her flowing gown shimmered like moonlight on sacred waters, the fabric reflecting the faintest traces of illumination as she moved. Symbols of ancient wisdom seemed to whisper in its folds—echoes of a power older than the stars. Her steps glided over the terrain, untouched by the destruction around her, as though the earth itself honored her passage. There was something both celestial and eternal about her, the quiet embodiment of balance, of intertwined mercy and judgment. A presence not of force, but of absolute authority—a guiding light in the darkness.

Beside her stood a young girl of about twelve, her appearance a striking contrast to the devastation that surrounded them. Her large, soulful brown eyes took in the scene with a mixture of wonder and quiet sorrow, focusing intently on the fallen warrior before her. Her dark, wavy hair cascaded loosely over her shoulders, framing her delicate features, and in her small hands, she clutched a woven pouch, her fingers gripping it tightly as though drawing comfort from its familiar texture.

The girl appeared unsure, her eyes revealing a hint of hesitation as she looked up at the woman, who regarded her with a gentle patience. In that instant, the girl's innocence became even more pronounced, a fragile yet steadfast beacon amidst the ashes of battle. Her presence, though tentative, held a strength of its own.

Sensing the young girl's reluctance, the woman placed a hand on her shoulder, offering comfort and reassurance. She leaned down slightly, her serene gaze meeting the girl's uncertain eyes. "Go on, child," the woman encouraged, her voice warm and soothing in the quiet atmosphere. "Say hello to the young man."

The girl glanced back up at the woman, her fingers clenching the woven pouch a bit more firmly as she inhaled deeply to steady herself. She nodded, albeit with some hesitation, and turned her attention back to Riichi, who lay weakened and bloodied on the ground before her. Gathering her courage, she took a step forward, moving carefully but with purpose.

As she approached, her eyes held a quiet compassion, though a trace of wariness remained in her look. She knelt beside Riichi, her small frame seeming almost out of place against the backdrop of ruin. For a moment, she just looked at him, her face showing a mix of curiosity and empathy, an innocence that couldn't be extinguished by the unnatural landscape or his injuries.

The young girl crouched next to him, her actions tender and unexpectedly soothing amidst the destruction. She leaned closer, speaking in a quiet, hushed tone. "Hello," she murmured, her large, expressive eyes scanning his battered form. A slight tremor in her voice betrayed her own fear, though her gaze remained fixed on him, a blend of sympathy and intrigue in her eyes.

"You look hurt," she said softly, her words laced with a quiet sadness. "Are you...are you okay?"

Riichi, feeling the pain pressing against him from all sides, managed to muster a faint, reassuring smile, wanting to shield her from the full weight of his suffering. "I'm fine," he replied, his tone as gentle as he could make it. "I don't feel a thing." It was an instinctive answer, a kindness born from years of shielding those around him, even now, even here. He wanted her to feel safe, despite everything.

The girl blinked, absorbing his words. Emboldened by his response, she looked at him with a newfound bravery. "Are you...going to die?" she inquired, her innocent question piercing straight through his resolve, highlighting the fragility of life and the finality he was now facing.

For a moment, he didn't answer, his gaze drifting up to the darkened sky. With a soft sigh, he replied, "I think I might." His voice was calm and even, carrying a newfound acceptance he hadn't known he possessed, yet tinged with the faintest sorrow—a sorrow not for himself, but for all he had lost, for the family and the life that would now slip away from him.

The girl furrowed her brow, melancholy casting a shadow in her eyes, yet her curiosity remained undeterred. "Why?" she inquired, her voice no more than a whisper.

Riichi's eyes softened as he looked back at her, taking a slow breath. "I fought to defend my family...my village. It was my duty as a samurai," he explained, his words carrying a sense of purpose, though edged with regret. He couldn't help but feel he had failed them, that his wrath had tainted his intentions.

The girl listened intently, her expression changing as she took in his words. Her eyes filled with admiration, and after a moment, she gave him a small, earnest nod. "You're very brave," she whispered, the reverence in her tone reaching a part of him that had begun to fade. Her simple declaration touched something deep within him, easing a fraction of the guilt that had settled on his heart.

The woman stepped forward, her movements fluid and calm as she placed a comforting hand on Riichi's shoulder. Her touch was warm and comforting, prompting him to look up at her. Her gaze exuded a quiet strength that made him feel anchored. "I am Eileen. Your journey does not end here, Riichi," she said, her voice carrying both compassion and a conviction that left no room for doubt. "You are still needed—to protect others, to combat a darkness that extends far beyond this world." Eileen gestured to the little girl. "You are needed to protect her. You will see each other again."

The young girl, seeming to draw courage from Eileen's words, extended her small hand toward him, her expression both tender and determined. Her dark eyes shone with innocent trust, a belief in him so pure it stirred a hidden emotion deep in his weary heart. "You can still protect those who need you. And you'll be my own personal superhero. I'd like to see you again," she spoke with a gentle but firm voice, a quiet strength flowing from her that was both unexpected and reassuring.

The simple faith in her words rekindled a small glimmer of hope within him, reminding him of the guardian he used to be and the honor that had guided him before rage had clouded his path. Moved by her courage, Riichi reached out, his hand trembling as he took hers, feeling her warmth seep into his cold fingers.

The moment their hands met, a surge of energy flooded through him, filling every corner of his being with light. Her touch seemed to calm the storm within, a sense of peace settling over his troubled spirit for the first time since the battle had begun.

As the warmth spread through him, Riichi felt his mortal wounds begin to fade, a strange, weightless sensation replacing the pain that had gripped him. The harsh aches softened, and his vision began to dim, though not with the darkness he had expected. Instead, a gentle, encompassing light surrounded him, pulling him away from the broken world he was leaving behind.

Within that radiant glow, something awakened—a presence both ancient and wise. A whisper of invisible branches wove through the light, the air rich with the subtle scent of blossoms and earth after rain. Strength unfurled in his core, quiet yet unyielding, as if roots had anchored him in unseen soil. The warmth coiled around his soul, fierce as the hawthorn's protective thorns, yet balanced by the quiet resilience of its bloom. As Eileen's power settled into him, it carried an unspoken truth: he would endure, shaped by the trials ahead, standing between the worlds of shadow and light—both guardian and warrior, like the tree that now lived within him.

In the silence that followed, the last sound he heard was the young girl's soft, heartfelt whisper. "Thank you."

The words resonated within him, an expression of gratitude that eased the last lingering burdens on his heart. With a sense of calm, he let himself be engulfed in the light, the final traces of his mortal life slipping away as he took his first steps on a new path, his journey as a Fallen just beginning.

Hibernia, Ireland, November 1274

Riichi's first breath in his new existence filled his lungs with crisp, unfamiliar air. Gone was the battlefield, the stench of blood and steel, the oppressive burden of his wounds. Instead, he lay upon a simple bed in a dimly lit room, the warmth of a crackling hearth casting long shadows along the wooden walls. His body felt… whole. No pain, no weakness. He sat up slowly, testing the strength in his limbs, flexing his fingers as if to confirm they were truly his own. The pull of death no longer clung to him.

Yet something heavier did.

The silence pressed in, suffocating in its unfamiliarity. No battle cries. No dying breath of a fallen comrade. No voice calling his name. They were gone. His family, his people, his past—reduced to bloodied bodies and fading memories. His hands curled into fists against the coarse fabric of the blanket, muscles tensing as a sharp breath forced its way through his clenched teeth. His chest rose and fell, too quickly, too unsteady.

He should be dead.

His fingers trembled. He willed them still.

He had committed a sin. A grievous one. He had broken the honor his family had instilled in him, only to survive while they perished. His failure, his shame, was absolute.

His breathing slowed, controlled now. Emotion threatened to claw its way to the surface, but he did what he had always done—what duty demanded of him. He locked it away, sealed the grief behind unshakable resolve. His shoulders squared, his spine straightened, and by the time the door creaked open, his expression was indecipherable.

A tall woman with golden hair stepped inside first, her natural authority was evident. Eileen. She exuded elegance and striking beauty, dressed in a long, flowing léine of deep blue, the fabric rich yet practical, cinched at the waist with an intricately woven belt. Over it, a heavy brat of dark wool draped over her shoulders, fastened with a silver brooch engraved with swirling Celtic patterns. Piercing blue eyes met his with an unreadable intensity, a gaze that saw more than she spoke. She carried herself with a deliberate grace—unshaken, always in control.

A man trailed behind her—a solid presence of broad shoulders and dark, curling hair. Oak. His rugged features were carved in quiet defiance, his brown eyes carrying the weight of a man who had long since stopped questioning fate. Unlike Eileen's polished composure, Oak stood with a warrior's unshaken poise, arms crossed over his chest, as though he had been waiting for this moment longer than he cared to admit.

A third figure entered, her presence softer but equally captivating. Hazel. Long, blonde waves framed her face, complementing the warmth in her green eyes. There was an easiness to her stance, a quiet observation behind the way she studied him. She wasn't curious or impatient—simply present, as though she had already accepted the inevitability of his arrival.

But someone was missing.

Riichi sat up further, scanning the room. A memory flashed through his mind—a little girl barely past childhood, with soft curls and knowing brown eyes. She had reached for him in the light, a tether between his fading soul and something beyond his understanding. That moment had felt genuine. More authentic than any dream.

He looked at Eileen, his voice calm even as anxiety began to build within him. "Where is the little girl?"

Eileen's face remained unchanged, though her eyes held an enigmatic quality. "She is not here."

A muscle pulsed in Riichi's temple. That was not an answer. "I saw her. Before I woke up. Who is she?"

For the first time, Eileen paused. Then, with a measured breath, she spoke. "Your future soulmate."

The words settled over him, both strange and unavoidable. His future... soulmate. He had spent his life with no illusions of fate or destiny, believing only in the choices men made. And yet, that girl had been there, undeniable in the final moments before his death.

"She came to your turning in her dream," Eileen continued. "That is why you are here, and she is not. That is why you live."

His hands curled into fists against the blanket. The significance of her statement hung heavily in the air. "What am I?"

Eileen stepped closer, her presence unwavering. "There are rules to what you are now. You are Fallen—neither mortal nor truly part of the afterlife. You exist between worlds, given this chance to atone. You were born on the night of a full moon. You have committed only one act of sin. The Celtic Hawthorn tree grants you your supernatural abilities, but it is she—your soulmate—who binds you to the earth itself."

Riichi exhaled sharply, his mind catching on the word. Fallen. A warrior stripped of his fate, neither alive nor entirely dead. Atonement. It had never been a concept he considered for men like himself.

"Bound?" he asked, his voice remained calm even as uncertainty pressed heavily on his chest.

"Without her, you would fade," Eileen clarified. "You are tethered by something greater than yourself. Without that bond, you would dissipate to a place worse than death."

He searched her expression for deception, but there was none. He had always believed death was the final reckoning—yet here he stood, given another chance. "Why?"

Eileen's gaze was unwavering. "Because it is the law of what we are."

Silence stretched between them. Riichi turned his thoughts inward, evaluating the words against his own instincts. If this was truth, then he had been spared for a reason. He had been chosen for something beyond a warrior's death.

She lifted her hand slightly, her voice firm but measured. "From this moment forward, you will be known as Hawthorn."

Riichi's spine straightened. "No."

Eileen's eyes sparkled with intrigue.

"My name is Riichi. My parents carefully selected this name for me. I will not abandon it. I will not answer to another."

Briefly, Eileen studied him, assessing. Then, with a slight nod, she relented. "Very well."

Satisfaction settled in Riichi's chest, though it was short-lived. Eileen raised her hand, fingers tracing deliberate patterns in the air. Before he could react, an unnatural heaviness settled over him. His body wavered, his thoughts blurred.

"You will not remember that your soulmate was at your turning until the time is right," Eileen murmured, her voice distant yet absolute.

His mind fought against the fog creeping over his thoughts, but the spell was already taking hold.

"You will never question my presence or my power. It is not for you to know."

The world darkened, his limbs sinking into stillness. Before unconsciousness took him, he glimpsed Eileen turning toward Hazel. Another murmured spell. Another veil cast over memory.

Then, nothing.

When Eileen turned to Oak, however, the air shifted.

The broad-shouldered man stood firm, arms crossed, expression inscrutable, as he met her stare without flinching.

Eileen lifted her hand. "Close your eyes."

Oak didn't move, his jaw set and his eyes unblinking.

A tense silence crackled between them. Then, his lips parted, voice low but absolute. "You will not alter my memories, Eileen."

A challenge. Not a plea, not a question. A statement.

Eileen narrowed her eyes.

"I am not your pawn."

Eileen paused, her gaze sharpening. Oak knew more than the rest, saw further than the others. He lacked a soulmate to tether him, yet he possessed something just as rare—understanding. He had revealed truths to her that she had not seen, broadened her perception in ways no other had. He had been the first.

She lowered her hand.

Oak did not smile. He simply nodded, as if he had expected no less.

Eileen looked away, deciding to let him keep his knowledge. She would have need of a second-in-command for the war ahead, and his understanding of her may prove useful. Oak, despite his defiance, would say nothing.

Chapter One
Old Memories, New Adventures

Donnelly's was never this quiet at night. By day, though, it felt like a secret hideaway, a retreat tucked away from the city's relentless rhythm. The bar now sat empty and still, its stools lined neatly along the counter, the air carrying the faint scent of polished wood and echoes of last night's laughter. With the café still under construction after the fire, Rowan's bar had become an unofficial clubhouse for Takoda, Rain, Aislinn, and Ariel—a tranquil, sunlit retreat where they could unwind together, away from the usual hum and activity of the city.

They'd gathered around a corner table, their chatter filling the otherwise silent room as they made themselves at home. Rowan kept the place closed during the day, leaving it free for them to use as they pleased, and it had quickly become a sanctuary of sorts. The sunlight filtered softly through the windows, casting a warm glow that caught on their glasses, giving everything a cozy, familiar feel. Even Ariel, the only one actually working there, had pulled up a chair, joining them with a contented smile as she leaned back, perfectly at ease.

Aislinn set her glass down, fingers absentmindedly tracing the rim as she spoke, her voice soft with thought. "It's going to take a few more months, at least," she murmured, glancing at the others. "But the café will be better than ever. There's something surreal about rebuilding from scratch, you know? Like an opportunity to make it even more ours."

Takoda grinned, throwing her friend a warm look, her eyes bright with both amusement and pride. "And you've got Rowan right upstairs, too," she teased lightly, the corners of her mouth quirking up. "Couldn't ask for a better setup, really."

Aislinn blushed just a little, a slight smile breaking through. "Rowan's been incredible, honestly. With his help and the insurance, it's not as overwhelming as I thought it would be. I'm just… grateful." Her voice softened as she spoke, and a gentle smile spread across her face, her gaze drifting as if lost in some fond thought.

Rain grinned, leaning back in her chair with a stretch. "Grateful, huh? Well, sounds like you've got a project, a place to stay, and, let's face it, one very attractive roommate."

She laughed, throwing a playful glance at Aislinn. "Meanwhile, Takoda and I are here as official daytime residents of Donnelly's, working on perfecting the art of doing nothing."

Takoda snorted, nudging Rain with a grin. "Hey, lounging around a bar all day has its perks, right? Free drinks, prime seating." She shrugged, her grin widening. "But yeah, the novelty's wearing thin. If I'd known we'd have all this free time, maybe I'd have picked up a new hobby—or ten."

Rain, ever the instigator, turned to Takoda with a knowing grin. "Hey, at least you got to enjoy two weeks alone with Riichi after everyone else was gone."

Takoda's smile faltered ever so slightly, her fingers stiffening around her glass for the briefest second before she forced herself to roll her eyes and disregard the remark.

Aislinn, catching the shift, quickly nudged Rain with her foot under the table. "You two can always find something to do, trust me," she said, smoothly redirecting the conversation. "Or," she added with a mischievous look at Ariel, "I'm sure Ariel could always put you to work here."

Ariel chuckled, picking up on Aislinn's cue, and rested her chin on her hand with a smirk. "Oh, believe me, I could come up with a few things. But let's be honest," she added with a wink, "the two of you aren't exactly cut out for bar life. Takes a certain kind of charm."

Rain held up her hands. "Hey, don't lump me in with Takoda. I could totally do it. You know, pour drinks, flirt shamelessly for tips…"

Ariel arched a brow. "You mean get distracted and forget to actually serve the customers?"

The girls' laughter spilled out, echoing through the silent room, their spirits lifted despite the waiting and uncertainty.

Takoda laughed along with them, but her mind kept circling back to Rain's comment. *Two weeks alone with Riichi.* It sounded so simple when said aloud, just a casual remark, something to tease about. But Rain didn't know what those two weeks had *felt* like.

The quiet moments. The push and pull. The way I had started to see past the layers he so carefully held in place.

And the way he had left, without a word since.

She inhaled slowly, forcing the thought away. *Not now.* This wasn't the time to think about him.

For now, she focused on the warmth of laughter, the ease of friendship, and the comfort of knowing that—at least here, in this sunlit bar with her friends—she didn't have to think about Riichi at all.

Even if, deep down, I already am.

The door to Donnelly's swung open, and Rowan stepped inside, surveying the animated scene around the corner table. His easygoing smile softened when his gaze fell on Aislinn, seated comfortably among her friends, laughter lighting up her face. He made his way over, folding his arms with a relaxed stance as he took in the lively group, amusement sparking in his eyes.

"Should I even ask what's got you all so wound up?" he asked, his tone warm with curiosity.

Aislinn's face lit up the moment she saw him, her smile broadening as she leaned back slightly to look up at him. "Oh, you know, just the usual—plotting our next world-shattering adventure," she replied with a mockingly grand wave of her hand.

Rowan chuckled, reaching out to brush his hand lightly over her shoulder in an easy, familiar gesture. The warmth between them was almost tangible, as if they shared their own private world in the midst of everyone else.

Takoda and Rain exchanged a knowing look, both of them clearly enjoying the sight of their friend so blissfully wrapped up in this new chapter of her life with Rowan. *She deserves this,* Takoda thought, watching the way Aislinn's entire demeanor relaxed around him. *After everything, she deserves someone who looks at her like that.*

"Well," Rowan began, looking around the table with a thoughtful expression, "if you're all in need of some excitement, why not take a trip? Shake things up a bit."

Ariel perked up, sitting a little straighter as her eyes sparked with instant interest. "Now that is a suggestion I can get behind!" She leaned forward, her excitement contagious. "Seattle. It's almost Halloween, and what better way to spend it than exploring haunted places? Ghost walks, the haunted underground—it's perfect!" She grinned, throwing a sly look at Takoda. "And who knows? Maybe you can figure out why you've been ghosted, too."

Takoda rolled her eyes, though she couldn't help the small laugh that escaped her. "Seattle's a big place, Ariel. I doubt we'll just run into Riichi on the street."

Ariel arched her eyebrows, giving Takoda a knowing look. "Oh, I don't know. Stranger things have happened," she teased, clearly enjoying every second of it.

Rain, quickly warming to the idea, leaned in with an eager smile. "Seattle sounds like a blast," she said, her eyes shining as she began imagining the possibilities. "A haunted Halloween adventure is exactly what we need." She turned to Aislinn, curiosity brightening her expression. "You in?"

Aislinn hesitated, her eyes briefly meeting Rowan's before she answered. "I think I'll stay behind this time," she said with a small smile, casting another glance at Rowan. "With the café rebuild, it's best if I stick around to keep an eye on things." Her cheeks pinked slightly as she added, "Besides... I have some other things to take care of, too."

Takoda and Rain groaned, immediately picking up on the implication in her voice.

Ariel leaned forward, her eyes glinting with familiar mischief. "So, Aislinn, these 'other things' you're staying behind for... care to share?" She raised an eyebrow, her grin promising no mercy.

Aislinn's cheeks deepened to a shade of crimson, and she stammered slightly, brushing off the question with a laugh. "Not a chance, Ariel."

Ariel laughed, leaning back with a smug little flourish. "Fine, fine," she said, shooting Rowan a playful wink. "You two lovebirds go ahead and enjoy yourselves. We don't need Aislinn to have a good time—we've got each other, after all," she added with a dramatic gesture. "And let's be real, I'm plenty of fun."

The group burst into laughter, the sound filling the empty bar as they all agreed that Ariel's vibrant energy was one of the best things about their time together. She beamed, clearly proud of her title as the group's lively instigator.

With Aislinn staying behind, the girls turned their focus to planning the Seattle trip, talking excitedly as they jotted down notes on napkins and mentally ran through what they'd need.

"Alright, hotel reservations first," Takoda said, tapping a pen against the table thoughtfully. "And costumes. We can't do Halloween without dressing up, right?"

"Of course," Rain agreed, a grin spreading across her face. "And we'll need to pack for the weather. Nothing ruins a ghost tour like freezing to death."

Ariel's eyes sparkled as she looked over at Rowan with a knowing smile. "Hey, Rowan, got any recommendations for where to stay?"

Rowan raised an eyebrow, catching her drift. Ariel's matchmaking schemes were as subtle as a storm, and he knew exactly what she was hoping for—a place conveniently close to Riichi. Suppressing a chuckle, he played along. "Any place in Pioneer Square would work," he offered casually, his tone neutral enough to keep the suggestion's hidden meaning under wraps.

Ariel nodded with a satisfied grin, clearly delighted by his answer. Meanwhile, the others continued chatting, blissfully unaware of the silent exchange between the two conspirators.

While the group laughed and made plans, Takoda felt a sense of excitement bubbling up within her. Seattle suddenly felt like more than just a getaway—it carried the promise of change, an energy that stirred anticipation in her chest.

"This is going to be great," Takoda remarked. She genuinely looked forward to a change of scenery and the thrill of Halloween night in a haunted city. "Ghost walks, the underground… it's just the distraction we need."

Privately, though, she couldn't deny the tiny, stubborn hope tucked away in the back of her mind. *Maybe—just maybe—we'll run into Riichi while we're there.*

She missed his calm, formal presence. She'd eventually gotten him to stop calling her *Miss Takoda* during his two-week recovery, but she could see him easily slipping back into it if they did run into him.

Would he still be the same?

She couldn't shake his presence from her mind; it was a mix of intrigue and an indescribable attraction.

Takoda let out a soft sigh, brushing the idea away as she returned her focus to the group, her smile lifting as the anticipation for their trip grew.

The peaceful afternoon atmosphere enveloped Donnelly's, the soft clink of glasses and murmur of conversation filling the empty bar as the group sat at the table, sharing their plans.

Ariel's eyes sparkled suddenly, her face lighting up with a new idea as she leaned forward, grinning with excitement. "We should go shopping before Seattle!" she declared. "We'll need costumes for the ghost tours, plus coats and maybe a few extras," she added with a mischievous gleam.

Rain's face lit up immediately. "I'm in. What's a trip without a little prep spree?" she agreed, her enthusiasm infectious.

With that, Ariel and Rain started gathering their things, chatting excitedly about which stores they absolutely had to visit. Throwing a grin at Takoda and Aislinn, Ariel added, "Come on, you two, this shopping spree will be epic!"

Aislinn shook her head, a gentle smile playing on her lips. "Tempting, but I promised I'd call my mom today. It's been a while."

Takoda adjusted her bag, glancing at Aislinn before turning back to Ariel. "I think I'll hang back with Aislinn, keep her company. I'll catch up with you two before we head out."

Ariel narrowed her eyes, mock suspicion dancing on her face. "Sure you're not just avoiding us so you can skip out on shopping?"

She turned to Rowan, who was sorting through some paperwork behind the bar. "How about you, Rowan? Feel like tagging along for some fashion advice?"

Rowan looked up, a wry smile tugging at the corners of his mouth. "Thanks, but I think I'll pass. Besides, you knew I'd say no," he teased, "but it's good of you to think of me."

Ariel laughed. "Just didn't want you feeling left out." With a final grin, she led Rain out the door, already deep in discussion about which shops to hit first.

As the door swung shut, Rowan glanced at Takoda, noticing the subtle way she shifted her posture, her fingers tracing the edge of her glass absently. There was clearly something on her mind, and he suspected she didn't want to share it in his presence. Sensing she needed some private time with Aislinn, Rowan gave a knowing nod to both girls.

Just as he was about to excuse himself, his phone buzzed in his pocket. He pulled it out, unlocking the screen to find a text from Ariel:

You should call him. We'll be there in 3 days.

Rowan smirked, shaking his head slightly. *The little pixie. She's at it again. Of course she's already making plans.* He wasn't surprised—Ariel didn't leave things to chance, especially not when she saw an opportunity to push things forward.

Without hesitation, he tapped out a reply:

I'll call him when you're on the road.

Sliding his phone back into his pocket, he glanced at Takoda once more before stepping back. "Well, I'll leave you two to it. Paperwork calls," he said with an easygoing smile, disappearing through the backroom door that led to his office.

Once they were alone, Aislinn wasted no time, leaning forward with a look of encouragement. "Okay, spill it. What's on your mind?"

Takoda's lips twitched with a faint smile, but it quickly faded as she looked down, searching for the right words. "Honestly... I'm wondering if going to Seattle is the best idea, considering Riichi's there."

Aislinn tilted her head, understanding sparking in her eyes. "It's been a while since you've seen him, hasn't it?"

Takoda nodded, her fingers fidgeting slightly with the edge of her sleeve. "Two months. And in that time... nothing. No texts, no calls, not even a message through you." She exhaled, her jaw tightening slightly. "I know Rain and Ariel tease me, but I can't help it—I've been thinking about him a lot. And... since he's part of your world now, I thought maybe you'd have some advice or... perspective?"

Aislinn's expression softened as she placed a gentle hand on Takoda's arm. "Takoda, it makes sense you'd think about Riichi. You two spent two weeks alone, even if it's… complicated. Are you worried about seeing him again?"

Takoda hesitated, her gaze drifting to the window as she spoke. "It's not just about seeing him. It's the way things ended. The last time I saw Riichi, he told me he felt something between us. There was this moment—he hugged me, kissed me on the cheek before he left, and for a second, I thought maybe…" She trailed off, shaking her head. "But then he was gone. And I haven't heard from him since."

She ran a hand through her hair, frustration creeping into her tone. "I don't know what I expected. I told myself I was okay with the way things were, but I guess I thought he'd at least reach out. Maybe that was naïve."

Aislinn studied her carefully. "Do you think he just forgot about you?"

Takoda let out a dry laugh, though it held no real amusement. "No. That's the thing—I don't think he did. And that might be worse." She looked back at Aislinn, a hint of doubt crossing her face. "Riichi doesn't do things on impulse. He's deliberate. Strict. If he's stayed silent, it's because he chose to."

Aislinn nodded, thoughtful. "And what do you think that choice means?"

Takoda exhaled slowly. "That's the part I can't figure out. Maybe he decided whatever was between us wasn't worth pursuing. Or maybe he's just that good at compartmentalizing, like everything that happened was some temporary thing that ended the moment he left."

She frowned, her hands curling slightly in her lap. "I keep replaying things in my head. The way he looked at me when I bandaged his wound. The way his voice softened when he said my name. That moment on the porch when he hugged me like he didn't want to let go." Her voice dropped, almost unsure. "The way his fingers lingered after he kissed my cheek. I know I wasn't imagining it. I *felt* something."

Aislinn's gaze was steady. "And you think he felt it too."

"I *know* he did," Takoda admitted, her voice barely above a whisper. "But if that's true… why hasn't he done anything about it?" She leaned back, exhaling sharply. "Maybe I misread everything."

Aislinn gave her a knowing look. "Takoda. We both know Riichi isn't the kind of guy to give mixed signals. He wouldn't have let himself get that close to you if he didn't feel something real."

Takoda's throat tightened. "Then why push me away?"

Aislinn was quiet for a moment before she said gently, "Because sometimes wanting something and allowing yourself to have it aren't the same thing. Riichi has spent his entire life following discipline and duty. Feelings like this? They probably terrify him."

Takoda let that sink in, absently tracing the rim of her glass. "So what am I supposed to do? Just walk into Seattle and pretend none of it happened?"

"Not at all," Aislinn said softly. "But you don't have to chase answers, either. If you see him, just be honest with yourself. You don't have to figure everything out right away."

Takoda let out a small, thoughtful sigh, a faint glimmer of hope edging into her expression. "Maybe you're right. I just don't want to set myself up for disappointment. But… I guess I'll just have to wait and see."

Aislinn squeezed her arm reassuringly. "If Riichi is anything like I think he is, you won't have to wait forever."

They shared a quiet moment, Aislinn's presence easing Takoda's doubts—if only a little.

★★★

Later that evening, while Takoda was alone in her bedroom, a profound stillness settled over her. She'd spent the afternoon laughing with the others, swept up in the excitement of the Seattle trip, but now, in the calm of her room, her thoughts began to drift, taking on a more reflective, somber tone.

She reached over to her nightstand, her fingers instinctively finding the small, worn pouch she'd had for as long as she could remember. She picked it up, feeling the rough, familiar texture under her fingertips. There was nothing remarkable about it—just a simple, weathered pouch—yet somehow, it felt like it held a part of her own story, something quiet and significant. The worn fabric was fraying slightly at the edges, but she held it gently, as though it might provide her an answer she struggled to find.

As she held it, a hazy, distant memory surfaced, the kind of memory that felt more like a dream. She could picture herself as a young girl, clutching the pouch tightly in her hands, looking up at someone's face, her own personal superhero. The details were blurred, like a reflection on water that rippled just as she tried to focus on it, but an inexplicable sense of familiarity. She could almost feel the weight of someone's hand on her shoulder, a comforting presence, yet she couldn't bring the image into full focus. Takoda shook her head softly, letting the memory fade, though a slight feeling of restlessness remained.

And, almost naturally, her thoughts drifted to Riichi.

All day, he had occupied her thoughts, seamlessly threading through her mind just as he had during the two weeks they had shared after the battle with Lucifer—after he had nearly lost his life. She could still see him lying there, unconscious, his face unnervingly still, the usual tension in his features momentarily absent. He hadn't known she was watching, unaware of how long she had sat beside him, unwilling to leave, memorizing the rare calmness of him before the world intruded once more.

It was hard to reconcile that image with the man she had first met—the one who leapt over the wall on to Haight Street with effortless grace, his coat billowing behind him, his expression focused and intense. She had watched him from a distance, drawn in by the quiet control he exuded, the way he commanded his surroundings with barely a word. There had been something captivating about his composure, something unshakable about the way he carried himself, as if nothing could break through the iron discipline that held him together. He had seemed untouchable. Indestructible. A figure equal parts mystery and protector.

But she knew better now.

She knew the man who had instinctively placed himself between her and danger, who had pulled her and Rain to the ground during the café explosion, shielding them from the blast. She remembered the heat, the debris, the ringing in her ears—and then, suddenly, the weight of his presence anchoring her, solid and unwavering. Afterward, his steady gaze had found hers, assuring her that she was safe. That look had stayed with her, a stabilizing force she hadn't fully understood but had learned to trust.

And then there was that last moment between them.

It had been two months since she had last seen him—since he had stood in that doorway, katana in hand, his dark eyes locked onto hers. Since he had thanked her, his voice full of gratitude. Since he had pulled her into a firm embrace, held her just long enough to make her heart stumble, and then stepped away. Since he had kissed her cheek and told her, *There's something here. Even if I don't know what it is yet.*

And then… silence.

No calls. No messages. Nothing.

Takoda exhaled slowly, frustration curling at the edges of the quiet ache in her chest. *Was she reading too much into it?*

She didn't want to be the kind of person who overanalyzed every moment, who let unspoken words and what-ifs take up space in her mind. But resisting wasn't easy. Not when *whatever this was* had woven itself into the quiet pauses in their conversations, into the intensity of his eyes when he looked at her, into the barely-there hesitation in his touch when she passed him the katana.

She traced the edge of the pouch as more memories surfaced, each one threading into the next.

The way he had bristled when Eileen assigned her to stay with him. The way he had tried—at first—to keep her at a distance, only to realize she wasn't going anywhere.

The wordless exchanges they shared, when the strain eased into an unnameable attraction.

The time he had stiffly insisted on helping her unpack the groceries, only to let out an unguarded confession—*I don't want to feel… like I'm useless.* His voice had been so low, so uncharacteristically vulnerable, that it had knocked the breath from her for a second.

Or that night in the bathroom, when he had struggled to change his bandages. He had snapped at her when she offered to help, sharp and cutting in a way that wasn't like him at all. She had almost left—almost walked away—but he had stopped her.

And when he had caught her wrist, his fingers warm and firm against her skin, and murmured *I'm sorry* in that quiet, restrained way of his…

That had been the moment she knew he wasn't as indifferent as he wanted her to believe.

It had been there, simmering beneath every glance, every careful word, every small gesture. The way he had listened when she told him about her heritage. The way he had matched her in their game of favorites, subtly letting down his guard. The way he had surprised her with sunflowers because she had mentioned once, during their game, that they were her favorite.

She could still remember the slight brush of his fingers against hers when he handed them to her.

And yet, despite all of that, he had still left.

Her grip on the pouch tightened.

Did he regret it? Was that why he hadn't reached out?

Or had she imagined everything?

Takoda let out a quiet sigh, feeling the familiar warmth and complexity of each memory settle around her. She couldn't help but wonder if Seattle would bring more clarity or simply deepen the questions that had lingered since those first moments. There was something undeniable between them, a quiet thread woven through each memory, and though neither of them had ever spoken of it, she felt its pull now more than ever.

Maybe that was why Seattle unsettled her. It wasn't the idea of seeing him again—it was the uncertainty of what would happen if she did.

Would he act like those two weeks had never happened? As if they had been nothing more than a temporary circumstance, a fleeting moment between two people caught in the same space?

Or worse… what if he still looked at her *that* way?

What if that pull between them was still there, just as undeniable as before?

With a deep breath, she stood and carefully placed the worn pouch into her suitcase. Whatever this small piece of her past carried—fragments of memory, whispers she couldn't yet decipher—it felt destined to come with her on this journey.

As she closed the suitcase, her mind lingered on each shared moment, the spoken and unspoken, each one drawing her toward Seattle with a quiet, insistent pull.

The evening stretched on, and Takoda found herself clinging to the hope that, just maybe, their paths were meant to cross again. The thought filled her with both excitement and a strange apprehension, as though whatever awaited her in Seattle might hold more than she'd anticipated.

Chapter Two

A Hand to Hold

Eileen had just gotten off the phone with Aislinn, who had apologized for calling later than planned. She had been helping Takoda work through something at Donnelly's and had just seen her off.

It wasn't the late call that unsettled her—it was the silence that followed, dense and stagnant.

She set the phone down, her fingers brushing against its cool surface. *I love you, Mom.* Aislinn's voice echoed in her mind—tentative, vague. She had responded in kind, but even now, those words weighed heavily in her heart, feeling foreign and burdensome. Leaning back in her chair, she exhaled slowly. The house stretched quiet around her, deep and unbroken, save for the measured ticking of the antique clock on the wall. Silence had never unsettled her before. It had always been an ally—constant, and reliable.

But tonight, it felt suffocating.

Her thoughts tangled, refusing to settle. *Aislinn. The Fallen. Soulmates. Archdemons.* She had sensed the approaching change for ages, an unavoidable war creeping toward them, slow yet inevitable. The divine whisper that had guided her for lifetimes had been silent of late, but she did not need prophecy to know—it was beginning. The pressure of it grew, subtly and persistently. Almost without thinking, she reached for her phone.

She dialed the number she knew by heart.

The line barely rang twice before Oak answered.

"Eileen." His voice was calm, yet there was an underlying hint of awareness—an edge of knowing. He always knew. "Has the Golden Dawn done something?"

"No," Eileen replied. "But I just got off the phone with Aislinn. It looks like we'll be heading to Seattle soon."

A brief pause. "I see." Then, after a beat, "That's not why you called, though, is it?"

"No… it's not," Eileen admitted, almost reluctantly.

Oak didn't respond right away, as if considering the sincerity of her words. "I can tell something's wrong. What is it?"

She turned toward the window, the darkened trees swaying beyond the glass. *What is it?* Even she wasn't entirely sure. It wasn't just one thing—it was *everything*. Aislinn's cautious words. The impact of choices that could never be undone. Soulmates appearing among the Fallen, one after another. The war she had spent lifetimes preparing for, finally on the horizon. She shouldered many burdens, but tonight, they felt more overwhelming than usual.

Finally, she admitted, "I need to have a conversation."

Oak let out a slow breath, a hint of dry amusement slipping into his tone. "That much I gathered. Try giving me a little more than cryptic riddles, Eileen."

She closed her eyes briefly. Of course, he wouldn't let her be vague. He never had. "I need someone to talk to. *You.* And I would like you to come to my home in California."

She knew he was considering it before he even spoke. Could picture him standing outside his home in Arizona, the vast land stretching around him, carefully pondering her words the way he always did.

"Eileen," he eventually spoke, his voice gentler now. "Is this important? I'm in Arizona. It would take at least a day to get a flight to San Francisco."

"It is important." She paused, frustration quivering in the back of her mind. "…to me. I can retrieve you."

Oak didn't answer right away, but that alone told her he understood.

Eileen didn't ask for personal conversations. She didn't *need* anyone—not in the way most did. But, for the first time in hundreds of years, she found herself reaching out. And she chose him.

Oak exhaled, his voice thoughtful. "Must be important if you're willing to use your powers."

"Yes."

She heard him moving around, the faint rustle of fabric, the scrape of a chair as he stood. "I'll text you when I'm ready. Understood?"

"Yes."

"Eileen, I mean it. If you show up before I text you, the deal's off. I won't come."

She almost smirked. *As if he wouldn't come if she truly needed him.* "Understood."

There was another noise on his end, the low creak of wood settling. "I'm going to take a shower, then I'll text. Give me twenty minutes."

She hesitated, then finally said, "Thank you, Oak."

No response, but just before the call disconnected, she caught the barely perceptible sound—a low hum of acknowledgement.

The call ended.

Eileen set her phone down on the table, watching the screen as though willing it to light up. She knew she should move, should consider what she wanted to say—but instead, she simply sat there. Waiting.

And in Arizona, Oak dragged a hand through his hair, exhaling slowly. He already knew—twenty minutes or not—she'd come for him the second the clock hit nineteen.

★★★

Oak stepped out of the shower, running a towel over his damp hair. He checked the clock. Five minutes to spare.

With a quiet sigh, he moved toward his nightstand where his phone rested, intending to text Eileen back. His fingers hovered over the screen, but his attention drifted to the duffel bag resting beside his bed.

He always kept a bag packed.

Experience had taught him that leaving home unprepared was a mistake he wouldn't make twice. The Golden Dawn had been striking more frequently, their movements unpredictable. The next attack could come at any time, any place. And if Eileen had called him for a personal conversation, it meant something was troubling her.

Something important.

This would take time. Tucking his phone into his pocket, he grabbed the bag's strap and slung it over his shoulder. He carried it with him into the living room, setting it down near the couch before pulling his phone out again. His thumb hovered for a fraction of a second before he typed out the message:

I'm ready.

Oak barely had time to set the phone down and start counting in his head. *Five… four… three—*

Eileen appeared.

She materialized without warning—one blink, one heartbeat, and she was simply *there*, the air bending around her like the universe had adjusted to accommodate her presence. Teleportation had always been second nature to her, effortless in a way that felt almost divine.

He huffed out a quiet chuckle, shaking his head. "You only got to three." Folding his arms across his chest, he studied her. "Were you staring at your phone waiting this whole time?"

A faint pink rose to her cheeks. "Do not tease me."

Oak smirked. "I'm not teasing. Just pointing out the truth."

Eileen shot him a look—one that told him he was treading close to a line she wasn't in the mood to cross. He let it go, adjusting the strap of his bag as she stepped forward, placing a hand on his arm.

A quick blink. Reality folding and unfolding.

And then they were standing in her home in California.

The air smelled different here—crisp, layered with the clean scent of damp earth and distant pine. The sort of silence that only came from seclusion wrapped around them, serene and untouched.

The house itself was new, or at least, new to Eileen. Oak hadn't been here before, and as she stepped away, he took his time looking around.

His bag dropped soundlessly beside the couch, but he didn't sit. Instead, he wandered, his gaze trailing over the details of the space. Sparse, but refined. Classic, but practical. Every choice intentional.

Eileen's home.

She didn't settle so much as she placed herself on the couch with careful intention, her posture straight, as if keeping it that way would help hold something else together. Only when she seemed ready did he finally turn to her.

"All right." His voice was composed and even. "Tell me what's on your mind."

Eileen maintained eye contact, though her expression faltered slightly. He didn't push. She would speak when she was ready.

She sighed heavily, looking past him toward the window. "Did I make the right choice?"

Oak frowned slightly, sitting on the other end of the couch. "You're going to have to be a little more specific."

She was quiet for a moment, then, "Faking my death. Leaving Aislinn."

Oak studied her. He had known Eileen for nearly two thousand years. She didn't regret decisions—she made them and moved forward.

"You believed it was necessary," he said.

"Yes," she replied, her voice was measured, though he detected a slight tremor. "Now that she knows the truth… I see the damage it caused. I knew there would be pain, but I never considered the struggles Aislinn would face alone…" She shook her head slightly. "Aislinn is trying to rebuild something between us, but I don't know if it's possible."

Oak watched her carefully. "You think she won't truly forgive you."

Eileen didn't answer immediately. *She wasn't someone who second-guessed herself, yet here she was, picking apart a choice made twelve years ago.*

"She says she wants to move forward," she admitted, "but I see the hesitation. The uncertainty. Even if she forgives me, will she ever trust me again? Will she always see me as the mother who abandoned her?"

Oak exhaled, leaning against the arm of the couch. "That isn't something you can control."

"No," she agreed. "But I wonder if I could have handled it differently."

Oak considered his next words carefully. "Would you have?"

She met his gaze again. Something flickered in her eyes—something he recognized. "…No."

Oak nodded. "Then there's no use dwelling on it."

Eileen tilted her head somewhat, as if assessing the weight of his words. "And if I fail her again?"

He sighed. "You're asking the wrong question."

Her brow lifted slightly. "Am I?"

"Yes." He crossed his arms. "You're looking at this as a mistake to atone for instead of a relationship to rebuild. She isn't trying because she has to, Eileen. She's trying because she *wants* to."

Eileen sat back a tad, her gaze dropping to the floor. Oak let the silence settle, knowing she needed space to process.

Eventually, Eileen spoke again, quieter. "I still have to tell her who I really am."

Oak nodded. "And you don't know how she'll take it."

Her jaw tensed slightly. "I've already given her insight, but I see it happening—she's changing. Becoming more like me."

Oak studied her. "And that worries you."

"Yes." Her fingers curled subtly in her lap. "She isn't just growing stronger. She's… shifting. Her presence, her power—it's becoming otherworldly. She's becoming like me." Her voice dropped slightly. "What if she is meant for something more? What if she is required to take on greater responsibilities as I have?"

Oak let the words settle, his expression thoughtful. "And if that's the case?"

Eileen's lips pressed together. For a long moment, she said nothing, but he could feel the answer in the weight of her silence.

Oak didn't push. He had spent millennia learning how to read her, knowing when to speak and when to wait.

Finally, she exhaled, her voice quieter. "If I had never allowed her to be pulled into this world… maybe her powers would have stayed dormant. Maybe she would have never had to experience any of this."

Oak looked at her intently. "You couldn't have stopped her from becoming part of this world, Eileen."

Her fingers flexed slightly, but she said nothing.

He continued, voice calm, certain. "She was always meant to be Rowan's soulmate. She would have become part of this world whether you did anything or not. Her powers would have surfaced eventually. That was inevitable." He leaned forward a little. "The difference is—now, you're here. You can guide her. Teach her. If she's meant for something more, at least she won't have to figure it out by herself."

Eileen let his words settle, but the tension in her shoulders didn't fully ease.

"I know," she said finally, though the burden of it still pressed against her.

They let the conversation settle there.

Oak let out a breath and adjusted his stance. "That isn't the only thing bothering you."

Eileen glanced at him with a keen, assessing look, as though she were considering whether to continue. He held her stare, waiting. He had known her long enough to recognize when she was calculating her words, deciding how much to reveal.

Finally, she spoke. "I fear I will fail them."

Oak didn't ask who. He already knew.

"The Fallen," he said.

Eileen gave a small nod, looking away. "In the beginning, they were just soldiers." Her voice was measured, but there was something beneath it—something heavier. "But now… they are my warriors, yes, but they are also my children." Her fingers curled subtly in her lap. "I have guided them, trained them, watched them grow into who they are now." A rare flicker of vulnerability crossed her expression. "And I cannot lose them."

Oak studied her. "You've lost Fallen before."

She exhaled, her jaw tensing. "I have." Guilt edged the words, barely audible. "And I told myself it was necessary." A breath, slow but unsteady. "The first who fell never lasted long enough for me to mourn them." Her hands tightened in her lap. "But this is different. I have spent lifetimes ensuring *these* Fallen survive long enough to find redemption." Her voice dipped lower. "And what if—" She stopped, inhaling sharply, as if forcing the thought back before it could take hold.

Oak didn't let her retreat. "What if what?"

Her gaze met his again, and for a fleeting instant, a raw vulnerability flashed across her face. "What if I lead them to their deaths instead?"

Oak held her stare. No amusement, no sarcasm. Just a quiet understanding.

"You won't."

Her lips pressed together. "You don't know that."

"No," he admitted. "But I know you." He leaned against the arm of the couch, arms crossing loosely over his chest. "You aren't reckless. You don't make decisions without considering every possible outcome. If there is a way to keep them alive, you will find it."

Eileen studied him, considering his words. Then, after a moment, she admitted, "We almost lost Riichi."

Oak exhaled slowly, nodding. "But we didn't."

She narrowed her eyes as a vein throbbed in her temple. "Because I intervened. I made sure he got the help he needed. But what if—"

"You'll do the same for the others if it comes to it," Oak said smoothly, cutting off the thought before it could gain momentum. "But I don't think it will be necessary."

Eileen lifted a brow. "You sound certain."

"I am." His voice was calm, unwavering. "That was the first battle against an archdemon, Eileen. There will be more. We both know that." His look was steady and knowing. "But don't underestimate the Fallen. They are smart and determined. They'll make sure that never happens again."

Eileen didn't respond immediately. Oak could see her mind working, processing his words, comparing them against the storm of thoughts still moving behind her eyes.

Finally, she gave a slow nod, though the tension in her shoulders hadn't fully eased.

"They're more prepared than you give them credit for," Oak added. "And they'll continue to prepare. Because that's what you've trained them to do."

Eileen exhaled, though the stress in her gaze remained. Oak didn't expect her to let go of the thought entirely—*she wouldn't be Eileen if she did. But she would think about what he said.*

Oak quickly broke the silence. "That's still not everything, is it?"

Eileen sighed, glancing away. "I fear I have made a mistake."

Oak frowned. "Go on."

"The soulmates." she said in a controlled tone, but there was an underlying nuance. A hesitation only someone like Oak would recognize.

"You knew they would be part of this," he pointed out. "You're the one who introduces them to each Fallen."

"I did." She exhaled, fingers pressing lightly against her knee. "But what if I chose wrong? What if, by introducing them to their soulmates, I unintentionally took away their free will?"

Oak's frown deepened. "Eileen, you didn't take away their free will."

She didn't answer right away. Instead, she inhaled, her gaze distant. "I don't want to believe it," she admitted, "but I can't ignore the possibility."

Oak shook his head. "That's not how it works."

She looked at him again, searching. He met her gaze, his voice even.

"Fate and destiny aren't the same," he said. "Their soulmates are their destiny. That was decided long before you ever entered their lives. You didn't *choose* their soulmates—you *found* them."

Eileen studied him carefully. "And what happens after that?"

Oak didn't waver. "That's fate. And fate is determined by the choices they make. You didn't take that from them." He let the words settle before adding, "You gave them a tether to this world, so they didn't fade. But what happens after they meet their soulmates? That's theirs to decide."

Eileen sat with that. He had given his answer—what she did with it was up to her.

After a long moment, she spoke again, her voice now a gentle whisper. "There's one more thing."

Oak remained silent, a statue of patience.

Eileen inhaled slowly. "I still don't understand why you don't have a soulmate."

He remained motionless, his expression a mask that revealed nothing.

Her gaze held his. "Or why you're still here."

Oak released a slow, measured breath, yet his eyes never strayed from hers.

For the first time in the conversation, words eluded him, lost in the vast silence between them.

She had voiced the one question that had haunted the recess of his mind for centuries—the question he had never been able to answer.

Eileen's voice had softened to a whisper. "I have spent centuries introducing the Fallen to their soulmates. And yet... you remain alone."

Oak shifted slightly, his fingers pressing lightly against the arm of the couch. She wasn't demanding an answer. She wasn't even looking for one. She was *worried*.

He let the silence stretch before finally speaking. "I don't have an answer for that." His voice was even, careful. "But whatever the reason is, it's not something you did."

Eileen didn't respond immediately. The weight of everything they had discussed pressed down on her, but *this*—this was what broke her.

Her hands clenched imperceptibly in her lap, and when she finally spoke again, her voice was even quieter than before, fragile and trembling. "I fear I failed you."

Oak's brow furrowed, a shadow of concern crossing his features.

Eileen drew in a sharp breath, tilting her head away, as if trying to keep her composure. "I have looked for almost two thousand years," she admitted. "And I still cannot find your soulmate."

A silence settled between them, more oppressive than any before.

Oak watched her intently, scrutinizing her words, her expression, the barely contained emotion she rarely let show.

When he finally spoke, his voice was calm and resolute. "I would never believe that you failed me."

Eileen's breath hitched, though she forced herself to remain still.

"Maybe you've been looking for the wrong thing," Oak continued. "Something has kept me tethered to this world when every other Fallen without a soulmate faded. Maybe we should be looking for *that* instead of a soulmate that doesn't seem to exist."

Eileen stared at the floor, her fingers tightening in her lap. She finally answered, muttering. "Yeah… maybe."

Silence stretched between them.

Oak didn't move, simply watching her. Despite their conversation, despite everything they had worked through tonight, she was still holding onto all of it. He saw it in the way she sat—shoulders rigid, hands twisting subtly in her lap, gaze unfocused yet troubled. Her lips pressed together every time another thought surfaced, and the restless movement of her fingers told him she was still unraveling all the weight she carried.

He had seen her like this before—*many* times before.

For nearly two thousand years, he had watched Eileen bear burdens no one else could fathom. He had seen her in quiet contemplation, in absolute command, in bitter solitude. And for almost just as long, when the weight became too much, he had been the only one she turned to.

She had been the one to teach him how to fight, how to wield the power of the Fallen, how to navigate the wars that stretched through time.

But *he* had been the one to teach *her* something else entirely—what it meant to be human.

His thoughts drifted back to the beginning.

To the night she had sat outside that house, watching candlelight flicker through an open window, studying the couple inside with detached curiosity. She had seen them embrace, had observed the way they disappeared into the privacy of their home. And then, with that same clinical detachment she applied to everything, she had turned to him, seeking answers.

Oak had explained. Marriage. Intimacy. The way love could lead people to one another.

And Eileen, with no hesitation, had simply asked, *Would you show me?*

Even now, after all these centuries, he remembered the moment with absolute clarity. The way she had looked at him—not with doubt, not with hesitation, but with unwavering certainty. He had questioned it, of course. Had warned her it wasn't something to be taken lightly. And she, in the same matter-of-fact way she approached everything, had responded, *If you do not wish to, I can find another.*

That had been the moment he knew.

She hadn't understood yet—not the dangers of people, not how trust could be manipulated, not how someone could take something from her she hadn't meant to give. And he hadn't been able to let that happen.

So, without another word, he had reached for her hand and said, *Come on.*

And that had been the start of something that lasted centuries.

Eileen had never sought him out for emotional connection. Not in the way most would expect. But whenever the weight of her existence pressed too heavily on her shoulders, whenever the silence stretched too long, whenever she needed to feel something beyond the relentless demands of leadership—she had come to him.

Sometimes it was after turning a new Fallen, but more often, it was simply when she needed a moment to forget.

Oak had never asked why. He had never needed to.

He had told her once, long ago, that intimacy could make someone forget—even if just for a little while.

Maybe that was why she sought him out.

Maybe that was why he never turned her away.

For so long, that had been their unspoken arrangement—one that neither of them questioned.

Until Rowan's turning changed everything.

At the time, Oak hadn't known why. He had only recognized that after she turned Rowan in 1847, she never sought him out again. He hadn't asked. He hadn't pushed for an explanation. Their relationship had never been built on expectations. It had always been something they allowed, never something they demanded.

And so, without question, Oak had let her go.

It wasn't until Aislinn entered the picture that he understood.

That night, when she turned Rowan, Eileen had met her daughter.

She hadn't known it then—not fully—but something in her had shifted. For the first time, she was no longer looking for an escape. She was looking for something else.

And so, she had stopped coming to him.

Now, across the years and all that had shifted between them, he watched her—watched the weight that pressed against her shoulders, the burdens she refused to lay down. He couldn't take them from her. He couldn't give her the answers she sought.

But he could give her what he had always given. He could let her forget—for a little while.

The thought settled in him, quiet and certain.

So he crossed the space between them and offered his hand. "Come on."

Eileen's gaze lifted, slow and deliberate. Her eyes flicked to his hand, then up to his face, as if searching for any trace of hesitation. But there was none. His purpose was clear, his resolve steady.

It had been a long time since he had offered this to her. Longer still since it had been possible.

She studied him, gauging his intent, but he revealed nothing beyond the calm assurance in his posture.

Then, he gave a single, answering nod.

Her fingers hovered, just for a moment, before settling into his.

Oak's grasp was firm but unhurried, his touch neither demanding nor hesitant. He drew her gently to her feet, his presence centering her more than she would ever admit aloud.

Without a word, he led her toward the bedroom.

The door closed softly behind them, sealing them in quiet. But it was not the quiet of restraint, nor the space left by words unspoken.

It was something else.

Recognition.

A choice.

Eileen stood near the edge of the room, her fingers still curled from where they had lingered in his grasp. Across from her, Oak turned to face her fully, his gaze steady—not expectant, not uncertain, but clear and assured.

They had stood like this before, long ago, in times when words weren't needed. When neither of them questioned the arrangement or the reasons behind it. It had always been uncomplicated—a need met, a temporary escape from the weight they both carried.

But tonight, the air between them felt different.

She exhaled slowly, the tension in her shoulders loosening as she stepped toward him. Oak remained where he was, making no move to reach for her, offering neither invitation nor resistance. He allowed her to decide the pace.

When she reached him, she lifted her hand, fingertips brushing the familiar lines of his jaw. The simplicity of the touch stirred something within her—a memory of warmth, of comfort that had waited quietly beneath the surface all this time.

His hand came up in response, catching hers. He held it there, against his cheek for a breath, before trailing his fingers down the inside of her wrist and settling them at her waist.

Eileen drew in a breath, slow and grounding, as she let herself sink into the familiarity of their closeness. Then, with the quiet resolve that had always defined her, she leaned in, resting her forehead against his.

Oak exhaled, his breath deep and even, and softly spoke her name. "Eileen."

Her name held more than recognition. It was a question, an offering, and an answer, all at once.

Her gaze searched his, her voice barely a whisper. "Are you sure?"

Oak's thumb brushed along her wrist, a gentle answer in itself. "I wouldn't offer if I wasn't."

She closed her eyes briefly, then tilted her chin, closing the space between them.

The kiss unfolded slowly, deliberate in every movement, carrying the memory of choices made long ago. But the instant Oak responded, a subtle part of her gave way. She pressed closer, and his hand at her waist tightened, drawing her to him as the space between them disappeared.

There was no rush in his movements, no urgency. His touch was deliberate, gentle, filled with an understanding that ran far deeper than the physical.

This wasn't about desire. It wasn't about loss or filling an unnamed emptiness.

It was something far more profound.

She felt it in the way Oak's hands moved over her, tracing familiar paths with patient intent. In the way he kissed her—not out of expectation, but because she welcomed it.

She felt it, too, in the way her body softened into his, her hands relearning the shape of him, following familiar lines as though rediscovering a language long forgotten.

Together, they undressed each other slowly, every movement a silent exchange. There was nothing to say—nothing that hadn't already passed between them in the quiet moments leading here.

When Oak guided her back to the waiting bed, she yielded without hesitation.

As he settled beside her, he met her gaze, his voice low and roughened by something deeper. "Let me help you forget."

Her reply came as a breath. "Just for a little while."

For the first time in what felt like a lifetime, she released the tension that had gripped her so tightly.

And in that same breath, Oak let down his own walls, not in words, but in the quiet vulnerability of his touch.

The night unfolded around them, seamless and unhurried, neither of them holding back, neither pulling away.

For hours, Eileen allowed herself to let go of the weight waiting beyond that room, surrendering fully to the moment shared between them.

And for the first time in what felt like ages, she let herself be held by him, finding solace in the quiet strength of his embrace.

I t had taken three days for the girls to prepare for their trip to Seattle. Ariel and Rain managed to drag Takoda to the shopping center on one of those days. While they hunted for new outfits, exclusively to wear in Seattle, Takoda focused on grabbing ingredients to make some snacks for the trip. She moved through the aisles efficiently, scanning the shelves for things she knew they'd all enjoy.

Then she saw it—red bean paste and powdered rice.

Her fingers hovered over the packages before she grabbed them, placing them in her cart without thinking. It wasn't until she rounded the corner into the next aisle that she realized what she had done.

Mochi. *Riichi's favorite.*

A quiet exhale slipped from her lips, and she tightened her grip on the cart handle. *You're overthinking it. It's just a snack.* A completely normal thing to bring on a road trip. That's all.

Still, as she stood in the checkout line, she glanced down at the ingredients. Her stomach twisted. She knew better.

But she bought them anyway.

Three days later, Takoda and Rain's apartment was a maze of open suitcases, half-folded clothes, scattered travel essentials, and trays of freshly baked goodies laid out on the kitchen counter. The scent of vanilla and sugar lingered in the air, mixing with the crisp breeze drifting in from the open window. A hum of pre-trip excitement filled the air, but beneath it lurked something more subtle—a quiet restlessness, a nagging sense of anticipation that had nothing to do with their travel plans.

Takoda turned, eyeing Rain's growing mountain of layers. "Are you sure you need three sweaters?" she called from the closet.

"Seattle's rainy season is no joke, you know," Rain replied matter-of-factly, tucking another scarf into her bag. "Besides, you can never have too many cozy options." She grinned, winking as she added yet another layer, clearly enjoying the preparations.

Their packing fell into an easy rhythm, years of friendship making the process second nature. Takoda's side of the room was neatly stacked, a careful balance of practicality and minimalism. Rain's, on the other hand, was an explosion of bold patterns, eclectic colors, and a handful of sentimental keepsakes she never traveled without.

After a while, they took a break, settling in with cups of tea. Rain, ever the mischief-maker, peered into the depths of her mug, swirling the dregs with a dramatic flourish. She raised her brows, turning to Takoda with an exaggerated air of mystery.

"I see... unexpected encounters," she mused, squinting at the shapes. "Perhaps... a familiar face in a strange setting?"

Takoda's fingers tightened around her mug before she could stop herself.

For a split second, her mind conjured an image she had been trying to avoid—standing on the porch with Riichi, wrapped tightly in his arms, feeling his warm breath as he whispered in her ear, '*There's something here.*'

She forced a laugh, shaking her head. "Oh, please, Rain. Last time you tried reading tea leaves, you said I'd meet my 'tall, dark, and handsome' by the grocery store's frozen section."

"And I was right!" Rain defended, feigning offense but grinning anyway. "That store clerk definitely had a 'tall, dark, and handsome' vibe."

Takoda rolled her eyes, willing her pulse to slow. Rain wasn't wrong—her readings did have a strange way of coming true. But Takoda refused to acknowledge that Rain's words had struck a nerve.

Rain leaned closer, inspecting the mug with exaggerated focus. "I'm serious, though. I have a feeling about this trip. I'm not saying it's anything romantic or that you'll meet him at Trader Joe's this time, but... you know. My readings have a certain accuracy."

Takoda took a slow sip of tea, masking the discomfort curling in her stomach. She refused to entertain the thought.

She had no reason to believe she'd run into Riichi. And if she did...

Would he even care?

She exhaled quietly, setting her mug aside just as Rain pulled out her phone, scrolling through the Seattle weather.

"Alright, it's official—cool and rainy all week. Just how I like it." She nodded in satisfaction, tossing another sweater into her bag.

Takoda zipped her suitcase closed before glancing at Rain's growing pile. "Maybe we should throw in a few outfits for warmer or colder weather, just in case." She shrugged at Rain's questioning look. "And maybe even our bathing suits. You never know if we'll stumble across a heated pool or something."

Rain raised a brow, giving her a long, knowing look. "Your gut feeling again?" she asked with a smirk, though her tone held genuine curiosity.

Takoda hesitated.

Normally, she trusted her instincts without a second thought. She'd always been in tune with those quiet nudges, the ones that told her when an important shift was coming. But lately... doubt crept in too easily, making her question whether those instincts were still reliable.

"Maybe. Or maybe it's just me overthinking," she said, brushing off the feeling with a light laugh. But as she turned back to her suitcase, a persistent weight settled in her chest—a restless anticipation, like standing on the edge of something just about to unfold.

As Rain continued packing, a sharp honk from the street made both her and Takoda jump. Peering out the window, she spotted Ariel waving exuberantly from her white Cadillac convertible, her brown hair catching the light as she signaled them to hurry.

Rain grabbed her suitcase, nudging Takoda with her shoulder. "Our chariot awaits," she quipped, laughing as she led the way down the stairs.

They barely managed to fit their luggage in the trunk, but Ariel somehow made it all work, rearranging bags with the ease of a seasoned road-tripper. As Takoda and Rain secured their bags, Ariel pulled out her phone and fired off a quick message.

Ariel: Leaving now.

A moment later, her screen lit up with a reply.

Rowan: Alright. Have fun. I'll make the call.

Ariel smirked, typing one last response.

Ariel: =)

Putting her phone away, she clapped her hands. "Alright, let's go!"

With one last check to ensure they hadn't forgotten anything, Takoda slid into the backseat as Rain settled in beside Ariel. The engine roared, and Ariel flashed them a playful grin, cranking up the volume on her playlist.

"Ready for the best two weeks ever?" she asked, her voice full of energy.

Takoda smiled, forcing herself to match the enthusiasm in Ariel's tone. "Ready as we'll ever be!"

The car rolled down the street, the wind tugging at their hair, music blasting. Seattle stretched ahead, two weeks of adventure waiting.

And yet, as they sped off, a quiet part of Takoda's mind whispered that this trip would bring new experiences, meaningful connections, and discoveries she was ready to embrace.

★★★

Back at Donnelly's, Rowan leaned against the bar, pulling out his phone and scrolling through his contacts. When he found Riichi's number, he hit call and lifted the phone to his ear.

It barely rang twice before Riichi answered. "Hey, Rowan."

"Riichi." Rowan kept his tone casual. "How are things going on your end?"

"Fine." There was a pause before Riichi added, "Is this meant to be a casual conversation? You don't normally do that."

Rowan smirked, rubbing his jaw. "Well… since Aislinn's come into my life, I'm learning to live a little more and try new things." His voice held a hint of dry amusement. "But you're right. I don't." He exhaled, shifting gears. "Last I heard, Eileen sent you on a mission. How'd that go?"

Riichi let out a short chuckle. "Good you're trying new things." He paused. "Mission? Still going, actually. I'm continuing to gather intel on the Golden Dawn. They've been causing unnatural weather patterns near the Washington–Canadian border, but the patterns have recently started shifting, slowly moving down the coast." His tone turned more serious. "I suspect the Golden Dawn is on the move. And they're headed straight for Seattle."

Rowan didn't like the sound of that. His jaw tightened. Seattle. That's exactly where the girls are heading.

"How long until they reach Seattle?" Rowan asked. "And where are you now?"

"I'm at my apartment," Riichi replied. "At the rate the weather patterns are moving, they should hit the city by the end of the week. Maybe sooner."

Rowan frowned. If Riichi was at his place, keeping watch without needing to relocate, then the Golden Dawn were close. Too close.

"Shit…" Rowan muttered. "Looks like you're going to have a complication then, my friend."

Riichi hesitated. "What does that mean?"

Rowan exhaled. "Ariel, Rain, and Takoda are actually on their way to Seattle as we speak."

Silence.

Rowan gave Riichi time to process, though he could almost hear the shift in the other man's breathing, the subtle change in energy. When Riichi finally spoke, his voice had unconsciously slipped into a more formal cadence—an old habit resurfacing under pressure.

"Seattle's security is compromised," Riichi said. "Why have they chosen to venture here?"

Rowan shook his head. "Really? You're giving me formal?" He let that sink in for a second before continuing. "Guess that one hit a bit. Anyway, they wanted to soak in Seattle's Halloween atmosphere. And I think…" He dragged out the words. "They were hoping to run into you. Takoda, especially."

Another long pause.

Rowan could picture Riichi's reaction—the mix of emotions he was no doubt trying to suppress.

Riichi sat stiffly in his chair, his grip tightening around the phone. Takoda is coming to Seattle.

His heartbeat kicked up, an automatic response he couldn't control.

She's hoping to see me.

His mind raced through everything that had happened between them—two weeks of cautious closeness, unspoken moments heavy with meaning, the warmth of her touch when she pressed fresh bandages to his skin. And then the two months of silence that followed. His choice.

She'll be in danger.

His jaw clenched. Seattle wasn't safe. The Golden Dawn was moving, and the city was about to become a battleground.

And she was walking straight into it.

Riichi's voice, when he finally spoke, was taut. "Seattle is not safe right now, Rowan. If anything happens to her—" He caught himself. "Them."

Rowan couldn't hold back a laugh. "Good to know you haven't lost interest. And that you actually have a legit reason for ghosting her."

"Rowan," Riichi snapped, irritation creeping into his tone. "This is not a joke. You know as well as I do that they're walking into danger."

"Yeah, yeah." Rowan waved off the warning, though he took the concern seriously. "Alright, look. I'll call Ariel and see if I can get them to turn around. But I'm telling you now—those girls are as stubborn as you. They're dead set on this trip." He sighed. "Them turning around? Not gonna happen."

"Still worth a shot," Riichi said immediately. "Tell me where they plan to stay."

Rowan smirked. "Embassy Suites in Pioneer Square."

There was a beat of silence. Then, a flat, knowing, "You told them to stay there."

"Yeah, well, someone needs to get your ass in gear, so you stop hiding behind duty."

"I don't—"

"Yeah, you do." Rowan didn't let him finish. "Anyway, they should be there around four."

"Understood."

"I'll call Ariel now," Rowan said. "In the meantime, plan for them to be there, and call in the Fallen at the first sign of trouble. Good deal?"

A long pause. Then, begrudgingly— "No. But fine."

Rowan chuckled. "That's what I thought."

Riichi could hear the smirk in his voice before the call ended. As he lowered his phone, he let out a slow breath.

Rowan had changed. Aislinn's done him some good. He was still sharp, still one of the best warriors Riichi had ever fought beside—but he wasn't as moody anymore. There was a lightness to him now, a balance.

And for that, at least, Riichi was happy for him.

★★★

The white Cadillac convertible zipped along the coastline, glinting in the mid-afternoon sun. With the top down, the wind whipped through the car, carrying strains of music and bursts of laughter as Ariel, Rain, and Takoda leaned into the road trip vibe. The early autumn landscape sped past in swathes of amber, russet, and hints of lingering summer green, each mile drawing them closer to Seattle's misty, moody horizon.

Ariel grinned, glancing over at her friends. "Alright, Halloween costumes," she declared, raising her voice over the music. "We're going all out this year. I'm thinking... dark fantasy, or maybe a modern fae theme. Something with mystery, magic—totally Seattle."

Rain's eyes sparkled as she turned in her seat to face Ariel. "I love it! Seattle's practically begging for something mystical. Count me in."

Takoda laughed, feeling the contagious excitement as she nodded along. "Alright, I'm game. Modern fae, dark fantasy... what did you have in mind?"

Ariel's face lit up. "I'm going full pixie," she announced, tossing her hair with a mock haughty air. "Glamorous, sparkly, and completely over-the-top. Think shimmery fabrics, metallic colors, fairy wings… I'm talking glittery face paint and neon accessories. Life of the party, here I come! We can pick up everything we need in Seattle and go full-on enchanted together."

Takoda and Rain exchanged amused glances. Ariel's energy was as effervescent as ever, and there was no denying she'd pull off a pixie costume with ease. She continued, "You guys can be my entourage of forest fae or woodland goddesses. Imagine it—together, we'll look like a crew straight out of an enchanted forest."

Rain clasped her hands together in excitement. "I'll be a forest nymph, then! Greens, browns, vines in my hair, maybe a wreath crown." She closed her eyes, already picturing the look. "It'll be subtle but glowing, like a spirit of the woods. We'll find some faux vines or maybe even those tiny twinkle lights to wind through my hair."

Ariel grinned. "Oh, that would be *so* perfect. And with your red hair? The twinkle lights would literally make it look like it's on fire."

Rain's eyes lit up. "Ooooh, now I *have* to do it."

Takoda watched as Rain's face softened, her expression serene and thoughtful, almost as if she'd stepped into a hidden part of herself. She couldn't help but think how perfectly the costume fit her friend's love for nature, grounding her in the calm presence she carried.

As they drove, Takoda looked down, toying with the edge of her sweater.

"Alright, Takoda. Tell us your costume plan," Ariel said, raising her brows.

Takoda caved. "Alright, I've been thinking about going as a modern sorceress. I want to get a black kimono with a red floral pattern, and we can look for accessories in Seattle, too—maybe some smoky makeup, glitter, and a temporary tattoo to tie it all together." She smiled, a touch self-conscious but warming to the idea. "I was even thinking of a lotus and dragon tattoo. Something striking."

Rain gave her a gentle smile, clearly loving the concept. "It's perfect," she said, the sincerity in her tone bringing a warm flush to Takoda's cheeks.

Ariel, however, wasn't about to let the moment pass without her usual teasing. She tilted her head, giving Takoda a sly grin. "Very mysterious and enchanting. That'll catch someone's eye."

Takoda rolled her eyes, but she couldn't shake the feeling that the costume might carry more significance than she initially thought. She added, almost as an afterthought, "The lotus and dragon thing just feels right. Resilience, strength, transformation… maybe it's a sign." The words echoed in her mind, staying with her.

The excitement of costume planning drifted into a relaxing silence as they continued up the coast, the air growing cooler as they drove north. Ariel turned the music down just a notch, settling back with a contented sigh.

Rain, however, had other plans. She turned to Takoda with a playful grin.

"So, Takoda," Rain began, drawing out her name in a sing-song tone. "Are you sure this trip will only bring ghost stories and Halloween parties?" She winked, a mischievous glint in her eyes. "Or is there someone special you're hoping to bump into?"

Takoda scoffed, swatting Rain's hand on the headrest. "Oh, please. It's just a Halloween trip," she said, though her words came out a little more forced than she intended. She shifted her gaze to the blur of landscape passing by, hoping neither of them noticed the flush creeping into her cheeks.

Without intending to, her thoughts drifted to Riichi again. They hadn't spoken in what felt like ages, and she had no reason to think she'd just bump into him. Seattle was a big place. Yet, a faint glimmer of hope tugged at her, as if some part of her wondered if their paths might somehow cross again.

She chided herself, mentally brushing the thought aside. He'd probably moved on by now. And anyway, that strange pull she'd felt back in San Francisco... it was probably just her imagination.

Ariel's phone buzzed from the center console. She glanced down, and her carefree expression flashed with concern before reappearing.

Rowan: *SOS. Call me.*

She clicked her tongue, tilting the screen away from Takoda and Rain so they wouldn't see.

Ariel exhaled sharply and sat up, tapping her fingers against the steering wheel. "Alright, ladies," she said, forcing lightness into her tone. "We're making a pit stop."

Rain groaned. "Already?"

Ariel shrugged. "Blame my bladder. I need to hit a travel center."

Takoda didn't think much of it, stretching her arms as the car veered toward an upcoming exit.

As Ariel pulled into the travel center, her fingers hovered over her phone. Whatever Rowan had to say, she had a feeling it wasn't good.

Ariel parked near the gas pumps, putting up the top and turning off the engine as Rain and Takoda unbuckled.

"I'll be back in a sec," she announced, grabbing her phone before either of them could question her. "Go grab snacks or something."

Rain shot her a curious look but shrugged. "Want anything?"

"Nah, I'm good."

Ariel offered her usual carefree smile, but the moment she stepped out of the car, the expression faded. She walked into the travel center, heading toward the restrooms. As soon as she stepped into the ladies' room, she pulled out her phone and dialed Rowan.

He picked up on the first ring. "Took you long enough."

Ariel scoffed. "Oh, I'm *so* sorry I couldn't drop everything and sprint to my phone the moment you texted *SOS*." She leaned against the tiled wall, lowering her voice. "What's up, Rowan? You don't do emergency texts unless there's actually an emergency."

"There is." Rowan didn't waste time. "I just got off the phone with Riichi. The Golden Dawn is on the move, and he thinks they're heading for Seattle."

Ariel's stomach dropped, but she recovered quickly. "Okay. And?"

"And?" Rowan repeated, exasperated. "And you need to turn around."

Ariel *actually* laughed. "Yeah, no."

Rowan sighed. "Ariel—"

"Nope." She cut him off without pause. "We've got plans, we're going, and a little thing like the Golden Dawn isn't going to stop us from having fun."

There was silence, and Rowan's voice dropped slightly. "This isn't a joke, Ariel."

"I *know* that," she said, rolling her eyes. "And I also know that if things get too messy, the rest of the Fallen will show up. You *know* they will. We're safe."

Rowan didn't sound convinced. "Just because we *might* show up doesn't mean you should waltz straight into trouble."

"I'm not going to let danger keep me and my friends from living life to the fullest," Ariel pointed out, her tone light but unwavering.

Rowan muttered something under his breath before shifting tactics. "Fine. But listen—Riichi was *not* okay when I told him Takoda was coming."

Ariel arched a brow. "Define *not okay*."

"He got *formal*."

That caught Ariel's interest. "Ooooh." A grin tugged at her lips. "So, he *does* still care."

"That's not what I—"

"It *is* what you're saying," she countered. "He still cares, which means Takoda's got a shot, and you're telling me that the Golden Dawn thing is actually serious."

"Yes," Rowan said flatly. "Both of those things."

"Then I really don't see a downside here," Ariel mused, inspecting her nails. "Takoda gets to see Riichi, we get our Halloween trip, and if the Golden Dawn shows up, well—at least we won't be bored."

Rowan sighed. "Why do I even bother?"

"Because you love me," Ariel teased.

Rowan didn't dignify that with a response.

Ariel smirked, checking herself in the bathroom mirror. "Relax, Rowan. We've got this."

"You better," he muttered. "And you call me the minute you notice anything unordinary."

"Aye, aye, captain," Ariel scoffed.

She hung up, tucked her phone back into her pocket, and stepped toward the sinks. Turning on the faucet, she let the cool water run over her hands, composing herself before heading back out.

★★★

Riichi sat in his apartment, elbows resting on his knees, gaze fixed on the city beyond the window. The sun hung high, casting a hazy glow over the skyline, its light cutting through the ever-present mist that clung to Seattle. The hum of traffic below was steady, distant—a dull backdrop to the thoughts pressing against his mind.

A hotel across the city. A woman he hadn't seen in two months.

Takoda was coming. She would be here in a matter of hours.

He had known she would be in Seattle before Rowan's call. He had felt it—that unshakable awareness that had never truly left him since their time together. But knowing it and hearing it spoken aloud were two different things. Now, it wasn't just a quiet, lingering thought in the back of his mind—it was real.

And he had no idea what to do with that.

The truth settled deep in his chest, pressing against the part of himself he refused to examine—the part that wanted her here.

Two months had passed since he left San Francisco, since he walked away from the quiet certainty she had brought into his life. He had thought distance would help, that space would give him clarity. Instead, it had done the opposite.

The moment he admitted—to himself and to her—that he cared for her, it was as if he had unlocked a force he could no longer contain. He had spent his existence forging himself into a man of discipline, structure, control. Emotions were distractions, weaknesses to be pushed aside in favor of logic.

But deep down, he knew that was a lie.

The truth was, he had never stopped thinking about her and couldn't push his feelings aside no matter how hard he tried.

She had unraveled his carefully built composure, exposing feelings he wasn't sure he knew how to handle. For centuries, he had built walls, locking away the parts of himself that felt too much, that longed for connection beyond duty and discipline. And yet, in two weeks, she had slipped past every single one of his defenses.

And now, after all this time, she was coming here.

Did she want to see me?

Rowan seemed to think so, but was that just wishful thinking? Or had she spent the last two months wondering why he disappeared? Had she been waiting for him to call, only to be met with silence?

Would she be disappointed? Angry?

Would she look at me the same way she had before?

That last thought unsettled him most of all. Takoda had seen *him*—not just the strategist, not just the warrior, but the man underneath it all. She had seen him injured, vulnerable, stripped of the control he clung to like armor. And despite it all, she had *stayed*.

But she hadn't seen everything.

She hadn't seen the darkness beneath the surface, the rage that coiled deep inside him, waiting for the wrong moment to break free.

Wrath. His sin. His curse.

If Takoda saw that side of me, if she ever witnessed what lay buried beneath my control… would she still want to see me then?

The thought dug its way under his skin, sharper than it should have been.

This was not about what *he* wanted though. This was about protecting her.

Seattle was dangerous right now. The Golden Dawn was moving, their presence growing stronger with each passing day. The weather patterns alone were evidence that something unnatural was brewing. If Takoda, Ariel, and Rain were walking into that… then *he* needed to be there.

That was the only reason he was going to see her.

Not because he had spent two months fighting the urge to pick up the phone. Not because her absence had left a hollow ache inside him that he had no idea how to fill.

This was about *duty*. It *had* to be.

He wasn't going to the hotel the moment she arrived. That would make it too obvious that he had been anticipating this moment. He would give them time to settle, to adjust.

And then, once night fell, he would go to her.

Takoda needed to understand what she was walking into. That was all. That was the only reason he would go to her.

Because Seattle was dangerous. Because the Golden Dawn was closing in. Because no matter how much it terrified him…

He *could not* stay away.

★★★

The car sped along the coastal road, Seattle's allure waiting on the horizon.

As they entered Pioneer Square, the city unfolded before them, its misty air thick with the scent of rain. Rain inhaled deeply, taking in the damp aroma of old brick and wet earth. Around them, cobblestone streets wove between historic buildings, their weathered facades softened by fog, giving the city a mysterious, almost haunting charm.

Ariel pulled up to the curb in front of the Embassy Suites, whistling as she took in the mix of modern architecture against the city's old-world backdrop. "Looks like the perfect blend of luxury with a hint of old Seattle magic," she remarked, nudging Takoda and Rain as they climbed out of the car.

Inside, the hotel lobby was bright and inviting, a stark contrast to the streets outside. Sleek furnishings, polished marble, and abstract artwork filled the space, creating a blend of contemporary design and warmth.

Rain turned in a slow circle, taking in the details. "Honestly, I half-expected cobwebs and candelabras. Guess we're not quite in a haunted mansion," she mused.

Ariel sighed dramatically. "Let's not rule anything out," she said, a teasing glint in her eyes. "Spooky season is just getting started."

The desk clerk handed them their room keys, and they made their way down the carpeted hallway toward the elevators. The moment felt *real now*—the trip, the city, the possibilities stretching ahead of them. Yet, as Takoda followed behind, suitcase rolling quietly behind her, she couldn't shake a strange sense of familiarity, as though she had been here before. *Or maybe*, she thought, *I was always meant to be here.*

She brushed the feeling aside as they reached their suite.

The room was just as modern as the lobby, with sleek furnishings, warm lighting, and floor-to-ceiling windows offering a rain-streaked view of the Seattle skyline. Rain immediately claimed the window seat, pressing her nose to the glass, lost in the city's glow.

"Oh, look at this!" Takoda announced, pulling a glossy hotel brochure from the nightstand. She flipped it open to a page featuring the indoor pool, its water sparkling under soft, ambient lighting.

Rain's eyes lit up, and Takoda smirked. "See? I *told* you we'd need our bathing suits."

Ariel peeked over her shoulder. "Perfect way to unwind after a day of spooky exploring," she agreed before tossing her bag onto the nearest chair. "But first, I say we hit up some Halloween-themed spots. This city's practically begging for it."

Rain nodded, excitement gleaming in her eyes. Takoda walked over to the window, watching the mist roll in over the rooftops below. The feeling from earlier returned—the pull of Seattle, the weight of the air, the whispers in the rain—it felt *like a city holding its breath, waiting for a moment to unfold.* She took a slow breath, pushing the thought away, and turned back to her friends with a smile.

"Alright," she said. "Let's see what Seattle has in store for us."

★★★

As dusk settled over the city, Japantown came to life under the glow of lanterns swaying overhead. The warm hum of voices filled the streets, mingling with the scent of fresh taiyaki and grilled yakitori. Boutique shop windows displayed delicate paper fans and intricate kanji calligraphy, while the soft flicker of candlelight danced over painted silk screens.

Takoda walked at an easy pace, letting herself sink into the atmosphere. Everything here felt vibrant, alive—like the city itself was breathing beneath the misty sky.

Her eyes landed on a display of silk kimonos outside a boutique. One, in particular, caught her attention—black, with red floral embroidery woven through the fabric. *Exactly what I imagined for my costume.* She could already picture it with smoky makeup, a lotus-and-dragon temporary tattoo curling along her shoulder.

A flicker of movement caught her eye—a group of kids running past, toy katanas in hand, laughing as they staged an impromptu battle. A faint smile touched her lips before an unexpected thought slipped into her mind.

Riichi.

Her heart gave an uneasy lurch at the thought of him—of his quiet intensity, his presence that seemed to command the space around him.

She had tried not to think about him, but it seemed like everything reminded her of him, especially now that they were in his city.

Did he even think of her at all?

The question popped into her mind, and she hated how much it *mattered.*

She shook her head, scolding herself inwardly. "He's just… someone I met once, stop thinking so much about him," she muttered.

And yet, the city wrapped around her with a strange ease, as if every step pulled her closer to an unspoken connection—threads of the past and present weaving together, drawing her toward a realization just beyond her grasp.

Ariel nudged her with a knowing grin. "Deep in thought over there?"

Takoda forced a laugh. "Just soaking in the sights."

Rain didn't say anything, but Takoda caught the glance she gave her—understanding, patience.

She let the conversation drift, let herself sink back into the soft lights of Japantown's lanterns and the hum of the city, but beneath it all, a quiet pull remained—a feeling she couldn't ignore, as if a truth buried deep within her was waiting to surface, no matter how much she tried to push it away.

The girls returned to the hotel, their laughter echoing down the hall as they recounted the evening's best moments.

As they passed through the lobby, the front desk clerk suddenly called out to them. "Excuse me—Miss Redcloud?"

Takoda blinked, turning at the sound of her name.

The clerk gestured toward the front counter. "You have a visitor."

Takoda's breath caught.

Her gaze followed where the clerk had nodded, her heart lurching before she even fully processed what she was seeing.

Riichi stood at the counter, back to them, his posture sharp and indecipherable.

A beat of silence passed. Then, as if steeling himself, he took a slow, steadying breath.

And then he turned.

The moment his gaze found hers, everything else—the lobby, the sounds, the world itself—seemed to still.

She could only stare as his dark eyes locked onto her, inscrutable yet resolute.

And then he spoke.

"Miss Takoda."

Chapter Four

A Step Forward

"Miss Takoda."

T akoda's breath caught, the words landing harder than she anticipated.

The way he said it—so formal, so careful—felt like a wall slamming between them. It had been months since he last used her name like that. Back then, his voice had softened, his words losing their distant edge. Now, he was stiff again, polished and composed, as if the time they had spent together had been nothing more than a brief, passing moment.

A dull ache settled in her chest, but she refused to let it show.

She lifted her chin slightly, gathering her composure. "Riichi."

He didn't react, not outwardly, but the way he held himself—too controlled, too still—gave her pause.

Ariel let out a low whistle, her voice breaking the thick silence. "Well. Guess we *did* run into him after all."

Takoda barely registered her words. Her attention was fixed on Riichi, her pulse a little too fast, her mind scrambling to process the fact that he was here, standing in front of her, looking at her like nothing had changed.

But everything had changed.

Two months. No calls. No messages. Just silence.

And now, suddenly, he was here, waiting for her.

Takoda inhaled slowly, forcing her voice to stay level. "What are you doing here?"

Riichi looked directly into her eyes, his face giving nothing away. "I need to speak with you." He hesitated. "Alone."

Her fingers curled slightly. *Alone.*

She faltered, doubt creeping in, twisting with the quiet sting of being ignored for so long.

Two months ago, she wouldn't have thought twice about following him anywhere. She would have trusted, without a doubt, that if he needed to talk, it was important. But now, she wasn't sure.

She had spent weeks convincing herself that whatever she had felt between them had only been in her head, that the way he had let her in—let her see *him*—had been a mistake he never intended to make. That had to be the reason he disappeared, right?

But if that were true, then why was he here now?

Aislinn's advice drifted through her mind.

"Get the answers you seek—even if it's just to understand your own heart."

She sighed, her eyes returning to Riichi.

He was still watching her.

And then she noticed it.

The way his throat moved—an almost imperceptible swallow, as if bracing himself.

Takoda's fingers tightened around the strap of her bag. *He's nervous.*

The thought unraveled a knot inside her.

Riichi never got nervous. He was always controlled, always certain, always knowing exactly what to say and when to say it. Yet here he was, waiting for her answer, not quite as composed as he wanted to be.

That—more than anything—made her decision for her.

She nodded. "Alright."

Ariel glanced between them, then let out a dramatic sigh. "Glad that's settled. Rain and I are going to the room, maybe check out that indoor pool."

Rain shot Takoda a quiet, reassuring look before following Ariel toward the elevator.

As their footsteps faded, Takoda turned back to Riichi. For a brief instant, neither of them spoke. The significance of his presence, the reality of him standing there after all this time, made her heart feel constricted.

Riichi adjusted his position, briefly scanning the lobby before returning his gaze to her. "May we go somewhere more comfortable?"

Takoda paused briefly before giving a nod.

Wordlessly, she led him through the lobby and out onto the veranda. The cool night air met her skin as she took a seat at one of the small outdoor tables. She could hear the distant hum of the city beyond the hotel's courtyard, the quiet rush of passing cars and the occasional murmur of other guests inside.

Riichi remained standing for a moment before sitting across from her, his posture as precise as ever.

Takoda rested her hands on the table, watching as Riichi took the seat opposite her. The space separating them felt denser than it should, thick with unspoken words and two months of silence pressing between them.

She willed her tone to remain calm. "Alright," she said, gentle yet assertive. "You have my attention. Start talking."

Riichi hesitated briefly, his posture as composed as ever, but something about him felt more rigid—like he was holding too much in, like he wasn't sure how to begin.

"If I've made you angry, I—"

"I'm not angry," Takoda interrupted, her fingers brushing absently over the wood grain beneath her palm. Her chest rose and fell in a slow, deliberate rhythm. She chose honesty over defensiveness. "I'm… hurt."

A brief shadow passed over Riichi's expression, but he didn't look away. Instead, he nodded once, acknowledging her words.

The sounds of the city drifted in and out—cars rolling over asphalt, the faint clang of a closing door, the echo of distant conversation. The world moved on around them, yet here, between them, everything remained suspended, waiting.

Then, finally, he spoke.

"I came to tell you that you, Ariel, and Rain should leave Seattle." His voice was level, but something beneath it felt personal, almost reluctant. "The Golden Dawn has been expanding their influence. They've been moving south, gaining power. I don't know their full plan yet, but I know a threat is coming. It's not safe for you here."

Takoda studied him, waiting for more, but it didn't come.

That was it? That was why he was here?

She searched his face, trying to understand, but the restraint in his features made it impossible to read him. "Is that really the only reason you came?"

His posture didn't shift, but his shoulders tightened almost imperceptibly. For a moment, she thought he wouldn't answer.

Then, quietly, he said, "No."

Takoda's breath stilled, her heartbeat, an uneven rhythm against her ribs.

She glanced down at her hands, her voice dropping to a mere whisper. "Then why did you come, Riichi?" She faltered, gathering the courage, forcing herself to ask the question she had been too afraid to say aloud. "I haven't heard from you in two months. You just... disappeared without a word. I thought you... did I imagine it?"

He didn't answer right away.

Instead, he sat still, his gaze holding hers, before finally shaking his head. "No. You didn't."

The confirmation should have made her feel better, but all it did was make the ache in her chest settle deeper.

She lifted her eyes back to him, trying to find something—anything—that would make this make sense. "Then why?" Her voice quivered a bit before she regained control. "Why didn't you call? Why did you just vanish?"

Riichi didn't look away.

For the first time since he sat down, he exhaled—not slow and measured, but like someone carrying something too heavy for too long. "Because I don't know what to do with it."

The words landed between them, simple but significant.

Takoda sat there, absorbing them, forcing herself to really *hear* what he was saying.

"I didn't know what to say," he admitted after a pause. His hands curled loosely together, his fingers pressing against one another as though grounding himself. "I've been working the same mission Eileen sent me on when I left San Francisco. That was my focus. That was what I knew. And for a while, I convinced myself that if I stayed focused, if I threw myself into the mission, into discipline, into duty—then the feelings would go away."

The silence stretched between them.

"But they didn't."

Takoda's throat tightened.

She allowed the silence to stretch on before softly saying, "So you ran."

A muscle in Riichi's jaw flexed, but he didn't argue.

"I didn't run from you," he said, quieter now. "I ran from *us,* from the feeling."

She pursed her lips, as the ache within her twisted into an uneasy feeling.

"I didn't know how to handle it," he admitted, his voice calm despite the enormity of the words. "And in trying to avoid it, I hurt you." His eyes held hers, open in a way she had never seen before. "I'm sorry, Takoda."

She swallowed against the lump in her throat.

She should say something. Anything.

But all she could do was sit there, looking at the man who had vanished without a word, now admitting that he had felt it too.

That he had run.

Not because she had imagined it. Not because it had meant nothing.

But because it had meant *too much.*

There was still one more question. "Do you really want me to leave Seattle?"

A muscle in his jaw flexed. He hesitated—just for a second.

Then, finally, his answer came.

"No."

Her knuckles brushed the edge of the table before she curled her hands into loose fists, unease threading through her like a taut string waiting to snap. The words sat heavy in the air, demanding space. She wet her lips, giving them a moment to settle.

No.

It wasn't just a word—it was a choice. A quiet admission that whatever had happened between them, whatever had made him run, wasn't something he wanted to erase.

She nodded, slow and thoughtful. "Then I'm staying."

Riichi didn't look surprised. If anything, he seemed to have expected that answer. His hand hovered near the table's edge for a brief moment before relaxing. "Even with the Golden Dawn here?"

"I wouldn't have left anyway." No doubt laced her words. "I can't live my life avoiding danger just because it exists."

Understanding deepened in his gaze, edged with what might have been admiration.

Takoda let a beat of silence pass before asking the question that had been forming in the back of her mind. "So, where do we go from here, Riichi?"

He didn't respond immediately. Instead, he studied her, his brow furrowing in the smallest way, as if searching for the right words.

"I don't know," he admitted. There was no hesitation in his voice this time, only honesty. "But I think… running wasn't a solution. It was an excuse." His gaze held hers, confident and sure. "I don't want to run anymore. But I don't know where to begin."

A small, thoughtful smile ghosted across Takoda's lips, barely there but genuine. "Maybe we start with breakfast."

Riichi blinked, just slightly caught off guard.

"And coffee," she added, lifting a brow. "At a café somewhere. Nothing complicated."

For the first time since she had sat down, the rigidity in his posture eased—not much, just a fraction, but it was enough. He gave a small nod. "That... sounds reasonable."

Takoda reached for her phone, unlocking the screen before sliding it toward him. "Here."

He paused before taking it, glancing at her in question.

"So, you don't have an excuse next time," she said simply.

A trace of something—amusement, maybe—touched his expression. He took the phone, his fingers moving over the screen as he typed. A moment later, a quiet vibration came from his pocket.

He had entered his number and sent himself a message. Now, they had no way to lose contact again.

He set the phone back down between them. "No more excuses. No more running."

Takoda held his gaze, the quiet promise settling between them.

His voice dropped slightly, softer now. "I really am sorry, Takoda. I never meant to hurt you, and I don't like that I did."

She believed him.

She had spent two months thinking she had imagined it all, wondering if the significance of that last night had been hers alone to carry. But now, looking at him, hearing the honesty in his voice, she knew—she hadn't been alone in it at all.

"I know," she said, her voice quiet but sure.

And this time, it didn't hurt so much.

Takoda pushed back her chair, "Come on. I'll walk you out."

Riichi nodded and stood, the quiet agreement between them turning into something more tangible now that they had made their plans for the morning.

There was no faltering, no trace of doubt—just an unspoken agreement that this was a step forward, even if neither of them knew exactly where it would lead.

They walked together through the hotel, moving past the subdued murmur of late-night conversation from the lounge, their steps unhurried. Neither of them spoke, but for once, the silence didn't feel heavy.

As they reached the entrance, Riichi turned to her, his expression thoughtful. He seemed to consider his words before speaking. "I'll see you in the morning."

Takoda nodded. "Yeah."

A beat passed, and just for a breath, it felt like he might say something more, but instead, he simply inclined his head, offering her a quiet sense of finality. Then, without another word, he stepped outside, disappearing into the night.

Takoda watched the doors slide shut behind him before letting out a slow breath.

This time, watching him walk away didn't hurt.

Turning on her heel, she made her way to the elevator and up to her hotel room, where she knew Ariel and Rain would be waiting.

The instant Takoda stepped inside, Ariel and Rain were already waiting, their eyes locking onto her like two detectives ready to interrogate a witness.

"You good?" Rain asked, scanning her expression as if searching for any sign of distress.

A nod was all Takoda managed before Ariel flopped dramatically onto the bed. "Okay, good, because we had already made plans to hunt Riichi down if you came back crying."

A quiet laugh escaped as she shook her head. "I appreciate the backup."

Ariel propped herself up on her elbows, eyes glinting with curiosity. "Are you gonna spill, or do we have to start guessing?"

Rain folded her arms. "We're obviously going to guess regardless."

Rather than argue, Takoda crossed the room and sank into the chair near the window. "He came to tell us to leave Seattle."

Both Ariel and Rain frowned.

Rain's brow furrowed. "Because he doesn't want you here?"

Her stomach twisted slightly at the assumption. "No. He told me to leave because of the Golden Dawn."

Some of the tension in Rain's shoulders eased. "Oh."

Ariel sat up, her attention sharpening. "What did he say about them?"

Stretching her legs out in front of her, Takoda leaned back. "He said their influence is growing. They're moving south, gaining power. He doesn't know their full plan yet, but he's sure it isn't safe."

A scoff echoed from the bed. "Pfft. Rowan tried to pull the same thing on me at the travel center earlier," Ariel said, waving a dismissive hand. "Told me we should turn around, that it was too dangerous." A smirk tugged at her lips. "I told him no."

Takoda gave a knowing nod. "I told Riichi the same thing."

"Of course you did," Ariel said, flashing an approving grin.

Rain let out a thoughtful sigh, leaning against the headboard. "Not exactly comforting news, but at least he's looking out for you."

The words settled in the room for a minute before Takoda traced a loose thread on the seam of her jeans. "That's not all we talked about."

Both heads snapped toward her, unrestrained curiosity flashing in their eyes.

"Oh?" Ariel leaned forward. "Do tell."

A beat passed before Takoda bit the inside of her cheek and finally said it. "He told me that he still has feelings for me... but he doesn't know how to deal with them."

The reaction was instant.

Ariel and Rain squealed in unison, the energy in the room changing from tense to electric in an instant.

"I *knew* it!" Ariel declared, punching the air.

"I *told* you," Rain chimed in, practically beaming.

Lifting a hand, Takoda tried to calm their enthusiasm. "We're taking things slow. I made plans to have breakfast with him in the morning."

Rain clapped her hands together. "That's a good start."

Ariel nodded sagely. "Breakfast is an excellent first step. No pressure, no drama, just food. Smart move."

A quiet laugh slipped past Takoda's lips. "Glad you approve."

"Now, the real question," Ariel said, eyes gleaming mischievously. "What's the plan for breakfast? What's the *vibe*? What's the *strategy*?"

An eyebrow arched in response. "Strategy?"

Rain nodded, completely serious. "Obviously. Do you go for easy conversation? Deep, meaningful eye contact? Test the waters with light teasing? Or"—she pointed at Ariel—"do you go with *her* usual method?"

Ariel grinned. "Shameless flirting."

Pressing her fingertips to her temples, Takoda exhaled. "You two are unbelievable."

Ariel smirked. "Listen, we just want to make sure you're prepared. The man *did* admit he didn't know how to handle his feelings. That *screams* unresolved tension."

Rain tilted her head. "She's not wrong."

Takoda let out a breath—not quite a sigh, not quite a laugh. "I'm just going to have breakfast and see what happens."

Ariel and Rain exchanged a knowing look.

"Uh-huh," Ariel said, unconvinced.

Rain grinned. "Just remember, whatever happens, we expect *full* details when you get back."

Rolling her eyes, Takoda shook her head, but the small smile lingering on her lips betrayed her amusement.

Ariel stretched out on the bed, hands behind her head, eyes flashing between Rain and Takoda. "Alright, so we've got Takoda going to breakfast with Riichi in the morning." She smirked, clearly enjoying the phrasing. "What do *we* want to do after that? Because, ladies, let's not forget—we came to Seattle to get our *Halloween on*."

Rain perked up instantly. "Seattle Underground."

Takoda nodded. "And Pike Place Market."

Ariel sat up, grinning. "Yes! That's the energy I need. We're diving headfirst into spooky season—history, hauntings, and overpriced fall-themed drinks."

Rain laughed as she leaned back against the pillows. "I mean, I do want to see the Underground. It's got hidden passageways, ghost stories, and literal buried history. We can't *not* go."

Ariel pointed at her. "Exactly! The whole city-under-a-city thing is fascinating. When Seattle burned down, they just… built over it. Can you imagine? Whole streets, abandoned buildings, forgotten tunnels—just left behind while everyone moved on like nothing happened."

Takoda tilted her head thoughtfully as she moved to sit on the bed with the other girls. "I wonder how much of it still feels alive down there."

Ariel's grin widened. "*That's* the spirit! I love it."

Rain nudged Takoda's foot with her own. "You know, I bet there's plenty of residual energy underground. Maybe we'll sense something."

Ariel's eyes lit up. "Ooooh, maybe Takoda will get a ghostly vision, and we'll finally confirm she's secretly psychic."

Takoda laughed. "I'm not psychic."

Ariel shrugged. "That's exactly what someone who is psychic would say."

Rain snorted into her drink before sitting up. "Alright, so Underground tour first. Then Pike Place?"

"Yes!" Ariel flopped back against the pillows. "I'm hoping they have some cute Halloween stuff out. We should check for accessories for our costumes."

Takoda smiled at the idea. "They probably will. I wouldn't mind finding a few extra pieces."

Rain's face lit up. "Ooh, and quirky souvenirs! I love getting random stuff from places like that."

Ariel tapped her chin, already brainstorming. "I want something either totally adorable or ridiculously haunted. No in-between."

Rain laughed. "So, either a pumpkin candle or a cursed doll?"

"Exactly."

Takoda chuckled, shaking her head. The idea of wandering through the crowded market, sipping something warm, surrounded by the scent of roasted nuts and fresh flowers, felt like the perfect way to spend the day.

Ariel drummed her fingers on the blanket, suddenly shifting gears. "Hey, Takoda, if you want, you could always invite Riichi to come with us when you see him at breakfast."

She barely paused before shaking her head. "Nah."

Ariel raised a brow, intrigued. "Oh?"

"This trip is for *us*." Takoda gestured between the three of them. "Besides, Riichi's still on Eileen's last mission, keeping an eye on the Golden Dawn. He'll probably be busy with that since they're getting closer to Seattle."

A slow smile spread across Ariel's face. "Girl Power. I like it."

Rain nodded. "Agreed. This is a *girls' trip*. Let the Fallen handle their Fallen business. We've got hauntings to explore."

Ariel clapped her hands together. "Okay, then it's settled. We'll meet up after Takoda's breakfast date and dive into some spooky Seattle history."

Takoda rolled her eyes at the word *date* but didn't bother correcting her.

Rain stretched, already looking content just thinking about the next day. "This is going to be fun."

Ariel yawned and pointed at them both. "Alright, we're going to bed before we ruin Takoda's big breakfast date by staying up too late. If she oversleeps, I *will* personally drag her out of bed."

Takoda shook her head with a laugh. "Noted."

Rain grinned. "Goodnight, future *psychic ghost whisperer*."

Takoda threw a pillow at her, laughing as she settled into bed. For the first time in a long time, she actually looked forward to the morning.

Chapter Five

Secrets in Bloom

The quiet noises of the hotel room surrounded Takoda as she blinked awake, the heaviness of sleep still clinging to her limbs. The air was cool, the subtle aroma of fresh linens mixing with the remnants of the citrus-scented shampoo Ariel had used the night before. The steady rhythm of Rain's breathing came from the other bed, undisturbed by the first hints of morning.

Takoda turned onto her side, her eyes landing on the sliver of sky visible through the gap in the curtains. A muted gray, still tucked in the quiet stillness of dawn. She inhaled deeply, letting the cool air calm her mind.

Last night's conversation with Riichi lingered in her mind, sharper now that she had space to fully process it.

He hadn't denied their connection. Hadn't brushed it off or deflected.

"I ran from us, from the feeling."

The confession had settled like a stone in her chest—heavy, undeniable. She hadn't imagined what happened between them in San Francisco. He had felt it, too. He just hadn't been ready to face it.

And yet, here he was.

Takoda exhaled slowly and ran a hand through her hair. No matter how she turned it over, the truth stayed the same. He'd come back. That had to mean something.

Pushing back the covers, she sat up, stretching the stiffness from her shoulders before sliding her feet to the floor. Rain barely moved. Ariel, as usual, was sprawled sideways across her bed, one arm dangling like she'd lost a fight with gravity.

Takoda shook her head, biting back a smile, and grabbed her toiletry bag before slipping into the bathroom.

The shower was quick. Hot water cleared away the last fog of sleep, but her thoughts kept drifting.

They'd agreed to breakfast—but never actually picked a time. A small detail, but it echoed so much of what lay between them. Always moving in sync, but never quite saying the things that mattered.

Tugging her hoodie into place, she reached for her phone and hesitated a second before typing.

Takoda: *I guess we're bad at this whole planning thing. We never actually set a time for breakfast.*

She hit send, ignoring the small flutter of nerves that tightened in her chest.

By the time she finished lacing up her boots, her phone buzzed.

Riichi: *Agreed. What time works for you?*

She smirked slightly. So very him. Straight to the point.

Takoda: *I'm almost ready. How soon can you be here?*

His reply came back fast.

Riichi: *Fifteen minutes.*

She let out a slow breath and locked her screen.

Fifteen minutes. She could handle that.

She scribbled a quick note for Rain and Ariel, left it on the nightstand, and capped the pen.

Left for breakfast with Riichi. I'll bring back coffee.

She glanced once more at the room—Ariel still flopped sideways across the bed, Rain buried under a blanket mountain—and then grabbed her jacket and stepped into the hall.

The elevator ride to the lobby was silent.

She leaned against the wall, her reflection in the polished doors barely moving.

He hadn't just come back. He was choosing to stay.

And somehow, that made all the difference.

When she stepped into the lobby, she scanned the open seating area, spotting a pair of older business travelers near the fireplace and a family wrangling their toddler near the entrance. No sign of Riichi yet.

Takoda adjusted her stance and checked the time. He still had a few minutes before his self-imposed deadline. She tucked her hands into the front pocket of her hoodie, inhaling the faint scent of coffee from the hotel café.

The distant sound of the sliding entrance doors caught her attention. She turned just as Riichi walked inside, his steps as measured and composed as always. Even in something as simple as dark jeans and his signature trench coat, he had the kind of presence that drew notice—not by demanding attention, but by the sheer quiet control he carried himself with.

She stared at the outline of his coat for just a moment more than needed. He always hid his katana beneath his coat. She had seen him do it before.

Is he carrying the katana I gave him in San Francisco?

His eyes landed on her immediately, and she caught the briefest flash of joy in his expression before his usual restraint settled in.

"Miss Takoda."

The formality made her laugh, the sound escaping before she could stop it. She shook her head, amused. "Riichi, I think we're past that."

His brow lifted, and for a half-second, it seemed like he might argue the point. Then, with a small, almost imperceptible nod, he corrected himself. "Takoda."

She smiled in approval. "Much better."

If he had an opinion on the matter, he didn't voice it. Instead, he gestured toward the door. "Shall we?"

"Yeah. It's not far, right?"

"Less than ten minutes."

They stepped out into the cool morning air, the city just beginning to shake off the last traces of dawn. The walk to the café was awkward but not entirely uncomfortable. There was still tension filling the gaps—uncertainties neither of them had figured out how to navigate—but the silence wasn't heavy like it had been the night before.

The café was warm, the scent of fresh coffee and baked goods wrapping around them as they stepped inside. A few customers sat scattered at the small wooden tables, some lost in their laptops, others engaged in low murmured conversations.

Takoda followed Riichi to the counter, glancing at the menu even though she already knew what she wanted.

She placed her order—a bagel with cream cheese and a latte—before turning her attention to the tray the barista set in front of Riichi.

A plate of fresh fruit and a croissant.

Her stomach flipped briefly at the familiarity.

That's the same breakfast I used to make for him back in San Francisco.

She didn't comment on it, but something about the detail made the morning feel… substantial. Like she had stepped into something significant without meaning to.

They settled at a small table by the window, the quiet sounds of the café filling the distance dividing them.

For a few minutes, they sat in silence. Takoda focused on spreading cream cheese across her bagel, and Riichi stirred his coffee with slow, deliberate motions.

Eventually, she broke the silence. "So… any recommendations? You've lived in Seattle for a while."

Riichi glanced up, considering. "For what, exactly?"

She took a sip of her coffee. "For things to do."

A pause. Then, as if deciding something, he set down his mug. "There's an exhibit at the Asian Art Museum on Japanese history and samurai culture. You may find it meaningful. I could take you to it."

A flicker of surprise ran through her. *He wants to take me to an art museum?*

She tilted her head, intrigued. "I think I'd like that. When would you want to go?"

"Three o'clock tomorrow," he said, no indecision.

Takoda nodded, a small smile tugging at her lips. "That works. Today, I'm exploring the city with Rain and Ariel—Seattle Underground and Pike Place Market."

Riichi's brow lifted, as if assessing the plan. "Pike Place Market?"

She grinned. "Yep. Ariel's on a mission to find something either completely adorable or ridiculously haunted. No in-between."

A barely-there hint of amusement crossed Riichi's expression. "That sounds… fitting."

Takoda smirked. "It really is."

The conversation carried on from there, the awkward edges smoothing out as they ate. He still wasn't completely at ease, but he had stopped *overthinking* his words, and that was a start.

When Takoda finished her coffee, she sighed. "Alright, I need to grab some to-go cups for Rain and Ariel before I head back."

Riichi set down his coffee mug. "I'll walk you."

She blinked, caught off guard. "You don't have to do that. I can manage on my own."

A faint pause, the briefest sign of hesitation in his expression. He didn't like the idea—she could tell. But he also wasn't going to argue.

"If you insist," he said finally, his tone carefully neutral.

Takoda smirked. "I do." Then, standing, she gestured toward the door. "But first, I'll walk you out."

An almost imperceptible flash of disappointment passed through his gaze before he inclined his head in agreement. "Very well."

As they stepped out of the café, ready to go their separate ways, Riichi's gaze moved to the opposite side of the street. A figure lurked there, watching him with cold, unblinking intent. Recognition flickered in the man's eyes—a Golden Dawn operative.

Riichi narrowed his eyes, a hint of familiarity passing between them, and the man's expression changed to alarm.

Before Takoda could react, the figure raised a hand, summoning a sudden burst of energy. The air crackled as Riichi moved instinctively, pulling her to his side, dodging just as the blast tore past them and struck the wall behind.

Fury surged through him, sharp and consuming. The sight of Takoda nearly caught in the blast shattered his usual restraint. Without sparing her a glance, he dropped his voice to a low, clipped command. "Stay here."

The words left no room for argument, and then he was gone, charging down the street in pursuit.

Takoda didn't stay. She darted after him, weaving through narrow streets, her eyes locked on his back as he moved like a shadow ahead of her. Her pulse hammered in her ears as she finally caught up—only to see him stop at the end of a dead-end alley, fists clenched, eyes fixed on a wall where the attacker had clearly scaled and escaped.

She slowed, breathless, approaching carefully.

Riichi turned sharply, fury flashing across his face. "I told you to stay where you were!" he snapped, his voice raw, frustration radiating from every tense line of his body.

She flinched at his tone but didn't back down. Her gaze stayed on him, watching the way he paced, sharp and agitated. The storm beneath his surface had broken through, and she'd never seen him this shaken. His control—always so precise—was gone.

"Riichi," she said softly, stepping closer. "Look at me. Talk to me."

But he didn't stop. His breath came too fast, fists flexing and releasing at his sides, the anger in him refusing to settle. She took a slow breath, reached out, and caught his arm.

The instant her fingers touched his skin, a faint orange glow flared around her hand. She gasped—energy rushed through her, alive and electric, pulsing with every beat of her heart. It wasn't just light. It *moved*. It *felt*.

She staggered slightly, overwhelmed by the wave of emotion pouring through her—his anger, raw and scalding, but deeper than that was fear. And under all of it, threaded between the cracks, was desire. She didn't understand how she knew—but she did. Instinctively.

I can feel what he's feeling. I can shift it. Change it.

"You can't keep this bottled up," she said, her voice steady but edged with urgency. She focused, grounding herself. "You have to let go."

He didn't seem to hear her. His chest rose and fell with shallow breaths, muscles tight beneath her touch, mind tangled in the chaos.

She made a decision.

"Riichi, kiss me."

His head snapped toward her, eyes wide. "What?"

"Kiss me," she repeated, firmer this time.

His breathing hitched. She felt the hesitation in him—then the shift. His restraint wavered. She pushed his fury lower, focusing on the connection between them, turning it into the desire that had sparked between them moments ago.

He felt it. She saw the moment he gave in.

Without another word, Riichi pulled her into him, crashing his mouth against hers. The kiss was fierce and unrelenting. A release. She tasted all of it—his frustration, his fear, the unspoken things buried under his silence.

His hands gripped her waist, grounding himself in her. Each second deepened the kiss, his need pouring into every touch, every stolen breath. And Takoda didn't hesitate. She kissed him back, just as fiercely, her hands tangled in his hair, holding him close as the heat surged between them.

What she hadn't expected was the way his emotions would pass through her—raw and unfiltered. Every shift she pulled from him stirred something in her, too. She didn't just sense it. She *felt* it. Matched it.

The kiss deepened. Everything blurred—his touch, her breath, the way their bodies responded without thought. The more he released, the stronger the pull between them grew. Each kiss more desperate. Every heartbeat louder.

His hands slid over her hips, anchoring himself to her like she was the only thing keeping him from slipping away. And it worked. She felt the difference. The fire in him dimming, steadying. The storm inside him finally breaking.

Then, just as quickly as it started—he stopped.

Riichi ripped himself away, breathing hard, guilt crashing over him like a wave. His hands curled into fists again, his shoulders tight with shame.

"I'm sorry," he said. "That wasn't right. I shouldn't have—"

Takoda didn't let him finish.

She grabbed his face, firm but gentle, and forced him to meet her eyes.

"No," she said, her voice clear. "You don't get to apologize. I told you to. I wanted you to. You have nothing to apologize for. Alright?"

He hesitated. His jaw clenched, and his eyes searched hers. But there was no space to argue. Slowly, the tension in his frame loosened, guilt slipping away.

"You good now?" she asked, letting her hand fall.

He nodded. "Yes," he murmured, his breath still catching. His gaze dropped again.

A silence settled between them—heavy, charged. Long enough to feel like it might crack if either of them spoke.

Finally, Takoda broke the silence with a small, playful smile. "So… does this cancel our plans for tomorrow?"

He looked up, surprise flickering in his eyes. "You… still want to go?"

Her gaze held steady, certain. "I do. Unless you'd rather cancel?"

He studied her face, a trace of wonder crossing his expression as if he were trying to understand her. "No," he said finally, his voice softer, "not unless you want to."

"Good," she replied, her tone light and easy, as though her heart hadn't just skipped at his words. "I don't want to cancel."

She gave him one last look, checking that he was truly alright, then added with a hint of amusement, "I should go grab those coffees for Rain and Ariel," breaking the tension with a knowing smile.

Riichi didn't smile back. His expression remained unreadable for a moment, then he exhaled, steady but firm.

"I'm walking you back."

She arched a brow. "Riichi—"

"No arguments." His tone was even, but the resolve behind it was absolute. "After what just happened, I won't let you walk alone."

She considered pushing back, just for the sake of it, but one glance at him told her it was useless. She sighed, giving in with a small shrug. "Alright. But first, coffee."

They returned to the café, where the morning rush had died down, leaving only a few lingering customers. Takoda ordered a caramel macchiato for Rain and a black coffee for Ariel while Riichi stood beside her, arms crossed, scanning the room like a sentry.

When the drinks were ready, she lifted the tray and turned to him with a smirk. "Want to carry one?"

Riichi barely spared her a glance. "No."

She huffed, amused, adjusting her grip on the cup tray. "Fine, bodyguard mode it is."

The walk back to the hotel was subdued, the earlier tension no longer pressing, yet an implicit feeling still a palpable strain. Neither of them acknowledged it, but it was there—beneath the silence, beneath the casual rhythm of their steps.

When they reached the entrance, Takoda turned toward him, balancing the tray in one hand. "Thanks for walking me—"

Riichi's fingers brushed against her wrist, stopping her mid-step.

Before she could react, he drew her back gently, guiding her to lean against one of the smooth stone pillars near the entrance. The movement wasn't forceful, but there was deliberation in the way he placed her there, as if he needed her to stay just a little longer.

Takoda arched a brow. "Are you trying to stall?" she teased, a playful lilt in her voice.

He didn't answer right away. Instead, he studied her, the city's muted hum filling the void that stretched out.

A trace of nerves crept up her spine. "I was just kidding," she added lightly. "You don't—"

"I think a part of me *is* stalling you," Riichi interrupted, his voice quieter now, measured.

Takoda blinked, her amusement fading. "Why?"

Riichi exhaled through his nose, gaze moving toward the street before coming back to hers. "I need you to promise me something."

Her stomach tightened. "Promise what?"

"When you're out today," he said, his voice firm but not overbearing, "you, Rain, and Ariel do not separate. Not even for a second."

The intensity in his expression made her pulse jump. "Riichi—"

"Promise me." His tone wasn't demanding, but there was no room for negotiation. "The Golden Dawn is still out there. I need to know you're safe."

She let out a slow breath, absorbing the magnitude of his concern. He wasn't being overprotective just for the sake of it. He had seen firsthand how close things had come this morning.

"I promise," she said softly.

A hint of relief passed across his features, but he wasn't done. "And if anything happens—if you even suspect something—you call me. Immediately."

Takoda's lips twitched. "You want me to call my very intimidating, katana-wielding backup if I run into trouble? Noted."

He didn't react to her teasing, and the lightness in her expression dimmed. She reached out, fingers grazing the edge of his sleeve.

"I mean it," she told him. "I'll call."

The last of his tension seemed to unravel at her words, but neither of them moved. The air around them altered, charged with silent emotions neither had voiced aloud.

Riichi's gaze stayed on her face, searching, as if trying to come to a decision. His eyes traced hers, dipped briefly to her lips, then back again.

And then—he made his choice.

His fingers lifted, brushing against the curve of her jaw with surprising gentleness, and before she could process the movement, his lips found hers.

Takoda's breath caught, the warmth of the kiss different from the one in the alley. This wasn't frantic or fueled by raw emotion—this was intentional, slow, a quiet claiming.

She leaned into him, her free hand resting lightly against his chest, feeling the steady thrum of his heartbeat. He kissed her as if he had all the time in the world, savoring the moment rather than rushing through it.

Her fingers curled into the fabric of his coat, pulling him closer. He responded in kind, his hands pressing against her waist, firm but unhurried, as though memorizing the shape of her beneath his palms.

Takoda barely noticed the world around them. The passersby, the city sounds, the crisp morning air—all of it faded into irrelevance.

The only thing that existed was him.

Behind them, Ariel and Rain stepped out of the hotel, then suddenly Ariel nudged Rain with her elbow, pointing in the direction of Riichi and Takoda as they kissed. Quickly, Ariel's hand shot out shoving Rain back through the entrance, a wide grin on her face.

And then, Riichi pulled away, just enough for their foreheads to nearly touch, his breath mingling with hers in the air surrounding them.

He didn't speak right away. Neither did she.

Finally, his hand slipped away from her waist, though his touch lingered for a fraction longer than necessary. "I'll call you tomorrow about the museum."

Takoda nodded, voice steady despite the way her heart still raced. "Okay."

She turned, heading toward the hotel doors, still feeling the warmth of his lips against hers.

As she stepped inside, Ariel and Rain were pretending to just be descending the stairs from the second-floor suites.

Ariel flashed her an innocent smile. "Oh hey, you're back."

Rain, ever more subtle, took the macchiato from the tray and lifted it in thanks. "Appreciate the coffee."

Takoda squinted at them.

Something about their casual entrance seemed too well-timed.

Then she caught the way Ariel bit her lip, barely containing a grin—and it hit her.

They had seen everything.

And Ariel was going to be insufferable.

"Well?" Ariel drawled, leaning against the counter with a slow grin. "How was your breakfast *date*?"

Takoda rolled her eyes, handing her the other coffee. "Oh, don't even try to play dumb. I know you two saw me kissing him."

Ariel clutched her chest in mock offense. "Us? Spying? I would *never*."

Rain took a long sip of her macchiato, offering nothing but an arched brow.

Takoda folded her arms. "So, you just *happened* to be coming downstairs the moment I walked in?"

Ariel shrugged, completely unapologetic. "Timing is everything."

Rain finally chimed in, her tone casual. "So, *was* it a date?"

Takoda hesitated for half a second as she led them to the lounge seating area. "No," she said, "it was just breakfast."

Ariel gasped dramatically. "I *saw* that kiss, Takoda. That was not a 'just breakfast' kiss."

Takoda groaned, sinking onto the couch. "Can we *not* do this right now?"

"Absolutely not." Ariel plopped down beside her, eager. "Spill."

Takoda sighed, knowing there was no way out. "Fine. We had breakfast. It was…" she searched for the right word, "*nice*."

Ariel gave her a flat look. "That is the *worst* description of romantic tension I have ever heard."

Takoda laughed, shaking her head. "It *was* nice! We talked. He invited me to the Asian Art Museum tomorrow. And *yes*, I kissed him—well, he kissed me."

Ariel smirked. "*Long*."

Takoda ignored her. "Anyway, the only other thing worth mentioning is that I promised Riichi we'd stick together today—*no separating*, not even for a second."

Rain nodded, setting her coffee down. "Makes sense. Rowan and Riichi both said the Golden Dawn was headed to Seattle."

Takoda glanced toward the large windows overlooking the city. Sunlight poured in far too warm for October, casting an unusual glow across the skyline. "The weather's off," she muttered.

Ariel followed her gaze and frowned. "Yeah, it is weirdly warm."

Locals outside moved about in short sleeves, some pausing to comment on the heat-wave. The air felt thick, heavy in a way that wasn't just Seattle's usual humidity.

"The Golden Dawn must be close," Rain murmured. "They've already started manipulating the weather here."

Ariel exhaled, shaking off the unease. "Well, nothing we can do about it now. We *do* still have plans, right?"

Takoda nodded. "Seattle Underground and Pike Place Market."

Ariel clapped her hands. "Then let's go explore some haunted tunnels, shall we?"

★★★

The entrance to Seattle's historic Underground was marked by a set of narrow steps leading beneath the city streets. Their guide led them down into the dimly lit tunnels, where old storefronts and passageways lay untouched beneath layers of dust and history. The air was thick with age, a mix of damp wood and old stone, a ghostly reminder of the city buried beneath the city.

As their footsteps echoed against the uneven floors, the guide recounted the history of fires, floods, and reconstruction, his voice bouncing eerily off the stone walls. Ariel whispered excitedly about ghosts, while Rain studied the glass sidewalk windows above them, where slivers of daylight barely trickled through.

Takoda tried to focus on their surroundings, but her mind kept pulling her back to the way Riichi had looked at her before he kissed her. The warmth of his hands on her waist. The certainty in the way he held her.

She swallowed, pushing the thought away.

This wasn't the time to be distracted by the way her heart still beat too fast whenever she thought about him.

The tunnels stretched into a maze of forgotten streets, remnants of a city long left behind. The flickering bulbs overhead barely illuminated the narrow passageways, their dim glow casting long, exaggerated shadows along the walls.

Takoda's fingers brushed over her wrist absently.

She hadn't told Ariel and Rain about what happened in the alleyway—the first kiss, the chase, the strange power that had flared to life at her fingertips. Not because she didn't trust them, but because… she wasn't sure what to say.

She wasn't even sure what had happened.

Until she knew for certain, she'd keep it to herself.

As they continued through the underground, a faint unease prickled at the edges of her awareness. It wasn't fear, exactly—just an odd sense of something being slightly off.

Should she call Riichi?

The thought struck her out of nowhere, tightening her grip on her phone. Would he even be able to do anything from where he was? Or would she just be worrying over nothing?

She hesitated, then shook it off. There was no real danger.

Still, she knew Riichi wouldn't be able to relax until he heard from her.

The moment they stepped outside and the blinding sunlight hit them, Takoda reached for her phone. She typed out a quick message.

Finished the Seattle Underground tour. Everything's fine. Nothing unusual.

She sent it before she could second-guess herself.

At least this way, Riichi wouldn't be left wondering.

As she slipped her phone back into her pocket, the heat pressed down on them, thick and stifling.

Rain slipped off her jacket, shaking her head. "Feels more like July than October."

Ariel tucked her coat under her arm, frowning. "I know, right? You'd think we'd be freezing by now."

Locals passing by were commenting on the heatwave, some pulling at their collars, others muttering about how unusual it was for this time of year.

Takoda glanced toward her friends, they could all feel the flash of unease. They knew what this meant.

The Golden Dawn was getting closer.

Ariel clapped her hands together, cutting through the tension. "Alright, enough with the doom-and-gloom. We're going to Pike Place Market, we're going to eat something amazing, and we are going to enjoy ourselves."

The festive atmosphere of Pike Place Market offered an odd contrast to the sweltering summer heat.

Pumpkins sat stacked in decorative piles, dried-leaf wreaths hung from vendor stalls, and the scents of cinnamon, cloves, and cider drifted through the air.

Despite the warmth, the lively energy of the market had its effect. The tension from earlier began to ease as they moved through the crowded walkways, letting the vibrant energy pull them back into the moment.

Ariel stopped abruptly, eyes lighting up at a stall filled with handcrafted fall decorations. "Okay, *we all* have to get something to remember today."

Rain lifted a skeptical brow. "That's your excuse for buying random things, isn't it?"

Ariel grinned. "Obviously. But this time it applies to *all of us.*"

Takoda chuckled, scanning the nearby booths.

She browsed through one vendor's display of hand-carved wooden charms, drawn to the delicate craftsmanship. Her fingers traced over the smooth grain of one in particular, its intricate pattern catching her attention.

Without overthinking it, she bought it.

It was only after buying it that she realized why it felt so meaningful—it reminded her of Riichi more than anything in Seattle. As she slipped the charm into her pocket, she let herself relax into the easy rhythm of the market, following her friends as they drifted among the stalls, their laughter mingling with the buzz of the crowd.

★★★

After Riichi had walked Takoda back to her hotel, he returned to the alley where the Golden Dawn operative had vanished, his thoughts narrowing into sharp, deliberate focus. He didn't expect to find the man still lurking—anyone working for the Golden Dawn knew better than to remain in one place for too long.

But there were always traces.

His gaze swept the alley, pausing on the weathered bricks and faint scuff marks, dissecting the scene with a trained eye. *Why had the operative been here?* What had drawn him to this particular location?

Yet, despite his best efforts, his mind refused to stay entirely on task.

Takoda.

She surfaced in his thoughts uninvited, unshakable.

The breakfast itself had been… pleasant. More than pleasant. She had teased him about his formality, disarmed him without even trying. The easy back-and-forth, the way she had smiled at him—it had felt like something dangerous in its simplicity.

And then, there had been the kisses.

His steps slowed as the memories flashed behind his eyes.

The first had been a reckless lapse in control. Not calculated, not planned. He hadn't even thought. One moment, his anger had been burning beneath his skin, and the next—

The moment her voice cut through the haze, the moment her fingers curled against his arm, something inside him had snapped. He had turned, barely seeing her, only feeling the pull—the overwhelming need to claim her, to ground himself in something real.

That kiss had been heat, raw and consuming, like trying to quench a fire with gasoline.

And it had left him shaken.

Riichi didn't lose control. Ever.

His hands curled into fists at his sides before he forcibly relaxed them. *Why had it happened like that?* Why had he let himself be swept up in something so unchecked?

Then there was the second kiss.

That one had been… different.

Not heat, but warmth. Not desperate, but intentional.

Steady.

He had known exactly what he was doing when he kissed her outside the hotel. He had taken his time, allowed himself to memorize the feel of her, the way she responded, the way she leaned into him like she wanted more.

The fire was still there—but this time, he had been the one in control.

He exhaled sharply, pushing the thoughts aside. *Now wasn't the time for this.*

With a slow breath, he reset his focus, stepping toward the wall the operative had scaled. *Answers first. Everything else could wait.*

The early morning light had shifted into midday, the sun casting sharp angles through the alleyways. Seattle's unnatural warmth clung to the streets, but Riichi barely noticed. His attention remained fixed on the subtle hints left behind—a scuffed rock, a faint footprint in the dust, the smallest shift in the grime on the pavement.

The Golden Dawn operative had been careful.

But not careful enough.

The trail led him into an older, neglected part of the city, where abandoned buildings and boarded-up windows made for the perfect hiding places. Riichi moved with quiet precision, his senses tuned for anything that felt out of place.

And then—he saw it.

Near the edge of an alley, a thin line of displaced dirt led to a narrow doorway, half-hidden beneath a tattered awning. Barely noticeable. But noticeable enough.

As he approached, he felt it—a faint hum of energy lingering in the air.

The operative had been here. Recently.

But he wasn't here now.

Riichi scanned the buildings one last time, committing every detail to memory. He'd need backup to investigate further—possibly Rowan. For now, he had confirmation that the Golden Dawn was actively operating in Seattle.

Just as he turned to leave, his phone vibrated in his coat pocket.

He pulled it out, Takoda's name flashing on the screen. A text.

Finished the Seattle Underground tour. Everything's fine. Nothing unusual.

A slow breath slipped out without him realizing.

She was safe.

He didn't text back—there was nothing to say. But he was glad for the message. It gave him peace of mind.

Sliding his phone back into his pocket, Riichi turned and started toward his antique shop, his thoughts already piecing together his next steps.

Chapter Six
A Night Unfolding

A soft hush lingered in their room at the Embassy Suites in Pioneer Square, the air still thick with early morning quiet. The city was waking—distant footsteps and the hum of passing cars drifted through the walls. Takoda stirred first, stretching beneath the heavy comforter before rolling onto her side. Across the room, Rain remained curled up, her red hair a vivid contrast against the white pillowcase, while Ariel lay sprawled out, one arm flung dramatically over her eyes like she was shielding herself from a day she wasn't ready to face. A groggy groan escaped her as she shifted. "Five more minutes," she muttered.

Takoda smirked, pushing herself upright. "You said that fifteen minutes ago."

Ariel peeked from under her arm. "Did I?" With a dramatic sigh, she threw the blankets off and sat up, her hair a wild mess. "Alright, I'm up. Where's the coffee?"

Rain stirred at the commotion, blinking as she stretched her arms overhead. "Good morning," she said, voice still soft with sleep. "Are we still going shopping?"

"Of course we are!" Ariel shot up, suddenly full of energy. "We need to get Takoda the perfect outfit for her big date—" she wiggled her brows, ignoring Takoda's immediate protest "—and Rain and I need to find our Halloween costumes."

Takoda groaned but smiled, already knowing there was no escaping Ariel's enthusiasm. "It's not a date."

Ariel gasped in mock offense. "You're meeting a ridiculously handsome samurai to spend the afternoon admiring art together. That sounds suspiciously like a date."

"It's not a—" Takoda exhaled sharply, cutting herself off. She wasn't going to win this argument. Instead, she swung her legs off the bed. "Fine. Let's just go."

By the time they were dressed and out the door, Pioneer Square was already bustling. Crisp autumn air carried the scent of coffee and fresh pastries from nearby cafés as they made their way toward the department store.

Inside, the store buzzed—racks lined with vibrant colors, shimmering fabrics catching the overhead lights, the murmur of shoppers weaving through displays. Ariel dove in first, eyes alight. "Yes!" she cried, snatching a silver, shimmery top. "This is it!" With gleeful confidence, she grabbed glittery leggings and oversized, iridescent fairy wings, fully committing to her glam pixie look.

Rain moved with her usual quiet grace, fingers trailing soft fabrics in rich, earthy tones. She plucked a delicate faux vine crown from a display and placed it atop her head, adjusting it thoughtfully. "I want my costume to feel like I'm bringing a bit of the forest with me," she said, voice serene as ever.

Ariel turned, grinning as she held up a glittery palette. "Both of you have to sparkle with me—it's non-negotiable." Before Takoda could protest, Ariel dabbed glitter across her cheek, then turned to Rain, who simply laughed and let her swipe a shimmering streak along her cheekbone.

As Ariel admired her reflection and Rain tested glowing makeup, Takoda slipped away to browse. Her fingers traced rich textures before her gaze landed on a long white dress with lace along the neckline. Simple yet elegant, it flowed with quiet strength—grounded and graceful. It reminded her of home—of her heritage.

Just beyond it, her eyes caught on a deep indigo silk wrap embroidered with subtle cranes. She reached out, brushing her fingers over the intricate design. Poised and timeless, the cranes stirred quiet reverence. They reminded her of Riichi.

An idea formed—one that blended both their worlds. She could wear the wrap over the dress, a quiet but meaningful nod to both their heritages.

"Oh, Takoda!" Ariel's voice rang out as she hurried over, arms still full of silver fabric and glitter. She took one look at Takoda's choice and grinned. "That's stunning. It's like… you're blending both of you into one look." She nudged her playfully. "Just imagine Riichi's face when he sees you in this."

Takoda rolled her eyes but couldn't deny the thrill sparking in her chest. This outfit felt like more than just something to wear—it was a quiet statement. A reflection of who she was and the connection growing between them.

The three regrouped at the checkout, each carrying pieces that reflected their unique styles. Ariel practically vibrated with excitement, twirling in place as she chattered about their Halloween plans. "We're going to be the most magical trio in town," she declared, giving a dramatic flourish of her shimmery wings.

Rain, serene as ever, adjusted the vine crown in her hands, smiling softly.

Takoda clutched her dress and wrap, a quiet anticipation settling inside her. This wasn't just about an outfit—or even Riichi. It was about stepping into something new, embracing the change unfolding around her.

Outside, the city pulsed with motion. Ariel skipped ahead, lost in animated conversation with Rain, who listened with patient amusement. But Takoda felt the need to step away, to clear her head.

Back at the hotel, she quietly slipped to the lobby and onto the outdoor balcony. A cool breeze brushed her skin as she inhaled deeply, centering herself. The day ahead held more weight than she'd realized. And despite Ariel's teasing, maybe—just maybe—it really did feel like a date.

And that thought? It was terrifying. But it also made her heart race in a way she wasn't prepared to acknowledge.

The early afternoon sun warmed the city, a breeze tugging at Takoda's hair as she leaned against the hotel balcony's cool railing. The hum of traffic and chatter below settled her as her thoughts drifted back to yesterday—to Riichi. That first kiss in the alley had been raw, instinctive, sparked without hesitation. She hadn't questioned it then. But now, as the rush faded, unease crept in. *Had he regretted it? Had I pushed too hard?* She'd told him not to apologize, but knowing Riichi, he was probably still overthinking it.

Then there was the second kiss. Deliberate. Thoughtful. The contrast sent a ripple through her chest, a feeling she couldn't name. *Was he trying to reassure me? To test the waters? Or had he wanted it just as much as I had?*

She glanced down at her phone, thumb hovering over the screen. A simple call might ease both their minds—or make things more awkward. Exhaling sharply, she hit the call button before she could overthink it. As the line rang, she tightened her grip on the railing, bracing herself against the swirl of nerves. *Had that kiss changed something between them?*

After three rings, the line clicked.

"Hello, Takoda."

His voice was calm, steady—providing stability amidst the uncertainty pressing in on her.

"Hi, Riichi," she replied, hating the slight hitch in her voice. She cleared her throat. "I just wanted to… uh, confirm our plans. For this afternoon."

A quiet chuckle followed. "Yes, I'll pick you up at three. We'll go to the museum together."

The ease in his tone loosened the knot in her chest. No hesitation, no tension—just certainty. She smiled. "The Asian Art Museum… sounds perfect."

A pause followed, less uncertain than unspoken. Then, quietly, Riichi added, "I've been looking forward to it."

The words sent a flutter through her. She pressed her lips together, surprised by how much strength they gave her. *Me too,* she admitted, as anticipation overtook her doubts.

They confirmed the time, and when Takoda hung up, she set her phone down with a breath. The city moved around her, still alive, but somehow everything felt a little lighter. Riichi's voice had quieted the unease inside her. She was ready.

Across the city, Riichi sat in his apartment above the antique shop, midday noise filtering through the walls. Sunlight stretched across the polished floor, but his thoughts were elsewhere.

Yesterday's attack replayed sharply—the way Takoda stepped toward him without hesitation, the vulnerability in her eyes, and the unexpected protectiveness that gripped him.

That reaction unsettled him. It wasn't the detachment he'd honed through centuries of discipline. It was something deeper. He wasn't supposed to feel like this.

She'd slipped past his defenses before he noticed. For centuries, he had kept his distance. Attachments made people vulnerable. Attachments led to loss. And yet, the idea of pulling away from her now felt… unnatural.

He glanced at his phone, thinking of the call. She'd sounded nervous, but not unsure. Sincere. That, oddly, had reassured him. She reached out despite her doubt.

He exhaled, eyes drifting to the clock. The museum exhibit had long held personal meaning—samurai artifacts, echoes of a life he rarely shared. And yet today, he wanted her to see it.

He wasn't sure why.

Caution tugged at him. The Golden Dawn was still a threat. Any bond beyond his world carried risk. But the thought of walking away from this—whatever it was—felt just as dangerous.

He'd let the afternoon unfold slowly. Carefully. On his terms.

Riichi arrived at the hotel right on time, posture composed as always. But when Takoda stepped outside, his expression faltered—just for a second. She wore a flowing white dress, simple and elegant, with a silk wrap draped across her shoulders. Cranes stretched their wings across the fabric, each one embroidered with quiet grace.

This wasn't just an outfit. She had chosen it with purpose—a blend of her heritage and his. *This means something.*

An unfamiliar tension tugged beneath Riichi's usual reserve. He didn't name it—didn't need to. Whatever it was, it rooted deeper than formality. He extended his arm, masking the pull winding through him. "Shall we?" His voice was even, but a quiet intensity lingered beneath—more anticipation than hesitation.

Takoda paused, then slipped her hand into the crook of his arm. The gesture was cautious, as if they were both testing fragile ground. As they walked, Riichi became acutely aware of her warmth beside him. Caution still hummed in the back of his mind, but for once, he chose to silence it. Just for a little while.

Their walk carried a subtle charge—not silence, not discomfort, but the tension of questions that hadn't found words yet.

Takoda, too, noticed the shift. Riichi wasn't distant now, not fixed on duty or veiled in restraint. These past months had changed that. He had changed that. Still, questions pressed at the edge of her thoughts. *What does this mean? Where are we now?* She wasn't ready to ask.

Instead, she broke the tension with a smile. "Just a warning… I probably still have glitter somewhere. Ariel was determined we all sparkled." She swiped her cheek, as if undoing her friend's mischief.

Riichi glanced at her, an amused flicker rising—just short of a smirk. "That sounds fitting."

Takoda blinked. *Was that… teasing?*

"You think glitter suits me?" she asked lightly.

A pause—then, "Yes."

Her stomach flipped. *That's new.*

Emboldened, she teased, "You don't seem like the sparkle type."

"I prefer things with less…" He searched for the word. "Distraction."

She huffed a laugh. "That doesn't surprise me."

Their eyes met briefly, and though he looked away, the shift between them stayed. It wasn't forced or awkward—just easy.

She exhaled, voice softer now. "It's nice. Just walking with someone again."

"I appreciate that you're here."

Simple. Honest. No grand gestures. Just truth.

Takoda turned to him, surprised by the ease in his words. He kept his eyes ahead, expression calm, but the warmth in her chest said enough. *Maybe I don't need to ask. Maybe he already answered.*

Inside the Asian Art Museum, the world hushed further.

Takoda had always loved museums—the way history echoed through stillness. But this time, it felt more personal.

Riichi's focus sharpened as they stepped into the samurai exhibit. He moved with quiet familiarity, drawn to the preserved relics like they weren't just artifacts… but fragments of memory.

They stopped in front of a samurai's armor, lacquered plates catching the glow of the overhead lights.

"This belonged to a samurai lord during the Edo period," Riichi said, his voice more reflective than instructional. "Every layer was built for protection without limiting movement."

He studied the armor in silence for a moment before adding, "Honor and restraint weren't just expected. They were everything."

Takoda watched him more than the display, drawn to the softened edge of his expression, the reverence in his tone.

"They lived with purpose," she murmured.

Riichi inclined his head. "And the discipline to uphold it."

She hesitated. "Do you miss it?"

He was quiet. Then, "I miss the clarity."

The word struck her—clarity. Certainty. Knowing your place and path. She understood it more than she wanted to.

Her fingers brushed the fabric of her wrap. "I think certainty's overrated," she said lightly. "If everything were clear, we wouldn't have room to change."

His gaze flicked to hers. There was no clear answer in his expression—just the flicker of thought. Then he nodded. "Perhaps." Not agreement exactly, but not rejection either.

She doesn't avoid truth, he thought. Even when it's uncomfortable.

They moved on through the exhibit. His voice stayed soft, explanations slower now, more thoughtful. The way he shared this part of himself—openly, without hesitation—wasn't casual. It was a quiet kind of trust.

And her willingness to receive it—without pressing, without judgment—carried its own meaning.

By the time they stepped outside, dusk had settled over the city, streetlights flickering to life.

Takoda should have said goodbye—thank him, walk away, end it on a polite note.

But neither of them moved.

Riichi's gaze shifted toward the street ahead. "There's a restaurant nearby." The offer was careful, measured. "If you'd like to continue."

He wasn't asking out of obligation. He wasn't offering because it was expected.

I want to stay in this, he realized. I want to know where this leads.

Takoda exhaled slowly, warmth blooming through her chest. "I'd love that," she said, her voice quiet but certain.

A small nod was his only response before they turned, walking in step once more. The questions between them hadn't vanished, but they no longer felt like hesitation.

They felt like permission. A door cracked open. And neither of them seemed in a rush to close it.

The restaurant Riichi chose was small and tucked away, its dim lighting casting a warm glow over dark wood tables. The scent of grilled fish and miso filled the air, blending with the low murmur of conversation to create a cocoon of privacy.

Takoda slid into the booth across from him, adjusting her wrap as she reached for the menu. Riichi studied his with his usual focus, but the silence between them wasn't cold. There was an undercurrent there—curious, attentive. Present.

This feels different, he admitted silently. *Not duty. Not rhythm. Something closer to peace.*

She watched him a beat longer than necessary. They'd shared meals before, fallen into quiet routines over tea in San Francisco. But tonight, the air between them felt charged—settled, yet brimming with the unspoken.

She broke the silence. "Anything you'd recommend?"

His eyes lifted, meeting hers. He paused, then nodded. "It's been a while, but they're known for their miso cod."

The way he said it—calm, open—felt like an invitation.

"Then I'll trust you," she said with a soft smile, setting her menu aside.

He didn't respond right away, only watched her. Then, subtly, his shoulders eased.

Their conversation flowed with the familiarity built over two weeks in San Francisco. Takoda was drawn to how he listened—not just with patience, but with attention. His eyes didn't drift. He didn't fill silences with noise.

He stayed with her.

Not long ago, she had wondered if the pull she felt was one-sided. *Was I mistaking my own feelings for something that wasn't there?*

But now? She didn't wonder anymore.

And neither, it seemed, did he.

They lingered longer than necessary, neither rushing to finish. When the check came, Riichi handled it without a word, sliding the receipt to the edge of the table. Then he looked at her.

"Would you like to walk for a while?"

The question caught her off guard, though it shouldn't have. It was simple. Deliberate. She nodded. "I'd like that."

The cool night air greeted them as they stepped outside, the city's hum softening with the later hour. Riichi led her through a quieter district, his pace unhurried, posture composed—but looser. They turned onto a narrow street, glowing lanterns casting golden reflections across the pavement.

"Nihonmachi," Riichi said, the name slipping from him naturally. "Japantown."

Takoda glanced up at him, noting the way he spoke the name—not as a passing fact, but with reverence. "I've been here before," she murmured, taking in the warm glow of the shops and the gentle sway of fabric banners hanging from doorways. "But it feels more alive now."

He didn't respond, but his gaze lingered on her for a fraction longer than necessary. *She sees it. Feels it.*

They moved through the quiet streets at a slow, even pace. It wasn't that neither of them knew what to say—it was that nothing needed to be said.

As they passed a small shop, Takoda stopped. In the window, a black kimono was displayed, embroidered with red flowers, each petal stitched with elegant precision. She had noticed it earlier with Ariel and Rain, drawn to its quiet beauty. Now, without realizing it, she lingered again, her fingers brushing the edge of the glass.

She hadn't expected Riichi to notice.

But he did.

She hesitated, he thought, *but her eyes didn't. She wants this.*

She didn't hear him step away. Didn't realize he had left until he returned, stopping beside her with a neatly wrapped package in his hands.

"You seemed to like it," he said simply, extending it toward her.

Takoda blinked, her breath catching slightly as she looked down at the bundle. "Riichi…" Her fingers brushed his as she took it, warmth blooming in her chest. "I don't know what to say."

"Then don't." His voice was quiet, but sure.

They continued their walk, Takoda holding the kimono close, her heart still fluttering from the gesture. Riichi's usual stillness wasn't gone, but something in him had shifted—he was letting her in.

As they strolled, a prickling sensation crept over Takoda—like a faint current brushing across her skin each time they passed someone. She tried to ignore it, not wanting to lose the peace of the moment. But it kept pressing at her awareness—subtle, insistent—like the air around her was suddenly tuned too sharp.

Near Pioneer Square, a quiet reluctance settled between them. Neither wanted the night to end. She glanced up, caught his gaze, and saw something unguarded there—a flicker of admiration he hadn't meant to show. Maybe he had been unsure, too.

They shared a soft, mutual smile, a recognition of the quiet connection forming between them. Hope stirred in her chest. Something had shifted tonight—subtle but real. And for Riichi, there was a rare, unspoken contentment—a quiet acknowledgment that this was worth exploring.

But just as the air grew easier between them, a throb bloomed behind Takoda's eyes. The emotions around her—excitement, frustration, fatigue, sadness—rose in a sudden, crashing wave. She tried to breathe through it, but the noise swelled, pressing in. Each passerby left an echo, and the din grew unbearable. Her steps faltered, a tremor rippling through her.

"Takoda?" Riichi's voice cut through the haze, grounding and clear. She couldn't answer. Her head pounded too fiercely, her thoughts splintering. She stumbled, reaching for the wall beside her. The rough brick scraped her palm, anchoring her for a moment.

"I… I don't know." Her voice shook, her fingers trembling as she looked down. "My head… it hurts so much." Her vision wavered—and then, to her shock, her hands began to glow with a faint orange light.

Riichi's attention snapped to her hands. His posture stilled, his senses narrowing. *That's not normal. Not for her.*

"We can't stay here," he murmured, already shrugging off his jacket. He wrapped it around her shoulders to conceal her hands, his movements swift and precise. He unstrapped his katana, holding it out. "Hold this," he said, voice calm, grounded. "Keep your hands hidden in the coat."

Takoda gave a faint nod, clutching the blade to steady herself. Riichi's arm circled around her, guiding her forward, shielding her from view.

She leaned into him, her legs weak beneath her, her senses dulling beneath the pounding in her skull.

Each step felt like a weight dragging her down. She tried to focus on Riichi's presence, the calm force surrounding her, but the storm inside her raged louder. Her body thrummed with energy she didn't understand—raw, wild, rising beyond her control.

After what felt like forever, they reached his apartment above the antique shop. Riichi unlocked the door with one hand, steadying her with the other. Once inside, he guided her to the couch and crossed the room in a flash, filling a glass of water.

Focus, he told himself. *Observe. Adapt. Shield.* The man she'd come to know might seem calm, but now, the warrior within him stood fully awake.

Takoda sat on the couch in a haze, vision flickering, hands trembling beneath the coat. The pain in her head spiked again, sharp and pressing—like something ancient had been buried deep inside her, and now it wanted out.

Riichi returned with a bottle of water, his face lined with worry. He knelt beside her, watching helplessly as she took it, her fingers shaking so badly she could barely hold on. Her wide, fearful eyes met his, and her voice escaped in a whisper, almost pleading. "Please… make it stop." Her hands moved to her head, pulling at her hair in desperation as tears pricked her eyes.

For the first time, Riichi felt a helplessness he couldn't ignore. He didn't understand this strange, raw magic, but he knew one thing—he had to help her. Kneeling in front of her, he took her shoulders in a firm, calming grip.

"Breathe through it, Takoda. Just focus on my voice. It will pass." His voice stayed low, soothing, though the unfamiliar glow from her hands left him with more questions than answers.

She clung to his arms, breathing quick and shallow, her voice barely audible. "Please, Riichi. Take it away." It cracked, and in a desperate, instinctive move, she pressed her glowing hands to his chest, eyes pleading, hoping he could somehow stop the storm inside her.

The moment her hands met his chest, a surge of energy exploded between them, sharp and consuming, pulling every suppressed emotion into a single, undeniable force. Riichi's breath hitched, his entire body tensing as her emotions flooded into him—not just fear or chaos, but raw, unfiltered need twisting through her, igniting a deep emotion he had buried too long. Her gaze locked on his, wide and burning, her panic drowned beneath a deeper intensity—one that called to him, dragged him under.

Desire.

There was no hesitation, no restraint. Just instinct.

Takoda moved first, her breath quivering as she surged toward him, her lips brushing his—testing, seeking. Riichi answered without thought, without question. Their mouths met in a rush of heat and urgency, his hands finding her waist, pulling her closer as the flood of emotion consumed them both. There was no room for control, no space for second-guessing. The sensations crashed through him—all of her—amplified by his own. There was no longer a difference between what was magic and what was real. It was just them.

Her hands roamed his chest, his shoulders, pressing into the solid warmth of him, fingers trembling as they explored the sharp edges of restraint he had once held so firmly. But there was no restraint now. His fingers tangled in her hair, tilting her head as he deepened the kiss, pouring everything into it—the need, the hunger, the ache that had simmered beneath the surface for weeks, now ignited into something uncontrollable.

Takoda gasped against his lips, her body arching into his, hands desperate, fierce, pulling at the fabric between them, tearing down every wall they had left. Then—her fingers found his belt buckle.

Riichi froze.

The haze of sensation clawed at him, raw and insistent, urging him to give in—to let go completely. His grip tightened. The fire burned through him, relentless, his body screaming for more, but somewhere in the depths of it, his mind fought back. *Not like this.*

With a sharp exhale, Riichi moved, shifting his grip on her wrists and turning her in his arms. Takoda barely had time to react before her back pressed to his chest, his arms locking around her, keeping her there—close, secure, contained. His breathing was rough, uneven against her ear, but he needed to slow it. Needed *her* to slow it. For a moment, he hesitated, his lips brushing the curve of her neck as if pulled there by instinct. The heat between them hadn't faded—it wouldn't fade, not yet—but he had to break through it. He had to pull them both back.

"Breathe," he murmured, his voice rough, tight. "With me."

Takoda trembled against him, her head tilting slightly, exposing more of her throat—a silent plea for more, for now, for anything but stopping.

Riichi squeezed his eyes shut. His fingers flexed against her hips before he forced himself to still. He pressed his forehead against the side of her head, his breath still uneven, still too much. "Breathe, Takoda."

She made a quiet sound, somewhere between protest and surrender, her body still tense with lingering need. But he held her there, grounding her, refusing to let her slip back under.

Slowly, deliberately, he guided her hands to rest over his, wrapping their fingers together where they pressed against her abdomen. He let his chest rise, expanding with a controlled, measured inhale.

"In through your nose. Hold." His voice dropped lower, anchoring them both. She shuddered, her breath hitching, but she tried.

"Now, release."

His breath fanned against her skin as he exhaled slowly, pushing the tension out, willing her to follow. Takoda inhaled again, still shaky, but her body loosened, her muscles losing their rigid pull. Riichi repeated the pattern, again and again, until the heat between them dulled—until the sharp, uncontrollable edge of need softened into something bearable. Until they were here, not lost in the storm, but rooted.

Takoda sagged against him. Her hands slipped from his, her body losing the last of its tension as exhaustion crashed into her all at once. Riichi caught her easily, his arms tightening around her waist as her knees gave out.

"Takoda—"

She barely stirred. Her breathing had evened out, but her body felt too slack against his. He turned her slightly, enough to see her face—her lashes fluttering once before her eyes closed completely.

Unconscious.

His jaw tightened. He'd known the power drain would hit her hard, but seeing her so completely worn out sent a foreign flicker of worry through his chest. Without another word, he scooped her up, lifting her effortlessly into his arms. The room was quiet now, the storm between them settled—but the remnants still clung to his skin, still burned low beneath his ribs.

He carried her into the bedroom, lowering her carefully onto the bed. Dim light from the window cast soft shadows across her face, her expression peaceful now, despite everything. For a long moment, Riichi didn't move. He simply looked at her, studying the delicate lines of her features, the faint traces of exertion still visible even in sleep. A deep breath left him, slow and steady. Reaching up, he ran a hand through his hair, dragging his fingers down to the back of his neck, exhaling again, clearing his mind. *This woman is going to be the death of me.*

His lips pressed into a firm line, but he didn't deny the truth of the thought. He would've lost himself in her tonight. If she had pushed a little harder, if he had hesitated even a moment longer—

Riichi closed his eyes briefly, then exhaled one last time, stepping back. Letting her rest.

Takoda stirred, the haze of sleep still clinging to her as she slowly drifted toward wakefulness. The warmth of the blankets wrapped around her like a fragile cocoon, but something felt different. The air was too still, too heavy, as if she had woken into a moment already unfolding without her. She blinked against the dim light and saw him.

Riichi sat at the edge of the bed, posture rigid, elbows braced on his knees, fingers pressed together in thought. His head was bowed, eyes fixed on the floor, his expression unreadable. But it was the way he sat that made something in her chest tighten. There was no ease in his form, no trace of the careful restraint he wore so well. He looked like a man on the edge of a decision—caught between holding back and stepping forward.

She swallowed hard, pushing herself upright, her limbs heavier than they should've been. "Riichi?"

He didn't react right away, but she caught the slight shift in his shoulders—a sign he'd heard her.

A thread of guilt wove itself through her, tangled between her own thoughts and his. The memories of earlier were hazy but undeniable—the flood of emotions that hadn't been hers alone, the way she had slipped too far, sinking into the depth of what he felt but never voiced. She had touched them—his thoughts, his guarded emotions, the pieces he kept locked away. And in doing so, she had taken something that should've only ever been given.

Her fingers curled against the blanket. "I—" She hesitated, forcing out words too small for the weight in her chest. "I'm sorry. For earlier."

Riichi still didn't look at her, but she saw his hands flex against his knees—a flicker of movement before he stilled again.

"I shouldn't have let it get that far," she admitted. "I don't know what came over me, but I—" She exhaled hard, shaking her head. "I shouldn't have done that to you."

Silence stretched between them. The longer it lasted, the more she felt it pressing down on her, suffocating in its uncertainty. Her gaze dropped, her hands tightening in the fabric pooled over her lap. "I should probably go."

Riichi moved. His hands unfolded, pressing against his knees as he finally lifted his head. When his gaze met hers, she expected hesitation, expected discomfort. But there was none.

"You don't have to go."

Takoda blinked. "You must think I'm a horrible person," she murmured, the words slipping out before she could stop them.

He shook his head, slow, deliberate. "I don't think you're horrible." His voice was steady. Certain. Like there had never been a doubt. "If anything," he continued, "you just helped me see what I truly want."

Her breath caught.

The air shifted—subtle, but undeniable—as the weight of his words settled deep in her chest. He wasn't speaking out of politeness or obligation. He meant every syllable. They landed with quiet finality, anchoring her in a way that made it impossible to look away.

Her fingers flexed against the blanket, her pulse drumming in her ears. "What do you want, Riichi?"

The question hung between them, thick with anticipation.

Riichi's gaze flickered. A shadow crossed his expression—not doubt, but restraint. A hesitation rooted not in uncertainty, but in years of self-denial. Years of setting emotion aside for control.

And then, for the briefest moment, Rowan's voice echoed in his mind. *You hide behind duty. Maybe it's time to stop overthinking and do something about it.*

He had dismissed it then, convinced it couldn't be that simple. But now, sitting here, staring at Takoda—who was watching him with careful hope—he knew Rowan had seen the truth before he had.

He'd spent too long holding himself at a distance, mistaking solitude for strength, clinging to logic like armor. But what use was logic when what he wanted—what made him feel alive—was sitting right in front of him?

Riichi exhaled slowly, as if an internal barrier had finally fallen away. The choice had always been there, waiting for him to stop pretending it wasn't.

He rose to his feet, the movement quiet but purposeful. Takoda's gaze followed him, drawn in by a pull she didn't try to resist. She stayed still, breath shallow, as he crossed the space between them. Each step was deliberate, steady, but the air between them grew dense with energy—undeniable and rising, like the moment before a storm breaks.

When he stopped at the side of the bed, his gaze met hers. In the soft light, his eyes held nothing back. No barriers. No distance. No hesitation.

"I want you to stay."

His voice was low, but the conviction in it stirred through her like a current. Then, softer—barely above a whisper, but meant only for her:

"I want *you*."

Her pulse stumbled.

She had known—of course, she had known. She had felt it all night, seen it in the moments where his emotions had slipped through the cracks he usually kept sealed. But hearing it aloud, spoken with quiet certainty and no retreat, unraveled the breath in her lungs.

Her throat tightened, words caught just behind them. She should say something, acknowledge the shift pulling them closer. But in that moment, words felt useless. The truth had already passed between them.

So, she moved instead, her fingers brushing his wrist—slow, tentative, not pulling, not demanding, just grounding.

That was all it took.

Riichi sank onto the bed beside her, and she turned toward him, drawn in by his warmth, by the quiet gravity of his presence. Her knees brushed against his, and she couldn't tell if it was her heart or his that was pounding between them. His hand lifted with a deliberate grace, fingers tracing the delicate line of her jaw, gentle and assured. His touch sent a shiver through her, not from uncertainty but from the profound significance of what it meant—what this meant.

And then, he kissed her.

There was no hesitation in his movement this time, no caution or restraint. It was slow, deep—a quiet unraveling of self-control, of the distance that once separated them, of everything they hadn't said out loud. Takoda inhaled sharply against his lips, her fingers fisting in the fabric of his shirt as he pulled her closer, anchoring her to him. His hands slid down her waist, tracing the gentle curve of her back, his grip firm yet imbued with a sense of awe. There was no urgency, no desperation, only lingering touches and the slow press of his body against hers.

She let herself sink into the embrace, let herself learn him the way he was learning her. Hands exploring, mapping, memorizing. She traced the broad lines of his back, felt the quiet strength coiled beneath his skin, the way his body responded to her gentle touch. Clothes slipped away like whispers in the night, each layer removed with quiet reverence, a slow unveiling.

Riichi's touch wasn't just seeking—it was deliberate, a study of every reaction, every shiver, every unguarded moment that passed between them. He was learning her, unraveling her essence with gentle persistence.

And she let him.

She wasn't sure when she ended up beneath him, but when she did, he paused. His breath came in shallow, uneven waves, his forehead resting gently against hers, as if anchoring himself in this moment before there was no turning back. His fingers traced the outline of her ribs, slow, reverent, his palm resting against the curve of her waist.

"I don't want to stop," he murmured, his voice a mere whisper that brushed against her lips.

Takoda's pulse thundered in her ears, but there was no doubt, no fear—only clarity. She cupped his face, tilting his chin up until his eyes met hers. There was no teasing, no second-guessing, no room for hesitation.

"Then don't stop."

Riichi drew in a sharp breath, his gaze locking onto hers as something primal flared beneath the surface. His grip tightened against her side—possessive, anchoring.

"I've never wanted anything like this before," she whispered.

His restraint shattered quietly, in the space between her words and his breath.

And then, everything gave way.

The last of his control burned away, dissolving into a fiery passion that erupted between them. Every movement was intentional. Every shift an exploration. It was a slow surrender, a gradual revelation of something deeper. Takoda felt the way his hands masterfully traced the contours of her body, fingers gliding over her delicate skin like he was committing it to memory. The warmth emanating from her was like an irresistible magnet, drawing him closer.

She gave her own hands the freedom to roam, finding pleasure in the solid strength he exuded. She reveled in the tautness of his muscles and delighted in the way he trembled beneath her fingertips as she lightly grazed them over his chest, down his abdomen and thighs. There mouths met hungrily, lips brushing against one another while tongues danced together in a passionate frenzy.

It wasn't just passion—it was a shared discovery, slow and unhurried, as if they had all the time in the world. His fingers sent shivers down her spine as they melded together into one.

And when dawn arrived, casting soft light through the window, illuminating their entwined bodies. Neither of them questioned what had happened.

There was no trace of regret, only a comforting warmth that enveloped them, only the undeniable presence of just the two of them in that serene moment. The quiet stretched between them—not heavy or uncertain, just the contentment of two souls who had truly connected.

Riichi didn't immediately pull away. His arms remained wrapped around her, his fingers trailing slow, absentminded patterns along her back. Takoda exhaled softly against his skin, her body still humming from the night they had unraveled together. She whispered his name, testing the weight of it. He hummed softly in response, a gentle vibration that blended seamlessly into the quiet between them.

She hesitated, then pressed her forehead against his chest, feeling the steady rhythm of his heartbeat beneath her skin.

"Are you alright?" he murmured, his voice lower, quieter than usual, carrying a tenderness that wrapped around her like a warm embrace.

It wasn't a question of regret. It was a question of whether she would take this back. Whether she would wake up and pretend nothing had changed.

Takoda smiled, a soft, tired smile that spoke of contentment and gentle acceptance.

"You really think I'd let you do all that and not be okay?" she replied, her voice laced with a playful hint of assurance.

The tension in Riichi's body eased slightly. His chest shook with something close to amusement, though he didn't quite laugh. Still, he nodded, brushing his thumb over the back of her hand in a slow, rhythmic motion, like a silent promise.

A comfortable silence settled between them once more. Then, gently, he pressed a lingering kiss to her temple, his lips a soft brush against her skin.

"Good," he whispered against her skin, his breath a gentle caress.

They didn't move for a long time, remaining entwined in the quiet comfort of each other's presence. Takoda fell asleep first, her body nestled against his, the soft rhythm of her breathing evening out. Riichi stayed awake, his gaze drifting over her peaceful face, memorizing the way she looked like this—unburdened, at peace, entirely real.

Because for the first time, he wasn't overthinking. He wasn't analyzing.

He was just here.

Chapter Seven
A Shifting Fate

Oak took a leisurely sip of his coffee, the warmth spreading through his chest as he leaned back in his chair. His time at Eileen's home had stretched longer than expected, to the point where he was running out of clean clothes. Setting his mug down, he turned toward her, his tone casual but deliberate.

"I need to go home today. You can either take me back, or I'll call a cab to the airport." He lifted his cup again, taking another sip before adding with an amused glint, "You've kept me prisoner long enough."

Eileen, standing near the counter, stilled for half a breath before answering, her voice calm and even. "I have not kept you prisoner. You have been free to leave whenever you chose."

Oak chuckled, shaking his head. "Eileen, it was a joke. You shouldn't be so serious all the time. I imagine that's why all your stress builds up." He smirked, lifting a brow. "Although, I don't mind relieving it."

Eileen didn't so much as blink. "If I am not stressed, then I would not need to call you."

Oak sighed, rolling his eyes. "Fair point." His gaze remained on her for a beat before he added, "But you'd probably call me for another reason."

His words weren't a question, though they left room for an answer.

Eileen didn't give him one.

He observed her for a heartbeat, but she was already turning away, shutting down whatever path he'd been trying to open. He didn't press it.

Instead, he started to take another sip of coffee but froze, an instinctive tightness settling in his chest. It wasn't the usual awareness that came from years of battle or experience—it was more profound, more definite, a resonant tug beneath his ribs. His fingers curled around the mug, grip firming as he breathed out.

"I'm getting a gut feeling," he murmured, his voice soft and tinged with an indistinct emotion. "Do you feel that? Something's happening." His gaze darted toward Eileen, his instincts already narrowing in. "Is it Riichi?"

Eileen's face changed, her attention turning inward as if reaching beyond what the present allowed. Silence stretched, heavy with something unseen. When she spoke, her voice carried a sense of absolute conviction.

"Yes. Riichi has discovered his soulmate."

Oak continued to watch her, fully aware that she couldn't see him. The knot in his chest remained. "That's not all of it, though."

Eileen remained distant, searching. Then, after another pause, her gaze sharpened. "No." A hint of a hidden understanding passed over her features. "The Golden Dawn has arrived in Seattle. The Fallen will need to gather."

She shook her head, clearing the last remnants of the vision, and turned to Oak, regaining her composure once more.

"I'll take you home to retrieve more clothes," she said, even now thinking ahead. "You'll need a bigger bag."

Oak let out a slow breath, running a hand through his hair. "Then we'll come back here and start making plans."

Eileen nodded. "We need to determine why the Golden Dawn is manipulating the weather—and how they are doing it."

Oak frowned, absentmindedly tapping his fingers against the side of his mug. "They wouldn't be doing it without a reason. It's either a consequence of a larger scheme, or it's a setup for whatever they're planning next."

"We'll also need to determine where they are in Seattle," Eileen continued. "And how the Fallen can find them."

Oak leaned forward, his voice turning more focused. "Do you want me to call the same people who came to San Francisco?"

"No," Eileen replied immediately. "I want more of us present this time. Call Vine, Reed, Elder, Ivy, Willow, Birch, Ash, Rowan, and Aislinn."

Oak studied her for a passing instant before asking, "You anticipating trouble?"

Eileen's fingers barely twitched against the counter. "I foresee a complication with Riichi's initial participation."

Oak absorbed that, rolling it over in his mind. He didn't ask what she meant—if she suspected a particular outcome or if it was simply an inevitability. Either way, she wasn't wrong.

He exhaled and pushed back his chair. "I'll make the calls."

Eileen inclined her head. "Once we return, we strategize."

She turned, lost in thought. Oak trailed behind her, a familiar heaviness settling over his shoulders.

Whatever was waiting for them in Seattle, it had already begun.

Seattle, Washington

Takoda began to stir, the warmth still clinging to her skin as her senses slowly adjusted to wakefulness. The room held the faint scent of him, a reminder of the night they'd shared—of the closeness, the honesty, the way neither had held back.

She turned her head, finding Riichi already watching her intently. There was no hint of apprehension in his gaze, no doubt between them. They both knew exactly where they stood.

She stretched, the slow pull of her muscles working out the last remnants of sleep. "Did you even close your eyes?"

The corner of his mouth lifted. "A little."

Her brow arched. "That's a no."

His amusement deepened, but he didn't argue.

She rolled onto her side, propping her head against her hand. "You're thinking."

"I always think."

"About?"

His thumb traced a slow arc along the edge of the blanket, as if considering his words before speaking them aloud. "Last night."

Takoda let the gravity of that settle briefly, watching him. "Good thoughts, I hope."

He looked directly into her eyes, unwavering and calm. "Yes."

A deep, rich warmth unfurled in her chest—not from relief, but from an emotion far more intense, more profound. Not because she'd been unsure of where he stood, but because hearing it from him made it real in a way that nothing else could.

She let her fingers brush against the fabric beneath them, her thoughts turning over the calm assurance that had settled in the space they shared. "I used to think I wasn't good at waiting."

Riichi's brow lifted slightly, curiosity evident in the slight tilt of his head. "Used to?"

Her lips curved, thoughtful. "Turns out... some things are worth the time they take."

His gaze held hers for a beat, a muted understanding passing between them. Then, with deliberate intent, he reached out, his fingers wrapping gently around her wrist. His touch was warm and purposeful.

"And this?" he asked, his voice low.

Her breath caught, but her answer was immediate. "This was worth it."

Takoda's pulse quickened, not because of nerves, but because this had never been a choice to second-guess.

A gradual smile pulled at her lips. "I'm glad I waited."

His hand slid to her waist, guiding her closer. The change in their closeness felt destined, as if they had reached this moment long before words ever touched the air.

Riichi leaned in and met her halfway, his lips gently brushing against hers in a slow, intentional kiss—a promise, a continuation, an acknowledgment that neither of them wanted to walk away from whatever they were building.

Takoda melted into him, fingers threading through his hair as the warmth of his touch sent a ripple of heat through her. There was nothing uncertain about this—no hesitation, no need to question.

The sudden trill of her phone shattered the tranquility. She groaned, flopping back onto the pillows. "If that's Rain—"

Riichi reached over, glanced at the screen, then smirked. "It's Rain."

She dragged a hand over her face. "Of course it is."

"You should probably answer before she gets worse ideas."

Takoda sighed and rolled away, grabbing the phone off the nightstand.

"You're alive!" Rain's voice rang through the receiver before Takoda even had a chance to say hello. "I half-thought I'd have to send a search party by now. Where are you?"

Takoda closed her eyes, shaking her head. "Relax, Rain, I'm fine. Had a late night… and an early morning wake-up call from you."

"Late night, huh?" Rain's tone turned speculative. "Should I be concerned?"

Takoda glanced at Riichi, mischief flashing in her eyes. "Only if you have a problem with happiness."

Riichi let out a soft breath with a hint of amusement, shaking his head.

After a few more reassurances, she ended the call and tossed the phone onto the bed. She sat up, running a hand through her hair before reaching for her clothes. She turned back to Riichi, who had propped himself up on one elbow, watching her with complete admiration—thoughtful, focused, and wholly present.

"You and Rain have an interesting connection," he remarked.

"She's like my unofficial big sister," Takoda explained, stretching before pushing herself upright. "She worries. A lot."

Riichi gave a small nod, though a shadow passed through his expression—an echo of something long buried, a reminder of the sister he couldn't protect.

Takoda reached for her shoes, but before she could slip them on, his voice cut through the quiet. "You're lucky."

She paused, fingers curling gently around the laces. When she looked up, his expression remained the same, but his words conveyed more than what was spoken aloud.

"Yeah, I am," she admitted, voice softer now. "I don't say it enough, but I know I am."

He didn't respond, only cleared his throat. But she could tell he heard her.

Slipping her shoes on, she rose, collecting her belongings. As she stepped toward the door, she felt it—the momentary awkwardness before a goodbye, the silent connection that briefly linked two people in a shared understanding.

She turned, sensing the question before he spoke.

"Will you be back?" His voice was even, but it wasn't just casual curiosity.

She smiled, positive. "Absolutely."

His shoulders relaxed, and without a word, he lifted the bag from the nearby chair and held it out to her.

Takoda accepted it, fingers brushing over the fabric through the bag. "Thank you."

Riichi didn't move away. Instead, his hand rested on the small of her back, holding her in place. The kiss he gave her wasn't rushed or uncertain. It was confidence wrapped in action, a silent confirmation of everything left unsaid.

When he pulled back, his forehead rested briefly against hers, his breath warm against her skin. His thumb absently traced the curve of her hip.

Takoda closed her eyes and smiled, the moment stretching, filling the space between them with more than words could hold.

Riichi took her hand, turning it over and examining the lines of her palm before he murmured, "If anything changes with your magic… call me."

She smiled, reassuring him. "You'll be the first to know."

One last glance, one final touch, and then she stepped into the hallway.

She didn't need to look back to know this wasn't an ending.

It was only just beginning.

After Takoda's departure, Riichi found himself alone in the quiet of his apartment, a stillness settling around him that usually brought comfort but now left room for the thoughts in the back of his mind to surface. The space still carried traces of her—a faint warmth against the cool air, a presence that hadn't fully faded.

He leaned back, letting his mind replay the events from the night, each one filled with a warmth he hadn't expected. It wasn't just the intensity of what they'd shared—it was the depth beneath it, a profound connection that was solid and unshaken. Takoda had woven herself into him, settling there with the certainty of a bond meant to last, something that had always been waiting for him to see it.

I want to keep exploring this.

The thought didn't come with second-guessing or doubt—it settled with calm resolve. He had always relied on discipline, a foundation that kept his world structured and controlled. But this felt different. Less like an intrusion, more like the ground beneath his feet finally feeling solid.

His mind drifted to her magic, the way it had surfaced—raw, untamed, yet distinctly hers. It fascinated him, the way she embodied an energy he couldn't quite define, a force he wasn't sure either of them fully understood yet. He had spent years keeping his distance from magic and relationships alike, but with Takoda, both had become impossible to ignore.

And it wasn't just her magic. *It was her.*

A hint of protectiveness stirred within him, a feeling older than instinct, an ingrained reaction. It wasn't just about her power—it was about who she was, what she meant. This connection had already taken root. He wasn't going to ignore it.

But just as quickly as that conviction filled him, another thought followed. *The Golden Dawn.*

They had arrived in Seattle, their movements deliberate, their presence calculated. Whatever they were planning, it wasn't random. He hadn't pinpointed why they were manipulating the weather, but it was only a matter of time before their intent became clear. A deeper scheme was unfolding, like a storm forming over distant cliffs.

This can't wait.

His jaw tightened as he considered his next steps. Rowan had always trusted his instincts—and Riichi trusted Rowan's. His friend had already experienced a soulmate bond with Aislinn, previously walked the path Riichi now found himself on.

If anyone could offer insight—not just about the Golden Dawn, but about Takoda—it was Rowan.

Reaching for his phone, he made the decision. It was time to bring Rowan into the loop.

He hit call, and after a couple of rings, Rowan's familiar voice came through.

"Hey, Riichi! You're calling early—everything alright?"

"Didn't mean to wake you," Riichi replied, a bit apologetic.

Rowan chuckled. "Nah, you're good. Aislinn and I are just finishing up breakfast."

Riichi's tone changed, leaning into the straightforwardness they both preferred. "It's the Golden Dawn," he began, voice calm. "They're here in Seattle. I tracked one of them two days ago; their movements feel... focused."

A pause, then Rowan's concern broke through. "Did you get close?"

Riichi faltered, the memory of the encounter flashing in his mind. "Close enough. There was... a complication. But I know where they are."

"Alright," Rowan said, his tone shifting to match Riichi's. "Aislinn's going to see Eileen, I'll go with her and then call in the other Fallen."

"Thank you," Riichi responded, the gratitude understated but genuine.

A brief silence passed before Rowan's voice returned, laced with a teasing edge. "By the way, did you happen to run into Takoda yet?"

Riichi blinked, caught momentarily off guard by the shift. "Yes...I have."

"Ah," Rowan laughed, "so she was the 'complication'?"

Riichi exhaled, feeling a faint warmth of embarrassment that he quickly tamped down. "Yes... unintentionally."

Rowan's laugh softened, but he didn't press. He was waiting. Letting Riichi decide how much more he wanted to say.

Taking a centering breath, Riichi confided the rest, trusting Rowan to listen without judgment. "There's something else. Takoda has... developed a power."

"She has?" Rowan asked, his tone became more serious now. "You're certain?"

"I am," Riichi replied, keeping his voice level. "Her magic—it's tied to her emotions. I'm not sure what it means or how to help her control it."

Rowan replied with calm assurance, "That sounds familiar. I've got your back. It's... different, but I think you already have a pretty good idea of what that means."

Riichi's shoulders relaxed slightly as he let out a sigh. Rowan's words settling any doubts within him. "Yes," he murmured. The response wasn't just agreement—it was acknowledgment. The thought had been circling in his mind since last night, but now, spoken aloud, it settled into something more concrete.

Takoda's power means she is my soulmate.

That truth had been waiting, just beneath the surface.

"Meet me at the Embassy Suites in Pioneer Square," he continued, moving back to logistics. "I'll arrange a secure place for us to regroup until we're settled."

Rowan's answer was immediate. "Got it. We'll be there before sundown."

Riichi thanked him, a quiet reassurance settling over him. Admitting he needed backup wasn't easy, but with Rowan, it felt almost natural.

The call ended, leaving him with the magnitude of everything that had just been confirmed.

The Golden Dawn was moving. That was urgent.

But Takoda was permanent.

And for the first time in longer than he could remember, this fight felt personal.

San Francisco, California

Rowan slipped his phone back into his pocket and looked over at Aislinn, his expression resolute. "Looks like we're going to Seattle," he said, nodding. "Let's pack a bag."

Aislinn glanced up from where she was stirring her tea. "Who was that?"

"Riichi." Rowan grabbed his jacket, already running through logistics in his head. "The Golden Dawn is in Seattle. He's securing an Airbnb now."

Aislinn set her mug down and straightened. "Are you coming with me to my mom's, then?"

"Yeah." Rowan gave a short nod. "I want to tell her in person that the Fallen need to mobilize."

Aislinn exhaled, moving toward their bedroom to grab a bag. "If she doesn't already know."

Rowan smirked faintly. "I'd be surprised if she didn't."

They packed quickly, moving with the simplicity of people used to preparing for sudden departures. Aislinn shoved clothes into her duffel with a practiced hand, tossing in an extra jacket just in case. Rowan packed light—essentials, weapons, and whatever else might prove useful.

As they finished, Aislinn glanced over. "Do we know who else is coming?"

Rowan shook his head. "Not yet. That's something we'll figure out when we get to Eileen's."

Aislinn slung her bag over her shoulder. "Then let's go."

By the time they arrived, the heavy iron gate had already been buzzed open, allowing Rowan to pull into the long, winding driveway. The house stood secluded, quiet, and unwavering as ever, nestled among the towering trees like it had existed there for centuries.

Aislinn stepped out of the car, stretching her arms before glancing up at the house. "I was hoping today would be a little more normal."

Rowan shut the car door and huffed a quiet laugh. "Yeah, well, normal doesn't really exist for us."

Aislinn sighed. "Figures." She adjusted her bag and started toward the door. "Let's get this over with."

They walked up the steps, but before they could knock, the door swung open. Eileen stood just inside, her gaze sharp and impassive.

"You're here sooner than I predicted," she noted, stepping aside to let them in.

"Figured you'd appreciate the initiative," Rowan said as he passed.

Aislinn followed, but as she stepped inside, her gaze caught on someone standing near the far end of the room—Oak.

Her brows lifted a little. "How did you get here so fast?"

Rowan tensed briefly at the question, but Oak barely missed a beat. "Eileen and I were already monitoring the Golden Dawn yesterday. We suspected they'd move soon." He gave a casual shrug. "When we confirmed their presence in Seattle this morning, we started reaching out."

Aislinn frowned, glancing at Eileen for confirmation, but her mother's expression remained indecipherable. That explanation made sense... but something about Oak already being there felt off. Still, she let it go—for now.

"Riichi's securing an Airbnb," Rowan said, getting them back on track. "I told him we'd be there by sundown. If that's not enough time for the rest of the Fallen, at least Aislinn and I will be there."

Eileen nodded. "That should be sufficient. We've already contacted the others."

Rowan's posture straightened minutely. "Who's coming?"

"Ivy, Willow, Birch, Ash, Reed, Elder, and Vine." Eileen's gaze moved toward the large map spread across the table—various locations marked in precise red ink. "All of them are taking direct flights within the hour. Vine is already on the road."

Rowan crossed his arms. "That should give us enough numbers to work with."

Aislinn's glanced at Oak once more, the unanswered question still hovering in the back of her mind. But for now, there were more pressing matters.

She turned back to Eileen. "So, what's the plan?"

Seattle, Washington

Takoda walked back to the hotel, her steps light against the pavement in the early morning hush. The city around her was still waking, but her thoughts were elsewhere, pondering the quiet warmth of the night before. Memories of Riichi surfaced easily—his constant presence, the quiet strength in his every movement, the moments of unexpected tenderness that had unraveled between them.

She had always sensed there was more beneath his composed exterior, a depth beyond the sharp focus and discipline he wore like armor. Last night had proved it. The way he had reached for her, the way he had held her—not just with purpose, but with meaning—had settled into her in a way that caught her off guard. And when morning came, there had been no awkwardness, no doubt. Only understanding.

A small smile tugged at her lips as she thought of his hand resting against her back, the subtle way his fingers had traced along her skin, as if memorizing the moment. There was something different about him, about what they had started. A difference she wanted to hold onto a little longer.

But reality pressed in as the hotel came into view, pulling her from the quiet space she and Riichi had carved out for themselves. Rain and Ariel were no doubt waiting—alert, inquisitive, and fully prepared to demand details. Rain's concerned call from earlier played through her mind, and she let out a soft chuckle, already imagining their expressions.

They'll be relentless, she thought with amusement, picturing Ariel's sharp, knowing stare and Rain's mix of amusement and concern. They would push, not because they were nosy, but because they cared. And while Takoda loved them for it, there was a part of her that wanted to keep some things private—not out of secrecy, but out of respect for the quiet space she and Riichi were still figuring out.

I'll give them just enough.

Her grin deepened as she planned her strategy—enough to satisfy their curiosity but nothing too personal. She could share his humor, how he'd surprised her with the kimono, how the night had unfolded in a way that had felt both natural and inevitable. But the deeper moments—the quiet confessions written in touch rather than words, the way it felt to be truly seen—those were hers to keep.

As her thoughts shifted, something heavier stirred beneath the surface. The magic.

It pulsed at the edge of her awareness, unfamiliar but undeniably part of her now. A force waiting to be understood, to be controlled. It wasn't just a thrilling new ability—it came with weight, with responsibility. And with it, a quiet uncertainty crept in. *What does this mean for my future? What is expected of me?*

Aislinn's name surfaced in her mind, instinctive and sure. Aislinn had walked this path before, had faced the wonder and the significance of magic head-on. She would understand.

She'll know what I'm feeling, Takoda thought, feeling a bit steadier in her decision. The first chance she got, she would reach out. She needed guidance, not just for herself, but for whatever was waiting ahead.

As Takoda stepped into the hotel lobby, she barely had a second to take in her surroundings before Rain and Ariel appeared, their expressions a mix of impatience and anticipation.

Rain placed her hands on her hips, letting out a dramatic sigh. "Look who finally decided to rejoin the land of the living! We were this close to filing a missing person's report."

Ariel smirked, arms crossed. "Locator spell, anyone? Might be faster next time."

Takoda laughed, shaking her head. "Alright, alright—clearly I was missed," she teased as her friends flanked her, already firing off questions.

"So, are you going to tell us about this mysterious night of yours?" Rain asked, eyes gleaming with curiosity. Ariel nodded in agreement, both of them watching her with elated grins.

"Maybe I'll just keep you both in suspense," Takoda mused, feigning nonchalance as she dodged their probing glances. She tossed out a few lighthearted details—like Riichi's completely unexpected gift of the kimono—but kept the deeper, more personal moments to herself, just as she had planned.

Seeing an opportunity to redirect, she flashed a grin. "How about we discuss this over breakfast? I'm starving. Hotel restaurant sound good?"

Rain huffed but relented with a quick shift in focus. "Fine, but don't think this is over." She looped her arm through Takoda's, already steering her toward the restaurant. "I'm thinking pancakes, maybe eggs. Ooh, or waffles!"

Ariel laughed, shaking her head. "As long as there's coffee," she said, her tone mock-serious. "I need it after somebody had me worrying all morning."

Takoda chuckled. "Coffee's on me, then." Her plan had worked, their interrogation taking a backseat to food debates as they approached the restaurant.

Just before they stepped inside, she paused. "You two go ahead and grab a table. I just need a minute to freshen up. I feel like I've been dragged through the morning." She winked, earning laughs and nods from her friends before they headed inside.

Back in her hotel room, she shut the door and leaned against the dresser, exhaling slowly. The morning had moved fast, sweeping her from one thing to the next, but now that she had a moment alone, her thoughts settled on the night before, the quiet sincerity in Riichi's gaze, the warmth in his touch. She closed her eyes briefly, letting herself sink into the memory before another sensation pushed to the forefront.

The magic.

It was there, humming beneath the surface, neither overwhelming nor ignorable. A presence she still didn't fully understand.

The thought of calling Aislinn surfaced again, stronger now. She needed guidance—someone who knew what it was like to stand at the edge of something new and unknown. *Aislinn would understand.*

First things first, she thought, eyeing the bathroom. *A clear mind before anything else.*

Stepping under the warm spray, she let the water relax her, mentally sorting through what she wanted to say. By the time she was dried off and dressed, a renewed sense of purpose strengthened her. She picked up her phone, ready to reach out for the answers she was beginning to crave.

The phone barely rang before Aislinn answered, her voice a familiar comfort. "Hello?"

"Aislinn?" Takoda replied, her voice carrying the reluctance she couldn't quite shake.

There was a pause, and Takoda could almost picture Aislinn's brows drawing together in concern. "Takoda... what's wrong?"

"Um. Are you alone?"

Aislinn's voice softened. "No, I'm with my mom... and Oak. Rowan is here too, but he stepped out to make a few calls. Hang on."

Takoda waited as Aislinn excused herself, the faint sound of footsteps followed by a door clicking shut. When Aislinn's voice returned, it was even more reassuring. "Alright, tell me—what's going on?"

Takoda faltered, then took a steadying breath. "I, uh... I ran into Riichi."

"Oh, did you?" Aislinn's tone turned playful, a knowing lilt in her voice. "See? Rain and Ariel were right. How'd it go? Did it... go the way you thought?"

Takoda let herself smile, something wistful slipping into her voice. "Yes. Maybe even better than I thought."

Aislinn laughed softly. "Well, that's good, right?"

"Yeah, it is," Takoda murmured, but her voice quivered. A tightness built in her chest, and she felt the unexpected sting of tears. "But I think there might be a problem..."

The change in her tone didn't go unnoticed. Aislinn's gentle teasing vanished, replaced by quiet urgency. "Oh no. Tell me what's wrong, Takoda. Did he hurt you? Because if he did, I can be there in a few hours, ready to blast him with some kinetic energy."

A faint laugh escaped Takoda, her tears breaking into a shaky smile. "No, no. He didn't hurt me. I'm fine. He's fine... we're fine. I'm just... overwhelmed, I guess."

Aislinn let out a breath, some of the tension smoothing from her voice. "Alright, that's good to hear. Take your time and tell me. I'm here to help."

Takoda fell silent just for a breath, then finally voiced the fear that had gnawed at her since last night. "I think... I might've unlocked a power."

She explained everything—the sudden headache, the rush of emotions that weren't hers, and how her hands had glowed a soft orange. She mentioned how Riichi had helped her, though she kept the deeper moments between them to herself, holding them close.

"Is that magic?" she asked quietly. "Or did I somehow get infected with something? I'm scared, Aislinn. I don't want to hurt Rain or Ariel… I don't know what to do."

"Takoda, it's alright," Aislinn reassured her, her voice calm and steady. "No, you're not infected with anything. It sounds like you did unlock a power. But I'm not sure what it is. I'd have to ask my mom… if that's okay with you?"

Takoda exhaled, pressing her fingers beneath her eyes to dry the tears gathering there. "Yes, that's fine. If you think it'll help." She paused, glancing at her own hand as if expecting the glow to return. "Aislinn?"

"Yeah? Is there something else?"

Takoda's voice dropped to a whisper, quieter, more uncertain. "Does that mean… Riichi and I might be like you and Rowan?"

There was a warm smile in Aislinn's voice when she answered. "Yeah, sweetie. I think it does. Are you okay with that?"

Takoda murmured softly, "I think… I don't know. What if he's not?"

Aislinn's tone softened even further. "Takoda, listen. I'll be there soon. Actually, Riichi called Rowan to let him know about the Golden Dawn in Seattle. We're planning to be there before the day's over. Oak has already contacted the others, and Rowan's checking on them now. Once we're there, I'll help you figure it out, okay?"

Relief swept through Takoda, her voice more even now. "Thank you. That makes me feel a lot better."

"I'm glad," Aislinn said, warmth threading through her voice. "I've got you, Takoda. See you soon, okay?"

"Okay. Love you."

"Love you too."

Takoda ended the call, taking a deep breath as the relief settled in. It wasn't an infection or a curse, and with Aislinn on her way, she felt more grounded. But the questions still lurked at the edges of her mind.

How would Riichi react? Would he pull away from her, or was this the beginning of something deeper?

Back in San Francisco…

Aislinn slipped her phone back into her pocket and returned to the room where Eileen and Oak were waiting. Her mother looked up, her expression composed yet carrying an air of quiet knowing.

"Sorry, that was Takoda," Aislinn murmured, an unspoken apology in her tone.

Eileen's gentle smile held firm, but there was something behind it—something vast, as though she were looking beyond the present moment. "I know."

Oak, sensing Aislinn needed a minute alone with her mother, pushed back his chair. "I'll get some coffee."

Aislinn barely registered his departure. A slight chill prickled at her skin as she studied her mother's face. Eileen had always possessed an aura of wisdom that felt both grounding and distant, as if she saw threads of fate woven where others saw only frayed edges. But this morning, that feeling was stronger—an echo of something larger stirring just beneath the surface.

She paused before speaking, keeping her voice low. "Takoda… something happened to her last night."

Eileen's gaze sharpened, though her expression remained blank, her silence carrying a gravity that Aislinn had long since learned to recognize. "Tell me."

Aislinn described it—the sudden headache, the emotions overtaking Takoda, the soft orange glow that had pulsed in her hands. "It sounded different from my magic," she admitted. "Like it was fueled by something else. It was… raw."

Eileen laced her fingers together, considering. When she finally spoke, her voice carried the same quiet authority Aislinn had heard countless times before—words spoken not just with knowledge, but with understanding rooted in something far older. "It sounds like emotional alchemy."

Aislinn's stomach tightened. "You're sure?"

Eileen gave a slow nod, a contemplative thoughtfulness flashed across her expression. Then, almost absently, she added, "That would be a very useful skill for Takoda to unlock."

Aislinn stiffened as another chill swept through her. It wasn't just the words. It was the way Eileen said them.

A change was occurring. She could feel it in the immensity of her mother's stare, in the way the air itself seemed to hum—subtle but unquestionable, like the remnants of a presence too vast to fully comprehend.

Aislinn swallowed, her voice barely above a whisper. "Is there something I should know?"

Eileen's distant gaze held for a second longer, as if she were seeing beyond the room, beyond the moment. Then, she exhaled softly, her expression warm yet touched by an unspoken weight—an awareness both timeless and inescapable.

"Not yet, my love," she murmured. "But it seems… fate is moving quicker than I anticipated."

S eattle, Washington

After her conversation with Aislinn, Takoda was feeling much more confident. She left the hotel room and headed to the restaurant where Ariel and Rain were waiting. As she entered the hotel's restaurant, the warm twinkle of jack-o'-lanterns cast restless shadows along the walls. Cobwebs stretched across the ceiling beams, their delicate strands catching the soft glow, while a faint mist curled along the windows, blurring the world beyond. The air carried the comforting spices of cinnamon and nutmeg, mingling with the distant hum of Seattle's morning rush.

Rain and Ariel were already nestled in a booth by the fogged-up glass, laughing over pumpkin-spiced lattes. At Takoda's approach, Rain waved her over with an eager grin.

Sliding into the seat across from them, Takoda barely had a second to get comfortable before Rain leaned in, mischief dancing in her eyes. "Ah, Cinderella returns after her enchanted evening," she teased, her tone dripping with playful accusation.

Ariel's grin widened as she nudged her mug aside. "Come on, spill! You can't just breeze in here like you didn't have a midnight rendezvous."

Takoda opened her mouth to respond, but the waiter arrived, setting down plates of pumpkin waffles drizzled in syrup, crisp maple-glazed bacon, and steaming mugs of apple cider. The rich, autumn scents curled around them, offering Takoda a brief reprieve as she wrapped her hands around her coffee. She took a slow sip, letting the heat fill her before answering. "It was just a night out," she said finally, keeping her tone breezy—though the small quirk of her lips didn't go unnoticed.

Rain arched a brow. "Just a night out?" she echoed, dragging out the words with skepticism. "So, what, you were just innocently wandering Seattle under the stars?"

Ariel smirked over her latte. "Did you two disappear somewhere off the map?"

A hint of mischief sparked in Takoda's eyes as she tilted her head to the side. "Seattle's full of surprises. You just have to know where to wander." She leaned back, arms crossing in a way that made it clear she wasn't about to elaborate.

Rain groaned but laughed, shaking her head. "Fine, fine. Keep your secrets—for now."

Ariel tapped her fingers against the rim of her cup, her expression shifting with sudden inspiration. "Since it's Halloween, I found this place that serves a 'witches' brew' tea.

Whole café's decked out like a proper witch's lair—crystal readings, drying herbs, spell books stacked in the corners. Sound like our kind of morning?"

Rain perked up instantly, her excitement evident. "Yes! And then we hit the Halloween market at Seattle Center—spooky crafts, haunted treats, booths packed with fall goodies." She shot Takoda a knowing look. "I bet you'll end up with at least three pumpkin candles before we leave."

Takoda chuckled. "Bold of you to assume it'll only be three."

Ariel grinned. "And we should top it off with one of those haunted history tours. Maybe we'll get a guide who's actually seen a real ghostly encounter." She waggled her brows. "You never know what lurks in the dark."

Rain gave an approving nod, instantly sold on the idea. Takoda, sipping her cider, felt a familiar thrill at the thought of unraveling the city's haunted past—an appropriate lead-in to the night she had ahead with the Fallen.

With Rain and Ariel caught up in their conversation, Takoda pulled out her phone, her fingers hovering over the screen before she typed a quick message to Riichi.

Takoda: *Spending the day with the girls. Just wanted you to know.*

Her phone buzzed a second later.

Riichi: *Noted. Did you tell them anything?*

She glanced up to see if Rain and Ariel were still deep in discussion before responding.

Takoda: *No. Thought I'd check with you first.*

A pause. Not long, but enough to make her wonder what he was thinking. Then his reply came through, strategic as always.

Riichi: *I appreciate that. But they should know about your ability. It'll keep them from worrying, and it's safer that way.*

His practicality was familiar, but beneath it, she recognized what he wasn't saying outright—his concern. He was always looking ahead, weighing risks she hadn't even considered yet.

Takoda: *Alright. I'll tell them that much.*

She kept her gaze on the screen, sensing he wasn't finished. Another message arrived.

Riichi: *Say what you feel is right. I trust you, Takoda.*

Her fingers curled slightly around the phone. He rarely used that word—*trust*—and when he did, it was intentional, carrying a significance that hovered far beyond the words themselves. She understood how rare it was coming from him.

Takoda: *Thank you for giving me your trust, Riichi.*

The conversation could have ended there. He'd been reassured that she was safe, and she'd carry his words with her, knowing he was always in the background, constant.

But this time, the silence stretched, unanswered thoughts hanging in the air.

Riichi stared at her last message, his thumb motionless over the keyboard. He could let it go. Keep the careful balance between them intact.

Instead, he exhaled slowly and typed.

Riichi: *Takoda, just so you know—you're important to me.*

Her breath hitched. Not from shock, but because it was him. He never said things like that without purpose, never gave away meaning lightly.

Her heartbeat felt erratic as she typed her reply.

Takoda: *You're important to me, too. XOXO*

She tucked her phone away, a quiet reassurance settling in—a steady warmth she carried with her, like the lingering glow of twilight.

Rain and Ariel continued chatting, oblivious to the change in her thoughts. But Takoda held on to the conversation, the magnitude of his words securing her as she stepped into the day ahead.

After breakfast, the girls lingered at the table, sipping the last of their coffee as the restaurant buzzed around them. The scents of cinnamon and roasted beans hung in the air, mingling with the subtle hum of conversation. Rain and Ariel, relaxed and laughing, seemed blissfully unaware of the thoughts tugging at Takoda's mind.

She set her mug down, exhaling slowly before meeting their eyes. "I wanted to tell you both the truth about something important." The gravity of the words remained in her chest, but she pressed on. "I think… I think I have a power."

The lighthearted ease between them shifted instantly. Ariel's smile faded into wide-eyed curiosity, while Rain's expression turned thoughtful.

Ariel leaned in, brows knitting. "Wait—are you saying this is like what happened to Aislinn?"

Takoda hesitated, turning the thought over in her mind before shaking her head. "I don't know. Aislinn's mom is Eileen, so it makes sense for her. My family… we're just normal." Saying it aloud made it sound even stranger, as if she were trying to convince herself.

Rain tapped her fingers against her mug, thinking. "Maybe it's connected to your Native American heritage? There could be a deeper connection—some kind of gift."

The thought sent a ripple of sudden emotion through Takoda—pride, maybe, though it was tangled with doubt. She hadn't considered that possibility before.

She went on, telling them about the strange experience she'd had the night before, though she left out the details of Riichi's involvement. "He told me to call him if it happens again. He knows how to help."

At his name, Rain and Ariel exchanged a quick glance, their curiosity obvious, but to their credit, neither pressed. They let the moment breathe, giving her the space to say more if she wanted.

And after a brief pause, she did.

"And… we spent the night together." Her voice was calm, matter-of-fact. Not an admission, just a truth she wasn't hiding.

Ariel grinned, and Rain gave her a look of warm approval, both of them reading between the lines but letting her set the boundaries.

Takoda lifted a hand before they could fire off any questions. "Nothing more than that. It's… private, but I feel a connection with him. A pull I don't fully understand."

Ariel's smirk grew. "Sounds familiar. You sure you're not pulling an Aislinn and Rowan?"

Takoda felt a blush creep into her cheeks but laughed, shaking her head. Their easy acceptance put her at ease, releasing an anxiety she hadn't noticed until it was gone.

Now that they knew about her power, the tension in her shoulders loosened. If anything happened while they were out, Rain and Ariel would be there. She wasn't alone in this—not with them by her side.

With the heaviness of skepticism finally lifted, she felt lighter, more present—ready to enjoy the day without reticence.

Leaving the warmth of the hotel restaurant behind, the trio made their way toward Seattle Center, where the Halloween market buzzed with life. Crisp autumn air carried the scent of caramel apples and spiced cider, weaving through the lively crowd. Stalls brimmed with handcrafted jewelry, pumpkin-scented candles, eerie décor, and tempting fall treats, all under the golden glow of string lights.

They browsed at a relaxed pace. Rain made the first purchase—a dramatic witch hat with an absurdly wide brim that nearly swallowed her face. She struck a pose. "What do you think?"

"It's a look," Ariel smirked.

"Perfect," Rain said, dropping it into her bag.

Ariel followed her instinct to a silver bracelet strung with tiny moon charms. As she fastened it around her wrist, she admired how the metal caught the light. "I'm embracing my inner celestial goddess," she said with a grin, handing over her payment.

Takoda drifted ahead, drawn to a stall draped in indigo. A matching hairpin and bracelet caught her eye—carved from dark wood and inlaid with turquoise and silver filigree. The delicate curves of mother-of-pearl reminded her of flowing water, of home. There was also a pull toward Riichi she didn't fully understand—but it felt right. She purchased them without hesitation, carefully tucking the bundle into her bag.

"You okay?" Ariel asked, nudging her shoulder.

Takoda nodded, still holding the wrapped pieces. "Yeah," she said, and this time, she truly meant it.

A sudden gust of wind ripped through the market, sharp and cutting. The three of them froze.

"Okay, this wasn't happening when we left," Rain muttered, clutching her sweater.

Ariel glanced skyward, watching heavy clouds drift in like a curtain being drawn. "Seattle's unpredictable, but this feels... off." She looked toward Takoda. "You think it's them?"

They didn't have to say the name. The Golden Dawn.

Rain exhaled. "The timing's too weird. Maybe they just arrived."

The chill between them deepened, untouched by the wind.

"Let's hit the café," Ariel said, adjusting her coat. "At least it'll be warm inside."

Inside the Witches' Brew Café, warmth greeted them along with the scent of dried herbs and tea. Dim lighting flickered across shelves of glowing potion bottles, crystals, and weathered books. Bundles of rosemary and sage swayed gently from the ceiling.

At the counter, they each chose a seasonal tea—Takoda picked "Golden Harvest," Rain "Ghostly Green," and Ariel, true to form, "Midnight Fog." Mist curled from the rims when their drinks arrived, adding an extra charm to the experience.

Once seated, Ariel leaned in. "So... how are you feeling? Since last night?"

Takoda took a beat. The intensity she'd felt—the crushing flood of emotions—was gone. What remained was still present, but distant, no longer consuming. "Better," she said. "I can still feel it, but it's not taking over."

Rain nodded. "That's progress. And if anything shifts, we'll deal with it."

The reassurance anchored Takoda in a way she hadn't realized she needed.

Ariel's attention flicked toward a display near the counter. She plucked a temporary tattoo from the stand—a dragon coiled protectively around a lotus blossom, drawn in elegant black ink. "Didn't you say you were thinking about a dragon for your costume?"

Takoda's breath caught. The design was perfect. The lotus symbol—resilience and renewal—made it feel personal. Not just decorative. It felt meant for her.

"This is perfect," she said, reaching for her wallet.

"Nope. My treat." Ariel smirked. "You have to wear it. It's, like, fate slapping you in the face."

Takoda laughed. "Guess I don't have a choice," she said, sliding it into her bag.

They lingered a while longer. Rain signed up for a crystal reading, while Ariel picked out a smoky quartz pendant. She held it up with satisfaction. "Supposed to ground me," she said. "Probably good for my inner witch."

By the time they stepped outside again, the cold had deepened. The wind cut straight through their layers, stinging and unnatural.

Rain yelped. "Okay, this is insane. It dropped thirty degrees in an hour."

Ariel's eyes scanned the street, her voice low. "That's it. It's them."

No one questioned it. The Golden Dawn had arrived.

Takoda exhaled through the creeping unease. "We should grab our coats before we head to the tour."

Rain and Ariel both nodded in agreement.

As they walked back toward the hotel, a delicate awareness came over Takoda, subtle yet distinct. The emotions of the people around her brushed against her senses—flashes of excitement, impatience, contentment. Nothing overwhelming. No sharp spikes of pain or dizziness like before. The energy of the city flowed around her, present but manageable.

Maybe it was because she was growing used to it.

Or maybe it was because she knew, without a doubt, that if her power flared up again, Rain and Ariel would be there to help her.

That certainty blanketed her like a shield, bringing a sense of relief she readily embraced.

Back at the hotel, the abnormal chill still clung to the air, pressing against the glass doors as they stepped inside. Wasting no time, they made their way to their room to grab extra layers—because whatever was happening with the weather, it wasn't normal.

Takoda pulled open the closet and reached for her coat, slipping it on before tossing a glance over her shoulder. "Aren't you both glad I suggested we bring our coats—just in case?"

Rain, yanking a thick sweater over her head, grinned. "The Takoda instinct strikes again." She grabbed her winter coat and tossed Ariel's at her. "I swear, do you have some secret weather-sensing ability?"

Ariel smirked, wrapping a scarf around her neck. "Or she's just an over-preparer."

Takoda shrugged, amusement flashing in her eyes. "And yet, you're both warm and thanking me."

Ariel sighed dramatically as she pulled on her gloves. "Fine. You win this round."

Bundled against the cold, they headed back through the lobby and out onto the street.

The icy air bit at their skin, sharp and deviant, but it did nothing to dampen their energy. Takoda wrapped her coat a little tighter, the anticipation of the evening vibrating beneath her skin.

Ariel and Rain had immediately launched into an animated debate over the best ghost story they had ever heard, their voices lifting in playful challenge.

Laughter threaded through their words, warmth cutting through the chill.

Just as they reached the sidewalk, Takoda's steps slowed. A familiar figure moved through the bustling street with effortless grace. Even among the crowd, Riichi commanded attention without asking for it. His pace was unhurried, his presence solid, as if the chaos of the city simply adjusted around him rather than the other way around.

Before she could react, her phone buzzed in her pocket.

She pulled it out to find a quick message from Aislinn: *"Be there in 15."* Tucking her phone away, Takoda decided to keep the news to herself for the moment, savoring the quiet thrill of knowing she'll see both Riichi and Aislinn soon.

Ariel spotted Riichi approaching and nudged Rain, her eyes gleaming with mischief. "You know what sounds amazing right now? Coffee," she announced, giving Rain another nudge. Before Rain could question her, Ariel turned back to Takoda with a bright, innocent smile. "Come on, let's grab some for everyone. Takoda, we'll be back in about thirty minutes, okay?"

Takoda caught the unquestionable wink Ariel tossed her way and fought back a knowing smile. "Sure, that sounds great."

Rain glanced between them, brow furrowing in confusion. Clearly, she hadn't caught on to whatever Ariel was up to, but before she could question it, Ariel was already half-dragging her down the street. She barely had time to look over her shoulder before they disappeared around the corner, leaving Takoda standing alone as Riichi reached her.

He hesitated for a fraction of a second, searching her face, as if looking for an invitation. Takoda met his gaze, tenderness spreading through her as she offered a quiet, reassuring smile. That was all he needed. Stepping closer, he leaned down, brushing a soft kiss to her cheek.

"Hi," he murmured, his voice low, gentle. His eyes searched hers, as though confirming she was truly alright. She let the sincerity of the moment comfort her.

"How are you?" His concern was subtle, but she could hear the quiet thread of worry in his tone, the way his gaze lingered, watching for any sign that her powers might still be overwhelming her.

"Better now that you're here," she admitted softly. "But really, I'm fine. Nothing… unexpected." She held his stare, willing him to believe her.

A hint of relief crossed his face, though she could still sense the tension he hadn't quite let go of. With a quiet laugh, she nudged his arm. "You need to stop worrying so much. I promised I'd call you if anything changed, remember?"

At her words, he finally exhaled, his shoulders easing as a small, genuine smile curved his lips.

Takoda let the instance rest before tilting her head with a knowing look. "By the way," she said, her voice teasing, "Ariel practically dragged Rain off to get coffee, which, conveniently, gives us about thirty minutes alone."

Riichi's smile deepened, a hint of intent sparking behind his eyes before he reached up, tucking a stray piece of hair behind her ear. "Then we shouldn't waste it," he murmured.

Before she could respond, he leaned in, closing the small space between them with an unhurried kiss. There was no rush, no urgency—just a calm, thoughtful connection, as if the moment had been waiting for them to claim it.

Takoda melted into it, her fingers curling against the front of his coat as heat spread through her. The world outside faded—the surprising cold, the weight of the morning, the mysteries still lingering ahead. For these fleeting minutes, it was just them.

When they finally pulled back, Riichi didn't move far, his forehead resting lightly against hers. "So," he said quietly, his voice a little softer than before, "tell me about your morning."

Takoda let out a breathy laugh, her pulse still humming with the thrill of the kiss. "Well," she began, settling comfortably against him, "it started with Ariel and Rain trying to get details out of me about last night…"

As they waited for Rain and Ariel to return, she recounted the morning, describing the Halloween market at Seattle Center, the Witches' Brew Café, and the assortment of spooky teas they had tried. She told him about Rain's ridiculous witch hat, Ariel's fascination with her smoky quartz pendant, and the way the Halloween market had felt like stepping into a world where autumn never ended.

Riichi listened attentively, his expression shifting with each detail, absorbing her words in that way he always did—fully present, never distracted. His quiet smiles were small but real, his subtle reactions telling her that he was just as much a part of the events as she was.

At some point, without thinking, their hands found each other. It wasn't planned, but it felt natural, effortless—a tacit understanding forming in the space where their fingers met. The warmth of his palm against hers sent a faint pulse through her senses—solid, genuine.

Then she saw it.

The soft orange glow shimmered at the edges of their joined hands, a delicate aura pulsing gently, like embers stirring to life. Her breath caught as unease coiled in her chest. *Was she influencing him? Manipulating his emotions without realizing it?*

Instinctively, she moved to pull her hand away.

Riichi tightened his grip before she could.

"It's okay," he said calmly, his voice composed, steadfast. "I don't feel anything changing." His thumb brushed lightly over the back of her hand, grounding her before she could spiral. "It doesn't feel like you're pushing anything onto me. More like…" His eyes held hers, inscrutable for a brief instant before softening. "Like your magic recognizes me."

She swallowed, searching for any sign that he might be hiding discomfort or doubt, but all she found was quiet confidence. The glow remained, shimmering between them—gentle, unintrusive. Not influence. Not control. Just… bonding.

She let out a slow breath, allowing herself to accept it. Whatever this was, it wasn't a mistake.

They stood like that for a heartbeat, letting the quiet settle between them. Just as Takoda parted her lips to speak, the low rumble of engines rolled through the air, breaking the moment.

Her head turned instinctively toward the street as a line of cars pulled up in front of the hotel. One by one, the doors opened, and familiar faces stepped out.

Rowan. Aislinn. Oak. Eileen. Vine. Reed. Elder. Willow. Ivy. Ash. Birch.

One after another, the Fallen arrived.

Eileen stepped gracefully from her car, the air around her shifting with quiet authority. As her eyes swept the scene, she immediately took note of Takoda and Riichi's joined hands, the faint glow of orange still hovering between them. Her eyes sharpened, not with disapproval, but with the keen assessment of someone who recognized significance when she saw it.

Riichi caught her look but didn't let go. Instead, with a subtle motion, he slipped their joined hands into the pocket of his coat, shielding the glow from view. Takoda hesitated but followed his lead, tucking her free hand into her own pocket as affection curled through her chest.

A gust of wind cut through the group, biting and unnatural.

Vine hunched his shoulders against the cold, exhaling dramatically. "Man, Riichi, would it have killed you to give us a heads-up? Some of us weren't prepared for a surprise ice age."

Riichi offered a mild shrug. "It was eighty degrees yesterday."

A collective silence followed.

They all knew this wasn't a coincidence.

Eileen looked at Oak, a silent exchange passing between them, carrying a gravity that needed no words. Almost in unison, they lifted their eyes toward the sky. Oak's focus sharpened, his connection to the natural world attuned to the unseen shifts rippling through the air. A single dark cloud drifted overhead, its presence supernatural, laced with a force that had nothing to do with the weather.

Oak extended a hand, his fingertips flexing as if sifting through invisible threads. Snowflakes began to descend, weightless and deliberate. He pointed upward, his expression indecipherable.

Eileen followed his line of vision, her celestial awareness narrowing in on the disturbance. The glint of recognition in her eyes was immediate.

Snow continued to swirl lazily around them, light but persistent.

"This is the work of the Golden Dawn," she said quietly.

As she stepped forward, the rest of the Fallen followed, their presence like an unspoken shield as they moved toward Riichi and Takoda.

Takoda, sensing the shift in focus, pulled her hand from Riichi's pocket and tucked it fully into her own coat, a trace of self-consciousness settling in.

Eileen's tone remained even, but the urgency beneath it was evident. "Let's keep this brief. Oak detected a thin layer of magic in that cloud, which confirms the Golden Dawn is actively manipulating the weather. Now we need to determine why."

Her eyes moved to Riichi. "Did you secure a place for us?"

Riichi nodded, his expression resolute. "Yes. Just outside the city. Another Airbnb—big enough for more than a few of us."

Eileen studied him for an instant before giving a single nod of approval. "Good."

A familiar burst of chatter broke through the pressure as Ariel and Rain returned, arms full of steaming coffee cups. Their conversation had been lighthearted as they approached, but Rain visibly lit up the second she spotted Elder.

"Nik?" she called, grinning as she strode toward him. "Hey! Long time, no see." Without a second thought, she wrapped him in a quick, familiar hug, her energy as bright as ever.

Elder—caught between amusement and the awareness of Eileen's watchful stare—let out a low chuckle, his posture briefly loosening. He straightened almost immediately, schooling his features into neutrality.

Ariel handed Takoda and Riichi their coffee before glancing over the gathered Fallen, her brows lifting slightly. "So… if all of you are here, I'm guessing things just got serious?"

Eileen met her gaze. "Yes. Riichi spotted a Golden Dawn member two days ago. Oak just confirmed they're behind the sudden weather changes."

Ariel's eyebrows shot up. "Seriously?" She glanced at Rain before both of them turned to Takoda, waiting for some kind of confirmation and a reason why she didn't say anything earlier.

Takoda merely shrugged, a casual, knowing smile tugging at her lips, as if Riichi spotting a Golden Dawn member was hardly worth mentioning.

Before Ariel could press further, a soft laugh broke through the air.

They turned to find Aislinn standing nearby, her warm, easy smile softening the friction. Ariel and Rain lit up at the sight of her, rushing forward in a burst of excitement. The next minute was filled with familiar laughter, eager embraces, and the kind of energy that made it seem like they hadn't seen each other in years rather than a week.

As Ariel and Rain stepped back, still grinning, Eileen turned her attention fully to Takoda. "You, Ariel, and Rain will need to come with us," she said, her tone calm but leaving no room for debate.

Ariel froze mid-step, blinking in surprise. "Wait, what? Why do we have to go?"

"It's not safe for any of you to stay here," Eileen replied evenly. "We're not taking any chances."

Rain paused, glancing back at the hotel. "But we're paid up for two weeks…"

Ariel, unfazed, waved off the concern with a calculated grin. "Rain, I'm sure Eileen will pay us back. Won't you, Eileen?"

Eileen didn't flinch. "If you request it."

Vine bit the inside of his cheek to keep from laughing at Ariel's boldness, his amusement barely contained.

Ariel tilted her head, a smirk playing at her lips. "Alright then, here's the deal. We'll agree to go—but only if we get to decorate and celebrate for Halloween. That *is* why we came here after all."

Ivy, clearly trying to contain her amusement, failed miserably, unlike Vine, as a soft snort escaped.

Eileen cast her a sharp, sidelong glance, though the faintest hint of reluctant amusement ghosted at the corner of her mouth before she turned back to Ariel. "Fine. You may decorate, but you are not to leave the house without my permission."

Ariel beamed, holding out her hand. "Deal."

Eileen clasped her hand in a firm shake.

"Nice doing business with you," Ariel quipped before grabbing Rain's arm, the two of them laughing as they dashed back inside to gather their things. Just before disappearing through the door, Rain called back over her shoulder, "See you soon, Nik! Hope there's a pool table—you owe me a rematch!"

Elder, thrown for a split second, let out a quiet laugh before quickly composing himself under Eileen's watch. He cleared his throat, straightening as if the occurrence hadn't happened.

Once Ariel and Rain were out of earshot, Eileen turned back to Riichi, all business. "Do you have the address written down?"

Riichi nodded, retrieving a folded slip of paper from his pocket and handing it to her. She scanned it briefly before passing it to Oak, who tucked it into his jacket with the careful precision of a warrior storing a vital message.

Eileen's focus returned to Riichi. "You'll ensure they're packed and get them there safely?" Though phrased as a question, there was no doubt in her tone.

"Yes," he replied, steady and certain.

Eileen nodded. "Good. We'll see you there. And don't take too long… Hawthorn."

The use of his Fallen name carried a significance beyond mere urgency—a reminder of the duty entrusted to him, of the path he still walked.

Riichi inclined his head, understanding the message without the need for further words.

With that, Eileen turned, stepping back toward the vehicles. Oak pulled out first, the others' cars falling into place behind him with an ease that spoke of long-forged unity. Even in a city of steel and glass, they carried the quiet, staunch presence of warriors from an older world.

As the engines rumbled to life, Riichi watched them go, the weight of what lay ahead anchoring him in place. There was no uncertainty—only focus.

Riichi turned back to Takoda, lifting the coffee Ariel had left him and taking a sip. Before he could swallow, Takoda muttered playfully, "Geez. What, is she PMS-ing or something?" referring to Eileen's intense tone.

Riichi choked instantly, sputtering as a cough racked his chest. Takoda gasped, then burst into laughter as she patted his back, her shoulders shaking. "Sorry! I keep doing that to you, don't I? First dinner back in San Francisco and now here."

He coughed again, then managed a laugh between breaths. "I'm fine," he assured her, his smile breaking through as he caught his breath.

As the laughter faded, his expression changed, turning serious, his look steady as he studied her. "Are you ready for this?" The question felt like he meant more than just their run-in with the Golden Dawn.

Takoda met his eyes, her nod filled with certainty. "Yeah, I'm ready." The words carried an emphasis that matched his own—a commitment, a choice, spoken with the quiet conviction of someone who knew exactly what she wanted.

Riichi nodded, giving her hand a reassuring squeeze before releasing it and stepping toward the hotel doors. Together, they walked inside, a shared sense of purpose preparing them both. Whatever came next, they would face it side by side.

As they crossed the hotel lobby, Riichi instinctively reached for Takoda's hand, their fingers linking with an ease that no longer felt surprising. A soft orange glow sputtered to life, illuminating their joined hands with a quiet pulse—gentle, yet irrefutably present.

Noticing the glow, Riichi faltered, lifting their hands, his brows furrowing. His gaze searched hers before he tipped his head toward a secluded corner of the lobby, a silent request. Takoda caught the implicit need for privacy and nodded, allowing him to guide her away from any prying eyes.

They sat on a plush couch in the hotel lounge, far from the low hum of conversation filling the space. The dim lighting cast soft shadows across the room, reflecting off the faint orange radiance between their joined hands. Takoda shifted a little, turning to face Riichi, watching as his gaze lingered on the light pulsing between them.

His expression was thoughtful, unreadable in a way that made her heart pick up speed. After a slow breath, he met her eyes.

"Are you… alright with this?" His voice was steady, but there was a careful edge to it, as if bracing for unwillingness.

Takoda paused, not because she didn't know her answer, but because she wasn't entirely sure which part he was asking about. She glanced down at their hands before meeting his eyes again. "Do you mean… am I okay with suddenly having magic? Or are you asking if I'm okay with what having magic might mean for us?"

His brows lifted slightly, as if her response had uncovered a layer he hadn't put into words yet. "Both," he admitted. "I want to know your thoughts on both."

She took a breath, letting the importance of the question settle before answering. "It's scary," she admitted. "Having a supernatural ability I don't understand… not knowing how to control it, what it means, or even what I'm supposed to do with it. But…" she paused, the flickering light between their hands shifting a bit, as if responding to her confidence. "I know I'll figure it out."

Riichi's eyes remained locked on hers, his thumb brushing absently over her knuckles, a small, supportive motion that stopped more than just her hands from shaking.

"And for what it might mean…" Takoda faltered only for a breath before pressing forward, her voice quieter now. "If I'm being honest, I think—no, I know—I had feelings for you long before this happened." She let out a short, almost embarrassed laugh, shaking her head. "The glow just… makes it stronger. Clears out any doubts I tried to have. And I'm okay with that, too."

Riichi didn't speak at first. The light softened between them, pulsing gently in the space where their hands met. His gaze searched hers, not in question, but as if memorizing every word she had just given him.

"But what about you?" she asked gently. "Is this a path you would have wanted?"

The question caught him off guard. He hesitated, his thumb brushing absently over her knuckles as he considered it. His gaze drifted downward, stopping on their intertwined hands, as if the quiet warmth between them held an answer he hadn't yet put into words.

After a moment, he exhaled, looking back at her. "What I want... is for you to be happy," he said, his voice steady, cautious. "I'd never want to bring you into this world if it's not a life you truly want." His grip on her hand remained firm, not possessive but centering, a presence rather than a claim. "Your happiness means more to me than anything, and I'd never want you to feel like this was forced on you or beyond your control."

The words settled between them like a quiet vow, unspoken yet deeply understood.

His gaze held even, but she saw an unspoken worry behind his eyes—not hesitation from doubt, but the quiet vulnerability of offering her a truth that left him unguarded.

"But..." he continued, his voice quieter now, "if I'm being honest, I had feelings for you long before any of this—probably since the café fire. I spent a long time trying to deny them, convincing myself it wasn't the right time. But if you're open to it, I'm ready to acknowledge them—and I'd like to see where this takes us."

The confession wasn't grand or dramatic, but it carried a depth that made her heart tighten. There was no pressure in his words, only a willingness, a quiet hope woven through the restraint of someone who would never demand more than she was willing to give.

Takoda's lips curved into a small, genuine smile as compassion spread through her chest. "I'd like to see what happens with us, too."

Riichi smiled softly at her words, a quiet understanding passed between them, deepening their connection in a way that felt both new and deliberate—a choice they were making together, unfolding with each shared moment.

Then, without overthinking it, she leaned in.

Riichi didn't question it.

Their lips met in a kiss that was tentative but sure—an acknowledgment, a choice neither of them had to put into words. The passion of it curled through her, sinking beneath her skin, steadying her more than any certainty ever had.

The spark between them flared once, then softened, like an ember finding its warmth, perpetual and enduring.

When they pulled back, Riichi's eyes lingered on hers, impassive in the way that always made her heart race.

But this time, she understood the look completely.

After a brief pause, Riichi released her hand, watching as the last spark of light dimmed. "I'll be here, waiting in the lobby," he told her, his voice calm but unerring. The firmness in his words carried the quiet promise of someone who would remain, no matter what.

Takoda rose to her feet, nodding in gratitude before turning toward the stairs. Halfway up, she glanced back. His eyes were already on her.

No words passed between them, but the moment held its own conversation, one that required no explanation.

Then she turned and disappeared up the stairs.

Riichi's gaze lingered on the empty space she left behind, a subtle tightness rising in his chest. The lobby's stillness seemed almost too quiet, as if the air itself was bracing for what was to come.

He cast a glance toward the door, instincts stirring. The road ahead would hold no easy choices, no simple paths.

But one thing was certain.

Whatever came next, he wanted to face it with Takoda by his side.

Chapter Nine

Gathering Trust

The late afternoon sun streamed through the hotel lobby's windows, gilding the space in warm light. Polished floors reflected the glow, while long shadows stretched across the room. Takoda, Ariel, and Rain descended the staircase, their suitcases rolling behind them. Anticipation buzzed among them, pressing at Takoda's ribs with a restless energy, fueled by more than just nerves.

Near the lobby's edge, Riichi stood with the kind of patience that made him impossible to ignore. He had always carried himself with purpose, a presence shaped by discipline rather than display. When they reached him, he handed a folded slip of paper to Ariel. She scanned the address, a hint of curiosity crossing her face, before tucking it into her pocket.

"So, this is where it all happens, huh?" she mused, her tone light but thoughtful.

Takoda nodded, then glanced at her friends. "Do you two mind if I ride with him?" She kept her voice casual, but her grip tightened slightly on the handle of her suitcase.

Ariel's smirk barely concealed her amusement, while Rain playfully nudged Takoda's shoulder with a knowing look. "You go on ahead," Rain said. "We'll catch up with you there."

Takoda exhaled, shaking her head as she pulled them both into a firm hug. Their presence grounded her more than she had anticipated. "See you soon."

Ariel and Rain headed for the doors, their conversation already transitioning to their own plans. Takoda turned back to Riichi, sensing the change in the atmosphere around them. "Alright. Let's get moving."

They stepped outside, any warmth of the day giving way to the cool bite of early evening. Their footsteps fell into sync without effort, the rhythm of the walk familiar in a way that surprised them both. The silence between them wasn't heavy. It gave them space to reflect, even as thoughts pulled at the edges of their focus.

Takoda glanced sideways, watching Riichi's calm, purposeful gait. He always moved like he knew where he was going—not just physically, but in life. As if every step was part of a plan he had already committed to.

A few blocks passed before he finally broke the silence. "You still have time to change your mind," he said, his voice even but carrying a deeper note—offering her an exit she knew he didn't want her to take.

She slowed half a step, surprised by the softness beneath his words. "I'm not changing my mind," she said, her voice quiet but sure. "I chose this. No one forced me. I want to be there."

He nodded once, but didn't look at her. "It's not about pressure. I just want to make sure you're doing this because you truly want to—not because it feels expected."

"I don't do things out of obligation," she replied gently. "If I didn't believe in this—believe in you—I wouldn't be here."

At that, Riichi finally glanced her way. There was no smile, but there didn't need to be. The shift in his expression said enough.

"I believe in you too," he said after a beat. "That's why I keep wondering if I'm giving you everything you need to feel safe in this."

She looked ahead again, her pulse picking up. "You are," she whispered.

When they reached his apartment, he packed quickly, efficiently. She had seen this place before, but this was the first time she really noticed how curated it felt. Shelves arranged with sharp precision. Books lined up by size. No clutter. No color that didn't match the others. It felt like walking into a perfectly drawn line—clean, straight, and self-contained.

"How long have you lived like this?" she asked, her voice quiet, eyes scanning the room.

He zipped his bag before answering. "Since the beginning," he said simply. "It helps me stay focused."

She trailed a finger along the edge of a small wooden table, her thoughts drifting. "Focused is good. But... does it leave room for anything unexpected?"

He paused by the doorway, studying her. "I never thought it needed to. Until now."

Takoda looked back at him, the words landing deeper than she expected.

"I'm ready," she said, without him needing to ask again.

A flicker of emotion passed behind his eyes—quiet acknowledgment, maybe something more—and he gave a small nod before guiding her outside.

The car ride passed in silence at first, but it wasn't the same kind of silence. It buzzed with unspoken thoughts, charged with everything they hadn't said aloud. The city blurred outside the window, streaks of gold from the setting sun sliding across the dashboard.

Takoda shifted in her seat. "It still feels surreal," she admitted. "Leaving everything behind and stepping into this... whole other life."

Riichi's hands stayed steady on the wheel. "It felt like that for me too. But then I realized—sometimes the only way forward is to burn the old road behind you."

She let out a short breath, part-laugh, part-nerves. "Dramatic. But not wrong."

"You don't have to burn everything," he added. "Just the parts that keep you standing still."

Her voice softened. "And what if I don't know what those parts are yet?"

He looked over at her then, just briefly. "Then we find out together."

That was when her composure began to slip. The further they drove, the tighter her chest became. Her fingers twisted in her lap, a habit she couldn't shake. Words threatened to surface, but tangled before reaching her lips.

Riichi noticed. His gaze flicked toward her again, then to the road ahead. Without speaking, he guided the car off onto a quiet stretch of roadside, gravel crunching beneath the tires as they eased to a stop.

The sunset painted the field beyond them in warm gold and burnished amber. He turned off the engine and faced her fully.

"You're holding something back."

Takoda hesitated, her throat tight. "I don't know how to say it," she admitted. "I don't want you to think I'm doubting you. I'm not. It's just—this world, this life—I'm scared I won't be enough."

"You don't have to prove anything to me," he said gently. "But you can tell me what's on your mind. All of it."

She reached for his hand. The moment their fingers touched, a sense of grounding steadied her. She closed her eyes, letting her emotions move through the connection. Not to manipulate—just to share. The choice to be vulnerable was hers, and she trusted him with it.

"I want to be in this," she said quietly. "I just… worry that I'm going to mess it up. That I won't be strong enough for what's ahead."

He tightened his grip, his palm warm against hers. "I've doubted myself too," he said. "But I've never doubted you."

Takoda's eyes stung, emotion catching in her throat. She blinked down at their joined hands.

"You don't have to carry this fear alone," he added. "And you don't have to be perfect. Just be honest—with me, with yourself. We'll figure the rest out."

She nodded slowly, her voice almost lost. "Okay."

And this time, she believed it.

Then, after a moment's thought, he let go, pushed open his door, and stepped out of the car.

Takoda was taken aback for a moment as he moved around to her side, opening her door. The evening light caught in his dark hair, shadows brushing over the sharp angles of his face. He looked down at her, watching her closely, his presence as steadfast as the roots of the Hawthorn tree that had shaped him—strong, immovable, patient.

He extended his hand. "Do you trust me?"

The question hung in the air, soft but definite, carrying more significance than the words alone.

Takoda met his eyes, her pulse racing as she slid her fingers into his. His firm hold enveloped hers, providing a sense of solidity and reality.

And for the first time in miles, the pressure in her chest finally eased.

He led her into the open field, where the last light of day cast a golden glow over the landscape, the sky melting into deep hues of violet and indigo. The air carried the hush of dusk, still and undisturbed, as if the world itself had paused to listen.

When they reached a spot beyond the car, he released her hand and moved behind her, his presence close enough that she could feel the warmth radiating from him. The air between them thrummed with a silent yet powerful energy, his concentrated attention providing her with stability.

Gently, he placed his hands over hers, his touch firm yet steady.

"We're going to try something," he murmured near her ear, his voice carrying the calm patience of a teacher, a guide. "An exercise to let go of anything you don't need to carry. Just follow my lead."

Takoda nodded, closing her eyes and centering herself on the warmth of his hands.

He began guiding her through a series of slow, controlled movements—each one fluid, deliberate, like a silent rhythm etched into the earth itself. His touch barely pressed, encouraging her to release the burdens she carried, to let her fears slip away with every motion.

"Breathe with each movement," he instructed softly, his voice low, anchoring. "Inhale, draw in calm. Exhale, let go of whatever doesn't serve you."

Takoda obeyed, releasing a slow breath. She pictured her nervousness as a dark mist unraveling with every exhale, thinning and dispersing into the fading twilight. The tension in her shoulders eased, the knots in her chest loosening as she allowed the movement to take hold, guiding her deeper into stillness.

They moved together in quiet synchronicity, their hands sweeping through the air in seamless arcs. Riichi's movements remained calm, composed, a force both firm and fluid—protective and resilient. The rhythmic flow calmed her, easing the restless hum of doubt that had followed her from the city.

As the exercise came to a close, their hands lowered in unison, and with it, the last remnants of unease faded. A newfound lightness settled over her, quiet but certain.

Takoda turned to face him, gratitude warming her chest. "Thank you," she murmured, her voice softer now, more assured. "I didn't realize how much I needed that."

A flicker of relief passed through his expression, though he didn't voice it. Instead, he lifted his hand, brushing his fingers along her cheek in a touch so gentle it barely skimmed the surface of her skin. Yet there was an unspoken sentiment in the gesture—an acknowledgment, a reassurance, a quiet kind of care.

Then, without a moment's pause, he leaned down, pressing his lips to hers in a lingering kiss—unshaped by anything but trust. It was intentional, unhurried, a wordless promise exchanged in the fading light.

As they pulled apart, the sun dipped below the horizon, the world folding into twilight's embrace.

They made their way back to the car, the silence between them was no longer heavy, but once again comfortable. As Riichi started the engine and they resumed their drive, Takoda watched the scenery skim past the window, her thoughts quieter, her heart lighter.

The tension from before had loosened its grip, replaced by a steady sense of belonging she hadn't known she was waiting for.

As they neared the Fallen's temporary base, a grand mansion rose ahead, its dark roofline cutting cleanly against the dusky sky. Unlike the estate in San Francisco, this one felt curated rather than lived-in—an elegant property with pristine hedges, tall wrought-iron gates, and a sweeping driveway designed more for appearance than permanence. Its size was impressive, its structure refined, but there was no history pressing in from the walls—just the quiet stillness of a place meant to impress, not remember.

Takoda swallowed, the sight filling her with both awe and anticipation.

Riichi parked, casting a glance her way. "Ready?"

She exhaled, nodding. "Yeah."

Together, they stepped out, the cool night air brushing against her skin as they crossed the threshold.

Inside, the mansion opened into spacious rooms filled with rich textures and soft, ambient light. The scent of polished wood and new fabric lingered in the air, subtle hints of lavender and citrus from a diffuser tucked near the entry. Everything was arranged with purpose—the furniture stylish but untouched, the artwork chosen for cohesion rather than meaning. It was comfortable in a way that felt temporary, like stepping into someone else's curated calm.

Even so, warmth met her as they stepped further inside. Voices carried from the sitting room, quiet conversation and laughter easing the edges of her nerves.

They entered a spacious sitting room off the main hall, where the glow of a television illuminated the faces of the Fallen, along with Rain and Ariel. The tension that had pressed against Takoda's ribs eased at the sight.

Vine looked up first, a smirk playing on his lips. "About time you two showed up."

Ariel turned, flashing them both a mischievous grin. "Now the party can really start!"

Her voice carried the same lightness Takoda had come to rely on—a playful ease that made even the most intimidating places feel like home. The air around them shifted, and just like that, the burdens she'd been carrying felt a little easier to bear.

Riichi nodded toward the stairs. "Let's find our rooms," he said quietly, guiding her down a hallway and up the sweeping staircase.

He chose the right side of the second floor, where he found two empty rooms directly across from each other.

Pushing open the door to one of them, he stepped aside to let her in. "I'll be right across the hall," he said simply, setting her bag down inside.

Takoda felt a strange combination of relief and anticipation. The space was welcoming in a way she hadn't expected—warm, quiet, untouched yet not unwelcoming. Moonlight filtered through the window, casting a faint silver sheen over the walls and softening the weight she hadn't realized she'd been carrying. She traced her fingers over the fabric of the bedding, grounding herself in the simple, tangible details.

After setting her things down, she took a calming breath before stepping back into the hallway.

They walked downstairs together, the space between them lighter after the long drive. Halfway down, a voice echoed from below.

"Riichi, Takoda. I need to see you in my office. Now."

Takoda's steps faltered a little at Eileen's tone, sharp and commanding. She glanced at Riichi, catching a hint of doubt in his expression before they both nodded and continued toward the base of the stairs.

Vine's chuckle drifted from the sitting room.

"Shouldn't have taken so long, huh?" he teased, his usual smirk in place.

The remark earned a small smile from Takoda, easing the tension tightening in her chest.

Inside Eileen's office, the atmosphere shifted. She closed the door behind them, her gaze sharp and assessing. The rich scent of parchment and old wood lingered in the air, a contrast to the weight of the moment. The walls bore no unnecessary decoration, only what was functional—maps, reports, and the faint scent of aged ink, a reflection of the mind that commanded this space.

"What kept you?" she asked, her voice brisk, her keen eyes narrowing slightly.

"There were things to take care of," Riichi replied, his tone composed, meeting her scrutiny without wavering.

Eileen's expression sharpened. "What things?" she pressed, her intensity steadfast.

Takoda's patience thinned. Irritation flared as she watched Eileen's sharp tone directed at Riichi. Before she could stop herself, the words left her lips.

"It doesn't matter what things there were. We're here now, aren't we?" Her voice held an unmistakable edge, making it clear she didn't appreciate the interrogation.

Eileen's expression softened, a knowing warmth breaking through the scrutiny. "Thank you, Takoda," she said, the change in her tone catching Takoda off guard. "You've always struck me as kind and gentle. I wasn't sure how you'd adjust to the supernatural world, but now I see you'll be just fine."

Takoda raised an eyebrow, irritation still simmering beneath her ribs. "You were *testing* me?" she asked, disbelief threading through her voice. "You could have just asked without the attitude."

Eileen's lips curled subtly, amusement flickering at the edges. But she gave a slow nod, acknowledging the truth in Takoda's words.

Then, just as smoothly, she switched back to business.

She leaned back, her presence filling the space—not through force, but with a quiet intensity that made it impossible to look away. It wasn't just authority—it was an innate power, a force woven into her very being. "Let's talk about your power," she said. "Based on Aislinn's reports, it seems you have a latent ability. Willow, who specializes in magic and energy manipulation, will be training you. She'll help you learn how to manage and understand what you can do."

Takoda glanced at Riichi, relief washing over her at the mention of Willow's guidance. She had known her ability was manifesting, but the thought of navigating it alone had been daunting. Now, with someone experienced helping her, the stress on her chest eased.

Eileen's gaze moved between them. "The timing of your power surfacing isn't random," she continued. "It's a direct result of the bond between you and Riichi."

The words settled between them like an indisputable fact. Takoda had already sensed it—this growing connection, the way she could feel Riichi in ways she hadn't before. Now, hearing it spoken aloud, the realization took root.

Eileen turned to Riichi, her expression steady. "For you, this will mean adjustments as well," she said. "You've spent a long time keeping others at a distance. But this connection requires change. As you grow closer, Takoda's abilities may develop in ways we don't yet understand. Whatever form they take, they will be a source of strength, not a weakness."

Riichi absorbed her words in silence, giving a small nod. He didn't need to speak for Takoda to know he was already turning over the implications, weighing what this meant for both of them.

Eileen watched him for a moment, then softened, a faint smile tugging at her lips. "For now, I want you both to relax. Join the others and get settled. Tomorrow morning, we'll discuss the latest developments with the Golden Dawn. Takoda, you'll need to be present."

They stood to leave, and Eileen led them back toward the sitting room, where Rain, Ariel, and the Fallen were still gathered. As they entered, she addressed the group.

"We'll be getting settled tonight," she announced, her tone light but carrying that same quiet authority that made it impossible to ignore. "Tomorrow, we meet to discuss everything we know. Take the night to rest."

A few murmured agreements passed through the room.

The air still held a hush, but not from secrets—it came from newness, the adjustment of settling into an unfamiliar space. In the flicker of lamplight and the soft sounds of the others nearby, Takoda felt a sense of grounding take hold. It wasn't home, but it was enough for now—a place to rest, to prepare, to begin.

Aislinn turned to Takoda, nodding toward the hallway. "Want to find a quiet spot to talk?"

Takoda pushed up from her seat just as Willow approached, a warm smile lighting her features. "Mind if I join you two?" she asked, curiosity flashing in her gaze.

Aislinn glanced at Takoda, who nodded enthusiastically. "Sure! The more, the merrier."

The three of them slipped out of the sitting room, their footsteps fading into the hall as a quiet sense of anticipation built between them.

Back in the sitting room, Rain stretched with a grin and shot a challenging look toward Nik. "Alright, who's ready for a rematch?" A playful edge laced her tone. "Last time was pure luck, and I'm about to prove it."

Nik didn't look at her right away. He finished the page he was reading, then set the book aside with deliberate care.

"You can try," he said simply, his tone unreadable. But as he rose, there was a flicker of awareness in his gaze—subtle, brief, but unmistakably directed at her.

Vine and Ariel exchanged a knowing glance, their eagerness unmistakable.

"We're in!" Ariel declared, already grabbing her things.

Laughter trailed behind them as the group headed toward the game room, the easy rhythm of their banter filling the hall.

Once the others had gone, Rowan turned to Riichi, tilting his head toward the door. "Feel like taking a walk?"

Riichi met his gaze, considering for a brief moment before giving a small nod. Without another word, the two of them stepped out, leaving behind the hum of conversation for the quiet hush of the hallway.

Near the corner of the room, Reed, who had remained unbothered by the changing energy around him, watched as the groups scattered. A faint smile ghosted across his lips.

"Looks like everyone's running off. Feels like being the last one picked in dodgeball," he muttered.

No one answered, but the room settled into a rare stillness, the kind that only came in the peaceful intervals between battles, between decisions, between the tides of something larger moving beneath the surface. Oak rose quietly and headed silently towards Eileen's office.

★★★

The kitchen was a cozy haven, bathed in soft light, with the rich scent of herbs and spices filling the air. The warmth of the space wrapped around Takoda the second she stepped inside with Aislinn and Willow, offering a familiar sense of comfort. This was her kind of place—anchoring, calm, filled with quiet purpose. A space where she could breathe.

As they gathered around a small wooden table near the window, Takoda glanced at her friends. "Eileen explained that Willow's here to help me with my new power," she said, strengthening her voice as she spoke. "Just in case you didn't already know." She exhaled, alternating her gaze between them. "It seems I can feel what others are feeling… and I can turn one emotion into another. But I ended up absorbing everything around me, and it got overwhelming."

She didn't mention how Riichi had helped her release it. That part she wanted to keep to herself.

Willow's eyes brightened with understanding. "That sounds like emotional alchemy," she mused, leaning in a bit. "I can do something similar with energy manipulation, which is why Eileen thought I'd be a good fit to help you. I think we'll make a solid team."

Aislinn nodded, her smile warm. "I can help too! I work with kinetic energy—still figuring it out, but if you need backup, I'm here."

Takoda felt a rush of gratitude, warmth pooling in her chest at their easy support.

Willow grinned, the trace of excitement in her expression evident. "Sounds like a plan. Magic like this is best developed with trust. The more we support each other, the stronger we'll be."

They talked a little longer, tossing around ideas for training, until Willow glanced at the clock and pushed back from the table, brushing her hands off lightly.

"I should get back," she said, amusement glinting in her eyes. "I don't want to leave Ivy alone for too long with just Birch, Ash, Oak, and Reed."

She cast a knowing look at Aislinn and Takoda.

"Besides," she added with a smirk, "I think you two have more to talk about."

With a quick wave, Willow slipped out, leaving Aislinn and Takoda alone in the warmth of the kitchen.

Aislinn turned to Takoda, amusement dancing in her eyes. "So," she said, leaning forward with a curious grin. "What's really going on with you and Riichi? I saw the way you two looked at each other earlier."

Takoda let out a slow breath, her gaze drifting toward the window. "It's complicated," she admitted. "I feel this pull toward him, like he makes me feel safe in a way I haven't before. But there's this nervousness I can't shake. I'm scared of what it all means."

Aislinn nodded, understanding clear in her expression. "I get that. When I started feeling things for Rowan, it was overwhelming. You want to trust those feelings, but opening up can feel like too much sometimes. Vulnerability is terrifying."

Takoda pressed her lips together, pausing before she spoke. "Riichi is so… reserved and focused. Eileen mentioned he might have to make adjustments because of our bond, and I can't help wondering—what if he doesn't want that? What if he doesn't want more than what we already have? What if he sees this bond as an obligation, not a choice?"

Aislinn tilted her head. "You're worried he might not want to pursue the connection?"

"Exactly." Takoda's voice dropped to a whisper. "What if he thinks it's too much? I don't want to push him into anything, especially if he feels like he's losing part of himself in the process."

Aislinn reached across the table, her touch light but reassuring. "It's natural to feel that way. But remember, he cares about you. He wouldn't be putting effort into this connection if it didn't matter to him. Riichi doesn't do anything without a reason. Give him a chance to show you how he feels—he's earned that space."

Takoda met Aislinn's gaze, indecision still remaining in her chest but easing slightly. "I just want to embrace this new reality without losing myself or pushing him too far. I want him to stay true to who he is."

Aislinn's smile softened. "You're not going to change him in a bad way. Relationships aren't about *losing* who you are—they're about *growing* into who you're meant to be. If this bond is real, he'll find a way to adapt without losing himself."

Takoda exhaled, some of the tension in her shoulders easing. "I hope you're right."

"I know I am," Aislinn said confidently. "And if you ever need to talk, I'm here."

A small smile tugged at Takoda's lips. "Thanks, Aislinn. That means a lot."

Aislinn nudged her playfully. "Come on, let's go find the others before they start the party without us."

Takoda let out a small laugh, shaking her head as they pushed away from the table and headed for the hallway, their footsteps light against the worn wooden floors.

★★★

The back patio was quiet, the cool evening air carrying the crisp scent of pine and damp earth. A gentle breeze rustled through the trees, and the occasional chirp of crickets broke the stillness. The warmth of the mansion hung back behind them, but out here, beneath the open night sky, the space felt clearer—unburdened.

Riichi stepped forward, his hands resting on the railing as he took in the darkened landscape. The peace of the night settled around them, yet the heaviness in his heart persisted. He had chosen Rowan for this conversation for a reason, but finding the right words still felt like wading through unknown terrain.

After a long moment, he finally spoke.

"I wanted to talk to you about the bond I've formed with Takoda," he said, his voice even, though a trace of doubt betrayed his usual composure.

Rowan leaned against the railing, his sharp gaze collected. "What about it?"

Riichi exhaled slowly, his eyes fixed on the distant tree line. "I care about her. A lot." The admission came easier than expected, but the emphasis behind it remained. "But I keep wondering how this bond is going to change things. Eileen said adjustments would be necessary, and I'm…" He hesitated. "I don't know if I'm ready for that kind of change."

Rowan studied him for a beat before nodding. "That's fair," he said. "It's a lot to take in."

Riichi's grip on the railing tightened. "What if I'm not capable of being more open?" he asked, voice quieter now. "I've spent so long keeping things in order, focusing on what needs to be done. What if this bond makes me into something I'm not?"

Rowan tilted his head slightly. "You think being with Takoda means losing yourself?"

Riichi didn't answer immediately. He wasn't sure he liked the way that sounded, but deep down, the thought had taken root. "I don't know," he admitted. "I just—there's comfort in control. In knowing where I stand. This bond… it makes me question everything I thought I had figured out."

Rowan let that sit between them for a moment before speaking. "You know, when I realized I had feelings for Aislinn, I fought it at first. I didn't want to acknowledge how much she meant to me. I told myself I had too much responsibility, too many things to focus on." He let out a dry chuckle. "It didn't change the fact that I still wanted her."

Riichi listened, taking in Rowan's words.

"I get it, Riichi. You've spent years structuring your life a certain way. But letting someone in doesn't erase who you are. It just… adds to it." Rowan glanced at him, his expression thoughtful. "You don't have to have it all figured out today. Just be honest with her about where you are now."

Riichi's brow furrowed as he processed that. He wasn't used to uncertainty—he didn't like uncertainty—and yet, this entire situation had placed him right in the middle of it.

"And what if that's not enough?" he asked, his voice lower. "What if she realizes this bond is more than she signed up for?"

Rowan met his gaze, unwavering. "Then that's her choice to make. But from what I've seen, Takoda isn't the type to walk away just because something's complicated."

Riichi exhaled slowly, his mind running through every interaction, every moment he'd spent with her.

"You can't control how she feels," Rowan continued, "but you can be honest about your own feelings. If this bond is real, she deserves to know where you stand."

A thoughtful silence stretched between them, only broken by the rustling of the trees. Riichi let out a slow breath, feeling Rowan's words settle.

"You're right," he said at last. "I need to trust in our connection. And I need to be willing to open up—without overthinking what it means."

Rowan smirked slightly, clapping him on the shoulder. "Now that's progress."

A hint of amusement flickered in Riichi's expression. "I wouldn't go that far."

They stood there a moment longer, the night stretching quiet and vast around them. Eventually, without a word, they turned back toward the house, ready to rejoin the others. The conversation might have ended, but the thoughts it had stirred lingered.

Riichi didn't have all the answers.

But maybe, for now, he didn't need to.

★★★

The mansion had settled into stillness, the energy of the evening fading as the Fallen retreated to their rooms. Only the occasional creak of the old wooden beams and the distant rustle of wind against the windows hinted at movement beyond the quiet halls.

Knowing Eileen had planned an early start for the Fallen meeting, Riichi walked Takoda to her room, his presence as dependable as ever.

"I'm right across the hall if you need anything," he said, his voice even, but the reassurance in it definite.

Takoda met his gaze, warmth fluttering in her chest at the simple but meaningful gesture. "Thanks, Riichi."

With one last glance, she slipped into her room, shutting the door softly behind her.

She changed into an oversized T-shirt, climbing beneath the covers, but sleep refused to take hold. Her mind spun with the bulk of everything—the celebration of Halloween, the sheer presence of the Fallen around her, the unfamiliar energy of the mansion, the awareness of the changes unfolding in her life.

The minutes stretched. She turned onto her side, then her back, then her stomach, but no position gave her peace of mind. Each attempt to close her eyes only pulled her deeper into the tangle of her own thoughts, the enormity of what she was stepping into pressing against her ribs like an unseen force.

After nearly an hour, she exhaled sharply, frustration bubbling to the surface. Lying here, restless and alone, wasn't helping.

Before she could overthink it, she slipped out of bed and crossed the hall, her bare feet making no sound against the cool floor. Her heart picked up as she raised her hand and knocked softly on Riichi's door.

A moment later, the door opened, and Riichi's expression softened when he saw her standing there in an oversized T-shirt, a nervous look in her eyes. "Is something wrong?" he asked, his tone laced with genuine concern.

She bit her lip, her voice quivering. "I… I couldn't sleep. I was wondering if it might be alright for me to stay with you?" Her words came out barely above a whisper, her need for comfort evident.

A trace of surprise passed through his gaze, but there was no hesitation in his answer. "Of course." He stepped aside, holding the door open. "Come in."

Takoda stepped into the room, the dim lighting casting soft shadows along the walls. The space reflected him perfectly—structured, deliberate, uncluttered. Every item had its place, no unnecessary distractions, no signs of impulsive living. And yet, beneath the precision, there was warmth.

She made her way to the bed, slipping beneath the blanket, and Riichi followed, settling beside her. The moment his arm wrapped around her, the tension in her body started to unwind.

"Thanks for this," she murmured, pressing her forehead lightly against his shoulder. "It's easier to breathe when I'm with you."

His arm tightened slightly, his thumb brushing against her arm in a slow, absent motion. "I'm glad you're here."

They lay together, the silence between them calm, undisturbed—neither burdensome nor heavy, just present. Yet beneath it, an unspoken pull stirred, pressing against the words they hadn't yet voiced.

After a while, Takoda stirred, her fingers smoothing over the fabric of the blanket, tracing idle patterns. "I'm afraid I won't be strong enough for this world," she admitted. "What if I can't control my abilities? What if I end up holding you back?"

Riichi exhaled slowly, his thumb brushing absently along the edge of the sheet, thoughtful. "I understand that fear," he admitted. "But I worry about the opposite." His voice dipped slightly, lower than usual, as if speaking the words out loud made them more real. "I don't want to be the reason you feel held back. I've spent so much of my life… contained. I don't want that to become a burden on you."

Takoda tilted her head, watching him. There it was—the restraint beneath his control, the conflict between who he was and who he was learning to be.

"We both want this, don't we?" she murmured. "I don't want to be the only one reaching for it. I want you to feel like you can lean on me too."

He took a deeper breath, as though the idea was only just beginning to take hold in his mind.

"You're right," he said after a pause, the quiet weight of those words carrying a decision. "We'll figure it out. Whatever comes next, I want to be someone you can trust."

Takoda exhaled slowly, feeling the constant warmth of his presence beside her.

Her pulse quickened as she met Riichi's eyes. There was no hesitation. No restraint. Just them.

She leaned in again, and the moment their lips met, the world outside of this room ceased to exist.

The kiss intensified in a heartbeat, unfolding slowly yet with an undeniable insistence, brimming with all the emotions that words could not express. A warm, tingling heat spiraled in her stomach as her fingers glided over his broad shoulders, exploring the firm, sinewy strength beneath her touch. The composed restraint he usually maintained was now unraveling, surrendering to the moment.

Riichi's fingers tightened at her waist, then glided up her back, his touch steady yet full of undeniable intent. There was nothing hesitant about the way he pulled her against him, the way he met her kiss with a hunger that matched her own. An intense fire was building between them, one they had both been holding back for too long.

Takoda gasped as his lips traveled to her jaw, down the elegant line of her throat, slow, deliberate, committing the texture and warmth of her skin to memory, savoring every inch beneath his touch. Her fingers tangled into his hair, gripping just enough to make him exhale sharply against her skin.

The atmosphere between them had always been like a quiet storm, brewing with unspoken intensity. A crackling tension simmered beneath the surface, like the charged air before a thunderclap, waiting for the inevitable moment when it would be unleashed.

Now, neither of them restrained themselves, and the storm was finally allowed to break free, sweeping everything in its path.

There was no fear. No doubt.

Only this.

Takoda shifted slightly, pressing herself closer, her breath catching as desire surged beneath her skin. A quiet ache stirred deep inside her, steady and consuming. Riichi's breath skimmed along her collarbone, warm and uneven, the sound of it brushing against her like a vow.

His hands slid up her back, fingers threading into her hair before tracing down her spine, anchoring her as their bodies aligned. Every movement spoke of certainty—how he held her, how he responded to every shift with quiet urgency.

The way he kissed her—slow, consuming, deliberate—set her alight. His lips lingered over hers, then moved lower, trailing heat along her neck, over the curve of her shoulder. Her fingers curled against his skin, holding on as if letting go had never been an option.

The connection between them deepened with each breath, each touch. He explored her with a reverence that sent shivers across her skin, his hands drawing paths that left her trembling beneath him.

There was no resistance in her. No need to hold back.

She leaned into him fully, her heartbeat syncing with the rhythm of his hands, the press of his mouth, the quiet force of what passed between them.

She wasn't just falling—she was choosing to fall.

And Riichi met her with full acceptance, steady and sure, giving her no reason to doubt the space they shared.

Time dissolved around them, lost in the hush of whispered names, the press of lips, the heat of skin against skin. What they created in those hours was not fleeting—it was grounded, lasting.

By the time they finally settled, their bodies tangled beneath the sheets, Takoda rested her head against his chest, his heartbeat steady, strong, a rhythm she knew she would never forget.

His hand smoothed over her back, slow, absent, as if grounding himself in the feel of her.

Neither of them spoke.

They didn't need to. The silence between them spoke volumes.

Sleep pulled at her, but before she gave in to it, she let herself fully sink into the moment—the warmth of him beside her, the way he held her like he never wanted to let go.

And for the first time in longer than she could remember, she didn't feel like she had to hold back either.

Outside, the wind picked up, stirring the thick clouds that had rolled in unnoticed. The air had shifted, an unnatural weight pressing against the quiet city beyond the mansion's walls.

But inside, wrapped in the warmth of Riichi's arms, Takoda felt nothing but the undeniable certainty of what they had just created between them.

Chapter Ten
Paths of Purpose

The tranquility of morning enveloped the room, bringing with it the serene stillness that came with the earliest hours. The dim glow of dawn traced along the edges of Riichi's window, brushing soft outlines across the space. Takoda remained still, listening to the even rhythm of Riichi's breath beside her. The silence between them wasn't empty—it was rich and meaningful, carrying the unspoken potential of what was beginning to take shape between them. No assumptions. No expectations. Only a growing trust, building with each peaceful moment.

She closed her eyes, allowing the thought to sink in. It wasn't about defining anything, not yet. It was about acknowledging what was there—the stability he brought, the way he made space for her without asking for anything in return. The way she wanted to do the same for him.

Finally, she turned to him, voice quiet, testing the words before she spoke them. "Last night... it felt different, in the best way." A pause. She chose her next words carefully. "It felt like us."

Riichi gently intertwined his fingers with hers, taking his time. His eyes softened, steady in the morning light. "I felt that too," he murmured. "It was... clear. Grounded." He exhaled, his voice slipping into something quieter, more reflective. "I appreciate you saying that. For being honest about it. About us."

The silence they shared wasn't indecision—it was a mutual understanding. There was no rush, no need to push the conversation further than where it naturally settled.

Riichi adjusted his position, his expression thoughtful. "The meeting with the Fallen is soon." His tone was practical but held the same gentleness he had offered her moments ago. "Eileen will go over the agenda and the team's objectives for the Seattle missions. The Golden Dawn's ability to manipulate the weather is worse than we've seen before—more dangerous, more unpredictable. We'll strategize, but there's no way around the risks."

Takoda listened, absorbing his words. He wasn't warning her—he was including her. Preparing her, just as he would any other member of the team he trusted.

"And since I'm leading strategy," he continued, "they'll expect me to take point, or at least be heavily involved." He looked her in the eye, a thoughtful expression in his gaze. "I want you to know I'm committed to this, but I also want to make sure you're comfortable with it. If you have any concerns, tell me. I'll listen."

She took in a slow breath, maintaining eye contact with him. "I get it, Riichi. This is who you are, and I don't want to stand in the way of that. I'll support you—always." A hint of a subtle but profound emotion glimmered in her eyes. "Just promise me you'll be careful."

His lips curled into a small, grateful smile. "That, I can do."

The conversation settled between them, a quiet acknowledgment of what lay ahead. Then, inevitably, morning pulled them forward. Takoda slipped from his room and crossed the hall to hers, her steps light.

When she emerged, freshly dressed and ready, Riichi was already waiting in the hallway. Their eyes met, a silent understanding passing between them, and without a word, they moved in step down the stairs.

As Takoda adjusted the hem of her shirt, an idea sparked. "How about breakfast?" She glanced at Riichi. "Something simple—fresh croissants, fruit. Just like San Francisco. A little comfort before the day kicks off."

His face relaxed, a gentle and appreciative look in his gaze. "Sounds perfect. Let me help."

Takoda set about gathering ingredients, pulling out the dough she'd prepared the night before. As she began shaping it, she glanced at Riichi. "Want to give it a try?"

He studied her hands for a moment before stepping in, rolling his sleeves back with quiet determination. She guided him through the motions, her touch light as she corrected his grip. He mimicked her movements carefully, but his first attempt ended up more of a misshapen lump than a crescent.

They both halted, staring at his creation. Suddenly, they burst into laughter, light-hearted and genuine. Riichi held up the doughy attempt with a mock sigh. "Maybe I should stick to the fruit."

"Maybe," she teased, handing him a knife.

They fell into a steady rhythm, slicing apples and berries side by side. Every glance, every soft chuckle, built on the quiet closeness between them, a growing familiarity that neither hurried nor resisted. In that instance, they weren't warriors or strategists, just two people preparing breakfast, letting the demands of the day hold off a little longer.

Once the platter of croissants and fruit was ready, they carried it to the table. The others trickled in, the scent of fresh pastries drawing appreciative murmurs.

Reed's face lit up as he reached for a croissant. "I've missed these," he said, voice lined with genuine appreciation. He glanced at Takoda, a flicker of something lighter in his typically inscrutable face. "You have no idea how happy I am to see you making them again."

Takoda returned his smile, feeling a comforting warmth in her chest. There was a quiet sense of home in moments like this, in shared meals and effortless conversation before the day's responsibilities took hold.

As they ate, Ariel nudged Rain, a mischievous glint in her eyes. "So, since Eileen's fine with decorating for Halloween, we figured—why stop there? We're throwing a party."

Vine arched a brow, but amusement tugged at his lips before he could protest. "If Eileen's on board, I'm in. A Halloween party might be exactly what we need."

Ariel's smirk widened. "Oh, don't worry about Eileen," she said breezily. "I have my ways."

Vine let out a short laugh, shaking his head. "Good luck with that," he said, skepticism laced with humor.

The energy around the table brightened, the idea of a party remained in the air like a silent promise—something to hold onto before things got more serious. Reed slipped one last croissant into his hand and shot Takoda a knowing look. "One for the road," he said with an easy tilt of his head.

With the last sips of coffee and the soft rustle of chairs pushing back, they gathered their things. The warmth of the morning stayed with them as they made their way toward the meeting room, camaraderie lingering in their steps.

The meeting room held a different kind of energy—charged, expectant. As the Fallen took their seats around the long table, the easy atmosphere from breakfast faded.

Eileen stood at the forefront, the kind of presence that made silence fall naturally around her. There was no need for theatrics or commands—when she spoke, they listened. A quiet current of something deeper seemed to pulse beneath her calm demeanor, an echo of the power she rarely let them see.

"We have a problem," she began, her voice edged with urgency. "The Golden Dawn's latest activities in Seattle suggest they've moved beyond surveillance and minor disruptions. They're manipulating the weather—on a scale we haven't seen before. This isn't a few scattered anomalies. It's calculated. Purposeful." She let that sink in before continuing. "I want theories. Why now? What's their goal?"

Rowan, ever the pragmatist, leaned forward. "If they're controlling the weather, it might be to create barriers around the city," he said. "Limit movement. Cut off communication. Make sure no one gets in—or out."

Vine gave a small shake of his head as he pondered the situation. "The energy required for weather manipulation like this isn't small. If they just wanted to block us, there are easier ways." His fingers tapped absently against the table. "This feels... bigger."

Aislinn frowned in thought as Vine's gaze flicked toward her. "It could be interference," he suggested. "Messing with electromagnetic fields, maybe. That kind of disruption could weaken abilities that rely on energy flow—like your kinetic manipulation."

Ivy, arms crossed, regarded him with measured skepticism. "There are simpler ways to weaken us," she countered. "If they wanted to disrupt powers, they wouldn't waste this much energy on something so broad." A pause. "No. This feels like concealment."

Reed gave a slow nod. "Weather like this would make it easier to move unnoticed, especially in chaos. If they're creating constant storms, it's the perfect cover for moving something—or someone—without detection."

A brief silence followed as possibilities stacked themselves, pieces moving into place but not quite forming a full picture.

Riichi, who had been listening intently, finally spoke. His tone was contemplative, deliberate. "What if they're target is something structural?" His gaze swept across the table, assessing each reaction. "If they're using this to weaken the veil between the human and supernatural realms... then the weather isn't the goal. It's merely a consequence."

Rowan frowned, skeptical. "Weakening the veil?" He shook his head. "That's dangerous. If they aren't careful, they'll end up inviting forces they can't control."

Willow, however, tilted her head, her expression thoughtful. "But if they're looking
to create a major crossover… weather manipulation would make sense. Destabilizing
natural energy patterns could be part of the process." She exhaled. "If that's their aim,
then whatever's coming… this is only the beginning."

The room fell into a heavy silence. The implications stretched far beyond Seattle.

Eileen folded her arms, gaze sweeping across the table. "Then we'd better be ready."

The room remained still as Riichi's theory unfolded before them, each possibility
peeling back another layer of the Golden Dawn's intent. But it was clear—they were only
scratching the surface of what they were truly up against.

Eileen let the silence hold for a breath longer, allowing the gravity of the moment to
root itself before she spoke. "Our primary objective is clear," she said, her tone leaving
no room for doubt. "We need every piece of information we can gather on the Golden
Dawn's activities in Seattle. Surveillance, reconnaissance—anything that gives us insight
into their motives and strategy. If we're lucky, we might uncover something that reveals
their plan before they set it into motion."

Her gaze swept across the table, pausing on each Fallen in turn, as if assessing their
preparedness. "Weather manipulation on this scale suggests a far-reaching agenda. We
need to understand not just the 'what' but the 'why.' The only way forward is to approach
this from every angle—follow every lead. No detail is too small."

A quiet ripple of agreement moved through the group, their curiosity transforming
into a keen, intentional awareness. The atmosphere in the room became charged with
collective focus. This wasn't just observation—it was the kind of mission where a single
overlooked detail could mean the difference between stopping a disaster or standing in
its aftermath.

Eileen nodded once, satisfied with their readiness. "Here's how we divide our efforts."

She straightened, her presence imposing but calculated, a force that did not demand
authority but simply possessed it. "First—training." Her gaze landed on Takoda. "Willow
and Aislinn, you'll work closely with Takoda. Mastering her ability needs to be a priority.
A deeper understanding of emotional alchemy may be critical if the Golden Dawn's plans
continue on this path."

Takoda exchanged a meaningful glance with Willow and Aislinn, a silent understanding connecting them. A promise. Whatever it took, she would sharpen her abilities—if
not for herself, then for the people counting on her.

Eileen turned next to Riichi. "Riichi, Reed, and Ash—you'll be heading to Georgetown
for recon. A Golden Dawn operative was last tracked there."

Riichi gave a short nod, but before he could respond, his gaze instinctively turned
toward Takoda. He wasn't sure why—maybe he just needed a silent confirmation that
she was good with this. That they were good. She met his glance with a steady, unshaken
nod, a small reassurance that eased something in him.

Eileen's sharp eyes caught the exchange, though she said nothing at first. Instead, a hint
of knowing passed across her face. "Riichi, is there a problem?"

"No," he answered smoothly, though there was a small change in his posture. "All good."

Eileen's lips quirked, amusement barely there but present enough to be noticed before she moved on.

"Oak, Elder," she continued, moving her attention to them, "monitor the weather and local reports in Seattle. If anything unusual crops up, Elder, use your geomancy to track energy shifts. I want to pinpoint the strongest sources of their influence."

Elder gave a slow nod. "If their power is tied to elemental forces, I'll feel it."

Oak leaned forward a bit, his voice calm as always. "If their storms become more volatile, I can reinforce key locations to prevent collateral damage. Even if we can't stop them outright, we can keep certain areas protected."

Eileen acknowledged their readiness before moving to the next group. "Rowan, Vine, Ivy, and Birch—perimeter scans. Focus on the outskirts of Seattle. Find any potential Golden Dawn bases. Ivy, if you can stretch your reality-warping abilities to expand the search, do it."

Ivy's expression sharpened with determination as she nodded. "That should give us a much wider range."

Rowan leaned back slightly, his focus narrowing on the bigger picture. "We'll need shifts. If we keep fresh eyes on the area at all times, they'll have no place to move unseen."

Eileen took in the last round of confirmations, letting the plan settle over them before she delivered her final warning. "This mission is high stakes. If Riichi's theory about the veil is correct, then the Golden Dawn may be attempting something more dangerous than we anticipated. This isn't just about Seattle. It's about the boundary between realms. If they succeed, we may be facing a threat we're not prepared for."

A hush fell over the room, but this time, it wasn't doubt or fear. It was understanding. The burden of their duty settled across each of them, but so did their resolve. They had faced impossible odds before. And they would face them again.

Eileen's gaze swept the room one last time. "Stay vigilant. Be ready for anything."

A final nod. A quiet dismissal.

The meeting room door swung open, and the Fallen began filing out, their expressions serious as they dispersed to prepare for their assignments. Ariel loitered in the hallway, standing just out of the way, waiting for the last of them to pass. She looked casual enough, leaning against the wall, though her fingers twisted in the fabric of her jacket as her mind raced through what she was about to say.

As Vine passed her, he caught her eye, a smirk spreading across his face. He patted her shoulder, the gesture playful yet knowing. "You're a brave girl, Ariel. Good luck," he said, his voice laced with both humor and intelligence. They both knew how firm Eileen could be, especially when focus was at stake.

"Thanks, Vine," Ariel murmured, though her grin was faint. When he finally walked away, she took a steadying breath, watching the last of the Fallen disappear down the hall.

Once the room was empty, Ariel approached the door, squaring her shoulders as she walked inside.

Eileen, still seated, glanced up and caught the quiet determination in Ariel's eyes, setting her pen down as she straightened. "Ariel?" Her tone was patient, her brow lifting slightly in question. "Is there something on your mind?"

"Yeah, actually," Ariel replied, feeling her confidence falter just a little as she closed the door behind her. "I wanted to talk with you about an idea I had."

Eileen nodded, watching her intently.

Ariel took another breath, as if gathering her thoughts into one last burst of courage. "Halloween's coming up," she began, her tone cautious but hopeful. "And I thought… maybe we could throw a little Halloween party. Just something here, for the Fallen. No outsiders, of course—just us." She gave a quick shrug, her voice softening as she added, "I mean, I don't even know anyone else in Seattle anyway."

Eileen's expression remained blank, though Ariel swore she saw the barest flicker of consideration in her gaze. But then, Eileen shook her head, her voice firm yet kind. "Ariel, I appreciate the thought, but now isn't the time for distractions."

Ariel had braced herself for this response, yet the emphasis of it still stung. She looked down for a minute, gathering herself. She wouldn't give up so easily.

"I know you're concerned about focus, Eileen," she replied, stepping forward, her tone more earnest. "But… I just think it could be good for everyone. We're all so wrapped up in missions and danger. A little break, even just for one night, could help us connect. Maybe even make us stronger as a group."

Eileen's gaze softened somewhat as she listened, nodding just once, as if acknowledging Ariel's conviction, but her resolve didn't falter. "I understand, but we're facing risks we haven't fully uncovered yet. I don't want to give anyone a reason to lose sight of what's ahead." Her voice was calm, but her tone was clear, each word firm.

Ariel's shoulders slumped, her earlier excitement now draining from her expression.

Eileen's eyes dawdled on her for a flash, scrutinizing her intent. It wasn't merely the look of a leader assessing a proposal; there was an underlying search for a deeper truth. Then, her voice softened, revealing an undercurrent that Ariel couldn't quite place.

"Ariel," Eileen said gently, "is this really just about a party for everyone else? Or is there something more you're not saying?"

Ariel's eyes darted away, a small, deflecting smile crossing her face. "No, I just thought it'd lift everyone's spirits a bit, that's all," she replied, though her tone held a slight edge of defensiveness.

Eileen's gaze didn't waver. "I think you're lying, Ariel."

Ariel's breath hitched, and her shoulders dropped a tad. She let out a small, resigned sigh, a wry smile tugging at her lips as she shook her head. "I can see where Aislinn gets it from," she admitted. "I couldn't fool her either."

Eileen's expression warmed, and her patience seemed to deepen. She watched Ariel silently, waiting for her to say what she truly felt. Ariel, feeling the significance of that silence, knew she was being given space to speak openly, and this time, she wouldn't let it pass her by.

She hesitated, the words catching in her throat as her gaze drifted to the floor. Taking a deep breath, she finally spoke, her voice soft, almost fragile.

"I didn't have much of a family growing up," she began, a hint of vulnerability breaking through her usual confidence. "It was… violent, unpredictable. Full of broken promises, empty words, and… no love." She let out a shaky breath, forcing herself to continue. "When I finally got out, I promised myself I wouldn't let that past define me. I wanted to live life fully, you know? To actually feel joy, to make memories that meant something."

She looked up at Eileen, her expression raw, her voice barely a whisper as she finished, "I just want… the family moments I never had. This party being one."

Eileen felt a pang deep in her chest, something old and knowing stirring within her.

The spark, the resilience, the way Ariel brought laughter to the Fallen—it all made sense now. She had built herself up from broken pieces, vowing to create a life she could feel proud of, despite all that had been taken from her. And in that moment, Eileen saw her not as someone asking for permission, but as someone standing in defiance of the life she had left behind—choosing to build something better instead of letting her past claim her.

She had seen warriors before. Fighters. Survivors.

But Ariel—Ariel was something else.

Eileen's gaze softened, and she moved closer, the warmth of her own motherly instincts rising to the surface in a way she rarely allowed. "You're brave, Ariel," she said gently, her voice steady with admiration. "It takes incredible strength to not let your past control your future. I know how much effort it takes to build a life from scratch, especially when it's easier to let yourself get pulled back into darkness. You've done something extraordinary."

Ariel nodded, her eyes glistening, emotions simmering just below the surface. Eileen's words touched her in a way she hadn't expected, and for a moment, she allowed herself to be seen as more than the lighthearted soul she always tried to be.

Eileen paused, understanding just how much this party meant to Ariel—not simply as a distraction, but as a chance to experience the sense of belonging she had been denied for so long.

She looked at Ariel, her own expression mellowed by realization.

After a thoughtful silence, Eileen finally spoke. "All right. You can have the Halloween party."

Ariel's eyes widened in surprise, her face lighting up as Eileen added, "But on one condition: it doesn't interfere with Fallen business."

A smile broke across Ariel's face, bright and genuine, her gratitude overflowing. Without a second thought, she wrapped her arms around Eileen, pressing her face into Eileen's shoulder. "Thank you," she whispered, her voice thick with emotion.

Eileen held her for a moment, a gentle hand resting on her back, feeling a surge of affection for this young woman who had carried so much and asked for so little.

She pulled away, giving Ariel a warm, steady smile as she reached for a box of tissues on the table. "Here," she offered, her tone light, "just in case."

Ariel took a tissue, dabbing at her eyes as she composed herself, her gratitude still clear in her expression. She stood to leave but paused at the door, glancing back at Eileen with a soft, sincere look.

"You're like the mom I always wished I'd had, you know." Her voice was quiet, carrying a depth of warmth and honesty that made Eileen's heart tighten. "Aislinn's lucky to have you."

Eileen's expression relaxed, a mixture of pride and affection filling her gaze as she watched Ariel leave.

She remained in the room a moment longer, her heart touched by Ariel's words, knowing that in ways both large and small, they'd forged a bond that would last far beyond that single embrace.

In a secluded corner of the mansion, away from the bustle of movement and preparation, Riichi and Takoda sat together, hands instinctively finding each other, fingers weaving in a way that felt both effortless and reassuring. The quiet around them wasn't merely absence of sound—it was a shared space, implicit yet valued, a moment carved out before the duties of the day pressed in.

Riichi studied her face, his gaze warm with a gratitude he rarely voiced. "Thank you," he said softly, his thumb gliding across her hand. "You never questioned me going on this mission… you've just been here. Steady. Supportive." He hesitated, then added, "I'm grateful—but I'd still like to know how you feel about it all."

Takoda's lips curved into a quiet smile. She squeezed his hand, grounding both of them with that one simple gesture. "I've seen your focus, your discipline. Back in San Francisco, it was in everything you did. This mission, your loyalty to the Fallen—it's part of who you are." Her voice was calm, resolute. "Of course I worry, but I won't stand in the way of that. I trust you. And I trust what we're building." She met his eyes without hesitation. "I handled it before. I can handle it again."

A calm settled over them—solid, reassuring.

Her fingers traced over his hand, a steady rhythm, less about comfort and more about connection. "You're a protector. That's never been in question. And I know you'll protect yourself too."

The truth in her words struck something in him. Not a sudden shift, but a quiet steadiness spreading beneath the surface. Her presence, her belief in him—it settled into the parts of him that had gone too long without anchoring.

Her alchemy pulsed faintly through the air, subtle and seamless, like sunlight warming skin through fabric. It wasn't overt magic—it was simply her. Calming. Centering. Something unshakable.

He'd always trusted his instincts, his planning, his skill. But her trust—unconditional and unspoken—reached further. It made space for him to be more than just prepared.

His grip tightened gently, reverently. He had felt connected to her before, but now it felt reinforced. Stronger. More defined.

He lifted her hand to his lips, pressing a slow kiss to her knuckles. "Thank you, Takoda," he said quietly. "Having someone who understands... who believes in what I do without needing proof... that means more than I can say."

She smiled, her eyes holding his with calm certainty, and neither of them moved, letting the silence stretch between them, steady and full.

Eventually, the moment gave way to the day.

He gave her hand a final squeeze before letting go, a private smile tugging at his lips. They rose together, a silent promise exchanged between them.

Whatever came next, they would carry this with them—not just trust, but something solid. Something beginning to take root.

***

Takoda stepped onto the worn stone of the back patio, Willow and Aislinn at her side. Today was a beginning—the first real step toward mastering her abilities.

The courtyard opened before them, quiet and cool, the scent of pine and damp soil clinging to the breeze. Leaves rustled like hushed breath, brushing over the garden paths that twisted through the space like ancient roots.

She took a slow breath, trying to draw in the calm. Nerves tugged at the edges of her focus, but beneath them was a flicker of something steadier—anticipation.

Willow turned to her with an encouraging smile. "We'll start simple," she said, her voice fluid and grounded. "Emotional alchemy begins with observation. Not reaction, not control—just awareness."

Takoda nodded, recalling Riichi's centering exercise. She closed her eyes, breathing deep. She pictured her anxiety as a cloud of ash, rising on her exhale, dispersing with each measured breath. Her hands moved in arcs, intentional and slow, echoing the movements he'd shown her.

"Good," Willow murmured. "That foundation will make everything else easier."

Aislinn stepped closer. "Now imagine a boundary," she said gently. "Not a wall. Just… a buffer. Something that lets the emotions pass through you instead of knock you over."

Takoda tried. At first, the quiet pulse of energy from Aislinn and Willow pressed in, unfiltered and overwhelming. It slipped under her skin, off-balancing her, but she caught herself. Anchored again. Let it pass. Breathe.

The pressure eased.

Willow watched her carefully. "Now," she said, "take that self-doubt—the one you carry too quietly—and try reshaping it into something else. Determination. Drive."

Takoda hesitated. Then she reached for it. The heaviness. The familiar drag of not being enough. She didn't push it away. She held it. Molded it.

And something inside shifted.

It wasn't perfect. It didn't last. But for a moment, she felt it—a clarity she hadn't expected.

Willow and Aislinn exchanged a glance. Willow's voice was quiet but firm. "That's the start."

Takoda nodded, surprised by the warmth swelling in her chest. Not pride, exactly. But hope.

They moved on. Willow asked her to redirect Aislinn's calm into sharp focus. Takoda tried. The emotion flickered, then faded. But Aislinn gave her a small nod anyway.

The progress was small. But it was hers.

As they paused, that familiar urgency returned, pressing at her ribs. Riichi was already out there. Facing danger. She needed to catch up. She needed to be ready.

Willow's hand touched her shoulder, grounding. "You're further than you think. Don't rush the roots. Power needs time to take hold."

They wrapped the session, and as they headed back toward the mansion, Takoda felt steadier. Not stronger. Not yet. But steady.

Still, a chill crept in as the great stone halls came into view.

Riichi was out there. Facing whatever waited in Seattle.

And no matter how far she'd come today, one question still clung to her:

Would it be enough?

<u>Chapter Eleven</u>
Uncovered Threats

The midday sun bore down on Georgetown, its harsh glare stripping the streets of their depth, leaving only a flat, washed-out landscape of decay. Cracked pavement stretched in uneven veins beneath Riichi's boots as he led Reed and Ash deeper into the industrial graveyard. Without the cover of darkness, they relied on meticulousness—slipping between skeletal remnants of rusting warehouses and jagged towers of forgotten machinery, their movements a whisper against the silence.

A low whirring vibrated through the air, a sound just beyond hearing but tangible in the way it pressed against Riichi's senses. The atmosphere thickened, the air laced with a charged energy that set his nerves on edge. A thin, unnatural haze coiled along the edges of the buildings, distorting their outlines like a mirage, warping the space between reality and whatever lurked beneath. The scent of old metal and oil clung to everything, but beneath it, something more insidious threaded through the air—like burnt herbs and damp earth, the persistent residue of rituals best left undisturbed.

He cast a glance at Reed and Ash. They felt it too. Even under the midday sun, the city pulsed with something that did not belong.

A quick gesture from Riichi sent them forward. He moved in seamless silence, a shadow against the rusted bones of the past. A glimmer of motion caught his eye—a lone figure weaving through the tangled alleyways near the Steam Plant, their dark coat swaying with each step. Golden Dawn. Riichi's brow furrowed. He signaled Reed to take the right flank, Ash to the left, and then they dispersed, shifting into position with the practiced ease of warriors who had spent centuries perfecting the art of unseen pursuit.

The Golden Dawn operative moved with motive, slipping between broken-down structures, the faint echo of his footsteps lost beneath the wail of distant machinery. Riichi kept pace, ghosting behind a stack of warped pallets, his senses keyed to the rearranging landscape. The industrial ruins sprawled before them in a labyrinth of rusting steel and skeletal scaffolding, the harsh sun casting sharp, angular shadows that cut across the ground like fractured sigils.

Reed had already disappeared into the slivers of darkness, his form barely more than a suggestion of movement where the light failed to reach. Ash, nimble and succinct, transformed into a smaller form, slipping through the narrow spaces between stacked crates and abandoned vehicles, his presence vanishing in the gaps where others wouldn't think to look.

As they rounded a corner, Riichi's gaze caught on a timid white mark near the edge of a crumbling wall—a chalked symbol, barely visible against the weathered surface but intentional in its placement. The scent of dried herbs ghosted through the air, too faint for human senses but distinct beneath the metallic tang of rust. Symbols and offerings. A familiar pattern. This was no arbitrary location; this was a working site, chosen for a reason.

Riichi crouched, tracing the symbol with a gloved hand, its rough edges telling him it had been drawn hastily but with purpose. A fragment of a larger design, its intention clear—to thin the veil, to fray the boundaries that held back whatever the Golden Dawn sought to call forth.

Reed materialized beside him, gaze sharp with unspoken recognition. "They're making moves out in the open now," he murmured, his voice edged with tension.

Riichi didn't look up. "They're either growing desperate," he said, reading the lines of the symbol like an unfinished puzzle, "or they believe no one will stop them."

A ripple in the air sent a shiver through the space between them. The subtle pulse of energy—faint, but enough to signal danger. Reed tensed beside him, his sharp eyes moving toward a narrow doorway, where the hint of unnatural magic clung to the threshold.

"Detection ward," Reed whispered, his voice barely a breath. The Golden Dawn wasn't just operating here—they were defending it.

Riichi studied the barrier, taking in the simple distortion around its edges. A crude but effective warning system. "Shadow-walk past it," he murmured to Reed. With a nod, Reed slipped into the shifting darkness, his form dissolving into nothingness as he passed through the shadows undetected.

Ash had already adjusted, his new form small enough to move unnoticed, weaving through the labyrinth of broken structures with the ease of a creature that belonged in such places.

With one last glance at the symbols behind them, Riichi moved. Each step was determined, an exact rhythm designed to bypass unseen threads of magic strung across the entrance. The air vibrated with static, the subtle sting of energy brushing against his skin, but the barrier remained untouched.

They slipped past the threshold without a sound.

Danger waited ahead.

The Steam Plant engulfed them in a breathless stillness, the kind that weighed on the senses rather than simply hovering in the air. They had cleared the first obstacle, but the mission was only beginning, the path ahead steeped in unseen dangers.

Dust clung to the stale air, thick with the scent of rust and neglect. Shafts of daylight pierced through fractured windows, casting jagged slashes of light across corroded beams and machinery long abandoned to time. The cavernous space yawned before them, each shadowed recess a possible hiding place, each corner holding the potential for something unseen.

Everything about the place felt... wrong. More than just the decay, more than the emptiness. It held a charged stillness, an expectation, as though the very walls waited for a force to stir beneath layers of dust and forgotten rituals.

They moved deeper. The remnants of past workings scattered across the floor told their own story—half-burned candles pooled in dried wax, faded symbols roughly chalked onto cracked concrete, relics crusted in filth but pulsing with a trace of old magic. A pattern, an intention. Riichi's mind worked swiftly, assessing the scene not just as a battlefield, but as a woven construct of purpose and power. Whatever the Golden Dawn had done here, it wasn't haphazard.

A whisper of unease curled through the back of his mind, a presence that wasn't quite there but watched all the same. The sensation threaded along the edge of his awareness, crawling beneath his skin. He motioned for Reed and Ash to stay close, every sense attuned to any hidden dangers.

Then—a scuff.

Soft, but distinct.

Riichi halted, lifting a hand in silent command. Another step—muted, cautious. A hushed murmur, barely more than a breath against the stale air. He didn't need to see his team to know they were poised, waiting, ready to strike.

They closed in.

The concealed chamber at the back of the plant came into view, its walls layered in chalk-drawn sigils, an intricate weave of symbols overlapping in a chaotic sprawl. A ritual in motion. A spell with weight.

In the center, a lone figure stood with his back to them, his fingers tracing a deliberate line over one of the symbols as he muttered beneath his breath.

Golden Dawn.

Riichi advanced, his voice sharp as steel. "Tell us what you're doing here."

The figure stilled but didn't turn. The silence stretched, taut and premeditated, before he finally spoke—low, unshaken. "Weakening the veil."

A chill coiled in Riichi's chest, but he didn't let it show. "What are you trying to unleash?" His words cut through the dim space, a demand, not a request.

The man chuckled, the sound hollow and knowing. "You'll see soon enough."

Before Riichi could press further, the air vibrated with a sudden surge of magic. The intensity of it hit like a physical force, a shockwave of raw energy that sent the space reeling. A burst of light seared through the chamber, blinding in its sudden violence. Riichi braced against it, his vision swimming as he fought to center himself. The sensation passed as quickly as it had come, leaving behind a charged emptiness, the ghost of its energy still hanging in the air.

When he could see again, the Golden Dawn member was gone—vanished into thin air, leaving only the fading echo of his words. Riichi clenched his fists, frustration simmering beneath the surface as he scanned the chamber for anything they could salvage from the abrupt encounter.

Reed moved beside him, his look fixed on the symbols that covered the walls. "They're amplifying something here," he muttered, his voice rigid. "It's not just weakening the veil—it's setting something in motion."

Riichi exhaled sharply, his mind fitting the pieces together. They weren't just standing in an abandoned ritual site. They were standing in a convergence point. A place willfully chosen, layered with intent, charged with power waiting to be released.

Ash studied the air, his gaze catching on a faint shimmer left behind—a residue of the spell's pulse. It loitered like a taunt, a whisper of something unfinished.

"Make note of everything," Riichi ordered, his voice edged with determination. "Eileen's going to want to see this."

They quickly cataloged the symbols, the chalk marks, and the eerie remnants of magic that still clung to the air. Each trace pointed to something predetermined, a design woven through the abandoned plant that hinted at forces they had yet to fully understand.

As they turned to leave, a heavy silence settled around them, broken only by the measured sound of their footsteps echoing through the structure. The tension carried with them into the sunlight, unspoken but undeniable. None of them needed to say it—they had uncovered only fragments, but it was enough to hint at a threat far deeper and more powerful than they had anticipated.

Riichi glanced at Reed and Ash, reading the same silent unease in their expressions. Whatever they were facing, they'd need Eileen's insight to decode it fully. Yet, even as they moved away from the plant, the sense of danger remained, a quiet reminder that the Golden Dawn was no longer operating in the shadows. They were making their move.

★★★

Rowan drove slowly along the Seattle perimeter, eyes scanning the landscape as the car crept through empty streets and past deserted lots. Birch, Ivy, and Vine sat with him, each watching for any sign of the Golden Dawn's presence. Their search had come up empty so far, but as they neared the expanse of Discovery Park, the dense, tree-covered landscape offered new possibilities.

"Nothing yet," Birch murmured, glancing back at Ivy and Vine. He then turned his attention to Rowan. "This might be our best shot at finding anything solid."

Rowan nodded and turned down a narrow road, guiding them toward the park's outer edge, where thick tree cover and a lack of foot traffic made it an ideal place for the Golden Dawn to operate unnoticed. He parked in a secluded spot just beyond the towering evergreens that marked the entrance. Ivy leaned forward, her fingers moving in a small, practiced motion. The car shimmered briefly before vanishing, its outline blending seamlessly into the surroundings.

"Good to go," she murmured, scanning the trees ahead.

Rowan stepped out, senses sharpened, and motioned for the others to follow. They moved in silence, adjusting their gear as they prepared to search the park on foot. The atmosphere felt different here, charged in a way that made the air feel thicker, heavier. This was no ordinary stretch of woodland. Rowan led them forward, weaving through the narrow, wooded path with careful calculation, each step sure. Shadows stretched between the trees, the wind barely rustling through the high branches.

As they moved deeper into the forested expanse, a low mist crept along the earth, curling around roots and stone. It moved unnaturally, clinging in slow, purposeful tendrils rather than dispersing like normal fog. Ivy halted, her gaze narrowing as she studied the shifting haze.

"It's infused," she whispered, her voice tight. "There's magic in the air."

Rowan nodded, unease pressing at the back of his mind. This wasn't a natural occurrence. It was a sign. They were drawing close to something intentionally placed, designed to mask whatever lay ahead. He signaled for silence, and they pressed on, their movements careful as they wove through the thickening mist.

The trees thinned near Fort Lawton's edge, revealing the outline of abandoned buildings in the distance. Just as Rowan adjusted his stance, movement caught his eye. He raised a hand, halting the others. Beyond the trees, figures in dark coats patrolled the grounds, their purposeful strides too practiced, too efficient, to be ordinary trespassers.

Golden Dawn.

They weren't just loitering. They were stationed. Watching. Controlling.

Vine let out a low whistle, his eyes sweeping the activity below. "That's not just a gathering. It's an operation."

There was a slight tick in Rowan's temple. This wasn't just another outpost—it was a central hub. He gestured for the others to move with caution, keeping their pace slow, pausing whenever a patrol drew near. They moved between the trees, crouching low where the paths opened up, their steps silent against the damp earth. The deeper they pushed, the more the fort's layout became clear—Golden Dawn members moved supplies in and out of the barracks, groups stationed at key points, a small cluster gathered around what looked disturbingly like a ritual site.

Rowan assessed their surroundings, then signaled for the team to split toward the barracks and officer's quarters. Ivy and Vine veered left, while Birch moved to flank Rowan's position. They kept close to the walls, slipping between stretches of darkness as they advanced. Nearing the nearest building, Rowan peered through a fractured window. The room inside no longer resembled a barracks—it had been transformed. Occult symbols lined the walls, crude yet purposeful, while shelves brimmed with ritual artifacts. The remnants of freshly cast magic still pulsed in the air, the energy clinging to the space like the last echoes of a fading incantation.

Ivy sucked in a sharp breath, drawing Rowan's attention to the doorway. "Detection ward," she mouthed. A flicker of concentration crossed her features as she reached out, twisting the energy around it to dampen its range. The shift was subtle, but enough. Rowan nodded and moved past her, slipping into the room without a sound. The others followed, their movements quick but accurate, their senses attuned to the peculiar stillness hanging over the space.

The atmosphere inside was thick with intention, as though the very walls had absorbed the weight of past rituals. This wasn't just a hideout—it was a preparation ground. A staging point. Rowan scanned the symbols etched into the surfaces around him, each one a thread in a larger weave of dark purpose.

"We're standing in the middle of their headquarters," he murmured, his voice low but certain. The stakes had just shifted.

Moving toward the old parade grounds, Rowan led the team through a dense stretch of trees, keeping low as they advanced. The area opened up ahead, but it wasn't the empty expanse he'd expected. Symbols had been carved deep into the earth, sprawling in intricate formations, their perfection unsettling. Ivy and Vine exchanged a look, a silent recognition passing between them.

"They're tapping into the ley lines," Ivy whispered, her voice barely audible. "These symbols… they're using the earth's energy to thin the veil."

A chill ran through Rowan. The Golden Dawn's reach wasn't just widespread—it was meticulous, calculated. If they had mapped the ley lines beneath Fort Lawton, they weren't simply experimenting. They were building something. He motioned the team to keep moving, his gaze flicking toward a group of Golden Dawn members clustered near a ward, their gestures methodical as they reinforced the enchantment.

Rowan signaled for cover, and the team dropped into the underbrush, pressing low against the damp earth as the patrol passed. Their hushed voices carried in the uncanny silence, their footfalls resolute, each step a reminder of how critical this site was to their operation.

Once the group had disappeared into the mist, Rowan gestured them forward. They moved cautiously, skirting the edge of the ritual site, staying within the shadows cast by the thick tree line. It was Vine who spotted the concealed entrance first—a section of debris and overgrown brush that looked too deliberately placed to be natural. His eyes narrowed, tracking the slight misalignment of branches and rubble. He signaled Rowan and Birch over, and together, Birch and Vine quietly shifted the debris aside, revealing a dark, narrow staircase descending into the earth.

Rowan took point, stepping into the hidden passage with careful precision. The air grew colder as they descended, thick with an eerie stillness that settled over them like a held breath. At the bottom, a small underground chamber stretched before them, dimly lit by a single candle that sputtered against the stale air. Shadows danced over an altar cluttered with forbidden books, arcane symbols, and ritual tools steeped in dark energy.

Artifacts littered the space, their surfaces worn smooth by repeated use. Some pulsed faintly, remnants of past enchantments still clinging to them. Rowan ran his fingers over the markings etched into the altar, tracing patterns that had been repeated countless times before. This wasn't the careless work of a faction grasping at power. This was the careful, ritualistic preparation of those who knew exactly what they were doing.

"This is beyond a base," he murmured, his voice grim. "They're staging something massive here."

The importance of the discovery settled over them, unvoiced but understood. Every symbol, every artifact, every line of chalk on the floor fed into a greater purpose—one meant to dismantle the barrier between realms. They exchanged tense glances before slipping back toward the stairway, careful not to disturb the ritual space.

Emerging from the chamber, they followed the pull of something strange in the air, an energy that hummed just beyond their senses. The cliffside loomed ahead, shrouded in thick fog that swirled in restless eddies, curling and shifting grotesquely. Rowan's instincts flared as they neared the edge. The mist was denser here, pooling low, concealing movement. Through the haze, shadowed figures stood positioned along the cliff, adjusting objects in deliberate, measured motions.

A subtle charge crackled through the air, a whisper of power that set Rowan's nerves on edge. They moved closer, keeping to the cover of the trees, their approach near soundless. From this vantage point, they could see it—a massive, intricately carved circle etched into the ground, runes spiraling outward in a design Rowan had never encountered before.

Ivy's brow furrowed as she examined the symbols, whispering just loud enough for them to hear. "They're using these runes to pull energy from the ocean," she explained, her tone measured, cautious. "They're amplifying the power of their rituals to reach farther, destabilizing the veil itself."

Rowan clenched his jaw. This was worse than he'd imagined. They weren't just weakening the barrier between worlds—they were dismantling it. He glanced at the others, the same realization settling over them. Fort Lawton wasn't a strategic outpost. It was the core of their operation.

A flicker of movement caught Rowan's eye—Birch shifting slightly, his foot nearly brushing against a barely visible sigil carved into the rock. The air around it purred, a ward carefully embedded into the cliffside, its magic poised to trigger the moment it was disturbed.

Ivy reacted instantly, her hand flashing out as she bent the perception around them, twisting reality just enough to distort their presence. Vine lifted a hand, sending a controlled pulse of electrokinesis to disrupt the ward's power just long enough for them to back away. Rowan gestured sharply, and they withdrew with careful accuracy, slipping back toward the woods before the effect wore off.

Once they were clear, they followed their path through the trees, each step purposeful. The return to the car felt longer, every shift of the wind, every distant footstep a reminder of what they had uncovered. When they reached the vehicle, Ivy lifted her hand, unraveling the illusion that had kept it concealed. Without a word, they climbed in.

Rowan started the engine, pulling away with quiet efficiency, their departure blending into the natural sounds of the park. The significance of the mission hung between them, thick with unspoken thoughts. Rowan's mind churned, working through the pieces, each revelation tightening the knot in his gut.

Fort Lawton served as more than a mere refuge. It was a command center. The Golden Dawn's reach stretched farther than they had anticipated, their intentions no longer just an encroaching threat but an immediate danger.

They had to warn Eileen. She would need to see everything.

★★★

The mansion's library was steeped in quiet, a silence that felt less like absence and more like a presence of its own. The only light came from the glow of laptop screens and the muted halos cast by reading lamps, illuminating worn leather chairs and the dark wood of the towering bookshelves. Oak and Elder sat among stacks of weather reports, maps, and ancient tomes, their focus unbroken as they sifted through layers of data, searching for the thread that would unravel the Golden Dawn's next move.

Elder bent over a ley line map, fingers tracing points of recent geomantic disturbances, his mind weaving patterns from the changing energy flows. Every so often, he would pause, jotting notes in quick, methodical strokes. Across from him, Oak scrolled through live weather data, his brows knitting with each anomaly he uncovered. They worked in silence, their understanding tacit, each aware of the stakes pressing down on them.

The quiet broke when Oak straightened, focusing intently on the digital map before him. "Elder, look at this," he murmured, his voice low but edged with urgency.

Elder leaned over as Oak pointed to a series of weather events lining up along ley lines—storms that had formed with unearthly precision, dense fog banks appearing without explanation, strange shifts in atmospheric pressure. Oak's finger traced a path across the screen, following the disturbances as they snaked through regions already marked by ritual activity.

Elder's eyes narrowed. The patterns weren't coincidence. "They're using the weather as a tool," he muttered, almost to himself. "It's like they're pulling at the veil, stretching it thin with each storm, using the elements to weaken the boundary between worlds."

Oak exhaled, grim. "That lines up with Riichi's theory. We've got physical proof now." He scrolled further, his fingers drumming lightly against the desk as more correlations appeared. Each storm, each surge in atmospheric energy, matched the ley line shifts Elder had been tracking. The alignment was too precise to be anything but intentional.

Then Elder stilled. His eyes fixed on the screen, brow furrowing as an energy spike flickered across his map—a faint but unquestionable disturbance just outside Seattle. "There," he said, voice taut. The readings were subtle, barely detectable, but the ripple in the earth's natural energy hinted at a ritual conducted recently.

Oak's eyes narrowed as he noted the coordinates. "That area was hit with sudden fog just hours ago," he said, suspicion heavy in his voice. They exchanged a glance, understanding the enormity of what they'd uncovered. The Golden Dawn wasn't just expanding their reach—they were amplifying it. And their ability to manipulate the natural world was escalating.

A shift in the room's atmosphere made Oak pause. The air thickened, pressing in—not oppressive, but charged. He glanced around, a slow frown settling over his features. "Do you feel that?"

Elder didn't answer immediately, his own awareness attuned to the shift. The room had changed. The air carried an energy that wasn't there before, something subtle yet obvious, a pressure that crawled beneath the skin. "The veil..." His voice was quiet but firm. "It's thinning." His gaze came back to the map, to the energy fluctuations forming an ominous pattern. "If the Golden Dawn keeps pushing, we might see a full breach sooner than expected."

The burden of that realization settled between them. Oak took a slow breath, pushing the tension into focus. "Then we don't have time to wait."

They moved quickly, organizing their findings into a concise report. Every weather anomaly, every map and ley line reading was compiled, the evidence building into something impossible to ignore. By the time Oak typed the final note, the picture was clear—this wasn't just a strategy. It was an assault.

As he finished, he glanced at the latest weather update. A storm was forming on the horizon. His chest tightened. Not just any storm—a controlled one. A convergence of elements shaped by unseen hands. He looked up, meeting Elder's steady gaze, the same understanding mirrored in his expression.

With a silent nod, they rose, determination settling over them like armor as they prepared to take their findings to Eileen and the rest of the Fallen.

A low rumble of thunder rolled through the mansion, reverberating through the quiet like an omen. The sound echoed through the vast library, a warning carried in the restless sky beyond the walls.

Oak clenched his fists. This wasn't just another confrontation on the horizon. This was the beginning of something far worse.

Outside, the storm gathered, dark clouds spiraling, building strength. And within the mansion, Oak and Elder braced themselves, ready to stand with their fellow warriors against whatever came next.

Afternoon shadows stretched long across the mansion's entrance as Riichi slipped inside, the scent of the city still clinging to him—sweat, dust, and the faint trace of smoke from Georgetown's grittier streets. The hours spent navigating its less welcoming corners had left their mark, smudges of grime on his sleeves, a tension in his shoulders he hadn't bothered to shake off. Fatigue etched fine lines at the corners of his eyes, his usually crisp movements carrying a rare heaviness.

Takoda was already waiting. There was nothing hurried in the way she stepped toward him, but the quiet steadiness of her presence always had a way of easing the sharp edges of his day. Without a word, she reached out and brushed a smear of dirt from his shoulder, her fingers pausing a beat longer than necessary—a silent question.

"Welcome back," she murmured, meeting his eyes without wavering. "You look like you've been through… well, more than just a routine afternoon."

A tired smile tugged at the corner of Riichi's mouth. "More than I'd like to admit," he said dryly. "Georgetown's not exactly a place to kill time."

A faint furrow appeared between her brows, concern lingering in the quiet that followed. She wasn't just asking—she was reading him, sensing the gaps, the weight he hadn't voiced.

"Did everything go as planned?" Her tone was even, but not impersonal. She had a way of asking that left no room for evasion, yet never demanded more than he was ready to give.

"Close enough." The answer was clipped, not careless—he wasn't ready to pull her into the depths of it. "Golden Dawn's stirring up more than we expected, but it'll have to wait. Eileen wants everyone back before we go over it."

Her shoulders loosened just enough for him to notice before she masked it again. "Alright," she said softly. Her hand settled lightly on his arm—not a request, not a question. Just presence.

Riichi held her gaze, letting the moment breathe. She grounded him in a way he hadn't learned how to name—an anchor in the storm without trying to calm it. The words came before he could think to stop them. "It's different when you're here. Easier."

The shift between them wasn't loud or dramatic, but it lingered, threading itself into the quiet where words often fell short.

The hum of voices cut through, drawing their focus toward the sitting room.

Inside, Ash and Reed had already claimed their spots, their silence heavy with the kind of weariness that didn't need explanation. Ash sat back, arms crossed, his expression unreadable but distant. Reed, more restless, drummed his fingers against the armrest, a quiet rhythm that never quite stilled. The television flickered, murmuring low across the room, just noise filling space no one intended to occupy.

Riichi dropped into a chair, his posture loose but never quite at ease. Takoda took the seat beside him, their quiet connection settling into the background like the room's stillness.

The front door creaked, and Rowan's team stepped inside—Rowan, Ivy, Vine, and Birch, each bearing the day's toll in ways only the Fallen could. Rowan's presence landed first, calm and commanding, a quiet steadiness that never needed to ask for space. Ivy's sharp-eyed focus swept the room, her movements precise and guarded. Vine, poised and polished, carried his usual arrogance with ease, but the tension in his jaw betrayed the calculations turning behind his eyes. Birch remained silent, grounded, as if the earth had shaped him and not the other way around.

Aislinn entered from the opposite hallway, steps slow, gaze scanning until it found Rowan. She crossed the room without hesitation and sank onto the couch beside him with the kind of ease born from deep familiarity. Willow followed, slipping onto the cushion near Ivy, her posture deceptively relaxed. Always watchful, she swept a glance across the room like she was reading the air pressure before a storm.

Silence settled, thick but not oppressive. They'd all made it back, but the echoes of the day clung—not in the dirt on their boots, but in the gaps between their words. The television hummed on, casting restless light across their faces, but no one watched. The tension wasn't fatigue.

They were waiting.

The heavy quiet fractured as Ariel and Rain swept into the room, their energy cutting through the tension like a burst of fresh air. Ariel paused, sharp eyes scanning the somber faces and unspoken weight in the air.

"Wow," she said with a grin, leaning against the doorframe. "Who died? You're all brooding like a bunch of Gothic novels in here."

A few faint smiles stirred, tension cracking just enough for her to wedge herself into the space it left behind. Sensing the shift, she straightened with a glint of mischief. "Listen up. I have good news. The Halloween party is officially happening, so you all need to get moving on your costumes."

Vine arched an eyebrow, the corner of his mouth lifting. "So, Eileen actually signed off on this?"

Ariel tilted her head, feigning innocence. "Of course."

Reed leaned forward, curiosity brightening his gaze. "How'd you manage that?"

"Told you—I have my ways." Pride flickered in her expression, a trickster pleased with a well-played hand.

Vine chuckled. "You're sly, Ariel."

Rowan, quiet until now, exhaled a sound that might've been amusement. "She's always been a bit of a pixie, haven't you?" His voice carried unmistakable warmth—fondness born of years spent watching her be entirely herself. "I don't know how she does it."

Ariel's grin widened, cheeks flushing under the rare acknowledgment. She straightened, clearly pleased.

The heaviness in the room eased. Shadows that had pressed in began to recede, replaced by talk of costumes and decorations. Voices lifted with the rhythm of something close to normal—however fleeting.

Reed turned toward Takoda, his seriousness softened by a teasing grin. "Hey, Takoda. You going to cook up anything special for us? You know how I love your food."

Takoda crossed her arms, amusement lighting her features. "I suppose I could whip up a few things. Can't have a party without treats, right?"

Laughter rippled through the group—small but genuine. They tossed around ideas, debated costumes, imagined decorations. It was a fragile reprieve, but they took it, leaning into the rare comfort of shared simplicity. For a little while, they weren't warriors or Fallen—just people stealing time from the storm.

The hum of conversation softened as Eileen entered the room, Oak and Elder at her side. The space didn't fall silent, but a quiet focus settled. Ariel's influence lingered in the loosened shoulders, in the way Vine murmured something to Reed that earned a faint smirk, in the ease returning to Takoda's posture.

Eileen's gaze swept over them with the kind of attention that missed nothing. She didn't speak, but her presence had always been the quiet gravity they revolved around. And yet, she saw it—what Ariel had done. A small, approving smile tugged at her lips as her focus settled on the trickster.

"Seems someone's brought some life back into the room," she said, her voice carrying the barest thread of warmth.

Ariel's grin brightened, satisfaction gleaming in her eyes. "I couldn't let everyone sit around brooding. And since we're all here, I figured we might as well start talking about the Halloween party."

Eileen gave a slow nod. "Good thinking." The words were simple, but meaning resonated in her tone—a quiet acknowledgment that Ariel had done what even she hadn't managed.

Ariel clapped her hands, already shifting the mood. "Alright, everyone—back to work! We'll iron out the details later." She shot Eileen a playful wink, and in the glance they exchanged, a quiet understanding passed between them.

At Eileen's signal, the group rose, moving toward the conference room in pairs and small clusters. The tension had eased, but anticipation still pulsed beneath the surface. Ariel had softened the edges, but the steel remained—threaded through them in every step.

The Fallen took their places around the conference table. Though unfamiliar, the space felt like countless others—another temporary war room, another borrowed battleground where strategies were whispered before being written in blood. The polished, unmarked table bore no history of their struggles, but their presence alone made it feel like all the others.

Eileen stood at the head, her authority unspoken yet absolute. An ageless intensity clung to her—a presence forged through eras of battle and endurance, like an ember that refused to die. As she surveyed the group, the air thickened, each of them acutely aware of what was at stake.

When the last murmurs faded, she spoke. "Thank you all for returning safely. The findings from today's missions are critical. Let's go through each team's discoveries to build a clearer picture."

Her gaze landed on Riichi. He rose, posture unshaken despite the wear carved into his features. "We found symbols, herbs, and wards placed strategically around Georgetown," he reported, each word deliberate. "But the most disturbing part was our encounter with one of their members. He didn't hesitate to tell us they're weakening the veil—and claimed we're already too late to stop it."

A ripple of unease passed through the room. Riichi's jaw tightened. "They weren't subtle. Their goal is to dismantle the veil, and they're moving fast."

Ash leaned forward. "There was… a disturbance in the air, like static," he said, scanning the room. "It felt unstable, like the veil was unraveling. The energy wasn't just off—it was wrong."

Willow's fingers drummed against the table. "If they're destabilizing the veil, they're either incredibly confident or incredibly desperate."

"Confidence and desperation go hand in hand for them," Vine muttered. "They'll see this through, no matter the fallout."

Eileen absorbed their words, saying nothing as she measured more than readiness—she measured resolve. Then she turned to Rowan.

Rowan stood, composure tinged with the burden of what they'd uncovered. "Fort Lawton is a central hub for the Golden Dawn. They've carved symbols directly into the earth, tapping into ley lines. They're even siphoning energy from the ocean."

He scanned the table. "They aren't just weakening the veil—they're doing it with precision. These storms are part of a grid. Every lightning strike targets key points to erode the barrier. Every ritual is a thread in a web designed to dismantle it."

Ivy leaned forward. "The magic there is layered. It's in the symbols, the air, the land itself. The entire place is a conduit."

Aislinn's grip tightened on her sleeve. "If they're forcing the veil open without knowing what's on the other side… they're playing with forces they can't control."

Rowan met her eyes, offering no promises—only certainty that they'd face whatever crossed that threshold.

At the head of the table, Eileen remained silent, calculation etched into every line of her expression. Then she turned to Oak and Elder.

Oak stood, movements precise. "Elder and I have been tracking supernatural disturbances. Storms, heatwaves, fog—they align with disruptions in the ley lines. The Golden Dawn isn't reacting to these shifts. They're causing them."

He let that settle. "A surge of magical energy hit the outskirts of Seattle—Fort Lawton again. Every anomaly, every ley line fluctuation, converges there. Our findings match Rowan's. They're amplifying natural forces, using them to tear at the veil."

Elder, watching the room, added quietly, "Rowan's right. These disturbances aren't random. They've mapped the ley lines, pinpointed weak spots. Every storm is another strike against the barrier."

Across the table, Reed exhaled. "If they keep this up, the veil won't just thin—it'll collapse. And they don't even know what's coming through."

"They don't care," Willow said. "This isn't about control anymore. They'll break the world open just to see what comes out."

A hush followed—not silence, but the kind of stillness that settled when words failed to match the scale of the threat.

Eileen let it breathe before responding. "Thank you, Oak and Elder." Her words carried rare acknowledgment. "The Golden Dawn's efforts are accelerating. Fort Lawton is confirmed as a primary target."

She studied the room, her expression unreadable. The impact of their findings pressed against each of them. They had uncovered the how—now they had to confront the why.

"We know their method," she said. "Now let's consider their motive. What do they gain from this destruction?"

Silence stretched. Riichi spoke first. "If they destroy the veil, dark forces cross over unchecked. We'd be overrun. No defenses. Just war."

"That's madness," Rowan said. "Even for them. They'd be caught in the fallout too… unless they think they'll benefit from the chaos."

Ivy's eyes narrowed. "What if control isn't the goal? What if chaos is?" She glanced around the table. "A world unbalanced. Unpredictable. The Golden Dawn thrives on instability and shifting power. They don't need control—just the edge in a world they understand better than anyone else."

Vine leaned in, unease flickering beneath his usually composed demeanor. "If that's true, they're not after temporary gain. They're trying to remake the world—collapse the barrier between realms. Reshape everything into a state we can't come back from. Gods, they're completely unhinged."

Ash nodded. "A world without protection. One where only those with their kind of power survive."

Stillness followed, heavier this time. The possibility no longer felt like theory.

After a brief pause, Eileen spoke. "Then we need more information—now. Their actions are escalating, and we can't afford to fall behind. Tonight, we split into recon teams. Fresh eyes might catch what we've missed."

A quiet murmur passed through the room.

"Riichi, take Birch, Vine, and Ash to Georgetown. Rowan, take Ivy, Willow, Reed, and Aislinn to Fort Lawton. Oak and Takoda, monitor weather patterns here. Elder, track geomantic fluctuations from the mansion."

Rowan nodded. "I'll make sure the team's prepared." He glanced at Aislinn. "And if we need Radiant Surge, we'll use it."

Aislinn met his gaze, voice steady despite the nerves beneath. "I'm ready. I'll follow your lead."

Eileen's composure softened just slightly. "This is dangerous ground. Trust each other. Stay aware. I need every one of you back safely."

The meeting ended. Chairs scraped back. Teams rose with quiet purpose. There was nothing left to say.

As they filed out, a silent understanding bound them. The risks were undeniable. The consequences, catastrophic. But hesitation had no place here. They would face the Golden Dawn head-on—ready for whatever darkness came next.

★★★

The front lobby of the mansion buzzed with quiet urgency, a pulse of controlled energy running through the space as teams made final preparations. Small groups gathered, double-checking weapons, maps, and comm devices, every movement executed with the precision of warriors who had done this far too many times. The low murmur of conversation blended with the rustle of gear, underscoring the shared intensity of what lay ahead.

Despite the sharp focus, anticipation lingered—a charged stillness woven through the air like the hush before a storm.

Takoda's attention found Riichi near the edge of the room, adjusting the strap on his vest with a soldier's meticulousness. His thoughts were clearly fixed on the mission, but a quiet strain remained in the set of his shoulders, the subtle furrow between his brows—proof even he wasn't immune to the gravity of the night.

She approached, her steps light, expression softening. Even in a room full of warriors preparing for battle, he was the only one she saw.

Riichi looked up, catching her eye—and for an instant, the rest of the room faded.

"I know you'll be fine out there. You're one of the best," she said quietly, her voice intimate. She hesitated, glancing down before meeting his gaze again. "But... with everything happening, it's hard not to worry."

Her words stirred an ache in his chest—one untouched by the weight of battle. Duty had always ruled his steps, but the quiet sincerity in her concern slipped past his defenses, loosening a feeling he wasn't prepared to face: the need to be seen for more than a soldier.

"You know I'll be careful," he said, his voice steady, warm beneath the surface. "I'll come back. Promise."

A faint smile curved her lips. It was the same reassurance he'd given her in San Francisco, but this time, she believed it. Without hesitation, he took her hand, their fingers interlocking with a natural ease. No fanfare—just the simple, grounding press of skin against skin.

Takoda exhaled, her grip tightening slightly. His touch always quieted the noise in her mind, pulled her into the present. He had been her constant, long before she realized how much that meant.

"I know you'll be careful. You always are." Her voice softened further. "Just... don't forget there are people waiting for you here."

Simple words, but they carried more than she expected. As she looked at him, something shifted—not a revelation, but a recognition of what had already taken root.

Riichi adjusted the final strap on his vest, movements as precise as ever. But when he turned back to her, his expression had changed—open, decisive.

Before either of them could question it, he leaned in and kissed her.

It was quick, measured—yet unmistakably deliberate.

The room hadn't disappeared. The mission still loomed. But for the space between breaths, none of it mattered. This wasn't impulse. It was choice.

Takoda's breath caught, warmth blooming in her chest as the shock hit her. She met his eyes, her expression a mixture of surprise and quiet wonder. *Do you realize what you've just done?*

Riichi held her gaze, a small smile playing on his lips. He knew.

And he'd done it anyway.

It wasn't a mistake, or a fleeting impulse he'd brush aside later. That small, deliberate act felt like a promise—a step beyond the unspoken truths they'd been holding back.

Takoda's heart swelled, the realization settling deep in her chest. She hadn't planned to love him. But she wasn't blind to the truth.

She already did.

Riichi gave her hand one final squeeze before stepping back, his fingers lingering for just a second longer before he let go. His expression sharpened as he rejoined his team, but the moment between them remained, unbroken.

Takoda watched him go, a quiet storm of emotions rising—pride, affection, and the undeniable thrill of something growing into more.

Around them, recon teams completed their checks. The hum of preparation faded as they turned toward the doors, ready to step into the night.

As the lobby stilled, a charged silence settled over the space, the weight of the mission closing in. But Takoda held onto that one small act—a gesture that had somehow changed everything.

★★★

The streets of Georgetown were blanketed in a dense, unnatural silence, as if the city itself held its breath. Riichi, Birch, Vine, and Ash moved with precise caution—shadows among shadows. The usual hum of city life was gone, replaced by an eerie stillness that sharpened their focus and set every nerve on edge. Riichi scanned the alleyway ahead, senses heightened. *The city feels like it's bracing for a storm.* His instincts buzzed. *This is no ordinary mission. Every sense is telling me we're about to uncover a threat far more dangerous than what we've faced before.*

Keeping low, they slipped deeper into the heart of Georgetown, every step drawing them closer to the Golden Dawn's energy source. Dim lights flickered in vacant windows like distant beacons, barely cutting through the oppressive fog clinging to the streets. Up ahead, faint voices drifted toward them, carried by the thick night air.

Riichi raised his hand, signaling a halt. Just beyond the alley, a courtyard emerged, shrouded in mist, where Golden Dawn members moved with quiet efficiency. Their faces were hidden beneath hoods, intent on their preparations. The Fallen crouched behind a crumbling wall, eyes fixed on the ritual site unfolding before them.

"Look at the scale of those symbols," Vine whispered, barely audible, gesturing to the intricate markings carved into the ground. Each line pulsed with unnatural energy.

Birch's jaw set. "This isn't a test run. This is the real thing."

Candles were placed in a wide circle, their flames casting eerie light that wavered in the mist. Small containers brimming with herbs and unfamiliar ingredients marked the boundary of the site, the air thick with volatile energy.

Riichi motioned for them to edge closer. They crept forward, just within earshot of the figures at the center of the courtyard. The leader—a tall figure with commanding presence—spoke in a low, authoritative tone that gripped the attention of everyone around him.

"The veil is thinning, just as we need it," the leader said, satisfaction threading through his voice. "With every strike, we're one step closer to releasing the storm. A typhoon born of our own power—a force no one can control but us."

A murmur of agreement rippled through the group, their fervor approaching reverence.

Another member leaned in, voice eager. "Once the veil is weakened enough, the supernatural storm will break through, cleansing this world and bringing power to those who wield it."

Riichi's jaw clenched. *A storm. A force of nature, created purely from dark energy. They aren't just cracking the veil—they're planning to unleash a force powerful enough to reshape the world.*

Beside him, Ash's expression tightened, hands flexing with quiet fury. The scale of destruction was staggering—more than reckless. It was catastrophic.

A tense glance passed among the Fallen as another cultist described the ritual's mechanics, their voice buzzing with excitement. "The heatwave, the fog, the lightning… they're all part of the storm's energy. Weakening the veil lets us pull in forces from beyond. When the storm hits, it will be unstoppable—a bridge to the other side."

Their eyes widened as the implications settled. *They're not just harnessing the weather—they're weaponizing it. Pulling in dark forces, feeding them through the storm, creating a passage between realms.*

Birch's grip tightened on his weapon. "They're insane if they think they can control this."

Riichi gave a small nod, expression grave. *This isn't just about thinning the veil—they're building a doorway. And once it's open, there will be no way to shut it.*

Just as Riichi was about to signal retreat, one of the Golden Dawn members froze, eyes narrowing in their direction.

Every muscle in Riichi's body locked.

The cultist's gaze sharpened, scanning the darkness.

Ash's pulse pounded. *Another second and we're exposed. His breath hitched. If they catch us now—*

Riichi moved, his hand issuing a slow, deliberate signal.

Not retreat. An order.

Ash understood instantly. He exhaled, his form rippling as he shifted—body shrinking, bones reforming in a smooth, seamless blur. Moments later, a sleek black cat darted from the shadows, knocking over a discarded glass bottle. It clattered across the pavement, sharp against the night.

The cultist spun toward the noise, shoulders tense. But when they spotted the cat slinking along the alley, its tail flicking lazily, they relaxed. With a muttered curse, they turned back to their preparations.

From the shadows, the cat's yellow eyes met Riichi's before Ash shifted back and rejoined the team.

One by one, they slipped away, silent and precise. They didn't breathe fully until the courtyard was far behind them.

They regrouped several blocks away, hearts still pounding but resolve solid. Riichi scanned his team, locking eyes with each of them. No one needed to speak.

Their pace quickened as they left Georgetown, urgency trailing them like smoke.

They carried more than intel now. They carried a warning.

The Golden Dawn's intentions were clear.

But one question loomed larger with each step:

Could they stop this storm before it was too late?

★★★

Under the cloak of night, Rowan, Aislinn, Ivy, Willow, and Reed crept toward Fort Lawton, each step deliberate, each breath measured. The air felt thick and electric, charged with an energy that hummed beneath the surface. Even from a distance, they could feel the power building—like the calm before a storm. They moved cautiously, sticking to the shadows, hyper-aware that they were approaching a place of intense magical activity.

This air… it feels like another realm, Rowan thought, instincts tightening in his chest. A warning, ancient and unrelenting, thrummed through his veins—as if his very blood recognized the wrongness of this place. He glanced at Aislinn, noting her furrowed brow. *Every instinct is screaming at me—this is dangerous. Volatile.*

"Let me go in first," Reed whispered, voice barely audible. "I can shadow-walk closer, stay hidden in the dark." He met each of their eyes with a nod. "I'll relay what I hear through the comms."

Rowan gave a tight nod, watching as Reed slipped into the shadows, his form blending seamlessly into the darkness until he vanished—like a specter slipping between worlds, unseen and untouched.

Aislinn watched him go, a mix of admiration and worry stirring in her chest. He was their link, their eyes and ears in the heart of the enemy.

The team remained low, static crackling softly through their commlinks. From his vantage point, Reed had a clear view of the ritual site where Golden Dawn members moved with practiced precision, carving symbols into the very bones of the earth. Candles flickered along the cliffs overlooking Puget Sound, their placement methodical—amplifying the power they intended to wield.

"Symbols are set up along the cliffs… they're using containers filled with herbs and a dark, potent essence," Reed's voice murmured through the commlink, tension threading each word. "Fort Lawton's definitely a key point for them."

The team listened, muscles taut, as the leader's voice rose—carried by the wind, laced with conviction, as if he stood right beside them. "The typhoon will originate here, in Puget Sound, where the energy is strongest. The Georgetown ritual will feed it, creating a channel that extends its reach. Once the veil is thin enough, nothing will stop us from tearing it open completely."

A reverent murmur swept through the Golden Dawn members.

"When the storm hits," another voice added, "it will wash away the old order and bring our power into the open."

Rowan's jaw tightened. *The storm isn't just a threat to the veil—it's a threat to everything in Seattle. They aren't just testing magic; they're forging a path to devastation.*

"Fort Lawton is the epicenter," Reed continued, calm but clipped. "They're using the ley lines and water to amplify the storm. Georgetown's just support—this is where it all comes together."

The realization hit like a hammer. This wasn't an experiment. It was a full-scale attack. The Golden Dawn was preparing to shatter the veil and flood the city with forces beyond understanding.

Just as Reed finished, Rowan noticed movement near the ritual site. A Golden Dawn member paused mid-step, scanning the shadows. His gaze drifted toward their position, suspicion sharpening in his narrowed eyes. He murmured to the others, their posture shifting with unease.

Rowan's pulse quickened. Too close.

If they moved, they'd be seen. If they stayed, the shadows wouldn't be enough. He turned to Ivy. "Bend reality—veil us."

She nodded, fingers twitching as magic curled through the air like a wavering mirage. The space around them warped, the light bending—just enough to distort how they were seen.

The cultist squinted, hesitating.

Rowan reached for Aislinn's hand, their fingers locking in silent agreement. They didn't activate the Shield of Ages, but stayed connected—ready if the illusion failed.

The cultists stiffened, eyes scanning the fog as Ivy's magic deepened. The shimmer twisted like moonlight swallowed by mist.

"Almost there… hold still…" Ivy whispered.

One of the cultists muttered, "Did you see that?"

Another shook his head. "Probably just the fog shifting," he said, uncertain.

Rowan remained still, body taut.

After a long few seconds, the cultists turned back to their work—clearly unsettled, but no longer alarmed.

Only when Reed reappeared at their side did Rowan signal their retreat. They slipped away, whispers in the mist, leaving nothing behind but silence.

At a safe distance, Rowan met his team's eyes. No words were spoken—none were needed. They all understood.

This was only the beginning.

The storm wasn't coming.

It had already begun.

★★★

Takoda sat in the quiet sitting room, fingers loosely clasped in her lap, gaze fixed on the doorway leading to the conference room. Riichi and his team had returned tense and silent, their expressions hard to read, but their energy heavy with whatever they'd uncovered. Even the way Riichi moved—his usual composed exterior taut with restraint—made her pulse quicken with unease.

She waited, minutes stretching too long, the silence making it worse. She tried to stay still, to be patient, but her fingers tapped absently against her thigh, restless. *What did they find?* The thought gnawed at her, each moment making it harder to shake. *What could have him this distant?*

At last, footsteps echoed. The conference room door opened, and the team emerged one by one, their postures tight, their expressions shadowed. Riichi stepped out last, his stare distant, as if his mind hadn't returned from wherever they'd been.

Takoda rose instinctively, reaching out to brush her fingers against his arm. "How about a walk?" she offered gently. "Clear your head a little?"

For a second, she thought he might say yes. His eyes met hers, a trace of emotion stirring behind them—but then he shook his head. "I need some time alone, Takoda."

The words landed like a stone in her chest—unexpected and jarring. She hadn't expected him to turn her away.

But she forced herself to nod, stepping back even as the unease rooted deeper. "All right," she said evenly, though the ache of it settled deep.

Riichi turned and walked down the hall, disappearing into the dim corridors, silence trailing behind him.

She remained where she was, staring after him, fingers curled slightly at her sides. This felt off. He wasn't just lost in thought—he was shutting her out.

Ariel and Rain wandered in shortly after, their energy cutting through the tension like a gust of fresh air. Ariel, sharp-eyed as ever, caught the look on Takoda's face immediately. Without missing a beat, she swept her into a lively conversation about Halloween decorations and costumes, her tone deliberately light.

Takoda let herself be drawn in, nodding along, even offering a few suggestions. She appreciated the effort—the way they pulled her into a space that felt warmer, more grounded.

But her mind kept circling back to Riichi.

Time slipped by. He still hadn't returned, and her unease only grew. She didn't want to hover or press if he truly needed space—but this didn't feel like him.

After nearly an hour, she exhaled, letting go of any pretense of patience. "I'll be back," she murmured to Ariel and Rain before excusing herself.

She wasn't going to wait for him to shake whatever this was.

Moving through the mansion's dim corridors, she searched for any sign of him, passing unfamiliar rooms and quiet spaces—each shadowed hallway a reminder that this place wasn't home. It wasn't as if she knew where he'd go—none of them had been here long enough to have habits—but instinct told her he wouldn't just be in his room waiting for clarity.

Eventually, she stepped onto the patio and paused when she saw him.

He sat alone on the edge of a wooden bench, elbows on his knees, fingers loosely clasped as he stared into the night. His posture was stiff, but his eyes were far away, as if he were watching something only he could see.

Takoda approached slowly, her voice quiet. "Riichi?"

No response. He didn't even blink.

She frowned and stepped closer, waving a hand in front of his face. "Earth to Riichi."

He blinked, startled, as if only now realizing she was there. "Takoda," he murmured. Her name carried a softened edge, but his voice still felt distant—like part of him hadn't quite returned.

She eased down beside him, watching closely. "What's going on?" she asked, voice warm but firm. "You've been carrying a weight since you got back. Talk to me."

Riichi's gaze dropped. His posture turned inward. "It's nothing," he muttered, low and dismissive. "Nothing you'd be interested in."

Her brow furrowed, frustration threading through concern. "Nothing I'd be interested in?" she echoed, sharper now. "You're clearly troubled, and you're just brushing it off?"

He exhaled, tilting his head toward the dark sky. "It's complicated, Takoda. I don't want to burden you with it."

The words struck harder than she expected.

She stood abruptly, arms crossing over her chest, voice tight. "If you don't trust me, that's fine. But don't expect me to believe it's nothing when it's so clearly not."

She didn't wait for a response.

Turning on her heel, she strode toward the garden—her steps brisk, her expression composed, though her mind reeled.

Riichi remained seated, her words hanging in the silence around him. The weight of them settled deep, threading through the spaces he'd kept carefully guarded. He hadn't meant to hurt her, but he had. He could see it in the way she walked away, feel it in the ache left behind. He exhaled slowly, pressing his palms to his knees. Regret was an unfamiliar companion, but it had taken up residence in his chest tonight.

After a stretch of silence, he rose. He couldn't leave things like this.

Moving swiftly, he followed her into the garden. The scent of damp earth and night-blooming flowers cut sharp in the cool air. His footsteps were quiet against the stone pathways as he wove through the hedge maze, his pace quickening with each turn.

Then, he saw her.

Takoda sat on a stone bench, knees drawn up, her head bowed. The quiet tension in her form struck him harder than expected. This wasn't just frustration—this was pain. And he had put it there.

He slowed his approach, moving with the same deliberate care he used when stepping into a fight where the next move mattered most. Taking a seat beside her, he hesitated before placing a tentative hand on her arm—a silent apology.

She tensed, then shrugged him off, her gaze still locked on the ground.

He sighed, running a hand through his hair. Words had never been his weapon of choice, but silence wouldn't fix this.

"You're right," he said at last, his voice low but steady.

Takoda didn't look at him, but he knew she was listening.

"I shouldn't have brushed you off. My mind's been tangled with the mission, with worry for you, for everyone. And then… there's my past and this bond between us. I didn't want to burden you with it all."

Takoda lifted her head, eyes sharp with both frustration and hurt. "It isn't about you burdening me, Riichi," she said, quiet but firm. "It's that when you shut me out, it makes me feel like I'm just someone on the sidelines. Like you don't trust me enough to let me in." Her throat bobbed, but she held his gaze. "And that hurts."

Her words hit like a strike he hadn't seen coming—not because they were unexpected, but because he finally felt their full force.

"You matter to me more than I've shown," he admitted, his voice rough. He glanced away, jaw tightening. "But I'm afraid of you seeing my darker side. I've done things I'm ashamed of, Takoda. Terrible things." His fingers flexed against his knee. "And I'm terrified to tell you… because I don't want to lose you."

The truth hung raw and exposed.

Then, he forced himself to look at her. "The truth is… I think I'm falling in love with you. And that scares me more than anything I've ever faced."

Takoda's expression softened. The tightness in her posture eased, though her eyes still searched his. Slowly, she reached for his hand, her grip warm and steady. "I know I'm falling in love with you."

His breath caught.

"I don't need you to tell me everything," she continued, gentle but unwavering. "Just… don't shut me out. Let me know when you're not ready. That's all I ask."

The knot inside him loosened, the tension slipping from his shoulders. He turned his palm up and laced his fingers through hers, grounding himself in her quiet strength. "I can do that," he promised.

They sat in silence, hands entwined. The distance that had separated them was no longer a chasm, just a space they were learning to bridge.

After a while, they rose together, hands still clasped, and followed the winding path in silence. The cool night air whispered between them, but neither spoke. Whatever tension had lived between them before had been replaced by something rawer, more real.

As they rounded a bend in the garden, Riichi slowed. The hedges opened into a quiet clearing, lit only by moonlight and the faint shimmer of magic lingering in the air. He turned to her, his expression unguarded for the first time all night.

"I don't have the right words yet," he said softly, brushing a thumb across her cheek. "But I meant what I said."

Takoda tilted her head into his touch, her eyes steady on his. "You don't need the right words. I already heard you."

His breath caught. Slowly, deliberately, he leaned in. Their lips met—not in haste or uncertainty, but with the quiet weight of everything left unsaid. The kiss deepened for a moment, then softened again, a rhythm born of mutual trust.

As they pulled back, their joined hands lit with a familiar glow—brighter this time, burning softly along their arms like the first sparks of a fire finding breath. Takoda drew in a quiet breath, watching the light spread with wide, astonished eyes.

"It's not stopping," she whispered, watching it ripple gently between them.

Riichi stared at the glow, then back at her, wonder bleeding into a slow smile. "Neither are we."

She huffed out a breath of laughter, the sound light and warm. "Was that supposed to be poetic?"

"Maybe. Did it work?"

"A little," she teased, though her fingers curled tighter around his.

They stood there another moment, letting the glow pulse between them, before turning back toward the mansion. Their steps were slow, synced. The light between them faded to a quiet hum, but the shift lingered.

By the time they reached the doors, the silence wasn't empty—it was full. Full of everything that had changed, and everything still waiting.

Chapter Thirteen
Awakening Forces

Morning stretched lazily through the room, weaving quiet bands of golden light that cast soft, warm traces across the rumpled blankets as Takoda stirred gently from sleep. The air carried a tranquil hush, the kind of stillness that settled comfortably between two people who had learned to coexist seamlessly in each other's presence, without the need to fill the silence with words or noise.

Beside her, Riichi was already awake, his gaze tracking the shifting sky beyond the window. He lay motionless, exuding a calm presence, and his face showed a rare tranquility found only in moments like this.

She nudged him playfully, breaking the quiet. "So, the 'orange glow' last night…" A teasing lilt crept into her voice. "Didn't peg you for the dramatic type."

His mouth twitched, amusement glistening in his dark eyes. "Neither did I." He let the thought settle before adding, "But you seem to bring it out of me."

Takoda arched a brow. "Oh? Should I be worried?"

His gaze drifted back to her, considering. "Not unless you mind seeing sides of me I'm still figuring out." His voice was calm, but she heard the weight beneath it—the quiet admission of change, of newness, of finding unfamiliar ground in a life that had once felt rigid.

She studied him for a moment, then shook her head. "I don't mind," she said simply. "Not at all."

Silence stretched between them, comfortable, broken only by the distant rustling of leaves beyond the window.

Riichi exhaled, tilting his head a tad as if debating whether to continue. Then, with careful deliberation, he spoke. "It's easier with you. Not just… talking. Existing."

The words weren't dramatic, but they resonated deeply, stirring a feeling that rooted itself in her chest, stable and certain.

Takoda gave a small nod. "Good," she murmured. "Because I don't plan on going anywhere."

His eyes locked with hers and held. For a man who had spent so much of his life guarding himself, it was significant.

A shift in the morning rhythm pulled them forward. As Takoda folded a shirt, she cast him a sidelong glance. "So, for today's meeting," she said, keeping her tone light but open. "Anything I should know beforehand?"

Riichi paused, fingers stilling against the fabric he was smoothing out. A beat passed before he answered. "Not much I can't say in front of the others," he admitted. Then, after the briefest hesitation, he added, "Just pay attention to how people react—especially when Eileen speaks."

His voice was calm, but there was a quiet undercurrent of strategy in it. He wasn't warning her—he was preparing her. Not everyone in the room would speak their mind, but their silence would say enough.

Takoda's fingers brushed his arm, her touch remaining just long enough to acknowledge what he wasn't saying. "Sounds like a plan."

A faint smile tugged at his lips, softening his features, and for a brief second, there was nothing but the serene quiet, the world seeming to pause around them—the kind of silence that was rich with meaning.

As they made their way toward the door, Takoda's fingertips lightly grazed Riichi's hand, sending a gentle spark through the air. Neither of them withdrew, allowing the warmth of the unexpected contact to linger, binding them in a silent, shared moment.

They walked in step, side by side, ready for whatever came next.

As they made their way downstairs, the scent of freshly brewed coffee and cooked bacon drifted through the air, mingling with the quiet noise of conversation from the Fallen already gathered. The mansion's kitchen and dining area carried a rare sense of ease, the morning light catching on polished surfaces and casting a soft glow through the open space.

Takoda veered toward the kitchen, Riichi falling into step beside her. She moved with practiced efficiency, gathering the ingredients they'd prepped the night before and rolling out the croissants with a steady hand. Though he wasn't much for baking, Riichi assisted where he could—fetching a tray, adjusting the oven's settings, ensuring everything moved smoothly.

As the croissants baked, warmth from the oven curled into the kitchen, filling the space with the rich, buttery scent of pastry. Takoda leaned against the counter, her hands resting on the cool surface as she glanced at Riichi.

"You know," she mused, tilting her head, "for someone who claims not to have a sweet tooth, you're remarkably invested in this process."

Riichi, standing close, rolled up his sleeves with careful movements, a subtle smirk tugging at his lips. "I wouldn't call it an investment," he replied, voice calm, reasonable. "Just... quality control. And I prefer to contribute rather than stand idle." His gaze skimmed toward the croissants, then back to her. "If I'm here, I might as well be useful."

Takoda scoffed. "Is that what you call hovering?"

Instead of answering, he leaned in, brushing a slow, thoughtful kiss against her jaw. The warmth of it sent a pleasant purr through her senses, and she turned toward him, catching the edge of his smirk before she stole a kiss of her own.

"If you're trying to distract me from my work," she murmured against his lips, "it's not going to—"

Riichi kissed her again, cutting off her teasing with a slow press of his mouth to hers. It was brief, but enough to make her exhale a quiet laugh when he pulled away.

"Not going to what?" he asked, his voice low.

Takoda huffed, nudging his chest lightly before turning back toward the oven. "You're lucky these are almost done, or I'd make you knead the dough for next time."

Riichi raised a brow, but she caught the hint of amusement in his expression as he leaned back against the counter, watching her pull the croissants from the oven. She arranged them carefully on a tray, their golden layers crisp and flaking at the edges. The inviting aroma filled the kitchen, wrapping around them in a comforting embrace.

She lifted the tray, casting him a small, pleased smile. "Think they pass your quality check?"

Riichi didn't answer immediately. Instead, he took one, broke off a piece, and popped it into his mouth, chewing thoughtfully before giving a single nod.

"Acceptable," he said.

Takoda rolled her eyes, but the warmth in her smile remained as she nudged his arm. "Come on, let's go feed everyone before Reed starts hunting us down."

With that, she led the way into the dining room, Riichi following at her side.

The moment she stepped in, the scent caught the attention of the Fallen scattered around the table. A few glanced up, their conversations pausing briefly as Takoda set the tray down on the long wooden table, the warmth from the fresh pastries still radiating into the air.

Reed, predictably the first to reach for one, took a generous bite, his usually stoic features softening in approval. "Perfect as always, Takoda. You're spoiling us," he said, his voice holding a rare note of warmth.

Takoda shrugged, but there was no mistaking the quiet pride in her eyes. "Just keeping everyone fed."

A few other Fallen murmured their thanks as they reached for their own, and soon, the easy rhythm of breakfast resumed. The air felt lighter now, a welcome reprieve from the usual burden of their responsibilities.

Riichi sank into a chair, his presence a quiet constant even in the relaxed atmosphere. Takoda sat next to him, filling her cup with coffee as the conversation around them flowed effortlessly.

Before long, Ariel bounded over to where Eileen sat, her energy unmistakable. Perching on the edge of a chair, she leaned forward, her hands gesturing animatedly. "Eileen, we need Halloween decorations for the mansion! I'm talking full-on spooky—cobwebs, jack-o-lanterns, the whole haunted vibe." Her grin widened as she painted the vision with clear enthusiasm.

Rain, standing nearby, smirked. "She's not wrong. A little festive spirit wouldn't hurt. Things have been heavy around here lately."

Eileen arched a brow but didn't immediately dismiss the idea. A slow smile ghosted across her lips, an indulgence she rarely showed outside of moments like these. For all her authority, there was a softness in the way she regarded Ariel, as if humoring her was as much a choice as it was a necessity.

Finally, she nodded, her voice carrying both warmth and its usual unwavering authority. "Alright," she allowed. "Just stay aware of your surroundings while you're out. And keep it tasteful—I don't want the mansion looking like a haunted carnival."

Ariel's victorious cheer echoed through the room. "You got it, boss! We'll make this place look amazing."

There was a subtle change in the room, a near-tangible exhale, as if Eileen's approval had granted everyone permission to embrace the lighter mood. Conversations brightened, laughter weaving into the buzz of morning chatter.

Ariel's excitement was infectious, and as she and Rain prepared to head out, she grinned at Reed. "So, what do you say? Maybe a knight in shining armor for Halloween? You've already got the brooding warrior thing down."

Reed exhaled, unimpressed but not entirely unaffected. "I'll pass, thanks."

Vine, never one to resist a chance for banter, smirked. "I see Ariel as more of a mischievous fae."

Ariel tossed him a wink. "Only if you're a wicked warlock."

Laughter rippled through the table as the teasing continued, the mood staying light as Ariel and Rain grabbed their things. A few Fallen called after them—warnings not to get sidetracked at the mall met only with Ariel's dismissive wave.

Before they could go, Takoda stepped forward, handing Ariel a neatly wrapped bag of croissants. "For the road," she said, her tone knowing.

Ariel beamed, squeezing Takoda's arm in thanks. "You're the best. This just made today even better."

With one final wave, Ariel and Rain disappeared down the hall, their laughter fading as they left.

As the room settled, Reed glanced at Takoda, offering a subtle nod. "You keep things moving around here," he murmured, his words simple but sincere.

Takoda's expression softened, a quiet satisfaction warming her features. "It's the least I can do."

As Ariel and Rain's departure faded down the hall, the atmosphere in the room transformed. The spark of their enthusiasm still echoed, but duty took hold, sharpening the focus in the air. Conversations quieted, and the ease of breakfast faded into a shared understanding—there was work to be done.

Eileen's gaze swept over the table, her posture adjusting, her presence controlling without effort. The shift was subtle, but immediate.

She rose, her face composed yet firm. "Let's move to the conference room."

Chairs scraped lightly against the floor as the Fallen stood, their actions fluid, methodical. A few topped off their coffee, Takoda covered the remaining croissants, and without need for further direction, they filed out. The transition was seamless, driven by routine and implicit urgency.

By the time they reached the long, dark wood table in the mansion's conference room, the levity of breakfast had faded entirely. Sunlight cut pale patterns along the walls, but no one noticed. Each seat filled quickly, shoulders squared, expressions taut with focus.

At the head of the table, Eileen stood, her gaze sweeping over the team. "Let's begin."

Riichi was the first to speak, his voice low and certain, setting the tone. "We went into Georgetown expecting the usual—small rituals aimed at weakening the veil. But this… was far beyond that." His expression darkened, his words calculated. "They've escalated. What we found was a ritual designed for large-scale destruction."

Birch's jaw tightened as he nodded. "This wasn't about carving symbols or scattering minor charms. They were manipulating the city's natural forces—the shifting heat, the fog rolling in at night, the lightning storms. They're weaponizing Seattle's climate."

Vine leaned forward, his gaze impassive but charged with unease. "The storm they're summoning isn't natural. It's supernatural. They're conjuring a typhoon powerful enough to shatter the veil completely, tearing it apart so forces from the other side can pour through."

A heavy silence settled over the room before Ash exhaled, his posture tense. "They're using the weather as a conduit to pull energy from beyond. This isn't just about weakening the veil—it's about ripping it open. They think they can control whatever comes through, but…" His voice trailed off, the implications speaking for themselves.

Riichi's tone hardened. "The Golden Dawn members we overheard were confident. Too confident. They believe this typhoon will cleanse the world, wiping away whatever stands in their way while feeding their power. And they don't care about the consequences."

Across the table, Elder frowned, his fingers tapping lightly against the wood in thought. "They're sacrificing control for speed. That makes them reckless… and even more dangerous."

Willow nodded, her voice thoughtful but laced with concern. "They're pushing to complete the ritual as quickly as possible. That means they're close… and desperate. Desperation makes people sloppy, but it also makes them willing to take risks they shouldn't."

Riichi inclined his head, his words steady but urgent. "We barely made it out without being detected. But from what we saw, they're ready to make a decisive move at Fort Lawton. If we don't act now, they'll create a breach we may not be able to close."

Eileen's gaze swept across the table, absorbing every word. She nodded, her tone even, yet leaving no room for doubt. "Thank you, Riichi. The urgency is clear. We need to act before this ritual reaches completion."

Rowan's voice broke the silence, his tone grim. "Fort Lawton is the focal point. They've been setting up along the cliffs overlooking Puget Sound, marking every step with care. They aren't just casting spells—they're constructing a full-scale ritual site, one designed for the cataclysmic event."

Reed's features betrayed nothing, his tone controlled, carrying a quiet edge. "I had a clear view from my position. Carved symbols, ritual candles arranged in intricate patterns, containers filled with blood-soaked herbs and charred bones. The energy was overwhelming. Their leader spoke openly about tearing the veil apart and letting darkness flood the city."

Aislinn shifted, her brows furrowing. "This isn't just about breaking through. They're creating a channel—one that could open a permanent gateway, allowing entities from beyond to enter unchecked."

Ivy's voice was unbroken, but a hint of concern sharpened her features. "They're amplifying the water's natural power and channeling it through the ley lines to make the typhoon unstoppable. Georgetown's ritual is designed to support the main one, feeding power into it so the storm spreads across the entire city. Fort Lawton is where they intend to tear the veil wide open."

Willow leaned forward, her words heavy with the gravity of what they had overheard. "We heard them say the typhoon would 'wash away the old order.' This isn't just about accessing more power. They want to rewrite everything."

Rowan's gaze swept over the team, his voice calm but edged with warning. "We stayed hidden with Reed's shadow-walking and Ivy's reality bending, but it was close. Their security is tightening. Their confidence is growing."

Reed didn't hesitate. "If this typhoon happens, it won't just destabilize the veil—it will destroy it. And if that happens, we may not be able to contain what comes through."

A hush fell over the room, his words sinking in like a final verdict. No one spoke. The danger was clear.

Eileen exhaled slowly, the only outward sign of the calculation running behind her eyes. Her gaze swept the table, landing on Rowan's team before shifting to the rest of the Fallen. "Thank you, Rowan." She straightened, shoulders squared with quiet resolve. "We now understand the full extent of their plans. And it's clear that our response must be swift and decisive."

Her focus sharpened, shifting between each member of the team. The room stilled, the gravity of the moment pressing in. "Our objective is clear: we must stop the ritual at Fort Lawton before they can tear open the veil. So, I want us to consider every angle. What are our options?"

Riichi spoke again, his voice level but carrying the quiet authority of a strategist who had spent lifetimes perfecting the art of war. "Their setup relies on distinct power points, each one sending energy directly into the veil. If we target those sources—disrupt just enough to throw them off balance—they won't be able to maintain stability. We don't need to destroy everything, just fracture their foundation."

Vine nodded, fingers tapping absently against the table as he considered. "That's workable. If I get close enough, I can short-circuit their equipment with electrokinesis. Breaking their power supply won't just slow them down—it'll force them to waste time recalibrating." His expression darkened slightly, sharp as flint. "They won't recover quickly from that."

Aislinn leaned forward, determined but thoughtful. "If I anchor a shield around their main ritual space, I could sever their connection to the veil entirely. A strong enough barrier would trap their energy inside, forcing them to burn through their reserves without achieving anything."

Across the table, Oak inclined his head, a quiet understanding passing between them. "I can reinforce the shield, strengthen it against outside interference. If we do this right, they'll drain themselves before they realize their ritual isn't working." His voice was steady, grounded in the certainty of one who had stood watch over the old world long before this battle began.

Willow, ever detailed, spoke next. "If I manipulate the energy flow beneath the ritual site, I can siphon power into the earth before it reaches critical levels. If the energy disperses into the ground, they'll be scrambling to compensate, and that's where we press our advantage."

Ivy folded her arms, considering. "I can warp the landscape around them—shift the alignment of their symbols just enough to fracture their intent. If their setup is even slightly misaligned, their power won't funnel properly. A ritual this complex demands accuracy, and we can deny them that."

Reed's voice was low but sure. "I'll shadow-walk close to their positions, track movements, and pinpoint who's directing the ritual. If we take out their key players, the rest of them will fall apart faster."

Ash inclined his head in agreement. "I can take it a step further. If I shift into one of their own and slip into the outer circle, I can feed them misinformation—lead them to second-guess their own timing." He smirked slightly. "Nothing derails a ritual faster than doubt in their own ranks."

Rowan, ever direct, leaned forward. "If it comes down to brute force, I'm ready to dismantle their setup by hand. Knock out their staging, scatter their components—whatever forces them to start over." There was no hesitation in his voice, only the steel resolve of a warrior who had spent centuries tearing through enemy lines.

Takoda hesitated for only a breath before speaking. "I may not have complete control over my abilities, but I'll support any of you if things get tense. If emotions start to rise, I can stabilize the team—especially you, Riichi." Her gaze found his, a quiet thread of understanding passing between them. She didn't elaborate. She didn't need to.

Elder, who had been listening intently, finally nodded, his voice as grounded as the earth itself. "I can shift the terrain beneath them, create tremors to fracture their alignment. Even a minor quake could throw them off just enough for us to act."

Eileen, who had been silent until now, absorbed each plan with the patience of one who had seen countless battles unfold. When she finally spoke, her voice carried both the command of strategy and an authority that ran deeper than time—an unshakable force that echoed beyond mere experience. "These are strong tactics—disruptions, shielding, misdirection, and direct interference." Her gaze swept across the table, inscrutable, yet as steady as the roots of an ancient tree. "If anyone has refinements to suggest, now is the time. We'll use every advantage we have."

Willow's sharp eyes flicked to Takoda. "She's been showing promise in emotional influence. If she hones it, she could affect the Golden Dawn's leadership during the ritual—introduce hesitation and confusion. A moment of doubt at the right time could derail their focus."

Takoda blinked, surprised, before straightening. "If that would help, I'll do it. I'll train, whatever it takes."

Eileen nodded, considering. "It's an option we'll keep in play. If we determine it's viable, we'll integrate it into the plan." Her focus returned to the room, command settling over her like a mantle woven of resolve and quiet inevitability—an unspoken presence that bound the Fallen to their purpose, whether they fully understood it or not.

"Our primary strategy is clear—dismantle the ritual's critical points before they complete their work. Precision and timing will be everything." She let that sink in before concluding, her voice calm but edged with steel.

"Our plan is simple. We stop them at Fort Lawton. We do not let them breach the veil."

Eileen let a moment of silence settle before addressing the first team.

"The mission will unfold in stages. First, the Surveillance and Misdirection Team will infiltrate." Her voice was calm, but the emphasis behind it carried no less authority. "Reed and Ash, position yourselves for intel and deception. Reed, you'll shadow-walk to track their movements, undetected, and relay real-time updates. Your priority is ensuring the Disruption Team isn't caught off guard. Ash, infiltrate their ranks—shapeshift, spread misinformation, fracture their focus from within. If they hesitate, they lose momentum. I need you feeding intelligence directly to me."

She met Ivy's sharp gaze. "Ivy, shift the environment before they realize what's happening. Alter the terrain just enough to throw off their symbols. A warped ritual site will weaken their control over the power flow, making it harder for them to reach the critical threshold."

She moved to the second team without pause.

"Once the setup is confirmed, the Disruption Team moves in." Her gaze settled on each of them. "Riichi, you lead. Pinpoint the weakest points and dismantle them before they can react."

She continued without hesitation. "Vine, Elder—target their power sources. Vine, short-circuit their amplifiers and disrupt their energy flow—anything that throws their balance off. Elder, use geomancy to fracture the ground, disrupting their symbols and breaking their ritual alignment."

Her attention shifted to the next pair. "Rowan, Aislinn—you're our core physical force. If this turns into close combat, be ready to shut them down immediately. Radiant Surge will be our strongest fallback—use it to reinforce our team and press the advantage if needed."

She let her words settle before finishing, her presence unwavering. "This team will be at the heart of the Golden Dawn's ritual. You will face direct confrontation. Be prepared to strike swiftly and with certainty."

Her focus then moved to the third group.

"Meanwhile, the Emotional Manipulation and Magical Support Team will reinforce from a safe position." She met their eyes in turn. "Takoda, Oak, and Willow—your job is to weaken their resolve and stabilize our forces."

"Takoda, influence the emotions of key Golden Dawn members. If you can instill hesitation, doubt, or fear, it may be enough to break their concentration. Oak, reinforce her efforts while shielding the Disruption Team from magical retaliation. They'll be deep in enemy territory—they will need protection."

She turned to Willow. "Willow, you'll handle energy manipulation—redirect excess power into the earth before it reaches the veil. Keep the ritual unstable. If they lose control of their energy flow, they'll collapse their own work."

Her gaze settled on Birch last. "Birch, you'll act as secondary support. Cover any team that needs reinforcement—whether it's providing shields, scouting, or acting as a fallback if Reed or Ash are compromised. Your adaptability will be key."

Straightening, Eileen's presence anchored the room.

"I will oversee command and coordination." No embellishment, just conviction. "I'll be in constant communication with each of you, adjusting our strategy as new intel comes in. Reed, Ash, and Ivy—you will be my eyes in the field."

She allowed a beat of silence before issuing her final directives.

"At my signal, all teams will pull back. The Surveillance Team will cover our retreat to ensure the Golden Dawn remains too disoriented to recover quickly."

Her final words came with quiet, unwavering certainty.

"Each of you has a crucial role. Train for your assignments. Sharpen your skills. Be prepared for anything." A pause, then the words that carried undeniable finality.

"We end this before they have the chance to complete it."

After the meeting, a quiet intensity filled the mansion as the Fallen prepared for training. Anticipation pulsated through the hallways, each member absorbed in thoughts of their role and the mission ahead.

In a secluded corner, Riichi found Takoda standing by a window, her gaze fixed on the courtyard where they would soon begin. The sunlight caught in her dark hair, highlighting the pensive look that shadowed her face.

He approached, his steps measured but deliberate. "Takoda." His voice was soft, steady, an anchor against the gravity of their task. "I wanted to check in—see how you're feeling about your role." His eyes held a quiet warmth, though his posture remained reserved, careful. He needed to know she was truly okay with being assigned to another team.

Takoda turned to him, her eyes settling into calm resolve. "I'm ready, Riichi." There was no hesitation in her tone, no uncertainty. "I trust the plan. Eileen put me where I'm needed, and I know you'll have everything under control. We'll both do our part."

A faint smile touched his lips, gratitude flickering in his gaze. "Thank you," he said, voice low, carrying an unspoken promise. "I'll be careful. I just... wanted you to know."

A quiet understanding passed between them in that moment—silent, resolute, unshakable. It was a tether, a connection forged not through words but through trust and recognition.

Soon after, the Fallen gathered in the courtyard behind the mansion. The field stretched beneath an endless sky, open and quiet, yet charged with the focused energy of warriors preparing for battle. Riichi met Takoda's gaze across the space, nodding to her in silent encouragement before moving to join his team.

Takoda turned toward Oak and Willow, who stood near her training area. Across the field, several targets pulsed with faint, shifting hues, each color holding a distinct emotional resonance. Oak gestured toward the closest one, its glow flickering between crimson and violet.

"Each color represents an emotion," he explained. "Red for anger, blue for fear, green for confidence. Your goal is to change them—guide them into doubt or confusion."

Takoda inhaled slowly, centering herself before focusing on the first target. She extended her hand, steady but hesitant, willing the deep red to fade into a muted shade of doubt, its certainty unraveling at the edges. Her fingers tensed as she pushed her energy outward, her brow furrowing with effort—but the color held, resisting the shift.

Exhaling sharply, she let her hand drop.

Oak's voice remained calm. "Take it slow. You're not forcing the change—you're leading it."

She gave a small nod, refocusing. This time, she envisioned the red unraveling, its sharp edges blurring into insecurity. For a moment, she thought she felt a shift, a hint of indecision in the color—then, just as quickly, it snapped back, vibrant and unmoved.

Willow stepped closer, her voice gentle. "Try anchoring the feeling first. Don't just think about doubt—find it in yourself, then extend it outward."

Takoda took another breath, drawing the feeling to the surface, shaping it into intent. She reached toward the target once more, picturing the color softening, unraveling from its rigid form. This time, it wavered—but only slightly, before stubbornly snapping back into place.

Her frustration flashed at the edges of her focus. She scanned the field absently, her gaze drifting across the courtyard until it landed on Riichi.

He moved through a reflex drill with practiced exactitude, each strike calculated, controlled—but she could see the strain beneath it. There was limitation in the way he moved, his aura pulsing with restless energy, streaks of deep blue and ember-red flickering like a fire waiting to ignite.

She knew that feeling.

He wasn't just training—he was directing. Pouring his frustration into every motion, every strike was a tacit battle against the forces threatening them.

Takoda's fingers flexed at her sides, awareness narrowing to the energy surrounding him. She could feel it—the unsaid tension in his thoughts, the rigid discipline he imposed over himself.

Instinctively, she reached toward him—not physically, but with the part of her that had begun to awaken, the ability she was only starting to understand.

A single, quiet thought rose within her.

A wish for him to let go.

To find clarity.

Her hands glowed—soft, warm, a muted orange that felt natural, intuitive.

The glow extended outward, reaching him, though she barely registered it happening.

Across the field, Riichi paused mid-strike. A sense of calm washed over him—not forced, not intrusive, just... present. Like an unseen current had strengthened him from within. The tension that coiled at his core unwound, his movements sharpening, his focus settling into a rhythm that felt normal, fluid, accurate.

He looked up, locking eyes with Takoda from across the courtyard.

For a heartbeat, neither moved.

She felt the connection between them like a current in the air, a silent recognition passing between them. He didn't need to speak, didn't need to question it. He simply acknowledged her with a trace of warmth in his gaze and a nod before turning back to his drill, his movements now effortless, unburdened.

Takoda exhaled slowly, a deep, unfamiliar satisfaction subsiding in her chest.

Nearby, Oak and Willow exchanged glances.

Oak's expression remained unreadable, but his voice was laced with quiet realization. "We've been teaching her wrong."

Willow nodded, realization settling in as she watched Takoda. Until now, they had instructed her to focus on the visible aura surrounding a person, teaching her to manipulate the outer emotional layers. But in doing so, they had unknowingly limited her.

This outward focus made her influence detectable—a visible magical signature in the air. But watching her now, it was clear: Takoda's strength came from within, shaped by the connections she forged rather than the energy she projected—much like Birch with his endurance manipulation.

"It's her connection to him," Willow murmured, observing how Takoda's gaze softened when she looked at Riichi.

Oak folded his arms, his expression contemplative. "She's not just influencing emotions at the surface—she's reaching into the core of a person's feelings. That's why it's undetectable. She's working from within, not imposing from the outside."

With this new understanding, Oak and Willow approached Takoda.

"Try a different approach," Oak suggested, his tone even but determined. "Don't focus on the aura. See beyond it. Connect to the emotion itself, not the colors. Imagine each one as a person—someone real, someone you're reaching out to."

Takoda absorbed his words, understanding settling into her expression. Determination glinted in her gaze as she turned back to the targets.

She took a slow, stable breath.

This time, she didn't see glowing orbs pulsing with color—she saw people. She felt their emotions, the way anger simmered beneath the surface, the way fear clenched in the chest, the way doubt wavered, fragile and uncertain.

She focused on the red target, the embodiment of anger. But instead of simply willing it to fade, she imagined the emotion itself—the way someone might grip onto their rage, the moment it began to waver under the pull of self-doubt.

What if I'm wrong?

The red flickered, dimming at the edges.

Slowly, it changed, softening to a murky gray.

Takoda's breath hitched, but she didn't stop.

She turned to the blue target, picturing someone lost in fear, their mind consumed by doubt, breath ragged, thoughts spiraling into panic. Instead of forcing the fear away, she offered an anchor—a quiet sense of security, the supporting presence of someone standing beside them, unwavering and constant.

The blue lightened, trembling between hesitation and reassurance before resolving into a soft, steady glow.

Her confidence grew with each turn, the colors responding not to force, but to consideration. What had once felt like struggle now flowed naturally.

When she reached the final target, she didn't doubt herself. She trusted in what she had begun to realize.

By the time she finished, a quiet sense of accomplishment settled over her. Not just because her ability had finally responded—but because she comprehended it now.

She glanced toward Riichi across the field. His movements were sharp and exact, his energy constant, no longer weighed down by frustration.

She knew now.

The bond she shared with him had done more than strengthen her abilities—it had revealed the truth of them.

She wasn't just influencing emotions.

She was bridging them.

★★★

Eileen sat alone in her office, maps and reports spread across her desk as she refined the final strategy. From the courtyard, the faint sounds of training drifted in—a quiet rhythm of movement, muted voices, the occasional sharp clash of effort meeting resistance. The house was calm, though a pulse of anticipation pressed beneath the surface.

She exhaled slowly, centering herself in the present. Pride stirred beneath the magnitude of duty, the staunch knowledge that the Fallen were preparing themselves for the battle ahead. But even as the air remained still, an unseen force stirred at the edges of her awareness.

Her vision fractured.

The walls of her office faded into a thick, smoldering haze, heat curling at the edges like invisible hands pressing inward. The air felt charged, heavy, a pulse thrumming beneath her skin as the space around her gave way to shadows.

Before her, a tattered scroll materialized, its brittle edges curling in an unseen wind. A whisper of movement sent flakes of parchment crumbling away.

Then, words seared themselves onto the surface—raw, jagged, as if clawed into existence.

I am watching you.

Eileen's gaze hardened, but she did not react.

A second mark burned below the message—a twisted, familiar symbol etched deep into the parchment. Her breath remained calm, though a slow tension coiled in her chest at the sight of it. The last time she had seen this mark, it had been on the note Rowan and Aislinn discovered—one they later learned had come from Lucifer himself.

The voice came—low, resonant, too close.

I'm watching you… and I'll be there soon.

The presence loomed, hidden yet oppressive, circling her thoughts like a predator playing with its prey. Then, a pause—calculated, taunting.

Have you checked on Takoda and Riichi lately?

The final words curled through her mind, a whisper laced with dark amusement. A rasping chuckle followed, stretching into a sound not entirely human before the vision shattered.

Eileen gasped—a sharp inhale as reality snapped back into place. Her office stood as it had before, the scent of parchment, ink, and steel grounding her in the present. But the manifestation lingered, its absence almost more unsettling than its arrival.

Her fingers curled against the desk's edge, but she remained still, letting the enormity of what she had seen settle down. Then she stood.

Her movements were swift but soundless as she crossed the room, the warning still burning at the forefront of her mind. She had seen countless threats before, faced enemies who thought themselves untouchable. But this one had marked its targets, and it was watching.

When she reached the courtyard, she slowed, her steps gauged as she took in the scene before her.

Oak and Willow stood near Takoda, guiding her through the final stages of her training. Their words carried an evident rhythm—a balance between patience and meticulousness, the kind of teaching passed through ages, meant to root power deep rather than force it to surface.

Takoda stood between them, her focus sharpened. The colored targets before her responded to the flow of her intent, shifting beneath her will. The training had changed—uncertainty had faded, replaced by understanding.

Across the field, Riichi moved through his drills, his strikes determined, his stance more grounded than before. His actions weren't just efficient—they were fluid, each motion refined in a way that had not been present earlier.

Eileen's gaze moved between them, a realization landing with quiet finality. Their bond was not just emotional—it was sharpening them, forging them into a force greater than the sum of its parts. Takoda's energy wove seamlessly through the targets, her influence growing stronger with each attempt. Riichi's combat carried a newfound fluidity, his strikes no longer edged with frustration. They weren't just training. They were elevating each other, their strengths interwoven like threads in an unbreakable weave. They were getting closer to Radiant Surge with each passing hour.

The vision's words pressed against her thoughts. *Have you checked on Takoda and Riichi lately?*

Her fingers curled at her sides. The warning had not been vague. It had not been a mere threat. It had been a statement of intent.

She stepped forward, her voice carrying across the field. "Fallen." The training stilled. "That's enough for today."

A ripple of acknowledgment passed through the courtyard as weapons lowered, movements slowed. One by one, the Fallen turned toward her, reading the change in her presence before nodding in quiet consideration.

She met their gazes—each of them, one by one, an implicit acknowledgment of their effort.

"You've all made excellent progress. Take the rest of the day to recover and prepare for what's ahead."

Her tone remained even, but an undercurrent of tension ran beneath it, subtle yet definite. She saw the way a few of them hesitated, how some exchanged glances before offering quiet nods of acknowledgment. They had felt it too—the shift in the air, the concealed presence pressing closer, waiting.

As the group dispersed, Eileen approached Oak, lowering her voice.

"I need to see you when you get a moment. It's urgent."

Oak's eyes glinted with awareness, reading what she didn't say. He gave a brief nod. "I'll find you soon."

She turned back to the courtyard, watching as the Fallen moved away. Takoda and Riichi remained a moment longer, speaking in quiet tones, their energy still intertwined in a way that had drawn the warning in the first place.

The presence from the vision had not left. It was still there, still watching.

A cold realization took root in her chest. It wasn't a question of *if* it would strike—only *when*.

Chapter Fourteen
Haunting Moods

As the training session concluded, Oak took a final, assessing look across the courtyard before turning toward the mansion. His steps were fixed, deliberate, his thoughts swinging from the day's drills to the unexpected summons that had drawn him away.

The corridors stretched quiet in the mid-afternoon, the hush carrying an air of watchfulness rather than stillness. Sunlight traced the ancient stone in muted bands, illuminating the worn edges of history itself—walls that had witnessed centuries, yet remained unyielding.

He reached Eileen's office and knocked once, firm and resolute.

A pause. Then her voice carried through the door—controlled, measured, but a tension beneath it pulled at the edges, fraying the calm she fought to maintain.

"Come in."

Oak stepped inside, his piercing gaze sweeping the space in an instant. Her office, always lined with ancient texts and fragmented maps, looked more disturbed than usual. Parchments lay open across the desk, ink smudged where fingers had traced hastily over words. Symbols lingered in the margins, half-formed thoughts recorded before their meaning could be lost.

Eileen sat behind it all, fingers ghosting over a brittle page—not reading, just touching, as if the worn texture could tether her to the present. A candle flickered low beside her, wax pooling in uneven drips, the air marked with the faint scent of charred parchment and aged ink—older than fire itself.

She met his eyes, gesturing toward the chair opposite her. "Sit, Oak."

He did, leaning forward slightly, the silence stretched tight with implicit meaning.

"I had a vision earlier," she began, her voice smooth but deliberately chosen. "It was… different."

That alone was enough to set him on edge.

She exhaled slowly, her tone carrying a discomfort that refused to relax, heavy and unshaken. "It didn't begin the way they usually do. I wasn't drawn into the past or cast forward into an omen. This time, it felt as though an unseen force—someone deliberate—dragged me into it."

His eyes flickered with an acute intensity, but he remained quiet, listening.

She continued, her words carrying an unnatural precision, as if the memory refused to fade. "Everything around me—unmade itself. The air thickened, burning against my skin like heat rising from scorched earth. I was trapped in it. Not watching. Inside it."

Her fingers, still resting on parchment, pressed down slightly. "And then... a scroll appeared."

A slight pause.

"Old. Worn. But left there—for me."

Oak barely moved, but his focus had honed into razor-edged precision, locked onto her every word.

"The message written across it read: *I am watching you.*"

It shouldn't have rattled her—not her. But the hesitation in her voice, the way she shaped the words, told Oak that this was different.

"Then a mark formed. At first, I thought it was Lucifer's—a sigil mirroring his past attack." She shook her head, her expression clear-cut. "But no. This was deliberate. Wrong. Not corrupted—crafted to be this way from the very beginning."

His jaw tensed, a flicker of calculation passing through his gaze.

"And then," she said, quieter now, "a voice. Not Lucifer's."

The way she said it sent a slow, creeping sense of awareness through him.

"This voice—it wasn't hissing, it wasn't taunting. It carried weight, each word deliberate, as though spoken by a force that had existed long before us, an unseen presence reaching toward present." Her tone dipped, barely above a breath. "It said: *I'll be there soon.*"

The air felt heavier, pressing inward. Eileen sat unmoving, her eyes dark with thought.

"And then," she continued, her voice unbroken but colder, "it asked me: *Have you checked on Takoda and Riichi lately?*"

That—*that*—was what made Oak's shoulders square, the entire atmosphere around him transforming. He didn't react outwardly, but Eileen saw it—the way his presence sharpened, honed like a blade sliding into place.

"The symbol," she continued, fingers tightening subtly, "it holds a different energy. I don't believe we're dealing with an archdemon." Her eyes met his, cold and definite. "This... seemed distinct. More deliberate. A force that has taken interest."

Silence stretched, heavy with recognition. Not doubt. Not hesitation. Confidence.

Oak gave a slow nod, his voice calm, absolute. "Then we find out who it is. And we make sure they never reach Takoda and Riichi."

Eileen glanced up at Oak, her gaze steadfast. "There's a possibility this entity is drawn to a specific connection," she said, her tone careful. "It could be the bond forming between Riichi and Takoda—much like Lucifer was inexplicably drawn to Rowan and Aislinn."

Oak considered that, his mind refocusing back to what he had observed during training. "I noticed it myself," he admitted. "Their bond is strengthening—quickly. Takoda was able to collect herself today by balancing Riichi's emotions, centering them both. And Riichi... he moved as if he could sense her without needing to see her."

Eileen tilted her head slightly, listening.

"After that, Takoda's control over emotional targets became more refined. Almost instinctive. And Riichi—" Oak's brow furrowed with thought. "It was as if a restraint had been lifted, a hidden limit erased. His movements became more accurate. His speed—his focus—everything realigned with an exactness I hadn't seen in him before."

Eileen pressed her lips together, absorbing his words. "I sensed it too," she admitted. "But I didn't detect a Radiant Surge. Which means the bond is still forming. That buys us time—but it also means the energy it generates could be acting like a beacon."

Oak nodded, weighing the implications. "If this entity is drawn to the bond, it might be waiting for it to fully mature before making a move."

Eileen's shoulders tensed, the strain almost imperceptible. "Then the message—*I'll be there soon'*—suggests exactly that. It's watching, waiting for the right moment. The instant their connection reaches its peak."

Silence put down roots over them, weighted and knowing. Then Oak spoke, cautious but firm.

"We could consider keeping them apart, at least for now. If their bond is drawing this entity closer, delaying its full formation could buy us more time."

Eileen shook her head. "No. The bond has to form naturally. If it's meant to play a role in confronting this demon—like Rowan and Aislinn's did with Lucifer—we can't interfere. It has to evolve on its own terms."

Oak didn't argue. He understood.

Still, the change in Eileen's countenance, the way her fingers curled slightly against the edge of the parchment, sent a whisper of agitation through him.

He studied her in the dim candlelight, the flickering glow tracing the intense angles of her face. To anyone else, she might seem entirely composed, as impenetrable as always. But Oak had spent nearly two thousand years at her side. He recognized the subtle signs—the way her breaths came just a fraction deeper than usual, the tension held in her shoulders, the careful control in her voice that only surfaced when she was hiding a deeper irritation.

He shifted slightly, his voice quieter now, edged with a rare softness. "You've had visions before, Eileen. But this one shook you in a way the others never have."

She didn't answer right away.

Oak waited.

When she finally spoke, her voice was softer, but no less resolute. "It was different. It didn't feel like a vision being *shown* to me." Her gaze lifted to meet his. "It felt like I was being *dragged* into it."

Oak held her stare, his features indecipherable, but a flicker of concern darkened his eyes. "And you haven't stopped thinking about it since."

She exhaled, the motion small, controlled. "I don't have the luxury of pushing it aside."

Oak frowned a tad, two millennia of understood burdens settling in the space they shared, a weight neither acknowledged. She had carried so much for so long—never questioning, never pausing. But that didn't mean it hadn't left its mark, etched into her in ways only he could recognize.

His voice was composed, quieter than before. "You don't have to carry it alone."

Eileen's composure faltered, just barely. A hesitation so brief most wouldn't have noticed it.

But Oak did.

She ignored him, moving the conversation forward before he could press further. "We need to focus on research. We've identified archdemons through their markings before. If this one shares any similarities with known entities, we might find a match."

Oak inclined his head slightly, accepting the turn, even as a quiet worry lingered at the edges of his thoughts. "I'll reach out to my contacts. There are scholars who specialize in archdemon symbols. If anyone has records of a mark like this, they will."

Eileen nodded, determination settling into her features. "Good. The more information we have, the better."

She exhaled, and though it was quiet, it carried weight. "For now, we keep this between us. No need to burden Riichi and Takoda with it until we're sure of what we're dealing with."

Oak's jaw tightened minutely, but he nodded. "Understood." His voice carried an edge of steel. "I'll keep a close watch over them. Both during training and tomorrow's mission. If there's even a hint of this entity making its presence known—I'll be ready."

Eileen offered a faint nod, a silent flicker of trust passing between them.

As Oak rose to his feet, a sense of purpose built in his chest. A familiar, collected resolve—but beneath it, a quiet realization, a pull toward a consideration just out of reach. A feeling he wasn't quite ready to accept.

Eileen watched him go, her gaze lingering a heartbeat longer than necessary.

Oak left her office, the conversation still pressing against his thoughts. They had faced Lucifer. They had faced the darkness of the Golden Dawn. But this—*this*—felt different.

And for reasons he couldn't yet explain, it didn't sit well with him.

The enormity of their discussion pressed down on him, yet as he neared the common area, the low hum of laughter and relaxed conversation met his ears, breaking through his thoughts. A hint of relief crossed his face, the familiar warmth of the late afternoon drifting through the halls, carrying the scent of old wood and a trace of cinnamon and spice from the kitchen.

Before he could reach the doorway, a burst of energy and noise filled the air as Rain and Ariel swept into the room, arms laden with bags, their voices bright and excited. Oak paused, watching as they made a grand entrance, effortlessly drawing the attention of every Fallen member present. He chose to stay near the doorway, out of sight, observing.

Rain and Ariel, each carrying an armful of bright orange and black bags, paused dramatically in the center of the common area, faces lit with excitement. Rain cleared her throat, catching the attention of everyone around.

"Listen up, everyone!" Rain called, her voice bright with anticipation. "We come bearing Halloween decorations, and we're here to give this place a proper Halloween vibe!"

A ripple of amusement spread through the room, a few chuckles escaping as the others took in Rain and Ariel's enthusiasm. Their bags overflowed with faux spiderwebs, carved pumpkins, fabric bats, and twinkling orange-and-purple string lights—a level of festivity the Fallen hadn't seen in a long while.

With practiced ease, the two honed in on Vine and Nik, who sat off to the side, watching with a blend of wariness and reluctant amusement.

"Vine, Nik—you're with us!" Ariel declared, eyes gleaming with mischief.

Vine and Nik exchanged a look, the silent awareness clear in their eyes. *We're doomed.*

"Do we really have a choice?" Vine asked dryly, raising an eyebrow.

"Nope!" Rain responded cheerfully. "You're officially on Halloween duty."

A round of laughter echoed through the room as the two men resigned themselves to their fate, much to the amusement of the watching Fallen and Oak.

Undeterred, Ariel tossed a catalog onto the nearby table, filled with costume ideas ranging from the ridiculous to the downright absurd. "By the way," she added with a wicked grin, "everyone's picking out a costume this year. No exceptions."

"And if you don't choose, I'll pick for you," she added, her smirk daring anyone to argue.

Rain nodded, backing her up. "That's right! This year, it's a *full-on* Halloween experience. We expect participation."

A few groans and laughs followed, but the combined forces of Ariel's scheming and Rain's enthusiasm left little room for argument. Oak smirked then turned, walking in the opposite direction back to his room, avoiding any confrontations.

"Alright," Rain continued, rubbing her hands together. "We're splitting into teams to decorate. Nik and I will handle one wing, and Ariel and Vine can take the other."

Vine opened his mouth to protest, but Ariel cut him off with a raised hand and a smirk. "It's for the *spirit* of Halloween, Vine."

Another round of laughter rippled through the room as the groups separated.

The quieter halls of the mansion seemed warmer beneath the soft glow of flickering lanterns as Rain and Nik strung up the decorations. Tiny, carved pumpkins with mischievous grins dangled from the rafters, casting playful shadows along the walls.

Rain paused mid-task, glancing at Nik as he adjusted a line of lights with defined movements. A slight smile curved her lips.

"You know," she mused, voice light, "you're a lot less intimidating when you're hanging pumpkins."

Nik paused, tilting his head a tad before looking at her, one brow lifting. "I wasn't aware I was intimidating to begin with."

Rain let out a laugh. "Oh, please. You've got that whole brooding, *'I don't talk to people unless absolutely necessary'* thing going on." She nudged him lightly with her elbow. "All serious, all mysterious."

Nik exhaled in a sound close to a chuckle, shaking his head. His usual impassive mask softened slightly, amusement flickering at the edges of his expression. "Maybe."

Rain's grin widened at his non-answer. "But I think there's more to you than the strong, silent act."

Nik didn't reply immediately, but the corners of his lips tugged ever so little upward. "And yet, I'm still not wearing a costume."

Rain gasped in mock offense, hand on her chest. "You wound me," she declared dramatically.

Nik gave her a dry look, but there was a trace of warmth beneath it now, a change just barely visible.

"Fine," Rain relented, waving a hand. "You *think* you're not wearing a costume. But that doesn't mean I won't pick one for you." She smirked, turning back to the decorations, already forming a plan. *He'd see soon enough.*

Meanwhile, in the opposite wing, Ariel and Vine had fallen into their own rhythm of decorating.

Ariel held up a massive decorative spider web, stretching it between her hands as she surveyed the walls with a calculating eye. "I'm thinking we go big. Make it look like a real haunted mansion—dark, moody, the works."

Vine, standing a few steps behind her, crossed his arms and smirked. "Just remember what Eileen said," he quipped, his voice laced with amusement. "No haunted *carnival* vibes. We don't need the place looking like a spirit-infested funhouse."

Ariel rolled her eyes, but the grin tugging at her lips betrayed her amusement. "Fine, fine. I'll dial it back." A pause. "A little."

Vine chuckled, watching as she continued contemplating the perfect placement.

"But we're *still* going all out," Ariel added with a pointed look. Then, without missing a beat, she turned to him. "Have you thought about your costume yet?"

Vine lifted a brow, considering. "You mentioned wicked warlock earlier, didn't you?" His smirk deepened. "I could probably pull that off."

Ariel's eyes gleamed. "Oh, look at that. You *do* pay attention."

Vine inclined his head slightly, as if conceding the point. "Which would make you…a mischievous fae, right?"

Ariel laughed, pleased. "Glad you're catching on, Vine. I *already* had that one picked for myself."

Their banter wove effortlessly into their work, Vine's dry humor tempering Ariel's boundless enthusiasm. They moved along the hallway, debating placement choices—Ariel constantly pushing for grander, more dramatic designs, while Vine countered with understated practicality.

"I'm thinking cursed portrait gallery in this hall," Ariel suggested, gesturing vaguely.

Vine gave her a sidelong glance. "You *do* realize that's a nightmare waiting to happen, right?"

"Exactly," Ariel shot back with a wink.

More than a few amused glances flickered in their direction from passing Fallen, their back-and-forth dynamic drawing quiet chuckles. It was easy—natural. And neither of them seemed inclined to change that.

Across the room, the Fallen tossed around costume ideas, laughter bubbling up as they playfully teased one another with increasingly absurd suggestions.

Riichi, however, remained on the sidelines, observing the chaos with his usual quiet reserve.

Takoda nudged him, her eyes glinting with amusement. "Come on, Riichi, you're not getting out of this. There has to be a costume you'd at least consider."

Riichi arched a skeptical brow. "Costumes aren't really my thing," he replied, his tone dry but not entirely dismissive.

"Oh, come on," she pressed, a knowing grin tugging at her lips. "Nothing dramatic—a little mystery, maybe?"

Briefly, Riichi hesitated, as if debating whether or not to humor her. Finally, he exhaled, a barely-there smile breaking through his usual stoicism. "Alright," he muttered. "Something understated, then."

Takoda laughed approvingly and gave him a light pat on the back. "*That's* the spirit."

Nearby, Reed leaned back in his seat, smirking. "Guess I'll stick with the easiest option. A ghost, maybe?" He shrugged, already imagining himself disappearing into the shadows.

Aislinn snorted. "Of *course* you would, Reed. You just want an excuse to wrap yourself in a sheet and call it a costume."

Rowan leaned closer to Aislinn, his expression turning mischievous. "We could always go as a matching set," he suggested. "What do you think? Haunted couple?"

She smirked, pretending to consider it. "Hmm… tempting," she mused, tapping her chin. "Or maybe I'll go as a vampire and make you my unsuspecting victim."

Ivy, listening to their exchange, rolled her eyes in mock exasperation. "Just don't go as zombies," she warned. "I'm not dealing with moaning and dragging feet all night."

The room erupted in laughter, and Birch, always ready to add to the fun, leaned in with a grin. "Then how about zombie hunters?" he proposed. "Think about it—tactical gear, toy weapons. We'd be prepared for anything."

Before anyone could respond, Ariel, having overheard, turned toward the group with a pointed look and an impish grin. "Remember, if you don't decide on a costume, *I* will pick for you," she warned.

A collective groan rose from the group, quickly followed by another round of laughter.

Ariel clapped her hands, gathering everyone's attention. "Alright, listen up! We're heading out tomorrow to grab more decorations," she announced, her voice carrying that familiar playful authority that no one dared ignore. "That means you all have until then to pick your costumes. And don't even *think* about slacking—Halloween is a *serious* affair around here, people. I expect commitment."

A mix of excitement and mild dread spread through the room as glances were exchanged. The mansion buzzed with an infectious energy—a rare lighthearted moment amid the constant strain of their responsibilities.

Even Vine and Nik, despite their initial reluctance, had been fully pulled into the atmosphere, their normally passive expressions subtly softening as they watched the antics unfold.

★★★

As the sun dipped lower, the mansion hummed with lingering warmth, laughter still echoing faintly through the halls as the Fallen finished their preparations. For a brief, rare whisper of time, the burden of their battles eased, replaced by an easy lightness—a sense of family, of shared celebration.

Now, as the evening relaxed into quiet, the halls grew still. Most of the Fallen had retired for the night, leaving only the distant flicker of lanterns casting soft pools of light against the stone walls.

Takoda and Riichi walked side by side through the dimly lit corridor, their steps leisurely, unhurried. The silence was charged, humming with awareness, each of them attuned to the other's presence without effort, without need for words.

As they neared their rooms, Riichi veered toward his door first, stepping inside with a natural ease. He unfastened his katana, the blade catching a sliver of lantern light as he placed it onto its stand, his touch prolonged —a practiced ritual that anchored him in the moment.

Takoda hovered in the doorway, watching as Riichi placed his katana on its stand with careful accuracy. He moved as he always did—deliberate, sure, his presence constant even in quiet instances like this.

When he turned, their eyes met, and she hesitated only for a breath before saying, "I thought we could stay in my room tonight."

Riichi studied her for a fraction of a second, not because he was doubtful, but because he recognized the quiet import in her words, a meaning that ran deeper than what she'd said aloud.

Takoda let out a soft breath, transferring her weight a bit. "I don't think I could sleep anymore without knowing you're beside me." The admission came easily, without embarrassment—just honesty.

His features remained guarded for a second longer before his expression eased. He stepped toward her, closing the distance with quiet conviction. "Then let's go."

She didn't have to ask twice.

He followed her into her room, their movements fluid, comfortable—like this had already become their natural routine.

Inside her room, the soft glow of a single lamp cast warm light over the space, wrapping it in a sense of quiet intimacy. Takoda shut the door behind them, turning back just as Riichi pulled his shirt over his head. He discarded it with little thought, moving as he always did—with effortless meticulousness.

Her eyes dipped—not away, but downward. Noticing.

A faint scar ran across his chest, barely visible now, a lingering mark from San Francisco. A remnant of the time Lucifer had nearly taken him from her.

Takoda stepped closer, her hand lifting instinctively, hovering just above his skin. The scar was faint now, but she remembered when it was fresh—when she had traced the edges of the wound with careful fingers, when she had changed his bandages and kept him from pushing himself too hard. Those two weeks had been the beginning of a bond neither of them had been ready to acknowledge then.

She glanced up, searching his face, and when Riichi gave a small nod, she let her fingers trace the mark.

Her touch was light, but the memory behind it carried influence.

"You never talk about this," she murmured, her fingertips gliding over the scar that had once been a raw, brutal wound.

Riichi's attention dropped briefly to where she touched him, but when he met her eyes again, his expression remained cool. "Because it's in the past."

Takoda huffed softly, her fingers still resting against his skin. "That doesn't mean it doesn't matter."

His lips parted slightly as if to argue, but then he stopped, reconsidering. He studied her—really studied her—and in that moment, she knew he wasn't just thinking about the scar. He was thinking about San Francisco. The long days she had stayed with him, making sure he didn't push himself too hard, offering quiet company when he refused to rest. The way she had refused to leave him alone, even when he hadn't asked her to stay.

His voice was quieter when he finally answered. "I survived. I got stronger." He exhaled, as if acknowledging the truth of it. Then, after a pause, his gaze softened. "But you're right. It does matter."

Takoda blinked, caught off guard by his admission.

Riichi reached for her hand, guiding it back to his chest, just over the faint scar. His touch was careful, deliberate. "This isn't just a mark from a battle," he murmured. "It's the moment I *saw* you—not just standing beside me, not just as another Fallen—but *you*."

Her breath hitched.

His fingers curled lightly over hers, keeping them in place. "When I was healing, you were there. Every day. Making sure I ate, making sure I didn't overdo it—even when I tried." A trace of a smirk ghosted his lips. "You didn't let me push you away. And I realized then… I'd found you."

Takoda swallowed hard, her heart beating faster. "Riichi…"

He held her look, his voice quiet but unwavering. "This scar isn't just a reminder of a fight I survived. It's the moment I knew I wanted you in my life."

Her fingers tightened against his skin, her throat suddenly too constricted for words.

Before she could find them, Riichi lifted her hand to his lips, pressing a slow, thoughtful kiss to her knuckles.

"You were with me then," he murmured against her skin. "And you're with me now."

Takoda exhaled shakily, her entire body humming with warmth. She stepped closer, her movements fluid, instinctive.

This wasn't hesitation or skepticism. It was everything that had built between them since that day.

Riichi reached out, his fingertips tracing a light path along the curve of Takoda's jaw, cautious yet gentle. He didn't rush—he never did. His touch was a whisper against her skin, yet the meaning behind it was evident.

Takoda sighed, tilting into his touch as if drawn by an instinct woven into the very core of their bond, an attraction she no longer questioned.

Then his lips met hers.

The kiss began slow, calm but within minutes, it deepened. His hand slid to her waist, anchoring her to him, while Takoda's fingers curled against his chest, then his shoulders, mapping the familiar strength beneath her hands.

Their movements were fluid, confident, each touch igniting a spark that burned hotter, a connection deepening with every action, every press of lips, every whispered breath.

But just as the intensity peaked, a mutual judgement passed between them.

They slowed.

They remained close, breaths mingling, the space between them shrinking into nothing. When their gazes met, there was only a quiet faith woven into the closeness they shared.

Riichi guided her toward the bed with an ease that felt natural. She nestled beside him, her head finding its place against his shoulder as his arm came around her, solid and secure.

For a long time, they simply lay together, the silence heavy with meaning—not with words left unsaid, but with a complexity that needed no explanation. A bond still strengthening, still becoming.

Takoda's voice was quieter when she finally spoke. "Tomorrow's mission… My abilities are still changing. I don't know if I'm ready."

Riichi's response was immediate. "You don't have to be."

She glanced up at him, searching his face.

His gaze held fixed, unwavering. "You don't have to be ready for everything, Takoda. That's why I'm here." His thumb brushed lightly over her wrist, bracing her. "We'll handle it. Together."

A breath shuddered from her lips, the tension in her shoulders easing as his words sank in, pacifying her in a way nothing else could. She believed him. She always had.

"Together," she echoed, softer now.

The warmth of his arm around her remained, solid and sure. Wrapped in that quiet strength, Takoda allowed herself to relax fully, letting his firmness eclipse the ambiguity of tomorrow.

They drifted into harmonious sleep, full of trust. And beneath it all, a belief—unshaken, unbreakable—took root between them.

★★★

The mansion was cloaked in silence, its halls dark and still, each Fallen deeply asleep in the dead of night. In their room, Aislinn lay curled against Rowan, his constant warmth comforting her as she drifted between sleep and wakefulness. Then—her breath caught.

Her eyes snapped open, wide and unfocused, as a vivid, almost tangible vision crashed into her mind. A figure emerged from the darkness—a demon, yet disturbingly human in appearance. His features were severe, refined, his presence exuding an unnatural stillness. His piercing eyes gleamed with an eerie, calculating intelligence, their depth revealing a danger that ran deeper than brute strength—cold, methodical, precise. His power wasn't chaotic or unchecked; it was controlled, intentional —not the kind that shattered recklessly, but the kind that struck with unnerving accuracy, shaped with purpose.

He stood over Takoda, his presence a quiet, suffocating force. There was no need for fangs, for grotesque deformities, for the chaotic rage so many demons carried. This one didn't need brutality to be terrifying. His expression was composed. Measured. But in the way a blade was measured before a killing stroke. The vision lasted just long enough for Aislinn to feel the unsaid threat radiating from him before it snapped away.

She gasped, lurching upright, her chest heaving.

"Aislinn?" Rowan's voice was low and rough from sleep, but instantly alert. His hand found her back, comforting her. "What happened?"

She turned to him, her breath shaking. "It was a vision," she stammered. "Not a nightmare—real. I saw a demon… and it was a warning about Takoda."

She didn't wait for him to respond. The urgency in her chest burned too hot. Throwing off the covers, she bolted from the bed, her pulse hammering. She had to get to Takoda—*now*.

She reached the hallway at a sprint—and then she wasn't running anymore.

For an instant, space folded—a warping of motion, a change of presence that sent the world tilting. Then—she was there. Right in front of Takoda's door.

The jolt of disorientation barely registered before—

"AISLINN!"

Rowan's voice roared from down the hall, his panic snapping through the quiet. She turned just as he skidded to a stop beside her, eyes wide, his chest rising and falling with adrenaline.

"What the *hell* just happened?" His gaze darted between her and the distance she'd somehow skipped. "You—" He pointed at where she had been. "You just *teleported*."

Aislinn blinked, her body still humming with a sensation she couldn't quite place. "What?"

Rowan gestured behind him, his tone astute with realization. "You were way back there. Then you just—vanished. And now you're here." His brows furrowed, disbelief cutting through his concern. "Did you know you could do that?"

Aislinn shook her head, but the question barely registered. Her pulse was still racing with the vision, her focus locked on the door in front of her.

"It doesn't matter," she breathed. "Not right now."

Without another thought, she pounded on the door, urgency tightening her voice.

"Takoda! Wake up! *Please—open the door!*"

The pounding echoed through the halls, loud enough that doors creaked open one by one, the Fallen stirring from their sleep. Shadows moved in the dim light as wary figures stepped into the corridor, their eyes keen, bodies tense—already bracing for trouble.

Inside, Takoda startled awake, throwing off the blankets before rushing to open the door. Aislinn stood there, breathless, pale, shaken. Behind her, Rowan hovered, but his focus moved past Takoda—to Riichi.

Riichi, bare-chested, reaching for his shirt.

Rowan's expression flickered—immediate, abrupt recognition. His mouth started to open.

But then—Riichi's look stopped him cold. *Not now.*

Rowan's jaw flexed, but instead of saying anything, he pressed his lips together and gave Riichi a short, curt nod.

The pressure in the hall didn't go unnoticed. The Fallen exchanged glances, wary energy rippling through the group.

Then—Eileen arrived. The change in atmosphere was instant.

She moved through the gathered Fallen with quiet authority, assessing the situation before lifting a hand. A simple gesture, but a command nonetheless.

"There's no immediate threat," she said, voice composed yet firm. "Stand down. This matter is in hand. Return to your rooms."

Her words seemed to unwind the group, and the other Fallen exchanged glances before nodding and retreating, trusting her judgment. As doors quietly shut and the tension in the air began to thin, only Aislinn, Takoda, Riichi, Rowan, and Eileen remained in the dimly lit hallway, Aislinn's vision hanging over them, unexpressed but heavy.

Eileen's voice, calm but firm, broke the silence. "Let's continue this conversation in private." She gestured for Aislinn, Rowan, Takoda, and Riichi to follow her into Takoda's room, closing the door behind them.

Once inside, they stood in a loose circle, the flickering light from a nearby lamp casting faint shadows across their faces. Eileen's gaze landed on Aislinn, stable and expectant. "Tell us everything you remember about the vision," she prompted, her voice gentle but focused. "Any details about this demon's appearance will help us later."

Aislinn took a slow breath, pressing a hand to her chest as if to steady the lingering adrenaline coursing through her veins. "His face was… striking. Too human. His eyes—dark, piercing—they felt like they saw everything. Not just in a way that was observant, but deeper. Like he was peeling back every layer, exposing every flaw, every vulnerability, and deciding whether or not to exploit it."

She shivered slightly, the intensity of the vision still gripping her. "His features were severe, almost elegant, but his presence… it was controlled in a way that made it more terrifying, like the silence before a predator strikes. It felt like standing in front of a force held in check—not caged, just waiting for the right time to break free."

Silence stretched in the room as the impact of her words landed.

Eileen's demeanor remained blank, though there was a keen perceptiveness in her eyes as she absorbed the description. "This level of clarity is rare, Aislinn. The details you remember will be invaluable when we begin identifying him." She inclined her head slightly, her composed presence reducing Aislinn's lingering discomfort.

Takoda listened, her heart thudding with worry. *Why her?* She had no doubt Aislinn's vision was real—she'd seen too much to dismiss it—but why was she the focus? She stole a glance at Riichi, who remained silent beside her, his posture impassive but his gaze locked onto Aislinn, absorbing every detail.

Then, after a pause, Eileen's attention moved towards Rowan. "Rowan, explain what happened in the hallway."

Rowan, still somewhat tense, exhaled and turned to Aislinn. "You teleported," he stated bluntly. "One second, you were running down the hall, and the next, you just—" He gestured vaguely between the door and the far end of the room. "—appeared in front of Takoda's door. No transition. No movement. You weren't there, and then you were."

Aislinn blinked at him, the reality of it setting in, but she only shrugged, still too rattled by the vision to fully process it. "I don't know how I did it," she admitted, her voice distant. "I wasn't thinking about it. I just… needed to get here."

Eileen studied her for a while, an inscrutable glance passing through her features. But rather than press, she nodded. "We'll address it before training tomorrow. For now, it isn't the priority."

Takoda, still trying to push aside the apprehension clawing at her, looked to Eileen. "This demon—do you think he's after me?" The words felt strange coming out of her mouth, as if acknowledging it made it more real.

A muscle twitched in Eileen's temple. "I had a vision as well," she admitted. "Earlier today. A cryptic message, a tattered scroll, and a symbol that resembled Lucifer's mark but carried an entirely different energy." Her attention flicked briefly to Riichi before returning to Takoda. "Oak and I discussed it at length. Given the timing of Aislinn's vision and what we've already suspected, we believe this demon is drawn to a force within you both. Much like Lucifer was drawn to Rowan and Aislinn's bond."

Takoda felt her stomach squeeze. She swallowed, glancing at Riichi.

His jaw clenched marginally, a flicker of anxiety passing through his gaze. His bond with Takoda—a connection that had been growing, one he had guarded instinctively without fully putting into words—was now a beacon. A target.

He didn't like it.

But beneath the intense awareness of what this meant, a deeper commitment took hold—calm, unwavering, and absolute.

Eileen continued. "The bond isn't fully formed yet," she assured them, her tone even. "That buys us some time to prepare. This warning is serious, but you're not in immediate danger."

Takoda exhaled, some of the tension in her chest easing, but the nervousness still lingered beneath the surface.

Eileen's gaze swept over them, her tone altering somewhat. "Tonight, rest. In the morning, we'll consult the ancient texts and see if we can match this demon's face and symbol to any of our records. Panic won't serve us right now."

Aislinn, still shaken but alleviated by Eileen's calm, reached for Takoda's hand and gave it a firm squeeze. "I know what it's like to feel like a target," she murmured, meeting Takoda's eyes with quiet reassurance. "But I promise you, Takoda—you won't go through this on your own. We're all here, and we're going to protect each other."

Takoda felt a wave of gratitude wash over her and managed a small smile, comforted by her friend's unwavering support.

In the corner of the room, Rowan and Riichi exchanged a few quiet words, their voices too low for the others to hear.

Rowan met Riichi's look, his expression knowing, evaluated. "Don't shut her out to keep her safe," he advised quietly. "I tried that with Aislinn—I thought keeping my emotions in check would protect her. But all it did was create distance." His voice remained low but definite. "Bonds are strongest when built on honesty. If you start holding back now, you'll only make it harder for both of you."

Riichi absorbed his words, recognizing the truth in them. He had already felt the instinct to shield Takoda, to carry this danger alone, but Rowan was right—closing himself off wouldn't protect her, it would only weaken what they were building.

He exhaled, his focus resolute. "I understand."

And he did. Rowan wasn't just offering advice—he was warning him from experience. And Riichi wasn't about to make the same mistake.

With a final glance exchanged, Aislinn, Rowan, and Eileen left Takoda's room, the heaviness of their conversation still haunting. Eileen lingered briefly in the hallway, her sharp eyes trailing Aislinn as she walked beside Rowan. She had just unlocked a new ability—one powerful enough to shift the battlefield in an instant.

And yet, Aislinn wasn't thinking about that right now. Her thoughts were still on Takoda, on the vision, on the looming danger.

Eileen exhaled silently and followed them a few paces behind, ensuring they reached their door safely. Only when Rowan ushered Aislinn inside did Eileen allow herself to turn away. One crisis at a time.

Inside Takoda's room, the door clicked shut with quiet finality.

Takoda stood there, her hand resting lightly against the wood, as if anchoring herself in the present. The dim glow of the lantern cast long shadows across the space, but it was nothing compared to the rigidity constricting her chest.

When she finally turned, her eyes were brimming with unshed tears. "A powerful demon… and it's after us," she whispered, her voice barely audible. "I don't know how to make sense of that." Her throat stiffened. "What if—" She hesitated, her breath catching. "What if I'm not ready? What if I can't do this?"

The second the words left her lips, the dam broke.

Riichi was beside her instantly, wrapping his arms around her, his hold firm, sure. She clutched at his shirt as a sob broke free, everything—the fear, the vagueness, the crushing realization of what they were up against—crashing over her all at once.

He didn't tell her not to be afraid. He didn't tell her to be strong.

Instead, he simply held her.

Her breaths were uneven, jagged against his shoulder, but Riichi remained calm, unmoving, his presence reassuring her in a way words never could.

After a moment, he lifted her chin, his fingers warm against her skin, his gaze staunch. "Takoda," he said, his voice quiet, cautious. "You don't have to fight what you're feeling. Fear isn't weakness. It means you comprehend what's at stake."

She swallowed hard, struggling to catch her breath, her pulse still erratic. But he didn't let her look away.

"I'm not going to tell you it'll be easy," he continued, his voice sturdy, committed. "But I know you. And I know that when it matters, when the time comes, you won't hesitate. You never do."

A shaky breath left her lips, his words sinking past the fear.

His thumb brushed the dampness from her cheek, a meditative, careful motion. "I won't promise that we'll always be ready for what comes next. But I do promise this—when it happens, I will be there, always beside you."

The firmness in her chest didn't fully disappear, but it eased. The panic lost its grip, replaced by a steadiness that anchored her, soothing her for the time being.

She let herself lean into him, her forehead resting against his shoulder, feeling the balanced rhythm of his breath, the quiet certainty in the way he held her.

They stood there for a long while, the night pressing in around them, the shadow of the demon's presence still lingering at the edges of her mind.

But here, in this space, with Riichi's arms around her, fear no longer dictated her next breath.

In the hallway, Eileen moved silently toward her room, her mind sifting through everything they had uncovered tonight. Aislinn's power. The demon's warning. The bond forming between Riichi and Takoda. It was all coming too fast.

She passed a door—and a hand shot out, catching her wrist.

Before she could react, she was pulled into the darkened room.

Her back met the cool wood of the closed door, and a firm palm covered her mouth before she could speak. Instinct flared in her muscles, but she halted—not out of hesitation, but recognition.

Oak.

The dim light illuminated his sharp features, the faintest gleam catching in his golden-hazel eyes. He was bare-chested, wearing only a pair of loose pajama pants, his grip firm but not forceful.

He didn't waste time on explanations. Didn't ask. Didn't preface.

"Take us to your house," he murmured, his voice quiet but absolute.

Eileen held his gaze for a long moment, the air charged with an awareness neither could ignore. Then, without a word, she gave a single nod.

And in the next instant—they vanished.

Chapter Fifteen
Fortifying the Walls

Woodside, California

As soon as they reappeared, Oak surveyed the room. The bedroom lamps cast a dim glow over dark wood furnishings, an unlit fireplace, and neatly stacked books. The air carried the scent of aged paper, ink, and Eileen—cool and pristine, with a tense undercurrent. Her presence filled the room, as if the room had already begun to vibrate with a quiet energy that was uniquely hers. But more than that—she hadn't moved. His body remained pressed against hers, caging her against the door, his hand still over her mouth.

His eyes darted to hers, an edge of amusement stirring despite everything pressing down on them like an impending storm, heavy and inescapable.

"Presumptuous, don't you think?"

Eileen arched a single brow, her stare fixed, unflinching. She didn't need to respond. She never did.

Oak exhaled slowly, watching her. The silence between them deepened, oppressive and suffocating, as if the very air had become charged with her unspoken thoughts. Close enough to feel the heat of her body, he could see the faintest tension in her—her jaw clenched, the slight flare of her nostrils, her carefully controlled breathing. She wouldn't admit to being overwhelmed, wouldn't allow the strain to show—but Oak could sense it, in every meticulous inhale, every minute detail she tried to conceal.

He dropped his hand from her mouth to give her the space to speak. She didn't. Instead, she held his gaze, steadfast, her calm unreadable as always. Oak held her focus, unmoving, his demeanor adamant. Neither of them blinked.

After a long moment, she looked away.

It didn't take much for Oak's mind to catch up with the pieces—Aislinn's vision, the demon after Takoda and Riichi, the threat closing in, the uncertainty of who this demon was, and now Aislinn's teleportation. And then there was the fact that Eileen had teleported them to her bedroom. She was carrying more than anyone should have to. She just wouldn't say it.

So, Oak said nothing. Not yet.

His palm grazed down her jawline, tracing the smooth arc of her throat before drifting lower, following the sharp curve of her collarbone. Each touch was slow, measured, deliberate. He was patient, watching for any response, waiting for her to break the calm exterior she'd so carefully constructed.

She didn't pull away.

That was all the invitation he needed.

Oak dipped his head, his lips brushing the delicate curve of her neck just below her ear. His breath was warm against her skin, the pressure of it pressing in with an intensity that mirrored the storm in his chest. "Let me," he whispered.

No command, no question—just understanding.

Eileen's chest rose and fell with a slow, methodical inhalation, but her shoulders didn't tense. She didn't resist. That was enough.

Oak lifted her effortlessly. Her hand slid up to his bare shoulder, nails pressing lightly into his skin, a fleeting but telling connection. She didn't push him away, didn't attempt to regain power. Instead, she allowed him to carry her, his steps slow, intentional, each one measured as he walked across the room. Though tense and unused to leaning on others, Oak sensed her quiet resistance fading as she gradually let go.

He lowered her to the bed with care, as though setting down a weapon with its edge still gleaming—dangerous, disciplined, never fragile. Her hair fanned across the pillow, a dark contrast against the pale sheets, her attention still unwavering—assessing, impassive. Still, she said nothing.

Oak braced himself over her, waiting. One last chance for her to stop him, to pull away, to retreat. To close off and pretend none of this was happening.

She didn't.

Instead, her breath deepened, and her hand slid from his shoulder to the back of his neck, fingers threading into his hair, anchoring herself to him.

He kissed her—not with urgency, but with intent. His lips brushed over hers, soft at first, testing, as though asking permission, yet demanding more with each gentle press.

Pleasure wasn't the goal. Relief was.

Oak's focus never faltered; his eyes never left hers. Every touch was thoughtful —slow, careful, calculated. His touch skated over her skin, tracing every curve, every dip with a feather-light movement. Eileen's breath stuttered in her throat, her skin rising in goosebumps beneath his hands.

He took his time, exploring her with purpose, not as a conquest, but as a revelation. His lips ghosted over her skin, slow as though memorizing her, as though giving her time to fall apart, piece by piece, until there was nothing left but the connection between them. He tasted the salt of her sweat, the lingering sweetness of her perfume, the heat of her skin as he inhaled deeply. With every breath, she consumed him more completely.

As his lips brushed against her core, she took in a sharp intake of air, a mix of surprise and anticipation apparent in the way her lungs filled. "What are you doing?" she breathed, a hint of curiosity lacing her words.

Oak glanced up with a playful smirk, his eyes twinkling with mischief. "Trust me," he murmured confidently, "You'll enjoy it."

For centuries, she had held herself together, building walls no one could breach. But now, as Oak's touch traced the lines of her body, she let go. For the first time in ages, she let herself fall.

He followed the changes in her breathing—the subtle tremor in her body, the way her muscles relaxed, the way she ultimately surrendered to him. Until there was nothing left but the two of them.

Her and him.

The quiet surrender she had never allowed herself to embrace.

And when it was over—when her body had finally given in, when the strain of everything had been stripped away—Oak didn't let her retreat. He held her close, as though he, too, was holding on to the fragments of whatever they had just shared.

They lay facing each other, the room steeped in quiet, the soft glow of the bedside lamp casting shadows along the curves of their bodies. The space between them was minimal—just enough for Oak to notice the slight tension in Eileen's form as she fidgeted with the edge of the sheet. Then, she moved.

Slowly, intentionally, she began to roll away, turning onto her side, creating space where there had been none.

Oak didn't allow it. His hand caught her waist, firm but gentle, holding her close, making it clear—he wasn't letting her withdraw. Not from this. Not from him. Eileen stilled, her body taut under his touch.

He pressed a kiss to her temple, lingering briefly before pulling back just enough to look at her fully, his hands braced on either side of her. "Tell me how you're feeling."

Eileen's lids remained half-closed, the intensity of her strategic thought cutting through the exhaustion beneath her focus. "About what?"

Oak huffed a quiet laugh, low and knowing. "Don't do that."

She arched a brow, feigning innocence. "Do what?"

"Deflect." His voice was even but not unkind. "You can't keep everything bottled up, like a bomb waiting to explode. I know you. You won't talk to Aislinn, and you sure as hell won't talk to any of the Fallen. But that doesn't mean you don't need to. And whether you like it or not, it's safer to talk to me."

Eileen's expression remained composed, but Oak noticed the subtle changes—her breath hitching ever so slightly, a flicker of tension buried beneath her restraint.

Oak's features softened, his hand moving gently along her wrist, feeling the pulse beneath her skin. "You don't 'feel,' is that it?"

Eileen's look sharpened, but before she could speak, Oak shook his head. "You're lying." He traced along her forearm slowly, methodically. "You spent fifteen years with Aislinn and her father. You wouldn't have done that if you didn't feel."

A hint of awareness flickered across Eileen's face, a brief flash that most would have missed. But Oak didn't.

"You told me once that the Fallen are like your children." His thumb brushed over the delicate skin of her wrist, slow. "That wasn't strategy. That was feeling."

A brief pause. Oak studied her, reading the unreadable. He had spent centuries watching her, understanding her in ways even she refused to acknowledge. And before he could stop it, before he could think better of it, the words slipped out.

"The only person you don't feel for is me."

Eileen's gaze snapped to his, her defiance burning beneath the surface, a challenge in her eyes.

Her voice, cold as ice, cut through the moment. "You're the one pretending. You don't know everything about me."

Oak didn't back down. Didn't move. Didn't let her retreat. The silence between them was thick, unyielding, heavy with things neither was ready to say.

"You may think I don't know everything about you," he continued, his voice quieter now, "and maybe I don't. But I know enough." He hesitated briefly before adding, "And I want to be the person you confide in."

Eileen's brow furrowed slightly, a faint challenge hidden beneath her calm demeanor. "Why does it matter so much to you? Why do you care if I confide in you?"

Oak hesitated, not expecting the question but not surprised by it. He absorbed her scrutiny, feeling the full force of her attention, as if she were trying to peer straight through him.

He cleared his throat, shifting his weight, trying to keep his tone even. "You're my leader, Eileen. I can't lead if I don't know how to support you. And I've seen what happens when you carry everything by yourself."

His words faltered slightly, but he pressed on. "If you don't speak up, if you keep bottling everything in… it'll wear you down. We need you strong. If I can help keep that from happening, I will. I'll do whatever I can."

Eileen's lips parted, but she didn't speak immediately. She paused, her silence heavy. Finally, she murmured, "I do confide in you. You're my second in command."

Oak let out a soft chuckle, shaking his head. "That's not the same thing, and you know it. That's business. I mean personally."

Eileen's expression sharpened, but Oak pressed on before she could argue. "Holding everything in doesn't make you stronger. It makes you a weaker leader." He let his words sink in before continuing, "If you keep bottling everything up and acting like nothing's wrong, the others will notice. And when they do, they might start to lose faith in you."

His words landed, and Eileen's shoulders stiffened, her lips pressing into a thin line as she processed them. Oak knew this wasn't about pride—it was about control. About never showing cracks. About keeping her people from seeing any vulnerability.

After a long pause, Eileen exhaled slowly. "It's too much at once. Aislinn's vision. The demon hunting Takoda and Riichi. Their growing bond. The Golden Dawn. The mission tomorrow." Her voice was steady, but Oak could hear the tension beneath every word. "And now Aislinn unlocked teleportation. She didn't even realize she could do it until it happened, which means she still doesn't have control over it. Another unknown. Another risk." Her jaw tightened. "And now I'm wondering if I've been too hard on the others."

Oak shook his head. "You haven't."

The tension in her posture unraveled just slightly, a measured release. "If they've noticed I'm struggling—"

"They haven't. Not yet," he reassured her. "But they will if you keep carrying everything alone."

She was silent, her face giving nothing away, but Oak knew she was processing, weighing the truth of his words.

He adjusted his stance, absently tracing along her forearm. "I suspected it was too much," he admitted, voice quiet but steady. "That you were feeling overwhelmed, even if you wouldn't say it." He exhaled slowly, his focus steady on hers. "That's why I'm telling you—whatever I can take off your plate, I will."

Eileen didn't respond, but Oak could feel the change in her exhale, a deepening release, a sign she was listening.

"I'll take on Riichi, Takoda, and their growing bond. I'm already covering the Fallen's training, and I'll step in more during strategy meetings. Whatever you need, I'll do it." His thumb brushed her wrist again, a quiet reassurance. "You don't have to keep everything in check alone, Eileen."

She studied him for a long while, her gaze narrowing with unreadable thoughts, her mind weighing options, deciding what to reveal, what to hide. A brief hesitation. A strategy forming. A silent debate she wasn't ready to voice.

Finally, she murmured, "If I ease up too much, they'll think they can slack off."

Oak smirked faintly. "I doubt that. You don't exactly inspire laziness." His voice grew more serious. "You don't have to ease up on them, but you might need to give them some breathing room." He tilted his head slightly, considering. "Rain and Ariel could help with that."

Eileen's brow furrowed. "How?"

"They're the two most extroverted people we have. They could boost morale." He paused. "You could rotate giving the Fallen a day off one at a time, and have Rain and Ariel spend time with them."

Eileen studied him briefly before nodding slightly, almost to herself. "I'll think about it."

Oak didn't press. She had opened up—more than she probably intended. That was enough for now.

Still, as she settled deeper into the pillow, her attention never strayed from his. She hadn't retreated. And Oak didn't let go.

Outskirts of Seattle, Washington

The mansion was quiet in the early morning, shadows resting in the hallway corners, softened by the muted glow from open doors. The stillness felt alive, as if the walls were bracing for the day's challenges. Oak walked purposefully down the corridor, his expression calm and focused, eyes alert as he searched each room for the others.

At the base of the sweeping staircase, Rowan and Aislinn appeared side by side, their steps synchronized, their faces alert yet tinged with curiosity. They noticed Oak immediately, and Rowan offered a brief nod, sensing the urgency in Oak's stare.

"Oak," Rowan greeted, his tone respectful, yet filled with unasked questions.

"Eileen wants us all in her office," Oak replied, his voice barely above a murmur, firm and direct. "It's urgent."

Rowan and Aislinn exchanged a glance, their earlier lightheartedness fading, replaced by a somber understanding. With a shared nod, they followed behind Oak, his unwavering presence guiding them through the mansion's quiet halls. The silence around them felt heavy, like a thick fog amplifying the soft shuffle of footsteps as they made their way toward the kitchen.

Inside, Riichi and Takoda stood by the counter, steaming mugs in hand. Riichi's posture was deceptively relaxed, his casual stance betraying the shrewd focus in his eyes as he noticed Oak's approach. Takoda, calm as ever, scanned the group with a swift, perceptive glance, sensing the change in the atmosphere.

"Eileen wants to see us in her office," Oak announced, his voice direct but underscored with urgency. "It's important."

Without hesitation, Riichi set his mug aside, his relaxed demeanor honing into readiness. Takoda followed suit, setting her coffee down and tucking a worn book under her arm before stepping into line with the others.

As they entered Eileen's office, the atmosphere shifted immediately. The room was orderly yet filled with quiet intensity—ancient books, maps, and scrolls scattered across the desk, fragments of wisdom waiting to be pieced together. Eileen stood near the window, her posture straight, a faint trace of tension evident in her stance.

Aislinn's attention swept over Eileen, a playful glint tugging at the edges of her face. "You look... refreshed."

Eileen's eyes narrowed ever so slightly, but she remained silent.

Eileen turned her attention to Takoda and Riichi, her gaze lingering just a moment before speaking. "We're facing an unknown threat, one that seems to have a specific focus." Her voice was firm, yet an underlying edge ran through it. "It's targeting both of you."

Her words hung in the air, and a ripple of unspoken concern passed through the group. Eileen looked at Aislinn. "Any information could give us an advantage—or at least a clearer understanding of what we're up against."

From a nearby stack, Eileen pulled an old leather-bound tome, its cover worn and softened by time, and slid it toward Aislinn. The book looked as ancient as some of the mansion's oldest artifacts, radiating an aura of power woven into its pages. Aislinn accepted it with a nod, carefully flipping through the faded ink and unfamiliar symbols.

For several minutes, the only sound was the soft rustling of pages turning as Aislinn searched. Then—

A distinct thud echoed through the room.

Takoda's book slipped from her grasp, landing on the floor with a soft slap. Aislinn's awareness shifted instantly, her scrutiny dropping to the book as it lay open on the floor, revealing a specific page.

She froze. Her focus sharpened.

Before Takoda could reach for it, Aislinn snatched it up, gripping the worn edges. "Where did you get this?" Her voice was clear, a note of urgency creeping in, as if the answer might alter everything she thought she knew.

Takoda blinked, startled by the abruptness. "The library," she replied. "It's The History of Japan."

Aislinn barely heard her. She turned the book toward Eileen, pointing to a detailed illustration on the page. "Mom. That's him." Her voice was unwavering, full of certainty. "That's the demon I saw."

The room fell into stunned silence.

Eileen took the book from Aislinn and studied the page. Her usually guarded expression faltered. She inhaled sharply, her lips parting, a sign of the change in her calm composure. Her grip tightened on the book, knuckles blanching, and when her attention lifted, it wasn't Aislinn she looked at.

She looked at Riichi.

"...Riichi."

His name escaped her lips like a sigh, but the tension of it hung between them.

Riichi leaned over her shoulder to examine the illustration. Instantly, his body stiffened, his breath catching before smoothing out. His jaw clenched, a cheek muscle twitching, revealing underlying tension. A storm brewed within him, and his presence shifted to a closed, impenetrable fortress.

The room seemed to freeze in anticipation.

Riichi's focus snapped up to meet Eileen's, fury unmistakable in his stare.

Eileen held his gaze, her voice unwavering. "Take a minute."

Riichi didn't argue. He didn't speak.

Instead, he turned and walked out.

Takoda stood frozen, her posture tense as she followed his retreating figure. Confusion knitted her brow. Whatever had just unfolded, she was missing a crucial detail, a connection just out of reach.

Eileen exhaled, slowly closing the book and resting it against the desk. She turned to Takoda, her face still unreadable. "Go after him. Make sure he's okay."

Takoda hesitated for only a heartbeat before following after him.

As the door closed behind her, Eileen's attention swung quickly to Rowan.

"Rowan."

He straightened, already attuned to the gravity of the moment.

"Follow her." Eileen's voice carried authority. "Keep your distance but stay close enough in case she needs you."

Rowan nodded, moving without hesitation.

Oak, having remained silent through the exchange, exhaled quietly. "I take it that means Riichi has history with this demon?"

Eileen's lips pressed together in a thin line, and when she finally spoke, her voice held a weight, deep and unyielding.

"The demon Aislinn saw…" She lifted the book once more, tilting it slightly so that the portrait of a man with piercing features seemed to stare back at them. "It's Kubla Khan."

A quiet, heavy pause filled the space.

Oak folded his arms, his attention flickering toward the door where Riichi had just exited. "Well… that's going to piss him off."

Eileen sighed. "It already did."

The atmosphere thickened, pressing in like an unseen force. Aislinn's brow furrowed with alarm as she glanced between Oak and Eileen. Her posture stiffened against the unspoken questions. "Alright, someone needs to start talking. Why was Riichi ready to tear the place apart? What makes Kubla Khan such a threat?"

Eileen exhaled slowly, setting the book back down with a quiet weight. She glanced at Oak before turning her attention back to Aislinn. "Because Kubla Khan's Mongol army was the one that attacked Riichi's village at Hakata Bay when he was still human."

Aislinn's jaw tightened, her lips parting as the revelation sank in.

Oak's voice remained steady but thick with meaning. "They destroyed his village. Killed his family. Riichi fought to his last gasp, but…" He paused, a sharpness edging his words. "He died from his wounds."

Eileen's gaze darkened further. "Kubla Khan's invasion is the reason Riichi is Fallen."

The room fell into an oppressive silence, thick and weighty, as the truth pressed down on them. Aislinn inhaled deeply, her focus darting toward the door where Riichi had gone. "Oh my god, Mom." She swallowed, her face tightening with worry. "Takoda…"

Eileen nodded. "Go. Check on them."

Without hesitation, Aislinn turned and quickly moved toward the door, her steps purposeful.

Once she was gone, the room settled into a heavy stillness. Eileen's attention lingered on the door Aislinn had just passed through. Slowly, her focus moved down to the book on her desk, and to Kubla Khan's face staring back at her.

A long sigh escaped her, and she ran a hand through her hair. Her fingers tangled into the strands before withdrawing. The weariness in the gesture didn't go unnoticed.

Oak locked the door with a soft click before walking over to Eileen. Without a word, he pulled her into his arms.

She didn't resist.

For once, she let herself be held.

★★★

Takoda moved swiftly down the corridor, her boots barely making a sound against the polished floor. Up ahead, Riichi disappeared into the stairwell at the end of the hall, his movements wary, but the tension in his posture undeniable.

When she reached the stairwell door, Takoda hesitated, listening. There was no sound of footsteps ascending. She turned her gaze toward the courtyard door, but before she could take a step, something in the shadows beneath the stairs caught her attention. The dim light barely reached the space, but there was a subtle move in the darkness, a small movement that suggested a presence hiding within.

Riichi.

He sat under the staircase, his back against the wall, legs bent with elbows resting on his knees. His head hung low, fingers knotted in his hair. The tension in his frame was clear—contained, yet barely.

Takoda exhaled softly, stepping closer. "Riichi."

He didn't respond. Didn't move.

She closed the distance between them and lowered herself onto the floor beside him. He lifted his head just enough for her to catch the intensity in his eyes— severe, raw anger simmering beneath the surface. But it wasn't just rage that tightened his jaw and stiffened his shoulders—there was something else. A quiet restraint, a force keeping the storm at bay. He was on the edge, fighting to hold himself together.

Takoda remained silent, allowing her presence to settle beside him, offering calm without intrusion. She extended her emotional alchemy gently—not to overpower him, but to create a space where he could breathe.

His shoulders stayed rigid, but Takoda could sense the subtle release in his grip, his fingers loosening slightly from his hair. A slow exhalation escaped him, a crack in the armor he'd so carefully built around himself.

"What happened?" she asked, her voice quiet, patient.

Riichi dragged his hand over his face, then rested his arm on his knee, his fingers flexing and relaxing in slow, deliberate movements. He took a moment to gather himself before speaking. "The demon in Aislinn's vision," he said, voice low but laced with cold fury. "Kubla Khan."

Takoda's breath caught, but she didn't interrupt. She'd suspected there was more behind his reaction, and now she knew.

His exhale left him in a slow release, his expression blank but tightly manipulated. "His army invaded my village. The night I died."

Takoda sat still, letting his words settle between them.

Riichi's posture was rigid, his jaw clenched. "The invasion destroyed everything. My home. My family. Everything." His voice was level, restrained, but it was clear it came at a cost. His fingers dug into his knee, a reflexive release of tension that could never be fully contained. "That was the night I became Fallen."

Takoda felt it—the checked precision of his tone, the careful pacing of his words. He was skimming the surface, but the depths were just below. This wasn't just about the name; it was about everything it unearthed. Everything he wasn't saying.

And she knew better than to push him for more.

She could feel it now—the hesitation, the emotions he was fighting to keep in check. This wasn't just about the past. It was about what he had done, the things he wasn't ready to share. But underneath it all, there was something deeper—fear, buried beneath the layers of control.

It wasn't fear of Kubla Khan.

It was fear of how she might react if she knew everything.

Takoda shifted slightly, turning toward him. "That's why you left the room."

Riichi's jaw tightened, but he nodded once. It was pointed, precise, a move entirely in check, but his eyes never wavered from hers. He was waiting. Watching. Hoping she wouldn't see through him.

Takoda did.

She felt it—the brief flicker of doubt in his composure. *If she knew the full truth, would she stay?*

Takoda didn't flinch. She extended her power a little more, letting it seep through the cracks in his restraint—not dulling his emotions, not erasing them, but helping him bear them.

"Whatever you're carrying, I'll stand by you," she said, her tone quiet but resolute.

For several seconds, Riichi held her stare before breaking it and looking away. Another slow breath, as if her words were sinking in.

She let the silence linger, then added, "And you won't lose me."

His expression hardened, but there was more there now—fury, yes, but also memory. He reached for her hand, his fingers brushing hers briefly before gripping her hand firmly, his hold tightening as if anchoring himself to her rather than to the storm inside him.

From the doorway of the stairwell, Rowan stood just outside, grounded and unobtrusive. He made no move to interfere but stayed watchful, a silent protector ensuring Takoda's safety.

Takoda didn't urge Riichi to speak again. She simply stayed.

And Riichi let her.

Aislinn stepped out of Eileen's office, spotting Rowan leaning casually against the wall at the end of the hall. His arms were crossed, and his face was neutral, though Aislinn could feel his eyes on her.

She approached him, tilting her head slightly. "Everything okay?"

Rowan gave a single nod. "Yeah." He didn't elaborate, but the way he was positioned, just outside where Takoda and Riichi had gone, spoke volumes.

Before Aislinn could respond, the stairwell door at the far end of the hall opened.

Takoda and Riichi stepped out, hand in hand.

Aislinn's focus moved over them, noting the ease with which Takoda carried herself, the quiet confidence etched in Riichi's features.

Takoda locked onto her, giving a small, reassuring nod. "We're good."

Aislinn exhaled softly, a tension she hadn't fully realized she was holding slipping away. "Good," she murmured, falling into step beside them as they made their way back toward Eileen's office. Rowan followed behind, his pace measured, unobtrusive.

When they reached the office, Takoda knocked lightly. A second later, the lock clicked open.

Oak swung the door wide, stepping aside to let them in.

As they entered, Eileen's attention immediately altered, zeroing in on Riichi. She didn't ask questions. She didn't need to.

Riichi gave her a single nod, his face composed once again.

That was all Eileen needed.

Turning toward the desk, her presence moved into strategy mode, commanding and focused. "We don't know when Kubla Khan will strike first," she began, her voice calm but laced with urgency. "And that puts us at a disadvantage. We need to be ready for any scenario."

She glanced around the room, her eyes astute. "That means additional, focused training. We'll concentrate on three key areas: connection and synchronization, emotional and aura manipulation, and combat readiness."

She turned to Oak, Rowan, and Aislinn. "Oak, you'll lead the emotional and aura work. Rowan, physical training. Aislinn, synchronization."

Riichi straightened slightly, a flash of disapproval crossing his face. "Is that really necessary? Takoda doesn't need to be combat-ready for tonight."

Rowan crossed his arms, mirroring Riichi's skepticism. "We have a lot to cover already. Focusing on connection work might be enough, at least for now."

Eileen's stare remained unwavering. "We don't know when or where Kubla Khan will make his move. It's better for Takoda to be prepared now than be caught off guard later."

Aislinn, flipping absently through the book still open in front of her, muttered, "I wouldn't worry too much about Koda." There was a quiet confidence in her voice, a knowing edge.

Takoda caught the look and allowed the corner of her mouth to quirk, but she didn't speak.

Oak leaned forward slightly, his tone contemplative. "Kubla Khan will be drawn to strong emotions—especially anger. The question is whether that will repel him or draw him in."

Rowan's perception sharpened as he turned to Riichi. "That means you need to stay composed. If he feeds on anger, you can't give him any ammunition."

Riichi held his ground, his expression unreadable for several seconds. Finally, with quiet certainty, he said, "I won't make the same mistake twice."

The room fell into a brief silence, his words hanging in the air, carrying their own impact.

Takoda glanced at Riichi, sensing the restraint in his posture, the tightness in his voice.

She lifted her chin, her voice calm. "I'll refine my emotional alchemy skills to help—and do whatever else I can."

Riichi turned to her, meeting her steadfast hold with an intensity that softened just slightly.

He nodded, his response coming without hesitation now. "We'll handle it."

Eileen studied them both, her approval subtle but evident. "The stronger your bond becomes, the more likely Kubla Khan will sense it. This training isn't just preparation—it's protection."

A heavy silence settled over the room.

Aislinn, still standing near Eileen, reached out and gently closed the book on the desk—the book that held Kubla Khan's face.

Eileen straightened, signaling the close of the meeting. "Tonight, will be dangerous, but if you stay focused and grounded in each other, we stand a chance. Training begins in an hour."

As they left the office, Eileen's words lingered in their minds, the pressure of them pressing against the silence that stretched through the winding corridors like an unseen current. The upcoming mission loomed, its urgency unspoken but palpable.

Riichi gave Takoda's hand a final, meaningful squeeze, his intention locked onto hers, fierce with determination. Beneath it, however, there was a quiet gravity, a depth of feeling he rarely allowed to surface.

Takoda returned his look with a composed smile, her confidence unwavering.

They walked side by side down the corridor, each bracing for what lay ahead.

As they entered the common area, the Fallen were already gathered, preparing for the morning's training with quiet intensity. The atmosphere crackled with the weight of the task ahead, each movement reflecting the seriousness of the night's mission.

Aislinn's attention shifted to Takoda with a mischievous spark. "Guess we'll see what you've got, Koda."

Takoda grinned confidently. "Don't blink, or you might miss it."

Eileen and Oak moved to the center of the room, and with a nod from Eileen, the group fell into formation. Her presence commanded the room—subtle yet undeniable.

"Tonight's mission will demand everything from each of you," Eileen said, her voice firm with the weight of countless battles. "Hone your skills, trust each other, and stay focused."

With a brief nod, she gestured to the doors leading to the back courtyard. The Fallen moved as one, focused and determined.

Outside, morning light fractured through shifting clouds, casting rays across the grounds. The courtyard, framed by towering trees, offered seclusion for their preparations. The air carried the scent of damp earth, mingling with a sharp bite of wind.

The teams broke apart. Takoda exchanged a glance with Aislinn, offering a determined smile before joining the Emotional Manipulation Team.

At the far end of the courtyard, Oak and Willow arranged glowing targets pulsing with fear, anger, and doubt. The energy within them crackled, volatile and unpredictable, testing the mastery of those who sought to tame it.

Takoda grounded herself before extending her reach. A pulse of calm radiated outward, softening the chaotic glow into a muted blue.

Oak and Willow pushed her further, challenging her to refine her touch at greater distances. As the targets shifted, Takoda adapted, letting resistance flow through her rather than forcing control.

Birch stepped forward, offering himself as a live target. His mental defenses resisted her influence, but Takoda stayed focused. With a steady exhale, she connected with multiple disruptions, her hands glowing softly as she maintained control over the energy.

"Good," Oak said, his voice low. "Keep your composure, even when things get unpredictable."

Across the courtyard, the Disruption Team worked just as focused. Riichi led them through ritual-dismantling drills, each movement swift and purposeful, aiming to disarm key components of the Golden Dawn's ritual.

Rowan and Vine sparred nearby, testing each other's reflexes. Aislinn and Elder practiced targeted strikes, adjusting with Riichi's cues.

"Tonight, we go straight into the heart of their ritual," Riichi called out. "No hesitation. Hit your targets and keep moving."

The team transitioned into close-combat drills, refining their movements for confined spaces. Riichi's corrections were precise, methodical.

Aislinn, wiping sweat from her forehead, smirked at Riichi. "For someone who loves strategy, you're a hard-ass when it comes to combat."

Riichi didn't look up as he adjusted Vine's footing. "Strategy means nothing if you're dead before you can execute it."

At the shadowed edge of the courtyard, Reed moved like a shadow, leading Ash and Ivy through stealth drills. They practiced vanishing into the courtyard's natural concealment, weaving between bands of light and shadow.

Ivy manipulated perception, creating small distortions to make objects seem closer or farther than they were. Ash layered misdirection, adjusting their presence just enough to stay unnoticed.

Their final drill was silent communication. Quick, precise gestures flowed between them. Reed nodded in approval before murmuring, "Stay sharp. We're the eyes and ears tonight. Our job is to keep them safe."

The sky darkened as the training continued. Thick clouds rolled in, casting an eerie gray over the courtyard. The air grew heavy, the scent of impending rain lingering as thunder rumbled across the hills.

The teams pressed forward, each strike and counter measured with purpose. They were ready.

As the session neared its end, Rowan, Aislinn, and Riichi approached Oak. It was time.

"Training's over," Oak called, his voice ringing across the courtyard. "Get ready for tonight. We'll need every ounce of strength and clarity."

The Fallen dispersed, exchanging quiet words before heading inside.

Takoda lingered, rolling her shoulders. What lay ahead pressed against her, an unseen force. This session had been unlike the others, testing her in ways she hadn't faced before.

She turned toward Oak, toward Riichi, toward the unknown. She was ready.

The courtyard had fallen silent, the earlier bustle of training now a distant memory. Only Oak, Aislinn, Rowan, Riichi, and Takoda remained, the overcast sky pressing down like a weight, the air thick with the urgency of their task.

Riichi felt the pressure settle in his chest—it wasn't just about survival but maintaining focus. If he lost his concentration, he wouldn't just risk his own life, but Takoda's too. He glanced at her, steady and composed, a quiet certainty grounding him. *Tonight, I have to stay focused. For both of us.*

Oak stepped forward, his presence unwavering. "We'll start with emotional and aura mastery," he said, voice calm and firm. "Kubla Khan feeds on anger. Don't give him a foothold."

Riichi knew Kubla Khan would target the anger that always simmered just beneath his restraint—quiet, controlled, but never far.

Takoda nodded, centering herself. She understood—this wasn't just about control, but trust. Trust in herself and her bond with Riichi. *If there's anyone I can hold strong for, it's you.*

Oak motioned for them to face each other. "Takoda, project a calming aura toward Riichi. Keep it steady. Riichi, don't fight it, but don't let it overtake you."

Takoda closed her eyes briefly, grounding herself before releasing a pulse of calm. Riichi immediately felt the shift—a subtle yet calming presence that brushed against him. He acknowledged it but held his ground. *Stay focused. If you lose focus now, you might lose her later.*

Oak observed, his tone low. "Good. Now, connect. A true exchange."

They tuned into the bond taking shape, the air between them thickening with an invisible current. Their connection grew stronger, not through force, but through effortless synchronization. The outside world faded, leaving only the bond they built together.

Takoda felt it—Riichi's quiet resilience, the strength beneath his restraint. *With him, I'm balanced. With him, I'm… more.*

Without warning, a ripple of agitation swept through the air—Oak had sent it, a deliberate wave of unease meant to disrupt them.

Riichi tensed, anger flaring before he forced it down. He felt Takoda react immediately, her focus reinforcing the calm between them. Her silent reassurance grounded him, and the storm Oak conjured faded beneath their shared strength.

Oak nodded, approval in his voice. "This is what you hold onto tonight. If you can keep this, Kubla Khan won't break you."

Aislinn stepped forward, lighter but focused. "Now, let's work on synchronization," she said. "Nonverbal communication is a powerful tool."

She guided them through mirrored movements, starting simple before adding complexity. Takoda and Riichi adjusted effortlessly, attuned to each other's subtle cues—slight shifts, measured pivots. Hesitations melted away, their movements falling into sync, as if they shared the same rhythm.

As they moved, Riichi felt a new sense of composure—pride, not in himself, but in how they fit together. *If she can trust me, then I can be what she needs tonight.*

"Close your eyes," Aislinn instructed. "Match your breathing."

They obeyed, their bodies falling into a unified rhythm. The courtyard blurred, narrowing their awareness to only each other.

Takoda felt the night pressing in around them, uncertainty coiling just beyond their reach. But with Riichi beside her, she didn't fear what lay ahead. His presence was certainty, an anchor amid the shifting unknown. *Whatever we face, I won't hesitate. Not with him. Not tonight.*

"Now move," Aislinn said. "Without sight. Stay in sync."

At first, their steps were careful, but quickly they adapted, responding to each other instinctively. Aislinn positioned herself as an obstacle, forcing them to navigate around her without breaking their rhythm. Their movements were harmonious, moving through space with intuitive awareness.

Riichi felt a surge of confidence. *If we can do this blind, we can handle whatever chaos the ritual brings.*

Aislinn clapped lightly. "Not bad. You two are more in sync than you realize. Rely on this bond tonight, and you'll move through the fight as one."

Rowan approached, the faintest curve of amusement tugging at his mouth, though his focus remained sharp. "Time to test your reflexes," he said, his voice steady but expectant. "Combat is as much about anticipation as it is about skill." He turned to Riichi. "Approach Takoda as if in a mock attack. Takoda, respond as needed."

Riichi hesitated for a split second, silently questioning her. She returned a nod, calm and unreadable. Whatever she had planned, she was ready. With that, Riichi moved toward her, starting slow before picking up speed, calculating his steps as he closed the gap.

The change was immediate. Instead of retreating or dodging, Takoda shifted with seamless precision, her movement fluid and hypnotic. She met his advance head-on, using his momentum to deflect him. A swift redistribution of weight, and before he fully processed what had happened, Riichi found himself on the ground.

The world tilted as he stared up at the sky, the stone beneath him cool to the touch. Silence followed, charged with the shock of those watching.

Oak's brow lifted slightly, acknowledging her effort. Rowan let out a low whistle. Aislinn's laugh broke the silence, wide-eyed and delighted.

Riichi blinked up at Takoda, still processing. *When did she learn that?* The realization hit him like a second blow—there were depths to her that he hadn't considered. She'd caught him off guard, and though his pride and instincts bristled, respect followed, deep and undeniable.

A smirk tugged at his lips. "Where did that come from?" he asked, still recovering.

Takoda extended a hand, her grip firm yet easy. "I'm a lover, not a fighter," she said, tilting her head. "But I might have picked up a thing or two."

She let the silence linger before adding, "Jujutsu classes. They were... fun."

Riichi chuckled softly, shaking his head. *Of course, she has layers I didn't know.*

Takoda wasn't finished. "It's also where I learned to say 'thank you' and 'you're welcome' in Japanese," she added, a playful curve to her lips.

That earned a full laugh from him. "I should've guessed," he murmured, lingering on her a beat longer than necessary. *She never stops surprising me.*

Rowan shook his head, entertained. "You're full of surprises, Takoda. That skill will serve you well tonight. Staying composed is just as important as strength."

Oak's eyes softened, approval marking his features. "You've been holding out on us," he remarked, arms crossed. "Use that to your advantage. Those who underestimate you won't see it coming."

Aislinn grinned. "If Kubla Khan gets wind of this, he's in for a shock."

The atmosphere shifted, subtle but palpable. Confidence threaded through the group, reinforcing the shared understanding that they were ready for more than they realized.

Rowan's smile faded, his voice turning firm. "Tonight, we stick to the plan. But if things go sideways, trust your instincts and each other. We've got one another's backs."

A round of nods followed, a silent agreement settling between them like the final breath before a battle cry. As they moved toward the mansion, uncertainty still loomed, but a sharpened sense of resolve had taken its place.

Riichi fell into step beside Takoda, glancing at her. "You really are full of surprises," he said, softer now, with a quiet admiration that was rarely voiced—a recognition of strength he hadn't expected but respected.

She returned his look, a knowing glint in her eyes. "Just keeping you on your toes."

He exhaled a quiet laugh, shaking his head. *I won't take her for granted again.* "Consider me warned."

The session concluded with a shared sense of purpose. Each of them was more attuned not only to their own strengths but to what they could accomplish together. As they parted to prepare, the courtyard emptied, but the unity they shared lingered—a force humming beneath the surface, waiting to be unleashed.

Chapter Sixteen
Wrath Unleashed

The Fallen gathered in the mansion's main hall, preparing their gear, and exchanging final thoughts. The usual buzz of camaraderie was subdued, their attention drawn to the mission ahead. The air crackled with energy, thick with anticipation. Outside, a dense curtain of clouds muted the evening's glow, casting cool silver hues across the space. The mansion stood in solemn stillness, as if its very walls understood the gravity of what lay ahead.

Near one of the large windows, Takoda adjusted her gear, silently reviewing the steps Oak had guided her through earlier. A heavy pressure sank deep into her bones—not hesitation, but awareness. The enormity of the night loomed close, but she exhaled slowly, finding her balance in the present moment.

Oak approached with his usual calm dignity, moving like a breeze through ancient boughs. In his palm, he carried a small object. As he stepped into the dim light, its details became clear—the intricate carvings on the sword guard, an elegant blend of two worlds. Stylized waves and cherry blossoms, clearly Japanese in their precision, intertwined with the sacred imagery of her own heritage—feathers etched with reverence, mountain peaks carved with enduring strength.

A flicker of warmth softened Oak's expression as he extended the guard to her. "I made this for Riichi's katana. Thought it might offer him another layer of protection, a tether to the earth when the storm comes. But I was hoping you'd add a bit of yourself to it—your focus, your balance."

Takoda traced the delicate craftsmanship with careful fingers, her voice softer now. "It's beautiful, Oak." She turned the piece over, admiring the way the elements blended as if they had always belonged together. "He'll appreciate this. More than you know."

Oak stood beside her, his tone calm yet firm. "Take a moment. Let yourself be centered. Let what you carry flow into it."

She obeyed, exhaling as she closed her eyes. With each slow inhale, she gathered the calm she wished for Riichi—the stillness that steadied hands, the clarity that turned doubt into instinct. Beneath her fingertips, the sword guard hummed with magic, absorbing what she offered. A soft pulse echoed in her palm, unseen but felt. When she opened her eyes, Oak watched with quiet approval.

"That's good," he murmured, a glint of recognition in his face. "A piece of you with him. That's all he needs."

Takoda smiled, a deep understanding taking root in her chest. She tucked the guard into her gear, knowing that when Riichi wielded his sword tonight, a part of her strength would be with him.

Across the room, she caught Riichi's gaze. A silent exchange passed between them—a tether, invisible but adamant. He gave a small nod, then gestured toward the door. Without pause, she followed him outside, stepping into the cool hush of the evening. The air carried the scent of rain, the distant rustling of leaves the only sound beneath the heavy, cloud-laden sky.

Here, beneath the night's questions pressing in around them, she could center her thoughts on him.

Riichi turned, the corner of his mouth lifting in reflective admiration. "I have to admit, Takoda—you really surprised me back there. That Jujutsu move…" He let the thought linger before adding, more softly, "I never knew you had it in you."

Takoda's lips curled in a knowing smile. "I like to keep people guessing," she teased, her tone light despite the storm gathering on the horizon. "Wouldn't want you getting too comfortable."

A rare laugh escaped him, soft but genuine. Then, without pause, he reached for her hand, threading his fingers through hers with thoughtful certainty. A firm, reassuring squeeze. "Honestly? Seeing that strength in you… it makes me feel like we'll be okay tonight." His voice dropped lower. "Like we're truly unstoppable as one."

Her hold tightened in response, as resolute as ever. "We are," she assured him. "No matter what's waiting for us, we'll face it side by side."

She reached into her pocket, retrieving the sword guard Oak had crafted. The etched symbols caught the dim light, a gleam of purpose in the dark. Handing it over, she offered a small, knowing smile. "Oak made this for you. I, uh, added a little calm and clarity—for tonight."

A flicker of recognition stirred in Riichi as he turned it over, tracing the carefully blended motifs—waves alongside feathers, cherry blossoms meeting mountain peaks. He absorbed the meaning of it without words, then secured it onto his katana with quiet determination. "Thank you. Both of you."

When he looked at her again, his expression softened, carrying a depth of meaning clearly felt. He lifted her hand once more, squeezing not out of reassurance, but as a quiet promise.

Then, without preamble, he leaned in, his forehead touching hers. A silent communion. A calming action meant to give them strength.

The moment stretched, leisurely. Then, in a movement as effortless as the pull of the tide, he tilted his head and pressed his lips to hers. A kiss that filled with a quiet intensity that spoke of trust, desire, and a bond that had been forged over time. It was slow, certain, and undeniably real.

When they finally parted, they exchanged a look that conveyed everything they couldn't say aloud.

Riichi's voice came, low and undeterred. "Tonight, you're my rock. Just don't let go."

Takoda's smile was soft, but resolute. "I've got you. Always."

A last, meaningful glance passed between them—a promise sealed without words—and they turned toward the mansion, stepping inside with a shared sense of determination.

They were ready.

Whatever waited in the dark, it would not find them trembling.

Inside the mansion, the Fallen moved through the final moments of preparation with focused precision. Rowan inspected his blade, thumb grazing the steel in a practice as old as war itself. Across the room, Aislinn sifted through her protective charms, fingers brushing each one before securing them away.

Oak and Willow stood together, their conversation quiet but certain. Their words weren't second-guesses but confirmations—the exchange of those who had faced battle and understood what lay ahead.

The hall thrummed with anticipation, each Fallen steadying themselves before stepping into the unknown. Elder caught Vine's eye and gave a slow nod—a silent exchange of trust. Nearby, Reed leaned toward Ash, murmuring something low before adjusting his gear.

No fear, no hesitation. Only perseverance.

A shared pulse of energy moved through them.

Ariel and Rain wove through the room, their company supporting rather than intrusive. Ariel stopped near Rowan and Aislinn, a brief exchange passing between them before she moved on. Rain brushed Takoda's arm in passing, her glance toward Riichi carrying an understanding of what this night would demand of him. The Fallen women—Willow and Ivy—acknowledged them with fleeting but purposeful glances, a silent reinforcement of the bonds they carried into battle.

Rain found Elder near the doorway, his usual air of detachment wrapped around him like armor. Still, she didn't hesitate, stepping close enough that their shoulders nearly touched. "Try not to fade into the background too much tonight," she murmured, her tone edged with teasing. "I know it's your thing, but some of us like knowing you're actually here."

Elder exhaled, his attention shifting to her with the faintest glint of amusement. "I'll keep that in mind."

Nearby, Ariel approached Vine, hands in her pockets, demeanor sharp despite the ease in her stance. "You good?" The question was simple, direct.

Vine's lips quirked, though his eyes held a shadow beneath the surface. "I always am."

Ariel didn't call him on it, just tilted her head. "Right. Well, if that changes, try not to get yourself killed proving a point."

Vine huffed a dry chuckle, shaking his head as she walked past, slipping into the crowd with her usual restless vitality. But she didn't stop moving until she found Eileen, pausing just long enough to say, "Not usually the type to say this, but… good luck."

Eileen turned, momentarily caught off guard. Most approached her with reverence, with questions, with caution. Never like this. She lingered on Ariel for a moment, weighing the unexpected sentiment before she gave a small nod. "Thank you."

Ariel smirked. "Don't get used to it."

Eileen huffed the faintest exhale of amusement—gone as quickly as it came. "Noted."

Ariel's grin lingered as she turned. "I'll keep things from falling apart while you're gone."

Eileen studied her for a beat longer before replying, quieter, but firm. "I know."

Ariel arched a brow, as if surprised by the trust, then gave a casual salute and walked away.

The moment remained with Eileen longer than she expected.

Drawing in a slow inhale, she refocused and stepped forward. The air around her shifted—not because the light bent to her, but because the room recognized her authority.

Her attention swept over them—not just seeing but knowing.

When she spoke, her voice cut through the stillness.

"Tonight, we step into unknown territory," she said, each word a foundation rather than a rally. "You've trained, prepared, and proven yourselves. Your strength lies not just in skill, but in each other."

She let the words sink in, taking in each warrior, memorizing them in this moment.

"Trust your instincts. Trust the person beside you." A pause. "Each of you brings a strength that cannot be replaced. We need all of it."

Her attention lingered briefly on Riichi and Takoda, pride in them, though she didn't single them out. Their strength was for the team, not just themselves.

"We step forward together. Stay sharp. Keep each other standing. And above all—remember why we fight."

Beyond the glass-paneled windows, the sky churned, thick with gathering clouds. She turned toward it, a reminder of the forces waiting beyond the mansion walls.

"This darkness is not permanent," she said, her tone absolute. "We step into it now so that others won't have to. Let that be the thought that carries you through whatever comes tonight."

Her words settled over them—not a burden, but a reinforcement. She took one last look at the team—not as individuals, but as a singular force. "You're ready," she said without hesitation. "I couldn't ask for a better team." With a final nod, she ended the moment. "Gather yourselves. We leave in five."

Attention tightened across the room, final glances exchanged, laced with conviction.

One by one, they moved toward the exit. Not cautiously, but with clarity.

The mansion's heavy doors swung open, and the night greeted them with the scent of rain. Overhead, clouds churned, swallowing the last traces of moonlight. A distant rumble of thunder rolled through the sky—low but suspicious. A warning. A promise.

Beyond the horizon, Fort Lawton loomed, its presence stretching through the darkness like an unseen hand. They would meet whatever waited there as one, but the night had already begun to stir. As they stepped forward, Eileen's words lingered—*We step into it now so that others won't have to.* A vow carved into the storm itself.

Then, without hesitation, they pressed on.

Above them, lightning tore the sky apart—a jagged, unrelenting promise of what lay ahead.

★★★

The ritual site loomed ahead, its outline barely visible through the dense fog curling along the jagged cliffside. The land pulsed with a slow, unseen rhythm, mist slithering over the rocks as if whispering to the abyss below. The outcrop jutted sharply over the restless waters of Puget Sound, where the tide churned against the stone with a ceaseless, hungry pull. Salt and damp earth thickened the air, sharp and biting, while overhead, the sky pressed low—swollen with the promise of a coming storm.

Symbols carved into the rock pulsed with a sickly red glow. The light slithered through the ritual site, stretching clawed shadows across the uneven earth, warping them like sentient creatures. From shadowed alcoves, murmurs and chants drifted into the night, each word not meant for human tongues, laced with an otherworldly force that did not belong.

Reed moved with refined precision, dissolving into the mist, becoming a phantom within the shifting veil. Every step was measured, every movement deliberate. Shadow-walking wrapped him in the absence of light, letting him slip between the cultists' patrols unnoticed. Eyes sharp, he observed their positions—the fractured formations, the restless shuffling near the glowing runes.

Even the cultists could feel the power creeping into their bones. One guard prowled the cliff's edge, his gaze flicking nervously to the symbols, as if the slightest distraction could summon something worse. The red glow carved hollows into his face, sharpening his unease. Another stood rigid near the ceremonial core, grasping a talisman so tightly his knuckles turned white, bracing against the oppressive strength pressing down.

Fear was already in the air. It only needed a push.

Slipping back into the haze, Reed moved toward the tree line, where Ash and Ivy crouched. "Guards along the perimeter, several stationed near the enchantment's circle," he murmured. "We pull the outer ones into the trees, the rest will be too distracted to notice the Disruption Team moving in."

Ash nodded, every muscle twitching with resolve.

Reed signaled once, and Ash moved forward, silent as shadow, weaving himself into the fog. A low growl rumbled through the night—not an attack, but a warning, primal and chilling.

The nearest guard tensed, fingers twitching toward his weapon. "Did you hear that?" he whispered.

Ash deepened the growl, a sound that resonated into the bones of the earth, slow and cautious. Then, in a shift of smog, he stepped into moonlight—towering, inhuman, his stance radiating predatory intent.

One of the guards stumbled back, his chest rising and falling unevenly. "What is that?" he hissed.

The other hesitated, grip tightening, but no answer came.

Hidden deeper, Ivy lifted her hands, her motions exact and decisive. The mist thickened, folding and twisting into solid shapes—human in form, yet wrong in essence, distorting reality around them. The guards shifted uneasily, their senses on edge, the tension in the air thick. The haze was no longer a mere fog—it became a part of the world itself, warping and shifting with Ivy's will. It pressed in, moved with persistence, and watched as if alive. Ivy maintained her control, bending the very fabric of the environment to her command.

A cultist swallowed hard, barely whispering, "Did you see that?"

His companion nodded stiffly, his posture becoming rigid as he turned toward the shifting shadows. "This place is cursed. We should warn the others."

Reed allowed himself the smallest smirk, the unraveling beginning. The first guard spun around, panic edging his voice. "We need backup! There's movement in the woods!"

Panic was the quickest poison. Several cultists turned toward the trees, catching glimpses of spectral shadows that vanished when they tried to focus on them. A crack in their formation—that's all it took.

Ash struck. He erupted from the underbrush, not attacking but moving with an unreal swiftness, too massive to process. His sudden movement shattered their composure. The cultists scrambled backward, weapons raised, hands trembling. They were ready to fight, but how do you fight a nightmare?

Reed tracked their movements from the shadows. The trap had worked. The guards had taken the bait, their attention splintering as they turned toward the trees. Those left at the ritual site glanced over their shoulders too often, their footing less certain. The air buzzed with hesitation.

Reed exhaled slowly. It was time.

A flick of his fingers signaled Ivy, and she released her hold on the shadows—not vanishing, but lingering at the edges of perception, a distorted echo of the environment. Another nod sent Ash blending seamlessly into the mist, his towering form melting into the darkness once more.

The stage was set. The rite was no longer their priority. The guards were scattered, their attention divided. The battle had already begun—long before the first strike fell.

Riichi received Reed's subtle signal from within the smog, a nod that surged adrenaline through him. He gestured to his team—Rowan, Aislinn, Vine, and Elder—and without a word, they began their approach. Moving low and swift, they wove through the fog, their movements a practiced dance against the cliffside's jagged terrain. Each step was measured, the only sounds around them the rhythmic crash of waves below and the muted murmur of cultists distracted by Reed, Ash, and Ivy's diversion.

As they neared the arcane site, Rowan leaned toward Aislinn, his voice low against the charged air. "The energy's concentrated here," he murmured, his attention locked on the pulsing symbols carved into the earth. "We need to dismantle it fast. If they sense us, it's over."

Aislinn swallowed, centering herself as the air seemed to pulse, the symbols vibrating with a sickening rhythm. The charge prickled against her skin—a warning, an unnatural heartbeat in the earth.

Vine moved first, his senses sharp as he spotted smaller markings scattered along the incantation's edge. Tiny objects—bones, twisted metal—arranged to amplify the spell's reach. He knelt, hands swift as he scattered the components, severing the magic's flow with each disruption. The objects clattered to the dirt, their potency undone, his movements efficient and precise.

Elder positioned himself near the clearing's edge, barely distinguishable against the thick cloud of vapor. His awareness flicked between the shifting haze and the cultists beyond—ever watchful, silent.

As Vine finished, Riichi raised his hand, signaling the team to halt. From their crouched positions, they spotted a handful of guards near the occult core, their attention split between the growing unease in the air and the fog rolling through the trees. Riichi's eyes narrowed, senses attuned to the shifting balance of the sacred power. With a sharp gesture, he signaled the team into action.

Rowan moved first, slipping behind a guard with fluid ease. His steps soundless, he closed the distance, hand clamping over the cultist's mouth in a firm hold. With a swift motion, he pulled the man backward, executing a silent takedown that left him slumped to the floor without a sound. Rowan eased him down, scanning the area before moving on.

Vine was already in motion, gliding behind another guard just steps from the ritual's heart. His movements precise and poised. He barely disturbed the mist as he struck, his hand snapping out with a single calculated motion. The guard collapsed silently, his hands loosening as the ceremonial components scattered across the dirt.

Aislinn's pulse quickened as they neared the central symbols. Elder's hand rested on her shoulder, balancing her, offering comfort against the dread in the air. The weight of the moment pressed into her chest, but knowing Elder was with her, held her steady. She met his gaze, nodding, and he released his hold, shifting behind her as she remained close, focus locked on the arcane power.

Ahead, a cultist stood with his back turned, muttering low chants, absorbed by the invocation's pull. Before Aislinn could move, Riichi was already in motion. His approach soundless, a seamless shift through the haze, each step deliberate. In one swift motion, he clamped a hand over the cultist's mouth, pulling him backward with controlled strength. The man barely reacted before Riichi struck, grip unrelenting as he cut off any struggle. The guard's body went limp, collapsing to the ground.

Elder gave a small nod as Riichi eased the cultist to the dirt, ensuring no sound betrayed them. Aislinn exhaled, apprehension unwinding from her shoulders. She stayed close but out of the fight, attuned to the unseen forces around them, rather than the combat.

One by one, the Disruption Team executed their roles with seamless precision, their movements synchronized as if rehearsed for this very moment. The space around the spell's core fell silent, the last of the guards unconscious, their presence erased without a trace. The team gathered beyond the innermost symbols, each acutely aware of the might thrumming beneath their feet.

Riichi scanned the disrupted markings, scattered objects, and motionless guards who had once stood watch. The air thickened, the pulse of the dark crux growing louder, pressing into the silence they had carved. He inhaled, letting his mind briefly drift to Takoda, to the calm she had given him before the mission. That stillness anchored him now, holding him steady as the night coiled around them, heavy with intent.

He signaled to Rowan, who nodded silently, clutching his weapon firmly. They were close now, on the threshold of the ceremony's heart, where the symbols pulsed with twisted power, their influence bleeding into the mist. The team moved forward, their steps calculated, their breathing even. The charged air thickened as they neared the final phase of their approach.

Takoda felt pressure build as the Disruption Team dismantled the symbolic components. A ripple of awareness stirred among the Golden Dawn members at the cliff's edge, their unease threading through the heavy air. Closing her eyes, she centered herself, steadying her rhythm before extending her aura in a methodical wave. Her energy spread like smoke, weaving through the vapor, dulling the cultists' suspicion.

Their movements slowed, minds clouded by her influence. Takoda held it steady, though strain coiled in her chest, each passing second demanding more focus. As the weight threatened to slip beyond her control, Oak and Willow's presence brushed against hers. Oak's spells were firm, stabilizing her aura. Willow amplified it, carrying her influence deeper into the gathering cultists.

The effect enveloped them like fog. The cultists' expressions slackened, confusion lacing the air in disoriented murmurs. Their concentration wavered, their attention drifting into the smog. Oak nodded at Takoda, his presence steady, anchoring her as they wove their magic into a seamless net, holding the cultists in place.

In the shadows along the forest path, Reed caught movement. Another group of Golden Dawn members emerged from the trees, strides sharp and purposeful. Their attention was different—alert, driven. Some unseen signal had stirred them, and they were heading straight for the ritual site. His jaw tightened. They had to be stopped.

Ash, sensing Reed's shift, moved beside him, posture tense. Without a word, he shifted into the guise of a cultist. The transformation took moments, and when he turned, he *was* one of them. Reed gave a quick nod, his look edged with urgency.

Ash moved toward them, steps brisk. "Intruders in the forest," he hissed, voice laced with alarm. "They're trying to disrupt the ritual. You—go that way!" He gestured sharply toward the woods.

The cultists hesitated, exchanging wary glances, but Ash's urgency was convincing. One by one, they shifted toward the tree line, suspicion pulling them into the forest's depths.

Nearby, Ivy had begun her work. As the cultists stepped forward, she bent the shadows around them, twisting the very fabric of the path beneath their feet. The trail buckled, folding in on itself, warping their surroundings as though the landscape itself was shifting. The cultists pressed on, but the world around them blurred and reshaped, the earth beneath their feet unstable and unpredictable, swallowed by Ivy's manipulation of reality.

Ash let his guise fade, slipping back toward Reed and Ivy. Their stares met, tension easing slightly. They had bought the Disruption Team time.

At the cliff's edge, Riichi and his team were inches from the ritual's core. The force thickened, pulsing in slow beats, each vibration pushing against the air like an erratic heartbeat. The carved symbols glowed with an unnatural rhythm, flickering with the spell's power. Every muscle in Riichi's body was taut, his senses honed on the energy beneath his feet.

He signaled to the team. Rowan, Aislinn, Vine, and Elder shifted into position, their movements methodical, attention absolute.

Aislinn approached one of the central runes. Even without touching it, she felt its pull—*wrong*, like a wound festering beneath the surface. A sickly warmth radiated from its markings, curling beneath her skin, threatening to seep into her bones. She swallowed, forcing focus.

Rowan knelt beside her, hand steady as he traced the etched lines. When she turned to him, his nod was simple—*you can do this*.

She exhaled, calming her shaking fingers as she reached for the rune. Takoda's aura brushed against her mind—a pulse of calm, a stabilizing hand. Aislinn held onto that feeling, tracing the rune's lines and breaking its connection with practiced movements.

The effect was instant. The markings fractured, the rune's glow faltering, its magic flickering before bleeding into the haze.

Riichi's senses sharpened. He felt it—the shift in power, the mystical foundation crumbling beneath them. The air shuddered, symbols pulsing with uneven light. The earth trembled as the magic's center unraveled.

Sensing the cultists stirring beyond Takoda's reach, Riichi raised his hand, signaling the final push.

The team moved with practiced precision, dismantling the remaining symbols in swift strikes. Every erased marking cracked the ritual's groundwork, its momentum thrashing in protest. The tremors beneath them intensified, a deep vibration running through the cliffside as the ceremony splintered.

Takoda clenched her jaw, sensing the Golden Dawn's awareness sharpening despite her influence. Gritting her teeth, she pushed harder, sending out another wave of calm, holding them back a moment longer. The strain coiled through her, pulse hammering, but she held steady. Oak's energy pressed against hers, reinforcing her reach, blending seamlessly as they expanded control over the remaining cultists.

The ritual was collapsing.

And they were seconds from finishing the job.

"Almost there," Riichi whispered to himself. The supernatural intensity frayed beneath his fingertips, its final symbols weakening, their glow sputtering like dying embers. With one swift motion, he erased the last markings at his feet, severing the cryptic hub completely.

The air stilled. The weight that had clung to the cliffside collapsed in on itself, folding away into silence. A heavy stillness settled, unnatural in its abruptness. The ritual, once pulsing with dark magic, now left only ruined symbols, their power undone.

For a moment, the team exhaled, muscles tight with exertion, the rush of victory creeping into their limbs. But the quiet wasn't a relief. It was a warning.

A low rumble echoed through the haze, distant yet undeniable. It rolled over the cliffside like thunder buried deep beneath the earth, sending unease crawling up Riichi's spine. The spell had broken, but something stirred in its wake.

They exchanged tense glances. The invocation was undone, but a shadow lingered just beyond their senses.

Riichi tapped his commlink. "The ritual is down." His voice was steady, though his pulse thudded beneath his skin.

Through the commlink, Eileen's voice came sharp and urgent. "Teams, fall back. We're moving out."

Relief flickered on their faces, shoulders easing as the mission's gravity took hold. But the air shifted—colder, heavier, thick with an unseen force. The fog pressed in, constricting, as a sensation pricked at the edges of Riichi's mind. Ancient. Sentient. Watching.

Aislinn's chest tightened. Her posture went rigid, her wide eyes locked on the swirling mist ahead. "Kubla Khan..." she whispered.

His name carried weight, sinking into the air like a stone dropped into still water. A presence pressed against them—not sudden, but inevitable—like a tide that had always been rising.

Riichi's fingers closed around the hilt of his katana, tightening before forcing himself to relax. *Stay cool.* Every nerve screamed for him to be ready, but he kept his breathing even, holding control. Around him, his team tensed, weapons poised, instincts sharpening with the charged air.

Rowan moved closer to Aislinn, his hand closing over hers as they summoned the Shield of Ages. The shimmering barrier flickered into existence, its ancient power humming between them. It wouldn't hold against someone like Kubla Khan, but it would buy them time.

Eileen's voice crackled through the commlink again, low and commanding. "Reed and Ivy, get close. Prepare to extract Riichi if needed. Stand by."

The air thickened around them, as if a heavy weight pressed down on their shoulders. Riichi's senses honed in, every rustle of wind, every heartbeat, striking sharp against the unnatural stillness. The influence wasn't attacking. It was watching. Analyzing.

Eileen's words came quick and sharp. "Oak and Willow, shield Takoda. Now."

Takoda's pulse quickened, Oak's stood beside her giving her strength. His enchantments anchored her, stabilizing her as the moment threatened to pull her under. She exhaled slowly, aligning herself, reaching for the connection she and Riichi had built.

"Vine," Eileen's voice continued, calm but edged with urgency. "Charge up your electrokinesis—be ready for anything."

Takoda inhaled sharply, centering herself, drawing on the memory of their training. She sent a pulse of calm through the bond, reinforcing their connection. Riichi's demeanor was strong, unwavering, but she felt the tension in him, the readiness coiled beneath the surface. *I'm here, Riichi.* The thought brushed his mind, and she sensed the subtle shift—his pulse slowed, his focus sharpening, his grip tightening with pure intention.

Then, from the fog, a figure emerged.

Each step was considered, smooth. The smog recoiled from him, as though unwilling to touch him. His silhouette took shape slowly, as if the world itself hesitated to reveal him all at once.

Kubla Khan moved with absolute command. He did not hurry—he had no need. The space bent to him the moment he entered. His dark robes, embroidered with gilded patterns shimmering faintly in fractured light, did not touch the earth. It was impossible to tell if he walked or if the world beneath him bent to his will.

His behavior wasn't brute force. It was inevitability.

His dark, shrewd eyes took in the Fallen, the subdued intensity of a man who had already conquered and was now observing. His expression didn't linger long on anyone, as if none were worth his full attention. His mouth curved, but it wasn't a smile. It was a thought, incomplete and unreadable.

Khan's power wasn't in dominance, nor fiery wrath. It was in the silence, in his mere existence, knowing others would bend before him.

When he spoke, his voice was deep, smooth—polished like river stones worn down by centuries of currents.

"You are… persistent."

The words weren't praise. They were fact. A statement, delivered as if already written in history, and he was merely acknowledging it.

The smog coiled tighter, the energy shifting subtly—not an attack, but a gradual change in the game board. A move had been made.

Khan surveyed them, his blank expression heavy with the silent scheming of a man who had shaped empires with nothing more than his will. There was no urgency in the way he regarded them, no sign of perceiving them as threats—only inevitabilities.

A slow, knowing smile tugged at his lips, as if indulging in private amusement. "All of this effort…" His voice carried through the thick air with the certainty of one unchallenged, not arrogant, but absolute. Smooth, composed, intentional. "For me?"

Takoda's pulse quickened, her stomach coiling against the unnatural stillness that followed.

The words hung, stretching the silence taut. She pushed herself to stay steady, locking her attention on Riichi and sending another pulse of calm toward him. He was ready. His aura, a wall of resolve, stood strong in silent defiance. But she could feel it—the storm just beneath his surface, held back by willpower alone.

Khan shifted his attention, observing each Fallen not as opponents, but as pieces in a game already won. His focus rested for a moment on Vine, as if measuring an unspoken variable, before moving to Rowan and Elder with idle curiosity.

But when his focus landed on Riichi, the moment thickened.

A calculated glint surfaced beneath his composed exterior, the flicker of recognition restrained by the patience of one who had razed empires and would do so again.

"Ah," he murmured, tone almost reflective. "The strategist himself."

Takoda felt Riichi's aura shift, his manner constant, unmoving. He locked onto Kubla Khan, jaw clenched, movements deliberate and restrained. Every part of him resisted the urge to react.

Taking a single step forward, Kubla Khan's movement was so structured it barely disturbed the air. "I've been looking forward to this meeting."

Riichi's hand tensed around the hilt of his katana, stable and cautious. He pushed himself to stay rooted in the present, to ignore the pull of history snapping at his resolve.

But Khan was in no hurry.

He studied Riichi as a ruler might consider a fallen warrior at his feet—not with pity, not with disdain, but with detached curiosity, as one who had seen men break beneath far less.

The air shifted, thickened.

Takoda pressed more of herself into Riichi's energy, reinforcing the calm between them. But even she could feel it—the slow constriction of space, the suffocating press of an unseen force closing in.

Stepping forward, the Reborn Conqueror moved through the fog, which curled at his feet like an extension of his will. He didn't need to raise his voice. He did not need to demand dominance.

It was already his.

The terrain beneath them thrummed, a pulse vibrating through the stone, as though something long buried had begun to stir. The past lingered—woven into the very earth beneath their feet, waiting to be remembered.

Watching.

Testing.

Takoda felt her aura fraying at the edges, Kubla Khan's presence pressing into her mind like an encroaching tide. It slithered past her defenses, creeping into spaces where doubt and fear threatened to take hold. *Don't lose focus.* She centered herself, reinforcing the tether that bound her to Riichi. *He's holding on—for now.*

His smile remained unchanged, the curve of Khan's lips a study in undeniable, effortless dominance. He took in the Fallen, indifferent as a ruler surveying a kingdom already conquered. Power radiated from him, pressing outward, thickening the air as if the space itself bowed to his authority.

"It's been some time since I've received a welcome quite like this," he mused, amusement curling through his words, smooth and unhurried. "It almost makes me feel..." His dark eyes flickered, a brief shift revealing a glacial sharpness, history and conquest bleeding through in a single sigh. "Nostalgic."

Takoda's stomach twisted. That single word wrapped around them like a closing fist, suffocating in its intent. The mist swirled at his feet, curling as if it, too, was listening.

The Shield of Ages flickered as Rowan and Aislinn reinforced it, a shimmering barrier enclosing the Disruption Team. Rowan tightened his grip on his sword, his eyes narrowing. "Shit," he muttered, barely audible. He knew what this was—Kubla Khan wasn't here to fight. He was here to push Riichi past the edge.

"Riichi," Rowan said, his tone even but edged with warning. "Don't let him get to you. We've got your back."

Riichi didn't respond, but his hands around his katana flexed slightly, reaffirmed by the company of his allies.

Khan's attention fully settled on Riichi, his behavior indecipherable, stance unshaken. "Ah, Riichi," he murmured, his voice slipping into a tone that almost feigned familiarity yet carried an unmistakable edge of satisfaction. He stepped forward, the fog coiling away from him, unwilling to touch what it could not claim. "I've often wondered," he continued, each word smooth, purposeful, "if you remember that night as clearly as I do."

A tremor pulsed through the earth beneath them—subtle, but undeniable, a whisper of ancient power shifting beneath the surface. Takoda felt it like tightening pressure, an unseen force pressing in from all sides. Riichi's fingers flexed over his katana's hilt, his stance unwavering, control absolute, yet the storm inside him gathered, restless and waiting.

With effortless precision, Kubla Khan tilted his head slightly, his expression unreadable. Then, he spoke the words designed to cut the deepest.

"Hakata Bay."

The name was not a question. It was a blade, unsheathed and set between them.

Rowan inhaled sharply. Vine shifted slightly, bracing. Aislinn's hand twitched over her charms but said nothing, her presence a steady support.

Taking in the Fallen's reactions, the Reborn Conqueror observed with the patience of one who had seen countless battles before this one. His attention lingered most on Riichi. "A fleet landing beneath the cover of night," he continued, his voice as smooth as the tide against the shore. "The clash of steel against wooden gates. The scent of burning thatch."

The words sank like lead into the air between them.

Riichi had not moved. Had not spoken. But he didn't need to. Kubla Khan already knew.

"The cries of those who fell," Kubla Khan murmured, each word slow, intentional, pressing into Riichi's chest. "The smoke thick in your lungs as fire devoured everything you swore to protect. The land slick beneath your feet—not just from the rain, but from the blood of the fallen."

Takoda pressed harder, sending a pulse of calm into Riichi's storm, but she felt his confidence fraying under the weight of history clawing its way into the present.

Khan's voice didn't waver, nor did he press, provoke, or demand. The damage had already been done. "The night you lost everything." His focus sharpened, studying every movement, every flicker of restraint struggling to hold Riichi together. "The night you fell into wrath."

The words clung like iron into Takoda's stomach. Rowan exhaled sharply, tension vibrating through his frame as his knuckles whitened around his sword.

The powerful demon remained impassive, patient. "A shame," he murmured, as though the memory belonged to another lifetime, another empire. "Such a waste of fine warriors."

The storm inside Riichi coiled tighter. The pressure radiated inward, contained by sheer will. Takoda felt it pressing against her aura, testing the edges of her influence, and she pushed harder, anchoring herself to him. *Hold on to me, Riichi.* She pressed every ounce of calm into the bond between them, her energy threading through his, grounding him before the dam inside him could break.

Watching the exchange with the detached air of a strategist, Kubla Khan knew the pieces were already set in motion. No strike was necessary; he only needed to wait.

Then, as if the conversation had never happened, his attention shifted elsewhere. "The Golden Dawn?" he mused, almost bored, as if their movement held no consequence. "Consider them… preoccupied." He did not blink. "I've kept them out of the way," he continued, unconcerned, "so we can enjoy this… uninterrupted."

The implication settled like a slow-turning blade, twisting deeper with each passing second. Kubla Khan observed Riichi with clinical curiosity, his conduct betraying no urgency, no aggression—just patience. He tilted his head slightly, studying him as if assessing an artfully crafted weapon.

"Not much of a conversationalist, are you?" Kubla Khan's tone was light, almost idle, but satisfaction edged his words. His smirk deepened, an echo of victory already won. "A shame. I do enjoy good conversation. Though," his dark irises gleamed, "perhaps you prefer action over words."

A muscle tightened in Riichi's jaw, holding his katana tighter. Every instinct screamed to strike, to silence the voice coiling around him like a vice. But he didn't move. The only sign of his turmoil was the slow, ordered exhale through his nose. *Don't give him anything to latch onto.* He forced the mantra through his mind, holding onto it as tightly as the blade.

Rowan broke the silence. "What do you want, Kubla Khan?" His voice was clear, direct.

Khan chuckled, indulgent and unhurried. He turned to Rowan, nodding slowly. "Ah, a voice of reason. A warrior who knows when to ask the right question." His focus shifted back to Riichi, sharpening with intrigue.

"I'm only here to introduce myself." He observed Riichi, noting every disciplined action, every flicker of restraint. "Riichi." His voice was smooth, edged with certainty. "You know who I am. A man once bound by mortal limits, now freed by the afterlife's... offering, a Reborn Conqueror."

His words coiled around Riichi's ribs, constricting. Kubla Khan wasn't here to fight; he was here to leave a mark, plant a seed, ensure his presence echoed long after he was gone.

Riichi's grip tightened, knuckles going white. He fought against the storm clawing at his restraint, every inhale pushing back the anger swelling beneath the surface. His jaw clenched, eyes narrowing as he refused to speak, offering only silent defiance. He wouldn't give Kubla Khan any opening to manipulate him further.

The Reborn Conqueror's smirk barely shifted, but a deeper glint of satisfaction appeared in his demeanor. The reaction wasn't unexpected—it had been anticipated. Calculated.

In the distance, Takoda felt the tremor of anger pulse through their bond, sharp as a blade against her senses. She clenched her fists, forcing her inhales to slow, pushing every ounce of focus into steadying him. *Stay with me, Riichi. Don't let him pull you under.* She sent another pulse of calm, but it frayed at the edges, barely making it through the storm within him.

Through the commlink, her voice came, tight, strained. "I'm trying, but he's slipping. He's close to breaking."

Eileen's voice followed, sharp and commanding. "Stay with us, Riichi. Hold your ground."

Takoda's heart pounded. She could feel the fight inside him, the war between command and fury. *Come on, Riichi.* She drove another surge of calm into their bond, willing him to anchor himself to her.

But Kubla Khan had already seen the crack in Riichi's armor, and like any conqueror, he pressed forward with unshaken confidence.

"Why resist, Riichi?" His voice was quiet, even. Not a taunt, not a provocation—just a statement of inevitability. "You've done it before. You let it take you once. Who knows, maybe you'll choose differently this time."

The words slipped into the silence like a dagger into flesh.

Riichi's fingers twitched over his katana's hilt, his body tense, restrained—but fraying. His voice came low, tight with restraint. "I am not like you."

Kubla Khan exhaled, the sound carrying finality like a blade sliding into its sheath. "Ah. So, you do speak." Amusement was light, but an edge crept beneath it. "I was beginning to wonder if Takoda favored the silent type."

The air around them sharpened.

Takoda stiffened at the sound of her name.

Rowan swore under his breath.

Khan's smile remained, impassive, as if he'd anticipated the shift in Riichi's energy. He watched the tension coil in his frame, restraint fraying, control stretched thin beneath the pressure of unspoken words. "I'll have to get to know her myself," he mused, almost absentminded. "She seems… intriguing."

The image struck before Riichi could stop it—Takoda, caught in the shadow of this man, forced into the same suffocating space he now occupied. Rage surged, white-hot and immediate, demanding an outlet.

He won't touch her. The thought was fire in his veins, a promise as much as a warning.

Already turning, the Reborn Conqueror exuded the effortless certainty of a man who had already won. "You and Takoda… not quite ready, but close." His focus shifted back to Riichi, satisfaction settling there. "When you are, I'll be back. Don't make me wait too long."

Then, as though he'd never been there, Kubla Khan stepped back into the mist, his form dissolving into the swirling fog, leaving only the echo of his existence.

Rowan, seeing the strain in Riichi's frame and the dangerous flicker in his expression, spoke urgently into the commlink. "Shit—he's lost it. We need to pull him out."

Instantly, Eileen's voice cut through the haze, sharp and demanding. "Reed and Ivy, get Riichi to Takoda now! Everyone else, retreat immediately."

The words barely registered, drowned beneath the fury consuming him. Kubla Khan's memory still clung to him, stirring old fire and pain. Then, a firm hold locked onto his shoulder—Reed, securing him. Ivy's fingers curled around his arm, her energy coiling like unseen threads. In a rush of motion, the world blurred around them.

When his boots hit solid ground, the storm inside him didn't still. He fought against the restraint, muscles taut with raw aggression, but Reed's hold was unyielding. Takoda was already there, cutting through the chaos like a blade of light.

She felt his emotions before even touching him, the bond between them humming with his barely contained wrath. Her hand found his arm, warmth against stress, her soothing touch settling into his skin. "Riichi," she murmured, her voice threading through the storm inside him. "I'm here. Just breathe."

He turned to her, his look fierce but distant, as if staring beyond her into a battlefield that no longer existed. Kubla Khan's words and the ghosts of memory weighed heavily on him.

Takoda didn't flinch. She only stepped closer—solid, unwavering.

"You're not there," she said, her voice strong, each word an anchor against the tide pulling him under. "You're here. With me."

His fingers tightened around the hilt of his katana, muscles locked in a grip he refused to loosen. Takoda didn't look away. She placed her hands gently on his face, re-centering him with her touch. "Look at me," she whispered, quiet but resolute. "I'm here. I'm safe."

His muscles knotted, but the tension in his frame refused to ease. Reed's grasp remained firm, holding him back, unwilling to release until Riichi loosened his own hold. The katana stayed clenched, an extension of his fury, unwilling to be set aside.

Takoda exhaled slowly, shutting out the world around her. She reached deeper, sensing his anger—wild and barely contained. She didn't suppress it; instead, she wove herself into it, countering the chaos with waves of calm, anchoring him to her, to their connection.

A flicker of recognition passed through him, the sharp edges of his fury dulling. His awareness shifted—not entirely, but enough. His hands loosened. The katana slipped from his hand, hitting the dirt with a muted thud. Reed nudged it away before cautiously releasing his hold.

The storm inside him didn't vanish. It never would. But as Riichi exhaled, the rigidity in his body eased, and without a word, he reached for Takoda, pulling her close.

She didn't hesitate. She wrapped herself around him, her touch firm yet gentle, a silent promise that she wasn't letting go. He buried his face in her shoulder, his body still trembling from the aftershocks of the fury that had nearly consumed him. The fear, frustration, and the raw edges of everything Kubla Khan had unearthed still simmered beneath his skin, but she was there, keeping him from sinking too deep.

Takoda moved instinctively, her hands running steady lines down his back, her presence easing the last of the stiffness from his muscles. She let her own energy settle, guiding him with each breath, each movement a calming reassurance. The fury inside him was still there, buried beneath the surface, but for now, it no longer held power over him.

Through the commlink, Eileen's voice was measured, understanding the vulnerability of the moment. "Oak, put a protective wall around them. Now!"

Oak raised a shield around them, the barrier solidifying into an opaque enclosure, cutting them off from the world beyond. Takoda immediately reached up, unfastening her commlink and then Riichi's, silencing both with deliberate precision. The stillness enveloped them, leaving only the sound of their quiet exhalations between them.

She held Riichi closer, her voice low, certain. "I'm here," she murmured, pressing her hands into his back, focusing him. "Whatever comes next, we stand against it." Her words held no reluctance, no doubt—she needed him to feel that, to believe it.

The last threads of fury unraveled in her embrace, replaced by a heavier weight—not wrath, but raw exhaustion. Riichi pulled back just enough to meet her stare, his eyes still burning with the embers of everything Kubla Khan had awakened in him. His hand cupped her face, firm and anchoring. Then he leaned in, capturing her lips in a kiss that was more than release—it was a claim, a turning point in the chaos that had nearly consumed him.

Takoda didn't flinch. She met him where he was, letting him pour the remnants of his turmoil into her, into them. But she wouldn't let him drown in it. As the kiss broke, she rested her forehead against his, her hands sliding up to his shoulders—firm yet reassuring. "You have to let go of this," she said softly, her voice carrying the same resolute strength that had supported him before.

A slow, uneven sigh escaped him. "I know," he admitted, his voice reluctant. "But when he mentioned you…" He stopped, jaw clenched, fingers tightening on her waist before he forced himself to loosen them. "I couldn't stop it."

Takoda's hands moved, cradling his face, her thumbs brushing the tension from his jaw. "That's exactly why he said it," she reminded him evenly. "Because he knew you'd react." She didn't soften the truth, didn't coddle him with reassurances he wouldn't believe. Instead, she met his frustration with unwavering confidence. "But you didn't lose control, Riichi. You pulled back. You're still *you*—I see it. I see *you*."

His jaw tightened, but she didn't pull away, didn't look at him with doubt or fear. There was no hesitation in her expression, no indecision. Just *her*—the same Takoda who had stood beside him before all of this, who wasn't about to step back now.

He pressed her against the wall Oak had conjured, fingers trembling where they held her waist, his hold desperate in a way he couldn't name. The fracture inside him deepened—she could feel it, the sharp edges of his frustration dulling, the restless energy shifting. He loosened his hold, his body calming as her presence wrapped around him, securing him in something real.

Finally, he turned to her again, the storm within him beginning to subside. His forehead dropped to her shoulder, arms circling her waist, and she felt the last of his resistance slip away. He still burned, still carried the fire Kubla Khan had stoked in him, but he wasn't drowning in it anymore.

Takoda wrapped her arms around him, one hand sliding into his hair, supporting him. "Your anger doesn't scare me," she whispered, her lips brushing his temple. "It never will."

His exhale was long, meticulous, forcing out the last of his turmoil. He held onto her for a moment longer, letting the final remnants of fury dissipate.

They stayed like that until she felt the conflict fully leave him, until she was sure he had steadied. Then, pulling back slightly, she searched his face, fingers trailing along his cheek in a quiet, affectionate touch.

"Are you ready?" she asked, her voice soft but sure.

He nodded, easing his grip on her as he straightened, fierce resolve returning to his stance. "Yeah," he said, quieter, but with certainty.

Takoda retrieved her commlink, fastening it back into place before securing Riichi's. With a subtle nod to Oak, the barrier dissolved moments later.

As the protective shield faded, Riichi caught Eileen's attention, her inscrutable stare meeting his. He didn't flinch. He didn't waver. His character remained steady, his purpose sharp.

He was ready.

"Let's go," he said, his voice carrying the steel of someone who had been tested—and come out the other side.

From the shadows, Kubla Khan lingered, his presence coiled in the mist, patient and knowing. A slow smile curved his lips, the glint in his gaze reflecting a thought left unsaid.

"Perfect," he murmured, his tone dark and amused. "A few more moments, and they will be exactly where I need them." His voice was smooth, every word laced with ominous intent.

Radiant Surge was nearly within his grasp.

And the game had only just begun.

The mansion's main hall lay in a heavy silence as the Fallen drifted in, exhaustion trailing them like shadows. An oppressive stillness clung to the air, thick and unrelenting, the strain of the night etched into their bodies. Kubla Khan had appeared, his taunts laced with a venom that refused to fade, wrapping around the team like a lingering frost. The hall—usually a place of refuge—felt cavernous, its vastness amplifying the quiet turmoil each of them carried.

At the center stood Eileen, constant and adamant, the axis around which the team naturally gathered. The quiet authority she carried provided stability, offering a presence that was both reassuring and determined. She let the silence stretch, allowing them a breath before she spoke, her voice thoughtful, laced with comprehension.

"Tonight, each of you faced more than the mission itself. You stayed strong, even when the battle turned inward."

The words hung in the air, cutting through the oppressive stillness. They were straightforward, offering no comfort or embellishment. Just recognition—the kind that didn't seek to soothe but to remind them of what they had endured.

She looked intently, stopping at each team in turn.

"Reed, Ash, Ivy—your vigilance bought us the time we needed."

Reed gave a clipped nod, his usual sharpness dulled by fatigue. Ivy and Ash exchanged a fleeting glance, a quiet pride glimmering beneath the strain of the mission.

She shifted her attention to the Emotional Manipulation Team.

"Takoda, Oak, Willow, Birch—you held us secure when our own emotions could have unraveled everything."

Takoda's lips curved into a faint, weary smile. Beside her, Birch pressed a hand to Oak's shoulder in silent recognition, their shared experience needing no words.

She finally focused her attention on the Disruption Team—Riichi, Rowan, Aislinn, Elder, and Vine. They stood slightly apart, the echoes of Kubla Khan's taunts still rippling through them. Eileen's gaze rested on Riichi, her nod carrying an unspoken acknowledgment, a reassurance meant solely for him.

"You dismantled the ritual with precision, even in the face of a force designed to break you."

The weight in her tone made it clear—she saw what had gone unexpressed, what they wouldn't yet say aloud.

She drew a slow breath, then let it out, her final words firm, steadfast.

"This mission tested more than our strength. It tested who we are together. Tonight, you proved that what we build here—this unity—is our greatest weapon."

The sentiment didn't erase the strain in the room, but it wove through it, reinforcing what mattered most. Even after a night like this, they weren't standing alone.

As the team began to disperse, Eileen remained fixed on Takoda and Riichi. A subtle nod. Stay.

She inclined her head toward her office, the gesture quiet but distinct. There was more to say—more to address—but she would give them a moment to collect themselves first.

As the other Fallen filtered out of the main hall, Vine remained by the window, his eyes fixed on the darkness beyond. His usual easy confidence had dimmed, replaced by a quiet rigidity in his posture. He had held his ground tonight, but Kubla Khan's taunts toward Riichi lingered, sharpening the unease beneath his otherwise controlled exterior.

From across the room, Ariel caught his silence. Decisively, she crossed the distance between them, her usual energy tempered by an intelligence she didn't have to voice. She stopped beside him, leaning against the windowsill, her voice light yet sure.

"You good? The mission sounded… intense."

Vine pulled his focus from the window, offering a half-smile that barely reached his eyes. "Yeah. Just wasn't expecting Kubla Khan to show up. Not sure I was as sharp as I should've been." His tone remained even, but the way his fingers flexed at his sides betrayed the doubt beneath it.

Ariel nudged him with her shoulder, her smirk knowing yet composed. "You handled it. We both know you don't back down when it counts." She crossed her arms, arching a brow before breaking into a grin. "And if there's a 'Most Unshakable' award, you've got my vote."

He let out a slow breath, some of the stress bleeding from his frame. Her confidence wrapped around him like a balancing force, reminding him of what had been accomplished rather than what still lingered in his mind. His smirk turned sharper, more familiar.

"Appreciate it, Ariel. You always know how to keep things in perspective."

They stood there in comfortable silence, the kind that didn't require conversation. For the first time since the mission ended, Vine allowed himself to stop thinking and just be. Ariel met his gaze briefly before tapping his shoulder, her usual spark flickering back.

"Next time, I'll have snacks waiting. Or at least coffee strong enough to burn through whatever hell you walk into."

Vine huffed out a quiet chuckle, the last of his tension unraveling. "I'll hold you to that."

Down the hall, voices faded into the distance, leaving behind the kind of quiet Elder preferred. He stood with his arms crossed, staring down the dim corridor, his thoughts running over the night's events. He had no doubts about his role, no regrets about his choices—but Kubla Khan's presence changed everything. The demon wasn't just another opponent. He was a calculated force, one that wouldn't be easy to predict.

Footsteps approached, unhurried but careful. Rain stepped up beside him, her charisma calm and absolute. She didn't speak right away, giving him room to acknowledge her on his own terms.

"Long night, huh, Nik?" she murmured, her voice carrying the kind of ease that invited conversation without demanding it. A small, knowing smile tugged at her lips.

Elder turned, exhaling through his nose before answering. "Yeah." The word was simple, but layered beneath it was the gravity of what they had witnessed.

She didn't press. Instead, she met his gaze, her voice as steady as her presence. "You're always the one holding the earth beneath us. But you know… it's okay to let someone else support you, too."

The words landed deeper than he expected, though he didn't show it. Rain had a way of seeing past what people said—past what they allowed themselves to show.

She reached out, her hand resting lightly on his arm, her touch slow, thoughtful. Elder exhaled, his shoulders losing the last of their strain, the simple gesture cutting through the weight he hadn't realized he was still carrying.

They stood there, the silence between them easy, mutual understanding settling in, a quiet reassurance that no words could capture. Rain's hand stayed, her presence offering a silent promise—one of staunch support, a constant she hoped he could rely on.

After a moment, she gave his arm a firm pat and stepped back. "Get some rest. You're going to need it."

Elder huffed a low breath, neither agreeing nor arguing, but the rigid tension in his stance loosened slightly, his shoulders relaxing. "You, too."

Without another word, Rain turned and walked away, leaving Elder to his thoughts—but no longer weighed down by them.

★★★

In the quiet of her office, Eileen stood near her desk, her face soft yet definite as she welcomed Riichi and Takoda inside. The room, bathed in the glow of a single lamp, carried a tranquility that contrasted with the night's turmoil. She let the silence subside first, offering them a moment to breathe before she spoke.

"Tonight was more than any of us expected," she began, her voice both gentle and resolute. "And I saw each of you rise to the challenge with strength and focus."

Her eyes shifted from one to the other, her quiet pride evident, as if she could still see the enormity of Kubla Khan's taunts pressing against them.

"Kubla Khan didn't make it easy for either of you." There was no doubt in her words, only clear insight. "His tactics were calculated, designed to provoke, to throw you off balance—but you didn't back down." The appreciation in her tone was clear, offering validation she knew they both needed.

She turned to Riichi, her focus sharpening as she studied the tension beneath his otherwise composed exterior.

"Riichi, I know Kubla Khan aimed to strip away your control, to force you into doubt and anger. But you didn't let him." Her voice was firm, leaving no room for uncertainty. "That restraint, that focus you showed tonight? That's your strength, and it's greater than anything he tried to use against you. You didn't lose control—you proved just how unbreakable you are."

Riichi held her gaze, his shoulders easing slightly. His response was simple but filled with quiet gratitude. "Thank you, Eileen."

Eileen shifted her attention to Takoda, kindness filling her expression.

"Takoda, your focus kept him—and all of us—grounded tonight," she said, sincerity laced in every word. "It's a rare strength, one we all rely on more than you know."

Takoda gave a small, modest smile. "Thank you."

Eileen nodded, her tone shifting into a gentler resolve, firm yet reassuring. "These tests will keep coming, but you've already proven that you're more than capable. And if there's anything weighing on you from tonight, I'm here whenever you need."

A beat of silence passed before Takoda spoke, her voice quiet but considered.

"Kubla Khan… was he always a demon? Or was he human first?"

Eileen's expression flickered—not hesitation, but a careful deliberation. "He was human once," she confirmed, her voice steady. "Everything history records about him, as you know it, is true. He was a powerful warlord, ambitious and relentless, expanding his empire with an iron will."

She let the words land before continuing. "But history only tells part of the story."

Eileen's gaze sharpened. "When he died, his soul should have moved on. But it didn't. His hunger—for power, for excess—was too great. It clung to him, refusing to let go."

"And that is how he became what he is now." Her voice carried absolute conviction. "He didn't just fall into darkness—he was devoured by it. And in return, it shaped him into a force more monstrous than the man he once was."

The silence that followed was thick with understanding. He hadn't simply become a demon. He had been transformed by his own insatiable greed.

Takoda took in the answer, but it wasn't enough. She glanced at Riichi, cautious, thoughtful. She wasn't asking just for herself—she was asking for him, too.

"Then… why now?" She looked back and forth between the two of them, careful with her words. "If he's from your time, Riichi, why hasn't he appeared before? What changed?"

Riichi's jaw tightened, but his gaze remained locked. He hadn't asked himself that question—not yet.

Eileen exhaled, folding her arms. "Some demons don't move until the right conditions are met." She looked at Riichi, then back to Takoda, her voice even but edged with consideration. "Timing. Influence. Opportunity. Whatever's happening now—this is what he's been waiting for."

A heavier stillness filled the room, carrying a new realization. Kubla Khan's arrival wasn't a coincidence. It was premeditated. Calculated. And that meant he wasn't going to disappear quietly.

Takoda studied Riichi, her expression cool, no pressure behind it—just a quiet promise that when he was ready to speak, she would be there.

When they left Eileen's office, the hallway outside was dim, shadows pooling in quiet pockets along the walls, reflecting the magnitude of the night's challenges. Riichi and Takoda walked side by side, their steps restrained, silence hanging between them like an invisible thread they were each reluctant to break.

Riichi's posture was firm, eyes fixed forward, his expression set in a serious, thoughtful line. His hands clenched briefly at his sides now and then, as though reaching for control over doubts still present from their encounter with Kubla Khan. Beside him, Takoda kept her arms folded lightly across her chest, her gaze occasionally flicking toward him, her eyes filled with questions she wasn't ready to ask and a worry she couldn't shake.

They continued in silence, each caught in their own thoughts until, finally, Riichi broke it, his voice low and resolute. "Let's talk. In my room."

Takoda looked at him, nodding. A mixture of curiosity and apprehension played across her face, but she didn't press for more. She simply followed him, a silent agreement guiding each step.

When they entered Riichi's room, the soft glow of a single lamp stretched across the modest furnishings, casting warmth over the neatly arranged belongings and carefully made bed. Normally, the space reflected his quiet discipline—structured, controlled. Tonight, it felt more like a place to breathe.

Without a word, Takoda sank onto the edge of the bed, elbows resting on her knees, fingers loosely laced together. Riichi leaned against the table, arms folded, his features carefully guarded, the strain of the night sinking into the silence that stretched between them. It wasn't insecurity —just a moment they both needed before the discussion.

Takoda exhaled, her voice stable despite the uncertainty threading through it. "I feel like we're holding back… things that need to be said." She traced idle patterns against the fabric of her pants before looking up. "If I weren't here—if the bond hadn't formed—Kubla Khan wouldn't have come for you now." Her throat tightened. "Maybe it would be better for you if I walked away."

The words tumbled out before she could pull them back. She hadn't planned to say them—but the thought had been there, lurking at the edges of her mind.

Riichi stilled.

Not a flinch, not a recoil —a complete stop. She felt his reaction before she saw it, in the sharp inhale, the way his arms dropped from their folded stance, fingers curling into fists at his sides.

"Takoda." His voice was low, but the intensity behind it left no space for argument.

She swallowed, forcing herself to meet his gaze.

"Don't."

A muscle ticked in his jaw, his grip tightening against the table as if reining in the impulse to reach for her right then and there. "You think walking away would make this easier?" His voice remained even, but clear-cut frustration crept into the edges. "That it would change anything?"

Takoda's breath wavered, but she didn't look away.

"If you weren't here, he'd still come." Riichi shook his head, exasperation threading through his words. "The only difference is, I'd have to face him alone." He let the importance of that take hold before pushing off the table, crossing the space to sit beside her. Not rushed, not forceful— intentional. His voice softened, though the certainty in it didn't tremble. "I don't want that."

Takoda turned, watching him carefully, searching for hesitation. There was none.

Her fingers curled against the edge of the blanket. "I just… I don't want to be the reason things get harder for you."

Riichi exhaled sharply, rubbing his palms against his thighs before settling them on his knees. "You're not." His voice was firm, leaving no room for doubt. "Takoda, you being here isn't making this harder. It's the only thing making it bearable."

She looked up, her face reflecting a hint of doubt.

Riichi leaned forward, his voice lowering. "Kubla Khan doesn't scare me. But you leaving? That would be worse than dealing with him. I don't want to face him if it means doing it without you."

Her doubt faded, replaced with quiet resolve. She gave a small nod, her grip tightening in wordless agreement.

Only then did Riichi's jaw tighten, his focus shifting inward.

"But I am afraid of one thing."

Takoda leaned closer to him, brows drawing together. "What is it?"

His fingers trembled as he avoided her gaze. "You seeing me… the way he described."

She didn't need to ask what he meant. The man he had been before. The warrior who had let wrath consume him so completely that it had cost him everything.

Takoda didn't flinch. Instead, she reached for him, her fingers wrapping gently around his wrist. The affection in her touch pulled his attention back to her, rooting him in the present, in the truth of who he was now. "I told you—your anger doesn't scare me. I don't need you to be unshakable, Riichi." Her voice was quiet but sure. "I just need you here…with me. That's all I've ever needed."

The words settled deep. Riichi let out a slow breath, the tension in his shoulders easing. She wasn't afraid of who he had been.

And she wasn't going anywhere.

Takoda rested her hand on Riichi's arm, and warmth surged beneath her palm, rolling over her skin like a slow-moving current. A soft, orange glow expanded outward, illuminating their hands in a constant pulse. The light stretched up their arms, encircling them in a radiance that cast golden reflections along the walls. The room itself felt charged, as if the very air recognized what was happening between them.

The glow wasn't new, but this time, it felt different—stronger, more absolute. The energy binding them together didn't just flicker at the edges of their connection—it took root, deeper than before.

Takoda's gaze drifted along the soft shimmer tracing Riichi's skin. *But what if I'm not enough? What if I'm still not what you need?*

The moment she thought the words, a ripple moved through the glow. A sensation, not quite touch but just as real, tightened in her chest. Before she could make sense of it, she heard Riichi's voice—not aloud, but inside her mind.

You are.

Her breath caught. Her pulse jumped.

She jerked her head up, wide eyes locking onto his. Riichi sat frozen, his fingers twitching, his own shock evident.

"Did you just hear that?" she asked, though she already knew the answer.

Riichi swallowed, his throat working against the pressure. "Yeah. I heard you."

She opened her mouth, then closed it, testing the new awareness between them. Carefully, tentatively, she thought the words rather than spoke them.

I don't understand how this is happening.

Riichi's head tilted, his brows furrowing. His reply wasn't spoken. *Neither do I.*

The gravity of the realization took root between them. This wasn't just a bond. It was evolving, shifting into a connection neither of them had fully grasped until now.

The glow flared, pulsing with heat, but it didn't burn. It wrapped around them, pressing close, as if the energy itself was responding to the trust forming between them.

Takoda took a slow step forward, closing the space between them. Riichi remained still, letting her move at her own pace, but his eyes never left hers.

She reached for him again, her fingers grazing the edge of his sleeve before trailing down his forearm. The stiffness in his muscles was still there, coiled beneath his skin, but his breathing slowed.

This is real, she thought, half to herself, half to him.

Riichi lifted a hand, catching hers, their fingers pressing together. *It is.*

The glow cast golden light over his face, highlighting the sharp angles of his jaw, the quiet steadiness in his expression. Takoda studied him, searching for any lingering doubt, but there was none. He believed in this. In them.

Her throat tightened. *"I need you to know…"* Her voice faltered briefly, but she pushed forward, needing him to hear the words. *"No matter what happens, I'm here."*

Riichi exhaled slowly, as if releasing a tension he hadn't realized had taken hold. His grip on her hand tightened, just slightly.

"I know."

Takoda didn't hesitate. She leaned up, closing the final distance between them, her lips brushing his in a kiss that wasn't rushed, wasn't desperate—but carried the quiet certainty that she meant every word.

Riichi responded instantly. His free hand slid into her hair, fingers threading through the strands, his thumb brushing just behind her ear. There was no hesitation, no need for restraint—just the undeniable pull of wanting her closer.

Takoda inhaled, her hands drifting over his shoulders. He kissed her like she belonged to him, like he had no intention of letting go.

The kiss intensified, her fingers tangling in his hair as she pulled him closer, pressing into him without a second thought.

The glow between them surged.

Riichi let out a quiet breath against her lips, his arm slipping around her waist. She felt the shift in him—not just in the way he moved but in the way he allowed himself to feel.

By the time they pulled apart, their foreheads still close, the golden light had dimmed, leaving behind only the warmth it had woven into them.

Riichi was the first to speak, his voice low but steady. "We'll move forward, no matter what."

Takoda let her fingers trace down his arm, her hand settling into his, their fingers slotting together with practiced ease.

"We will."

The tenderness between them remained as they moved through the quiet motions of getting ready for bed. Riichi pulled a t-shirt from his dresser and handed it to Takoda without a word.

She took it, offering a small nod of thanks before peeling off her mission-worn shirt and tugging the fresh one over her head. The soft fabric settled around her, carrying the faint scent of him—clean, familiar.

Riichi changed just as easily, swapping his sweat-dampened clothes for a plain shirt and loose pants before turning back to her.

He led her toward the bed. The moment she slid beneath the blankets, he followed, wrapping an arm around her and pulling her close.

Takoda nestled against his chest, her head resting over his heartbeat. The perpetual rhythm beneath her ear eased the last traces of worry, rooting her in the quiet.

Beneath the blankets, their hands found each other, fingers lacing together naturally.

A calm stretch of quiet carried a clarity that spoke for itself.

Their breaths slowed in sync, adoration settling between them. And as the night deepened, they drifted off—not just in exhaustion, but in the quiet certainty of belonging.

★★★

The morning light filtered through the curtains, casting a soft glow over Riichi and Takoda as they lay wrapped in the lasting warmth of sleep. Takoda stirred first, her eyes drifting open to find him still resting, his features relaxed in rare stillness. For someone always so controlled, there was an openness to him like this, free of the weight he always carried.

A faint smile tugged at her lips as she let herself enjoy the moment before Riichi's eyes flickered open, meeting hers with a quiet familiarity. "Good morning."

"Good morning," she murmured, their words easy, woven into the peaceful space between them.

They lay there a little longer, neither rushing to move, but eventually, the pull of the day's responsibilities broke through the peace. As they got up, Riichi gave her a small nod. "I'll meet you in the hall."

Takoda smiled before slipping into her own room.

The routine of a hot shower and fresh clothes helped ground them, easing them into the day ahead. When Takoda stepped into the hallway a few minutes later, Riichi was already there, waiting. His eyes passed over her—not in assessment, not in expectation, but in quiet appreciation.

She patted her pockets, then frowned. "Oh—I forgot a hair tie. Be right back."

Riichi followed as she stepped back into her room. He leaned against the doorframe, his presence unintrusive but steady while she rummaged through her suitcase. As she dug through her belongings, her fingers brushed against a small white pouch. Without thinking, she pulled it free and handed it to him. "Hold this?"

He took it without thought.

The moment his fingers curled around the fabric, the air around him seemed to still. A memory rose to the surface, sharp and immediate, as vivid as the instant it happened.

He was standing on the battlefield where he had died, the scent of blood and salt thick in the air, the weight of wrath still coiled inside him, even as Eileen stood before him. But she wasn't alone. Beside her, a girl clutched the very pouch now resting in his palm. *Takoda had been there.*

The realization struck him hard, the past colliding with the present in a way he hadn't been prepared for. His grip tightened around the pouch, his posture going rigid.

Oblivious to his reaction, Takoda found her hair tie and turned toward him, only to pause. Her brows pulled together, her gaze flicking over his face. "Riichi?"

He didn't answer immediately, forcing himself to exhale, grounding himself in the present. The weight in his chest didn't fade. "This pouch... where did you get it?" His voice was calm, but an edge of careful scrutiny rested beneath it.

She blinked, caught off guard by the question. "Oh, this?" She smiled, rubbing her fingers over the fabric. "I've had it since I was a kid. It was a gift from my mother. I don't know why, but it's always brought me comfort. I even keep it nearby when I sleep."

Her answer confirmed what he already knew. This wasn't coincidence. Takoda had been there the day he became Fallen. She had been a constant comfort at a time he hadn't even realized he needed.

He schooled his expression as he handed the pouch back to her, his fingers lingering for a fraction of a second before he pulled away. "This... it's important." His voice carried quiet weight, but he didn't elaborate.

Takoda tucked the pouch back into her suitcase, curiosity flashing across her face. "Are you sure you're okay?"

Riichi straightened, nodding once. "I need to speak with Eileen."

She studied him but didn't push, offering him a gentle smile instead. "Okay...I'll be downstairs when you're ready."

He watched as she left, then exhaled slowly, pressing his fingers against his temple.

Takoda had always been part of his story.

Even before he had known her name.

★★★

The morning was quiet, sunlight stretching across the room as Aislinn stirred beneath the blankets. Rowan's arm rested heavily around her waist, the heat of his body holding her in place. She could tell by the steady rhythm of his breathing that he was already awake.

She turned slightly, meeting his gaze. "Morning."

His voice was rough with sleep. "Mornin'."

Neither of them moved at first, staying in the comfort of waking up together. Eventually, Rowan sighed and stretched, his muscles tensing briefly before he shifted onto his back. "I'm gonna grab a shower."

Aislinn hummed in acknowledgment, her eyes following him as he sat up and ran a hand through his already-messy hair. He pressed a kiss to her temple before pushing to his feet and making his way toward the bathroom.

She listened as the water started running, the uniform sound filling the room. A tender thought drifted through her mind—I could just join him.

And before she even processed the idea, the space around her lurched.

The warmth of the blankets vanished, replaced by a sudden rush of steam and scalding water. She gasped as the spray soaked through her clothes, her breath catching at the shock of heat against her skin. Rowan swore, his hand bracing against the tile as he blinked at her through the mist.

Aislinn stared back, water dripping from her lashes, the reality of what had just happened sinking in.

Rowan dragged a wet hand down his face, exhaling slowly. "Should I be flattered or concerned?"

She shoved her soaked hair back. "I didn't mean to! I was just thinking about—" She cut off, the realization hitting her like a punch in her chest. She had thought about joining him. And now she was here. She had teleported.

Rowan's brows lifted slightly, his voice as dry as ever. "Figured you'd wait till after breakfast to start ignoring personal boundaries."

Aislinn groaned, shoving the glass door open and stepping onto the tile, water streaming off her as she stripped off her soaked clothes. Rowan kept showering, his tone casual as he spoke over the water.

"We should probably talk to Eileen about this."

"No kidding," she muttered, wringing out her hair before reaching for fresh clothes.

She grabbed a shirt, but before she could even pull it over her head, the space around her shifted again.

The rush of water crashed over her for the second time, heat pouring down as she landed right back where she started.

Rowan let out a slow breath through his nose, bracing his hands against the tile as she appeared in front of him for the second time. "Right. So, flattered and concerned."

Aislinn let out a sharp breath, running her fingers through her hair in frustration. "I swear, I am not doing this on purpose."

Rowan caught her waist, securing her in case she decided to vanish again mid-sentence. "Yeah, I got that part." His fingers flexed against her damp skin, his grip casual but firm. "Maybe stay this time—just so I can keep an eye on you."

She sighed, frustration clear in the tightness of her shoulders. "I don't even know how to control it. It's like it just… happens."

Rowan nodded, his expression shifting from amused to focused. "Then we need to figure out what's triggering it. Could be instinct. Could be emotional."

Aislinn let out a dry laugh. "Great. So, I need to either suppress my thoughts or start wearing a tracking device."

His smirk was brief as he reached for the shampoo. "I'll settle for keeping you in arm's reach."

She sighed, leaning into the warmth of the water as she let the tension in her body ease. The lack of control over her ability gnawed at her, but Rowan's calm presence kept her grounded.

They finished showering, Rowan keeping deliberate contact every now and then—his fingers brushing her arm, the occasional touch to her wrist—subtle, but intentional. Once they were dressed and ready to head downstairs, he caught her hand, fingers lacing through hers as he pulled her close.

"You feeling stable, or do I need to tie you to me?"

Aislinn huffed a laugh. "I think I can manage."

"Mm." He didn't look convinced, but he gave her shoulder a light squeeze before taking her hand again as they started toward the stairs.

She sighed, pressing against his side for just a moment. "This is going to be a long day."

Rowan's grip tightened slightly, his thumb brushing over her knuckles. "Then let's get through it together."

★★★

Each step toward Eileen's office felt weighted with the questions Riichi couldn't ignore. The small white pouch had stirred memories he hadn't revisited in years, vivid and irrefutable, drawing him back to that day when he'd become one of the Fallen. Images of Eileen standing with the little girl beside her—Takoda, he now realized—flashed through his mind with startling clarity. Determination guided his every step, demanding answers he wasn't sure he was ready to fully confront.

He reached her office, opened the door, and stepped inside, closing it firmly behind him. Eileen looked up from her desk, her calm expression as familiar as it was unnerving, a small, knowing smile touching her lips as if she had been expecting him all along.

"You remember," she said simply.

Riichi nodded, the flicker of frustration in his gaze tempered by his respect for her. Eileen had always seemed to know what they wanted to discuss before they spoke, her intuitive foresight a mystery he'd learned not to question too closely. Her gaze held solid, inviting him to proceed.

"Who was the little girl, Eileen?" His tone was low but direct, cutting to the heart of his question.

Eileen's expression gentled, though her composure held firm. "I think you already know," she said, her voice calm yet carrying a quiet conviction.

A surge of realization passed through him, his analytical mind confirming what he'd suspected from the moment he held that pouch. He needed to hear it from her, though, to ground the truth in her words. So, it was Takoda.

"Why was she there?" he asked, searching her face for answers.

Eileen didn't respond immediately. Instead, she tilted her head slightly, her expression thoughtful. When she finally spoke, it was with a gentle but resolute question of her own. "Riichi, how do you feel about Takoda?"

His patience wavered, irritation tinging his voice. "That doesn't answer my question, Eileen. Why was she there?"

Her posture shifted, her tone subtly authoritative, a reminder of her role as their leader. "You need to answer mine first, Riichi. How do you feel about Takoda?"

Exhaling sharply, Riichi felt frustration simmering just beneath the surface. He sank into a nearby chair, running a hand through his hair to steady himself before meeting her stare, trying to rein in his impatience. Eileen's way of leading conversations always felt like a riddle, both insightful and elusive.

"I care about Takoda… deeply. Is that what you wanted to hear?"

Eileen's expression softened, though her gaze remained probing, as though she were urging him to go further, to unearth the emotions he was trying to sidestep. "No. I want to know how you really feel."

Riichi clenched his fists, realizing that Eileen wouldn't let him evade his own truth. Rising from the chair, he began to pace, tension gathering in his shoulders, each step charged with annoyance. A glance at Eileen showed her seated calmly, her patient expression only intensifying his restlessness.

Finally, he stopped, forcing himself to draw a deep breath as his gaze fixed on the bookshelf along the wall. He steadied himself, anchoring in the quietness of the room before he turned back to face her. "I think…" His voice was low, almost vulnerable. "I *know* I'm falling in love with her."

Eileen said nothing, her presence quiet yet unruffled, offering him space to continue.

"If I let that feeling grow," he murmured, his voice barely above a whisper, "it would only be right to tell her about my past, the terrible things I did… What if she hates me? I don't know if I could bear that. What if I lose myself, just as I did before?" His eyes dropped, the enormity of his confession sinking in. "And Takoda… if I tell her, would it hurt her? I can't do that to her."

Eileen studied him, her face filled with compassion but penetrating, absorbing the weight of his fears. "Riichi, love is as much a choice as it is an emotion. To truly love someone is to let yourself be seen, even in the places you wish to hide." She held his stare, her tone staunch. "She's already touched those shadows within you without realizing it. That's why you feel this way; she is already your light."

Eileen rose from her chair, stepping closer, her voice gentle, as if sharing a truth she knew he needed to hear. "I understand your fear—that sharing your past might change how she sees you, that she might pull away. But Riichi, concealing it is the greater risk. Holding onto those memories as if they're a poison will only keep you chained to them. She deserves the chance to see you as you are, and you deserve the chance to let her truly know you."

Riichi lowered his gaze, visibly torn by the thought of causing Takoda pain. His jaw clenched as he weighed the cost of honesty.

"If she cannot accept your past," Eileen continued, "then perhaps she's not the one to help you bear it. But consider this—do you really believe she would abandon you so easily?

This woman who, without trying, found her way into your heart, who unknowingly gave you strength even as a child?" Eileen's eyes softened, her voice filled with a quiet confidence. "Takoda possesses a quiet strength. It's not fragility—it's resilience. Trust in that and allow her to decide for herself."

Eileen paused, letting her words sink into the silence between them.

"And as for your fear of losing yourself..." Her tone softened. "You're not the same man you once were. The Fallen aren't bound to remain who they were. Each day since your turning, you've chosen a different path. Takoda, in knowing your whole truth, can help you stay focused. She can be your balance, just as you can be hers. And if, by some chance, you lose yourself again—which I don't believe you will—she would be the one to call you back, just as she did before."

A faint spark of hope glinted across Riichi's face, though the burdens of his past remained in his eyes.

"I brought her to you that day," Eileen said softly, "because I knew, even then, that you needed her—and that she needed you. It's rare to find someone whose heart aligns with yours, who strengthens you simply by being close. That kind of bond is worth any risk. But you can't truly keep her near unless you're willing to let her see you—completely."

She took a step back, her gaze unremitting, allowing him to process her words.

"Yes, she might be hurt by what you reveal. But Riichi, she'll be hurt far more if she discovers that you didn't trust her enough to share it." A gentle, encouraging smile touched her lips. "Love often brings pain, but it's a gift when that pain leads to understanding."

Her eyes held his, offering quiet reassurance. "And remember, you're not alone. I am here. She is here. You're surrounded by those who would stand by you, if you'd let yourself believe it."

Riichi stood in silence, Eileen's words settling over him like a balm, easing the fear he'd carried for so long. He clenched his fists, letting her insights sink in fully. Could he really let Takoda see all of him—the darkness and mistakes he'd hidden for years? Part of him had always thought he had to carry this weight alone, that exposing it would unravel the life he'd rebuilt. But he saw now that hiding it might only push her away in the end.

Takoda deserves to know the real me, he thought. And maybe... maybe I deserve to show her.

Finally, he cleared his throat, meeting Eileen's steady gaze. "Thank you, Eileen," he said quietly, his voice calm but tinged with vulnerability. "You've given me a lot to think about." He paused, summing up his realizations in a few measured words. "I see now that Takoda deserves to know who I really am, and maybe... maybe it's time I stop hiding from that, too."

A faint, self-deprecating smile touched his lips as he looked away briefly. "I'll try to trust in what you've said—that I'm not alone in this."

He held her gaze a moment longer, offering a small, respectful nod that conveyed the depth of his gratitude, even if he couldn't fully express it in words.

Eileen's words settled in Riichi's mind, their weight mingling with his own thoughts. He turned to leave, but before he could take a step, her authoritative voice called him back, her tone shifting to the composed command of the Fallen's leader.

"Oh, and Riichi, before you go, there's one more thing," she said. Her voice remained resolute, but a glint of tenderness softened her gaze. "I've been inspired by another to grant each of the Fallen time off whenever possible. It seems we often overlook that rest is as essential as duty."

Riichi raised an eyebrow, uncertain of her intent but nodding respectfully, waiting for her to continue.

"With that said, I am officially relieving you of all duties today. You are free to do as you choose, and I suggest you use your time wisely." She paused, letting her words sink in, then added with a subtle, almost playful smile, "Takoda has leave for the day as well. She's earned it."

Riichi blinked, momentarily caught off guard, though he masked his surprise quickly. *Takoda?* He glanced back at Eileen, his mind racing with possibilities. Her serene smile suggested she knew exactly what she was doing.

"Consider it a chance for both of you to find some peace—perhaps together," she added, her gaze softening, a motherly encouragement slipping through her composed exterior. "You are dismissed, Riichi."

He inclined his head, a trace of gratitude in his expression as he took in her words. As Riichi stepped out of Eileen's office, a subtle tension wove through his thoughts, the significance of her words persistent even as he took in the quiet of the hallway. Today was his to spend with Takoda, a chance to break the silence of his past and let her closer than he'd ever allowed anyone before. But the questions he hadn't yet answered—about what he'd share, about how much he'd risk—hung like shadows at the edge of his mind.

A single thought surfaced, equal parts thrilling and unsettling: *What would she see when he finally let her in?*

Morning warmth settled into the kitchen, casting soft golden hues over the countertops where Takoda worked, her hands moving with practiced ease as she chopped vegetables and stirred eggs. The constant rhythm reinforced her, offering a sense of calm against the quiet worry lingering in the back of her mind. Riichi's sudden departure to speak with Eileen had left her troubled, though she couldn't quite name why.

Ariel entered first, her sharp attention catching on Takoda's slight distraction. With a teasing grin, she bumped Takoda's shoulder. "What're you cooking up this morning? Breakfast or big thoughts?"

Takoda laughed, brushing a stray piece of hair behind her ear. "Maybe both."

Ariel hummed, studying her for a beat before turning to make coffee. Aislinn slipped in next, greeting them with a soft smile before reaching for a mug. She sat beside Ariel, her gaze drifting toward Takoda in quiet curiosity. Aislinn had always been observant—she wouldn't say anything outright, but the way her eyes lingered made it clear she'd noticed the tension in Takoda's features.

The soft murmur of the coffee machine filled the kitchen as Rain entered, her presence calm as she poured herself tea. She took a seat at the table, cradling her mug between her hands, occasionally glancing at Takoda. A slight crease formed between her brows, as if she were piecing together the subtle tension in the room.

Takoda kept her focus on the skillet, but the growing silence surrounding her made her shoulders tighten. By the time Ivy and Willow wandered in, drawn by the smell of coffee, the air had shifted. The usual morning chatter was subdued, their greetings warm but watchful.

Finally, Takoda let out a breath, setting down her spoon. "It's just… Riichi was distant this morning. We talked after the mission last night, and I told him how I was afraid *I* was the reason Kubla Khan showed up. He assured me that wasn't the case, but now… I don't know. What if he's changed his mind?"

Ariel scoffed, but there was a hint of awareness beneath her usual teasing. "Riichi changing his mind? That doesn't sound like him." She nudged Takoda's arm, offering a lopsided grin. "But if *you're* worried, then yeah, you need to talk to him. You're not overthinking this."

Rain exhaled, considering. "If he really believed you were the reason Khan showed up, he wouldn't have reassured you in the first place. Riichi's not the type to lie just to spare feelings." Her expression softened. "But he *is* the type to shoulder burdens alone. Maybe he's wrestling with doubt about his own decisions and doesn't want to drag you into it."

Aislinn concurred. "That makes sense. When he almost died fighting Lucifer, you stayed with him the whole time—even when the rest of us had to pull back. He knows you're strong enough to handle the truth, Takoda. If he's struggling with guilt or doubt, he just needs a reminder that he doesn't have to deal with it alone."

Ivy crossed her arms, thoughtful. "Riichi's always been the type to carry responsibilities by himself, but if his feelings toward you had changed, I don't think he'd be distant—he'd be upfront about it. He wouldn't shut you out unless he was trying to work through something specific."

Willow nodded, her voice quiet but firm. "In all the years I've known him, I've never seen him trust anyone like he trusts you. That hasn't changed."

Takoda absorbed their words, their meaning settling deep. Maybe they were right. Maybe Riichi wasn't doubting *her*—maybe he was wrestling with the lingering impact of last night's encounter, questioning whether he could have done more.

Before she could respond, Vine strolled into the kitchen, clearly in search of coffee. The room fell into a sudden hush. Raising an eyebrow, he took in the scene.

"Oh, don't stop on my account." He smirked as he poured himself a cup. "Sounds like I walked in on a full-blown Riichi appreciation meeting. Anything insightful you'd like to share with the class?"

The girls exchanged amused glances, barely containing their laughter. Ariel gave an exaggerated sigh, waving him off. "Sorry, Vine—classified info. Girls only."

Vine chuckled, raising his hands in mock surrender. "Fine, keep your secrets. I won't tell Riichi I stumbled into his personal analysis session." With a smirk, he took his coffee and disappeared down the hall, leaving them laughing in his wake.

The tenderness of shared memories enfolded Takoda, her earlier worries easing beneath the quiet reassurance of their support. Glancing at the friends who had become family, she smiled. "Thank you. All of you. I don't know what I'd do without you."

They returned to breakfast preparations, their laughter and conversation weaving through the kitchen like a familiar melody. The moment carried on in easy camaraderie—until the air shifted.

Takoda turned just as a familiar figure appeared in the doorway. Riichi. His look met hers, a quiet openness settling in his features—not hesitant, not distant, just concrete.

The others noticed immediately, trading knowing smiles and subtle bobs of encouragement. Takoda straightened, her heart calming. Whatever was on his mind, she was ready to hear it.

Riichi stepped into the room as the laughter faded, his focus resting on Takoda with quiet affection. He offered a polite bow to the others before turning his full attention to her, a gentle smile easing onto his face.

"Takoda, could I have a moment with you?" His voice was soft, but the quiet urgency behind it made it clear—he wanted privacy.

She nodded, falling in beside him as they stepped out into one of the mansion's corridors. The air carried the faint scent of aged wood and old stone, the hush of the expansive halls wrapping around them. Ornate moldings and rich tapestries lined the walls, relics of the past that spoke to the history held within this place. Normally, she might have taken a moment to admire them, but her focus remained on Riichi, on the measured quiet between them.

He was thinking. Choosing his words carefully.

They walked in silence until they reached a recessed alcove, where soft light traced the intricate patterns in the marble floor. He turned to her then, his face composed—calm, yet carrying an underlying resolve.

"I wanted to apologize, Takoda," he said, holding her gaze. "I know I was distant this morning, and I could see it worried you."

A quiet exhale left her lips, some of the tension in her chest easing. He hadn't missed it.

Riichi continued, his tone measured but open. "I needed to speak with Eileen about my past... parts I haven't fully shared with you yet." A flicker of hesitation passed through his eyes, but he didn't look away. "She was there when I turned. There are things she understands that I'm still trying to process."

His honesty carried no excuses, only quiet sincerity.

She searched his face, taking in the way a muscle ticked in his cheek before he went on.

"I didn't want you to think I was shutting you out," he said. "I want to share everything with you—I just need to do it right."

Takoda's fingers curled slightly at her sides, resisting the urge to reach for him. His restraint wasn't a rejection; it was careful, deliberate. A promise that he wasn't hiding, only making sure he didn't give her pieces of himself too broken to carry.

After a beat, he exhaled, a hint of a smile ghosting his lips. "Eileen gave us the day off." His voice lightened, the shift subtle but telling. "I thought we could spend it together—just us, if you'd like."

The simple offer steadied her, easing some of the tension in her chest, but the unease from this morning still clung to the edges of her thoughts.

Riichi noticed. Of course he did.

Without a word, his presence reached for her through their bond, constant and reassuring. His voice filled her mind, quiet but dedicated.

You weren't the reason Khan showed up. And I don't want you to leave. His thoughts blanketed hers, firm yet laced with a sincerity that softened the weight of his words. *I meant what I said—I don't want to face him alone if it means you're not there.*

Her breath caught, his words sinking in with quiet finality. He wasn't just comforting her—he was making it clear. He wanted her beside him. Not out of duty. Not out of necessity. But because she was the one he trusted to stand with him.

Warmth stirred in her chest, dissolving the last of her doubts. Their hands remained clasped, a soft glow beginning to radiate from their joined fingers, golden-orange light pulsing gently as it spread up their arms—a visible reflection of their bond.

They stood in silence, wrapped in each other's company, the last traces of tension dissolving between them. Then Riichi shifted slightly, his thumb brushing against her knuckles as a knowing smile played at his lips.

"Just us," he said, his voice carrying quiet enthusiasm. "No missions. No distractions."

Takoda studied him, reading the subtle eagerness beneath his composed exterior. This wasn't just about taking a break—it was about choosing each other, about grounding themselves in what they were before the next battle came.

She squeezed his hand, the warmth of his presence sinking into her. "Then let's make it count," she murmured, her voice even now.

His fingers curled around hers in agreement. "Of course."

As they turned to walk together, the closeness of their bond lingered—not just encouragement, but a sure sign of their strength in adversity. Whatever lay ahead, they were a team built on trust.

Elsewhere in the mansion, a different kind of quiet had taken hold. In the conference room, the Fallen gathered around the long table, the tension of the night's mission settling over them like a shadow that refused to lift.

Eileen stood at the head, her composed dignity setting a focused tone for the meeting. As the others settled in, Oak entered with a pen and notepad in hand. Without a word, he took the seat beside her. Eileen's gaze flicked toward him briefly, noting the change, but she said nothing.

Encircling the table sat Rowan, Aislinn, Elder, Reed, Vine, Birch, Ivy, Ash, and Willow, each Fallen displaying a blend of fatigue and composure after their efforts.

Eileen began with a steady nod, addressing the team with a tenderness that softened her usual formality. "Riichi and Takoda are excused today," she announced. "They need this time to recover and regroup after the events of last night." Her words carried a consideration that was met with quiet signs of agreement.

After a brief pause, she continued, "Let's go over the mission results."

Rowan rose first, standing in for Riichi to report on the Destruction Team's role. His voice was clear and confident as he described their actions. "The Destruction Team successfully neutralized the ritual site. We dismantled the symbols and removed all ritual objects, disrupting the Golden Dawn's setup without drawing attention to our presence."

Rowan glanced at Vine, Elder, and Aislinn, acknowledging them with a small bow. "Vine, Elder, and Aislinn showed exceptional precision. Each played a crucial role in keeping the area secure under pressure."

The team exchanged appreciative glances, recognizing the Destruction Team's ability to execute under tense conditions.

Next, Reed leaned forward, providing a concise debrief on behalf of the Distraction Team. "Our team used shadows, illusions, and Ash's transformations to divert the cultist guards. Ivy's illusions were particularly effective," he added, giving her a nod, "and Ash's ability to transform kept the cultists confused and off-balance, buying us the time needed to clear the site without being detected."

Ivy and Ash shared a quick smile, acknowledging their teamwork, while the others conceded in appreciation for the seamless way the Distraction Team had covered the operation.

Following Reed, Oak stood to report on the Emotional Manipulation Team's efforts. His tone was calm but carried a hint of pride. "Our focus was on the cultists themselves. By introducing emotions of fear and doubt, we prevented them from regrouping. Takoda's empathic support was crucial to our strategy, adding a depth to the emotional influence we needed to keep them scattered."

The other Fallen members concurred, their respect for Takoda's contribution evident as they absorbed Oak's words. Though she wasn't present at this debriefing, her impact on the mission was evident, woven into the team's overall success.

Then Rowan's voice took on a darker tone as he shifted to the topic that weighed heaviest on the room. "There's also the matter of Kubla Khan," he began, his tone measured but serious. "The moment he appeared, it was like a dark storm moved through the area. His aura alone was overpowering."

A hush fell over the room as Rowan continued, his gaze sharpening. "From the moment he materialized, his focus was locked on Riichi. It felt as if the rest of us were merely spectators. We could do little but watch, unsure if intervening would escalate things further. Riichi, though, handled it… with incredible composure. He faced Kubla Khan directly, without flinching."

Rowan's demeanor turned grave. "It was clear that Khan was testing him, gauging his reaction. He seemed to be probing, taunting Riichi in a way that made us feel almost powerless, like he was holding all the cards."

A shiver ran through the room as Rowan described Kubla Khan's parting words. "Before he left, he issued a warning—a message that hinted at deeper plans still in motion. It was unsettling. The way he spoke left no doubt that he's playing a game we've only begun to understand."

Eileen surveyed the table, taking in the gravity of what Rowan had shared. As contemplative silence filled the room, she noted Oak quietly writing detailed notes in his notepad, his features inscrutable.

Vine spoke up first, his usual humor absent. "The ritual symbols… they had a different energy to them, like they were accessing a deeper source of power. My guess is the Golden Dawn has tapped into a force beyond what they previously controlled—something unstable." His insight sparked a few murmurs, concern flickering across the faces at the table.

Oak nodded thoughtfully, adding to Vine's comment. "The dark energy lingering at the ritual site wasn't just residual. It felt like it was tied to an ongoing ritual or a direct link to Kubla Khan himself." He exchanged a glance with Elder, who leaned forward, his tone steady but serious.

"Whatever that energy was, it's possible it could be a conduit or an anchor to a larger network of power," Elder suggested. "It could mean there's a broader plan in place, one that extends beyond a single ritual."

Aislinn, her expression pensive, raised a question. "Could the dark energy be a kind of… signature?" Her voice was soft but filled with determination. "Maybe Khan wanted us to find it, to let us know he was there. A tactic to discourage us, perhaps."

Several Fallen members agreed thoughtfully, considering Aislinn's theory. As discussion continued, Eileen's attention flicked to Oak once more, catching sight of him jotting down another note. She didn't acknowledge it, but she noticed.

Eileen's focus swept over the group as she transitioned into follow-up assignments, her calm authority anchoring the team's attention.

"First, Reed, Vine, and Birch," she began, "I'm assigning you to investigate Fort Lawton. Focus on detecting any residual energy, symbols, or signs that the Golden Dawn may still have influence there." She met each of their eyes, her tone firm. "Work carefully—these sites could still be marked."

The trio consented, exchanging glances that conveyed mutual resolve.

"For Georgetown," she continued, "Ivy, Ash, and Willow, you'll handle the investigation. Your task is to search for traces of ritual power and identify any symbols linked to Kubla Khan. There's a chance the Golden Dawn is still watching these sites, so take extra caution."

Ivy's stance shifted to one of thoughtful determination, and Ash gave a curt nod, while Willow's calm demeanor held relentless. Eileen's careful division of roles left no doubt about the precision of each assignment.

Before she could continue, Oak closed his notepad and spoke, his voice cool. "Elder and I will research Kubla Khan's and his title—'The Reborn Conqueror.' He deliberately called himself that last night, and I want to know why. If there's any historical or supernatural significance to it, it could give us insight into his goals."

Elder agreed, his thoughts clearly turning over the implications. "Titles carry weight, especially with beings as powerful as him. There's a reason he chose those words."

Eileen gave Oak a brief look, noting the initiative. She hadn't assigned him this, but she didn't need to—he had already taken on the responsibility.

Oak continued, turning toward Rowan and Aislinn. "I want the two of you to monitor Nihonmachi. Cultists could regroup there, and we need eyes on the ground. If the Golden Dawn is trying to establish deeper roots in Seattle, Nihonmachi is a place they might target."

Rowan nodded, his features neutral, though there was a flicker of approval in his posture. "I'll see what connections I can make and keep you and Eileen updated on anything I find."

Eileen regarded them both, then added, "Be discreet. We still don't know the full extent of the Golden Dawn's reach here, and I don't want them catching on that we're watching."

Aislinn's thoughtful gesture reflected her comprehension of the responsibility. "I'll analyze any symbols or patterns we find, see if they match previous Golden Dawn movements."

Eileen studied them for a moment before offering a brief bow.

The team shifted into a logistical discussion, with Reed proposing a rotating schedule for the Fort Lawton and Georgetown investigations to ensure continuous surveillance without drawing attention. The others agreed, finalizing the details.

Finally, Eileen offered a closing reminder, her tone resonant with quiet confidence. "Adaptability and vigilance are our allies in this fight. Trust in your skills and in each other. The insights you gather will help us stay one step ahead of the Golden Dawn."

As the Fallen began to disperse, Eileen turned slightly, catching sight of Oak closing his notebook. He had taken structured notes throughout the meeting, each detail recorded with a methodical precision she hadn't expected but appreciated.

She hesitated briefly before speaking, her tone quieter, more personal. "I appreciate your help today. It didn't go unnoticed."

Oak regarded her, his usual restraint tempered by a rare hint of warmth. He inclined his head slightly. "I told you I'd take a more active role. Just making good on that."

A flicker of a rare, small smile crossed Eileen's lips before she shifted focus back to the room.

Then, just as Rowan and Aislinn moved to leave, a shift in the air caught her attention.

Aislinn's posture was slightly off—not enough for anyone else to notice, but Eileen did. And Rowan, who was usually more composed, had an uncharacteristic tightness in his stance, his grip on Aislinn's arm firmer than necessary.

Eileen's brows knitted together.

"Rowan. Aislinn." Her voice carried its usual command, but there was an added layer of intent behind it. "A word before you go."

Rowan stopped mid-step, his demeanor deadpan, but Eileen didn't miss the way his lips pressed into a thin line.

Aislinn looked up at him briefly before turning back to Eileen, ambiguity flickering behind her guarded expression.

As the last of the Fallen exited, Eileen remained at the head of the table, watching Rowan and Aislinn closely. The door shut behind the others, leaving the three of them in silence.

Rowan's arms were crossed, his stance rigid, tension in every line of his frame. Aislinn, though composed, held a quiet hesitation—like there was more to the story than what she was prepared to say.

Eileen shifted her focus between them before leaning against the table, her voice even but expectant. "I assume this has something to do with why Rowan won't let go of you."

Aislinn exhaled. "Yeah. Because I keep disappearing."

Rowan's tone was edged with frustration. "She's been teleporting. Not on purpose."

Eileen remained quiet, waiting for them to explain.

Aislinn hesitated just slightly before speaking. "It happened this morning. Every time I—" she paused, adjusting her wording. "—tried to leave the room, I ended up in the bathroom instead. Over and over."

Rowan let out a sharp breath. "Every damn time."

Eileen studied Aislinn carefully. She had already known teleportation would manifest—she had seen it that night when Aislinn appeared outside Takoda's door. She had hoped it would emerge gradually, giving Aislinn time to adjust before it became disruptive.

That hope had just been disproven.

"It's accelerating," Eileen murmured, straightening. "I was hoping we'd have time to ease you into this, but that isn't an option anymore. We need to address it now."

Rowan's stare hardened. "Address what, exactly?" His focus darted between them, sharp with suspicion. "Teleportation isn't a normal Fallen ability. And if it's happening to her, that means it's coming from *you*."

Eileen had expected that conclusion. Rowan was too intelligent not to question it.

"I need your word first," she said, her tone calm but laced with quiet authority. "Before I explain anything, you must swear that nothing we discuss regarding Aislinn's powers—or mine—leaves this room."

Rowan's jaw tightened. "And why would I agree to that?"

Aislinn tensed beside him. "Rowan—"

"No," he cut in, gaze still locked on Eileen. "You've kept me in the dark about plenty already. I want to know why you need my silence before I just hand it over."

Eileen held his stare. "Because you're smart enough to know that the wrong information in the wrong hands would put Aislinn in danger."

A sharp glint flashed in Rowan's eyes—cold, calculating. He didn't like being backed into a corner, but he wasn't reckless enough to deny the truth of her words.

Slowly, he exhaled. "Fine. You have my word. But you will explain."

Eileen gave a small nod of acknowledgment before shifting her focus back to Aislinn. "Your teleportation isn't random. It's connected to me."

Aislinn frowned. "Because you have teleportation?"

Eileen inclined her head. "Yes. My abilities go beyond what the Fallen are capable of, and as my daughter, you're beginning to develop your own."

Rowan's gaze sharpened. "Then it won't stop at teleportation."

"No," Eileen confirmed simply.

Rowan studied her, suspicion darkening his expression. "If your powers surpass the Fallen, then *what exactly are you?*" His voice remained even, but there was a weight behind it—an implicit demand for answers. "And why haven't you used them to stop the Golden Dawn? Or the demons suddenly crawling out of the woodwork?"

Aislinn's attention snapped back to Eileen at that, her brow furrowing.

Eileen didn't flinch. "Because using my powers for Fallen duties is forbidden," she said, her tone measured. "And when I *do* use them, there are consequences."

Rowan didn't react outwardly, but his fingers curled slightly where they rested against his arms. "For you?"

"Yes."

His attention flicked toward Aislinn. "And her?"

Eileen's answer was immediate. "No. Aislinn will not inherit the burdens I carry."

That answer landed, but Rowan wasn't done. "That still doesn't tell me *what* you are."

Eileen held his stare, her response deliberate. "It's not knowledge that concerns you."

Rowan exhaled sharply through his nose. "Convenient."

Eileen's lips twitched, just barely. "Necessary."

Aislinn, perhaps sensing that Rowan was seconds from pushing harder, cleared her throat. "So what now? Because I can't exactly keep teleporting into the bathroom every time I—" she cut herself off, shifting. "Every time it triggers."

Eileen didn't press her on the omission. Instead, she said, "I can place a temporary lock on the ability. It won't block it completely, but it will stop it from activating without your control."

Aislinn nodded quickly, eager to move on. "That works."

Eileen raised a hand, pressing her fingers lightly to Aislinn's temple while the other relaxed over her heart. A faint golden glow pulsed from her touch, divine energy weaving through Aislinn's core as she placed the restriction.

Aislinn inhaled sharply as the awareness spread through her, then let out a slow breath as it faded. "It's... *there*, but it feels distant. Like it's waiting for permission."

"That's exactly what it's doing," Eileen confirmed. "You'll regain access when you learn control."

Aislinn flexed her fingers, keeping her face neutral. "And how do I *do* that?"

Eileen lowered her hands, meeting her directly. "Whenever you have free time in your Fallen duties, come see me. We'll work on it until you can direct the ability properly."

Rowan exhaled, his posture finally easing. "Good."

Eileen studied them both for a beat, then stepped back. "That will be all."

Rowan hesitated for a fraction of a second, watching her. "This isn't over."

Eileen regarded him with steady composure. "No, it's not."

He gave a sharp bow and turned toward the door.

Aislinn lingered just a moment longer, a quiet understanding passing between her and Eileen. Then she followed.

Eileen remained where she was, listening to the door click shut behind them.

She allowed herself exactly three seconds to process the full impact of what had just been confirmed.

Then she pushed it aside and turned her mind to what came next.

★★★

The morning light was weak and colorless as Ivy, Ash, and Willow arrived in Georgetown. Overhead, dark clouds churned unnaturally fast, shifting in silent turbulence. The air carried a sharp chill, unseasonable and unnatural, wrapping the streets in a tension that didn't belong. Even without direct evidence, the lingering effects of the Golden Dawn's ritual were clear—warping the elements, twisting the balance of the city itself.

The three split up, each scanning their surroundings with quiet precision. Ivy trailed her fingertips along aged brick and weathered stone, her sharp eyes searching for remnants of ritual markings. Ash, his senses honed to the energy woven into the air, let his instincts pull him toward traces of lingering magic. Willow moved like a shadow through the streets, her awareness extending beyond sight, attuned to the invisible shifts in their surroundings.

Ivy's fingers stilled as she brushed over faint markings carved into the mortar between stones. Though weathered, the symbols still pulsed with residual power—like embers buried beneath ash, waiting to be stoked back into flame. A whisper of magic clung to her skin as she traced the patterns, and she signaled to Ash and Willow, her voice low.

"This wasn't erased properly." She pressed her palm flat against the stone, feeling the muted thrum of lingering energy. "There's still power here."

Ash's gaze sharpened. He inhaled slowly, focusing, letting the magic in the air settle over his senses. A thread of dark energy curled toward a narrow alley, an imprint left behind by those who had worked the ritual. He gestured subtly in its direction.

"There's a residue leading that way," he murmured. "It's recent. Unstable. Either they tried to restart the ritual, or they left it incomplete."

They moved as one, slipping into the alley's deepening gloom. The air was thick here, pressing close, heavy with the remnants of a ritual abandoned but not forgotten.

A shift in the energy sent a prickle up Willow's spine. She raised a hand in warning, her movements fluid but sharp with urgency.

She motioned them into the cover of a shadowed doorway just as two figures emerged near the alley's end. Their voices, low and edged with frustration, carried through the still air.

"The weather manipulation alone is exhausting—keeping this up while we rebuild is draining us," one of them muttered bitterly. "If Fort Lawton's guards hadn't failed us…"

The second cultist let out a sharp exhale. "We have to maintain it. If we let the energy break, everything we've built collapses. The ritual needs power, and we're not stopping the elemental manipulation until it's fully restored."

Ivy, Ash, and Willow exchanged looks, understanding settling between them like an implied warning. The Golden Dawn wasn't just maintaining the ritual's effects—they were fueling them, refusing to let the energy fully fade.

A shift in the air made Ivy's pulse spike. One of the cultists turned, his scrutiny sweeping the alley. His posture stiffened as he locked onto the space where Willow stood.

Ivy reacted instantly, weaving an illusion over their position. Shadows rippled, distorting their figures, making it appear as though nothing stood there but shifting darkness.

At the same time, Ash shifted seamlessly into the form of a lean, silver-furred cat. He darted across the alley, his movements deliberate, drawing the cultist's attention away from Willow. The man's frown deepened, his focus snapping to the stray, suspicion flickering in his gaze.

Willow seized the opening. She gestured sharply to Ivy and Ash before slipping through the narrow gap between buildings, her steps near soundless. They followed, keeping to the edges of shadowed corridors as she led them through winding alleys, moving with the surety of someone who had spent a lifetime navigating unseen paths.

It wasn't until they emerged onto an empty side street that she allowed them a moment to breathe.

Ash shifted back, his tone grim. "That was too close."

Ivy exhaled, her fingers still tingling from the residual energy in the symbols. "The magic here is… thick. Like it's seeped into the foundation itself." She glanced back toward the alley. "It hasn't dissipated. Whatever they're doing, it's still alive."

Willow folded her arms, her tone edged with certainty. "If they're this determined in Georgetown, Fort Lawton is going to be worse."

Ash let out a quiet breath, his thoughts difficult to read. "They're not backing down."

A silent agreement passed between them. This wasn't over. With a final glance at the swirling sky above, the three turned, their path leading them back to Eileen.

***

The library's grand shelves loomed over Oak and Elder, dust motes swirling in the dim midday light. Outside, dark clouds churned unnaturally fast, the mansion's thick stone walls muffling the wind's hollow wail. A creeping chill settled over the room—one that had nothing to do with the season.

Oak struck a match, touching it to the stacked logs in the fireplace. Flames crackled to life, their glow flickering over polished wood, but the mansion's library held nothing of value for what they needed.

Exhaling, Oak lifted a hand, fingers tracing unseen symbols. Energy pulsed in response. Across from him, Elder murmured an invocation, his voice a quiet thread of power. The air thickened, magic answering their call.

Books materialized from nothing—heavy tomes, brittle scrolls, pages inscribed with ink that had never faded. Their collection. Their knowledge. The scent of aged parchment filled the space, layered with candle smoke and pressed herbs.

Oak ran a hand over a worn leather cover and flipped it open. "Now we begin."

They worked in silence, methodically pulling scrolls and heavy tomes from their shelves, each searching for insight into the enemy before them. Kubla Khan. The Reborn Conqueror. The name alone carried a weight that pressed into the pages of history, but it was what lay beneath the legend that concerned them now.

Oak ran his fingers across the brittle pages of an aged volume, the script winding in elegant yet severe strokes. "He isn't just a warlord seeking conquest," Oak mused, eyes scanning the lines. "He's attempting to transcend death itself—to become an eternal god of war."

Elder, seated across from him, turned a page in his own text. The firelight cast shifting shadows over his face, sharpening the lines of his features. "And he's close," he muttered. "He discovered a ritual that anchors him to the physical world. As long as it remains incomplete, he exists in a state between worlds—unable to fully manifest, but impossible to banish."

Oak's brow furrowed, a shadow passing over his features. "A conqueror who never has to surrender. That explains the title."

Elder tapped a passage in the book before him, his focus sharpening. "There's more. His power doesn't come from sheer force alone—he feeds on wrath." He looked up. "Riichi's wrath."

A heavy silence stretched between them.

Oak leaned forward, his voice quieter but no less grave. "Every time Riichi succumbs to his anger… Khan grows stronger."

Elder concurred. "It's a cycle—one that Khan is counting on. He doesn't just want Riichi as an enemy. He wants to break him, twist him, reshape him into his greatest weapon." Elder's fingers tightened over the edge of the book. "If Riichi fully gives in, he won't be fighting for us anymore—he'll be fighting *for Khan.*"

The thought hung between them like an unspoken omen.

Oak exhaled slowly, shifting through another text. "He's not just targeting Riichi, though." His eyes skimmed over a passage written in a dialect few could still read. "Takoda," he murmured, his fingers drumming against the table in agitation. "Khan sees her as a tool."

Elder frowned. "For what purpose?"

"To gather followers," Oak said grimly. He pushed the book toward Elder, tracing his finger along the passage. "Her empathic abilities make her more than just a potential ally—she could be a weapon to amass an army. If Khan twists her gift, he could use her to sway warriors to his cause, bending them to his will."

Elder's frown deepened. "And worse—if he gets to her first, he could use her to break Riichi completely."

A heavy silence fell over them.

Elder turned another page, scanning the lines before his expression grew even more severe. "It's not just them, Oak. Their bond itself is a risk."

Oak's head lifted, his body stilling. "Explain."

Elder's voice was measured but tense. "Their Radiant Surge." He shifted the book slightly, letting Oak see the translation. "It says here that Khan's ritual requires a rare fusion of power—strength and destruction, control and persuasion. *War and conquest.*" Elder's voice dropped lower. "That's Riichi and Takoda."

Oak's brow furrowed, his fingers tightening on the edge of the book. "Not Rowan and Aislinn?"

Elder shook his head. "No. Their bond is built on protection—guardianship, endurance, stability. That wouldn't serve Khan's purpose. But Riichi and Takoda?" He tapped the page, voice firm. "He's a warrior. She's an empath. Together, they don't just wield power—they amplify it."

Oak's mind worked quickly. "If their power aligns with the ritual's requirements—"

Elder met him squarely. "—then their Radiant Surge could be the final piece Khan needs to bind himself permanently to the physical world."

The fire crackled, filling the silence as the truth took hold, inescapable.

"If that's true…" Oak murmured, his fingers drumming against the table. "Then their greatest weapon is also their greatest risk."

Elder nodded grimly. "If they use it at the wrong time, in the wrong way… they could *complete the ritual for him.*"

For the first time in centuries, a flicker of uncertainty passed through Oak's expression. He had seen war in many forms, fought alongside warriors of all kinds—but this was different. This wasn't just battle. It was a long, deliberate game. A war of patience, strategy, and manipulation.

And Khan was a master of all three.

Elder leaned back slightly, his voice measured. "We need more insight. This is bigger than we thought."

Oak consented. "Agreed. We'll need Eileen's perspective—and the others. If we're going to stop this, we need to understand *every* piece of his plan."

Elder closed the tome before him, his fingers resting on the aged cover. "Then let's make sure we do."

Gathering their notes, they rose from their seats, sharing looks of determination. Protecting Riichi, Takoda, and the Fallen from Kubla Khan would take more than strength.

It would take strategy.

Without another word, they left the library, prepared to share what they had uncovered—and to ensure that Khan's conquest ended before it could begin.

★★★

Rowan and Aislinn walked through the snowy streets of Seattle toward Nihonmachi, the city's Japantown. The cold air and heavy clouds created an eerie atmosphere, mirroring the tension Rowan sensed beneath the surface.

Their first stop was a small tea shop, where the elderly owner studied Rowan carefully as he spoke of the disturbances he'd observed. After listening quietly, the man directed Rowan to Nami, a young woman behind the counter.

Nami agreed to pass along any rumors about Golden Dawn activity and warned that Seattle's supernatural currents were shifting in ways even the Fallen hadn't yet noticed. Rowan left with a sense of accomplishment, the first step in building their network completed.

Their next stop was a bookstore, its windows fogged with warmth. Inside, shelves were heavy with knowledge—of Seattle, the world, and the supernatural. The proprietor, a wise and enigmatic man, listened as Rowan explained the threats facing the city.

The man's expression remained neutral, but his jaw tightened with certainty. "I've felt it," he said quietly. "The city's balance is shifting. There's a force pressing against it."

Rowan didn't need to ask if the man would keep watch; his silent nod confirmed it.

They continued their rounds, visiting a few other places, each conversation requiring patience and discretion. Trust wasn't easily earned in Seattle, but Rowan's steady approach laid the foundation for a promising network of contacts.

As they stepped back onto the street, a gust of wind whipped snow into the air. Aislinn tucked her hands into her coat pockets, casting a smirk at Rowan.

"Making friends already?" she teased, affection flickering in her look.

Rowan chuckled quietly, brushing snow from his shoulder. "We'll see if they're the right ones."

They walked on, the afternoon's stillness settling around them. For a brief moment, Rowan allowed himself to appreciate the progress they'd made.

But then, the air shifted. A ripple of energy rolled through the space, faint but unmistakable—familiar, yet wrong.

Rowan slowed, instincts sharpening as a sense of awareness prickled over him.

Whatever peace the afternoon had held, it was gone.

Something—or *someone*—was watching.

Rowan's steps slowed. The city moved as it always did—people weaving through the snowy streets, voices muffled beneath layers of winter clothing—but amid the shifting crowd, a presence stood out.

A man walked with deliberate ease, each step purposeful yet unhurried. The world seemed to move around him rather than the other way around, as if he belonged to a different rhythm entirely. Dressed in refined but timeless clothing, he carried himself with an effortless authority, one that didn't demand attention but commanded it nonetheless.

Then his attention locked onto Rowan's.

The recognition was instant. *Kubla Khan.*

He didn't stop moving, but his pace slowed just enough to make his intent clear. This was no coincidence.

Khan inclined his head slightly, the gesture as effortless as it was deliberate. "Rowan. Aislinn."

There was no theatrics, no overt hostility. Just knowledge.

Aislinn's chin lifted slightly, her tone casual despite the sharp awareness in her stance. "Didn't expect to see you here."

Khan acknowledged her words with the faintest flicker of a smile, just enough to suggest he found the situation amusing. "It would be negligent of me not to take an interest." His dark gaze flicked to Rowan. "Not many could have undone what the Golden Dawn built at Fort Lawton, and Lucifer's failure in San Francisco was… instructive."

Rowan didn't react, though the statement confirmed what he had already suspected. Khan wasn't here to fight. He was here to learn.

"Failure teaches," Rowan said evenly. "If you're paying attention."

Khan studied him for a moment before offering a slight tilt of his head. "Indeed."

The moment stretched in silence. Khan didn't fill it with unnecessary words. He didn't need to. Instead, he observed, the sharpness in his gaze betraying an active mind, one that evaluated every detail like a craftsman studying his materials before making a cut.

"You interest me," he finally said, not as a compliment but as an observation.

Aislinn's arms crossed, her expression impassive. "Glad to know we're memorable."

"Memorable?" Khan echoed, considering the word as though tasting it for the first time. Then, with a small, knowing smile, he corrected her. "No. I seek understanding."

Rowan understood exactly what that meant. Khan wasn't here to admire them. He was collecting data.

"What was it?" Khan continued. "Strength? Strategy?" His eyes narrowed slightly. "Or was it trust?"

Rowan gave him nothing.

Khan's interest sharpened, his scrutiny measured, as if unseen pieces were falling into place. "Yes," he murmured. "Trust."

Aislinn didn't move. "Sounds like you think that's a problem."

"Not a problem," Khan corrected, and this time, there was the faintest edge of amusement in his voice, like he enjoyed the conversation more than he should. "A factor." He regarded them with detached curiosity. "Trust is a weapon. But every weapon has a breaking point."

The words weren't a threat, just a fact, spoken with the certainty of someone who had tested the theory before.

Rowan didn't blink. "You're wasting your time."

Khan studied him for a moment longer, then exhaled through his nose—something close to a chuckle, though there was no real humor behind it. "Perhaps." He tilted his head slightly, as if finalizing an internal conclusion. "But every war is won before the first battle is fought."

There was no arrogance in the statement—only certainty.

Rowan and Aislinn remained impassive, giving him nothing further to work with. If he was looking for an exploitable weakness, he wouldn't find it here.

Satisfied, Khan turned and walked into the shifting crowd, his presence fading effortlessly into the city. No parting threats. No unnecessary gestures. Just strategy.

Rowan exhaled slowly, the cold air burning against his lungs.

Aislinn's voice was quiet. "He wasn't here to fight."

"No," Rowan agreed. "He was here to study."

Aislinn kept her focus on the space where Khan had disappeared. "Then we make sure he learns nothing more."

Rowan nodded and started moving again, his mind already turning toward their next step. Kubla Khan didn't engage in battles he wasn't certain he had already won.

And that alone made him dangerous.

★★★

Snow blanketed Fort Lawton in a thick, undisturbed layer, absorbing sound and muting the world beneath a heavy, frozen silence. The sky above was a vast, impenetrable void, dark clouds swallowing the moon, shrouding the landscape in shifting shadows. A sharp wind cut through the air, each gust carrying a frigid bite that settled deep into the bones.

Reed moved first, his steps calculated and deliberate. Having spent years navigating Alaska's brutal winters, he knew how to adjust his stride, ensuring each step left no sound, no sign of passage. Vine and Birch followed his lead, their movements careful as they weaved through the snow-laden ruins of the fort.

Ahead, flickering torchlight illuminated the remnants of the ritual site. Golden Dawn cultists moved in precise, deliberate patterns, their breath visible in the bitter cold. Fresh markings had been drawn into the snow, carved in intricate, swirling lines of ink and ash—symbols of renewal. Birch's gaze darkened. "They're preparing to restart," he whispered.

Vine knelt beside one of the symbols, tracing its edges with gloved fingers. The ink was still wet, the scent sharp in the frozen air. "They're not just determined," he murmured. "They're confident."

A sudden voice broke through the stillness.

"Do you realize the mess we're in because of you?"

The three of them froze, shifting deeper into the shadows as a Golden Dawn officer strode into view. The man's voice was sharp, his breath coming in visible bursts of cold. He stood rigid, his frustration barely restrained as he addressed two guards standing stiffly before him.

"The ritual disrupted. Progress halted. All because you failed to keep this site secure against the Fallen."

The guards cast nervous glances at one another, their postures defensive beneath the sharp intensity of his glare.

"We have no choice now," the officer continued, his tone cutting through the cold air like a blade. "We accelerate the weather manipulation. The storm must strengthen. The temperature must drop. This time, we will not fail."

The words hung in the night like a threat.

Hidden behind the thick underbrush, Reed, Vine, and Birch exchanged looks, grasping the full extent of what they had just heard. This wasn't just a method of concealment—the Golden Dawn was using the storm as a weapon.

The wind howled in response, a sharp, unnatural gust sweeping through the fort. Snow stirred in violent whirls, turning the world into an endless churn of white. The temperature plunged, the cold biting through layers of insulation, sinking deeper than winter's reach.

Reed signaled for them to move. Every second spent here was a risk. They needed to withdraw with the intel before the storm became impenetrable.

They began their retreat, adjusting their footing as they moved through the thickening drifts. The landscape had shifted; beneath the fresh snowfall, a layer of treacherous ice waited unseen.

Reed's boot skidded. Birch stumbled beside him, barely catching himself before Vine reached out, gripping his arm and steadying him.

"Careful," Reed murmured, his voice barely audible over the howling wind. "They've iced the earth beneath the snow. Watch your footing."

Their movements slowed, every step measured against the frozen terrain. The snow thickened, swirling in heavy sheets that shrank their visibility. Even the fort's towering structures blurred, disappearing into the storm's suffocating reach.

Then—a sharp crack overhead.

The accumulating snow proved too much for an old, ice-laden branch. It snapped, splintering through the silence with a sharp, violent crack.

Vine barely had time to react.

Reed lunged, gripping his jacket and yanking him back. The branch slammed into the ground where Vine had just been standing, snow and ice erupting in a blinding spray.

Silence followed.

The three of them stood still for a breath, then two, listening, scanning.

No alarms. No rushing footsteps.

Birch exhaled, his breath forming a thick cloud in the frozen air. "They're turning this entire place into a death trap."

Vine ran a hand over his face, brushing snow from his skin. "It's working."

They resumed their retreat, pushing forward with even greater urgency.

Only when they reached the perimeter of the fort, where the wind no longer cut like a blade and the snowfall thinned just enough for visibility, did they allow themselves to stop.

Vine's hands tightened into fists at his sides. "They're not just altering the weather. They're forcing it into submission."

Birch adjusted his scarf, his attention locked on the distant ruins slowly vanishing beneath the snowfall. "And if they keep this up, the entire area will pay the price—not just us."

Reed exhaled slowly, watching the storm thicken behind them, swallowing Fort Lawton in silence. His voice was quiet, but firm.

"This isn't just about completing a ritual. They're establishing control."

The weight of that truth settled between them.

Without another word, the three of them got in their waiting car and drove toward the Fallen base, their urgency doubled. If the Golden Dawn succeeded in completing their ritual, tonight's bitter chill would only be the beginning.

Chapter Nineteen
Radiant Devotion

The morning light streamed into Takoda's room, casting a golden glow over the space, warming the air between her and Riichi as they settled in for a rare day off. After the intensity of last night's mission, Eileen had ordered them to step back and recharge. While the rest of the Fallen continued their investigations, Takoda and Riichi were given something rare—breathing room. No orders, no battles. Just time.

Riichi stretched, rolling out the last traces of tension from his muscles. He leaned back in his chair, exhaling a slow breath. "A full day to ourselves," he murmured, a rare, easy smile forming. His attention fixed on her, steady and expectant. "So… what do you want to do, Takoda? Today's yours."

She grinned, mischief glinting in her eyes. "We both know I have ideas." Her head tilted, studying him. "But what about you? What do you want?"

His smile deepened, as if the answer had always been obvious. "I want to focus on you." The way he said it was simple, sure—as if there was nowhere else he'd rather be.

Affection flickered in Takoda's chest. She'd spent most of her life prioritizing others, making sure everyone had what they needed. The idea that today was about her—completely, intentionally—felt significant.

"Well…" she leaned in slightly, voice dipping into a playful hush. "Since you're giving me complete control…" A spark of excitement lit her expression. "I thought we could start with some cooking. It is my constant. When everything else changes, cooking is the one thing that always makes sense, and I'd like to share that with you." A pause, then, with a teasing lilt, "And Ariel and Rain found a hidden hot tub on the lower levels. I was thinking we track it down and claim it for the day."

Riichi let out a quiet chuckle, clearly intrigued. "Cooking and hot tubbing," he repeated, nodding in approval. "Not bad. But there's more on your mind."

The teasing edge in his voice softened as Takoda glanced toward the window, her posture shifting with quiet resolve. When she locked eyes with him again, her expression held no hesitation.

"There is," she admitted. "Last night… staying back, supporting from a distance, waiting for you to return to me—it didn't sit right."

Riichi's amusement faded as he listened.

"I don't want to be protected from the fight, Riichi." Her voice didn't waver. "I know Eileen places me at a distance for strategy, but I don't want to watch from the sidelines while you take every risk. I want to stand with you. Fight with you. If I'm stronger, she won't have a reason to keep me back."

Riichi exhaled, watching her carefully.

"Last night only made it clearer." Takoda's fingers curled against her knee. "You were out there, putting everything on the line, and I was waiting—hoping my power was enough to reach you in time if you needed it." Her jaw tightened. "But what if it hadn't been? What if I could've done more if I was there with you?"

Riichi's brow furrowed slightly, but his gaze remained level, weighing her words.

"I don't want to stay where it's safe while you carry the risk alone," she finished. "I want to be someone you can rely on—not from the other side of the battlefield, but beside you."

For a moment, Riichi said nothing. He simply studied her, taking in everything—the steadfast resolve, the fire in her eyes.

His fingers brushed over hers before he took her hand, his grip solid and warm.

"Takoda… you already are someone I rely on." The words were measured, quiet, but filled with certainty. "Your emotional alchemy—it keeps me stable when nothing else can. You don't need to prove your worth to me."

Her fingers tightened against his, but she shook her head. "That's not what this is about." Her voice was softer now, but no less firm. "I trust myself, Riichi. I know what I'm capable of. I just need to be better."

His thumb brushed absently against her knuckles, a silent trace of thought passing through him. A flicker of conflict danced in his gaze—not resistance, but acceptance edged with caution.

Finally, he exhaled, the tension easing just enough for a sounder resolve to take its place. "Alright," he murmured. "If this is what you want, then we'll train. I'll push you as hard as I push myself. But understand this, Takoda—" he lifted her hand slightly, not looking away, "I will always worry about you being in danger. That's not going to change."

Takoda's lips parted slightly, her breath catching—not at his concern, but at the quiet confession buried beneath it.

She squeezed his hand once, her grip firm. "Then we'll just have to make sure we walk out of every battle together."

A breath of silence passed between them—not heavy, not uncertain. Just assured. Rooted. Like a vow exchanged without words.

With their plans set, they rose to prepare for the day, a quiet steadiness carrying them forward.

***

Takoda and Riichi stepped into the courtyard, the morning air crisp against their skin. Overhead, fast-moving clouds churned in shades of gray, their shifting forms a silent reflection of the energy between them. The cold sharpened their focus, wrapping the moment in quiet intensity. They exchanged a glance—a wordless understanding. For Takoda, this wasn't just training. It was the first step toward proving she belonged beside him in battle. For Riichi, despite the protective instinct simmering beneath his calm exterior, it was a chance to help her grow. And he would see it through.

They started with warm-ups, their movements fluid and methodical. Takoda eased into familiar jujutsu stances, her posture specific, deliberate. Riichi followed, seamlessly aligning his Combat Reflex techniques with her rhythm. He didn't speak, letting the constant cadence of their footwork carry them into focus. Takoda's presence felt different today—stronger, sharper. She moved with purpose, her energy relentless, and he found himself watching her with a newfound respect.

As they transitioned into sparring, Takoda didn't hesitate. She met Riichi head-on, her jujutsu seamlessly blending with her emotional alchemy. She wasn't just reacting—she was claiming her place, pressing forward with quiet intensity. Her strikes carried the weight of her conviction, her movements guided by sharp concentration.

Then she moved. Fast.

A defined pivot. A seamless weight shift. In an instant, she had Riichi off balance, her grip sure as she swept his leg out from under him. He barely caught himself before hitting the ground, landing in a controlled crouch, but his expression flickered with surprise.

Riichi straightened, studying her with sharp interest. "What belt did you say you were?"

Takoda smiled. "I didn't."

His brow lifted.

She rolled her shoulders, stepping back into a ready stance. "Shodan."

A first-degree black belt.

Riichi blinked once, then let out a quiet, impressed breath. She hadn't just picked up jujutsu for self-defense. She had mastered it.

A slow grin tugged at the corner of his lips. "And you're just now mentioning this?"

She shrugged, feigning nonchalance. "It never came up."

His amusement deepened. "Convenient."

Takoda didn't respond—she simply moved.

He barely had time to react before she attacked again, her strikes faster, sharper. She wasn't just keeping up with him. She was pushing him.

Midway through their exchange, Takoda sent a solid pulse of supportive energy toward Riichi, the warmth of it threading through his limbs. The sensation wasn't overpowering—it was controlled, intentional. A quiet anchor. He exhaled slowly, feeling the immediate impact, the way it reinforced his own focus. When he caught her look, a flicker of understanding passed between them—a silent acknowledgment of the strength she offered not just to him, but to the entire team.

They broke briefly, catching their breath. Riichi studied her for a moment, his expression unreadable before it softened, edged with undeniable pride.

"You're stronger than I expected," he said, his voice even but firm. "You're ready for this."

Takoda stared at him, her pulse even, her confidence unwavering. His words didn't feel like approval. They felt like recognition. She wasn't being humored—he saw her as his equal now, as someone who could fight beside him. And that realization filled her with quiet pride.

As they moved together again, their strikes and counters blended into a seamless rhythm. Each attack met its mark, each step perfectly timed, as if they had been training together for years instead of just today. Unlike her past sessions with Oak and Willow, Takoda didn't hold back. She fought with the same intensity that Riichi did, matching his precision, his pace. And he noticed.

She was more at ease with him than she had ever been with anyone else—her movements fluid, her instincts sharper. Riichi could see it now. She wasn't struggling to keep up. She belonged here. The realization settled in him like an unquestionable truth.

Their sparring continued, their connection deepening in the quiet exchanges between them. Takoda felt it—the way Riichi adjusted, no longer testing her, but meeting her fully, as if he had accepted what she had always known. She could fight at his side. She would.

Snowflakes began to drift down, catching in their hair and clothes as they moved. The snowfall thickened, veiling the courtyard in white, adding an almost surreal beauty to the moment. But neither of them slowed. They were too focused, too locked into the rhythm they had found.

Eventually, they stopped, both breathing heavily from the exertion. Snow dusted Riichi's shoulders, clung to the strands of Takoda's hair. He exhaled, eyes sharp as he took her in—not as a protector watching over someone fragile, but as a warrior standing before her equal.

"You're more powerful than you realize, Takoda," he said, his voice low but smooth, conviction woven into every word. "You have everything it takes to stand beside me."

His words carried more than praise. They carried belief.

Takoda absorbed them, feeling their weight settle inside her—not as a burden, but as a foundation. His belief in her wasn't given lightly. She had earned it.

After a quiet moment, Riichi turned away to reset one of the training dummies, his back to her, leaving her a moment to savor his words.

With a spark of mischief, Takoda scooped up a handful of snow, molding it quickly between her fingers. Riichi was still focused on adjusting the training dummy when she let it fly, the snowball striking his shoulder with perfect accuracy.

He stilled, glancing down at the damp spot on his jacket before lifting his eyes to hers. Slowly, deliberately, he turned—expression unreadable, but the sharpness in his eyes betrayed his intent.

Takoda's grin widened.

She shifted back a step, already reaching for more snow.

Riichi arched a brow. A silent challenge.

Before she could react, he moved, scooping up his own handful in one swift motion. The moment she saw his fingers tighten around the snow, she darted sideways, laughter spilling out as she launched another shot.

The game ignited instantly.

Snow flew between them, quick and relentless, bursts of white scattering through the air as they dodged and fired. Takoda's aim was sharp, her reflexes keeping her just ahead of him—but Riichi wasn't far behind. His speed was an advantage, his instincts razor-sharp, anticipating her movements almost too well.

She barely dodged his next throw, twisting out of the way at the last second. "You're fast," she called over her shoulder, breathless with exhilaration.

He smirked. "You're predictable."

She gasped in mock offense. Another snowball left her fingers instantly, hitting its mark—his chest.

Riichi exhaled sharply, more from indignation than impact. "Alright." The single word carried a quiet warning.

Takoda recognized the shift too late.

He lunged.

Her feet barely had time to move before his arm wrapped around her waist, momentum sweeping them both to the ground. They landed with a muffled thud, snow kicking up around them, laughter tangled in the cold air.

The chill of the snow soaked into her back, but it barely registered.

The world had gone still.

Snow drifted around them, muffling the space beyond. The only sound was their breath, uneven from laughter, mingling in the cold.

Riichi braced his weight on one elbow, keeping himself from pressing fully into her, but he didn't move away. Snow dusted his hair, melting where it touched his skin, but Takoda barely noticed. His breath curled warm between them, a contrast to the cold settling beneath her.

Their playful energy hadn't disappeared, but a deeper undercurrent slipped in—a moment between moments, the kind that didn't need to be acknowledged to exist.

Takoda shifted slightly, fingers pressing into the snow, but she didn't pull away.

Neither did he.

Riichi's gaze flicked to her lips, but it wasn't a question.

She met him without hesitation, tilting up to press her mouth to his in a kiss that felt as easy as breathing.

It was a touch familiar, steady in the quiet rhythm they'd long since fallen into. His fingers skimmed along her jaw—not hesitant, not deliberate, just a slow, absent-minded touch, like second nature.

Snow clung to their skin, melting in the heat between them, but neither seemed to care.

When they finally broke apart, Takoda let her forehead rest against his for a breath before shifting back.

A small smirk flickered at the edge of Riichi's lips, a knowing glint in his eyes before he sat up.

A gust of cold air swept over them, sharp against Takoda's skin. She shivered, and Riichi took immediate notice.

He pushed himself to his feet and reached down, offering his hand. "We should get inside before you freeze solid."

His tone was light, but the tenderness in his eyes was unmistakable.

Takoda let her fingers slide into his, the grip firm as he pulled her up. His hand lingered for a fraction of a second longer than necessary.

"Good idea," she murmured.

Her gaze flickered toward the courtyard, snowfall erasing the marks of their chase, covering the footprints and scattered remains of their playful battle. Yet the moment still clung to her like warmth against the cold.

Side by side, they headed inside, leaving the snow behind but carrying the quiet weight of what had just passed between them.

After the snowball fight, Takoda and Riichi stepped into the warmth of the kitchen, brushing stray snowflakes from their clothes as the heat from the oven wrapped around them. The contrast from the cold outdoors was immediate, sinking into their skin, but it was more than just the heat of the room—it was the comfort of being here, together.

The space felt intimate in its simplicity—the constant hum of the stovetop, the faint scent of herbs already hanging in the air. Takoda let out a slow breath, rolling her shoulders as a quiet contentment settled inside her. There was a restful peace about this—about sharing a space with him where neither of them had to be anything but themselves.

She broke the silence with a playful challenge. "How about we make lunch for each other?" A mischievous glint lit her eyes. "I'll cook for you, and you cook for me."

Riichi stilled, his brows twitching together in hesitation. "Are you sure you want to try my cooking?" His voice was dry, edged with real concern.

Takoda laughed, shaking her head. "Of course." She nudged his arm as she passed. "Just surprise me."

He exhaled, the uncertainty in his expression lingering for a breath before shifting into firm determination. If she trusted him with this, he wouldn't disappoint her. Without another word, he moved toward the counter, rolling his sleeves up.

As they worked, they fell into an easy rhythm—each lost in their own process, but fully aware of the other's presence.

Takoda selected her ingredients, her movements practiced and sure. She skewered venison alongside small potatoes and carrots, seasoning each piece with care before sliding the tray into the oven. The scent of roasted herbs and slow-cooked meat filled the kitchen, a whisper of home wrapped in love.

For the Three Sisters salad, she combined roasted squash, corn, and beans—the balance of flavors an unspoken nod to tradition. Cooking had always been a way to connect with her roots, and today, it felt like sharing a part of herself.

Meanwhile, Riichi approached his own meal with quiet precision. He worked with intent, shaping onigiri with careful hands, pressing the rice into neat triangles, each one holding a tender bite of salmon.

Cooking wasn't second nature to him, but he respected the process.

The steam from his miso soup curled into the air, the rich aroma blending with the earthiness of Takoda's dish. It was simple. Humble. But there was meaning in simplicity.

As she turned to check on him, Takoda couldn't help but smile. Riichi was focused, almost too much so. His usual tactical intensity hadn't faded—it had simply transferred into an unexpected place.

"You look like you're planning an attack, not making lunch," she teased, laughter bubbling in her chest.

Riichi, still concentrating, muttered, "I'm trying not to mess this up."

She grinned. "We'll see if you're still saying that when I'm done judging your work."

He glanced up, one brow lifting in challenge. "We'll see if you're still laughing when you try it."

Their banter filled the space, light and easy, but beneath it was the quiet understanding that neither of them needed to say—this wasn't just passing time. This was them choosing each other, choosing to be here, and that choice mattered.

They weren't just making food. They were sharing something personal.

When the meals were ready, they set their dishes on the table, exchanging glances with quiet anticipation.

Takoda's venison skewers and Three Sisters salad were rich with color, simple yet full of meaning. Riichi's onigiri and miso soup were meticulously arranged, reflecting his natural sense of balance and control.

For a moment, they just looked.

Not at the food—but at each other.

A silent acknowledgment passed between them, the kind that didn't need to be spoken aloud: *I made this for you.*

They sat, and Takoda took the first bite of the onigiri. The saltiness was subtle, the texture soft yet firm—the kind of comfort food that didn't need to be elaborate to be satisfying. She glanced at Riichi, her expression shifting into quiet contemplation before she finally said, "This is really good."

A slow, pleased exhale left him, like he hadn't been sure she'd say that.

Riichi lifted a venison skewer, taking a bite. The flavor was rich, earthy—the kind of food that tasted like it belonged to the land itself. He chewed slowly, then nodded, setting it back down.

"I can taste the care in this," he murmured, setting down the skewer. "This meal—it's you. Your roots, your people, the land you come from. It carries their strength, their resilience. I can feel it in every bite."

Takoda stilled, fork resting lightly between her fingers.

She wasn't sure what she had expected him to say, but this—this was different.

He wasn't just complimenting the food. He was recognizing her in it.

The warmth of the kitchen pressed in, but the heat curling through her had nothing to do with the stove.

She searched for a response, but nothing seemed adequate. Still, Riichi didn't press for words.

They ate slowly, not just tasting the food, but absorbing the meaning behind it.

Takoda shared the story of the Three Sisters, explaining how each ingredient represented unity and balance—a reminder that nothing in nature thrives alone.

Riichi listened, quiet but focused, like every word mattered. And she realized it did.

In return, he told her about onigiri—the comfort in its simplicity, the way something so small could carry tradition and care.

Neither of them spoke in grand statements, but everything they said felt like another thread woven between them.

A silence stretched as they finished eating, but it wasn't empty.

Takoda glanced at him, feeling a deep, unshakable tenderness settle in her chest. A gratitude not just for this moment, but for him.

When Riichi met her gaze, there was kindness there—a quiet understanding.

★★★

As late afternoon faded into early evening, Takoda and Riichi made their way to the lower levels of the mansion, following Rain's directions to the hidden hot tub. The deeper they descended, the quieter the world became, the last remnants of the day fading behind them. The hallways grew dimmer, the air warmer, carrying the faint scent of mineral-rich steam.

After a bit of searching, they finally found it—a secluded, softly lit room, its warmth wrapping around them like a quiet invitation. The water shimmered under the glow of recessed lighting, gentle ripples breaking the surface, the entire space exuding a sense of stillness. Without a word, they stepped into the steaming pool, the heat sinking into their muscles, unraveling the tension of the day. The chill of the snowfall, the exertion of training—it all faded beneath the soothing heat of the water.

Takoda exhaled slowly, leaning her head back against the edge. The contrast between the cold air above and the heat below sent a pleasant shiver through her. She glanced over at Riichi, catching the way his shoulders finally relaxed, the sharp edges of his usual tension smoothing out. She smiled.

"Today's been… incredible," she murmured, her voice softer than she intended. She turned to face him fully, her expression open, unguarded. "I didn't realize how much I'd come to rely on these moments with you."

Riichi looked up at her, his brow easing as the usual guarded look in his eyes gave way to quiet longing.

"It's been a rare day," he agreed, his voice even, thoughtful. "One I hadn't thought I'd experience."

Takoda studied him for a moment. The honesty in his words settled in her chest—uncomplicated, yet meaningful.

Their conversation drifted naturally, and eventually, she found herself sharing pieces of her past she rarely spoke about.

"I was an only child." Her fingers skimmed the surface of the water absently. "My parents doted on me. Probably spoiled me a little." A faint, nostalgic smile touched her lips before it faded. "My mom passed from cancer four years ago. My dad… soon after. I think it was… maybe a broken heart."

The weight of those words settled between them, heavier than the steam rising from the water.

Riichi's face remained calm, his usual sharpness replaced with quiet understanding.

"I'm sorry," he said quietly.

Takoda lifted her head, considering him with a small, knowing smile. "Thank you. I've made peace with it." She let her fingers drift through the water, watching the ripples spread outward. "Now I have Rain, Aislinn, Ariel… and you."

The last words left her effortlessly, but the moment they reached the air, she felt them take root somewhere deeper than before.

Riichi said nothing at first, but when she glanced up at him, he was already watching her. His silence wasn't hesitation. He was listening. Absorbing.

She let the quiet stretch, comfortable and heartfelt. Then, softly, she asked, "Do you ever think about your family?"

The shift was immediate. The warmth in his eyes cooled, his gaze flickering downward for half a second before settling on the water's surface.

Takoda's stomach tightened as she realized she had pressed against a boundary she hadn't meant to cross. She reached out instinctively, fingers just barely brushing the surface of the water between them.

"You don't have to answer," she said gently. "I didn't mean to—"

Riichi shook his head, a small motion, as if pushing aside the instinct to retreat. His expression didn't harden, but a quiet distance settled into his features.

"It's alright," he said, though his voice carried the measured control of someone choosing each word with care.

He didn't say more.

Takoda faltered, studying him, a flicker of self-doubt creeping in. She hadn't meant to disrupt the moment, hadn't meant to pull him into the past if he wasn't ready.

I should have been more careful.

Before the thought could settle, she felt his voice in her mind—calm, comforting.

You didn't ruin anything. Just… give me a moment.

The sincerity of his words quieted the lingering worry in her chest. She studied him, watching as he pieced together the words he wasn't used to saying, his expression marked by the weight of a memory not yet spoken aloud.

She nodded, her touch light against the water.

A long silence stretched between them as Riichi stared into the swirling steam, his expression unreadable. But Takoda didn't need to decipher it—she could feel the shift, the way the air between them carried an unguarded truth he wasn't ready to say aloud just yet.

And then, finally, he spoke.

"I had a younger sister," he began, his voice quieter than usual, as if speaking the words required effort. "Aya." The name settled between them, carrying a love that flickered briefly before being swallowed by the weight of loss. "We lived in a small village by the water in Hakata Bay. It was peaceful, removed from the outside world. My family was everything."

Takoda remained silent, watching the way his fingers curled slightly against the stone edge of the tub, a reflex he likely wasn't aware of. He held himself with the same measured control he always did, but there was a tension beneath it—a restraint not fully concealed.

"One evening, we were having dinner together," he continued. "That was when they came." His grip tightened, his tone holding a quiet edge. "Kubla Khan's forces. The Mongols attacked. Their ships filled the bay like a storm, their soldiers pouring into the village before we even understood what was happening."

His jaw clenched. "I knew my family couldn't be in the open. I told them to hide—showed them a space beneath the floorboards." His fingers flexed, pressing into the surface beside him. "Then I left to fight. I thought if I stood with the others, if we held them back long enough, we could protect our home."

He swallowed, his throat working through the next words. "We never stood a chance."

The words settled between them, stark and final. "We fought, but they overwhelmed us. We weren't facing warriors—we were facing an army designed to conquer. Their weapons burned through wood, their arrows rained down before we could raise our defenses. We barely slowed them down." His breath came slow and measured. "And then, in the middle of the fight, I felt it. A pull. A warning. I knew before I saw it."

His grip on the stone edge of the tub tightened. "I ran. I didn't think, I just ran home as fast as I could, through the burning streets, past the bodies." His voice stayed level, but the effort it took was clear.

He drew in another breath. "By the time I got there... they were gone."

Takoda's chest tightened. She had known this was coming, but knowing wasn't the same as hearing him say it.

"The Mongols had found them." His voice was quiet, but not detached. He had lived with this truth for centuries, but speaking it aloud was not the same as accepting it. His hands stilled in the water, his posture rigid, but his face carried a depth of grief that had never faded. "Aya...she was only ten."

For a moment, he closed his eyes, as though he could still see her, frozen in time—the way she had clung to his sleeve whenever she was scared, the way her laughter had once filled their home. His voice, when he spoke again, carried a rawness that had been carefully buried. "She was everything to me. I promised her I'd always protect her. And I failed."

He didn't describe what he had seen. He didn't have to. The way his fingers curled, the way his gaze didn't meet hers, said more than words ever could.

"After that, I wasn't thinking anymore. I couldn't." His voice remained level, but there was a storm beneath it, like a fire still smoldering after centuries. "Everything—grief, failure, regret—disappeared. All that was left was rage."

Takoda stayed quiet, allowing him the space to speak on his own terms.

"I killed until my body gave out. I didn't care who was in my way. I just wanted to destroy." His jaw tensed. "And when I collapsed, I didn't care if I died."

His breath was shallow, as if reliving the memory pulled the exhaustion from that night into the present. "But I didn't."

His fingers flexed again, this time with clarity—not relief, not regret, but recognition. "When I opened my eyes again, Eileen was standing over me. She wasn't alone. There was a little girl beside her." His gaze lifted, meeting Takoda's with careful attention. "She was holding a small white pouch. Just like the one you showed me."

Takoda's breath caught.

"That's why I went to speak with Eileen," he continued. "I needed to be sure. You were that little girl, Takoda. What you remember as a dream… was reality for me."

The moment settled between them, thick with the weight of memories surfacing.

"You asked if I was hurt," Riichi said, watching her closely. "I told you I was fine."

The words echoed in her mind, distant yet familiar.

"Then you asked why I was hurt. I told you… I'd been trying to protect my family and my village."

Takoda inhaled sharply, her thoughts catching on a fragmented image—small hands clutching a pouch, a wounded man lying in the dirt, the scent of earth and blood mixing with the cold.

"You got a little bolder after that, asking if I was going to die." Riichi's voice remained composed, but there was a heaviness beneath it—raw but restrained. "Not wanting to frighten you or lie, I told you simply… I think I might."

Takoda felt a tightening in her chest, her heart bracing for what she now sensed was the true connection between them.

"Eileen told me she needed me to become a member of the Fallen," Riichi said softly, his eyes fixed on her. "And then you said…"

Takoda's voice emerged as a whisper, finishing his thought with words she hadn't fully remembered until this very moment. "You're very brave… You can still protect those who need you."

Riichi's breath caught, a faint, bittersweet smile crossing his face. "Yeah," he replied quietly, his voice thick with emotion. "You did."

Takoda didn't speak. The air between them carried the weight of everything that had just been unearthed.

Riichi exhaled slowly, running a hand through his hair, his fingers dragging through damp strands. "I kept this from you because… I was afraid. Afraid you'd hate me. That knowing this would change how you see me." His voice, always controlled, carried a rawness she hadn't heard before. "I didn't want to hurt you. I thought if you knew… you'd turn away."

Takoda reached for his hand, pressing her palm over his. He finally turned to her, the tension in his shoulders lingering, though not as rigid as before.

"I could never hate you," she said softly, each word carrying the fullness of her sincerity.

A shaky breath escaped him, his shoulders relaxing as her words lifted the heavy weight he had carried alone for so long. He felt a deep, unexpected peace settle over him, realizing that he didn't have to hide his past from her or fear her judgment anymore.

Overwhelmed with relief, he pulled her into a tight embrace, holding her close as though anchoring himself in her presence. A few unshed tears slipped down his face, a testament to the relief and gratitude he felt in her acceptance.

As he held her, he pressed a gentle kiss to the top of her head, finding comfort in the warmth of her presence. Takoda leaned into him, sensing the depth of his vulnerability and silently offering her own strength, a reassurance he didn't need to ask for.

They remained in the embrace, feeling the weight of everything they had just shared—the trust given, the fears laid bare, the quiet vow that neither would turn away.

In the silence that followed, they both knew they were truly safe with each other, a bond now strengthened by trust, acceptance, and the comfort of being fully seen.

After their heartfelt moment in the hot tub, Takoda and Riichi quietly made their way through the hallways toward her room, craving the privacy to savor this new depth to their relationship. They reached her door, and as she stepped inside, she glanced back at him with a soft smile as he closed the door behind them, watching her with affection in his eyes.

Letting her hair down, Takoda moved toward the bathroom. "I was thinking of taking a shower," she said, her voice soft yet inviting.

Riichi nodded with a small smile. "I'll take one too," he said, turning toward the door, but her hand caught his, stopping him.

"No, Riichi," she whispered, looking up at him, her face holding a quiet intensity. "I want to take a shower... with you."

His expression softened, tension easing from his features as she led him into the bathroom. Steam curled around them, thick and warm, cocooning them in a world of their own. As they stepped beneath the cascading water, his hands traced over her shoulders, gentle yet deliberate, drawing her closer. His touch held both reverence and restraint, a careful balance between tenderness and the quiet storm lingering beneath the surface.

She met his gaze, her hands sliding up to cradle his face, thumbs brushing over his cheekbones. "Riichi," she murmured, her voice clear and even. "Your past doesn't define you—it shaped you. And I love who you are." She took a breath, balancing herself before allowing the words to flow freely. "I love you, Riichi."

His grip on her waist tightened, grounding himself in the weight of her confession. His eyes, dark with emotion, never wavered from hers. "I love you, too," he murmured, his voice thick, raw. He laced his fingers with hers, holding onto her like she was the only solid thing in his world. The glow of Radiant Surge flared between them, a golden-orange light encircling their entwined hands, pulsing in time with their heartbeats.

The warm glow bathed the shower, illuminating the space with an ethereal light. Riichi exhaled, his fingers skimming over her arms, tracing the droplets of water that clung to her skin. Takoda placed her hands on his chest, feeling the constant rhythm of his heart beneath her fingertips. Slowly, she slid them upward, threading her fingers into his damp hair, guiding him toward her.

Their first kiss was slow, unhurried, an affirmation of everything unspoken. Then another, deeper, carrying the weight of every emotion left unsaid. Riichi's arms wrapped around her, his hands spanning the small of her back as he pulled her closer, their bodies pressed together beneath the falling water. Each touch, each lingering kiss, deepened the connection between them, the heat of their embrace mingling with the warmth of the water. Takoda's fingers traced the muscles of his back, feeling the tension melt beneath her touch as his lips found hers again, thoughtful, consuming. The glow pulsed in rhythm with their movements, intensifying as they held each other, breaths mingling in the steam-filled air. Every caress, every wordless promise passed between them, dissolving the space that had ever existed between their souls.

Hand in hand, enveloped by the vibrant glow of Radiant Surge, they moved into the bedroom, unable to part. The flickering light cast fluid, shifting shadows along the walls as they lay together, bodies drawn together in an unbreakable pull. There were no barriers left, no walls between them—only the raw depth of their love.

Each kiss was a promise, their hands exploring with devotion, tracing every contour, every curve, as if etching the memory of this moment into their very being. Their movements were slow, methodical, savoring every brush of skin, every soft sigh. Riichi's fingers traced along her spine with a quiet urgency, his lips following, pressing against her skin as though each kiss carried a whispered vow. Takoda arched into him, feeling the heat of his breath against her neck, the way he held her as if she were something precious—something irreplaceable.

As they surrendered completely to each other, the glow of Radiant Surge flared, burning brighter, a reflection of the fire that ignited between them. The air around them thickened, heavy with the raw intensity of their emotions. Riichi's hands moved over her with a tenderness that stole her breath, his touch exploring every inch of her as if committing her to memory through sensation alone. She held onto him, anchoring herself in the sheer depth of their bond, their connection surging like a tide that neither could resist. A quiet gasp left her lips, her body shuddering as they reached their climax in unison, energy pulsing through every shared breath, binding them in a force greater than themselves.

In that moment, their connection deepened, the glow of Radiant Surge pulsing in time with their racing hearts. Riichi's thoughts brushed against hers, carrying a weight that went beyond words. *You are everything to me.* His voice, silent yet undeniable, wrapped around her like warmth, sinking deep into places she hadn't known could ache for him.

Her response was immediate, instinctive. *And I am yours… always.* The thought was not just sent—it was felt, weaving with his as if it had always belonged there.

Not yet sated, their bodies continued to move together in perfect harmony, utterly consumed by one another, the glow of Radiant Surge illuminating the room in an unbroken rhythm. Their thoughts meshed, a seamless flow of whispered confessions and truths that wound them even closer.

As they lay together, Riichi's hand slid along her side, his fingers gliding over her skin with quiet devotion. His thoughts reached her, raw and unguarded. *I've waited so long to tell you,* he conveyed, his gaze fixed as he brushed a thumb tenderly along her hip. *You mean more to me than I ever thought possible.*

Takoda's response was immediate, her thoughts wrapping around his like a loving embrace. She moved in sync with him, her hand finding his as she intertwined their fingers, rooting herself in his presence. *I feel complete with you, Riichi,* she conveyed softly, her expression sure and filled with conviction. Her fingers tightened gently around his. *Nothing else matters but this, right here, with you.*

The glow pulsed around them, vibrant and alive, filling the space with a passion that mirrored the depth of their bond. Through the night, they shared their deepest thoughts, each telepathic whisper layering upon the next, until their connection felt boundless, infinite—something neither time nor fate could ever sever.

As dawn approached, the Radiant Surge began to soften, leaving a gentle warmth that wrapped around them. Exhausted but fulfilled, they lay entangled, hearts beating in perfect harmony. Riichi pressed a tender kiss to her forehead, his thoughts brushing over hers one last time that night: *I love you, Takoda. Every part of you.*

She held him closer, her thoughts soft but unwavering. *And I will love you always.*

They drifted into sleep, their bond now unbreakable, bound by a love fully realized and the silent certainty that they belonged to each other—completely, irrevocably—as the first light of dawn crept into the room.

***

Far away, in the depths of the unseen, a ripple stirred through the air—a shift so subtle, yet undeniable. Kubla Khan's head lifted, his senses sharpening as the disturbance reached him. He had been waiting for this. Watching. Calculating.

The energy of Radiant Surge pulsed like a beacon, confirming what he had long suspected.

A slow, knowing smile curled his lips. "It's time," he murmured to the darkness around him. "They're ready."

A layer of early morning frost coated the mansion grounds, shimmering under the pale sunlight that stretched across the snow-covered landscape. It was the last week of October, yet winter had arrived unnaturally early, a chilling testament to the Golden Dawn's growing influence. The contrast between the warmth of the crackling fire in the hearth and the frozen world beyond the window was stark, the room a small haven against the unnatural cold.

Eileen stood at the window, her gaze heavy with contemplation as she watched the untouched snow. She wore a wool sweater, its soft fabric a rare concession to comfort, though it did little to soften the authority that rested on her shoulders. Behind her, Ariel bounced on her heels, her knit hat and bright scarf adding a splash of color against the muted tones of the room. Rain stood beside her, her hands wrapped around a warm mug, watching the scene beyond the glass with quiet interest.

"Thank you both for coming." Eileen's voice carried the burden of unspoken responsibility, though a faint smile softened her expression as she turned to them. "It seems the Golden Dawn's reach is seeping into more than just our battles. Even the seasons are bending to their will."

Ariel let out a low whistle, her eyes bright with intrigue. "Twisted winter wonderland vibes, huh? I was expecting pumpkins and crunchy leaves, but instead, we get *this*." She gestured to the frostbitten landscape with exaggerated flair. "Not exactly prime Halloween weather, but I'll give them points for drama."

Rain chuckled, cradling her mug between her fingers. "I have to admit, it's beautiful in a way. Wrong for October, but still… I bet the Golden Dawn doesn't have a view half as nice."

Eileen studied them, their lighthearted banter a balm against the unrelenting weight she carried. She gestured for them to sit, her gaze sharpening with purpose. "I called you here because I need your help in a way that only the two of you can offer."

Ariel's excitement was immediate. She dropped into a chair, leaning forward with bright-eyed enthusiasm. "Ooo, mysterious. Is this a secret mission? Some kind of stealthy, sneaky operation? Because I have *always* wanted to—"

Eileen exhaled, a knowing look settling on her face. "Not quite."

Ariel deflated slightly but grinned. "Worth a shot."

Rain nudged her with her elbow before turning her focus back to Eileen. "How can we help?"

"With everything happening, the Fallen are being stretched thin—physically, mentally, emotionally." Eileen's voice held the same steady cadence it always did, but there was a rare note of concern beneath it. "I've seen what exhaustion does to warriors who have nothing to fall back on. Strength becomes brittle when it isn't given time to rest. So, I'm implementing 'days off.' They'll resist at first, but without it, we risk losing more than just battles."

Ariel's brows lifted, surprised. "Days off? You mean, like, actual time to... *relax*? Have you met them?"

Eileen's mouth twitched at the corners. "Yes, which is why I need your help. You both have a gift for lifting spirits, grounding people in the things that remind them why they fight. No grand gestures are required—just presence, conversation, a reminder that they exist outside of war. I need you both to check in, keep them engaged in something that isn't strategy or survival."

Ariel lit up as realization dawned. "Wait, you're saying we're *officially* the emotional support squad? *This* I can work with."

Rain grinned, resting her chin in her palm. "So... who's our first victim?"

Eileen allowed a rare smile, her gaze carrying a flicker of appreciation. "Vine."

Ariel gasped dramatically. "Oh, this is going to be *amazing*. Vine doesn't *do* relaxation. I bet he'll try to schedule his 'day off' down to the minute with *extensive* sword training."

Rain laughed, nudging her playfully. "Think we can actually get him to unwind? This might be our toughest mission yet."

Eileen's expression remained poised, but amusement glimmered in her eyes. "I trust you'll find a way. He may resist, but I have faith in your talents."

Ariel's grin turned positively wicked as she turned to Rain. "We *need* a name for this. Something with flair. What about... *The Spirit Squad*?"

Rain's smile widened, her eyes dancing with mischief. "Oh, that's *perfect*. Spirit Squad—it's got a ring to it. Way better than just 'Ariel and Rain.'"

Eileen exhaled through her nose, shaking her head slightly as she leaned back. "Spirit Squad, then. I believe it suits you both quite well."

Ariel beamed. "Consider the Spirit Squad officially *in action*! We'll make sure Vine gets the *full* relaxation experience."

Rain smirked. "We should probably start small—maybe just convince him to sit down for five minutes before he starts planning how to weaponize relaxation."

Eileen inclined her head, the warmth in her gaze quiet but present. "Your support is invaluable. True strength isn't just about what we can do alone—it's about the people who stand beside us."

Ariel huffed a dramatic sigh, placing a hand over her heart. "So poetic. But, uh, real talk—when do we get official Spirit Squad sashes? I feel like badges would also be acceptable."

Eileen shook her head, though there was a keen fondness in her expression. "No sashes, I'm afraid. But you've earned something far more meaningful—the respect of the Fallen."

Ariel exchanged a victorious look with Rain before they both rose, their excitement practically tangible as they playfully brainstormed their *first mission*. Their energy lingered long after they left, a burst of light against the ever-present reality of war.

Once Ariel and Rain were gone, Eileen turned back to the window, her gaze steady as she took in the unnatural winter draped over the land. Snow clung heavily to the trees, blanketing the world in an eerie stillness that did little to ease the tension in her chest. The sight should have been peaceful, but instead, it was a warning. A quiet, creeping testament to the darkness pressing ever closer. The unnatural frost was no simple shift in the seasons—it was the Golden Dawn's influence made tangible, a silent declaration of how far their reach had spread.

Turning from the window, she exhaled slowly and strode toward the conference room, arriving early to prepare for the meeting. Though the Airbnb was meant to be temporary, the space had become their central base for planning, its modern furnishings an odd contrast to the gravity of their discussions.

One by one, the Fallen entered, each taking their seats around the polished wooden table. Their movements carried the discipline of warriors who had seen too much and still shouldered more, yet none of them belonged here in the ordinary sense. The walls of this home had never seen battle, had never soaked in centuries of war like the places they once called their own. It was unfamiliar, but for now, it had to serve.

Takoda settled into her seat, her quiet presence grounded as ever. Beside her, Riichi sat in still, silent observation, his gaze moving over the room in measured sweeps. He was absorbing everything—the hushed conversations, the flickers of unease in his comrades' expressions, the way small shifts in posture betrayed exhaustion. Every detail mattered. Every unspoken thought carried weight.

At the head of the table, Eileen took her place, and beside her, Oak sat with his usual quiet presence. A worn leather-bound notebook rested in front of him, his pen already poised to write. He had promised to be more active in meetings, and though he spoke little, his sharp gaze followed every exchange, his notes capturing the essential details that might be needed later.

Eileen rose, her presence neither rushed nor softened as she addressed them.

"Thank you all for gathering early." Her voice carried effortlessly through the room, steady as a tide, unwavering in its command. "Our recent missions have confirmed what we feared—the Golden Dawn's reach is spreading, and now we have an even greater concern. Two nights ago, we encountered a new threat—Kubla Khan."

A ripple of tension passed through the room. Even among warriors who had faced the worst of the supernatural world, a name carried undeniable power.

Eileen let her gaze settle on each of them in turn. Kubla Khan's presence was unexpected, but it hadn't been random. They needed to understand why he had surfaced now, and more importantly, what his connection—if any—was to the Golden Dawn.

She continued, her voice measured. "We don't yet know his motives. His presence at the mission site may have been coincidence—or it may be something far worse. If he's working against the Golden Dawn, we may be facing a battle on multiple fronts. If he's working with them, we may be too late to prevent what's coming."

Beside her, Oak's pen moved steadily across the page, recording every word. His expression remained unreadable, but his focus was absolute.

Eileen gestured to Ash, Ivy, and Willow—the Georgetown team—to begin their report.

Ash leaned forward first, his voice clipped. "In Georgetown, we encountered residual energy—strong enough to linger well past the initial ritual. Signs of elemental manipulation were present throughout the site, and the cold wasn't just unnatural—it was calculated. A fog clung to the area, not rolling in from the water, but hanging heavy, held there by something deliberate. The Golden Dawn is pushing their control harder than ever."

Willow's expression darkened. "We found remnants of ritual markings—some left intentionally incomplete. Their placement wasn't random; they were meant to pulse, to sustain a presence. The magic was still active when we arrived, weaker than it had been, but not fading naturally. As we tracked the energy further, we overheard two cultists arguing. They were struggling to maintain the ritual, blaming setbacks at Fort Lawton but refusing to abandon the work."

Ivy's fingers drummed lightly against the table, the movement precise, measured. "The symbols we found didn't match anything we've seen before. The power bound to them felt volatile—unstable. Whatever they're building, they're pouring more into it than usual. They're not just experimenting. They're committing."

Takoda leaned forward, her expression thoughtful. "That kind of investment means they're closing in on something. If they're fighting this hard to hold their ground, it's because they know abandoning it would set them back in a way they can't afford."

Reed, his sharp gaze fixed on Ivy, gave a slow nod. "If Georgetown is part of a broader network, this won't be the last time we see this level of disturbance. They're testing how far they can stretch their influence."

Riichi absorbed their words in silence, a sense of foreboding building. The team's observations painted a picture of desperation, but desperation born from purpose. The cultists' fixation on these rituals suggested deeper stakes—stakes that might drive the Golden Dawn to escalate even further. His gaze lingered on the others, piecing together the hints of a broader strategy.

Eileen nodded solemnly, shifting her focus to Oak and Elder, the team that had spent the last day researching Kubla Khan.

Oak flipped open his notebook, his expression composed as he began. "Elder and I focused on uncovering what we could about Kubla Khan—his history, his abilities, and why he might have resurfaced now. What we found suggests he isn't just clinging to the past—he's trying to reclaim it."

A quiet weight settled over the table.

Elder leaned forward, his tone calm but firm. "Khan isn't a conventional enemy. He isn't here to lead another invasion or build an empire from the ground up. He's operating in a liminal state, caught between existence and oblivion. The only thing preventing him from fully returning is an incomplete ritual."

Oak continued, his pen tapping lightly against the page. "The problem is, he doesn't need to complete it alone. Every battle, every surge of emotion he stirs feeds into his return. And if he can manipulate the right people—use their strength instead of his own—he won't just come back. He'll come back unstoppable."

Elder's gaze flicked to Riichi. "You, in particular, are a key piece of this."

Silence stretched across the room.

Elder didn't soften the truth. "Khan thrives on wrath. The more you fight him, the more you fuel him. He doesn't just want to face you, Riichi—he wants to turn you. To mold your anger into a weapon he can wield."

Takoda's gaze flickered toward Riichi, subtle concern in her eyes.

Oak's voice remained level. "And it's not just Riichi he's watching. Takoda is just as valuable. Her abilities make her the perfect conduit for gathering influence. If he can twist the way she connects to others, he could build an army without lifting a blade."

A small crease formed between Takoda's brows.

Elder's voice was quieter but no less intense. "And then there's the matter of your bond." He glanced toward Eileen before continuing, his next words weighted with significance. "Khan needs a balance of power—two forces that together create something stronger than either one alone. If he finds a way to exploit that energy, he won't have to search for another solution."

Oak exhaled through his nose, his grip tightening slightly around his pen. "Which means Riichi and Takoda's Radiant Surge could be the missing piece of his ritual. If he forces them into a position where they have no choice but to use it…"

Elder finished the thought, his tone grim. "They'll complete it for him."

A heavy stillness filled the room.

Oak closed his notebook but didn't look away from the others. "That means we're dealing with more than just an enemy. We're dealing with someone willing to reshape fate itself. And whether he succeeds depends entirely on how well we understand the pieces he's trying to move."

Eileen's gaze shifted to Rowan and Aislinn, prompting them to share their findings from Nihonmachi.

Rowan's voice was steady but laced with a sharp edge. "In Seattle, we worked on establishing connections within Nihonmachi, securing contacts who could alert us to any Golden Dawn activity. We were making progress—several business owners agreed to pass along anything unusual. But while we were setting up those alliances, we weren't the only ones watching."

He paused, exchanging a glance with Aislinn before stating what they both already knew. "Kubla Khan."

The mere mention of his name settled over the room, unspoken but heavy.

"He approached us in the open," Rowan continued, his expression unreadable. "No attempt to hide, no theatrics. He knew exactly where we were, and he made it clear he had been expecting us."

Aislinn's tone was even, but a quiet tension in the way her hands folded in her lap—measured, restrained—hinted at deeper thoughts. "He greeted us by name. And then he acknowledged Fort Lawton."

Rowan's gaze darkened. "He said, 'Not many could have undone what the Golden Dawn built there, and Lucifer's failure was… instructive.'"

The room remained silent, absorbing the implications behind that statement.

Aislinn exhaled quietly. "It wasn't a compliment. It was an observation. One that implied he was paying very close attention."

Rowan's jaw tightened. "After that, he shifted the conversation. He started asking about Lucifer—specifically, how we defeated him. His questions were subtle, careful. He wasn't digging for obvious weaknesses, but he was looking for something. Testing for gaps we hadn't considered."

Aislinn nodded. "He wasn't just studying our tactics. He was measuring us."

Rowan leaned forward slightly, his tone lowering. "Then he turned to a different focus—our teamwork. He called trust 'a weapon—or a weakness.'"

Willow let out a slow breath, shaking her head. "If he's analyzing our relationships, that means he sees them as exploitable. We need to reinforce those connections now, before he finds ways to tear them apart."

Elder's voice was firm. "Kubla Khan isn't looking for a fight. Not yet. He's looking for ways to dismantle us before that fight ever begins."

Silence settled over the table.

Hearing Rowan and Aislinn's account, Riichi felt a prickle of unease. Kubla Khan's observation about the typhoon ritual struck him as more than a mere compliment. It carried an implication, a hint that Khan saw value in that power—a value he might seek to reclaim for himself. Silently, Riichi braced himself, the urgency to fortify their defenses heightening as he considered how the warlord could capitalize on their every move.

As Rowan and Aislinn's report concluded, Eileen turned her attention to Reed, Vine, and Birch, the team from Fort Lawton.

Reed's tone was steady but heavy as he began. "The Golden Dawn has resumed activity at Fort Lawton, accelerating preparations to restart their ritual. They seem focused on manipulating the weather to create barriers. When we arrived, a severe snowstorm was brewing—clearly unnatural. Even with winter gear, the intensity was almost unbearable."

Reed's gaze narrowed as he continued. "The ritual site had fresh symbols hidden under layers of snow, set up for a quick reactivation. We overheard a Golden Dawn officer pushing his guards to speed up the weather manipulation, insisting that they create 'a natural barrier' to keep intruders out. The snowfall intensified quickly, turning the entire area into a frozen trap. It felt like the environment was becoming their weapon."

Vine's voice held a rare edge as he spoke. "The weather was more than a deterrent; it was lethal. Snow and ice covered everything, and there were sheets of ice hidden beneath that made every step dangerous. Their manipulation of the elements was strategic, converting the landscape into a trap."

Birch added, a note of weariness in his tone. "We barely made it through without incident. The wind was strong enough to snap branches overhead, one of which almost struck us. It's clear that they're creating a deadly zone around Fort Lawton."

Elder's voice was solemn as he responded. "If they're using weather as a weapon, they're reaching a new level of threat. This ritual could evolve to other areas, pushing the environment itself against us."

Willow nodded grimly. "If they're willing to weaponize nature, they'll stop at nothing. Controlling the environment on this scale could harm anyone nearby, creating a deadly fortress around their ritual."

Listening to Reed's report, Riichi sensed a grim pattern forming. The Golden Dawn's strategy was becoming clearer: they weren't merely using elemental power—they were weaponizing it, transforming natural spaces into barriers that could decimate anyone trying to breach them. As he thought on the implications, he realized that this level of control might hold significant allure for Kubla Khan, a tool he could bend to his own designs.

Eileen's gaze swept over the team, a quiet intensity filling the room as she addressed them. "Based on your findings, it's clear the Golden Dawn's intentions are escalating. Let's discuss what their next moves might look like—and then we'll turn to Kubla Khan's potential motives." Her tone was focused, the gravity of her words resonating in the room. "Anticipating these moves will be critical if we're to stay ahead of both threats."

A stillness settled as the team absorbed her words. Seated beside Takoda, Riichi held a posture of deep contemplation, his fingers resting just below his nose, hands pressed together as he sat in silence. The room seemed to shift around him, the other Fallen members attuned to his quiet presence, recognizing his role as their lead strategist. He remained silent, his thoughtful demeanor signaling to the others that he was already piecing together the threads from their reports, finding connections hidden within each observation.

Birch spoke up, breaking the silence. "The Golden Dawn is likely to keep fortifying key locations, especially those with supernatural significance or influence. They'll use these areas as footholds to expand their reach—places they can entrench themselves without drawing too much attention."

Willow nodded, her voice thoughtful. "Those zones might also act as traps for us. They're probably creating protective barriers, or maybe even nodes in a larger ritual. If they're working toward something bigger, we could see an expanding radius around Seattle, bit by bit."

Elder's expression darkened as he added, "If they're linking these fortified sites, they might be creating a network to channel energy. This could be part of an overarching ritual, a way to amplify their power through these connected zones. Left unchecked, they could be building toward something massive."

Eileen's expression remained steady, though her gaze sharpened. "All signs point to the Golden Dawn prioritizing this network, but we need to stay vigilant on both fronts. Now, let's consider Kubla Khan and what he might gain from recent events."

Reed's brow furrowed as he leaned forward, his tone thoughtful. "If Kubla Khan is observing our moves or keeping tabs on the Golden Dawn's efforts, he could be learning how to target us effectively. By manipulating these situations, he might be trying to assess our unity, resilience, and any strategic flaws. It's like he's measuring us as much as he is building his own plans."

Vine leaned back, folding his arms as he considered Reed's point. "And he's already shown interest in powerful rituals like the typhoon. Maybe he's observing us to see how we handle it—maybe even looking for ways to leverage that type of power himself."

Takoda's gaze shifted, her voice quiet but resolute. "His focus on trust and teamwork tells us something about his intentions. He could be targeting our cohesion, looking for any insecurities or weaknesses that could fracture us. If he's paying that close attention to how we work together, he might see our unity as a vulnerability."

Through it all, Riichi remained silent, his eyes moving from one speaker to the next. Theories and speculations filled the air, each piece forming a potential part of the puzzle, but Riichi stayed focused, listening intently. As their strategist, he was sifting through every detail, piecing them together, shaping a comprehensive view of how to counter both the Golden Dawn's and Kubla Khan's separate strategies.

Eileen, sensing his thoughtful demeanor, turned to him with quiet respect. "Riichi, I know you've been listening carefully. What are your thoughts? Do you see anything we might have overlooked?"

All eyes turned to him, the room awaiting his insight, each member trusting in his ability to make sense of their observations and lay bare the next steps in their relentless pursuit to counter the dual threats of the Golden Dawn and Kubla Khan.

Adjusting his posture, he pressed his hands together, his expression composed yet intent. His tone was clear and calm, and the meticulous precision in his voice immediately drew the room's attention. He glanced at Eileen, who gave him an encouraging nod, her trust in his insight unmistakable.

"From our recent findings, it's apparent that the Golden Dawn is intensifying its efforts to reconstruct the typhoon ritual." His eyes moved over the gathered faces, each member drawn in by his steady delivery. "They're undeterred by our previous disruptions, and I believe they see this as their final chance to fully breach the veil."

His focus shifted toward Reed. "Your observations at Fort Lawton showed that elemental manipulation and unnatural cold are reinforcing key locations, creating barriers that hinder interference. Ash's team found lingering ritual symbols in Georgetown, their energy still active. The Golden Dawn is clearly preparing these sites with fidelity, each layer of reinforcement bringing them closer to weakening the veil enough for dark entities to cross over and secure a lasting influence."

A murmur of agreement ran through the room. The implications were heavy, and the tension hung thickly as he continued.

"However," he said, shifting smoothly into his next point, "there's more than just the Golden Dawn at play. We also need to consider Kubla Khan."

Locking eyes with Rowan, he referenced the Nihonmachi team's encounter. "Rowan and Aislinn's report indicated that Kubla Khan had a genuine interest in the Golden Dawn's typhoon ritual when he said, 'Not many could have undone what the Golden Dawn built there.' That wasn't just a compliment. He's not merely going to use their ritual—he's refining it, guiding it into something more effective, something that serves his vision rather than theirs."

His gaze swept across the room, reading the realization settling over the team before pressing forward. "I also believe Kubla Khan intends to shape the Golden Dawn into something far more dangerous than they were before. Then, there's the matter of him saying, 'Lucifer's failure was… instructive.' Both statements tell us he wasn't admiring our strategy—he was analyzing it, seeing us as a force capable of dismantling something powerful, as well as our ability to defeat Lucifer in San Francisco. He sees us as a threat."

His voice sharpened slightly. "His questions weren't about the cult's failure. He was testing the limits of what they created, studying its flaws so he could reshape it into something far more controlled and powerful. If the Golden Dawn failed with their first attempt at Fort Lawton, Khan won't repeat their mistakes. He's assessing, adapting, and preparing to make their next attempt unstoppable."

Letting a brief pause settle over the room, he shifted slightly, scanning their reactions before continuing. "Unlike Lucifer, Khan won't leave them in disarray. He will forge them into an actual force—an army, rather than a scattered faction. By the time they near the ritual's completion, they won't just be a cult grasping at power; they'll be a structured force with clear leadership and purpose. Khan isn't using them as disposable assets—he's refining them, ensuring they become an army that can serve his long-term goals."

As he presented each layer of his analysis, Takoda watched him intently, captivated by the way he connected details that others might overlook. She couldn't help but admire his intelligence, the precision in his deductions striking her with a sense of awe. The way he spoke, completely in control, so effortlessly commanding the room, sent a thrill through her. His voice, steady and deep, wove logic through chaos, drawing clarity from uncertainty, and she felt it in her chest, in the way her breath caught just slightly.

And gods, was it attractive.

Her gaze lingered on him, and the thought whispered through her mind before she could stop it:

If only we could find a private place right now...

Mid-sentence, he paused, then subtly cleared his throat, pretending to gather his thoughts. A slight smirk touched his lips as he sent her a lighthearted, internal message:

It seems I can hear you whenever your emotions are this strong, no matter where we are. I love that you find me attractive right now, but you're distracting me.

Caught off-guard, Takoda felt a warm blush rise to her cheeks, and she quickly covered her mouth with her hand, stifling a smile. She looked away, willing herself to remain composed, though a glint of amusement remained in her eyes. Riichi, clearly pleased by her reaction, resumed his presentation, his focus renewed.

Shifting to his next point, his voice took on a somber tone. "Kubla Khan's interest in both Takoda and me suggests he has specific plans for us. Takoda's ability for emotional alchemy wouldn't just amplify wrath—it could be transformed into something far more controlled, something he could weaponize with precision. Under his guidance, her power could be honed into an instrument of destruction unlike anything we've seen before."

He paused, glancing around the room to ensure everyone was following. "As for me, I believe he hopes to leverage my strategic mind and combat experience—not as a pawn, but as an ally. If he thinks I can be persuaded to see the logic in his vision, he won't rely solely on force. He will attempt to manipulate my reasoning, presenting his order as the only solution to the chaos. The Radiant Surge bond that we share could be a conduit—one he could potentially shape into something devastatingly effective in his control."

His expression remained serious, his tone unwavering. There was no need to elaborate on Kubla Khan's history of exploiting powerful bonds; everyone understood the gravity of what he was implying. But this wasn't just about understanding Khan's methods—it was about anticipating his next move.

"I suggested earlier that Khan's molding the Golden Dawn into something more structured, more effective," he continued. "But their rituals aren't just tools for him—they're a foundation. Every aspect of their magic, from the typhoon to their environmental manipulation, feeds into his long-term strategy."

After a brief pause, he moved on. "That brings us to their use of weather manipulation as a critical part of their defenses and as a method for weakening the veil itself. The Golden Dawn's manipulation of the elements serves a dual purpose: to create a natural barrier around their sites and to slowly prime the veil, making it more susceptible to their rituals."

Turning back to Reed's report, he continued, "The extreme, unnatural cold at Fort Lawton appears designed to repel interference, making it difficult for any of us to approach or disrupt their work. However, Ash's observations in Georgetown indicate that the Golden Dawn's weather manipulation isn't just a defensive measure—it's the source. Everything we've seen suggests that Georgetown is the central hub controlling these environmental effects, sustaining the unnatural cold and shielding their other site."

The room fell into a pensive silence as his analysis resonated, each member processing the layers of intent and strategy he had laid out, the threats that awaited them at every turn.

With the foundation set, he smoothly transitioned into strategy. "To start, I recommend targeting the weather manipulation rituals at Georgetown. This location isn't just another stronghold—it's the mechanism controlling their environmental defenses. If we dismantle their efforts there, Fort Lawton will be left exposed."

His gaze moved across the room, ensuring everyone followed. "By cutting them off at Georgetown, we don't just halt their ability to manipulate the weather—we strip Fort Lawton of its primary protection. With their defenses down, we'll have a direct path to disrupting the typhoon ritual itself."

He gauged their reactions before moving on. "Second, I propose we strengthen the Radiant Surge bond between Takoda and myself to guard against Kubla Khan's influence. If we fortify this connection, we can effectively create a barrier, ensuring it remains a source of strength rather than a vulnerability he can manipulate."

No elaboration was needed. The team understood the significance of protecting this bond from external threats.

"Next, I advise close surveillance of both the Golden Dawn and Kubla Khan," he said. "By tracking their movements, we can adapt our strategy in real time, identifying those critical moments where decisive action will have the greatest impact."

The room charged with focus as the team absorbed his words.

"We should also establish protocols to monitor and disrupt any alliance forming between Kubla Khan and the Golden Dawn. If he tries to leverage the cult as Lucifer did, preventing this cooperation will weaken both parties, creating opportunities for us to strike effectively."

Recalling the destructive potential of past alliances, he allowed the significance of this point to sink in before pressing forward.

"Finally," he continued, "we need to prepare tactical responses for potential confrontations at the Golden Dawn's ritual sites. Each of these locations will have unique environmental hazards and defenses, like those encountered at Fort Lawton. Anticipating and countering these barriers is essential to ensure we're fully prepared for high-stakes engagements at each site."

A quiet intensity settled over the room. Each Fallen's expression reflected their understanding of the challenges ahead and the clarity his strategies provided.

A faint stillness settled over the room, the air thick with contemplation as his analysis took hold. Riichi's thoughts flickered to the hawthorn tree—a symbol of both resilience and upheaval. Like the tree, he had learned to withstand storms, to bend without breaking, and to guide others through the thorns of war with unwavering resolve.

His gaze swept over his team, confident in their resilience and readiness. "By taking these actions, we not only disrupt their plans but strengthen our own defenses, ensuring that we're prepared for whatever they throw at us next."

As he settled back into his seat, Takoda's hand slipped into his, her fingers weaving between his in a silent gesture of connection. She kept her gaze ahead, but her voice reached him telepathically, laced with a subtle urgency.

"I think we need to go to my room after the meeting."

A quiet smile touched his lips as he glanced down at their joined hands. His reply carried a hint of warmth and amusement.

"If that's what my analysis suggests, we'd better act on it."

Takoda's fingers tightened around his, a spark of anticipation passing between them. Without a word, they both returned their attention to the meeting, the understanding clear between them: there was more to discuss—and perhaps an unspoken desire to explore further.

Eileen nodded thoughtfully as Riichi concluded his presentation, her expression a mix of respect and satisfaction. "Thank you, Riichi," she said, her voice carrying quiet authority. "Your insights have given us a clear picture of what we're facing and the best approaches we can take to counter it."

She glanced around the table, pausing just long enough to invite any last questions or comments, giving the team a moment to absorb Riichi's recommendations.

When no one spoke, Eileen's tone sharpened with decisive clarity. "Our primary objective is clear: disrupt the Golden Dawn's weather manipulation rituals at Georgetown. Their elemental manipulations are weakening the veil, leaving it more vulnerable to the ritual's effects. Disabling these defenses is our priority, and we'll divide into three specialized teams for this mission."

She gestured to the first group, her gaze settling on Reed, Vine, and Birch. "Reed, Vine, and Birch—you'll form the Distraction and Surveillance Team. Your objective is to create diversions along the Georgetown perimeter, drawing attention away from the primary ritual sites and monitoring cultist activity."

Reed nodded, and Eileen continued, "Reed and Vine, your task is to set up subtle disturbances that pull the cultists' focus from the main areas. Birch, you'll oversee surveillance, keeping track of any changes in cultist movements or reinforcements. Any activity you observe should be communicated to Riichi and the Disruption team immediately."

Birch gave a brisk nod, his expression focused, while Reed and Vine exchanged a quick glance, silently aligning themselves with the mission's needs.

Turning to Riichi, Eileen continued, "Riichi, Rowan, Aislinn, Ash, and Ivy—you are the Disruption and Combat Team. Your goal is to dismantle the ritual structures directly controlling the weather manipulation."

She looked at each team member in turn. "Riichi, Rowan, and Aislinn, you'll be responsible for breaking down key symbols, dismantling the ritual setups, and nullifying the elemental symbols to cut the ritual's power. Ash and Ivy, you'll handle any immediate threats in the area, allowing the Disruption team to work without interference. Riichi, I want you coordinating this team's movements and adjusting tactics as needed."

Riichi gave a curt nod, his focus matching Eileen's. Rowan, Aislinn, Ash, and Ivy exchanged determined looks, mentally preparing for the task ahead.

Eileen then turned to the third team. "Takoda, Oak, Elder, and Willow—you'll be the Support and Security Team. Your role is to provide reinforcements to the Disruption team and manage defensive spells to keep the area stable."

She continued, "Oak and Elder, your focus is on magical support. Counteract traps, shield the Disruption team from unexpected threats, and reinforce their defenses. Takoda and Willow, you'll secure the perimeter, keeping an eye out for cultists trying to interfere. Takoda, I need you countering any disruptive elemental effects from the ritual while Oak maintains a stable operational area."

Takoda nodded, and Willow shot her a quick, supportive smile. Oak and Elder exchanged a brief look, both prepared to ensure stability where it was needed most.

Eileen took a moment, then turned toward Oak as he leaned forward slightly, his presence steady but commanding.

"If Kubla Khan intends to involve himself with the Golden Dawn," Oak said, his voice measured and direct, "Fort Lawton is where he'll do it." His gaze swept across the room, his expression unreadable. "Riichi's analysis suggests he's still observing, waiting for the right moment to step in. If he sees value in their rituals, he won't waste time watching from a distance—he'll insert himself where they're strongest."

Oak let a beat of silence settle before continuing. "That means we need to keep a close watch on both the Golden Dawn and Khan's movements at Fort Lawton. Their activity there is too consistent to ignore."

His tone remained even, but there was an unmistakable edge of urgency as he continued. "I'm assigning teams of two to monitor these movements. If their forces start shifting resources or strengthening defenses, we need to know before we make a move in Georgetown."

His gaze flicked toward specific Fallen, pairing them based on their complementary strengths and field experience. "Each team will rotate shifts to ensure no gaps in surveillance. We can't afford any surprises."

Satisfied, he glanced toward Eileen, briefly seeking her approval before continuing.

Eileen glanced at Oak, who gave a small nod before turning to Rowan and Aislinn. His tone remained even, but there was an underlying weight to his words.

"I also want the two of you to continue checking in with your Nihonmachi contacts," Oak instructed, his sharp eyes settling on them. "These alliances are still new, but they could become a valuable source of intel on the Golden Dawn's movements. Establishing trust is key. If they notice anything unusual—new faces, incoming shipments, or strange activity—relay it immediately."

Rowan and Aislinn exchanged a nod, understanding the significance of their role beyond the battlefield.

Then Eileen shifted her focus to Riichi and Takoda, her expression softening slightly.

"Lastly, we'll arrange another private training session to strengthen your Radiant Surge bond. This bond will be essential in countering Kubla Khan's influence, ensuring it remains a barrier rather than an entry point." She glanced at Oak, Rowan, and Aislinn. "I'd like you three to provide guidance and oversight again."

Takoda gave Riichi a supportive look, while Oak, Rowan, and Aislinn nodded, prepared to assist.

With a final sweep of her gaze, Eileen reinforced the urgency of their mission.

"Our coordinated efforts here will be crucial in countering the Golden Dawn's defenses. Stay vigilant and connected to maximize our impact."

A moment of silence settled over the room as everyone processed the mission details, strategy and preparation looming over them. Then, Eileen's expression shifted slightly, her tone lightening just enough to signal a change in focus.

"Before we wrap up, I want to introduce a new plan —the 'Day Off' Initiative." She paused briefly, her gaze flicking to Oak, recognizing his suggestion with a small nod of acknowledgment before continuing. "This is a reminder that mental resilience is just as important as strategy. Pushing ourselves relentlessly without reprieve only makes us brittle in the long run."

Her attention swept across the team. "Ariel and Rain will be instrumental in this effort, offering morale boosts and providing a lighthearted reprieve when it's needed most. They're eager to support the team in their own way, and I know their dedication will make a difference. We can't underestimate the power of maintaining balance."

She turned to Vine. "To start, Vine, you'll have the rest of the day off. Use it to recharge," she added, giving him a small nod of encouragement.

Vine raised an eyebrow, crossing his arms as his gaze flicked around the room. "I get the first day off? Do I look like the one who needs it most?" His tone carried a mix of sarcasm and genuine curiosity, half-expecting to see more exhausted faces around him.

Eileen responded evenly, a faint smile playing at the corner of her lips. "I know you're used to keeping things moving, but trust me, Vine—everyone can benefit from some downtime, even you. Ariel and Rain will see to it that you actually enjoy it."

Vine let out a mock sigh, a smirk tugging at the corner of his mouth. "Fantastic. Just what I needed—quality time with Ariel and Rain and a forced break. I'll be sure to savor every second." His sarcasm was barely concealed, but there was no real fight in his acceptance.

Eileen's gaze swept over the team one last time. "That's all for now. Prepare your resources and stay sharp—we move forward with definitive purpose."

With that, she dismissed the team. Each member rose with intention, their focus set on the mission ahead. Though the atmosphere remained serious, there was an undeniable sense of unity as they moved to put their plans into action.

As the team began to leave, a quiet tension lingered in the room. Eileen's assignments had been clear, yet one decision stood out—the placement of Takoda on the Support and Security team. Though she held herself with quiet composure, her gaze remained unwavering, her steady posture masking the quiet determination beneath.

She belonged on the front lines.

Riichi sensed it before she had to say a word. Her thoughts brushed against his, unspoken but firm, and the resolve in her stance mirrored the certainty in his own mind. Stepping forward, he broke the silence.

"If I may, I'd like to propose a reassignment for Takoda," he said, his voice measured but firm. "Her skills are perfectly suited to the Disruption and Combat team. Her ability to harness emotional alchemy would be critical in countering the Golden Dawn's elemental manipulation—and in creating the kind of powerful disruptions we need to dismantle their rituals swiftly."

A few of the Fallen paused on their way out, turning back with interest. Riichi's words carried weight—not just because of his strategic insight, but because they knew he would never make this request based on personal bias. If he believed Takoda belonged on the front lines, it was because he had no doubt in her capabilities. Riichi would never compromise the Fallen as a whole if he sensed even the slightest weakness in her readiness.

Eileen's gaze sharpened as she listened, her respect for Riichi's tactical mind unmistakable.

He continued, his tone unwavering. "Takoda's recent training has been rigorous; she's adaptable and more than capable under pressure. With her on the frontline, we'd have a significant tactical advantage that could shorten the time required to neutralize their defenses."

Across the room, Oak, Rowan, and Aislinn listened closely. Subtle glances passed between them, their silent agreement clear. Oak gave an almost imperceptible nod, while Rowan and Aislinn exchanged a look that spoke of their trust in Takoda's abilities. Their support added weight to Riichi's proposal, further validating his perspective.

Eileen took in their reactions, her expression thoughtful but unreadable. She appreciated Riichi's reasoning and the quiet confidence the others clearly felt in Takoda. Yet, the conflict was clear in her eyes.

She weighed the mission's demands against the risks involved.

A pause settled over the room before Eileen finally inclined her head, acknowledging Riichi's argument.

"You make a strong case, Riichi," she admitted, her voice carrying both respect and caution. "However, this decision carries a level of risk that warrants further consideration." Her gaze moved between Riichi and Takoda, assessing them both before continuing. "I'd like us to discuss this in my office. Thirty minutes."

A quiet stillness followed. The depth of her words anchored the room in place, signaling both her trust in Riichi's analysis and the gravity of the choice before her.

As Eileen dismissed the team, her gaze lingered on Takoda for a moment longer, contemplative and unreadable.

The meeting had ended, but a decision still hung in the air, waiting to be made.

Chapter Twenty-One

Testing Limits

Rain stretched out on the couch, arching her arms above her head as she and Ariel lounged together, the murmurs of the TV filling the cozy room. The Fallen meeting had just wrapped up, leaving behind a rare pocket of quiet.

"So, Vine is first up for the Spirit Squad," Rain mused, a half-smile playing on her lips. "Think he'll make it easy on us, or should we be bracing for Vegas-style theatrics?"

Ariel let out a snort, rolling her eyes. "With Vine? Who knows. He'll probably go full spectacle—wouldn't surprise me if he asks us to charter a yacht."

Rain grinned, tilting her head in thought. "Oh, I can see it now—Vine sprawled out on the deck, sunglasses on, champagne in hand, soaking up the attention like he was born for it."

Ariel laughed, her eyes gleaming with amusement. "Or, plot twist—what if he asks for something completely low-key? Like, what if all he wants is to sit in a coffee shop and people-watch?"

Rain scoffed, shaking her head. "Vine? Sitting quietly in a café, latte in hand, reading a book? Yeah, that's the day I start believing in miracles."

Their laughter filled the room, dissolving into easy chatter about the rest of the team and their imagined 'day off' requests.

Ariel leaned in, a smirk tugging at her lips. "What about Elder?" she teased. "Or should I say, Nik? What do you think he'd want?"

Rain rolled her eyes, though her smile softened. "Please. Elder wouldn't know relaxation if it smacked him in the face. He'd probably just tell us to leave him alone."

Ariel nudged her. "Except, he doesn't seem to mind hanging out with *you*."

Rain shrugged, keeping her tone casual. "Only because I remind him he's not actually ancient. I swear, he's been brooding since the Fallen first showed up in San Francisco."

Ariel's lips twitched, intrigued. "Oh, come on. You've got to admit, he's got that whole 'mysterious loner' thing down. Maybe he's just waiting for someone to bring him out of his shell."

A blush crept onto Rain's cheeks, but she waved Ariel off. "Please. Nik's 'vibe' is just him being uncomfortable around people. He's more at ease when he's left alone with his own thoughts."

Ariel's grin sharpened. "Uh-huh. So you're saying there's absolutely no interest there? None at all?"

Rain huffed, crossing her arms in mock defensiveness. "Of course not. I'm just trying to get him to act his age."

Ariel chuckled knowingly. "Sure. If that's what you want to call it."

Shifting tactics, Rain leaned back with a mischievous smile. "Tell you what—if you let me off the hook for Vine's day, I'll take over when it's Nik's turn. Deal?"

Ariel eyed her, clearly entertained. "Wait. So I get Vine duty, and you get the brooding Russian all to yourself? Sounds like someone's got an ulterior motive."

Rain scoffed, waving a dismissive hand. "It's not like that! I'm just… doing you a favor."

Ariel gave her a long, knowing look before shaking her head. "Uh-huh. Sure. But fine, deal. I'll take Vine, and you can have the 'fun' of Elder's day."

Sealing their playful bargain, their conversation drifted to the rest of the team.

"What about Ivy?" Rain mused. "She strikes me as the type to go for something adventurous. Maybe a hike or rock climbing."

Ariel nodded, laughing. "Definitely. And Reed? He'd probably just ask us to leave him alone in the woods to camp for a day."

Rain snickered. "Totally. And Oak? I could see him wanting something completely out of left field, like a cooking class. Can you even picture him in an apron?"

Ariel's eyes lit up with delight. "Oh, absolutely. Oak, in an apron and a chef's hat, all serious about perfecting his soufflé. Would love to see it."

They both laughed, each imagining the ridiculous scenarios, a bubbling excitement growing between them. Ariel shot Rain a smirk.

"Think we can actually turn these Fallen into regular people for a day?" she challenged.

Rain grinned. "If we can't, no one can. Spirit Squad's got this."

Their laughter hummed through the room, carrying an undercurrent of anticipation. The challenge ahead promised entertainment, but as Rain leaned back, her thoughts flickered—briefly, stubbornly—to Nik. She wasn't sure what it meant, and she wasn't about to dwell on it. Not yet.

★★★

The air inside Eileen's office carried the weight of an impending decision. The Fallen sat in a deliberate silence, each aware of why they were there. The firelight cast long shadows along the bookshelves, flickering over worn leather bindings and ancient tomes.

Eileen sat behind her desk, her presence as immovable as the foundation of the building itself. She didn't lean forward, didn't adjust her posture—she simply was, commanding the space without effort. Her attention settled on Riichi first.

"You want her on the front line," she said, not a question, but a challenge. "Convince me."

Riichi, seated in the chair across from her, met her gaze without hesitation. He didn't shift, didn't fidget. When he spoke, it was with the certainty of a man who had already thought through every argument. "Takoda has earned her place in combat," he said, his voice measured but firm. "She's refined her emotional alchemy to the point where she can use it with intention, integrating it seamlessly into her techniques. In training, she's demonstrated both control and adaptability. I wouldn't push for this if I had any doubts."

Takoda sat on the couch beside Aislinn, her shoulders squared, her hands steady in her lap. Riichi's confidence in her wasn't new, but hearing it spoken aloud, in front of Eileen, solidified it in a way that settled deep in her chest.

She exhaled, centering herself before she spoke. "Eileen, I respect your caution, but I know my abilities. I believe I belong on the front lines." No doubt. No hesitation. "I've trained for this, and I trust myself to handle whatever comes."

Eileen didn't immediately respond, though her focus sharpened.

Aislinn leaned forward, elbows on her knees, her expression resolute. "Takoda's been through worse than training exercises. She's not just prepared—she's already been tested. I've seen her fight through circumstances that would have crushed most people. She doesn't break."

Eileen gave a slight nod, acknowledging Aislinn's words, but her thoughts remained impassive.

Rowan, standing near the bookshelf, crossed his arms. "I've only seen her fight once, but it was enough to see her potential. If she has the right guidance, she'll transition well."

Oak, seated in the chair opposite Riichi, regarded Takoda with the measured patience of someone who understood the gap between skill and true readiness. "She's disciplined. Controlled." His tone held a quiet certainty, each word grounded in years of battle-worn insight. "But stepping into a real fight isn't the same as training for one. The rhythm is unpredictable, the stakes unforgiving. It's not about ability—it's about adapting when everything shifts."

His words weren't discouragement, only truth.

Eileen's expression didn't soften, but there was consideration in her posture. "Your arguments hold merit," she said. "But skill alone doesn't decide a battle." Her attention darted to Takoda. "Once you cross into real combat, you don't return as the same person. Readiness isn't just about ability—it's about what you're willing to face."

Takoda absorbed the warning but didn't waver.

Riichi leaned forward, his composure steady. "Then let her step forward."

Eileen studied him for a beat before turning back to Takoda. "I'm willing to consider it," she said at last. "But I need to be sure." She steepled her fingers, her posture resolute. "By the end of the day, I'll have a test for you. One that will prove whether or not you're ready."

Takoda met her eyes directly. "I won't disappoint you."

Eileen nodded, expectation clear in her tone. "Then I look forward to seeing what you can do."

The meeting ended not with closure, but with momentum. Takoda left the office knowing this wasn't just a chance to prove herself to the team—it was a moment to define herself.

★★★

Laughter drifted between Ariel and Rain as they lounged near the hearth, the crackling fire filling the space with a lazy warmth.

Vine strolled over, hands in his pockets, amusement flickering in his expression. He'd clearly been waiting for this.

"Well, ladies, looks like you're in for a treat—you get to hang out with me today."

Rain didn't miss a beat, rolling her eyes with exaggerated exasperation. "Lucky me. Oh wait—" She shot Ariel a teasing grin as she slung her bag over her shoulder. "Actually, only Ariel's stuck with you. I, unfortunately, have other plans... like, I don't know, shaving my legs."

Ariel let out a laugh as Rain tossed her a wink and disappeared down the hall, leaving the room quieter, the warmth of their laughter still lingering.

She turned to Vine, eyes glinting with mischief. "So, Mr. Vegas," she teased, crossing her arms as she leaned back against the couch. "What's the plan? Or do you just expect me to entertain you?"

Vine shrugged, an easy motion, though his response was slower, as if he wasn't entirely sure how to answer. "Honestly? No clue. I don't really do 'days off.'"

Ariel tilted her head, watching him. Vine always carried himself with control, a sharp-edged confidence that rarely slipped, but now... there was a shift in him. Not reluctance, exactly—just unfamiliarity.

"Okay, fair," she said. "What about back home? What do you usually do in Vegas?"

A smirk tugged at his lips, the kind that hinted at a private joke only he understood. "Mostly investments, watching the market," he said smoothly, as if stating the obvious. "Sometimes I'll catch some live music. Or take a drive out of the city if I need a change of scenery."

Ariel listened, catching the subtle shift beneath his words. For all his easy charm, there was a part of him that needed distance, even in a city built for indulgence.

She grinned. "Want to do one of those?"

Vine let out a quiet chuckle, the tension in his shoulders easing a fraction. "Honestly? Anything that gets me out of here for a day sounds good to me."

Ariel's grin widened. "Perfect. I've got an idea." She pushed off the couch, dusting off her jacket with unnecessary flair before gesturing for him to follow. "Go grab your coat and keys. Meet me out front."

Vine raised a skeptical brow. "Should I be concerned?"

She tilted her head, eyes glinting with mischief. "Only if you don't trust me."

Vine scoffed but turned toward the stairs.

"Oh, and change into something normal!" Ariel called after him. "We're not going to a funeral—you can skip all the black."

A rare laugh slipped from him, low and amused, before he disappeared upstairs.

Ariel rocked on her heels, fingers drumming absently against her thigh as she ran through her plan. This wasn't about killing time. Vine lived in structure—discipline, control, order. Today, she wanted to give him the opposite. No strategy. No mission. Just a day that didn't demand anything from him.

A few minutes later, footsteps sounded on the stairs, and she glanced over to see him return. Dark jeans, a fitted black sweater, his usual combat boots. No weapons in sight, though she had no doubt he was still armed in some way.

A fleeting look of curiosity crossed her face. "Well, at least it's not all black," she quipped. "It'll do."

Vine shrugged. "I like black."

Ariel sighed dramatically. "Shocking."

A hint of a grin ghosted across his lips—subtle, but real. "Guess so. Lead the way."

Ariel threw open the door and stepped outside, the cool morning air crisp against her skin.

Today wasn't about the Fallen. Or battles. Or duty.

Today was about showing Vine what it meant to just be.

★★★

The courtyard, recently cleared of snow by the Fallen's elemental magicks, stretched wide before them, patches of slush and ice catching the morning light. Though the general training session had ended, Riichi, Takoda, Aislinn, Oak, and Rowan remained, all knowing this was where the real test began.

Riichi turned to Takoda, his expression edged with challenge. "How about we give them a preview?"

Takoda met his gaze, reading his intent before he even spoke. With a steady breath, she reached inward, activating their bond. The energy surged between them, alive and waiting. In an instant, a warm, molten glow wrapped around them both, Radiant Surge crackling to life in a pulse of deep orange light.

Aislinn's lips parted slightly before a grin took over. "So you two did it—fully bonded," she said, clearly impressed.

Oak observed them in quiet contemplation before offering a nod of approval. "That's strong," he remarked. Not just praise, but recognition of a connection that mattered.

Rowan crossed his arms, his sharp gaze assessing the energy around them. "It's solid," he said, then tipped his chin toward the glow. "But you'll need to get a handle on that. Glowing in battle isn't exactly an advantage."

Aislinn chuckled. "Trust me, took us a while to figure that out. Think of it like holding back a strike—power's still there, just not broadcasting itself to everyone."

Riichi and Takoda exchanged a glance. The glow softened—not gone, but drawn inward, no longer an exposed current but a force waiting beneath the surface.

Oak stepped forward, his presence centering the space between them. "Now show me you can use it."

Riichi's grip on their connection stabilized, the shift in his stance one of quiet antici-pation. "Let's make it count."

Takoda squared her footing beside him, the energy still humming through her. "We're ready."

With a flick of Oak's wrist, the training course changed. The terrain turned unpredictable. Ice patches disrupted footing, barriers forced agility, and shifting targets filled the space with movement designed to demand instinct, not thought.

The signal came.

Riichi was already in motion. His katana cut through the first target with effortless precision. Takoda adjusted a half-step behind, her body flowing into a defensive sweep, flipping the second target into the ground before it had a chance to strike.

Another attack from above. Riichi's blade shot up, deflecting the blow in one seamless movement. Takoda pivoted beneath him, countering with a strike of her own—her reflexes sharpening as the pulse of their bond filled the gaps in her timing.

From the sidelines, Aislinn let out a low whistle. "She's catching on fast."

Rowan barely blinked, his focus locked on them. "Not just catching on. She's adapting."

The course escalated. More targets, shifting terrain. Riichi moved with his usual lethal efficiency, his blade never lingering longer than necessary. Takoda adjusted alongside him, each movement smoother than the last. The energy between them carried her forward, refining her rhythm, drawing her into the unspoken cadence of Riichi's combat style.

A cluster of dummies activated in rapid succession. Riichi's katana slashed in quick, decisive strikes. Takoda moved seamlessly with him, filling in the spaces between his attacks, modifying to cover the openings instinctively.

The final sequence came faster than expected. A coordinated rush—multiple targets, no time to plan. Riichi was already moving, his blade carving through the chaos with honed accuracy. Takoda didn't think—she just moved. Her body responded, not to separate threats but to the rhythm of their combined attack, her jujutsu slipping into the spaces where Riichi's strikes had already landed.

By the time the last dummy fell, they were no longer just reacting to each other—they were moving together.

The orange glow around them pulsed steady and controlled, woven into their synchronization rather than existing outside of it.

The silence that followed carried the weight of what had just happened.

Oak stepped forward, watching them for a moment before speaking. "That's a start," he said, his voice even but carrying a deeper weight beneath it. "Keep training like this, and soon you won't just be keeping up. You'll be the ones setting the pace."

As training continued, Riichi and Takoda's rhythm became sharper, their movements more attuned, but the challenge remained. Their bond heightened Takoda's reflexes, allowing her to respond with near-instant reactions to Riichi's hyper-accelerated pace. Yet, the high-pressure conditions of the course demanded more than instinct alone.

At one point, while weaving through a rush of incoming targets, Takoda's concentration slipped—just for a breath. The bond wavered, her balance faltered, and she stumbled. She caught herself quickly, but the disruption was enough to drive home a critical lesson—staying in sync required more than just raw connection. It required control.

Rowan stepped forward, his gaze sharp as he studied her stance. "Try not to overthink it," he advised. "The bond is meant to guide you, not the other way around."

Aislinn moved beside her, offering a small nod. "You've got this. Just breathe—focus on Riichi. Let the bond center you."

Takoda steadied herself, exhaling slowly as she let the warmth of their connection settle her. The next round, she adjusted faster. Each sequence demanded more, but she moved with growing confidence, her instincts sharpening as she leaned fully into the bond.

As the final round concluded, the sound of approaching footsteps cut through the air, drawing everyone's attention.

Eileen stepped into the courtyard.

She moved with quiet precision, her presence alone enough to still the group. Gone was her usual leadership attire. Instead, she wore fitted black combat gear, her hair drawn back in a no-nonsense ponytail. The change was subtle, but unmistakable—this was not a conversation. This was a test.

Her gaze swept over them before settling on Takoda.

"Takoda," Eileen said, her voice even, controlled. "Let's see if you're ready. If you can best me in a sparring match, you'll have your place on the combat team. If not, you stay with support."

The words landed like a blade in the cold air.

Takoda's breath caught, surprise flared in her eyes before she schooled her expression. She glanced at Riichi. He didn't hesitate—just gave a small nod, his quiet confidence in her steady and unwavering.

A beat of silence stretched between them before Oak shifted uncomfortably, glancing between Eileen and Takoda. His expression was unreadable, but there was an edge of concern in the way he straightened, as if already questioning the necessity of this challenge. He took a step forward. "Eileen, I'm not sure—"

Riichi moved before he could finish, placing a firm hand on Oak's shoulder. His voice, though quiet, carried certainty. "Let's see what happens."

Oak hesitated, his jaw tightening. Even as he stepped back, the tension didn't leave his stance.

The courtyard grew still, anticipation thick in the cold air.

Takoda straightened, the weight of Eileen's challenge settling fully now. This wasn't just about securing her place in combat—it was about proving she belonged there. To Eileen. To the team. To herself.

The bond pulsed between her and Riichi, strong, steadfast, a silent force anchoring her resolve.

She lifted her chin, her expression shifting—no hesitation, only focus.

With a final glance at Riichi, Takoda stepped forward.

The group watched in silence as she and Eileen squared off, bracing for what was to come.

★★★

Vine stepped outside, casual yet effortlessly cool in dark jeans, black boots, and a fitted black knit turtleneck sweater. Ariel eyed him with an approving once-over, taking in his all-black attire.

"Don't you *ever* wear anything other than black?" she teased, crossing her arms.

He shrugged, unbothered. "I told you. I like black."

As they walked toward his car, Vine shot her a sidelong glance, his mouth quirking slightly. "Mind if I drive? Just in case I need a quick escape."

Ariel rolled her eyes. "Fine, but you're stuck with me today," she replied, sliding into the passenger seat of his sleek black Porsche. The car's quiet power suited him, and as he settled in, she caught the subtle ease in his posture, as if the day already felt different.

She refused to reveal the destination, instead feeding him turn-by-turn directions. As they navigated the streets, she made a point to tease him about his perpetually serious expression, tossing lighthearted jabs, while he countered with dry, effortless comebacks. Their usual guardedness thinned, peeling back in small moments, neither of them pushing, but neither resisting the natural pull between them.

When they finally arrived at a bustling indoor entertainment complex, laughter and flashing lights spilled out from the entrance. Vine took in the crowded scene and raised an eyebrow.

"An indoor playground?" His tone was skeptical, but not entirely dismissive.

Ariel grinned, undeterred. "Yep. Come on," she said, grabbing his arm. "Let's see if you can keep up."

Inside, she led him straight to the go-karts, her competitive streak surfacing instantly. "Think you're up for a race?"

Vine chuckled, his amusement clear despite his usual restraint. "We'll see."

They climbed into their karts, and the moment the race started, Ariel floored the gas. She laughed every time she surged ahead, barely skidding around the track's tight turns, her energy infectious. Vine played it differently, his movements measured, his approach calculated. He didn't rush—he studied, waited, then overtook her with infuriating ease.

By the time they pulled into the pit, both were breathless, their laughter lingering between them.

Vine gestured toward the next set of activities, his eyes settling on the rock climbing wall and strength-testing games. Without a word, he walked over to the punching bag machine, sizing it up before landing a precise, powerful strike that sent the marker high.

Ariel crossed her arms, grinning. "Bet you can't do it again."

He met her gaze, a glint of playfulness and challenge behind his cool exterior. "Challenge accepted."

They continued exploring the complex, moving from one game to another, exchanging victories and sarcastic remarks in equal measure. When it was Ariel's turn to pick, she led him to the arcade, her enthusiasm only growing as they competed across the machines.

At the claw machine, she watched as Vine studied the game with his usual sharp focus. He failed his first attempt, then the second, and she snickered at his narrowed gaze.

"You're really giving the claw machine the Vine treatment, huh?"

Without looking at her, he adjusted his approach and tried again. The claw descended, latched onto a stuffed animal, and—finally—dropped it into the chute. He retrieved it and handed it to her without ceremony.

"Sometimes persistence pays off," he said, feigning indifference.

Ariel smirked, tucking the plush under her arm. "Admit it. You got invested."

Vine only glanced toward the next section. "What's next?"

When she spotted the Halloween-themed escape room, her eyes lit up, and she grabbed his arm before he could protest. The dim lighting and eerie decorations created a spooky but fun atmosphere, and they moved through the puzzles together, Ariel's enthusiasm a perfect contrast to Vine's steady, methodical approach.

"Didn't expect you to be this good at an escape room," she remarked, watching as he scanned the room with keen attention.

His lips twitching at the corners. "Quick thinking has its perks."

As they worked through the challenges, the banter between them grew easier, laughter slipping in naturally, the guardedness from earlier now completely absent. By the time they solved the final puzzle, a quiet, mutual understanding had settled between them.

As early evening approached, Ariel glanced around before turning back to him, her grin confident. "Alright, I think we've conquered this place. How about we take the adventure somewhere else?"

Vine nodded, a glint of intrigue in his eyes. "Lead on, troublemaker."

Back in his car, Ariel directed Vine through winding streets until they pulled up to a dimly lit underground entrance decorated with faint Halloween touches. He scanned the scene, his brow lifting slightly in mild curiosity.

"A haunted basement?" he remarked, his tone unreadable.

Ariel flashed a knowing look. "Trust me."

Inside, the club was dark and cozy, the eerie lighting casting flickering shadows across the space. Low music thrummed beneath the murmur of conversation, the atmosphere laid-back but lively.

Ariel browsed the drink menu, grinning when she found a fitting choice. "Witches' Brew for me," she said, then handed Vine another option. "You get a 'Vampire's Kiss.'"

Vine gave her a skeptical look but took the drink without protest. "Naturally."

They clinked glasses, sharing a quiet laugh before settling in. As they sipped, Ariel took the opportunity to tease him about the over-the-top Halloween décor, pointing out the gaudy cobwebs and the occasional animatronic bat. Vine responded with his usual dry humor, his steady presence an easy contrast to her energy.

The balance between them felt natural, their interactions effortless.

When Ariel spotted the pool table in the corner, she nudged his arm. "Think you're up for a game?"

Vine set down his drink and stood. "I'll give it a shot."

It didn't take long for her to realize she was terrible at pool. She lined up her shots with confidence—only for them to veer wildly off course. Vine, on the other hand, sank each one with calm precision.

She scowled at the table. "I think you hustled me."

Vine leaned on his cue stick, amusement ghosting in his eyes. "If I were hustling, I'd let you win first."

Her next shot barely grazed the ball.

Vine exhaled a quiet chuckle, then moved behind her, adjusting her grip over the cue. The shift in proximity sent a slow awareness through her, his presence solid against her back, the warmth of his hands firm but easy.

"Try this," he murmured, guiding her aim.

Ariel focused, more on the weight of his touch than the game. She took the shot—it was better, but not by much.

Vine tilted his head slightly, his voice edged with dry amusement. "Progress."

She stepped forward, putting space between them even as a hum of tension lingered. "You sound so impressed."

"Wildly."

They played a few more rounds before Ariel eventually set her cue aside. "Alright, I concede. But we're not done yet."

Her attention cut toward the dance floor. The moment Vine followed her gaze, she grinned.

"Tell me you dance."

He exhaled, slow and measured. "I didn't say I don't."

"Then prove it." She grabbed his wrist before he could change his mind, tugging him onto the floor.

The music pulsed through the room, an upbeat rhythm thrumming beneath their movements. Ariel swayed effortlessly, her steps light and confident as she let the beat guide her. Vine remained composed, his movements measured, but he didn't resist when she met his gaze and stepped closer, her energy drawing him in.

Then the song shifted, the tempo slowing, the change coaxing them into a different rhythm. Ariel's hands drifted up to his shoulders, a natural adjustment to the new pace. Vine's grip settled at her waist, firm but unhurried, his warmth sinking through the thin fabric of her shirt. The shift between them was subtle but undeniable—an awareness deepening in the space they shared.

Ariel met his gaze, her lips parting slightly as they moved in sync, the tension curling between them like an unspoken challenge. Neither of them pulled away. Neither of them broke the moment.

As the song faded into the next, Ariel exhaled a quiet laugh and stepped back, letting her hands fall away. "Not bad."

Vine mirrored her, his expression unreadable, but the flicker of amusement in his eyes gave him away. "Likewise."

After a few more songs, they decided to call it a night. By eleven, Ariel was tipsy, her laughter carrying through the cool evening air as they left the club. Vine walked beside her, steady as ever, his usual composure unchanged but his gaze flicked to her more often than usual.

At the car, she leaned against the door and grinned up at him. "How are you still so sober after all that?"

Vine smirked, casting her a sideways glance. "Benefits of being Fallen—high metabolism. Takes more than a few drinks."

Ariel huffed, shaking her head as she climbed into the passenger seat. The drive back was quiet, the city lights blurring past, their earlier energy settling into an easy calm.

She stretched her legs, tilting her head back against the seat, exhaling slowly. The night had gone differently than she expected, and she had a feeling Vine wasn't quite expecting it either.

Vine glanced over at her, a faint smile softening his expression as he took in her contented look, knowing they'd both found a new sense of ease with each other.

★★★

Back at the mansion, the training grounds were quiet, the mid-afternoon sun casting long shadows over the field. A charge of anticipation lingered in the crisp air as Takoda prepared for her sparring match with Eileen. Off to the side, Riichi, Aislinn, Rowan, and Oak stood watching, their expressions a mix of encouragement and curiosity.

Takoda glanced between them before looking at Eileen, brow furrowing. "Are you serious?"

Eileen nodded, her stance relaxed but unmistakably firm. "Yes. This is how I'll test your skills."

Takoda searched the faces of the others, but no one seemed surprised by the challenge. Riichi stepped forward, resting a hand on her shoulder. His voice was low, meant only for her.

"You've got this, Takoda. Show her what you can do."

The quiet confidence in his words settled her nerves, grounding her. Aislinn, standing nearby, grinned. "You'd better be ready, Mom. Takoda just might surprise you." She turned to Takoda, mischief dancing in her gaze. "This is going to be fun to watch."

Takoda inhaled deeply, centering herself as she faced Eileen. The bond with Riichi pulsed steadily, a quiet reassurance strengthening her resolve.

The match began.

Eileen's movements were measured at first, her approach almost leisurely. She shifted with the kind of precision that came from experience, testing Takoda's reflexes rather than attacking outright. Takoda recognized the tactic and seized the opening.

She moved—fast. Closing the distance in an instant, she executed a flawless jujutsu maneuver, using Eileen's own stance against her. A sharp twist, a fluid motion, and Eileen was on the ground.

A breath of surprise passed through the onlookers. Even Eileen, as she rose to her feet, had a glint of approval in her eyes. She dusted off her sleeves and gave Takoda a small, approving nod.

"Looks like I'll need to give you a real challenge, then."

The shift was immediate. Eileen dropped lower into a balanced stance, her presence sharpening, the air around them thickening with focus. When she came forward this time, it wasn't to test Takoda—it was to push her.

Takoda exhaled, steeling herself.

The pace quickened. Eileen's strikes were precise, her footwork seamless. Takoda countered with agility, adapting, adjusting, responding to every move. The sparring became a relentless exchange, each clash revealing the depth of Takoda's discipline.

She could feel it now—what Riichi had meant when he told her to trust herself. The bond between them was steady, amplifying her awareness, helping her anticipate Eileen's movements.

Eileen landed a few clean strikes, but Takoda recovered quickly, her responses becoming sharper, more fluid. The more she leaned into the fight, the more confident she became, her movements no longer reactive but instinctive.

From the sidelines, the others watched in silence. Aislinn's eyes were bright with excitement, and Rowan's expression held a quiet respect. Oak, arms crossed, gave a small nod of approval.

Takoda barely noticed. Her focus was on Eileen—on the way their movements had fallen into sync, a rhythmic exchange of offense and defense. Her breath came faster now, but she didn't falter. She didn't hold back.

Then, finally, they reached a pause, both holding their positions, their breathing measured.

Eileen tilted her head slightly, then raised a hand, signaling the end of the match. A small, satisfied smile played at her lips.

"Welcome to the combat team, Takoda," she said, stepping forward. "You've earned it."

Relief and triumph swelled within Takoda. She glanced toward Riichi, whose nod carried quiet pride. Aislinn clapped, beaming, and even Rowan offered a brief but sincere, "Well done."

Eileen's expression softened slightly as she added, "Keep up this level of focus and commitment, and you'll be an invaluable member of the team."

Takoda straightened, her chest rising with steady breath. "Thank you, Eileen. I won't let you down."

Then, smiling, she turned to the others. "I think it's my turn to cook. Let's head inside, and I'll make us something to eat."

Laughter and light conversation filled the air as they walked back toward the mansion, the energy between them lighter than before. The day had been a victory for Takoda, one she had earned—not just in Eileen's eyes, but in her own.

★★★

Vine pulled up to the mansion, turning off the engine as he noticed Ariel fast asleep in the passenger seat. A quiet smile crossed his face as he took in her relaxed expression, her usual energy softened in sleep. He reached over, nudging her shoulder gently.

"Hey, we're back," he murmured.

Ariel stirred, her eyes fluttering open, and she gave him a sleepy smile. "Hmm? Already?"

They stepped out of the car and walked toward the mansion, the quiet between them comfortable. As they reached her door, Vine paused, glancing at her with a slight smile.

"I actually had fun today," he said, his tone softer than usual. "Thanks for the day off."

Ariel paused, her own smile brightening as she leaned casually against the doorframe. "Glad you enjoyed it." She hesitated for a moment, then shrugged. "Want to come in? We could watch some TV before you head out."

Feigning hesitation, Vine tilted his head slightly, his lips quirking. "I suppose I can grace you with my presence a little longer."

With a laugh, she opened the door and let him in, gesturing toward the bed. "Make yourself comfortable," she said, tossing him the remote. "Find something scary."

Vine shot her a dry look at the request but settled back on the bed, scrolling through channels with a faint grin as he searched for a horror movie. Just as he found one that looked promising, a flicker of movement caught his attention.

Ariel had started changing, casually slipping out of her clothes and into her nightwear.

Vine's gaze drifted over, interest flickering beneath his usual composure. "What exactly are you doing?"

Unfazed, Ariel glanced over her shoulder, her expression innocent. "Just putting on my night clothes," she replied with a shrug. "Or did you think I was doing something else?"

Vine chuckled, leaning back as he shot her a smug look. "Maybe. I am pretty good-looking, after all."

She rolled her eyes, muttering under her breath about his "massive ego" as she finished changing. Though he tried to keep his attention on the screen, Vine couldn't help but steal a few glances, his interest piqued by the way she carried herself—completely at ease, completely unbothered.

Once Ariel was done, she joined him on the bed, settling in close beside him. They sat shoulder to shoulder, their attention on the horror movie as it started, the screen casting flickers of light across the room. A tense scene built up, and Ariel flinched at a jump scare, instinctively hiding her face against his shoulder.

Vine chuckled, his tone slightly teasing. "That's not scary at all," he said with a grin. "It's completely fake."

Annoyed by his lack of sympathy, Ariel punched his shoulder playfully, earning a laugh as he grabbed her arm and tackled her back onto the bed. Their laughter mixed together, but as they landed, the atmosphere shifted. Their eyes met, the space between them disappearing as their faces drew closer.

Ariel's gaze darted to his lips, her breath hitching as she leaned in, her usual boldness tempered by the quiet intensity between them. She wasn't hesitating—she was choosing this. Vine didn't wait for second guesses. He closed the distance, capturing her lips in a deep, prolonged kiss that sent a slow burn through them both.

Heat curled through Ariel's veins as she melted into him, their connection electric and undeniable. Vine's hands slid along her waist, fingers splaying as if claiming the moment, the shape of her. She pressed closer, savoring the feel of his warmth, his strength—a presence that both consumed and held her firm.

Tracing a path up her spine, Ariel suppressed a gasp, biting her lip, her breath catching in a way that sent a rush of satisfaction through him. Something about that reaction stirred him, but he set the thought aside. Not when she was pulling him closer, just as eager, just as wanting.

Their kisses deepened, the space between them vanishing as touch and sensation took over. Ariel's fingers mapped out the muscles along his back, her need reflected in the way Vine held her, his grip tightening as if he couldn't get enough, both desperate for further contact. Neither of them wanted restraint—only the rush of feeling, the surrender to the tension that had been building between them all day, the intensity almost suffocating.

Breathless and urgent, every caress stoked the passion building inside them. Ariel barely registered the shift when Vine suddenly pulled away, hovering just above her, his breath uneven. His eyes—dark with hunger, edged with hesitation—searched hers.

"Are you sure about this?" His voice was rough, brimming with self-control.

Ariel barely managed a nod, her pulse thumping loudly in her ears. No need for words. The way she clung to him, pulling him back down, spoke volumes.

He kissed her again, his hand skimming over her hip, eliciting that sharp intake of breath and the way her teeth caught her lower lip. This time, he noticed. *That's a tell.*

His smirk deepened against her mouth. *Interesting.*

In their fevered need for closeness, their hands fumbled as they hastily removed the clothes creating a barrier between them. Clumsy hands and eager lips explored every bit of exposed skin as it was revealed until both stood naked, entirely consumed by their passion.

When they came together, Ariel experienced a sense of completeness like never before. Their bodies fit perfectly, moving in seamless rhythm as they lost themselves in the pleasure.

For Vine, it wasn't just release—it was grounding. A raw, undeniable moment where everything else fell away. No masks, no calculated distance—just her. The heat, the weight, the way they moved together felt familiar yet brand new, as if rediscovering something long forgotten but essential.

He wasn't used to feeling anything past the moment itself, but something about this—about her—stuck in a way he hadn't expected.

Vine's touch ignited a fire along Ariel's skin, setting her senses ablaze. Every nerve in her body seemed to tremble with anticipation as he explored her form with a fervent hunger. Moans of pleasure escaped her lips uncontrollably, surrendering to the overwhelming sensations enveloping her. She felt consumed by him, yet instead of fear, she embraced the pure bliss that coursed through her veins.

Their bodies moved together in perfect harmony, their connection deepening with each shared breath. As Vine's sounds of pleasure mingled with her own, the passion between them intensified, building like a crescendo in an orchestral masterpiece. A spark ignited under his fingertips, spreading through her, propelling her towards a climax that painted vibrant colors behind her closed eyelids.

In that moment of release, Ariel shuddered, her body tensing and then relaxing in euphoric waves. The explosion of pleasure left her completely spent yet utterly satisfied. As Ariel trembled beneath him, Vine felt the last of his control give way. His release hit hard, shooting through him with such force that he lost himself to it, his body seizing and then going slack as he collapsed, breathless, on top of her.

Breathing heavy and overcome with sensation, they lay intertwined for a few precious moments, basking in the lingering echoes of their lovemaking. Ariel's fingers threaded through Vine's hair, a gentle caress that spoke volumes in the silence between them.

After a moment, Vine let out a quiet chuckle, the sound warm and a little charmed. "Well, that was... unexpected."

Ariel smirked, shooting him a satisfied look as her fingers lazily trailed over his arm. "But fun. We're definitely doing that again," she added, a playful glint in her eye.

She propped herself up on one elbow, watching him thoughtfully.

*That **had** been fun. Better than fun, actually.* Her gaze drifted over his face, taking in the sharp angles and that ever-present trace of amusement. *Good-looking? Obviously. Confident? Too much. But there were worse things.*

They worked well together—no complications, no expectations. And that was exactly what she wanted. "So... how about friends with benefits?"

Vine's brow lifted slightly, his gaze flickering over her, considering. *Straight to the point. I like that. No strings, **and** she's hot? That works.*

His lips curved into a slow, knowing grin. "I can work with that."

Ariel stretched lazily, her lips curling with satisfaction. "Alright, but there have to be rules." She sat up, her tone light but decisive. "Rule number one: no kissing in public. We're not dating."

Vine nodded, feigning seriousness. "Fair. Rule number two: no hand-holding."

She shot him a look. "Were you planning to hold my hand?"

Vine arched an eyebrow, feigning innocence. "You never know. I can be affectionate."

Ariel snorted. "Yeah, sure."

"No talking about it with any of the Fallen," she added.

Vine tilted his head, a hint of teasing in his eyes. "Keeping it a secret?"

"Less drama that way," she shrugged.

He considered it for a second, then nodded. "Good. Our little secret." A glimmer of shared mischief passed between them.

"No jealousy," she added, her tone firm. "No matter what."

Vine's lips curved into a faint smirk. "Jealous? Please. That's not my style."

Ariel laughed. "Good, because I don't do jealous either."

"No talking about feelings," she said, her eyes gleaming.

"Definitely a rule I can get behind."

Vine chuckled. "Perfect. Emotions are overrated anyway." Their laughter mixed easily, keeping the moment light and boundaries intact.

Ariel stretched, then added, "No calling each other in an emergency either. No 'come save me' scenarios."

Vine's expression shifted slightly, and he shook his head. "Actually, scratch that one. If you're ever in trouble, especially with the Golden Dawn, I want you to call me."

Ariel met his gaze, her own impishness fading just enough to show she understood the weight behind his words. "Fair enough. Same goes for you. Deal?"

"Deal." A small, genuine smile flickered across Vine's face before vanishing.

"And one last thing—no pet names," she said with a grin.

"Oh, I'm definitely calling you something," he replied, mischief dancing in his expression. "But I can promise it won't be 'snookums.'"

Ariel laughed, rolling her eyes. "Good. Because I might call you names, too. But let's keep it to anything other than 'honey' or 'sweetheart'—and definitely not 'snookums.'"

They shared a look, amusement lingering as the ground rules settled between them.

Vine leaned back slightly, watching her with an interested glint in his eye. "You set those rules awfully fast. Do you have these on standby, or am I just special?"

Ariel grinned, stretching lazily. "Oh, definitely special. I handpick my business associates very carefully."

Vine let out a quiet laugh. "Good to know I meet your high standards."

"Alright, final rule," Ariel said, stretching and leaning back. "No spending the night. No rule-breaking here."

She nudged him with a smirk as she sat up. "Which means you need to get going."

Vine let out a quiet laugh, following her lead as they both got dressed, the mood easy and teasing. At her door, Ariel peeked out into the hall, scanning for any signs of movement.

"Use those Fallen skills of yours," she whispered with a teasing smile, "and don't wake anyone up."

Vine chuckled softly, but she quickly shushed him with a laugh, nudging him into the hallway. As he slipped out, she leaned against the door, a lingering smile playing at her lips. For a moment, she let herself bask in the energy of the night, feeling both content and recharged.

Meanwhile, Vine moved through the quiet halls, his steps near soundless as he made his way back to his room. Satisfaction flickered in his expression.

That was a very good day off.

But as he walked, her "rules" replayed in his mind—especially the *no kissing in public* one. Sure, he wouldn't push it in front of the other Fallen... but there were plenty of other places where that rule didn't necessarily apply.

Rules were flexible.

And he had every intention of testing hers.

The early morning light seeped through the curtains in Riichi's room, casting a warm, gentle glow that softened everything it touched. Takoda stirred first, blinking awake in the quiet stillness. She remained still, watching him sleep, his features unguarded, his breathing slow and steady. Moments like this felt like a rare luxury—a fleeting calm in the storm of their world. Warmth curled through her chest, a mix of gratitude and love that settled deep.

Riichi's eyes fluttered open, a faint smile forming as he met her gaze.

"You're making it impossible for me to get out of bed, aren't you?" she murmured, her voice thick with sleep, softened by affection.

His smile deepened. "That's the plan," he teased, voice low.

Their laughter blended with the hush of the morning, the easy warmth between them holding them in place before the day's demands could pull them apart.

Takoda shifted closer, resting her head lightly against his shoulder. After a moment, she exhaled, the words slipping out before she could second-guess them. "I still can't believe I'm on the combat team." Excitement colored her tone, but beneath it, a thread of uncertainty lingered. "I know I owe so much of it to you for speaking up."

Riichi brushed a strand of hair from her face, his touch deliberate, his voice laced with quiet pride. "You earned that place yourself," he said without hesitation. "I only made sure Eileen saw you were ready. The rest? That was all you, Takoda. And I couldn't be prouder."

She felt the strength behind his words, the staunch belief he had in her. It anchored her, reinforced everything she'd worked for.

After a pause, Riichi's expression turned thoughtful. "Georgetown's a different kind of terrain. It won't be like the open space at Fort Lawton," he explained. "It's tight, industrial. We'll need to move differently—stay aware of every corner, every shadow."

Takoda nodded, picturing the enclosed spaces, the shifts in movement they'd need to make. "And if I lose focus, you'll keep me in check?" she asked, tilting her head as a playful smile tugged at her lips.

His fingers tightened briefly around hers, his gaze unwavering. "Always."

Reassurance settled over her, quiet but absolute. A look passed between them—shared purpose, understanding, and a depth of feeling neither had spoken aloud, yet both acknowledged in the space between them.

Leaning back against him, Takoda let the anticipation settle, her mind already moving toward the next challenge. "I'm looking forward to working more with our aura control," she admitted with a laugh. "The last thing we need is to turn into a neon sign in the middle of a fight. And I want to keep up with you in combat."

Riichi's chuckle was low, edged with amusement. "One step at a time," he said, the warmth in his voice matching the confidence in his expression. "We'll make the Surge work for us—not the other way around."

His words lodged in her mind, solidifying her focus. In this quiet moment, their bond felt almost tangible—a promise threaded between them.

After a few more prolonged moments, they eased into the rhythm of the day. Moving around the room, Takoda caught a loose thread on his collar, brushing it off with a quick, instinctive motion. Riichi caught her hand as she did, lacing his fingers through hers, the contact brief but centering, a exchange of compassion.

Hand in hand, they descended the stairs in easy sync, the soft morning light illuminating their steps. At the bottom, they paused, still holding onto each other. Riichi turned toward her, and before a word could pass between them, he leaned in, capturing her lips in a slow, lingering kiss. There was no rush—just the passion of two people who knew each other deeply. It was an unspoken reassurance, a vow.

With one last squeeze of her hand, they parted—Riichi heading toward his meeting with Eileen, while Takoda made her way toward the kitchen, her mind already spinning with thoughts of breakfast preparations for the Fallen. Even as they stepped into their separate tasks, the steady pulse of their bond remained—constant, unshaken, carrying them forward into whatever the day would bring.

The kitchen was alive with the warm scents of freshly brewed coffee and sizzling breakfast. Rain and Ariel sat at the kitchen island, each with a steaming mug in hand, casually cutting up fruit as they chatted with Takoda, who moved around the kitchen, putting the final touches on breakfast. Their conversation was lighthearted, filled with laughter and easygoing remarks about the day ahead. Every now and then, Rain tossed in a playful comment that kept them all grinning.

As the chatter ebbed, Vine strolled in, pausing briefly in the doorway. His expression remained collected, unreadable as ever, his sharp gaze sweeping the room in a composed, almost absent assessment before he made his way to the coffee pot. His arrival brought a subtle shift in the room's energy—not an obvious change, but enough that Ariel noticed. She kept her attention on the fruit in front of her, outwardly indifferent but hyperaware of his presence. They'd agreed last night to keep things private, and she had every intention of making sure they stuck to it.

Rain glanced up from her coffee, curiosity sparking in her expression. "So, Vine," she asked casually, "how was your day off? Eileen's big 'day-off' experiment treating you right?"

Ariel raised an eyebrow, a smirk tugging at her lips as she joined in. "Yeah, Vine, spill," she said, her voice light but edged with playful probing. "Anything exciting?"

Vine's gaze shifted toward her, his expression betraying nothing—but Ariel caught the brief glint of amusement, the almost imperceptible gleam in his eyes before he responded.

"I had a lot of fun," he said smoothly, following the statement with a brief glance her way, just quick enough to be missed by the others. Then, looking back to the group, he added, "*Thoroughly* enjoyed myself."

Ariel's heart did a little flip at his choice of words, but she kept her cool. A faint, almost-hidden smile toyed at the edges of her lips, maybe even a hint of color creeping into her cheeks, but she focused on the fruit in front of her, slicing with practiced ease. The look in her eyes, however, held the satisfaction of someone who knew exactly what he meant.

Takoda, oblivious to the subtext, flashed a warm smile. "Glad to hear it, Vine," she said genuinely. "Everyone deserves a break every once in a while. It's good to see you get one."

Rain nodded, taking another sip of coffee, already shifting her focus toward the day's plans.

Takoda glanced at the time and set down her knife. "Rain, can you help me carry these out?" she asked, gathering a few plates.

"Yeah, got it." Rain grabbed a tray of fruit and headed toward the dining room, Takoda right behind her, leaving Ariel and Vine alone in the kitchen.

Vine shifted, moving closer. Ariel remained focused on the fruit, her hands sure and controlled, but her awareness sharpened as he leaned in, voice pitched low for only her to hear.

"Did I pass your test?" he murmured, the words laced with just enough challenge to keep her guessing.

Ariel chuckled, her lips curling in a knowing grin. "You did," she replied smoothly. "Smooth as ever."

He took a slow sip of his coffee, clearly satisfied. "Good," he said, his tone light, but the smugness was unmistakable.

Just as he began to turn away, Takoda and Rain reentered, carrying more breakfast items for the table. The moment was seamless—Ariel continued cutting fruit as if nothing had happened, and Vine, ever composed, showed no indication of their quiet exchange.

He took a slow step past her, reaching for his coffee on the counter. In the same motion, his fingers brushed against the curve of her hip before delivering a quick, deliberate pinch—so brief, so subtle, that no one else could have noticed. Ariel's breath caught, her grip on the knife tightening for half a second, but she refused to give him the satisfaction of a reaction.

Vine, of course, didn't need one.

He lingered just enough to murmur at her ear, his voice a hushed thread of amusement. "Not a rule," he mused. "Might have to test a few more."

Before she could retort, he was already stepping away, coffee in hand, slipping toward the exit with the same effortless composure he always carried.

Ariel watched him go, her expression neutral, but the glint in her eye told a different story—a thrill at their hidden understanding, the anticipation of a game neither of them had any intention of losing.

★★★

The conference room filled gradually as the team assembled, each member settling into their seats with focused expressions. At the head of the room, Eileen stood with her usual commanding presence, a quiet authority that set the tone before she even spoke. Beside her, Oak remained composed, a silent but supporting force.

Eileen's sharp gaze swept across the room, assessing their readiness. "Thank you all for being here," she began, her voice even and direct. "Today, we'll review the mission details for disrupting the Golden Dawn's rituals in Georgetown. Their efforts to manipulate weather patterns there have intensified, and we need to be prepared for close-quarter tactics. The industrial layout means confined spaces, tight passageways, and limited visibility. Adaptability will be essential."

Her words settled over the room as each team member absorbed the details, mentally preparing for the challenges ahead. She allowed the weight of the briefing to sink in before continuing.

"To maximize our strengths, I've restructured the teams based on specific skill sets," she announced, scanning the room. "This isn't about rank or seniority but about ensuring each of you is positioned where you'll be most effective."

A faint murmur passed through the group, though it quickly faded as they focused on her explanation.

Eileen began with the first team. "Distraction and Surveillance will include Reed, Vine, and Ash. Ash's shapeshifting ability enhances our flexibility in reconnaissance, which will be crucial for this mission."

Vine exchanged a glance with Reed, both nodding in awareness, while Ash gave a subtle nod from his seat, already absorbing his role.

"Next, Disruption and Combat. Riichi, Rowan, Aislinn, Takoda, and Ivy—you'll be our front line for dismantling the rituals directly." Eileen's gaze landed on Takoda. "This is your chance to put your training into practice."

Takoda met her eyes, resolve burning in her chest. She nodded, unwavering, but felt the quiet support of Riichi beside her, focusing her further.

"Lastly, Support and Security," Eileen continued. "Oak, Elder, Willow, and Birch—you'll secure the perimeter and provide reinforcements to maintain control of the area. Birch," she added with a nod, "your Endurance Transference will be vital here. Lending stamina when needed could mean the difference between success and failure."

With each team defined, Eileen clarified their objectives. "The Disruption and Combat team will dismantle active rituals and handle resistance as needed. Distraction and Surveillance will manage perimeter control and gather intel. Support and Security will reinforce and stabilize our position as necessary."

Her tone was sharp, efficient, each word cutting through the room with clarity. Across the table, everyone straightened, the gravity of their assignments sinking in.

Oak took this moment to step in, his voice calm yet authoritative. "Rowan, Aislinn," he said, his gaze shifting between them, "check in with our contacts in Nihonmachi this afternoon. We need updates on Golden Dawn's movements. Prioritize any information that suggests an escalation in ritual activity."

Aislinn gave a short nod, already processing the task, while Rowan absorbed the directive with the same composed focus he always carried.

Eileen's gaze softened slightly as she looked at Riichi and Takoda. "You two will conduct additional bond training after our group session. Your synchronized movement and awareness in combat give us an advantage. Strengthen that connection."

Her attention shifted to Oak, Rowan, and Aislinn. "Continue working with them. The better their coordination, the stronger our combat unit becomes."

Takoda glanced at Riichi, who met her gaze with a quiet but certain smile. This was their opportunity to sharpen their edge, to refine what they had already begun to build.

Oak's steady voice carried through the room. "Tonight, I'm assigning two teams for surveillance. Birch and Ash will cover Georgetown. Reed and Vine will monitor Fort Lawton. Stay sharp. Any sign of ritual activity or an increase in enemy presence needs to be reported immediately."

Eileen allowed a moment for the details to settle before giving a short nod, the finality in her voice leaving no room for doubt. "The success of this mission depends on your focus and adaptability. Prepare for today's training and stay sharp."

A few team members exchanged nods, murmurs of agreement passing between them. The atmosphere was charged with renewed purpose.

Then, Eileen shifted her attention to Elder, a faint but noticeable smile breaking her otherwise serious expression. "One last note—Elder, you have tomorrow off. Rest. That's not a suggestion."

A soft hum of amusement passed through the room at the rare but definitive order.

Eileen gave one last assessing look at the team. "Now, let's get to work."

With that, the team rose, their movements efficient, driven by purpose. They exited with the recognition that today's training wasn't just another session—it was preparation for the fight ahead, one they'd meet together.

The training area lay open to the elements, and a biting wind slashed across the field, cutting through layers of clothing and sinking deep into their bones. Heavy clouds loomed overhead, thick with the promise of snowfall, adding a sense of urgency to their drills. The cold was relentless, pressing in with every gust—a constant, gnawing reminder of the resilience they'd need in Georgetown.

As the teams assembled, focus sharpened, bodies tensing against the chill. The atmosphere turned gritty, the unyielding wind forcing them to adapt—movements crisp, breath visible in the frozen air. It became an unspoken endurance test, one they met without complaint, sheer determination in their eyes.

Reed, Vine, and Ash slipped into position as the Distraction and Surveillance team, diving straight into stealth drills. The wind, unpredictable and sharp, amplified every movement and sound, testing their ability to remain unseen. They moved with precise control, adjusting to the shifting elements, using cover with silent efficiency. Quick glances and subtle hand signals dictated their coordination, their communication stripped to necessity. The weather would betray them if they weren't careful, and they adapted, weaving through the training grounds with calculated accuracy.

Nearby, the Disruption and Combat team—Riichi, Rowan, Aislinn, Takoda, and Ivy—executed takedown drills, dismantling mock ritual symbols with relentless focus. The cold seeped into their muscles, slowing reflexes, but they compensated by attuning to each other's movements, falling into sync. Wind ripped across the field, carrying a stinging bite that made verbal commands useless, forcing them to rely on instinct and nonverbal cues. Quick nods, sharp gestures, and seamless footwork kept them in rhythm, each strike calculated. The bitter air and aching muscles were irrelevant—only efficiency mattered.

On the other side of the field, Oak, Elder, Willow, and Birch—comprising the Support and Security team—worked with the practiced efficiency that came from experience. They set up barriers, secured perimeters, and reinforced positions against the punishing wind. Cold stiffened their fingers, but they kept moving, refusing to let it slow them down. Birch's endurance transference proved vital, siphoning off their fatigue before it could take root, keeping them sharp. Every gust carried a new test, demanding swift adjustments and sharper reflexes, pushing them to anticipate and react with meticulousness.

Through every drill, the weather remained an unrelenting adversary, a force that pressed them together, binding them in shared struggle. Quick glances, brief nods, and fluid movements spoke louder than words—small but vital acknowledgments of trust.

The wind howled through the field as the session came to a close. No one lingered, yet no one rushed. Their movements were careful, bodies thrumming with residual energy, eyes reflecting a quiet readiness. They gathered their things without a word, the looming snowfall a final warning of the resilience they'd need in the days ahead. Bracing against the wind, the teams dispersed, each stepping forward with the unwavering determination to face whatever awaited them together.

The training area had been transformed into a replica of Georgetown's industrial maze, a network of narrow pathways, metal beams, and tight corners that demanded precision and adaptability. Cold wind sliced through the air, carrying the scent of snow, but neither Riichi nor Takoda acknowledged the chill. Their focus was absolute, attuned only to each other and the task before them. Everything else faded into the periphery of their intense practice.

With the wind whipping around them, their movements carried a striking elegance—grace entwined with lethal intent. Riichi moved with the fluidity of a sword dancer, his katana slicing through the air in thoughtful arcs. Each motion followed the rhythm of a kata, measured and honed, his body shifting like water, the blade an extension of his will.

Takoda stood motionless for a moment, absorbing the rhythm of his strikes. She didn't simply mimic him; she felt the movement, aligning herself with the current of his form. Her jujutsu background shaped the way she mirrored his stance—agile and fluid, every shift deceptively soft yet laced with controlled strength. Together, they balanced force and finesse, the contrast between them forming a seamless harmony.

Through the silence of their connection, Riichi's voice brushed against her mind. *Let the movements come to you. Feel the rhythm of the air, not just the blade.*

Takoda sharpened her focus, her thought answering in kind. *I'm listening to the wind. It carries your movements.*

Their telepathic exchange was effortless, deep with consideration. This was more than a matter of matching motions—it was about moving as one, allowing the rhythm of their environment and each other to dictate the flow.

As their warm-up progressed, their synchronization deepened, their pace gradually accelerating. The unhurried kata gave way to faster, more dynamic sequences, each movement a seamless transition into the next. Combat wove into the routine, shifting them from practice into the controlled intensity of a duel. Riichi maneuvered through the course with honed accuracy, his katana flashing between metal beams and tight passages. Takoda adapted with instinctive agility, anticipating his strikes and countering with quick evasions.

Riichi's blade swung toward her in a measured attack. Takoda spun with practiced grace, a whirl of movement that left her standing just behind him, ready to strike. In a swift motion, she sprang up, her foot soaring towards his back in a well-placed kick. He intercepted her leg in midair, skillfully twisting it into a controlled hold. But Takoda instinctively countered, effortlessly slipping out of his grasp and landing nimbly on her feet, moving like water flowing over rock.

The wind howled around them, but it did nothing to break their focus. Their telepathic conversation threaded through the clash of motion.

You're holding back, Takoda challenged, her tone edged with amusement. *What would this look like if I weren't here?*

Then I wouldn't be able to move with such fluidity, Riichi replied, his thought infused with respect. *We are only as strong as we are together.*

Their exchange was more than just words—it resonated through every strike and counter, a demonstration of trust, adaptation, and understanding. Each movement held weight, an unspoken recognition of the other's strength. Riichi's steadfast respect for Takoda's abilities was evident in the way he engaged her fully, and with each exchange, her knowledge of his style deepened. She wasn't just keeping up with him; she was learning him, refining her reactions to complement his own.

Their pace quickened again, escalating into full combat. Riichi's katana became a blur, his attacks swift, each strike honed for efficiency. Takoda kept ahead of him, her movements fluid as she wove through the obstacle course, every evasion calculated. Their fight was more than a clash of skill—it was a dance of attack and defense, an intricate display of balance and synchronization. The structures around them ceased to be obstacles; they became part of the fight, their surroundings shaping the rhythm of their engagement.

You're anticipating my moves now, Riichi thought, a trace of a smile threading through his mental voice. *You're almost reading my mind.*

I'm not reading your mind, Takoda countered, her thought firm, filled with certainty. *I'm feeling it. I can sense where you're going before **you** do.*

Their bond strengthened with every exchange, their combat evolving beyond conscious thought. It had become instinctual, a wordless trust dictating their reactions. They no longer had to think through each motion—their awareness of each other's presence had sharpened into an unshakable rhythm, allowing them to respond with seamless intuition.

As their movements intensified, they worked to dim their Radiant Surge, forcing the orange glow surrounding them to fade into a barely perceptible flicker. The energy still coursed through them, amplifying their strength and coordination, but they held it just beneath the surface, moving with quiet, controlled power. Their combat no longer relied on raw force—it was refined, deliberate, every motion an exercise in balance rather than excess.

On the sidelines, Oak observed with a measured gaze, studying the way they adapted to suppressing their Surge. His voice carried across the training ground, calm but purposeful. "You're pushing too hard to control it," he noted, the words guiding rather than correcting. "Let the energy flow through, but don't suppress it too much. The flow is your power—let it guide your next move."

Takoda took a centering breath, absorbing Oak's words. She shifted her focus, allowing the energy within her to settle into its natural rhythm rather than forcing it into submission. Immediately, she felt the change—an effortless current that carried through her body, sharpening her movements with newfound fluidity and power.

Through their bond, Riichi's thought reached her, steady yet gentle. *Let it flow—feel it. Trust the Surge, but don't overpower it.*

Her response came without hesitation. *I trust you. I trust this bond.*

The certainty in her thought deepened their rhythm, an unshakable confidence threading through their connection.

They pressed into the final phase of their training, testing the boundaries of their synchronization. Riichi's katana flashed through the air, each strike wielded with lethal precision. Takoda flowed around him, anticipating every movement before it fully formed. She flipped over him, landing behind him with practiced ease, using the momentum of his swing against him. With seamless grace, she dropped into a takedown, guiding him down without resistance.

In that moment, hesitation no longer existed. They weren't simply matching each other—they had fully attuned to one another's movement, reacting in complete harmony. They weren't two fighters working together. They had become one.

We've become one, Riichi's thought murmured through the bond, laced with wonder. *Keep moving like this.*

This is our rhythm, Takoda replied, the words carrying certainty. *We're ready.*

The final sequence of strikes and counters came to a close, their footwork slowing as the last echoes of movement faded. Breath misted in the cold air, but neither of them felt the chill. They stood together, chests rising and falling in unison, the satisfaction of perfect synchronization evident between them. Their bond had elevated them beyond individual skill—it had amplified their strength into a force neither could have reached alone.

From the sidelines, Rowan's usually guarded expression shifted, his sharp gaze softening with measured approval. For a long moment, he didn't speak, absorbing the effortless unity between them. When he finally broke the silence, his voice carried quiet awe. "You two are ready. That's exactly how it should look in the field." His gaze shifted to Takoda, respect glinting in his eyes. "I never thought I'd see anyone keep up with him like that... you're more than ready for what's coming."

The depth of Rowan's approval hit unexpectedly, his respect clear in a way that went beyond simple acknowledgment.

From a few steps behind, Aislinn smiled, her voice warm as she took them in. "That was perfect," she said, her gaze shifting between Riichi and Takoda. "You've both mastered it. Takoda, I honestly couldn't believe how fluid you've become. It's like you've always been a part of him."

There was an undeniable spark of admiration in her eyes, an appreciation for what they had just demonstrated—a bond that had evolved beyond technique, seamlessly woven into every movement.

Oak remained silent for a long beat, his usual composed demeanor tempered by a rare note of reverence. When he finally spoke, his voice carried an uncharacteristic depth. "You've found your flow," he said, his gaze assessing. "Your bond is… extraordinary. It's not just about skill anymore—it's the energy you share, the trust between you. Don't forget this. Keep that control." His eyes moved between them, weighing their potential. "You've become a force to be reckoned with."

There was no flourish to his words, no exaggerated praise—just quiet certainty, the kind that carried real meaning.

The cold wind swirled around them, but neither Riichi nor Takoda felt the bite of it. As they held each other's gaze, comprehension passed between them. They had crossed a threshold in their training, reached a level of connection that couldn't be undone.

Without another word, they stepped off the training grounds, the connection between them stronger than ever. Their bond wasn't just instinct now—it was a force, one that neither of them would question.

★★★

Nihonmachi thrummed with energy, its narrow streets lined with small shops and older buildings steeped in history. The cold wind sliced through the alleyways, carrying a sharp chill that settled deep, amplifying the tension humming beneath the surface. Rowan and Aislinn moved with intent, their senses sharp, attuned to the subtle undercurrent in the air. This district had always held secrets, but tonight, the silence felt heavier—like an unseen presence watched from the edges, just beyond reach.

They had come to meet new contacts, hoping to uncover any threads tied to the Golden Dawn's movements—especially rumors of a larger ritual forming in the shadows.

Their first stop was a small, tucked-away tea shop nestled between two taller buildings. Inside, the warmth wrapped around them like a protective cocoon, the delicate fragrance of steeped leaves and herbs offering a momentary reprieve. Behind the counter, Nami, the young shop owner, looked up warily, her eyes sharp with unspoken awareness. Rowan approached her with respect, offering a nod and a simple promise—to help keep the supernatural disturbances in Nihonmachi in check.

She hesitated only briefly before speaking.

"There's been a shift lately…" Nami murmured, her voice hushed but urgent as she prepared a fresh pot of tea. "The winds—they're different. Stronger. And people are acting strangely. I've heard whispers of gatherings, strangers asking questions they shouldn't be asking." She cast a glance toward the door, as if the walls themselves might listen in. "They aren't from here. They're pulling people in, spreading their influence like a slow-moving tide."

Rowan leaned in slightly. "Who are they? What are they after?"

Nami's fingers tightened around the teapot. "I don't know for certain… but it feels dark, powerful—an intrusion that doesn't belong." She lowered her voice. "There are rumors of a ritual being planned, one unlike anything I've heard before. They're reaching beyond elemental control. This is more than just storms."

Rowan thanked her, leaving her with a final warning to stay vigilant. He and Aislinn stepped back into the night, moving toward their next contact—a small bookstore tucked into a quieter corner of the district.

Inside, the scent of old paper filled the air, the dimly lit space lined with shelves of history and supernatural lore. The proprietor, a middle-aged man with wary eyes, greeted them with a curt nod. His attention darted toward the door before he spoke, voice low and cautious.

"I've heard strange things happening in the city," he admitted, watching them carefully. "New faces, gatherings… but it's more than that." He leaned forward slightly, his voice dipping lower. "There's a presence—a darker power. It's not from this world, and it's growing. It's… connected to them, in ways I don't think they even fully understand."

Aislinn's brow furrowed. "Do you know what they're trying to do? What's their endgame?"

The man hesitated, his fingers tracing the worn edge of the counter. "From what I've heard, this isn't just about manipulating the elements. They're reaching for a force far older than any of us, something that shouldn't be bound by human hands. They're trying to harness power that's been buried for centuries, the kind that refuses to be controlled." His eyes darkened. "They stick to places with history, sites where magic still lingers beneath the surface. Be careful if you go looking for them. They'll know you're watching."

Aislinn and Rowan exchanged a look. This was worse than they had expected.

As they left the bookstore, Rowan felt it before he saw it—a faint prickle at the back of his neck, the unmistakable sensation of being watched. He kept his pace even, barely tilting his head as he muttered, "We're being followed. Keep moving, but don't let them close in."

Aislinn's gaze remained forward, her voice just above a whisper. "Who?"

"One of their new recruits, most likely," Rowan murmured. "They've noticed us asking questions, and they don't like it."

Aislinn risked a quick glance back. A figure in dark clothing trailed them, hood drawn low, movements careful—casual to an untrained eye, but deliberate. Intentional.

Without hesitation, Rowan and Aislinn picked up their pace, weaving through the tight-knit streets, their steps precise but unhurried. Turning sharply down a narrow alleyway, they pressed themselves against the wall, silent, waiting. The figure strode past without hesitation, unaware of their hiding place.

Only when the street fell quiet did Rowan exhale. "We lost them," he murmured. "But this isn't over. The Golden Dawn isn't just gathering power—they're tracking us now."

Aislinn's expression hardened. "We can't afford mistakes. If they've started following us, it means they're looking for more than just information."

Rowan's attention snapped to the alley entrance, his jaw tightening. "If they find the mansion—"

"We can't let that happen," Aislinn cut in, her voice firm, leaving no room for doubt.

Rowan pulled out his phone and typed quickly: *Had a 10-foot shadow in Nihonmachi. Need to get some sunscreen.*

A response came almost instantly. His phone vibrated. Aislinn's did too.

Eileen's message was short but unmistakable. *The morning sun casts a shadow that must stay outside.*

It wasn't just for them—it was a warning to every Fallen. The Golden Dawn had started tracking their movements. No one could afford to lead them back. Every precaution had to be taken.

The wind cut against their faces as they resumed their path, urgency thrumming beneath their measured steps. The Golden Dawn wasn't just growing—they were watching. Waiting.

And now, the hunt had begun.

★★★

The Fallen gathered in the mansion's common area, unwinding after a long day of training and preparation. A rare sense of ease settled over the group, the usual tension lifting as laughter and conversation filled the space. Ariel and Rain, having schemed to inject some fun into the mix, stood beside a pile of orange and black bags, each one labeled with a name. The night's mission? Costumes.

Ariel's eyes gleamed with mischief as she lifted the first bag. "Alright, everyone, time to get into the Halloween spirit! Costumes are here, and there's no backing out. Everyone wears theirs, whether you like it or not!"

Scattered chuckles rippled through the group, but Rain, her tone playful yet firm, wasn't about to let anyone off the hook. "I swear, this is the best part of the day. If you didn't pick a costume, I took the liberty of choosing one for you—think of it as a gift. So, brace yourselves."

One by one, they distributed the costumes, starting with Riichi. Rain handed him a sleek black bag, a knowing smirk curving her lips. "Takoda said no ninjas, so we got creative. You're a Japanese dragon warrior—still powerful, but with a little more fire."

Ariel grinned. "And you're matching Takoda's sorceress look. You two will be the power couple of the night."

Riichi accepted the bag, his face unreadable, but a trace of approval flashed in his gaze. He nodded slowly. "It's... fitting."

Rain's grin widened. "You'll look sharp in this. Think of it as a duo costume—with a little extra flair."

Next was Vine. Ariel pulled a dark bag from the pile, her smile turning sly. "We made a deal, remember? Here's your 'wicked warlock' costume. Don't worry—I'm going all-out as your 'mischievous pixie.' We'll be the best duo there."

Vine took the bag, his lips quirking into a smirk. "Wicked, huh? This should be interesting."

Rain tossed him a few accessories with a chuckle. "Perfect fit for you, especially with that smug grin."

Aislinn handed Rowan his costume, satisfaction lighting up her face. "Went with a classic—vampire chic. You'll be the hunter, I'll be the vampire. Feels like a solid match."

Rowan inspected the costume with a measured glance before giving a small nod. "It's... appropriate."

Aislinn laughed, clearly pleased. "Just wait until we're in costume together—you'll make the perfect vampire hunter."

When it was Elder's turn, Rain passed him a bag with an expectant grin. "Alright, Elder, you're going as a wood elf. It'll match my forest nymph look perfectly—for, you know, extra support. Can't have you backing out on me now."

Her tone was light, teasing, but beneath it lay a subtle hope—that he wouldn't challenge the pairing.

Elder lifted a brow, a faint smile playing at the corner of his lips. "A wood elf? Not what I expected, but... I'll give it a try."

Rain nudged him playfully. "You'll look great—graceful, strong, just like the forest."

With each costume handed out, Ariel and Rain couldn't resist a few extra jabs and jokes. Ariel winked as she passed out the last of the bags. "Trust me, this is the best batch of costumes I've ever picked. Everyone's going to look amazing."

Rowan, dry as ever, murmured, "I'm sure we'll all be... unrecognizable."

Riichi leaned toward Takoda, his voice low, laced with amusement. "Let's hope the costume doesn't outshine the warrior beneath it."

Takoda smirked, nudging him back. "Don't worry. You'll still be just as intimidating—just don't let the dragon do all the work."

As everyone examined their costumes, laughter and lighthearted remarks filled the room. The effort Ariel and Rain had put into the selections didn't go unnoticed, and even Rowan, usually the most serious among them, cracked a rare smile.

"Well," he admitted, taking in the assortment, "I suppose this is one way to lighten the mood. I'll give you both credit—these are impressive."

Riichi gave a slow nod of approval. "You've outdone yourselves. But let's see how it all plays out at the party."

Beaming, Ariel clapped her hands together. "Alright, that's it! Everyone's set for the Halloween party! No excuses. Let's make this a night to remember—and no spells gone wrong, okay?"

Rain added with a laugh, "And no hexes turning people into frogs. Other than that, let loose! It's time for fun."

As the group dispersed, the air thrummed with renewed camaraderie. The costumes offered a rare reprieve from the weight of their responsibilities, a moment to indulge in the absurd before the battles ahead. Between the teasing, shared grins, and the occasional begrudging smirk of approval, the simple act of picking costumes had done more than just set the stage for the party—it had given them a fleeting moment of normalcy.

It was a reminder that even with a war looming, there was still space for laughter—for moments that made the fight worth enduring.

***

Riichi's room was dimly lit, the glow of the TV flickering across the walls, but neither of them paid it any mind. Wrapped in the warmth of each other's presence, the rest of the world had fallen away, leaving only the charged stillness between them.

Takoda traced slow, featherlight patterns along Riichi's palm, the touch absentminded but grounding. A slow heat curled through her, not from nervousness, but from anticipation, a deep-rooted need pressing at the edges of her restraint. They had built this bond carefully, piece by piece—but now, she wanted to know what it felt like to tear down every last barrier and let it consume them completely.

Riichi's dark eyes settled on her, keenly attuned to the shift in her energy. His voice came low, a quiet coaxing. "What's on your mind, Takoda?"

She met his gaze, lips parting slightly, but the words caught in her throat. Then, after a breath, she whispered, "Have you ever wondered what it would feel like… if I let my emotional alchemy enhance what we already have?" Her voice barely broke the silence. "Now that we're bonded—fully aware?"

The question hung between them, thick with possibility.

Riichi didn't speak right away. Instead, he studied her, his grip on her fingers tightening just slightly as his expression darkened—not with hesitation, but with a weight far more intentional. His voice, when it came, was barely above a murmur. "Tell me more."

Her heart pounded, but she didn't hesitate. "Back in Seattle, when I lost control… everything bled together. It was too much—too wild. But now, I can guide it. I want to feel that again, but this time, I want to be in it. I want to let go—with you."

His answer was immediate. No hesitation. No uncertainty.

"Then show me."

Takoda let her alchemy unfurl between them, a slow-burning pulse of warmth that wrapped around them, winding through the bond and pulling them deeper into each other's presence. This wasn't like before—there was no chaos, no loss of control. This was conscious, a slow and steady release of energy, lacing into every touch, every breath.

Then, as their lips met, the world vanished.

A sharp gasp spilled from her, swallowed between them, as sensation struck like a live current. Every touch ignited. Every breath burned. His hands, rough and warm, branded into her skin, their connection sinking into flesh and bone, a force neither of them could pull away from. Her energy didn't just brush against his—it merged, unraveled, tangled, his emotions bleeding into hers in a perfect storm of need, want, and aching depth.

Can… can you feel it? Her voice trembled through his mind, her body arching into his as the rush of emotion overtook her.

A low, rough sound rumbled in his chest as his grip tightened at her waist, pulling her deeper into him. *Yes…I feel….* His thoughts cut off as his lips trailed along her throat, his breath hot against her skin. *Closer than ever.*

Their movements fell into an effortless rhythm, drawn together in a way that transcended touch alone. Every barrier had fallen, every restraint shattered beneath the overwhelming force of feeling each other completely.

Takoda's breath hitched, her mind hazy with the sheer intensity of it. She could barely think, barely string together words—only raw sensation, only the aching need to be closer, deeper, more.

This… A gasp, a sharp inhale as his hands pressed against her back, guiding her closer. *This is what I wanted… So intense.*

His thoughts tangled into hers, breathless, rough-edged as a groan of pleasure escaped. *Feels… incredible.*

Takoda's power surged between them, amplifying everything—every brush of skin, every heartbeat, every soft sound lost between kisses. Their bond pulsed like a living thing, demanding more, pulling them deeper into the firestorm between them.

Her thoughts fragmented, barely holding onto coherence. *I can't—Riichi—I—*

I know. His voice wasn't just in her mind—it was everywhere, wrapping around her, filling her, pulling her under.

He quickened his pace. The energy between them swelled, crashing over them like a wave, consuming, relentless. They were no longer just two souls bound together. They were one. Completely, impossibly, inescapably one.

Time blurred, sensation overtaking thought until there was nothing left but breath, heat, and the quiet tremors of their shared climax.

When the storm finally softened, they remained tangled together, bodies warm, their bond still humming beneath the surface like an ember that refused to fade.

Takoda pressed her forehead against Riichi's chest, fingers tracing slow, lazy circles against his skin as their heartbeats gradually steadied. A soft, dreamlike contentment settled over her, warmth curling around every inch of her.

Silence stretched between them, not empty, but full—charged with the lingering pulse of everything they had just shared.

Then, Riichi's voice broke the silence, low and slightly rough at the edges, the faintest trace of amusement threading through his words.

"We're going to have to do that again."

Takoda let out a slow, breathless laugh, her fingers tightening against his. "Yeah," she murmured, pressing closer. "Definitely."

★★★

Late evening settled over Fort Lawton, the remnants of the old coastal defense installation overlooking Puget Sound cast in deep, shifting shadows. A biting wind cut through the cliffside, carrying the distant crash of waves below. Hidden among the skeletal remains of crumbling structures, Vine and Reed crouched low, watching the Golden Dawn's movements.

Below them, cultists worked methodically, etching new symbols into the ground, their voices a low murmur beneath the wind. Lanterns flickered, casting eerie light over the half-finished ritual site. Vine barely shifted as he scanned the scene, his voice a whisper. "They're rebuilding. If they finish whatever this is, it's not just a storm—it's going to be a disaster."

Reed gave a short nod, eyes sharp. "We need to hear more before we pull back."

Then, the air shifted.

A slow, rippling tension spread through the gathered cultists, a sudden awareness that an unfamiliar force had arrived. Vine tensed, instincts flaring. A tall, commanding figure stepped from the darkness—his presence alone silencing every voice, halting every movement.

Kubla Khan.

The Golden Dawn members froze, some instinctively backing away as the warlord's piercing gaze swept across them. He moved with absolute control, like a man who had already decided this was his territory and was simply waiting for the rest of them to realize it.

From their vantage point, Vine and Reed barely breathed.

Below, one of the Golden Dawn officers stepped forward hesitantly, his voice cautious but bold. "Who the hell are you?"

A sharp hum of amusement pulsed through the air. Khan didn't answer immediately. Instead, he studied the man—his expression impenetrable, his stillness absolute. Then, in a voice both calm and resolute, he asked, "What's your name?"

The officer straightened slightly, as if recognizing that he was being measured. "Gideon Kross."

Khan nodded once. "Are you the leader?"

Gideon gave a dry scoff. "No." He tilted his chin toward a nervous-looking man standing to the side. "That idiot over there is."

Khan barely glanced at the so-called leader. A flick of his wrist.

An invisible force hurled the man backward, sending him screaming over the edge of the cliff. A sharp crack sounded below. Silence.

Then, Khan turned back to Gideon, completely unfazed. "Well. Now you are."

The Golden Dawn members stared in stunned silence—but none protested. Some even exchanged glances, as if they had already been thinking the same thing.

Gideon didn't flinch. His lips pressed together briefly before he gave a sharp nod. "Fine by me."

The power shift was immediate. Khan tilted his head, considering him. Then, as if satisfied, he gestured toward the half-finished ritual site. "Tell me what this is."

Gideon exhaled, but his voice remained firm. "The Typhoon ritual. When completed, it will summon a storm with the power to decimate entire regions. But that's not the only purpose." He glanced at the other cultists. "We planned to use it to shatter the veil completely. Once it's gone, nothing will stand between us and the forces beyond. We will be the ones to shape what comes next."

Khan let the words settle before speaking. "No."

Gideon frowned. "No?"

Khan stepped forward, his presence suffocatingly close. "Your thinking is flawed. You believe you can stand against what comes through, that your magic will hold against the darkness beyond the veil?" His gaze swept the group, his disdain unmistakable. "Pathetic."

Several of the cultists looked down instinctively—not Gideon. He held firm, waiting for Khan to continue.

Khan exhaled slowly, almost as if disappointed. "You will not simply shatter the veil and expect to reign over the aftermath. Power does not belong to those who open the door—it belongs to those who know how to control what steps through."

A hush fell.

Gideon's expression darkened, but he nodded once. "Then tell me how to do it."

Khan's lips curved slightly. Yes. He had chosen well.

Vine's pulse pounded. This was worse than anything they had anticipated. This wasn't just about summoning storms or breaking the veil. The Golden Dawn thought they were orchestrating the fall of the barrier between worlds—but Khan wasn't just letting it fall. He was making sure he was the one who dictated what came next.

Reed shifted beside him and whispered, "We have to move. Now."

But before they could retreat, Khan's head snapped upward. A deep, prickling chill ran down Vine's spine. Khan wasn't just looking in their direction.

He saw them.

Vine barely had time to think before Khan raised a hand.

A violent wave of energy tore through the air, slamming into the cliffside. The impact sent Vine reeling, pain splitting across his forehead as something jagged grazed him. Warm blood spilled down his face, streaking past his temple.

"Move!" Reed hissed, yanking him back just as another shockwave tore through the space they had been crouching in. Vine barely got his bearings before they shadow-walked out of range.

The world snapped back into focus as they landed near the vehicle, breathing hard, adrenaline still spiking. Vine pressed a shaking hand to his forehead, feeling warm blood trickling down his skin. "Shit! That… could have gone better."

Reed exhaled sharply, throwing the car into gear. "You're lucky that's all you got."

The engine roared to life as they peeled away from the site, headlights slicing through the darkness. Vine's vision swam for a second as blood dripped onto his collar. Reed passed him a handkerchief without a word.

Vine took it, muttering, "I hate surveillance missions."

Reed huffed out a humorless breath. "Yeah. Try getting hit harder next time. Then you'll really hate them."

Vine scowled, pressing the fabric to his wound as he stared out the window, watching the city blur past. There wasn't much time. The rules had changed.

They pulled into the driveway, parking hastily before heading inside. The mansion was still, save for the faint murmur of the TV from the sitting room. Ariel and Rain lounged on the couch, laughter rising from whatever played on the screen, their easy amusement a stark contrast to the tension grinding against Vine's skull.

As soon as they stepped inside, Ariel looked up, her laughter vanishing the instant she spotted the blood trailing down Vine's forehead.

"Oh my God—what happened to you?" she asked, rising quickly, concern flashing across her face. "Let me look at that."

Vine barely spared her a glance. "I'm fine," he muttered, brushing past her.

Before Ariel could push further, Eileen stepped out of her office, her gaze snapping to them like a predator scenting blood. Her expression hardened. "What happened?"

Ariel reached for Vine's arm, intent on checking the wound herself, but the moment her fingers grazed his sleeve, he recoiled, frustration boiling over.

"I told you—I'm fine! Just let it go!" His voice came out sharp, his temper frayed from the night's events.

Without waiting for a response, he turned and strode up the stairs, disappearing down the hall with heavy, deliberate steps.

Ariel stared after him, her hand still half-raised before she let it drop. Hurt flashed across her face, but it vanished just as quickly, buried beneath a mask of sarcasm.

Reed let out a low sigh, shaking his head. "Vine can be a bit of an ass sometimes. Don't let him get to you."

Ariel huffed, crossing her arms. "Yeah, well, I'll just add 'grumpy' to his list of charming qualities. I'll survive."

Eileen barely acknowledged the exchange, her focus locked on Reed. "Tell me what happened."

Reed's expression was grim as he stepped forward. "Kubla Khan's taken over the Golden Dawn. He showed up at Fort Lawton tonight and made it clear—he's calling the shots now. They're still going through with the Typhoon ritual, but he's altering their plans. He told them they weren't thinking big enough." Reed's jaw tightened. "He's not just letting them shatter the veil. He's making sure he's the one in control of whatever comes next."

Ariel let out a dry laugh, shaking her head. "So, let me get this straight. A warlord demon just took over a doomsday cult, they're about to rip a hole in reality, and we're supposed to stop that? Without knowing what's coming next?"

No one answered. They didn't need to. The truth was as clear as the cold wind rattling the mansion's old windows—there was no plan, no clear path forward.

Eileen absorbed Reed's words, her expression unreadable, but the sharp glint in her eyes made one thing clear—this changed everything.

Chapter Twenty-Three
Under the Surface

The mansion was still, wrapped in the hush of early morning. Vine stood outside Ariel's door, the only sound in the corridor the faint hum of the heating vents. Dressed in black recon gear, he blended into the shadows, an extension of the darkness he so often embraced. Yet for once, he hesitated, his usual certainty tempered by uncertainty.

From the other side of the door, the low murmur of a television slipped through the gap beneath it. She was awake.

Still, he lingered. Reed's words replayed in his mind—direct, unfiltered. *"Vine can be a bit of an ass sometimes. Don't let him get to you."* The bluntness had caught him off guard, but he couldn't exactly argue. He'd heard worse. And, if he was being honest, Reed wasn't wrong.

Pride warred with the instinct to turn away, but he exhaled, shoving it aside, and knocked, his touch light against the wood, careful not to disturb the rest of the mansion.

Inside, Ariel paused, recognizing the knock immediately. A hint of irritation sparked beneath her ribs—his last words to her hadn't just stung; they had *dismissed* her. She'd felt foolish for showing concern, and that wasn't a feeling she was willing to entertain twice.

Still, curiosity won out. She pulled the door open without a word, meeting his gaze just long enough to make her point before turning away, leaving the door open in silent invitation.

Relief loosened tension in his chest, just a fraction. He stepped inside, nudging the door closed behind him with a quiet click. The TV cast shifting light across the room, a flickering glow that softened the contrast between them—his dark, tactical gear and her casual tank top and boxer shorts. The unspoken tension between them hung in the air, thick but undefined.

She turned, arms crossing over her chest, expression impassive. "Here to yell at me some more?"

The sarcasm was a thin veneer, but the edge of hurt in her voice cut through it.

Vine exhaled slowly, nodding once. "No. I'm not here to yell." The words came quiet, unguarded. "I heard Reed talking to you earlier, and… I know I can be an ass sometimes. He's right." Saying it out loud felt strange, awkward. He wasn't used to apologies—especially not ones that weren't layered in excuses.

Ariel's expression didn't shift. If anything, her response was even more indifferent. "It's fine." The words were casual, but an edge lurked beneath them. Dismissive.

She leaned against the dresser, gaze moving briefly to the TV before settling on him again. "If you do need to yell, go ahead. I'm used to it."

That stopped him cold. She said it so easily, like it didn't matter. Like she expected it. The realization settled deep, a pull of recognition. He studied her, searching for the meaning beneath the words.

"Used to it, huh?" His voice dipped, lower now. "What does that mean?"

Her shoulders tensed. "Just that I've been yelled at a lot before." A shrug, nonchalant. "Doesn't really bother me."

Liar.

Vine didn't press—he could recognize a line she wasn't ready to cross—but his stance shifted, less distant, more present. He stepped forward and lowered himself onto the edge of her bed, the movement casual but deliberate.

"Look," he said, meeting her gaze. "I'm sorry."

That was it. No backtracking. No deflection. Just a simple truth, as raw as he was willing to make it. "I shouldn't have snapped at you. I get that you were just looking out for me… even if I didn't show it."

The blunt sincerity caught her off guard. Her irritation eased, but she didn't let it show. Instead, her gaze dropped, narrowing slightly as she caught sight of the bandage above his eye. The edges were haphazard, barely holding.

Ariel exhaled sharply and shook her head. "Hold that thought." Without waiting for a response, she turned, disappearing into the bathroom.

Vine barely had time to process before she was back, a compact first aid kit in her hand. She didn't hesitate, flipping it open as she moved, already pulling out supplies with practiced efficiency.

She gestured toward the bed. "Sit still."

The authority in her voice was undeniable, but the way she squared her shoulders, her movements clipped and sure, struck Vine as familiar—too familiar. This wasn't just irritation. It was habit.

His smirk was automatic. "Not arguing."

"Good."

Ariel ignored the glint of amusement in his eyes as she soaked a cotton swab in rubbing alcohol. "This is going to sting," she warned, tone matter-of-fact as she brought it to his skin. "Try not to be a baby about it."

He scoffed, the sound dismissive. "I'll survive."

The second the swab touched the cut, a sharp burn radiated through the wound. His breath hissed between his teeth, fingers curling instinctively—searching for an anchor. His hand landed on her thigh, the warmth of her skin beneath his palm grounding him before he realized what he had done.

Ariel stilled.

For a fraction of a second, her focus wavered—not on the cut, but on the weight of his touch, the unintentional closeness. Then, just as quickly, she regained control. She finished cleaning the wound with precise movements, the tension in the air thickening with each second that passed.

When she finally leaned in and blew lightly over the cut, Vine's pulse stuttered. The cooling relief barely registered over the awareness of her breath ghosting over his skin. His fingers twitched against her thigh, but he didn't move, didn't speak.

She didn't either.

A heartbeat passed, then another. His eyes closed for a brief moment, the air between them too charged, too undefined to break.

Neither one pulled away.

Neither one spoke.

Once the wound was clean, Ariel pressed a fresh bandage into place, her touch lingering for a moment longer. "Better?" she asked, her tone softened by a subtle warmth.

He met her gaze and nodded. "Yeah. Thanks." The gratitude in his voice was quiet but genuine.

As she put the supplies away, her gaze drifted to his hands. Scrapes and bruises marked his knuckles, fresh and telling. Without thinking, she reached for his hand, lifting it gently for a closer look. "Let me guess… Kubla Khan did this too?" Her tone was light, almost teasing, though her eyes showed concern.

Vine smirked, though it was faint. "Actually… I ran into a wall in my room," he muttered, the excuse flimsy at best. He had clearly punched something—probably out of frustration.

She raised an eyebrow, amusement sparking in her expression. "Real smooth move," she said, voice laced with teasing. Her fingers brushed lightly over his bruised knuckles, her touch careful. "Let's fix these too," she added, already reaching for another antiseptic wipe.

As she cleaned his knuckles, she continued, "You know, there are other ways to handle anger," her voice playful but edged with consideration. "Next time, try punching a pillow. Or, I don't know, scream into it if you're feeling dramatic. Could be pretty satisfying."

He let out a short huff, almost a laugh. "Noted," he murmured, his gaze drifting to her face as she focused on his hand.

Her expression softened as she added, "Or… you could always talk to someone instead of the wall." She glanced up, her teasing fading into sincerity.

The suggestion settled between them, and he studied her for a beat. "Someone like you?" he asked, a hint of curiosity in his voice.

Her gaze didn't waver as she replied, "Yeah." The word was soft, an offer held without expectation as she finished tending to his bruised hand. Her fingers lingered just a little before letting go.

They fell into an easy silence, a mutual awareness settling between them—unspoken, but acknowledged. After a moment, Vine exhaled and stood, rolling his shoulders as if shaking off the weight of the conversation.

She walked with him toward the door, her steps casual, unrushed. Just as he reached for the handle, she hesitated. "You know…" she said, her voice lighter now, "you can stay if you want."

Vine stilled. Ariel barely had time to process the shift before he turned, backing her into the wall in a slow, deliberate motion. The movement was fluid, his body pressing against hers, but it wasn't aggressive—just controlled.

He let her feel him. His arousal was unmistakable, heat radiating between them, proof that his restraint had nothing to do with lack of desire.

His lips hovered near her ear, his voice a hushed murmur. "It's tempting," he admitted, the words slow, intentional. "But I want to keep things honest between us."

Pulling back just enough to meet her gaze, he continued, his voice low but steady. "I don't want this to turn into an outlet for frustration... or just a way to burn off steam. I want to enjoy you." His gaze dipped briefly, the corner of his mouth twitching before he added, "Every moment of it."

Ariel held his stare, her expression unreadable at first—but then, she nodded, her understanding clear.

Vine lingered for a second longer, his breath warm against her skin before he dipped his head. His lips brushed the side of her neck, slow and deliberate, a lingering touch that sent a faint shiver down her spine. A promise of restraint, not reluctance.

Then, he stepped back. "Goodnight, Ariel."

She exhaled, watching as he pulled the door open and slipped out, the quiet click of the latch following in his absence. A slow smirk tugged at her lips as she leaned back against the wall, fingers brushing absently over her thigh where his hand had been. *Yeah... this was going to be interesting.*

Out in the hallway, Vine released a slow breath and started toward his room. As he passed the mirror lining the corridor, he caught sight of the fresh bandage she had placed over his eye. He dragged a hand through his hair, shaking his head slightly, but there was no irritation—just muted amusement.

His pace didn't quicken, nor did he rush to shut the door behind him once he reached his room. For the first time in a while, he found himself looking forward to seeing where this would lead.

***

Nik's day off, and Rain hadn't seen him in the common room with the others. Not that she expected to—Nik wasn't the type to lounge around, engaging in casual conversation or wasting time in easy company. No, she knew exactly where he'd be.

Tucked away somewhere quiet, far from distractions, likely lost in a book.

Smiling to herself, she headed for the library, her steps light and confident.

Pushing open the heavy door, she let her gaze sweep the room until it landed on him. As expected, he was seated by one of the tall windows, a book in hand, completely absorbed in its pages. Sunlight streamed through the glass, catching in the edges of his dark hair, illuminating the sharp angles of his face. He looked entirely at ease in his solitude, perfectly content with a day spent in undisturbed retreat.

Too bad for him.

She strolled forward, her grin mischievous. "So, this is where 'Elder' spends his day off?" she teased, casting a glance at the book in his hands. "I was expecting something a bit more… exciting."

Nik looked up, mildly surprised but not particularly thrown by her sudden appearance. "It's quiet here," he said simply, his tone neutral. "I plan to read, maybe catch up on a few things I haven't had time for." He paused, his gaze sparking with subtle amusement. "Some people would call that relaxing."

Rain arched a brow, feigning disappointment. "Seriously, that's it?" She let out a small, exaggerated sigh, shaking her head. "You have an entire day to do whatever you want, and this is what you choose?"

Her eyes drifted toward the book in his hands, her interest piqued. *The Music of the Spheres*. She tilted her head, intrigued but keeping her expression light. "Didn't peg you as the cosmic harmony type," she mused, watching for any reaction. "Big fan of the universe's soundtrack?"

Nik gave no indication he had heard her at all, simply turning a page.

She smirked. *Alright, keep your secrets.*

Before he could redirect the conversation, she leaned in slightly, her grin widening. "Alright, you're clearly in desperate need of a better plan." Her voice carried a playful lilt, her eyes flashing with challenge. "Lucky for you, I've got just the thing."

Nik's brow furrowed slightly, though he didn't look entirely opposed. "And what exactly do you have in mind?" Skepticism laced with curiosity.

"You'll see." The excitement in her voice made it clear she wasn't going to explain. "But first, put the book down, or we'll be here all day."

With a casual shrug, she spun on her heel, tossing a final remark over her shoulder as she strode toward the door. "Come on, we're not spending your day off cooped up in the library."

She didn't wait for a response, leaving him little choice but to follow.

Nik watched her go, exhaling a slow breath before slipping a bookmark between the pages of his book to hold his place. With a small shake of his head, he closed it, realizing he'd been outmaneuvered yet feeling oddly amused by the turn of events.

As Rain stepped into the hallway, the Fallen were beginning to gather in the conference room for their daily meeting.

The conference room carried an undercurrent of tension as the Fallen gathered, each member settling into their seats with practiced focus. Morning light slanted through the windows, casting deceptive warmth over the serious expressions around the table.

Eileen took her place at the head, gaze steady as she absorbed the weight in the room. Whatever was reported today would determine their next move.

Rowan broke the silence first. "Nihonmachi is tenser than before," he said. "Nami—the tea shop owner—has noticed unusual activity. No specifics, but from what she described, the Golden Dawn is reconstructing the typhoon ritual. This time, on a larger scale."

A murmur rippled through the room.

Aislinn leaned forward. "We also spoke with the bookstore owner. He warned of a dark presence over the city. Based on his description…" She hesitated briefly. "It suggests Kubla Khan has taken an interest."

Silence fell.

Rowan's jaw tightened. "If they've aligned with him, we're facing more than just a storm ritual. He's shifting their focus toward something worse."

Eileen gave a slight nod, absorbing the implications.

Reed exhaled. "Vine and I scouted Fort Lawton. The Golden Dawn was already reconstructing their ritual site. Then Kubla Khan arrived, making his new leadership clear. From what we gathered, they're planning to break the veil between worlds entirely."

A heavy pause filled the room.

Vine's expression darkened. "It's worse. He isn't just breaking the veil—he's making sure he controls what steps through." His gaze swept the room. "And he's confident he can pull it off."

Reed nodded. "We barely got out unscathed. He knows we're watching. The cut above Vine's eye should be proof of how close we came to being compromised."

Eyes darted to Vine, who remained impassive.

"If anything," Reed continued, "we need to be more cautious than ever. Kubla Khan isn't just making the Golden Dawn stronger—he's reshaping them into something entirely different."

A weighted silence settled.

Ash leaned forward. "Birch and I focused on Georgetown. The Golden Dawn is manipulating the weather for a large-scale event, but we identified structural weaknesses in their setup."

Birch picked up where he left off. "There are flaws—both physical and magical. If we hit the right points, we can dismantle their network before it reaches full power. But it won't be easy. The sites are heavily guarded, some with magical barriers. Precision will be critical."

Ash scanned the table. "It'll be a challenge, but if we take out those weak points, we'll cripple their operation before it gains momentum."

The room fell silent, the pieces aligning into a single, grim reality.

Eileen let the reports settle before nodding, her gaze unreadable but resolute as she studied the team.

She straightened. "We can't allow the Golden Dawn to maintain their control through these weather manipulation rituals," she stated, her voice firm and unwavering. "Our priority is disrupting the sites in Georgetown. We execute this mission tomorrow night."

A ripple of determination passed through the table. No one spoke, but the shift in posture, the slight tightening of shoulders, made it clear—each Fallen understood the weight of her words.

"To ensure we're fully prepared," she continued, "we'll train as a single unit today. Each team will demonstrate their skills, and everyone will provide constructive feedback. This session will help us refine our coordination and eliminate any weaknesses. I expect every one of you to treat this seriously."

A few nods. A flicker of tension released as the focus sharpened, their minds shifting into planning mode.

Oak took the lead on assignments, his voice steady. "Willow, you're with me tonight. We'll handle recon in Georgetown. I want a full report on any last-minute changes in ritual activity or security before we strike."

Willow gave a short nod, already focused on the task ahead.

Oak's gaze shifted. "Aislinn, Rowan, Ivy—you're assigned to Fort Lawton. Keep tabs on any new movements or reinforcements. We can't allow the Golden Dawn to strengthen their defenses there."

Rowan exchanged a glance with Aislinn and Ivy, their expressions shifting into a shared understanding before he gave a curt nod.

Eileen took a measured breath before her next directive. "Considering Kubla Khan's alliance with the Golden Dawn, it's time we expand our forces." Her gaze settled on Oak. "Reach out to the rest of the Fallen. I want them here by the day after tomorrow, immediately following the Georgetown mission."

Oak held her stare for a beat, the weight of the request settling between them. A flicker of urgency crossed his expression before he nodded. "Understood. I'll start calling in the reinforcements."

With that, Eileen cast a final look around the table, her expression resolute. "Tomorrow night's mission is crucial. We cannot afford any mistakes. The Golden Dawn's hold is strong, but as long as we remain coordinated and precise, we can dismantle their plans. Dismissed."

The Fallen rose, their movements reflecting a collective resolve. As chairs scraped against the floor and murmured discussions sparked to life, Oak remained behind, stepping toward Eileen.

He studied her for a moment before speaking, a thoughtful edge to his voice. "Eileen… you might want to drop by Takoda and Riichi's training session later."

She arched a brow, catching the subtle shift in his tone. "Is there a reason?"

A knowing smile formed at the corner of Oak's lips. "You're going to want to see for yourself."

Eileen searched his expression, noting the quiet certainty behind his words. Slowly, she nodded, though anticipation curled in her chest.

Whatever Oak had noticed, it was worth paying attention to.

After the meeting, the Fallen headed straight for the courtyard to begin training. The morning air was crisp, carrying the faint scent of damp earth, while sunlight streamed in golden streaks. Seattle lay veiled in dense fog, dark clouds lingering on the horizon—a fitting reflection of the tension surrounding the mission ahead.

★★★

Across the city, in the ruins of Fort Lawton, another meeting was taking place—one that ensured the path ahead would not be so simple.

The air inside the abandoned structure was thick with damp rot, the scent of mildew woven into the crumbling walls. A single lantern flickered on a rusted metal desk, casting jagged shadows against peeling paint. This was Gideon Kross's command post—a crude but functional base where the Golden Dawn planned their next moves.

Kubla Khan stood across from him, his presence filling the room with a quiet but undeniable gravity. He exuded control—not through brute force, but through careful calculation, a predator that never moved without intent.

Gideon leaned forward, fingers steepled, his gaze sharp beneath the dim light. "The Fallen will come for Georgetown first," he said, his voice steady despite the weight of the conversation.

Khan smiled, a slow, knowing curve of his lips. "Of course they will," he murmured, rolling a silver ring over his knuckle. "They believe themselves predictable only to one another. But strategy? It is universal. Just as Riichi Miyamoto anticipates my movements, I anticipate his."

Gideon's expression remained unreadable. "You're certain of this?"

Khan tilted his head, as if amused by the question. "The Fallen are warriors, not aimless disruptors. They will dismantle our operations in a sequence—Georgetown first, Fort Lawton next. That is their nature." His fingers stopped moving, his gaze sharpening. "But we will not make it easy for them."

Gideon straightened. "What do you have in mind?"

Khan stepped closer to the desk, his voice calm but carrying the weight of command. "Strengthen the barriers at the ritual sites. They should not fall with a single disruption. Force the Fallen to exert themselves. The longer they fight to break through, the more vulnerable they become."

Gideon nodded. "And the acolytes?"

Khan's smirk deepened. "Give them power. Resistance. Purpose. I will lend them what they need." He extended a hand, and the air hummed—not with raw magic, but something deeper, older. An unseen force shifted, unseen but felt, pressing against the space between them.

Gideon exhaled slowly, understanding the unspoken offer.

"You want them to last longer in a fight."

Khan nodded. "More than that—I want them to test the Fallen's limits. Their pain, their endurance, their convictions." He turned, his dark coat sweeping the floor as he moved toward the exit. "Give them what they need to hold the line. Have it ready by tomorrow. When the time comes, I will give them more."

Gideon didn't ask for specifics. He knew better.

Instead, he watched as Kubla Khan disappeared into the night, leaving only the echo of his presence behind.

Tomorrow, the Fallen would come.

And this time, they would bleed for every step forward.

★★★

Back at the mansion, the Fallen gathered in the courtyard, preparing for the battle ahead—unaware that their enemy was already setting the stage.

Ivy had reshaped the courtyard, bending reality to create a near-perfect simulation of Georgetown's industrial sprawl. The ground cracked beneath their feet, rusted metal structures loomed where there had been open space, and stacks of crates formed barriers. Ritual sites pulsed with energy—not mere illusions but altered constructs, their presence as real as anything else. Figures in Golden Dawn robes moved in the shadows, reacting as if truly alive.

Oak stepped forward, taking his place as the session's leader. "Today's training is a mock mission," he announced. "Ivy has set the stage—treat it like the real thing. Each team will demonstrate their skills, and we'll provide feedback. Let's begin."

Ivy refined the last details of her construct, the space shifting, settling with a weight that made it clear—this wasn't just an illusion.

Oak divided the teams. Reed, Vine, and Ash were assigned to distraction and surveillance, tasked with gathering intel and creating diversions without revealing themselves. Reed moved like a shadow, slipping between obstacles, adjusting seamlessly as the landscape shifted under Ivy's manipulation. Vine controlled bursts of light and movement, redirecting attention with meticulousness, while Ash cycled through different forms, blending into the environment before relaying information back. Their coordination was sharp, adapting to the unpredictable terrain.

As their round ended, Rowan assessed their performance. "Reed, your stealth is flawless—exactly what we'll need."

Aislinn nodded at Vine. "Your diversions are clean and precise. The course reacts to them like real enemies—good sign."

Takoda smirked. "Nicely done. If you keep this up under real pressure, they won't know which way to turn."

Oak nodded in agreement, offering refinements to strengthen their coordination even further.

Next, Oak, Birch, and Willow stepped into position, focusing on protection and reinforcement. Oak layered barriers around the team, transparent shields flashing before stabilizing. Birch strengthened their endurance, ensuring no gaps in their energy output, while Willow wove stabilizing currents through the defenses, reinforcing weak points before they could be exploited. Ivy tested their response, sending a ripple through the environment that destabilized the ground beneath them. Oak adjusted immediately, recalibrating the barriers before the distortion could break them apart.

Ivy gave a small nod. "That'll hold against whatever they throw at us." Aislinn stepped forward, testing the perimeter. "It reacts quickly—exactly what we need." Oak took in the feedback, already considering refinements for stronger layering in high-risk areas.

Then, Riichi, Takoda, Rowan, and Aislinn took their positions. Their objective: dismantle the ritual sites while countering Ivy's reality shifts. The moment they moved, the battlefield warped. Walls stretched higher, pathways narrowed, and barriers pulsed unpredictably. Ivy forced them to adapt in real time, the ground shifting beneath them as they fought.

Takoda and Riichi moved in perfect sync, countering Ivy's constructs with seamless precision. These weren't projections—they reacted, struck back, adjusted to their movements. Rowan and Aislinn worked alongside them, dismantling the ritual sites as their energy resisted, forcing them to break through as they would in a real battle.

Ivy increased the difficulty, air distorting as adversaries formed, tangible as any living opponent. The pressure mounted, and Riichi and Takoda activated Radiant Surge, a faint orange glow sharpening their movements, strikes honed with perfect efficiency. Rowan and Aislinn followed suit, a soft blue light surrounding them as the Shield of Ages expanded, reinforcing the battlefield against Ivy's shifting terrain.

Then Ivy introduced a final challenge—a mock bomb at the center of the ritual site. The energy pulsed, reacting to their presence, primed to detonate. Without hesitation, Rowan and Aislinn expanded the Shield of Ages, its protective force wrapping around them and Riichi and Takoda. The field held, absorbing the would-be explosion, proving their ability to defend against large-scale magical attacks.

The other Fallen watched, their expressions a mix of admiration and assessment. Whatever doubts had surrounded Takoda's role in the fight had vanished. The evidence was in front of them—her connection with Riichi was seamless.

Oak gave a small nod of approval at their controlled use of Radiant Surge, while Ash and Birch discussed the potential applications of the Shield of Ages as a key defensive tool. Reed crossed his arms, analyzing the shield's reach. "That could be a game-changer if we get overwhelmed in Georgetown."

Oak stepped forward as the session wound down, his voice firm but laced with encouragement. "You all performed well today. Your skills will be essential tomorrow. Preparation is our best advantage." His gaze swept across the group. "If you need more practice, stay and refine anything necessary. Otherwise, continue with your assignments and stay sharp."

The Fallen began dispersing, some lingering in small groups to discuss tactics while others moved off to prepare for the mission ahead. Soon, only a few remained in the courtyard, making way for a private training session Oak had quietly arranged—one designed specifically for Riichi and Takoda.

Takoda and Riichi stepped into the courtyard, where Ivy's intricate obstacle course remained. The simulation of Georgetown's industrial sprawl stretched around them, filled with barricades, jagged surfaces, and the shifting figures of Ivy's conjured reality—phantoms of Golden Dawn members lurking, poised to strike.

Without a word, they activated their Radiant Surge, the faint orange glow beneath their skin barely visible. The subtle display spoke volumes about their control, a bond refined enough that they no longer needed the surge to flare to wield its power.

Moving forward, their synchronization was nothing short of extraordinary, as if they shared a single, unified mind. Takoda maneuvered through obstacles with expert finesse, twisting, spinning, and evading each strike effortlessly. Riichi remained by her side, countering attacks with clear-cut strikes, their coordination seamless. Every movement flowed into the next, creating a silent dance that transformed the battle into a form of artistry.

As they navigated the course, a telepathic exchange passed between them, blending accuracy with subtle, playful affection.

Two behind you, and one moving to your left, Riichi noted, admiration clear in his tone. *You're absolutely incredible, by the way.*

Oh, I know, Takoda replied with a smirk, her voice warm in his mind. *Watch my back—I'm going in.*

Always. He assured her. *I wouldn't miss watching you work.*

Takoda spun fluidly left, sweeping low to eliminate two adversaries swiftly. Riichi followed suit, dispatching another opponent and safeguarding her flank with pinpoint accuracy. Their rhythm remained unbroken, a flawless momentum that left no room for hesitation between offense and defense.

From the shadows, Eileen stepped onto the courtyard, drawn in by their display. She observed in silence, her gaze sharp with assessment.

"They've learned these skills in just four days?" she murmured, a note of disbelief in her voice.

Oak, standing beside her, corrected gently. "Actually, they only started syncing like this yesterday."

Eileen's attention sharpened as she took in the slight glow surrounding them. "They're not using Radiant Surge?"

Oak's restrained pride showed in his expression. "They are. Notice the faint orange tint? They've refined it to that level of control. Just thirty minutes ago, it was brighter."

Eileen raised an eyebrow, clearly impressed. "They're learning that quickly?"

Oak nodded. "I thought you'd be impressed."

Takoda and Riichi continued moving through Ivy's intricate constructs, their footwork and strikes weaving seamlessly through the fabric of reality itself. Ivy pushed them harder, shifting the course beneath them, but neither faltered. Their trust in each other held them steady amidst the chaos. Another telepathic exchange passed between them, their rhythm undisturbed.

You make this look so easy, Riichi, Takoda teased, her mental tone warm and playful.

Only because you're with me, he replied, amusement lacing his mind-voice. *Now, ready for the final move?*

With you, always, she answered, resolute.

In perfect harmony, Takoda executed a swift low strike to the left. Without missing a beat, Riichi followed with a powerful, forceful blow, his strength obliterating another construct into minute fragments. The surroundings quivered as the illusions crumbled away, leaving behind a profound sense of satisfaction that settled over them like a gentle mist.

Nearby, Rowan, Aislinn, and Ivy had been watching, their expressions a mix of awe and realization. Ivy's reality-bending constructs had been designed to challenge them, yet they hadn't struggled.

Rowan shook his head slightly, glancing at Oak. "Honestly, Oak, we have nothing more to offer. Riichi and Takoda are beyond us now."

Aislinn nodded, admiration in her eyes. "They've reached a level we haven't touched. Watching them is like seeing pure synchronicity."

Ivy, standing to the side, folded her arms, a slow smile curving her lips. "Their control is breathtaking. I couldn't challenge them even if I tried."

Eileen, still watching with approval, offered a suggestion. "Now that we have two bonded pairs, it would be good if they began training together. They could learn from each other."

Oak nodded in agreement. "My thoughts exactly. Moving Takoda to the combat team was the right choice." He glanced at Eileen. "Do you want them to continue?"

Eileen's lips curved slightly, a rare smile of approval. "No, end the training. Kubla Khan won't see them coming."

Oak signaled the end of the session, his expression carrying both pride and satisfaction as Takoda and Riichi finished.

★★★

Rain strode down the hall, fully expecting Nik to be right behind her. After a few steps, she glanced back—empty space. She sighed, rolling her eyes.

Of course.

A few moments later, Nik emerged from the library, his measured steps a stark contrast to her restless energy. She smirked. "Come on, Elder. Some of us don't have all day."

His brow lifted slightly, but he didn't rise to the bait, his composure as steady as ever. She waited until he reached her side before turning and falling into step beside him.

"We're taking your car, right?"

Nik cast her a sidelong glance, mild amusement flickering in his eyes. "That's fine."

Rain grinned. "Good. Otherwise, I'd have to ask Ariel to borrow hers." She tilted her head, feigning innocence. "Not that I have a driver's license or anything."

Nik's eyebrows inched higher. "Do you even know how to drive?"

Rain shrugged, barely containing a laugh. "Not really. I know you're supposed to keep both hands on the wheel, though."

Nik chuckled, shaking his head. "It's a little more complicated than that."

At the parking area, Nik unlocked the doors to a practical, no-frills black sedan. Rain took one look at it and laughed softly. "Yep, that tracks."

Nik glanced at her, but said nothing, simply climbing into the driver's seat. Rain slid in beside him, glancing around at the unadorned, spotless interior.

Nik started the engine, but didn't move.

Rain arched a brow. "Uh… why aren't we moving?"

He gave her a calm, steady look. "You need to tell me where to go."

"Oh. Right." She pulled out her phone, grinning as she tapped in the address. "Just follow these directions."

Nik's expression hovered somewhere between mild suspicion and restrained amusement. She was exaggerating her innocence—he could tell—but he didn't press. Instead, he shifted into gear and pulled onto the road.

As they drove, Rain leaned back, watching the passing scenery. "So, you were really planning to spend your whole day off in the library?"

"Yes."

Rain laughed, shaking her head. "You know, there are more exciting ways to spend a day off."

Nik remained quiet for a moment before finally answering, "Not everyone needs excitement to be content."

Rain wasn't deterred. She kept the conversation going, weaving playful questions between lighthearted observations. Bit by bit, she caught glimpses of his dry humor beneath the reserve, his responses losing their clipped edge. He wasn't exactly open, but he was engaging with her in a way that felt... natural.

By the time they'd been on the road for a while, their exchange had settled into a steady rhythm—easy, almost familiar.

Then Nik cast her a curious glance. "So... where are you taking us?"

Rain's grin widened. "You'll see soon enough."

A few minutes later, they turned onto a quiet country road, pulling up to a vast, open field dotted with bright orange pumpkins. Nik peered through the windshield, faintly puzzled but amused.

"A... pumpkin patch?"

Rain beamed as she unbuckled her seatbelt, practically bouncing out of the car, her red hair catching the sunlight in fiery streaks. She swung around to Nik's side and opened his door, tugging lightly on his arm. "Come on! It'll be fun!"

Nik raised an eyebrow, hesitating before letting himself be pulled along, his reluctance tempered by curiosity. "This... suits you," he remarked, a small smile tugging at his lips.

Rain laughed, her eyes shining. "That's the whole point!"

She led him straight toward the haunted house, flashing him a teasing smile. "Let's test your bravery, *Elder*."

Nik arched a brow. "I think you're the one who should be worried."

Undeterred, Rain grabbed his hand—without thinking—and pulled him inside.

Dim lighting flickered through the corridors as Rain narrated every exaggeratedly "scary" moment.

"Ooo, look, a spooky ghost. Should we be terrified?" she quipped, voice dripping with sarcasm.

Nik raised an eyebrow, unimpressed but entertained.

Then a figure leaped from the shadows. Rain instinctively grabbed onto Nik's arm, her fingers curling into the fabric of his sleeve. Her breath hitched before she laughed, shaking her head. "Okay, maybe I'm a *little* scared."

Nik smirked. "I thought you were fearless."

Rain scoffed, rolling her eyes. "I *am*. Just... less so in haunted houses." Her hand lingered on his arm a beat longer before she let go, warmth creeping into her grin.

After the haunted house, they breezed through the corn maze, Rain deliberately getting them lost just to prolong the fun.

By the time they reached the game booths, Rain's attention locked onto the prizes. "Think you can beat me at ring toss?"

To her surprise, Nik excelled—not just at ring toss, but nearly every game they played. His throws were calculated, his aim exact, and before long, he had racked up enough wins to claim a small plush toy.

Without a word, he handed it to her, his expression difficult to read, yet oddly soft. "For you."

Rain accepted it, the gesture catching her off guard. She held it close, then smirked up at him. "You've been holding out on me, Elder. Practicing carnival games in secret?"

Nik chuckled, shaking his head. "Just a bit of beginner's luck, I guess."

They shared a laugh, their playful back-and-forth settling into an easy rhythm. But beneath it, an awareness simmered—unspoken, yet unmistakable.

As the afternoon stretched on, Rain wandered toward a nearby field filled with wildflowers, her red hair catching in the breeze, strands glowing like embers in the late afternoon sun. She moved with easy delight, pointing out different blooms, plucking a few and tucking one behind her ear.

Nik watched, his gaze lingering. Without a word, he reached for a single flower and gently placed it behind her other ear.

Rain stilled, a soft blush warming her cheeks. She hadn't expected that. Her smile lingered, quieter now, touched by the unexpected sweetness of the gesture.

They walked together, their conversation shifting easily. At one point, Nik paused, gathering a few more flowers. Without drawing attention to his movements, he wove them together with a faint touch of magic, preserving their vibrancy. When he finished, he placed the delicate crown on her head, his touch light but deliberate.

"I think this will go well with your wood nymph costume," he said.

Rain's fingers brushed over the petals, her usual teasing absent. "It's beautiful," she murmured, looking up at him.

For a breath, neither moved. Then, with an easy exhale, Rain grinned and turned toward the pumpkin patch.

Back at the mansion, Rain and Nik carried their pumpkins to the back patio, setting them down with a quiet sense of anticipation lingering between them.

Inside, Rain gathered carving tools, pausing as she grabbed a cookie sheet. "Takoda's going to want these seeds," she noted. "She'll probably do something creative with them—seasoned or candied."

Nik glanced at her, noting the ease with which she considered others. A small smile played at his lips. "You think of everything, don't you?"

Rain shrugged. "What can I say? I'm a woman of many talents."

Nik chuckled. "I'll take your word for it."

They set up outside, the crisp autumn air carrying the faint scent of fresh pumpkin.

Rain shot Nik a playful glance. "Let's keep our carvings a surprise until the end. No peeking."

Nik arched a brow. "Fine, but no cheating."

As they carved, Rain kept the conversation light, tossing out Halloween stories and casual questions. Nik's responses started off brief, but soon, his guard loosened, and to her satisfaction, she coaxed a few chuckles out of him.

New goal: get Nik to laugh as much as possible tonight.

At one point, she scooped up a handful of pumpkin pulp and tossed it straight into his lap.

Nik paused, glancing down at the mess, then slowly lifted his gaze, unreadable.

Rain bit back a laugh. "Come on, lighten up! It's all part of the fun."

A long beat passed before Nik exhaled a quiet chuckle, shaking his head. "You're asking for trouble."

Rain grinned. "I'll take my chances."

For the first time that evening, Nik seemed at ease, his usual sharp edges softened by something rare—contentment.

After a while, they leaned back, satisfied with their work. Rain peeked at Nik's pumpkin but caught herself, holding up a hand in mock guilt. "No peeking! Let's reveal them together."

Nik smirked. "Fine, but no complaints when mine's better."

They turned their pumpkins at the same time.

Rain's was a lopsided mess, its crooked grin and mismatched eyes full of chaotic charm. She beamed.

Nik's, however, was a masterpiece—a wolf standing atop a jagged cliff, its head tilted back in a silent howl beneath a full moon. When the candlelight flickered inside, the carving seemed to breathe.

Rain's fingers traced the edges, admiration flickering in her eyes. "Nik, this is beautiful."

Nik didn't look at the carving—instead, he studied her. His voice was a whisper, low and certain. "Thank you. I was… inspired."

The words landed, heavier than expected, threading an unmistakable shift through the air.

For a breath, neither of them moved. The glow of the patio lights flickered between them, stretching the moment just long enough to be felt.

Finally, Rain smiled, breaking the quiet but not the tension. She turned back to admire their pumpkins, and Nik followed her gaze.

They sat there for a while, close but unhurried, the night settling around them, the space between them smaller than before.

★★★

Ariel lay sprawled on the floor in a large, empty room at the far end of one of the mansion's wings, surrounded by bags of Halloween decorations. Her knees were pulled up, her gaze fixed on the ceiling as she mapped out the vision in her mind. The room was still, the only sounds the faint rustling of plastic bags and the occasional footsteps echoing in the hallway.

As Vine strode past the open doorway, he slowed, spotting Ariel stretched out on the floor, utterly lost in thought. A smirk tugged at the corner of his lips. Without hesitation, he stepped inside and lowered himself to the floor beside her, mirroring her pose.

"Looking at anything interesting up there?" he asked, his voice laced with amusement.

Ariel turned her head, laughter slipping past her lips at the sight of him. "Just imagining where everything should go," she said, flashing a grin. "I've got a whole vision here, and you're lucky enough to be part of it."

Vine arched an eyebrow, his smirk deepening. "Am I now?" he mused, feigning skepticism, though the glint of warmth in his gaze betrayed his enjoyment.

They tossed ideas back and forth, bouncing between eerie silhouettes in the windows, flickering jack-o'-lanterns, and an excessive amount of fake cobwebs. Ariel gestured animatedly as she described the haunted scene she wanted to create, her excitement undeniable.

Vine rolled his eyes, though the amusement behind them was unmistakable. "You do realize this is a decorating project, not an exorcism, right?" he teased.

Ariel smirked. "If we do it right, maybe we'll summon an actual ghost."

Vine let out a low chuckle, shaking his head. "And you say I'm the dramatic one."

As they spoke, Eileen passed by the open doorway, pausing briefly to take in the sight—Ariel and Vine, lying on the floor, deep in conversation, laughter threading through the space between them. Her expression was unreadable, though she raised an eyebrow before continuing down the hall, leaving them undisturbed.

A few minutes later, Ariel and Vine got to their feet, diving into the decorating process. They worked in a steady rhythm, stretching cobwebs across the corners, positioning ghostly figures against the walls, and adjusting the flickering lanterns for maximum effect.

Ariel climbed onto a ladder, reaching for the ceiling as she tied thin strings to the plastic bats. Vine stood below, handing them to her one by one, his movements effortless, his smirk unwavering. The mood was easy—light, the kind of playful energy that came naturally between them.

Then, as Vine reached up to hand her another bat, pain slammed through his chest—sharp, searing, and sudden. His body tensed, his breath hitching as he instinctively doubled over, his vision tilting.

Ariel, still balanced on the ladder, caught the movement immediately. She stilled, her grip tightening around the rung. "Vine?" Her voice lost its playful edge, shifting into concern. "Are you alright?"

He forced himself upright, shoving the pain down beneath a smirk. "I'm fine," he muttered, rolling his shoulders as if shaking it off. "Probably just something I ate."

Ariel arched an eyebrow, clearly unconvinced. "Uh-huh." She crossed her arms. "Alright… but if you pass out, I'm leaving you here with the decorations." She tried to keep her tone light, but she didn't move back up the ladder, her gaze lingering on him.

Before Vine could throw back a retort, the pain struck again—deeper, sharper, unforgiving. His breath strangled in his throat as the world lurched around him. His knees buckled.

His body hit the floor.

Ariel's heart dropped.

"Vine!" She scrambled down the ladder, nearly tripping in her rush. Panic surged through her veins as she dropped beside him, her hands gripping his shoulders. "What's going on? Are you okay?"

His face was colorless, his chest rising and falling in uneven gasps. He barely seemed aware of her, his fingers digging into the floor like he was fighting to stay grounded.

Ariel shook him gently, her voice rising. "Vine, can you hear me? Stay with me!"

Her pulse pounded as she searched his face, desperate for any sign of recognition, of clarity—of him.

At that exact moment, Eileen, who had continued down the hall, stopped abruptly, her face tightening as a vision overtook her senses.

She saw fire. A young girl's face—someone she recognized.

The images vanished as quickly as they had appeared, leaving her breathless, tension tightening in her chest. A sudden urgency filled her. Something was wrong.

She spun around and sprinted back toward the room.

Eileen arrived to find Vine unconscious on the floor, Ariel kneeling beside him, shaking his shoulder gently.

"Vine, please. Can you hear me? Wake up," she murmured, panic threading through her voice.

Without hesitation, Eileen knelt beside them, her expression calm but intensely focused. She checked Vine's pulse, her sharp gaze assessing him with measured efficiency.

Ariel's voice wavered, edged with fear. "What's happening to him? Is it because of that Kubla Khan guy?"

Eileen shook her head slightly, her voice steady. "No, I don't believe this is Kubla Khan."

She tapped Vine's cheek, her voice low but firm. "Vine. Wake up."

He didn't respond.

Eileen turned to Ariel, her expression hardening as she met her gaze. "Ariel, you must promise not to mention what you're about to see."

Ariel stared at her, confused and overwhelmed. "What? I don't understand. What are you talking about?"

Eileen's voice became unyielding. "Promise me, Ariel. This is binding. If you try to speak of it, you won't be able to."

Ariel hesitated, worry clouding her expression. "I… I don't understand what you're talking about."

Eileen's gaze didn't waver. She softened just slightly, but her tone remained insistent. "If you care for him, you will promise now."

Ariel opened her mouth to protest but caught herself. She looked back at Vine, her concern for him overriding her confusion.

She nodded, her voice barely above a whisper. "I… I promise."

As soon as the words left Ariel's lips, Eileen placed her hand gently on Vine's shoulder.

For a moment, her expression softened, as if there were more to this moment than she was letting on.

In the blink of an eye—they vanished.

Ariel knelt motionless, her pulse racing as she stared at the empty space where they had just been.

The room fell silent, the weight of the moment settling heavily on her shoulders.

V ine lay on the leather couch, its chilled surface pressing against his skin, though it registered as nothing more than distant sensation. The space around him stretched into an unbroken void—endless darkness without walls, without form. A pale glow cut through the abyss, a single dim light casting thin illumination over him, tracing the sharp lines of his face and the faint shimmer of the figure kneeling beside him.

Eileen.

Draped in a flowing white dress and cloak that rippled like water in the hush of the dim light, she leaned in close, her expression calm yet tinged with sorrow.

"Vine… you need to wake up now," she murmured, her voice carrying an ethereal resonance, the sound stretching, fading, then vanishing into the silence. She reached out, her fingers grazing his cheek, her touch featherlight—an urging, not a demand.

Vine stirred. His eyelids fluttered open, his vision unfocused, struggling to latch onto the dim light, the figure above him, the strange hush pressing in from every direction. A crease formed between his brows as his mind clawed through the haze, grasping at fragments of awareness.

"Eileen?" His voice was hoarse with disorientation as he shifted slightly on the couch. Recognition flickered in his eyes—then alarm. His body tensed as he pushed up onto one elbow, movements jerky, muscles coiled. "What's going on? Where's Ariel?"

Eileen's lips pressed into a thin line, her stare unwavering but shadowed with sorrow. "Ariel is safe," she assured him. "She's at the mansion, unharmed." Her words lingered in the air like dust settling in stillness. Then, with quiet gravity, she added, "You, on the other hand… are not."

Vine went still. The statement lodged in his chest, cold and weighty. His gaze darted around the abyss, searching for answers in the void. "What do you mean?" His voice sharpened. "Where are we?"

"We're in the In-Between," Eileen answered, her tone unyielding yet soft. "Not a place for the living. Not a place for the dead. A threshold between both." The explanation carried an eerie finality, her voice swallowed by the abyss that stretched endlessly around them.

Vine's jaw tightened. His gaze darted across the empty space again, the endless blackness pressing in despite its vastness. "Why?" Frustration undercut his words, his confusion mounting. "Why are we here?"

Eileen's expression softened. "Vine, do you remember what happened in the room with Ariel?"

His breath hitched. His gaze went distant, searching. The fog in his mind thinned, fragments surfacing. "Yeah," he said slowly, his voice laced with thought. "We were decorating for Halloween." The memory sharpened, his brow knitting tighter. "Then I felt a sharp pain, but it faded. I ignored it, kept going. But when I tried to hand her another decoration, it came back—worse this time. And then..." His voice faltered. Realization struck, sending a ripple of alarm through his features. He snapped his gaze to Eileen, his throat tightening.

"Did I die?" The question left him in a sharp breath, laced with barely checked panic.

Eileen's lips curved in the smallest, almost sorrowful smile. "No, Vine," she said gently. "You didn't die."

Relief flashed through his expression, his shoulders loosening marginally. But it was brief. His gaze hardened once more, the tension creeping back into his frame as he studied her. "Then what's happening?" His voice was low, edged with insistence. "Eileen, tell me what's going on."

Her eyes lowered, glassy with unshed tears. She inhaled slowly, as though gathering herself. When she spoke again, her voice was quiet, but its significance settled like a stone between them.

"I had a vision tonight," she admitted. "There was fire... and a young woman." A hesitation. Then, softer—more final— "I believe there was a house fire. And I don't think she survived."

Vine stilled, the faint light casting deep shadows across his face as her words sank in. He straightened slowly, his movements deliberate, as though burdened by the gravity of her revelation. Leaning forward, he rested his elbows on his knees, his hands clasped tightly in front of him, his expression carved with disbelief and quiet dread.

A long, suffocating silence stretched between them. When he finally spoke, his voice barely rose above a whisper, raw with unease. "Who was the girl?"

Eileen's reluctance was palpable as she met his gaze. A slow, measured breath left her lips before she finally answered. "She was the one you were destined to meet... your potential soulmate."

Vine didn't respond immediately. His expression remained impassive, but his fingers curled inward, tightening until his knuckles blanched. The hollow ache in his chest deepened, pressing into him with an unbearable weight. Though his face revealed little, the enormity of her words echoed in the silence, reshaping the stillness between them.

Slowly, his fingers came together, forming a steeple in front of his face. His posture grew rigid, his thoughts coiling inward. After a long pause, his voice broke through, quiet and laden with thought. "Why does her dying put me here?"

Eileen's eyes held firm, her voice calm but edged with quiet sorrow. "Because even though you never met her, you were still connected. Now that she's gone... you are left with a choice." She let the words settle, giving them weight before continuing with quiet finality. "You must make this decision because you no longer have a soulmate. You cannot earn full redemption through her."

The faint echo of her words faded into the surrounding darkness, their meaning sinking deep into Vine's chest. His hands dragged through his hair before coming to rest over his face. His breath was slow and measured, but his body remained tense, his shoulders heavy with the enormity of her explanation.

Finally, his voice came, tinged with weary resignation. "And… what is this decision?"

Eileen's gaze softened. She waited a beat before answering, her tone gentle yet firm. "You must decide whether to remain Fallen, knowing you no longer have a soulmate or a guaranteed path to redemption. If you stay, the possibility of redemption still exists, but it will be harder." She studied him carefully before adding, "It will require you to find the person you choose to be with—the one who may or may not redeem you."

Her voice softened as she offered the alternative. "Or… you can choose to move on. To die." The words came quietly, but there was weight behind them. "Your actions since your original sin will be taken into account, but I can't tell you where you'll go. That's not my decision to make."

Vine lifted his head slightly, his expression strained, his voice quiet yet edged with desperation. "Has this ever happened to anyone else?"

Eileen shook her head slowly, her expression somber. "No. You are the first."

The silence that followed was thick, pressing in like a heavy shroud. Vine exhaled sharply, his fingers threading into his hair as he leaned forward, motionless for what felt like an eternity. Eileen remained beside him, steady, waiting without pressure.

At last, Vine glanced at her, resignation etched into the lines of his face. "I have to decide now, don't I?"

Eileen nodded, her expression compassionate but unwavering. "Yes."

A deep sigh escaped him, emptying what little resolve he had left. "And why should I choose to remain Fallen if my future is gone?"

Eileen leaned in slightly, her tone steady, encouraging. "Your future isn't gone. You just have to work harder to shape it." She paused, allowing the words to settle before continuing, her voice softer. "You may still find someone. It will take time, and there's no guarantee of what will happen."

Her gaze held his as she added, "The Fallen still need you. You can still protect others—the reason you became Fallen in the first place." A brief pause, then her voice took on a quiet insistence. "You can look at losing your soulmate as the end… or as a new beginning."

Vine's jaw tightened, frustration darkening his expression. A low growl rumbled from his throat as he raked his hands through his hair, gripping the strands tightly. The enormity of the choice bore down on him, visible in the shallow rise and fall of his breaths.

Eileen's voice gentled, becoming more personal. "There are people in this life who care about you. You would be missed if you chose to move on."

She listed them, her tone quiet but certain. "I would miss you. Oak, Rowan, Reed…" A beat. "Ariel."

At the mention of her name, Vine's hands stilled, his fingers tensing against his scalp. His jaw clenched, his breath coming in shallower. The name lingered between them, unspoken yet undeniable in its weight.

Eileen didn't press. Instead, she continued, her voice carrying quiet understanding. "If you choose to move on, you'll find peace. You won't have to fight anymore. But again… there is no guarantee of what that afterlife will be."

Vine exhaled sharply, a low, ragged sound, his shoulders rising and falling with the force of it. He sat motionless for a long moment, head bowed, wrestling with the decision that loomed before him.

Finally, his hands dropped to his sides, and he raised his head, locking eyes with Eileen. The storm of emotions flickering in his gaze—anger, grief, resignation—remained, but she held his stare, steady and unwavering.

Her voice was soft yet firm. "Vine, do you wish to remain Fallen?"

The question hung between them, thick with finality.

Vine's lips pressed into a thin line, his expression unreadable at first. But then, with a low, rough exhale, he muttered, "…Yeah." His voice was hoarse, reluctant. "Let's do that one."

The oppressive void around them began to shift. The darkness receded, peeling away like mist, and a warm glow seeped into the space. The familiar details of Eileen's office emerged—the soft leather of the couch beneath him, the towering shelves crammed with books, the faint scent of aged parchment and wood. Reality pulled him back, grounding him in the tangible world.

Eileen's flowing gown and cloak had vanished, replaced by her usual tailored attire. Yet she remained kneeling beside him, unchanged in her quiet steadiness.

Vine bolted upright, his breathing ragged, as if surfacing from deep water. His gaze skimmed around the room, taking in his surroundings before snapping back to Eileen. For a moment, he simply stared, tension coiled tight in every muscle.

Then, without a word, Vine stood, his movements sharp and deliberate. His steps carried force as he strode to the door. He yanked it open—then slammed it shut behind him. The echo rattled through the space, the finality of it cutting through the quiet.

Eileen remained kneeling beside the couch, her gaze fixed on the door. She didn't move, didn't call after him. Instead, she exhaled slowly, the breath measured, quiet. Relief and sorrow settled in the silence, sinking into the stillness around her.

Down the hall, Oak sat in the common room, idly flipping through the pages of an old book, though his focus had long since drifted. The soft murmur of the house pressed around him, steady and unintrusive—until the sharp crack of a slamming door shattered the quiet. His head snapped up just in time to see Vine moving through the common area, his steps hard, unyielding, his posture rigid with tension.

There was no hesitation as he climbed the stairs and disappeared down the hall, shoulders rigid with barely contained fury.

Oak didn't need to guess where Vine had just come from.

Setting his book aside, he pushed himself up and strode toward Eileen's office. He knocked lightly, a quiet tap against the heavy wooden door, then waited.

Silence.

His frown deepened. Eileen always responded—even if it was just a sharp, *"Give me a minute."* But this time, there was nothing.

That alone told him enough.

Oak turned the handle and stepped inside, shutting and locking the door behind him without pause.

Eileen was still kneeling beside the leather couch where Vine had left her, her hands resting in her lap, her head bowed slightly. She hadn't moved. Hadn't snapped back to her feet like she normally would. Hadn't pushed forward like she always did.

Oak exhaled softly, making his way toward her.

He crouched down beside her, reaching out. "Need a hand?" His tone was even, low—just for her. He took her arm, ready to help her to her feet.

Eileen pulled away sharply, twisting from his grasp before he could even get a hold. "I'm fine."

Her voice was firm, clipped. A rejection.

Oak didn't move, didn't react to the bite in her tone. He just studied her, his gaze skimming over the slight tension in her shoulders, the way she refused to look at him. Finally, he let out a slow breath. "No, you're not."

Eileen's fingers curled slightly in her lap, but she said nothing.

Still kneeling, Oak leaned in slightly. "Tell me what happened."

"I said I'm fine."

"And I said you're not."

Eileen's jaw tightened. With slow, measured movements, she pushed herself up from the floor, stepping away as she walked toward the window. The soft glow of the night bled into the room, catching against the sharp edges of her profile.

Oak stood as well, watching her. Then, without a word, he stepped closer and reached for her again.

Eileen shifted subtly, a movement so small most wouldn't have noticed—but Oak did. A withdrawal. A refusal.

He let his hand fall back to his side, but his voice remained level. "Eileen."

For a moment, she remained silent, her gaze locked on the darkness beyond the window. Then, finally, she spoke. "Vine lost his soulmate."

The words were quiet, but their weight was unmistakable. Oak's expression remained unreadable, but his stance shifted—firmer, more rooted.

"And?"

Eileen exhaled slowly, finally turning to face him. Her expression was composed, her usual restraint firmly in place, but her eyes carried an unspoken heaviness, a tension that settled deep.

"Without a soulmate, a Fallen is no longer tethered."

Oak absorbed the words without outward reaction, but deep in his chest, a silent certainty took hold.

He had never seen it happen himself—the unraveling, the slow decay of those who had nothing holding them to this world. But Eileen had. She had told him what it looked like, what it meant. Some unraveled, their existence simply fading from reality. Others…

decayed. It was slow, insidious. Their bodies held for days—weeks, if they were strong. But eventually, they all fell apart.

And now, for the first time, a Fallen was walking that path alone.

Vine would be the first.

"Will he unravel like the others?" Oak asked quietly.

Eileen shook her head. "I don't know. Most likely."

"How long does he have?"

Eileen hugged herself, gaze remaining fixed on some distant point beyond the glass. "I don't know."

Oak exhaled slowly, rolling his shoulders as he glanced toward the door. "Vine's pissed."

"I expected nothing less."

"You're going to talk to him?"

"Not tonight."

Oak's jaw tightened. "You can't ignore this."

"I'm not ignoring it."

"The hell you aren't!" Oak stepped closer, irritation pressing into his tone. "You're standing here pretending like this doesn't matter, but I *know* you, Eileen. You don't like firsts. You don't like not knowing what comes next."

Her eyes flashed with warning. *Back off.*

But Oak ignored her threat.

"This has never happened before," he continued, voice dropping lower. "Vine is the first. You don't know if he's going to unravel. You don't know if he's going to fade. Hell, maybe he won't." He let the words settle before adding, "Maybe he'll end up like me."

Eileen's expression froze.

"I don't have a soulmate," he reminded her. "And I'm still here."

Eileen's arms crossed, her posture hardening. "You don't know why you survived, Oak."

"I know." His voice remained measured, but an undercurrent ran beneath it—subtle, restrained, yet undeniable. "And neither do you."

For a long moment, neither of them spoke.

Then, finally, Eileen's voice dropped, quieter but sharper. "I can only go off what I know."

Oak's patience snapped. *"Bullshit!"*

Eileen's head turned sharply, eyes narrowing.

"You don't know," Oak pressed, voice cutting through the thick silence. "You don't know how long he has. You don't know if he'll decay or survive. And you don't know what you're supposed to do about it."

"And what do you expect me to do?" Eileen shot back.

"Take a break. Step back. Let yourself think."

"No."

Oak clenched his fists. "Eileen—"

"I said no!" Her voice cut through the space between them, absolute. "I don't have *time* for a reprieve. Tomorrow night's mission takes priority."

"Fine," Oak snapped. "You won't help yourself? Then at least help Vine."

Eileen's expression didn't change, but Oak saw it—the trace of hesitation, so brief it could have been missed.

"He's going to need support," Oak pressed, voice hard. "And you know damn well he's not coming to you for it."

Eileen stayed silent.

"Find someone who can reach him," Oak continued. "Someone who can relate. He's the first to lose a soulmate. He's not going to handle this well."

Eileen's gaze flickered slightly.

"Reed. Riichi. You know who'll handle him best."

The silence stretched taut between them, thick with tension. Finally, Eileen turned her gaze back to the window, her voice quieter. "I'll think about it."

"No. *You'll do it.*"

Oak stepped toward the door. "After tomorrow's mission, I'm coming straight back." He met her gaze, unwavering. *"And I'm not taking 'no' for an answer."*

Eileen said nothing.

Oak remained a moment longer before unlocking the door and stepping out, shutting it quietly behind him.

The moment she was alone, Eileen exhaled slowly. Oak's words lingered.

Her mind settled on one name.

Ariel.

With one last breath, Eileen turned from the window and strode toward the door.

She had a conversation to start.

★★★

Ariel paced the length of her room, her steps quick, restless. The soft glow of her bedside lamp cast warm light across the space, but it did little to ease the unease coiling in her chest. She paused by the door, glancing at it as if willing it to open. The moment Eileen and Vine had disappeared replayed in her mind—a whirlwind of confusion, fear, and frustration. She clenched her fists, torn between storming through the mansion in search of answers and knowing she'd likely find none.

A sharp knock shattered the silence. Ariel froze, her pulse leaping. Finally. Relief surged through her, and she hurried to the door, yanking it open in one swift motion.

"Vine—"

The name barely left her lips before her heart sank. Eileen stood in the doorway, calm and unreadable. Ariel's expression faltered, the relief draining from her features. "Where's Vine? Is he okay?" The words tumbled out, too quick, too desperate.

Eileen's lips curved slightly, knowing. "May I come in?"

Ariel wavered for a moment, then quickly stepped aside, pushing the door open wider. "Of course. Sorry. Of course, you can come in. I was just..." She gestured vaguely at the room, her thoughts still scrambled.

Eileen stepped inside, her gaze sweeping briefly over the cozy but cluttered space. "Expecting someone else?" One brow arched, amusement glinting beneath the question.

"Duh," Ariel said, crossing her arms, irritation slipping through. "So are you going to make me beg for answers? You two just d—just d—" The words caught, tripping over the impossible thing she had seen.

"It's the bond," Eileen said simply. "I told you you wouldn't be able to say anything."

Ariel scowled. "Yeah, well, that doesn't make it less annoying."

"Vine is fine… for now. I imagine he went to his room." Eileen lifted a hand before Ariel could press further. "And no, before you ask, I think he should be left alone for tonight."

Ariel let out a long breath, tension unwinding slightly. "You two scared the crap out of me. I've been worried out of my mind." She sat heavily on the edge of her bed, rubbing at her temples before gesturing toward the chair. "Sit, please."

Eileen settled into the chair, her movements as effortless as ever. "I know. I'm sorry."

Ariel blinked, thrown off by the unexpected apology. That alone softened her frustration, but curiosity quickly edged in. "So… what happened?" Her eyes narrowed slightly as she leaned forward.

Eileen's tone remained even, deliberate. "It was a supernatural event. Not Kubla Khan. Not a heart attack. Nothing like that." She hesitated for a fraction of a second. "He passed out. I took him to revive him." Her voice dipped lower, making it clear there was more she wasn't saying.

Ariel picked up on it instantly. She wasn't stupid. Her lips quirked into a half-smile. "I get it. You can keep your supernatural secrets. That's not my world." She exhaled, running a hand through her hair, expression softening. "I'm just glad Vine's okay."

Eileen inclined her head, watching Ariel thoughtfully. The quiet stretched a little too long, and Ariel shifted under her gaze. "But… I get the feeling you're here for something else," she said, tilting her head slightly.

Eileen's expression turned more earnest. "I do need a favor."

Ariel's mouth twisted into a smirk. "Oh, so you want me to take down Kubla Khan? Did you find out he's allergic to humans or something?"

Eileen chuckled, the sound light, amused. "I do enjoy your take on life, Ariel." Then her tone shifted, serious now. "But that's actually what I wanted to talk to you about."

Leaning back, she studied Ariel. "You and Vine are… friends, correct?"

Ariel mulled it over before responding. "I don't know if I'd exactly say we're friends… but I guess we get along."

Eileen nodded, her voice softening. "Vine has experienced a great loss tonight." Ariel's expression sharpened, but before she could ask, Eileen continued. "I won't say more than that. If you want to know more, you'd have to talk to him—but I wouldn't advise it."

Ariel frowned, lips pressing together, but she let it go.

"Given your past, Ariel, and despite it, you show resilience. You choose to embrace life." Eileen's words were deliberate, each syllable considered. "This perspective is exactly what Vine needs right now—what none of us can offer him."

Ariel let that sink in, absorbing it. After a moment, her lips pursed. "So what you're saying is… he's broken right now, and me, not being part of your posse, might be able to help put him back together?"

Eileen smiled, and a quiet laugh escaped her. "Yeah. Something like that."

Ariel nodded, determination settling in. "Sure. I'll give it a go."

Eileen rose, and Ariel followed, walking her to the door. Just as she reached for the handle, Eileen turned—and pulled Ariel into a hug.

The gesture was unexpected. Ariel stiffened for a half-second before slowly relaxing, sinking into the warmth of it. It wasn't just polite. It wasn't just a thank you. It was comfort. It was reassurance.

Eileen held her at arm's length, her hands resting on Ariel's shoulders. "Thank you." Then, with a motherly glint in her eyes, she added, "Now get some sleep. I can see the bags forming under your eyes."

She brushed her thumbs lightly beneath Ariel's eyes, smoothing away the exhaustion that wasn't physically visible but had settled deep.

Ariel blinked, caught off guard, too surprised to respond.

With one last reassuring smile, Eileen left, the soft click of the door settling into the quiet.

Ariel stared after her for a long moment before exhaling, tension leaving her body. She turned off the lamp, climbed into bed, and pulled the blankets tightly around her.

For the first time that night, she felt steady.

Her thoughts lingered on Vine.

And the quiet resolve that no matter what, she was going to help him heal.

★★★

The kitchen was filled with the warmth of brewing coffee and the comforting aroma of breakfast on the stove. Outside the window, a dense fog cloaked the landscape, lending the morning an eerie stillness. Aislinn stood by the window, arms crossed as she stared into the gray haze. The fog felt wrong—unnatural. It clung to her thoughts, thick and heavy, pressing in on her senses. She couldn't shake the feeling that the Golden Dawn was behind it, using the cover to mask their movements. Her chest tightened at the thought, the urgency of their mission that night rising within her. The weather needed to clear, and soon.

Behind her, Takoda moved fluidly between the counter and stove, flipping pancakes with practiced ease. At the table, Ariel and Rain sat sipping coffee, their quiet conversation blending with the subtle clink of silverware and the occasional sizzle from the stove. The warmth of the kitchen contrasted with the unnatural chill beyond the window, but Aislinn couldn't shake the unease prickling at the back of her mind.

The sound of footsteps broke the quiet as Ivy and Willow entered, their cheerful smiles cutting through the morning gloom. "Good morning!" Ivy greeted brightly, her eyes lighting up at the sight of the others.

"Morning," Willow chimed in, her voice soft but warm. They moved to join the group, their presence seamlessly blending into the cozy atmosphere.

Ivy clasped her hands together, excitement bubbling over. "I can't wait for Hazel and Holly to get here! We should bake cookies for Ariel and Rain's party. Sugar cookies, maybe? What do you think?" Her enthusiasm was infectious, and even Ariel and Rain couldn't help but smile.

"That sounds like a great idea," Ariel said, her grin matching Ivy's energy. Rain nodded in agreement, the suggestion lifting the mood in the room.

Willow turned to Rain, curiosity evident. "So," she began with a sly smile, "how did your day with Nik go?"

Ariel's grin widened mischievously as she jumped in, "Are you going to leave me alone during Fallen meetings once you and Nik start dating?"

Rain laughed, shaking her head, though a faint blush crept into her cheeks. "I doubt that will be happening anytime soon," she replied, her voice light but tinged with shyness.

Ivy leaned forward, a playful glint in her eyes. "You never know. Maybe Nik is secretly a hopeless romantic."

Willow snickered. "Or maybe he's an *Elder* statesman when it comes to romance."

The pun earned a chorus of laughter around the table.

Rain's smile faltered slightly as the teasing continued. She shifted in her seat, gathering her thoughts before speaking, her tone more serious. "I really wish you'd all stop calling him *Elder* and making those jokes."

The room quieted as the others registered the shift in her tone.

"Do you even know he prefers to be called Nik?" Rain continued, her tone unwavering but firm. "I think he sometimes acts the way he does because he's aware of all the *Elder* jokes. It's just… not nice."

Willow's face softened, genuine regret in her expression. "I'm sorry, Rain. I didn't realize he'd rather be called Nik."

Ivy nodded quickly, guilt flashing across her features. "Yeah, me too. I didn't mean to upset you."

Ariel, ever the mood-lifter, smirked. "Jeez, Rain. Way to be a mood killer."

Takoda, not missing a beat, turned from the stove with a teasing grin. "Aww, come on, Ariel. Leave her alone. *She's falling in love.*"

Laughter rippled through the group, breaking the tension. Even Rain couldn't hold back a smile. "It's not because I'm *falling in love*," she said, sticking her tongue out playfully. "I just don't like seeing people not being treated the way they want."

Aislinn grinned, leaning forward. "Yeah, yeah, whatever. So are you going to tell us what you and Nik did, or not?"

Rain laughed, fully relaxed now. "Fine, fine," she said, leaning back in her chair. "We went to the pumpkin patch and did the corn maze. It was hilarious—Nik kept trying to *map* out the maze like it was some big strategic mission." Her laugh bubbled up as she added, "But the best part was the pumpkin carving. Look!" She gestured toward the counter, where a lineup of pumpkins rested.

The group turned their attention to the pumpkins, eyes widening at the sight of Nik's intricate carving—a wolf howling at the moon, every detail carefully etched into the surface.

"Wow," Ivy breathed. "I didn't know he was so good at carving!"

"That's incredible," Willow agreed, leaning in to inspect it. "And no magic. He did this completely by hand." Her voice carried both respect and surprise.

"Definitely didn't see that coming," Ariel added with a grin.

Willow straightened, pointing a finger toward the pumpkins. A soft, shimmering spark of magic leapt from her fingertips and settled over them like a fine mist. "There," she said with a satisfied smile. "Now the pumpkins won't rot."

The small act of magic added a touch of wonder to the moment. "Nice touch," Aislinn said, nodding appreciatively.

Takoda glanced at the clock. "The meeting starts in five minutes."

The girls began gathering their things, exchanging lighthearted farewells as they prepared to leave. As they headed out, Willow called back to Rain, "We'll do our best to call him Nik from now on."

"Promise," Ivy added with an encouraging smile.

Rain nodded, her expression lighting up with gratitude. "Thanks. I appreciate it."

As the girls reached the doorway, Ariel paused, spotting Reed among the Fallen heading toward the conference room. She grinned and handed him a croissant. "I saved you one, freshly baked by Takoda."

Reed's face lit up, accepting the pastry with a cheerful, "Sweet!" He shot her a quick nod of thanks before disappearing down the hall.

Rain lingered beside Ariel, watching the others disperse. The air felt lighter now, the earlier tension melting into the easy warmth of camaraderie. The morning had started shrouded in fog, heavy with unease, but in the kitchen's glow, it felt like things were beginning to clear.

Ariel turned toward the hallway just as more Fallen began filtering in, their footsteps purposeful, their movements shifting the atmosphere from casual to focused. She crossed her arms loosely, scanning each face as they passed, exchanging quiet greetings. Across the hall, Eileen stood near the entrance to the conference room, her presence composed, acknowledging each arrival with a slight nod or a quiet word.

Ariel's gaze sharpened as she continued watching the stream of faces. Something was missing. Or rather, *someone*. Her eyes narrowed slightly as she searched the group again, a furrow forming between her brows when Vine didn't appear.

She glanced toward Eileen, who caught her gaze with a knowing look. Eileen gave a subtle shake of her head, an unspoken message passing between them. *Go upstairs. See if you can get him to join us.* Ariel straightened, nodding almost imperceptibly in response. A flicker of responsibility rose within her.

Rain's voice broke through her thoughts, light and teasing. "So, Ariel, do you want to try and finish decorating the room for the party?"

Ariel turned, her expression softening at her friend's easy smile. She gave a small, reassuring grin. "Sure, that sounds like a great idea." She hesitated briefly, her gaze darting toward the staircase before adding, "You go ahead and get started without me. I just gotta go upstairs and grab something first."

Rain shrugged playfully. "Okay, cool. Don't take too long. I might put the bats in the wrong place or something."

Ariel chuckled, Rain's lighthearted remark momentarily easing the tension coiling in her chest. "I trust you'll survive," she replied with a smirk, shaking her head.

As Rain strolled down the hallway, her steps relaxed, Ariel's smile loitered—but it didn't reach her eyes. She watched her friend disappear around the corner, her easy energy a sharp contrast to the knot forming in Ariel's stomach. Once Rain was out of sight, Ariel turned on her heel, her expression hardening with determination. She climbed the stairs two at a time, her thoughts focused, urgency propelling her forward.

Stopping outside Vine's door, she hovered for a moment, her hand raised just above the wood. The hallway was silent, save for the faint sounds of activity downstairs. She drew in a deep breath, shoulders lifting with the effort. *Okay, Ariel. You can do this,* she whispered under her breath. Steeling herself, she knocked firmly, the sound ringing with purpose.

Seconds stretched into what felt like minutes before she finally heard movement inside. The door creaked open just enough for Vine to appear.

The sight of him stopped her short.

He stood there in loose shorts and a wrinkled t-shirt, his hair a mess, strands falling haphazardly over his forehead. It was a stark contrast to his usual polished appearance. Ariel blinked, her thoughts catching up with the scene. *Jeez, Eileen could have warned me it was this bad. Vine's always dressed like he's ready for a photoshoot.*

"What do you want, Ariel?" His voice was clipped, edged with irritation. He leaned against the doorframe, his expression closed off.

Ariel forced a smile, her trademark lightness sliding into place like armor. "Hey, just stopping by. Checking on you. You kinda gave me a scare last night." Her voice was bright, almost cheerful, but Vine's stony expression didn't budge.

"Ariel, I'm not really in the mood right now," he said flatly. His eyes narrowed slightly. "Did Eileen send you?"

Ariel tilted her head, her grin shifting into a knowing smirk. "Would you believe me if I said no?" She kept her tone teasing, hoping to break through his walls.

Vine's jaw tightened. "Look," he said, sharper now, "I'm not up for games, Ariel."

Her smile faltered slightly, but she pressed on. "Aww, come on. You owe me an ex—"

"Ariel, *go!*"

The words cracked through the air, sharp and unyielding.

Ariel's smile vanished. She blinked, her eyes widening slightly, the sting of rejection hitting before she could brace for it. She swallowed hard, blinking rapidly to push back the sharp burn behind her eyes. *Don't cry. Not in front of him.*

Without a word, she turned on her heel, head slightly bowed, fighting to keep her emotions in check. Her footsteps were soft but purposeful, carrying her away as quickly as she could manage without outright running.

Vine watched her retreat, the realization of what he'd just done pressing heavily on his chest. "Shit," he muttered, raking a hand through his already disheveled hair. He took a step back from the door, then paused. His shoulders sagged, the full impact settling over him.

"Ariel," he called after her, his voice softer now.

She didn't stop. Her pace quickened slightly, and Vine cursed under his breath again. Gritting his teeth, he stepped into the hallway and moved after her, his longer strides closing the distance quickly. Reaching out, he caught her wrist, fingers curling gently around hers to halt her.

"Ariel," he said again, regret threading through his voice. "That was me being an ass again. I'm sorry. I didn't mean to yell."

She didn't look at him, her free hand lifting to swipe at her face with her sleeve. The motion was small, but it hit him hard. *Shit. She's crying?*

For a moment, he couldn't speak, the lump of guilt in his throat choking him. He held her hand a little tighter, his mind racing to figure out how to fix what he'd just broken.

His voice softened. "Ariel? Seriously, I'm sorry. I didn't mean to make you cry."

Ariel inhaled deeply, shoulders rising with the effort to compose herself. She turned to face him, forcing a small smile onto her lips. It wavered slightly, her emotions still raw, but she worked to mask them with a light tone. "No, it's fine. I'm fine. I'm a girl; we do that sometimes."

Vine's lips twitched into the barest smile, a flicker of relief surfacing at her attempt to brush it off. But the tension in her voice, the guarded look in her eyes, told him she wasn't entirely fine.

Her expression softened as she faltered briefly, then spoke quietly, her voice tinged with vulnerability. "It's just… some wounds are invisible, you know?"

The words settled between them, quiet but heavy.

Vine's faint smile faded, his expression shifting into a muted solemnity, perceptive and searching. His voice came out hoarse, barely above a whisper. "Yeah. I get it."

The air shifted. The unspoken gravity of shared pain settled into the silence. Ariel glanced down, her hand still in his, while Vine's gaze stayed locked on her, as if seeing a part of her he hadn't noticed before.

Without a word, he turned, keeping hold of her hand. His grip was steady but gentle, his voice low when he finally spoke.

"Come on. Let's talk."

Ariel blinked, surprised but willing, as Vine guided her back toward his room. His steps were quiet, but his grip remained firm, signaling his readiness to let her in—to share the weight he'd been carrying.

The dim light spilling from the open bathroom door cast soft illumination across the space. Ariel's gaze swept over the room, immediately noting how meticulously organized it was. Every item had its place, arranged with careful precision, but as she took it in, she realized what it lacked. No pictures. No personal touches. It was as if the space belonged to no one at all.

She couldn't help but think of her own room, full of bright colors and chaotic energy—a reflection of herself. This place felt sterile, empty, like a shell.

Vine walked past her without a word, heading straight for the bed. He didn't look at her, didn't acknowledge her presence. He simply lay down, stretching out on his back with one arm draped over his eyes. His posture was rigid, the silence pressing in just as starkly as the room itself.

Ariel lingered near the door, hesitating for a brief moment. But the ache in her chest urged her forward. She stepped toward the bed and sat on the edge. When Vine still didn't react, she slid further onto the mattress and lay beside him. The quiet creak of the bed seemed deafening in the stillness. Vine shifted slightly, making room for her without a word. The gesture was subtle but clear: she could stay.

For a long moment, neither of them spoke. The silence hung heavy between them, a tangible weight neither seemed willing to break. Ariel tilted her head back, gazing at the ceiling before finally speaking.

"You know," she said softly, a faint smile tugging at her lips, "lying down's great for thinking. Keeps the blood going to my head instead of my feet."

Vine didn't respond immediately, but after a beat, a soft, breathy laugh escaped him. It was faint, but it was real.

Ariel smiled at the sound and rolled onto her stomach, tucking her hands under the pillow. Her head turned toward him, her eyes scanning his profile. He stared up at the ceiling, his expression distant, his usual confidence nowhere to be found. This person beside her wasn't the sharp, composed Vine she knew. This was someone quieter, burdened by a weight he couldn't—or wouldn't—share.

She watched him for a moment longer before speaking again. "Okay," she said gently. "I'll go first."

That caught his attention. His head turned slightly, dark eyes sparkling with curiosity, cautious but present.

"I don't talk about this," Ariel admitted, her voice softer now. "Ever. But maybe it'll help."

She took a slow breath, steadying herself. "When I was a kid, things were… good. My dad had a great job. My mom stayed home with me and my little sister, Emily. It was perfect. Until it wasn't."

Her voice wavered slightly. "My dad lost his job when I was eight. Everything fell apart after that. The arguments started. Bills piled up. And…" She swallowed hard. "Other things."

She stalled briefly before continuing. "By the time I was twelve, I had my routine down. Every bruise had a story. Every hospital visit had an excuse. 'I fell off my bike.' 'I slipped on the ice.' 'I tripped down the stairs.'" She let out a humorless laugh. "I think I've broken almost every bone in my body."

Vine's gaze didn't waver. He turned slightly toward her, listening intently, though his expression remained unreadable.

"But the worst," Ariel said, her voice dropping to a whisper, "was when I was sixteen. I woke up in the hospital after being unconscious for two days. My face was so swollen, I didn't even recognize myself in the mirror."

Tears slipped down her cheeks, her voice cracking. "That's when I found out my parents had been arrested—for murdering Emily. She didn't survive what I did."

Her breath hitched, the words breaking apart. "She was only fourteen."

Ariel stopped, her chest rising and falling as she struggled to compose herself. The tears came faster, blurring her vision.

Vine moved. He rolled onto his side to face her, his hand lifting. With surprising gentleness, he brushed away a tear trailing down her cheek. His touch was soft, hesitant, but steady.

She inhaled sharply, her voice barely above a whisper. "After that, I went into foster care. I was angry at everything. At the world. At myself. I fell in with the wrong crowd, started stealing cars, doing things I'm not proud of."

Her lips curved into a faint, bittersweet smile. "Then I met Rowan. Two years ago, he pulled me out of it. He gave me a chance to start over. Without him… I don't know where I'd be."

The silence that followed was different now. Heavy, yes, but no longer suffocating.

Ariel wiped at her face, her breathing evening out. She glanced over at Vine, who was still watching her, his gaze carrying an unspoken depth that weighed between them.

Vine's fingers hovered near Ariel's cheek after brushing away the last of her tears. For a moment, he simply looked at her, dark eyes softening with quiet understanding. Then, moved by her vulnerability, he leaned forward and pulled her into a firm hug. His arms wrapped around her securely, his embrace solid, offering the comfort his words couldn't quite convey.

"I'm sorry," Vine murmured, his voice low and genuine. "For yelling at you earlier. I didn't realize how much it would hurt you."

Ariel's shoulders relaxed slightly, the tension from her story slowly easing. Vine's hold remained steady, grounding them both in the quiet connection they shared.

"Thank you," he said after a beat, his tone sincere. "For trusting me with that. I know it couldn't have been easy."

Ariel let out a small, shaky laugh against his shoulder. "It wasn't," she admitted softly, her voice still thick with emotion. "But it felt right."

They stayed like that for a long moment, their breathing steady, the silence between them no longer heavy but *settled*. Vine pulled back just enough to look at her, his gaze searching. "If you hadn't told me what you just did," he said quietly, "I never would have guessed. You always seem so carefree. Playful." He paused, tilting his head slightly. "How do you do it?"

Ariel's lips curved into a faint smile, her fingers absently tracing the pillow beneath her. "I made a choice," she said simply. "I decided that my past wouldn't define my future. I've been given a life—a chance to live—and I'm going to enjoy every second of it. I don't take anything for granted anymore."

Vine didn't respond immediately. He lay back slightly, eyes fixed on her as he absorbed her words. Their meaning settled deep, rooting itself in a way that felt undeniable. His gaze drifted toward the ceiling, his thoughts shifting in quiet contemplation.

Finally, he exhaled slowly. "I'll be back," he said.

Before Ariel could respond, he stood and disappeared into the bathroom. Moments later, the steady sound of water filled the air. She remained where she was, her fingers idly brushing the fabric of the sheets as she let the silence settle around her.

When Vine reemerged, steam curling behind him, he was wearing nothing but a pair of black boxer briefs. Ariel blinked, momentarily caught off guard. She had never seen him so undone, stripped of his usual polished exterior. He didn't seem to notice—or care—as he moved to his closet, retrieving his signature black Fallen attire.

"What are you doing?" Ariel asked, laughter laced through her words.

Vine glanced at her over his shoulder, smirking faintly as he buckled the straps of his combat gear. "I could hide if you want," he said, slipping into his usual dry humor. "But I thought we were beyond that."

Ariel shook her head, a chuckle escaping her. "No, I meant… what are you *doing*?"

Vine adjusted the cuffs of his sleeves, turning to face her fully. His voice held an even calmness, his expression unreadable, but a quiet resolve burned beneath the surface. "I'm living."

The words echoed back to her own earlier statement. Ariel's smile softened, recognition flickering in her gaze. Without another word, he strode toward the door and gestured for her to follow.

She didn't hesitate.

The walk down the stairs was quiet, but there was an unspoken understanding between them, a shift in the air. At the bottom, Vine paused. Then, without warning, he leaned down, pressing a soft kiss to the top of her head.

"Thank you," he murmured.

Ariel stilled, warmth spreading through her chest, the unexpected gesture leaving her momentarily speechless. She watched as he turned, moving toward the conference room with unhurried purpose.

Inside, Eileen paused mid-sentence as Vine entered. He didn't say a word, simply giving her a small nod before taking the nearest empty seat. Eileen held his gaze for a brief moment before nodding in return. No questions. No orders. Just quiet acknowledgment.

Ariel lingered for a moment, a sense of peace settling over her. Then she turned, heading down the hall toward Rain, who was already waiting for her. The sight of her friend, bright and expectant, brought a lightness to Ariel's step.

"Ready to keep decorating?" Rain asked, holding up a tangled string of bat-shaped garlands.

Ariel grinned, shaking her head. "Definitely." The morning had started heavy with fog, but as she settled into the moment, she realized—*things were beginning to clear.*

The Fallen meeting concluded, and as the members dispersed, Eileen crossed the room with measured steps. Her expression remained composed, though her thoughts lingered on one particular member of the group.

Near the doorway, Vine adjusted the cuff of his sleeve, his movements precise yet absentminded. Eileen approached, her voice quiet but firm. "You good?"

He looked up, meeting her eyes with a nod. "Yeah. I am. I'll be ready for tonight's mission." His tone held no hesitation, only certainty.

Eileen studied him, sharp enough to catch the shift in his demeanor. A small smile touched her lips, gratitude settling beneath the ever-present weight of responsibility. Whatever Ariel had said to him had made a difference. With a slight nod, she stepped back, allowing him to rejoin the others as they moved toward the training grounds in the backyard. Their voices faded into the hall, the mansion's silence creeping in behind them.

Eileen turned toward the far end of the corridor, her steps calculated, the soft echo of her boots against the hardwood the only sound accompanying her thoughts. As she neared the room Ariel and Rain had taken over for party preparations, the quiet was replaced by the faint rise and fall of laughter. Light chatter drifted through the door, a rare break in the tension that had settled over the mansion in recent days.

She pushed the door open and took in the scene. The room had transformed into a carefully curated blend of Halloween festivity and elegance. Strings of twinkling lights framed the walls, delicate webs stretched across corners, and clusters of bats hung from the ceiling as though caught mid-flight. The tables were set with centerpieces that balanced eerie charm with sophistication. She had expected an over-the-top spectacle, but instead, Ariel and Rain had created something tasteful, even refined. The realization was unexpected, and a flicker of approval warmed her chest.

Ariel adjusted a skeleton prop near the doorway while Rain stood perched on a small stepstool, struggling to secure a stubborn string of bats. Their easy laughter filled the space, the energy light, unburdened.

Eileen cleared her throat just enough to announce her presence. Ariel turned first, her face lighting up. "Eileen! Hey!"

Rain blinked, clearly startled. "Uh, hi," she said, stepping down from the stool. "What's up?"

Eileen allowed the faintest smile. "I was wondering… Can I help?"

Rain hesitated, glancing at Ariel, her expression caught somewhere between surprise and uncertainty. Ariel, however, didn't miss a beat. Grinning, she stepped forward and took Eileen's hand without hesitation. "I would love that," she said, tugging her toward the decorations. "Come on, we could use an extra pair of hands."

They fell into a rhythm quickly. Eileen focused on draping garlands along the walls with practiced efficiency, her precise movements a contrast to the girls' lively, animated efforts. Ariel and Rain weaved between the tables, setting props, arranging centerpieces, and exchanging quick-witted barbs that filled the room with a rare, infectious warmth.

"Rain, you can't just stick bats anywhere," Ariel chided, hands on her hips. "There's a system."

Rain huffed, waving a bat in her direction. "Oh, forgive me, your highness. I didn't realize we were aiming for bat perfection."

Eileen smirked faintly but said nothing, adjusting another garland with an ease that made her presence feel seamless rather than out of place.

As the room quieted for a brief moment, she stepped closer to Ariel, lowering her voice. "Thank you for checking on Vine."

Ariel barely glanced up from the candles she was arranging. "I was happy to help," she replied, brushing it off as if it had been nothing.

Eileen didn't press, only observed the girl beside her. Ariel had no supernatural abilities, no centuries of experience, and yet she had a way of shifting the energy in a room—of bringing a quiet, persistent light into the lives of those who had spent far too long in the dark. *The Fallen are lucky to have her,* Eileen thought, warmth stirring beneath the steel edges of her mind.

The decorating continued, their work punctuated by Ariel's exaggerated complaint that the room might be *too* spooky for certain Fallen.

Rain shot her a look. "You're just afraid they'll say you're bossier than Eileen."

Eileen arched a brow but said nothing, her amusement apparent as Ariel turned, scandalized. "Excuse me? I am *not* bossy, and neither is Eileen."

The conversation dissolved into laughter, the rare sound filling the space like an ember catching fire.

By the time the final touches were in place, the room felt complete. Stepping back, the three of them surveyed their work. The decorations struck the perfect balance of festive and eerie, neither overwhelming nor underwhelming. Ariel exhaled in satisfaction, hands on her hips. "We nailed it."

Rain grinned. "Yeah, we did."

Eileen glanced between them, her lips curving slightly. "Good work," she said, her tone simple, yet weighted with a quiet acknowledgment.

The moment stretched just long enough to be felt before they parted ways, the sense of shared accomplishment lingering in the air.

***

The evening air thickened with purpose as the Fallen moved through the mansion, each step measured, every movement driven by preparation. The once lively house had quieted, the faint clink of gear being secured breaking the hush. Shadows stretched across the walls as the last traces of sunlight surrendered to the creeping dark. A chill pressed in—not from the air, but from the knowledge of what awaited them. The unnatural shift in the weather hinted at forces beyond the ordinary.

In a dimly lit corner, slightly apart from the others, Takoda stood beside Riichi, their practiced synchronization evident as they secured weapons and checked their gear. She glanced at him, noting the ease in his posture, the unshaken focus in his movements. But beneath that composure, there was something different—a quiet softness that hadn't been there when they first met.

Tilting her head, a playful smile tugged at her lips. "You know," she murmured, "you've changed a lot since we met. The Riichi I knew wouldn't have dared to kiss me in public or speak casually to people like Rain and Ariel."

Riichi paused, setting down the katana he had been inspecting. He turned to her, the warmth in his expression unmistakable. "It's because of you, Takoda," he said quietly. "You've shown me that I don't have to keep hiding. That I can let others see who I really am."

He stepped closer, his voice lowering, as if admitting a carefully guarded truth. "For so long, I thought keeping my distance was the only way to protect myself. But you… you've taught me there's strength in letting people in."

Takoda chuckled softly, her fingers brushing the hilt of her weapon. "So what you're saying," she teased, "is that I've corrupted you? Turned you into a softie?"

Her teasing faded as she reached up to adjust the collar of his shirt, her movements slowing. "But seriously, Riichi. I'm proud of you. I know how hard it is to let people in. I know it's not easy for you."

His fingers brushed hers, his voice unwavering. "It's easier with you. You make everything easier."

For a moment, the rest of the room faded. Riichi leaned in, deliberate, savoring the space between them before closing it. His lips met hers in a quiet, unhurried kiss, the kind meant to be felt, not just shared. Takoda closed her eyes, letting herself sink into the moment, the warmth of it easing the tension that had gripped her shoulders.

When they pulled apart, she glanced around, catching the not-so-subtle glances from a few of the other Fallen. Some stole quick looks in their direction; others pretended not to notice. Amusement flickered in her eyes as she whispered, "You do realize everyone saw that, right?"

Riichi shrugged, a rare smirk ghosting across his lips. "Let them."

Takoda studied him, her chest tightening—not with worry, but with quiet admiration. He had come so far. Not just in opening up to her but in allowing himself to connect with the others. He was still the warrior she had met, still the man shaped by discipline and restraint, but now—now, there was more.

He bent to retrieve his katana, his movements sharp, purposeful. The shift was subtle but undeniable—his focus narrowing, his mind already stepping into the night ahead. Still, the warmth of their moment lingered, anchoring him. As he straightened, they exchanged a final look—a silent promise of strength, of unwavering support.

Takoda reached out, squeezing his hand briefly before stepping back. Without another word, they turned toward the mission ahead.

The common room was a hive of quiet motion as the Fallen finalized their preparations. Weapons were adjusted, gear secured, last-minute adjustments made with the efficiency of those who had been through countless battles. The air carried a hushed tension, the dense fog outside pressing against the windows like a living thing, its unnatural pull unmistakable.

At the center of it all, Eileen stood, her presence commanding without effort. She waited, letting the room still before she spoke.

"Tonight's mission is crucial," she said, her voice cutting through the quiet. "The Golden Dawn has been escalating, and we cannot afford to let them go unchecked any longer. This is our moment to stop them."

Her gaze swept over them—not just as warriors but as individuals she had shaped, guided, and trusted. Her tone softened just enough to carry the weight of her next words.

"Stay sharp. Stay focused. Watch each other's backs. We succeed together. Trust in what we've prepared for, and trust in each other."

A solemn silence followed, the unspoken unity of the group more powerful than any response could be.

Eileen gave a final nod before issuing the last set of instructions, ensuring every detail was understood. Slowly, the room shifted back into motion, the final steps before battle falling into place.

Rain and Ariel wove through the group, offering their goodbyes with an ease that belied the weight of the moment.

Ariel's grin was sharp as she approached Rowan, her tone laced with teasing. "Try not to make any stupid decisions, okay?"

Rowan arched a brow, the smirk that followed as confident as ever. "I don't do stupid. Risky, maybe. But never stupid."

Rain turned to Aislinn, her expression more serious. "Keep an eye on him for us."

Aislinn gave an exaggerated shrug, her grin unrepentant. "Don't worry, I've got him."

Across the room, Ivy and Willow exchanged lighthearted barbs with Rain and Ariel.

"You better have cookies ready when we get back," Willow warned, pointing a finger in mock severity.

"They better be the good ones," Ivy added, her deadpan delivery undercut by the glint in her eyes.

Ariel pressed a hand to her chest in mock offense. "Only the finest for our brave heroes."

As Reed passed, Ariel slipped a small pouch into his hand. He peeked inside and let out an approving hum. "Snacks? You're spoiling me."

"Someone has to," she quipped.

Reed chuckled, tucking the pouch into his pack before heading toward the entrance.

Toward the back of the room, Rain approached Nik, her usual confidence softened at the edges. She hesitated, just briefly, before speaking. "Promise me you'll be careful out there."

Nik's faint smile tempered the cool detachment he usually carried. "I always am," he said, the words easy, but the quiet reassurance beneath them meant only for her. "Besides, someone has to keep things running smoothly here. Think you can manage that?"

Rain rolled her eyes, though a small, fond smile betrayed her. "I'll try, but Ariel might make it impossible."

Nik let out a rare, quiet chuckle. "Then keep her out of trouble for me."

For a beat, Rain hesitated. Then, before she could second-guess herself, she leaned in, pressing a quick kiss to his cheek. Nik blinked, caught off guard, but the warmth that flickered in his smile was unmistakable. "You take care of yourself too," he murmured, his voice quieter now, the usual sharpness softened.

Nearby, Ariel found Vine tightening the strap on his pack. She stepped in close, resting a hand on his arm to catch his attention. "Hey, you sure you're good?" The casual edge in her voice couldn't quite disguise the concern beneath it.

Vine's movements stilled just slightly before he glanced at her, the usual steel in his expression tempered by sincerity. "I'm good," he said. "Thanks to you."

Ariel arched a brow, the teasing glint returning. "Me? Nah. You had it in you all along."

The corner of his mouth lifted, a rare flicker of amusement breaking through, and she gave his arm a quick squeeze before stepping back. "Just… come back in one piece, okay? Don't give me another reason to worry."

Vine met her gaze, the weight behind his nod saying more than words. "I'll be fine."

Ariel's smirk was light, but the warmth in her eyes didn't waver. "Good. Because if you're not, I'll have to hunt you down myself."

Vine's smirk widened, his head tilting just slightly. "Noted. Guess I can't let you down, then."

At the front of the mansion, the Fallen began to gather, their voices quieter now, movements more deliberate as they prepared to step into the mist-drenched night. Rain and Ariel followed them to the top of the front stairs, watching as engines roared to life, headlights cutting through the dense fog before disappearing down the winding driveway.

Rain folded her arms against the cold, her worry unspoken but evident. Ariel's hand landed lightly on her shoulder, her tone steady. "They'll be back before you know it."

Rain gave a small nod, though her gaze remained fixed on the road long after the last taillight faded into the night.

As the Fallen drove toward Georgetown, they would soon find that the new leader of the Golden Dawn, Gideon Kross, and Kubla Khan, the Reborn Conqueror, had prepared for their interference.

Earlier that afternoon, Kross and Khan were in his office at Fort Lawton, the former military base now repurposed into a war room for the Golden Dawn's operations. The air crackled with unseen tension, thick with the weight of the coming battle. Kross stood over a wide table, the map of Georgetown spread before him. Marked locations designated the strongest ritual sites, each fortified, reinforced, and waiting.

"The Fallen will come soon," Kross said, his voice even. "The barriers are in place. They'll have to fight harder to bring them down."

Khan stood on the other side of the room, near the boarded-up windows, his presence suffocating without effort. "Good," he murmured, his fingers tracing the silver ring on his hand. "They should struggle. I want them to bleed for every step forward."

Kross nodded. "Our acolytes are armed and in position. I've made sure they're prepared for sustained combat."

Khan's dark eyes gleamed with quiet satisfaction. "They are prepared for nothing," he corrected. He lifted a hand, and the air hummed with power—not raw magic, but an ancient force, a lingering presence that burrowed into the bones of those who swore their loyalty.

Outside, across the city, the first wave of empowerment took hold.

Golden Dawn acolytes staggered mid-step, gasping as the dark energy flooded through them. Their limbs steadied, their vision sharpened, the edges of pain dulled into nothing. The weak no longer felt exhaustion. The hesitant no longer feared the fight ahead.

Now, they would last longer. Strike harder. Withstand more.

Kross observed the shift, but his expression remained unreadable. He did not kneel before demons, nor did he follow blindly. But he knew power when he saw it. And he would use it.

"The Fallen will push forward regardless," he said. "We need to force them into prolonged fights. Keep them from advancing too quickly."

Khan turned from the window, his lips curving in a slow, knowing smirk. "Which is why I have strengthened the barriers. Let them claw their way through. Let them exhaust their precious energy trying."

Kross reached for the radio on his desk, his next command precise. "All squads, be advised—hold the line. Do not rush. Draw them in, wear them down. When the time comes, strike as one."

Static crackled in response, followed by swift acknowledgments from squad leaders stationed throughout Georgetown.

Satisfied, Kross met Khan's gaze. "When the time comes, will you give them more?"

Khan chuckled, dark amusement rolling through the air like a gathering storm. "Of course."

Outside, thunder rumbled, a low and ominous sound, as if the heavens themselves braced for what was coming.

The Fallen vehicles slowed to a halt, the industrial district of Georgetown stretching before them like a graveyard swallowed by mist. The air was thick with unnatural energy, each breath charged with the weight of dark rituals in motion. Fog wove between the skeletal remains of warehouses, their rusted frames jutting into the sky like the bones of a long-dead beast. The hum of something wrong vibrated through the pavement beneath them.

Eileen's voice crackled over the commlink. "Stay vigilant. Stick to the plan and keep each other safe. Every step matters."

The teams split, dissolving into the mist with practiced coordination.

Reed, Vine, and Ash took the perimeter. Reed's shadow walking veiled him in invisibility, a phantom lurking amidst the ruined streets.

"Patrol spotted near the south alley," he murmured over the commlink. "I'll trail them."

Vine crouched at a rusted power junction, his fingers crackling with sparks as he tampered with the streetlights. The fog seemed to pulse in response to his actions.

Vine's eyes narrowed. "That should have blacked out the whole block," he muttered. "But they've reinforced the grid."

Above them, Ash soared in raven form, his sharp vision cutting through the fog.. "Four cultists moving north. But the defenses—" his voice tightened slightly, "The wards are stronger than expected. They won't go down easy."

Closer to the ritual site, Riichi led the Disruption and Combat team through the narrow alleys with silent steps and unwavering focus. The sickly glow of runic symbols pulsed ahead, casting an ominous light that distorted the mist around them.

He signaled a halt, his voice firm over the commlink. "They've fortified the barriers," he informed Aislinn and Ivy. "Can you break them?"

Aislinn crouched near the glowing ward, her brows furrowing. "It'll take more effort than usual. This isn't just a basic defense—it's layered."

Takoda scanned the ground, her keen eyes catching slight depressions in the dirt. "They've set physical traps too," she warned.

"Ivy, start unraveling the wards," Riichi ordered. "Aislinn, be ready to defend. Takoda and I will cover you."

At the perimeter, Vine braced his hand against the transformer, sending a controlled burst of electricity through the power lines. The junction box overloaded with a sharp pop, sparks cascading onto the pavement.

"That got their attention," Vine muttered.

Reed's voice crackled over the comm. "Confirmed. Patrols are on the move toward your location. You've got an opening—but don't assume it'll last."

Ash's raven form swooped low, his report crisp. "Reinforcements incoming faster than anticipated. Stay cautious."

Riichi wasted no time in giving orders. "Move in."

The ritual site loomed ahead, an eerie vortex of pulsating elemental runes and chanting cultists. The fog thickened abnormally around them, amplifying the sickly glow emanating from the symbols.

Riichi raised his hand, signaling the team to spread out. His katana gleamed in the dim light, its polished steel reflecting the corruption before them. He met Takoda's eyes, their bond flaring to life as they activated Radiant Surge. A familiar heat surged through them, synchronized and seamless, their energy crackling in quiet harmony.

The cultists turned sharply, sensing the shift and immediately attacked without hesitation or fear.

They attacked in unison.

A coordinated sprint, not a reckless charge—tight formation, calculated movement. No wasted steps.

"Three incoming, left," Riichi sent telepathically. *"They're setting a barrier."*

"I've got this. Cover me," Takoda responded confidently.

With calculated precision, Takoda lunged towards her target—but before she could reach him, he twisted his hands and formed a barrier that unleashed a powerful wave of force towards her.

A wave of force slammed into Takoda, hitting like a battering ram. She was flung back, boots skidding hard across the pavement before she braced herself, flipping into a controlled roll to stay on her feet.

Riichi sprung into action, his katana slicing through a forming sigil with expert speed and accuracy, disrupting another incoming attack

Takoda steadied herself, breathing hard, eyes narrowing as realization clicked into place. *They're using the barriers as weapons now*—a dangerous twist that required a shift in tactics.

This realization fueled their determination as they prepared for the intense battle ahead.

Rowan and Aislinn activated their own Radiant Surge, their glow cutting through the fog. Rowan bulldozed into the enemy line, enhanced strength sending cultists sprawling. Aislinn fired kinetic blasts, shielding Ivy as she worked to break the ritual's core.

"Rowan, left! Aislinn, cover Ivy! Takoda and I will take the rest," Riichi ordered through the commlink.

Takoda, already back on her feet, surged toward the nearest caster, dodging a second forcewave and locking them into a brutal wrist throw. The cultist hit the ground hard, breath knocked from his lungs.

But instead of surrendering, he clawed at the ground, scrambling to keep fighting.

There was no fear in his eyes. No hesitation. Only fanatical determination.

They were not breaking.

Riichi barely had time to deflect another incoming strike before his katana clashed against a second cultist's dagger, sparks flying. The man's movements were fast—extraordinarily so.

They weren't just stronger. They had been reforged.

"They're fighting to the death," Takoda realized, her breath sharp with understanding.

"Then we end this fast."

Ivy's hands hovered over the symbols, her reality bending twisting their form—but the runes resisted, snapping back into place.

"This spell has layers," she gritted out. "I need more time."

Aislinn threw up a barrier just as a cultist hurled a searing projectile toward them. The impact shook her to the core, sweat beading on her temple.

Rowan barreled into the enemy line with enhanced strength, his power turning their momentum against them, breaking bones with every collision.

"Switch left, I've got the caster!" Riichi sent to Takoda, his voice cutting through the chaos.

"On it."

They moved in sync, Takoda intercepting two attackers as Riichi cut through the final defensive spell holding the ritual intact.

"NOW!" Ivy shouted.

She wrenched her hands downward with determination—and the final symbol shattered. The ritual's power snapped, unraveling into nothing.

The fog thinned. The weather manipulation collapsed. The ritual site was neutralized.

The remaining cultists fought on fiercely until their last breath, until there was nothing left of them to give.

As the final body hit the ground, Riichi exhaled heavily, the tension coiled in his muscles refusing to fully release. He glanced at Takoda.

"That wasn't normal."

She wiped her brow, her expression unreadable. *"No. It wasn't."*

Rowan pulled Ivy to her feet. The first site was down. But whatever awaited them at the next one… it would be worse.

The team moved cautiously toward the final ritual site, a clearing hidden deep within the industrial wreckage. The energy pressing against them was thicker than before, darker, heavier. The symbols etched into the ground pulsed erratically, the cultists' chanting layered with an unsettling resonance that vibrated through the fog.

Riichi lifted a hand, halting the group as his sharp gaze swept over the battlefield. This wasn't the same as before. The barriers were stronger, the ritual's energy surging in deviant waves. Elite Golden Dawn members flanked the perimeter, their presence a clear sign that this site held greater significance.

Takoda stepped closer, her voice barely above a breath. *This one's different.*

Before Riichi could respond, the first strike came.

Spells detonated the fog, bursts of fire and lightning ripping through the air. Riichi moved first, his katana cutting through a glowing arc of energy mid-flight, the force of the strike pushing him back a step. Takoda dodged low, rolling beneath a streak of fire before coming up into a fluid counterstrike that sent her opponent reeling.

A blast of raw energy hurtled toward Rowan, the air crackling with its charge. Before it could strike, a ripple of power surged behind him—Willow's energy manipulation twisting the attack, dispersing its force just enough to keep him on his feet. The residual impact still hit hard, forcing Rowan to brace, but he recovered quickly, using the momentum to slam into the nearest cultist, sending them crashing into a metal beam.

Aislinn moved in tandem, raising a shimmering shield just as a bolt of lightning shot toward Ivy. The strike exploded against the barrier, deflecting into the fog, scattering embers into the air.

Riichi and Takoda activated Radiant Surge, the glow of their bond flaring around them. Their movements synced, an unbreakable rhythm between them.

"I'll engage the caster upfront," Takoda sent telepathically.

"I'll handle the flanks," Riichi responded, shifting to intercept the approaching cultists.

She feinted toward the lead caster, forcing him into a defensive stance, while Riichi's katana sliced through a cultist's staff in a clean strike, severing its power mid-cast. Takoda capitalized on the opening, disarming the caster and forcing him into the ground with a swift strike.

Nearby, Rowan and Aislinn fought to hold the line, Rowan's raw strength plowing through guards as Aislinn kept her kinetic blasts precise, breaking their formations.

"Hold them steady!" Rowan called.

Aislinn didn't look up, her shield shimmering as it repelled another strike. "Just keep pushing," she shot back. "I'll take care of the rest."

Kneeling at the ritual circle, Ivy extended her hands over the symbols, her power stretching toward the runes. The moment she touched them, she stiffened.

They resisted.

Her teeth clenched. "These symbols are regenerating," she hissed. "It's fighting me."

Aislinn threw up another barrier as a series of projectiles rained down, aimed directly at Ivy. The force of the impact pushed Aislinn back a step, but she didn't falter.

"We don't have time for this," Rowan gritted out, planting himself in front of Ivy.

Ivy exhaled sharply. "Then make me time."

The ground trembled, a deep vibration rolling through the industrial wreckage. Riichi's grip tightened around his katana as a second wave of elite Golden Dawn cultists emerged from the shadows, their bodies outlined in pulsing, unnatural energy. The air rippled with power, the very presence of these warriors heavier, sharper.

"Oak, reinforce Ivy. Aislinn, move to the frontline." Eileen's voice came firm and direct over the commlink. "Birch, fortify Riichi, Takoda, Rowan, and Aislinn. Elder, Willow—disrupt their formation. Reed, Vine, Ash—hold the perimeter."

The battlefield shifted as the Fallen adjusted.

Oak moved swiftly to Ivy's side, raising a solid barrier around her as she continued working on dismantling the ritual. The moment his shield took form, Aislinn turned away, rejoining Rowan on the frontlines as instructed.

A pulse of reinforcing energy rippled through Riichi, Takoda, Rowan, and Aislinn as Birch channeled his endurance transference. The weight of exhaustion lifted slightly, muscles no longer burning with strain, their movements sharpening as strength returned.

Elder pressed his hand to the ground, sending jagged spikes of stone erupting beneath the advancing cultists. The first line stumbled, thrown off balance, but the second wave adjusted too quickly, leaping over the disruption with supernatural speed.

Before they could recover, Willow twisted the residual energy in the air, redirecting it back toward them. A sharp crack echoed through the battlefield as a bolt of purple lightning lashed across the cultists, striking several at once and forcing them back.

At the perimeter, Reed, Vine, and Ash engaged the cultists attempting to break through. Reed moved like a shadow, striking from behind before fading into the mist. Vine sent another crackling surge of electricity, but the energy dispersed harmlessly against the cultists' barriers.

"They're absorbing it," Vine snapped.

Reed's response came calm but urgent. "Switch to physical attacks. Electricity's useless."

The battlefield shifted again.

Elder's geomantic upheaval should have left the area wrecked, but the broken terrain snapped back into place, as if nothing had happened. Traps that had been disabled reactivated instantly, reforming beneath their feet.

"I thought you cleared these!" Oak's voice cut in, sharp but controlled.

"I did," Elder growled. "They're regenerating."

At the front, Aislinn held her ground, firing off kinetic blasts to force the cultists back while Rowan ripped through the nearest attackers with sheer strength.

Then, the ground beneath Takoda pulsed.

Riichi saw it first—the shimmer of a runic trap activating directly beneath her feet.

Takoda—!

Takoda reacted instantly, shifting her stance, but before she could escape, a bolt of condensed energy shot toward her.

And Aislinn vanished.

One moment she was at Rowan's side. The next, she was in front of Takoda, arms raised, her blue energy flaring in a split-second shield.

The attack struck hard, colliding against the barrier with a violent explosion. The force rippled outward, dust and debris whipping around them.

Takoda caught her breath, staring at Aislinn in disbelief.

Aislinn blinked, hands still raised, energy still flickering across her fingers. She had teleported.

She hadn't even thought about it. She had just moved.

Takoda exhaled, tension still coiled in her muscles. "You okay?"

Aislinn flexed her fingers, energy still faintly sparking over her skin. *...I think I just figured out how to control it.* Turning to Takoda, she said, "I got your back."

The battle raged on, the Fallen holding their ground, but the ritual site's defenses refused to break.

Riichi cut through an advancing cultist, his katana clashing against a spell-infused dagger before he drove forward toward Ivy. The ritual's glow pulsed brighter, resisting their efforts, its runes reforming the instant she severed them.

"Ivy, what's taking so long?" he called over the chaos, slicing through another incoming strike.

Ivy's fingers trembled over the shifting symbols, her voice strained. "I'm—" she exhaled sharply. "It's not stopping! I break it, and it just—restores itself!"

Nearby, Aislinn teleported to Rowan's side, blue energy already glowing around her hands as she pressed them to a deep wound at his ribs. The magic pulsed, sealing the gash before she turned toward the next injured ally. She was moving without hesitation now, teleporting between the Fallen as they fought, mending wounds in the space between attacks.

At the edge of the battlefield, Oak caught a flicker of movement through the thick mist.

Eileen.

She stood where the fog curled unnaturally, the remnants of magic thick in the air. But it wasn't just her presence that made Oak's chest tighten—it was the white cloak and dress she now wore.

A faint shimmer pulsed around her fingertips, threads of golden light weaving through the mist as she manipulated forces unseen. The shift was subtle, almost imperceptible, but Oak recognized it instantly—Eileen wasn't just watching. She was interfering.

Shit!

His head snapped back to Ivy just as the ritual lurched, the relentless energy faltering. For the first time since the fight began, the pulse of the ritual stuttered.

Just for a breath.

Just long enough for Ivy to seize control.

The symbols snapped apart, their connection severed. A sharp crack of energy fractured the air, and then—the spell collapsed.

The paranormal storm overhead raged instead of fading, lightning streaking erratically across the sky as if the world itself resisted letting go of Kubla Khan's influence. The wind howled, carrying the last echoes of the ritual's energy through the ruins.

The cultists did not flee. Even with the ritual broken, they fought on.

Riichi deflected another strike, his body moving in perfect rhythm with Takoda beside him. They didn't stop until the last cultist had fallen, Riichi's katana gleaming with the final flickers of Radiant Surge as he drove his blade into the last attacker.

Then—silence.

The ritual was broken. But the storm remained.

Aislinn stood motionless, fingers still curled as residual energy flickered over her skin. She stared at her hands, breath unsteady, as if the reality of what she had just done was only now sinking in.

Takoda exhaled, stepping closer. "You saved me."

Aislinn's nod was small, almost imperceptible. "I didn't even think. I just... moved."

Across the battlefield, Oak's gaze shifted toward Eileen. She hadn't moved. Hadn't spoken. But she was back in her combat gear.

As his eyes settled on her, she flinched—small, almost imperceptible, but undeniable. Her punishment for interfering was just received.

His jaw clenched. *Damn it, Eileen.*

They had won, but Kubla Khan's presence still lingered.

★★★

The mansion came into view, its silhouette standing against the fading night. The Fallen's vehicles pulled to a stop, their return marked by exhaustion and the weight of battle.

On the front steps, Ariel and Rain stood waiting. The relief on their faces was instant but quickly overshadowed by the sight of injuries.

As Vine stepped out of the vehicle, his gaze locked onto Ariel's. A smirk tugged at his lips as he gave her a quick wink—a silent acknowledgment of her earlier support. Ariel's grin widened, playful but warm, her look mirroring his unspoken gratitude.

The Fallen filed inside, some clutching wounds, others moving stiffly, their bodies bearing the toll of the fight. The usual hum of quiet conversation was absent, replaced by the low murmurs of pain and exhaustion.

Aislinn was already moving, blue energy flickering over her hands as she began healing the worst of the injuries. She crouched beside Ash, pressing her palms against his shoulder where a jagged wound tore through his jacket. The glow intensified, sealing the gash beneath the torn fabric.

Ash exhaled sharply as the pain dulled, then smirked. "Guess I owe you one."

Aislinn arched a brow. "Just try not to get stabbed next time."

Ash chuckled, rolling his shoulder experimentally. "No promises."

Nearby, Elder worked on the minor injuries, his green magic weaving through small cuts and bruises, mending them with quiet precision. His power was slower than Aislinn's, less intense, but steady.

One by one, the Fallen's wounds were treated. Though battered, they had survived.

As the others settled in, Oak caught a glimpse of Eileen. She didn't stop to check on anyone or offer a word of acknowledgment. Without hesitation, she turned and disappeared down the hall, her posture composed, her stride unwavering.

Oak's jaw tightened.

Without a word, he followed, his pace unhurried but deliberate.

She was heading to her office. Of course she was.

And he wasn't about to let her bury herself in work again.

Oak stepped into Eileen's office, closing the door behind him with deliberate finality. The quiet click of the lock echoed through the space.

Eileen didn't look up. She remained seated at her desk, flipping through reports, her focus unshaken. Her expression was unreadable, but Oak knew better.

"I told you I'd be back," he said, his voice even but carrying weight. "You're taking a break."

Eileen's pen scratched across the paper. "I don't have time for a break."

Oak crossed the room in a few strides and plucked the pen straight from her fingers.

Her gaze snapped up, cold and sharp. "Give that back."

"No." He twirled it between his fingers, watching her carefully. "You've been running yourself into the ground all week. It stops now."

"I have work to do." She reached for the pen, but he lifted it just out of reach.

Oak's jaw tightened. "Enough." Then he grabbed her wrist and pulled her up from the chair in one smooth motion.

"It's time for a break," he said firmly.

Eileen exhaled through her nose, reluctant. "Fine."

Then she moved first.

Her fingers curled into the front of his shirt, and she kissed him—hard, insistent. A clear distraction. A tactic.

Oak returned the kiss, his hands bracing her waist. He let her have this moment. Let her think she'd won—

Then she winced when his hand brushed her back.

He felt it. And his entire body went still.

He pulled back just enough to study her face. His voice was rough. "Turn around."

Eileen didn't move. "It's nothing."

Oak's eyes darkened. "Turn. Around."

She held his stare, her defiance solid as stone.

Oak exhaled sharply, then moved. He spun her gently but firmly, his fingers gripping the fabric of her shirt—and with one sharp motion, he ripped it open.

Eileen inhaled sharply, shoulders going rigid.

Oak didn't care.

Because there—across her back—was a deep, angry lash, still fading from the supernatural punishment she had taken.

His breath came slow, controlled—but his eyes burned.

"This is what you call nothing?" His voice was quiet, but thick with restrained fury.

Eileen exhaled through her nose, still composed. "It's already healing."

"That's not the point," Oak growled.

She tilted her head slightly, voice edged with impatience. "Then what is?"

Oak's nostrils flared. "That you won't even admit when you're hurting."

She rolled her shoulders, as if to prove her point. "I don't need to."

Oak went silent for a beat.

Then, without another word, he turned away, striding toward the small sink at the back of her office. The sound of running water filled the space as he grabbed a hand towel, soaking it under the cool stream before wringing it out.

"Sit on the couch," he said, his voice firm but quiet.

Eileen didn't move.

Oak stilled, then turned back to face her, eyes sharp. "I'm not arguing with you. Sit. On. The couch."

For a moment, he thought she might fight him on it just out of sheer stubbornness. But then, with an almost imperceptible sigh, she relented, moving toward the couch and sinking onto the cushions.

Oak crossed the room, kneeling beside her as he pressed the damp cloth against the laceration. His touch was firm, but careful, wiping away the remnants of dried blood.

Eileen stayed quiet, her shoulders gradually losing their tension as he worked.

Neither of them spoke for a long moment, the only sound the quiet movements of Oak tending to her. When he finished, he set the cloth aside and let his fingers ghost along the unmarred skin just above the gash.

Then, slowly, he leaned in and pressed a kiss between her shoulder blades.

Eileen let out a breath. Maybe the first real one since the mission.

Oak smirked slightly against her skin. "You're impossible."

She huffed, the corner of her mouth twitching. "And you're dramatic."

Before he could respond, she turned toward him, her hand sliding up the side of his neck. This time, when she kissed him, there was no deflection. No evasion. Just quiet, deliberate warmth.

Oak kissed her back, slow and deep, his hand slipping to her waist, anchoring her there.

No rush. No expectations. Just them.

For once, Eileen let herself stay in the moment

★★★

The storm over Fort Lawton raged, lightning splitting the sky as the unnatural fog began to fray at its edges. The desecrated battlefield lay in ruin, its rituals dismantled, but the Golden Dawn's war was far from over.

Kubla Khan stood unmoving, his gaze locked on a conjured projection flickering before him—an ethereal window to the battle that had unfolded in Georgetown. The last remnants of the ritual's energy allowed him to watch its unraveling, though the image was already beginning to distort.

Beside him, Gideon Kross stood rigid, arms crossed, listening intently as reports crackled over the radio. Faint, static-filled voices of cultists still stationed in Georgetown relayed the damage: Both ritual sites destroyed. Fallen forces still intact. The veil compromised.

Gideon's fingers tapped once against his sleeve, absorbing the information. "The Fallen dismantled both ritual sites," he reported. "The Typhoon remains active, but its defenses are failing."

Khan rolled a silver ring over his knuckle, his expression composed but unreadable. His voice, when it came, carried a quiet inevitability.

"Of course they did."

Gideon frowned. "You expected this?"

Khan's lips curved—not in a smile, but something colder. "The Fallen aren't reckless. They dismantle key structures first. Riichi and Takoda's bond was the key."

The flickering image before him pulsed once before vanishing, its energy spent. Khan finally turned to Gideon, his gaze sharp, all amusement gone.

"We will not let them continue unchecked."

Gideon gave a slow nod. "Fort Lawton is the last site. We still have the storm, and the defenses are holding. There won't be another failure."

Khan tilted his head, considering. Then, almost absently, he murmured, "They've grown stronger... but every bond has a breaking point."

He turned away, his coat sweeping over the damp ground as he moved toward the ritual circles. The symbols still pulsed with residual energy, the storm above swirling violently, refusing to dissipate.

"Let them think they've won," Khan said, lifting a hand toward the storm.

The winds surged in response, twisting into a controlled force at his command. "Their moment of victory will become their greatest mistake."

A final bolt of lightning split the sky, casting a jagged glow over Fort Lawton.

The Golden Dawn was not finished.

<u>Chapter Twenty-Six</u>
Foundations of Trust

Ariel lounged on her bed, sketchbook propped against bent knees, the TV murmuring in the background. She wasn't watching—just letting the shifting light and low hum fill the silence.

Her pencil traced slow, deliberate strokes, weaving abstract patterns across the page. No clear shape, no plan—just an outlet. She didn't draw every night, but when the hours stretched too long and old ghosts crept in, it was the one thing that steadied her.

She hovered over the page, searching the lines for meaning. Restless energy buzzed beneath her skin, an itch that refused to let her sleep.

A knock at the door cut through the stillness. The spell shattered. Her pencil slipped from her fingers, rolling off the bed and hitting the floor with a soft clatter.

"Rain?" she called, swinging her legs down. "Did you lock yourself out again?"

Her voice carried its usual teasing lilt, but when she pulled the door open, the words stuck.

Vine stood in the dim hallway, his silhouette framed by the low glow of the overhead light. His hair was tousled, and the usual sharpness of his features was dulled by exhaustion. Faint shadows clung beneath his eyes, a quiet admission of sleeplessness.

"Vine." Ariel's voice softened. She blinked, concern creeping in. "What's up?"

No words followed. He just looked at her, his expression guarded, a quiet strain tightening beneath his calm veneer.

"Is everything okay?" she asked, tilting her head.

Vine exhaled through his nose, barely more than a breath. "Yeah," he said, but it wasn't convincing. His gaze broke away for a second before returning. "I was walking around. Couldn't sleep. Heard your TV and thought I'd check on you."

Her brow arched. "Checking on me?" She crossed her arms, amusement threading through her voice. "You do realize I'm just a binge-watching insomniac, right?"

The corner of his mouth twitched, but whatever response he had, faded before it reached the surface. His eyes drifted past her, scanning the room, though he didn't seem to be looking at anything in particular.

Ariel sighed. "Did you… want to come in?"

A flicker of something crossed his face—relief, maybe, though it was gone too fast to tell. He gave a small nod. "Yeah. Sure."

She stepped back, letting him in, then closed the door behind him. The lock clicked into place. She didn't usually bother locking her door, but the motion had been instinctive, as if drawing a line between them and the rest of the world.

Climbing back onto the bed, she leaned against the headboard and patted the space beside her. "Make yourself comfortable."

Vine hesitated before perching on the edge, stiff, as if he wasn't sure whether to stay or go. Ariel's gaze flicked to her sketchbook still resting on the nightstand, but before she could grab it, Vine's eyes followed hers.

"What's that?" he asked, nodding toward it.

Ariel flushed and swiped the book off the table, tucking it under the bed. "Nothing," she said quickly. "Just… stuff."

One brow lifted. "Stuff?"

"Yes. Stuff," she said flatly. "And it's off-limits."

He raised his hands in mock surrender, but the smirk that had begun to form faded as silence crept in. Ariel studied him, then leaned forward, her eyes narrowing slightly.

"You're acting weird." She searched his face. "What's going on?"

His throat worked in a quiet swallow, but he didn't waver. For a moment, it looked like he might retreat, but then he met her eyes, quiet resolve settling over him.

"You told your secrets," he murmured. "I guess it's my turn now."

The shift in his tone sent a ripple through the air. Ariel straightened, the teasing edge in her expression fading into quiet sincerity. She gave him her full attention.

"Okay," she said gently. "I'm listening."

Vine leaned forward, resting his elbows on his knees. His fingers tapped against each other in a restless, unconscious rhythm. The room's quiet seemed to press down on him, amplifying the weight of what he needed to say. The words felt foreign—like something he'd never quite learned how to carry.

He stared at the floor, focus locked on a point that didn't exist, as if the right words might appear in the worn carpet fibers. The silence stretched, not uncomfortable but heavy with meaning left unsaid.

Finally, he exhaled. His voice was low, deliberate. "I had a soulmate," he said, the admission quiet but sharp, like speaking it aloud might crack something fragile. His eyes didn't leave the ground. "I passed out on you the other night because the woman I was meant to be with—my soulmate—died before I ever met her."

Ariel blinked, the weight of his confession sinking in. The lighthearted energy she carried so easily dimmed. "Vine…" she started, her voice soft with understanding.

He shook his head, cutting her off before she could say more. "Eileen told me last night," he continued, his tone clipped, measured. "The bond, the connection—it's gone. Just… gone."

Ariel stayed quiet, instinct telling her this was a moment for listening, not filling the silence. Her fingers twitched, the impulse to reach for him pulling at her, but she held back.

"I had to decide," he said, his voice tight. "Stay Fallen, keep fighting, or… move on." The words hung between them, almost tangible in the space they occupied. His lips pressed into a thin line, silence doing the talking for him. Then, quieter, almost as if to himself, he added, "I chose to stay."

Ariel didn't hesitate this time. She leaned forward, her hand resting lightly over his. "I'm glad you did," she said simply. Her voice was calm, no hesitation, no forced reassurance—just certainty.

Vine finally looked at her, his dark eyes guarded but not empty. He didn't pull his hand away, but his fingers remained tense under hers, his body coiled with restless energy. "You shouldn't be," he muttered, bitterness lacing his tone. "It wasn't some noble choice. I stayed because... I don't know how to do anything else. Fighting, surviving—it's all I know."

Ariel shrugged, the faintest smile tugging at her lips. "Still glad," she said, her tone just as even. "You're here, and that's what matters."

His brow furrowed, jaw tightening as his focus drifted past her. "She was supposed to be my future," he said after a long pause, his voice quieter now, rough around the edges. "The one who could've... I don't know, balanced all this out. Made it mean something."

Ariel narrowed her eyes slightly, the teasing glint in her expression softening into something quieter. She shifted closer, warmth threading through her voice. "And now?"

Vine let out a slow breath, dragging a hand down his face. The motion was unhurried, heavy, as if centuries of exhaustion had woven themselves into his bones. "Now it's on me, I guess," he said, dry and self-deprecating. "Whatever redemption I've got left to earn, I've gotta do it the hard way."

Ariel's fingers curled more firmly around his, her grip warm but without pressure. "You've been doing it the hard way for centuries, haven't you?" she mused, a spark of teasing beneath the words. "This is just another day at the office for you."

A faint smirk ghosted across Vine's lips. It didn't quite reach his eyes, but it was there, however fleeting. "Yeah," he muttered. "Something like that."

Ariel leaned in, her voice quieter now, no amusement this time—just certainty. "You've got people who care about you," she said. "Eileen, Rowan, the Fallen... and me."

Her words lingered in the stillness, settling in a place between them neither of them fully acknowledged. Vine's gaze flicked to her, searching her face for cracks in her sincerity. He didn't find any.

For a moment, he said nothing. Then, finally, he gave a small nod—subtle, but deliberate. The room settled into a quiet calm after Vine's confession. Ariel didn't press for more; she knew when someone needed room to breathe. Instead, she leaned back against the headboard, drawing her knees up as she glanced sideways at him.

Vine remained on the edge of the bed, elbows braced on his knees, fingers tapping a light rhythm against his thighs. The motion seemed unconscious, a glimpse of the restless energy simmering beneath his composed exterior.

"So..." Ariel broke the silence, her voice light, laced with mischief. "Do I get a trophy for this? Maybe a plaque?"

Vine glanced at her, one brow lifting. "A trophy?"

"Yeah, to commemorate this monumental event." She smirked. "'Ariel, Listener of Broody Fallen.' It'll look great on my wall."

A quiet laugh escaped him—so subtle she might have missed it if she weren't listening for it. "Don't push your luck."

Encouraged, she grinned. "Hey, I'm just saying. It's not every day you spill your soul. Big moment, Vine. Huge."

He rolled his eyes, but there was no real bite behind it. After a moment, he shifted back, easing against the headboard beside her. His movements were measured, deliberate, but not hesitant. When their shoulders brushed, Ariel tilted her head, studying him with a faint smile.

"Better?"

He shrugged. "Different."

"Different can be good." She leaned her head back against the wall, staring at the ceiling. "Sometimes you just need someone next to you who gets it, you know?"

Vine didn't respond right away, but the tension in his frame eased by degrees. Finally, he murmured, "Yeah. Maybe you're right."

Ariel turned to him, her smile soft, teasing. "I'm always right. You should know that by now."

He huffed a breath, shaking his head. "You're impossible."

"Impossible," she echoed, "but also extremely helpful. And funny. And very good at listening."

Vine shot her a sidelong look. "Is this your way of fishing for compliments?"

"Not fishing. Just stating facts." She grinned. "You're lucky to have me around. Admit it."

His lips twitched, almost smirking. "Unbelievable."

"Thanks." Ariel beamed. "I work hard at it."

Their banter flowed easily, a familiar thread weaving between them. Shifting, Ariel sat cross-legged to face him, her expression softening.

"You're going to be okay, you know," she said, quiet but sure.

Vine's dark eyes flicked to hers. He didn't respond immediately, but his shoulders relaxed further, the subtle shift saying more than words.

"Really," she added. "You don't have to handle it all alone. Not anymore."

The words settled between them, warm and sure. Ariel reached out, resting a hand lightly over his. The touch was unassuming, but it grounded the moment. Vine's focus dropped to their hands, and after a beat, he turned his palm upward, letting their fingers slide together. His grip was small, almost hesitant, but present.

When he spoke, his voice was low but certain. "Thanks."

Ariel studied him, her smile turning gentle. "For what?"

"For… this." The weight in his voice made the words feel heavier than they seemed.

Her smile brightened. "Anytime."

The quiet between them deepened, the shifting glow of the TV casting soft shadows along the walls. Ariel stayed close, watching him. He wasn't looking at the television—his gaze locked somewhere distant, lost in thoughts she couldn't follow. But his posture, the slight pull of tension in his frame, betrayed the weight of everything he'd laid bare.

"Hey," she said softly, nudging his arm. When he didn't respond, she reached up, fingers brushing lightly against his jaw. "Vine."

His dark eyes flicked to hers, hesitant but holding. "What?"

"You're here," she said simply, steady and sure. "That's what matters. You stayed. And that says more about you than you think."

His brow furrowed slightly, old defenses creeping back in. "It wasn't some grand choice," he muttered. "I stayed because I didn't know what else to do. Because it's all I know."

Ariel shook her head, her touch remaining gentle. "No. You stayed because you're stronger than you give yourself credit for. Because you know—deep down—you make this world better just by being in it."

A faint scoff left him. "You can't know that."

"I do," she replied without hesitation. "And if you can't see it yet, you'll just have to trust me. One day, you will."

Vine held her gaze, searching. She didn't waver. The silence stretched, thick with everything neither of them said, and for a moment, it seemed like he might deflect, retreat. But then, after a beat, he gave a small, almost imperceptible nod, his shoulders easing slightly.

Ariel let her hand drop from his jaw, resting lightly against his arm. "See? That wasn't so hard."

"Don't get ahead of yourself," he muttered, though the corner of his mouth twitched in what might have been a smirk.

"Too late," she quipped. Leaning back against the headboard, she let her fingers trail absently against his arm. "I'm putting 'emotional breakthrough guru' on my résumé."

He rolled his eyes, but the tension in his posture continued to dissolve, bit by bit. They sat in companionable silence, the night settling around them like a quiet embrace. Then, drawn by some invisible thread, Ariel shifted closer, her hand trailing down his arm until her fingers brushed his.

The contact sent a ripple through the air, and she felt him stiffen slightly beside her. Still, he didn't pull away.

"You don't have to keep it all locked up," she murmured. "Not with me."

He didn't answer right away. A slow breath left him, tension lingering in his posture. After a moment, his fingers flexed, then closed around hers—not hesitant this time, but deliberate. His hold carried a quiet weight of understanding, as though he had made a choice, even if he wasn't sure what it meant yet.

When he finally spoke, his voice was low, edged with truth. "You're not what I expected."

Ariel's lips curved, amusement dancing in her expression. "What's that supposed to mean?"

"You…" He hesitated, choosing his words carefully. "You surprise me. You don't back down. And you don't look at me like I'm some broken thing."

"That's because you're not," she said simply. "You're just figuring it out. Same as the rest of us."

Her words hung in the air, soft but certain. Vine's grip on her hand tightened slightly as he shifted closer, eliminating any space between them. Ariel's breath hitched as his eyes flicked to her lips, the air between them becoming dense, charged with a quiet intensity.

God, I want her.

Vine leaned in, and Ariel didn't resist.

The kiss was slow at first, tentative—a quiet question in the way his lips brushed against hers. Ariel's heart stuttered before she leaned into him, her hand sliding to his chest, fingers curling against the fabric of his shirt. His palm came up to cradle her face, firm yet careful, as if afraid of breaking the fragile moment between them. When the kiss deepened, it carried the weight of unspoken emotions that both understood but hadn't voiced.

The hush of the room enveloped them, broken only by the soft cadence of their breaths, the faint rustle of fabric as they drew closer. Ariel shifted, straddling Vine's lap, her hands gliding over his shoulders. He let out a slow, contented sigh, as if that one small act unraveled the last thread of tension he still held.

Then, with quiet purpose, he eased her onto the mattress, hovering above her. He hesitated, searching her face for permission.

He's so hot. Could I stop even if I wanted to?

She gave a slight nod, her voice barely above a whisper. "Stay."

He answered without words, only in the way his lips found hers again, the kiss shifting from tentative to certain. His hands skimmed over her skin with deliberate care, learning the shape of her like a quiet vow. Their bodies aligned, moving with an unhurried rhythm that spoke not of urgency but of understanding, of a need deeper than desire.

Ariel's fingers tangled in Vine's hair, drawing him closer, their connection raw and unguarded. The walls that had once separated them had slowly fallen away along with their clothes, leaving only this—a moment where nothing else existed but them.

This shouldn't feel this good. The thought hit hard, sinking deep, but Vine didn't pull away. He couldn't.

The night unfolded in a language of whispered touches and tender moans, of hands tracing familiar paths with newfound gentleness. They took their time, unhurried and undisturbed by the outside world—it was only them. Their bodies moved in slow, measured harmony, not seeking escape, not chasing oblivion, but finding solace in each other.

When the stillness returned, they remained entwined, their breathing slow and even. Ariel rested her head against Vine's chest, her fingers drawing light patterns along his skin. His arms wrapped around her, holding her close, as if anchoring himself in the warmth of her presence.

As sleep crept in, the weight of their shared confessions remained, but it no longer pressed so heavily. For the first time, neither lay awake, lost in the past. Wrapped in each other's warmth, the silence wasn't lonely—it was peaceful.

Soft light from the flickering TV stretched across the room, its glow shifting over rumpled sheets and scattered clothes. Ariel stirred first, her eyes cracking open to the muted illumination. For a fleeting moment, warmth wrapped around her, Vine's slow, even breaths beside her offering a deceptive sense of calm.

Then the muffled sound of voices in the hallway shattered it.

A knock at the door jolted her fully awake. Ariel froze, heart hammering.

"Ariel?" Rain's cheerful voice filtered through the door. "Are you in there? You didn't come down for breakfast."

"Shit," she whispered, bolting upright. Her elbow nearly caught Vine in the ribs as she scrambled, heart racing.

Beside her, Vine stirred, blinking against the dim light. His brow furrowed slightly as he took in her panic, then flicked toward the door.

"Morning," he drawled, voice low and edged with sleep. A smirk tugged at his lips, as if this was all mildly amusing.

"Not the time," Ariel snapped, shooting him a sharp look as she scanned the room for any damning evidence.

Vine stretched, utterly unbothered. "Relax. It's just Rain. What's she going to do, file a report?"

"Oh, I don't know—maybe tell the entire mansion?" Ariel hissed. She snatched his shirt off the floor and chucked it at him. "Get dressed and hide. Now."

He caught the shirt with infuriating ease, arching a brow. "You're really bad at mornings."

Another knock. Louder this time. "Ariel? Are you ignoring me? Should I be worried?"

"I'm fine!" Ariel called, voice a little too high. She yanked on her pants, glaring as Vine, still moving at a glacial pace, tugged on his jeans like they had all the time in the world.

He leaned back slightly, reaching for his boots. "Bathroom, huh?"

"Yes, bathroom!" she hissed, shoving his jacket at him. "Go! Now!"

Vine shrugged, clearly entertained, and strolled toward the bathroom as if he had nowhere better to be. "You're fun under pressure, you know." He disappeared inside just as Rain knocked again.

"Ariel, what's going on?" Rain's voice carried a teasing suspicion. "Why's the door locked? Are you hiding something?"

Ariel's pulse kicked up another notch. She snatched the remote and cranked up the TV to drown out any noise. "I stayed up too late watching true crime," she called, voice laced with mock exasperation. "Locked the door because I got spooked."

Rain laughed. "You locked your door because of TV? Really?"

"Yes!" Ariel groaned, pressing a hand to her temple. "Now go away! I need coffee before I deal with anyone."

From behind the bathroom door, she caught the faint sound of Vine laughing. Her jaw clenched. *If he thinks this is funny, I swear…*

Rain sighed dramatically. "Fine. But you'd better be downstairs in five minutes. I'm starving, and I'm not waiting around for you all morning."

Ariel held her breath, listening as Rain's footsteps faded down the hall. When she was sure Rain was gone, she exhaled, shoulders sagging.

The bathroom door creaked open, and Vine leaned lazily against the frame, arms crossed, smirk firmly in place. "That was fun."

"You're impossible." Ariel scowled. "This is why we don't break rule number one—no spending the night."

Vine stepped closer, voice low with amusement. "Maybe. But watching you panic was worth it."

Her glare deepened, but before she could retort, Vine reached out, brushing a strand of hair behind her ear. The gesture was brief, deliberate.

"One for the road," he murmured, pressing a slow, deliberate kiss to her lips.

Ariel stiffened for half a second, but his teasing warmth dissolved her resistance, and she leaned in. Her hands skimmed against his chest before she caught herself, pulling back abruptly.

Her cheeks warmed. "Go. And be quiet."

Vine chuckled, grabbing his jacket and slinging it over one shoulder. As he moved toward the door, he glanced back, smirk widening. "You're worth the trouble, you know."

Ariel rolled her eyes, but despite herself, a small smile twitched at the corner of her lips. She peered into the hallway before whispering sharply, "Take the back stairs. Don't get caught."

With a silent nod, Vine slipped out, moving effortlessly down the hall. Ariel waited until he vanished around the corner before shutting the door and leaning against it with a long sigh.

"It's Vine. Of course, he's a rule-breaker," she muttered, shaking her head.

She shut off the TV and moved to the mirror, smoothing her hair and adjusting her shirt. With a deep breath, she steeled herself for Rain's inevitable interrogation.

Here we go.

★★★

The common area buzzed with conversation and laughter, a rare moment of ease among the Fallen. Takoda and Riichi sat near the fireplace, murmuring quietly, while Rowan and Aislinn shared a loveseat, Rowan's arm draped lazily across the back.

On the floor, Ariel sprawled beside Rain, tossing around ideas for their Halloween party.

"We don't need anything over the top," Rain said, propping her chin on her hand. "Just something chill so people can actually relax."

Ariel nodded. "Good food, music, and everyone in costumes. That's enough of a push."

Rain smirked. "Especially since we need to make sure Hazel, Holly, and Alder actually have costumes."

Ariel snorted. "Oh, if they try to back out, we're calling them out. No exceptions."

"Absolutely no exceptions," Rain agreed.

Nearby, Elder and Ash spoke in hushed tones about last night's mission, while Ivy and Willow perched on the couch, their chatter weaving into the background. Vine stood by the window, posture easy but gaze distant. Reed and Birch exchanged quiet words by the doorway, and at the far end of the room, Oak and Eileen observed it all with amused detachment.

Then footsteps echoed in the hallway. The chatter stilled as the door swung open.

Ariel was the first to hop up. "Finally! You're late. What kept you?"

Hazel strode in first, arms wide as she took in the lively room. "Look at this—feels like a family reunion."

"Good to see everyone," Holly added, flashing a warm smile before moving to hug Takoda.

Alder followed last, his usual calm demeanor in place as he offered a polite nod. "It's good to be back."

"Uneventful trip?" Rowan asked.

Hazel nodded. "Nothing to report, but we're ready to dive in."

"Not yet," Ariel cut in, eyes gleaming mischievously. "More importantly—did anyone bring costumes? Or are Hazel and Holly carrying the team?"

Hazel smirked at Holly. "Of course, we brought costumes."

Holly grinned. "Oak made sure we did."

Rain's smirk widened as she turned to Alder. "Wait. *Did you* bring one?"

Alder blinked. "No. I thought Oak was joking."

A few snorts echoed through the room. Ariel folded her arms, grinning. "Don't worry! I think I have a ballerina outfit you can borrow. Tights included."

Rowan chuckled. "Should've taken Oak seriously."

Alder sighed, shaking his head. "Hard pass. I'll figure something out. And I promise—it won't involve tights."

Holly offered sweetly, "I could whip something up with illusions if you're desperate."

Alder's lips twitched. "Thanks, but I'll manage."

The laughter died down as Rain nudged Ariel, whispering something in her ear. Ariel's grin sharpened before she turned to Eileen.

"We need to talk about something important. Like, *critical-mission* important."

Eileen tilted her head, amusement flickering in her gaze. "Alright. I'll bite. What is it?"

Ariel clasped her hands dramatically. "We need to set a date for the Halloween party."

Rowan smirked. "For Ariel, that probably *is* critical."

Alder, deadpan, added, "Cookies, costumes, and world-saving. Totally on brand."

"Exactly," Ariel said, beaming.

Eileen took a moment to scan the group before nodding. "The night before the full moon. But just so we're clear, I'm not making it mandatory."

Ariel clapped her hands together. "Done! And Alder, if you need costume help, just let me know. I already helped everyone else."

Alder gave a faint smile. "I'll keep that in mind. But fair warning—I'm keeping expectations low."

Eileen's voice rose above the lingering chatter. "Now that everyone is here, we'll be meeting in fifteen minutes. Be ready."

The group murmured their acknowledgment as Hazel and Holly followed Ivy and Willow toward the guest rooms, their voices fading into the background.

Ariel, Rain, Takoda, and Aislinn drifted toward the kitchen, Ariel immediately grabbing a notepad. "Alright, let's get some cookie brainstorming done while we have time."

"Pumpkins and bats," Rain said, hopping onto a stool. "Non-negotiable."

"We should do something Fallen-themed," Ariel smirked. "It's too perfect to pass up."

Aislinn tilted her head. "What about flavors? Rowan's favorite is spiced. That could be a good addition."

"That's actually a great idea," Ariel said. "We should do a variety—match everyone's tastes."

Rain shrugged. "That's fine, but isn't sugar cookies kind of the whole Halloween vibe?"

"Basic can be good," Takoda added. "We don't need to go overboard."

Ariel grinned, sketching quick doodles of cookie shapes. "We can mix it up. Spiced, sugar, maybe a chocolate one. And shapes—bats, pumpkins, stars…"

Rain sighed dramatically. "Fine, but I'm *not* frosting the stars. Too Christmas-y."

Ariel laughed. "Alright, no overthinking. Let's just keep it fun."

Their laughter filled the kitchen, the simple act of planning cookies a welcome distraction before the meeting ahead.

Minutes later, the rain pattered against the windows as the Fallen gathered in the conference room, the crisp October chill creeping in at the edges. Eileen stood at the head of the table, her presence commanding as she straightened a page in front of her.

"Let's begin," she said evenly. "Last night's mission disrupted two of the Golden Dawn's major ritual sites. Thanks to your efforts, their weather manipulation network is down, and as you've probably noticed—" she gestured toward the window—"the storm has finally broken."

She let the moment settle before shifting her attention to the newest arrivals. "For those of you who weren't present, the Golden Dawn wasn't just reinforcing their wards. They were weaponizing them—testing new methods to sustain power past normal limits. The storm didn't dissipate immediately because Kubla Khan's influence extended beyond the ritual itself. His magic still lingers."

Alder leaned forward slightly, brow furrowed. "Do we know if that's Khan's direct power or something they've manufactured?"

Eileen's fingers tapped against the table. "Both. Khan's involvement is undeniable, but the Golden Dawn wouldn't rely solely on one entity for power."

She paused before continuing. "With Gideon Kross now in control, we have to assume their approach will be different. Kross isn't just leading them—he's restructuring them. They're moving from factions into an organized force. That means they'll strike with precision instead of reckless devotion. We need to be ahead of them."

A brief silence settled over the table.

Then Oak, who had remained quiet up until now, leaned forward. His voice was steady, measured.

"Our next step is recon." His sharp gaze moved to Reed, Vine, Hazel, and Alder. "We can assume Kross has made Fort Lawton his headquarters. Your job is to find it—locate exactly where he's set up his base within the grounds. The Golden Dawn reinforced barriers at Georgetown, so we need to see if they're doing the same here. If they are, we'll need a way to break them."

He turned to Hazel. "Use your weather manipulation. See if there are new traces of the Typhoon Ritual that weren't there before. If Kross is altering their plans, he may be shifting the way the ritual is structured."

Hazel gave a firm nod. Alder's expression remained unreadable, but his thoughts were already working through the possibilities. Reed, ever the shadow, gave a slight tilt of his head in acknowledgment. Vine, leaning back with arms crossed, simply observed.

Oak shifted his attention. "The second mission is in Nihonmachi. Rowan, Aislinn, and Holly—you'll be tracking their movements. If Kross is pushing for expansion, they'll need a secondary stronghold. If they've lost their primary sites, we need to know where they're regrouping."

Aislinn nodded, already thinking ahead. Rowan's eyes flicked toward her before he gave his own brief nod. Holly, her usual lightness absent, simply muttered, "Got it."

Before Oak could move on, Riichi leaned forward slightly, his voice controlled. "You haven't assigned Takoda or me to any recon."

Takoda tilted her head, smirking faintly, though her arms remained crossed. "Yeah. Feels like an oversight."

Eileen met their gazes evenly. "Not an oversight. A decision."

Her tone remained firm, but there was a weight behind her words. "You're both capable. That's not the issue. But Khan and Kross have already singled you out. If they're tracking anyone, it's you. Sending you into recon isn't strategy—it's exposure."

Takoda exhaled sharply, but she didn't argue. Riichi held Eileen's gaze for a moment longer before nodding once.

"Understood."

Eileen let the room settle before continuing. "Moving on to the next thing on the agenda. We're implementing new bonded training."

She turned to Riichi and Takoda, then Rowan and Aislinn. "If we're right about the connection between bonds and enhanced power, it's time we harness that intentionally."

Takoda and Riichi exchanged a glance, an unspoken agreement passing between them. Rowan leaned back slightly, rubbing the back of his neck. Aislinn nodded, her focus unwavering.

Eileen's tone sharpened. "We don't know how deep Khan's reach extends, but if he's targeting those with strong bonds, it means he sees them as a threat. And I want to make sure he's right to."

She paused, then glanced at Oak.

"One last thing before we adjourn."

Oak's gaze flicked toward her, unreadable, but she caught the faint shift in his posture.

"You're taking tomorrow off," Eileen said, tone even, decisive.

A beat of silence—small enough to go unnoticed by the others, but weighted between them.

A silent repayment—he had forced her to take a break last night, and now she was returning the gesture.

Oak's lips parted, the protest clear in his expression. "Just the rest of today."

Another pause. The air between them tensed, silent resistance meeting immovable authority.

Eileen didn't argue. Didn't press. Instead, she inclined her head, the smallest concession. "Fine."

Then, as if nothing had happened, she turned back to the room. "If there are no further questions, prepare for your assignments. Dismissed. Aislinn and Rowan, a word before you go."

As the Fallen rose, murmuring among themselves, the rain continued outside—a quiet reminder that the storm hadn't fully passed.

Not yet.

But they would be ready.

Eileen leaned against the conference table, arms crossed as the last of the Fallen filed out. She let the silence settle before speaking.

"Aislinn, let's talk about your new skill."

Aislinn met her gaze without hesitation. "I can control it now. It's not random anymore."

Eileen nodded. "Explain."

Aislinn exhaled. "I have to consciously decide when to use it. If I don't want to teleport, I don't allow myself to move. It's like… an internal switch. I can feel when it's there, and I either activate it or hold it back."

Eileen considered this. "Then you're ready for the next step—bringing others with you."

Aislinn straightened slightly. "I figured that would be next."

"Reed can give you pointers," Eileen continued. "Shadow-walking others works on a similar principle. And if you need more instruction, I'm available whenever we have a moment."

Aislinn nodded. "I'll start working on it."

Eileen turned to Rowan. "You're leading today's training."

He gave a single nod, already expecting it.

Her gaze settled on both of them. "Now, about teleportation. The Fallen saw it last night. They'll want an explanation."

Rowan's jaw tightened. "So we're just going to lie?"

"No," Aislinn corrected. "We'll tell them only what they need to know."

"That's still withholding the truth," Rowan muttered.

Aislinn held his gaze, her voice quiet but firm. "It's protecting my mom. If we don't give them an answer, they'll start looking for one."

Tension flickered in Rowan's posture. He didn't like it. But after a long moment, he nodded. "Alright. But we don't make a habit of this."

Eileen said nothing, letting the decision stand between them.

"Then we're done here," she said. "Go prepare for training."

Rowan nodded once and turned for the door. Aislinn followed but glanced back at Eileen.

"Thanks."

Eileen inclined her head slightly. "Don't waste the opportunity."

The rain tapped against the windows, soft but insistent.

They had work to do.

★★★

The hum of playful banter drifted from the mansion's common area, where Ariel and Rain lounged on the couch. Ariel sprawled sideways, legs draped over the armrest, while Rain sat cross-legged, gesturing animatedly as she recounted a story that had Ariel in stitches.

"You seriously said that to him?" Ariel gasped between laughs, clutching her stomach.

Rain grinned. "Of course! He deserved it. You should've seen his face—"

"Seen whose face?" Oak's calm voice cut in as he entered the room, his presence grounding without disrupting.

Rain turned, startled but smiling. "Oak! Sneaking up on people now?"

Oak smirked faintly. "Not quite. Just letting you know I'm taking my 'day off' this afternoon instead of tomorrow."

Ariel arched a brow, a mischievous glint in her eyes. "Taking the shortcut, huh?"

Rain tilted her head. "Is that even allowed?"

Oak chuckled, leaning casually against the doorframe. "Eileen approved it. Besides, tomorrow might get busy. No sense wasting time."

Ariel exchanged a look with Rain, her grin widening. "Alright, so... fishing? Hiking? Napping? Or is your idea of a day off just sitting in a chair and staring at the wall?"

Rain smirked. "He's probably going to read some ancient book about strategy or something."

Oak shook his head, amusement flickering beneath his composed exterior. "Actually, I was thinking of turning it into an opportunity for the two of you."

Ariel sat up, instantly suspicious. "Wait—your day off is about us? That doesn't seem right."

Rain's smile faltered slightly. "Yeah, we're not making this 'Rain and Ariel Day.' That's not fair to you."

Oak crossed the room, his voice carrying quiet warmth. "It wouldn't feel that way to me. This isn't just about taking breaks—it's about keeping morale up. You two are as much a part of this group as anyone else. If you don't take time to enjoy yourselves, the rest of us feel it too."

Ariel blinked, her usual sarcasm giving way to something softer. Rain murmured, "You're too nice sometimes, you know that?"

Oak gave a small shrug. "I'm old. I've learned a thing or two."

Rain chuckled, brushing a lock of hair behind her ear. "Well, since you're so insistent... what do you have in mind?"

Ariel narrowed her eyes in mock suspicion. "And don't say 'wall-staring.'"

Oak smirked. "It's your day now. You two decide."

Rain frowned slightly. "We didn't exactly have a plan for this."

Ariel's expression lit up. "Shopping. Definitely shopping."

Rain shot her a skeptical look. "Shopping for what?"

Ariel ticked items off on her fingers. "Ingredients for Takoda's cookie project, some last-minute party decorations, and—oh! A gift for Eileen. You know, a small gesture of appreciation."

Rain considered it, then nodded. "Okay, that's reasonable. Anything else?"

Ariel's grin turned devilish. "A Halloween costume for Alder."

Rain's skepticism returned. "Shouldn't we ask him what he wants to be first?"

Ariel waved a hand. "No, it should be a surprise. If he doesn't like it, we'll just tell him Oak picked it out."

Oak raised an eyebrow. "That's your strategy? Pin it on me?"

Ariel beamed. "You're the leader. It comes with the territory."

Oak exhaled, shaking his head. "Fine. But no ballerina costumes."

The trio laughed, the mood light and easy. Oak glanced at the clock and straightened. "Grab what you need and meet me outside in five minutes. You two handle the shopping list—I'll get my coat and keys."

As Oak left, Ariel and Rain exchanged a look, already brimming with ideas. Their chatter picked up again, the afternoon shaping up to be an unusual mix of Oak's steady presence and their infectious energy.

***

The crisp October air carried the scent of damp earth, remnants of the morning's rain still clinging to the grass. The Fallen had finished their group training session, but four remained behind on the obstacle course Ivy had set up, ready to push their limits further. Rowan, Aislinn, Takoda, and Riichi stood in a loose circle, the atmosphere thick with unspoken anticipation.

Rowan was the first to break the silence. "Since we're the only bonded pairs, we don't have much to go on. If we share what we've learned, maybe we can help each other figure out what's possible."

Takoda nodded, brushing a loose strand of hair behind her ear. "Our Radiant Surge has been improving. There's a faint orange tint now when it's active. It's not much, but it's progress."

"That happened when we started focusing on synchronization," Riichi added. "It wasn't something we planned—it just started happening when we became more in tune."

Takoda glanced at Rowan and Aislinn. "Have you noticed anything similar?"

Rowan and Aislinn exchanged a look. Rowan's brow furrowed slightly as he answered, "Not exactly. We haven't seen any color changes, but we've developed something defensive—a barrier we call Shield of Ages."

Takoda's expression remained neutral, but her interest sharpened. "We've seen it. How do you activate it?"

"It responds to intent," Rowan explained. "It isn't something we summon manually—it just appears when we focus on protecting others."

Riichi's brow creased slightly. "That's different from Radiant Surge. Ours is tied to synchronization. Have you ever tried calling on it deliberately?"

Aislinn tilted her head, considering. "Not exactly. It's more instinctive."

"That's interesting," Takoda mused. "If it only activates under certain conditions, maybe you could train yourselves to summon it on command."

Rowan exchanged a glance with Aislinn. "That's something we should try."

Aislinn nodded, her gaze thoughtful. "And we'll work on Radiant Surge without physical contact. If telepathy is possible for you two, it might be for us too."

The pairs fell into an easy rhythm of discussion, piecing together what they could about their bonds. Every new discovery was uncharted ground, every failure an opportunity to learn.

Eventually, talk gave way to action as they moved to the obstacle course. Rowan and Aislinn took their position first, standing side by side. Their hands brushed briefly before parting, a silent cue as Radiant Surge activated between them. A faint blue glow surrounded them, dim but steady. They moved through the course with synchronized precision, weaving through obstacles, their bond guiding each step.

Halfway through, Rowan paused, his brow furrowing slightly in concentration. A moment later, his voice resonated in Aislinn's mind. *Can you hear me?*

Aislinn faltered, her hand brushing against a low barrier as she snapped her gaze to him. *I can. This is... incredible.*

The connection felt fragile, like a thread stretched between them, but its existence alone sent a surge of excitement through their bond. Aislinn's lips curved into a grin, and Rowan matched it, their movements regaining momentum.

Across the training ground, Riichi and Takoda stood side by side, their gazes fixed on a wooden post at the far end of the field. It was a sturdy target, worn from past training sessions. Both took a slow breath, grounding themselves.

Let's focus on the target, Riichi's voice echoed in Takoda's mind, steady and calm.

Right. One step at a time, she responded, aligning her focus with his. The connection between them felt seamless, the rest of the world fading away.

Riichi's katana responded first. A faint vibration hummed through the hilt, subtle at first, then stronger. The blade shimmered with a faint orange glow, like embers caught in the wind.

Do you feel it? Riichi asked.

Takoda's grip tightened. *It's building. Keep it steady.*

The energy pulsed between them, growing stronger. Streaks of gold wove through the orange glow, the katana humming in time with their synchronization. Riichi adjusted his stance, the weapon thrumming with their shared intent.

It's time, he thought, his message clear and resolute.

With a fluid motion, he raised the katana and swung in a controlled arc, releasing the energy in a brilliant surge. The pulse streaked toward the target, leaving a trail of light in its wake. For a brief moment, it held—a clean, powerful strike hurtling with purpose.

Then, Riichi felt it—a shift, an almost imperceptible tremor. The pulse wavered. The energy's rhythm faltered, unraveling like a thread pulled too tight.

Takoda—move!

"Get down!" Riichi's voice rang out, cutting through the air as he dropped his katana and dove, shielding Takoda.

Across the field, Rowan reacted just as quickly, pulling Aislinn out of the blast zone.

The pulse fractured mid-flight, splintering into jagged shards of light that rained down in bursts of volatile energy. Each impact left faint scorch marks across the field, the air humming with residual static before fading into an uneasy stillness.

Riichi remained braced over Takoda, his arms protectively around her. Only when the last shard had settled did he exhale, shifting back to give her space.

Takoda sat up slowly, scanning the scorched earth. Her voice was tight with worry. "That could have seriously hurt someone."

Riichi shook his head, his tone firm but calm. "We took precautions. No one got hurt, and we learned something valuable."

Takoda hesitated, her gaze lingering on the katana lying still on the ground. The glow that had surrounded it moments ago had vanished, leaving behind only the weight of their unfinished progress.

"But if it happens again… if we aren't ready next time—"

Aislinn stepped closer, warmth in her tone but conviction in her stance. "When I first got my kinetic energy ability, I nearly hit Rowan. I barely managed to turn it in time, and the blast scorched the trees on either side of him." A small smile tugged at her lips, laced with both reassurance and understanding. "It's overwhelming at first, but it gets easier."

Rowan huffed a quiet laugh, dusting off his sleeve. "She's not exaggerating. I thought I was done for that day. And what you two are working on—it's beyond anything we've seen before."

Takoda exhaled slowly, her fingers curling slightly at her sides. "Thanks," she murmured. "I just don't want to be the reason anyone gets hurt."

Riichi placed a steady hand on her shoulder, his voice even. "That's why we keep training. We'll get there."

His fingers tightened briefly around the hilt of his katana. The glow had long since faded, but the remnants of their attempt lingered in his thoughts. *We'll figure it out. Next time, we'll be ready.*

From the stone wall bordering the patio, Vine observed the session, arms resting on his knees, his gaze sharp but distant. The energy that had gathered around Riichi's blade—wild, barely contained—had been powerful. But it wasn't the strength that held his attention. It was the moment it cracked apart, unraveling beneath its own force.

His fingers drummed lightly against his wrist as his thoughts circled. The connection between the bonded pairs wasn't just a weapon—it was trust. Unshaken, absolute. They moved together without hesitation, each relying on the other to hold the line.

How do you put that much faith in something that could break?

A strange tightness settled in his chest, one he refused to acknowledge. They had a force that made them stronger, sharpened them in ways he would never experience. *It's not just power. It's a connection that can't be replaced.*

And yet, he couldn't pull his focus away.

Inside the mansion, Eileen paused near a window, catching sight of Vine below. The tension in his frame, the way his expression hardened as he watched—it didn't escape her notice. She lingered for a moment, unreadable, before moving on.

The training session wound down. Rowan and Aislinn exchanged a brief glance, their quiet triumph unspoken. Riichi and Takoda remained by the scorched earth where their energy had fractured, their determination solidifying.

Vine exhaled through his nose and rose from the wall. He turned toward the mansion, his steps unhurried but his mind restless.

The others had *each other*. Had purpose. Had the kind of foundation that made them unbreakable.

What do I have?

The thought trailed him into the shadows, unanswered.

The streets pulsed with life, golden streaks of early evening sunlight spilling over the vibrant storefronts. Crisp autumn air carried the mingling scents of roasted chestnuts and warm spices, drifting from vendor stalls that lined the cobbled streets. The hum of conversation rose and fell, blending with the occasional clang of a shop bell and the rhythmic shuffle of passing footsteps.

Ariel darted ahead, energy as untamed as ever. She flitted between display windows, pausing just long enough to exclaim over whatever trinket caught her eye. "Look at this!" she called, lifting a pumpkin-shaped lamp with an exaggerated grin. "It's perfect for the party, right?"

Trailing a few paces behind, Rain smirked. "You're like a magpie. If it sparkles, you want it."

"Shiny things make the world better," Ariel quipped, already pivoting toward the next display.

Oak moved at a measured pace beside Rain, hands tucked into the pockets of his coat. His presence grounded their lively energy, his focus lingering on Ariel's unchecked enthusiasm. "Let's stay focused," he said, his tone even. "We're here for a reason."

Ariel whirled back, mischief dancing in her eyes. "Oh, come on, Oak. Can't I enjoy the scenery while we shop?"

His lips curved in the faintest smirk. "Enjoy it all you want, as long as we leave with a gift for Eileen."

They stepped into a boutique nestled between towering storefronts, its warmth wrapping around them like a soft scarf. Glass cases glowed under golden light, each display holding intricate pieces of jewelry. The faint scent of lavender wove through the air, mingling with the soft melody of instrumental music drifting from hidden speakers.

Ariel made a beeline for one of the cases, her gaze locking onto a pendant encrusted with shimmering gems. "What about this?" she asked, excitement lacing her voice. "It's bold, flashy—it screams Eileen!"

Rain folded her arms, unimpressed. "It screams you, Ariel. Not Eileen."

Oak approached with a glance at the pendant, his voice calm. "Rain's right. Think about what she'd actually wear."

Ariel groaned but moved on, fingers trailing across the glass as she searched for something else. Rain, meanwhile, stopped before a display showcasing a Tree of Life pendant encircled by thirteen small gemstones. Its design held an understated elegance, simple yet layered with meaning.

"This," Rain said, nodding toward it. "Simple but meaningful."

Oak studied it for a moment, then gave a single nod. "Understated. It suits her."

Rain turned to the shopkeeper. "Can you engrave the back? *'Neart agus Croí.'*"

Ariel tilted her head. "That sounds fancy. What's it mean?"

"Gaelic," Rain answered. "Strength and Heart. It fits her perfectly."

Ariel hesitated, her lips quirking in a reluctant frown before she sighed. "Fine. You're both right. Again."

While Oak and Rain finalized the purchase, Ariel wandered to a small stand near the register, her fingers brushing over a tray of delicate charms. She skimmed past stars and crescents, tiny lockets and etched runes—until her hand stilled.

A vintage-style key rested among them, its intricate detailing catching the light. She picked it up, turning it over in her palm, drawn less by its shape and more by the quiet pull it stirred in her.

She's been the mom I never had. The one who unlocked a part of me I didn't even know was closed.

Without hesitation, she carried it to the counter, slipping a few bills onto the surface before tucking the charm into her bag.

When she rejoined the others, her expression was as light as ever, but something deeper lingered beneath it.

With Eileen's gift chosen and safely tucked away, their next stop was clear. The costume shop burst with color and movement, racks of extravagant outfits stretching toward the ceiling in a chaotic display of fabric and embellishments. The scent of dye and adhesive clung to the air, mingling with the rustle of cloth as customers sifted through costumes.

Ariel wasted no time diving into the nearest section, yanking out a gold-accented druid ensemble with dramatic flair. "This is it!" she announced, holding it aloft like a trophy. "Alder will look like a forest god."

Oak's voice cut through her enthusiasm with effortless finality. "He won't wear that. You know that."

Ariel groaned, her face twisting in exaggerated disappointment before she shoved the costume back onto the rack. "Fine," she muttered, dragging out the word like a petulant child.

Rain, meanwhile, had been quietly scanning another section. She pulled out a Rune Warrior costume, its design an intricate blend of leather and metal accents, a dark cloak draping behind it. The fabric gleamed faintly where glowing runes had been etched into the armor and prop sword.

"Practical and mystical," Rain mused, holding it up with a smirk. "Perfect balance."

Ariel eyed it, clearly reluctant to concede, but after a moment, she sighed and nodded. "Fine. It'll do."

As they moved toward the register, Ariel's attention snagged on a display near the counter. Nestled among an assortment of impulse purchases sat a Rubik's Cube, its glossy surface reflecting the overhead lights. She picked it up, turning it over in her hands.

It's not much, but maybe it'll help. A distraction for when the quiet gets too loud.

Without a word, she dropped it onto their pile of purchases.

Rain cast her a questioning glance. "What do you need that for?"

Ariel's shrug was effortless. "Always wanted one as a kid. Never got one."

Rain accepted the response with an easy nod, but Oak's gaze flicked briefly to the cube before returning to Ariel. He didn't press her, but the slight shift in his expression suggested he suspected there was more to it than nostalgia.

They stepped back onto the bustling streets, a few shopping bags in hand. The warm glow of the setting sun stretched long across the cobblestones, the city alive with the soft hum of evening activity.

"I still think the druid costume would've been perfect," Ariel muttered.

Rain smirked. "And I think Alder would've torched it."

As the mansion came into view, Ariel's hand brushed against the Rubik's Cube tucked into her bag. A flicker of uncertainty crossed her mind, but she quickly pushed it aside. *It's just a little thing. Maybe it'll help. I guess I'll find out.*

Her focus shifted back to the lively conversation as they passed through the gates, the warmth of their camaraderie lingering in the cool evening air.

Back in Seattle, Rowan, Aislinn, and Holly made their way through Nihonmachi, the district alive with activity. Damp sidewalks reflected the muted light of the overcast October sky, while the crisp air carried the aroma of grilled skewers and fresh mochi. Locals and tourists drifted between shops and restaurants, their conversations blending into a lively hum.

Rowan moved with quiet purpose, hands tucked into his jacket pockets as he scanned the crowd. Aislinn stayed close, her attention shifting between storefronts and passing figures, alert but composed. Holly trailed behind with an easy stride, her relaxed posture betraying none of the sharp awareness in her glances.

"This place feels... different," Aislinn murmured, her gaze sweeping over the vibrant shopfronts. "Lighter, like the whole area is starting to breathe again."

"The weather can do that," Rowan replied, his voice calm but firm. "Just don't let it lull you. Stay alert."

Holly let out a quiet laugh, nodding toward a group of tourists snapping photos by a koi fountain. "Relax, *Aidan*," she teased, her smirk evident. "If we run into trouble, I think I can handle a few tea enthusiasts."

Rowan's expression remained unreadable, but his response was dry. "They're not the ones I'm worried about."

A wooden sign swayed above them as they reached a tea shop nestled between larger establishments. The kanji etched into its surface had been smoothed by time, the shop's warm glow inviting against the gray sky. Rowan pushed the door open, a soft chime ringing as they stepped inside.

The scent of jasmine and green tea wrapped around them, the air steeped in warmth. Glass jars lined the shelves, their labels inked in delicate calligraphy, while soft instrumental music played in the background.

Behind the counter, Nami greeted them with a composed smile. Her dark hair was pulled back, a streak of silver framing sharp features that missed nothing. "Aidan. Aislinn." Her voice held warmth, though her gaze flicked to Holly with quiet curiosity. "And I see you've brought someone new."

"This is Caley," Rowan said with a nod. "She's helping us out."

Nami inclined her head. "Welcome, Caley. Any friend of theirs is welcome here."

Holly returned the gesture with an easy smile. "Thanks. Your shop smells incredible. Might have to expand my tea collection."

Nami chuckled. "You wouldn't be the first to leave here inspired."

She led them deeper into the shop, her expression shifting as she lowered her voice. "The weather's improved—no doubt thanks to your efforts," she said, gratitude laced in her tone. "Business is better. People seem lighter. But not everything is back to normal."

Rowan gave a slight nod, prompting her to continue.

Nami's fingers traced the edge of the counter as she spoke. "There have been... strangers. They don't buy anything. They ask vague questions and watch more than they browse."

Rowan's posture remained still, his voice even. "What kind of questions?"

"They ask about the area, the locals," Nami said. "Nothing outright suspicious, but enough to notice. I overheard one mention their leader—a powerful man. He's furious about the disruptions. They spoke of retaliation."

Rowan's jaw tightened slightly, but his tone remained measured. "Thank you for telling us."

Nami cast a glance toward the back of the shop before lowering her voice further. "If you want more information, go to the herb shop near the corner. Fumiko knows more than most."

"We will," Rowan assured her.

Aislinn stepped forward. "Anything else? Anything unusual beyond their presence?"

Nami studied her for a moment before shaking her head. "Just... be careful. Whatever they're planning, they won't let this go."

As they stepped back into the cool night air, Holly exhaled, breaking the tension with an easy grin. "Well, I'll make sure I don't look too much like a tourist. Just in case."

Nami gave a faint smile, though the concern in her eyes lingered as the door closed behind them.

The streets of Nihonmachi remained as lively as ever as they stepped outside. Rowan's pace quickened, his movements precise, his focus sharpening now that they had direction. Aislinn matched him, her earlier curiosity shifting into quiet resolve. Holly kept stride, the usual ease in her posture tempered by the weight of their mission.

The bookstore was dimly lit, the scent of aged paper and leather hanging thick in the air. Towering shelves loomed around them, each crammed with well-worn volumes that whispered of history and hidden knowledge. Behind the counter, the gruff owner looked up, his expression shifting as recognition dawned.

"Aidan. Aislinn." He leaned back slightly, arms crossing over his chest. "Back so soon?" His eyes flicked to Holly. "And who's this?"

"This is Caley," Rowan said. "She's working with us."

The man gave a short nod, approval unspoken but evident. "Good. You've been bringing in capable people."

Holly leaned against the counter, her smirk laced with mischief. "Glad to know I'm making a good impression."

The owner gestured toward the shelves as he spoke. "Business has picked up since the weather changed. But there's been a shift—more strangers than usual. They linger, browsing without purpose, asking odd questions, watching people."

"What are they looking for?" Rowan asked.

The owner shook his head. "Hard to say. Their questions don't make much sense, but they're fixated on someone."

Holly scoffed, arms crossing. "Not exactly subtle, are they?"

The man let out a short, rough laugh before reaching beneath the counter. He retrieved a folded sheet of paper and slid it toward Rowan. "One of them left this behind. Figured it might mean something to you."

Rowan unfolded the page, revealing a series of symbols scrawled in dark ink. Aislinn stepped closer, her brow furrowing.

"This is part of a ritual," she said, voice steady. "It's directional—like it's channeling energy toward a focal point."

The owner studied her, nodding in approval. "You've been learning."

Rowan tucked the paper into his pocket, his expression unreadable. "Anything else?"

"Only whispers," the man admitted. "Whoever they're working for, he's furious—and he's got a plan."

Rowan inclined his head. "Thanks. We'll follow up on this."

As they turned to leave, Holly lingered by the counter, her smirk returning. "Next time, maybe they'll leave behind a roadmap instead of riddles."

The owner's dry chuckle followed them out, breaking some of the tension that had settled between them.

Back on the damp streets, the trio moved with quiet determination. Rowan's stride was measured, his focus shifting to the bustling crowd with every step. Aislinn walked close beside him, her expression thoughtful as she pieced together everything they'd learned. Holly trailed behind, her usual humor restrained but not entirely buried.

"We've got enough to act on," Rowan said, his voice low, decisive. "Let's make this count."

The streets of Nihonmachi remained lively, the scent of freshly made taiyaki and spiced tea mixing with the hum of conversation. Rowan's stride lengthened, his focus sharpening on a figure lingering near a vendor's stall. Their posture was too casual, their attention not on the wares but on them. Without breaking pace, Rowan adjusted his stance, voice low.

"We're being followed. Black jacket, twenty feet back. Don't look."

Aislinn's breath hitched, but she forced herself to keep walking. "What do we do?" she murmured.

Holly's smirk widened. "We give them something to wonder about."

Rowan steered them toward a quieter street, their movements unhurried but deliberate. As they reached a narrow alley, Holly brushed her fingers against the damp brick wall, the motion effortless. Shadows rippled unnaturally, bleeding into the stone until it looked as though the trio had vanished into it.

Rowan pulled Aislinn deeper into the alley while Holly lingered, smoothing the illusion. Their tail hesitated at the entrance, scanning the space. A long pause. Then a muttered curse before they turned back toward the main street.

Aislinn exhaled. "Did that actually work?"

Holly shot her a look. "Of course it worked. You're looking at a pro."

Rowan's attention remained fixed ahead. "Don't relax yet. That was one. There could be more."

As they slipped back into the crowd, Rowan's voice dipped lower. "You need an alias if you're going to keep running intel. Your name stands out."

Aislinn arched a brow. "Says the guy using his real name as an alias."

Rowan let out a quiet chuckle. "Fair. But I'm serious. You're not just a civilian anymore."

The weight of his words settled over her, her teasing edge fading. She nodded. "Fine. I'll think about it. Any suggestions?"

"We'll find one that fits," Rowan said.

They reached the herb shop nestled at the end of a quieter street, its earthy scent wrapping around them as they stepped inside. Shelves lined the walls, packed with labeled jars and dried herbs bundled with twine.

Behind the counter, Fumiko, a woman in her fifties with an air of quiet authority, watched them with assessing eyes. Her hands moved with practiced ease as she arranged small packets.

"Nami said you might have insights," Rowan said, inclining his head. "I'm Aidan. This is Aislinn and Caley."

Fumiko dipped her head in greeting. "Nami has a discerning eye. Welcome."

She listened as Rowan explained their purpose, her expression unreadable. "Strangers have been lingering," she said, tying off a bundle of herbs. "They make small purchases but watch more than they shop. It's clear they're looking for someone."

Rowan's voice remained measured. "Have they said anything specific?"

"They've been more visible in the last few days," Fumiko said. "Especially since the weather disruptions. Whoever they follow, their leader—he's not pleased."

Aislinn leaned in slightly. "Is there anything else you've noticed? Anything we can use?"

Fumiko considered for a moment before handing Rowan a small card. "If I learn more, I'll contact you. Be careful. They won't stay subtle for long."

Rowan accepted it with a nod. "Thank you."

As they stepped outside, Rowan's posture stiffened. "We've got another one," he muttered under his breath.

Holly's grin sharpened. "Let's make it interesting."

Without hesitation, Rowan guided them into the shadows, ducking into the narrow space between two buildings. They pressed against the cold brick, breath held as their pursuer stepped onto the street behind them.

Holly lifted her fingers, barely moving her hand. Just ahead, three shimmering duplicates of their group emerged from the alley and strode confidently into the open. Their tail hesitated, their gaze flicking between the real alleyway and the decoys before choosing wrong—trailing after the fakes.

Aislinn glanced back as they slipped away. "Do you think they recognized us?"

"They don't have to," Rowan said. "Watching is enough."

Holly leaned against a wall, her tone breezy. "Good thing they're terrible at spotting illusions. Let's hope that luck holds."

"Don't count on it," Rowan muttered. "We've pressed enough for one day. Let's head back."

They moved swiftly through the alleys, the fading light stretching long shadows behind them. By the time they reached the mansion, the sun had nearly set, the air sharp with the bite of encroaching night.

Inside, they found Eileen in her office, her demeanor calm but alert as Rowan delivered their findings.

"Golden Dawn members are patrolling Nihonmachi, disguised as tourists," he said, setting the paper with cryptic symbols on her desk. "They're looking for someone. We've confirmed it through multiple sources."

Eileen's gaze sharpened. "Not someone—us." Her tone was measured, but the weight behind it was undeniable. "They aren't searching blindly. They know we're there."

Aislinn stepped forward. "They're getting bolder. Whatever they're planning, it's escalating."

Eileen absorbed their report in silence, her fingers brushing briefly over the edge of the paper before she spoke. "If retaliation is coming, they won't hold back. We'll address this at tomorrow's meeting." Her voice remained steady, but a quiet intensity settled behind her words. "For now, stay ready. We may need to act quickly."

As the trio left her office, the weight of what lay ahead pressed down on them. Rowan met Aislinn's gaze, the unspoken certainty between them clear—this wasn't just a threat. It was a warning.

★★★

The evening air had cooled by the time Ariel, Rain, and Oak returned to the mansion carrying their shopping bags. Inside, the quiet halls carried an easy calm, the anticipation of the upcoming festivities lingering beneath the surface. A warm glow spilled from Eileen's office, a constant reminder of her unwavering focus.

In the common area, Alder lounged in a worn leather chair, a book in hand. He glanced up as they entered, his brow lifting as Ariel triumphantly raised a garment bag.

"Look what we got you!" she announced, her grin all mischief. "You're going to look like a total badass—or maybe just a really stylish tree warrior."

Alder set his book aside, eyeing her with mock suspicion. "Is this your way of telling me I'm not getting out of it?"

Rain smirked as she dropped her bags onto the floor. "You're not. We picked it, so now you have to wear it."

Alder's gaze flicked to Oak. "Did you at least veto the worst of it?"

Oak gave a measured nod. "They showed restraint. This time."

Rain grinned as Ariel unzipped the bag, revealing the Rune Warrior costume. "You're going to look great. Just don't complain when we make you wear it."

Alder stood, taking the costume with a critical glance. He turned it over in his hands, running his fingers over the fabric. After a moment, a flicker of amusement crossed his face. "Not bad. I'll give you that."

The group exchanged a satisfied look—Alder's approval, however begrudging, was as good as a win.

Ariel clapped her hands. "Mission accomplished."

As Alder returned to his chair, Ariel and Rain shared a look.

"We should add notes for Eileen's pendant," Rain suggested, pulling a small notepad from her bag.

"Good idea," Ariel agreed. "I'll write mine upstairs." She gathered her things and headed toward her room while Rain sat at the common area table, her pen already moving. Oak leaned against the wall, offering quiet input as she worked.

Upstairs, Ariel set her bags down and pulled out the Rubik's Cube she had bought earlier. She turned it over in her hands, studying its glossy surface. *It's not much, but maybe it'll help. He deserves something to focus on besides... everything else.*

Setting the cube on her desk, she reached for the small key charm she had purchased. Wrapping it carefully, she placed it in a small box, then hesitated before picking up a notecard. The blank surface stared back at her, but after a moment, she began to write.

Eileen, you're the key to everything good in my life—the mom I never had, the guide I didn't know I needed. I can never thank you enough, but here's a start.

Love, Ariel.

She swallowed against the lump in her throat before starting a second note, this one for the pendant.

For the woman who's the roots of this family tree—thank you for being our guide and our strength.

Love, Ariel.

Downstairs, Rain finished her note with a flourish. Oak glanced over her shoulder and nodded approvingly.

This tree reminds us of you—strong, rooted, and always reaching toward the light. We're so grateful for all you've done.

- Rain.

Rain set the note aside as Ariel returned. Together, they packed the notes with the pendant and made their way to Eileen's office.

Eileen looked up as they entered, setting her papers aside. "Well, this is a surprise."

Rain stepped forward, the box cradled in her hands. "We wanted to give you something to show how much you mean to us."

Ariel's grin was bright. "Yeah, but don't get all teary on us—you're supposed to be the strong one."

Eileen chuckled softly, warmth flickering behind her sharp eyes as she accepted the box. She lifted the lid, her expression shifting as the Tree of Life pendant caught the light. Slowly, she unfolded the notes, reading each one in silence.

When she finally spoke, her voice was quiet. "This is beautiful. Thank you. I don't know what to say."

"You don't have to say anything," Rain said, her smile small but sincere. "You deserve it."

Ariel waved a dismissive hand. "You can just say we're your favorites. We won't tell anyone."

Eileen laughed, the shimmer of emotion in her gaze unmistakable. "I'm so proud of you both," she said after a moment. "You've come so far, and it's an honor to have you in my life."

As they turned to leave, Ariel hesitated at the doorway, gripping the smaller box with the key charm. She took a breath, then stepped back toward Eileen's desk.

"I, uh... I wanted to give you something extra," Ariel said, uncharacteristically quiet. "You don't have to open it now. Just... thanks, Eileen. For everything."

Before Eileen could respond, Ariel slipped out, catching up to Rain in the hallway. Her heart pounded, but she masked it with a grin. "Well, that wasn't so bad."

Rain shot her a knowing look. "You're impossible."

Once alone, Eileen unfolded the second note, her fingers brushing the delicate key charm inside.

Eileen, you're the key to everything good in my life—the mom I never had, the guide I didn't know I needed. I can never thank you enough, but here's a start.

Love, Ariel.

Eileen leaned back, the quiet settling around her. She's endured so much pain, yet she still gives this kind of love.

She closed her fingers around the charm, holding it for a long moment before tucking it carefully into a small keepsake box on her desk.

Outside, Ariel's laughter rang down the hall, teasing Rain about something inconsequential. Rain's grounded presence and Ariel's unshakable spirit filled the space in a way Eileen wouldn't have traded for anything.

★★★

The night air was bitterly cold, October's sharp chill settling over the dense woods of Fort Lawton. Trees swayed gently in the breeze, their leaves rustling in hushed tones, while the distant crash of waves against the cliffs echoed through the stillness. The team moved carefully through the shadows, each step deliberate, their breaths forming faint clouds in the frigid air.

Fort Lawton's eerie isolation amplified the tension. The moon hung low behind thick clouds, casting just enough light to silhouette the forest against the dark expanse of Puget Sound. Ahead, the faint glow of the Golden Dawn's ritual site flickered between the trees—a foreboding beacon.

Vine crouched at the tree line, taking in the clearing with practiced precision. His sharp instincts cataloged every detail, tracking movement and possible points of entry. Behind him, Reed moved soundlessly, his keen perception attuned to the slightest shift in their surroundings. Alder followed, his focus unwavering despite the tight line of unease in his jaw. Hazel, bringing up the rear, exuded quiet control, her fingers flexing subtly in preparation.

Through a gap in the trees, the ritual site emerged. A faintly shimmering defensive ward encircled the cliffside clearing, its edges pulsing softly with magic. Inside, a brazier burned with unnatural brilliance, its flames casting long, restless shadows over uneven ground. The chime of an enchanted wind instrument echoed through the air, its melody threading through the site like a whisper. Near the cliff's edge, a spring shimmered, its glow resonating in harmony with the other anchors.

"Ward's strong," Vine murmured.

The group crouched lower, their presence masked in the dark. Hazel knelt beside him, fingertips grazing the damp soil as she closed her eyes. Her breath slowed, her awareness stretching outward. The elements responded, revealing the ritual's structure in an intricate weave of energy.

"The anchors—water, air, and fire," she whispered. "They're the key. The ritual draws power from all three."

Vine glanced at her. "How far along?"

Hazel's brow furrowed. "A week. Maybe less. The defenses are strongest around the brazier. It's the central point."

Reed's voice was barely audible. "If we disrupt one, what happens?"

"They're interconnected," Hazel replied. "Breaking one could collapse the whole thing."

Vine's expression darkened. "Good. Let's confirm the locations."

Reed slipped into the shadows, his movements seamless as he circled the perimeter, his route keeping him out of sight. Vine remained beside Hazel, his attention fixed on the energy humming from the ward.

Minutes later, Reed reappeared. "Anchors confirmed," he whispered. "The spring by the cliff, the wind chime in the tree, and the brazier dead center. All guarded."

Vine's jaw tightened, but his voice remained even. "We'll need to hit fast and hard when the time comes. No room for mistakes."

They regrouped at their vantage point, tension thick as Hazel's words hung in the air. The ritual's vulnerabilities were clear—but so was the danger. Reed and Vine exchanged a brief nod before preparing to retreat.

Alder suddenly halted. His breath hitched, body stiffening as if struck by an unseen force. The glow of prophecy ignited in his eyes, washing his face in an eerie light.

The others reacted instantly, forming a protective circle around him. Reed scanned the darkness, muscles coiled for an ambush. Hazel knelt beside Alder, her voice calm but firm. "He's having a vision. Stay close."

Alder's glowing eyes remained unfocused, but when he spoke, his voice carried the weight of prophecy.

"The flood will consume Seattle," he intoned. "A typhoon, vast and unrelenting, will drown the city in chaos."

The words hung in the frigid air, his voice an unshakable force.

"The veil will break. The realms will bleed together. Demons will pour through the rift, spreading destruction from the shadows of the city."

Hazel steadied him with a grounding touch while Vine and Reed remained poised for any threat.

Alder's voice sharpened. "Kubla Khan sits at the center, unseen but in control. He weaves the storm from the dark, his hand guiding the tide of destruction."

He inhaled sharply, his tone hardening. "Gideon commands the Golden Dawn, his followers emboldened with new power, gifted by their master. Their hands will spark the riots. Their whispers will spread the fire."

Alder's expression darkened. "Riichi will lead the demons. Takoda will bind them to him."

Silence pressed down on the group as the words settled.

"The army that crosses the veil will bow to him, his wrath binding them. He will not know himself. He will not remember his purpose. Only the call of war."

His breath hitched. "And Takoda—she will be the offering. Her gift, twisted. Her light, used to fuel the Surge. If Khan takes her, he takes everything."

The glow in Alder's eyes dimmed. His body sagged as exhaustion overtook him, breath ragged. Vine and Hazel caught his arms, steadying him as he tried to shake off the vision's toll.

His voice was hoarse but clear. "Gideon spreads the fire. Riichi commands the storm. And Takoda… she is the spark Khan needs to burn the world."

Vine straightened, his expression cold with resolve. "We've seen enough. Time to move."

Alder nodded weakly, still regaining his strength, while Hazel and Reed exchanged grim glances. Urgency pressed down on them as they slipped back into the cover of the woods, their retreat swift and silent.

They moved quickly through the dense terrain, their steps careful but urgent. Vine's sleek black Porsche waited where they had left it, its dark frame barely visible beneath the sparse moonlight. Vine slid into the driver's seat with practiced ease, his grip firm on the wheel as the others settled in. The engine purred to life, its low hum barely disturbing the stillness as they vanished into the night.

Minutes into the drive, Reed broke the silence from the passenger seat. "We've got company," he said evenly. "Two cars back. They're not even trying to hide it."

Vine checked the rearview mirror, catching the faint glint of headlights trailing them. His grip on the wheel tightened, and he pressed the accelerator. "Hold on," he said, his voice calm but unyielding.

The Porsche surged forward, its engine purring as it wove through the darkened streets with fluid precision. Behind them, the Golden Dawn vehicle held its course, persistent and unshaken. Vine maneuvered with ease, the tires hugging the pavement as he took a sharp turn. Hazel braced against the door as the car straightened, their pursuers unfazed.

"They're not backing off," Reed noted, his tone clipped.

Hazel exhaled through her nose, her focus sharpening. The humid air responded, gathering in a near-invisible haze over the asphalt. Within moments, the road behind them shimmered with a slick, unnatural sheen. The Golden Dawn car hit the patch—its tires skidding wildly before the driver managed to regain control.

"They're stubborn," Hazel muttered.

Vine's lips twitched faintly. "Not for long."

His fingers flicked toward the dashboard, and the headlights cut out, plunging them into darkness. Inside the car, a faint electric glow pulsed at his fingertips and eyes, his electrokinesis flaring to life. Signals, circuits, and motion painted the world in sharp clarity inside his mind, each road contour unfolding in a precise, pulsing grid.

"You sure about this?" Alder asked from the backseat, his voice hoarse but steady.

Vine didn't turn. "Watch me."

The Porsche cut through the night like a specter, its movements seamless under Vine's control. Hazel sent another slick patch across the road, forcing their pursuers into another violent swerve. Vine took the opening, veering into a narrow side street, his mind mapping the alleyways ahead.

The Golden Dawn vehicle struggled to follow, its headlights bouncing wildly as the driver fought to keep up. But Vine was already ten moves ahead. A sharp left, then right—his hands worked the wheel with precision, threading them through the city's hidden veins.

Their pursuers faltered. The distance widened. And then—darkness.

"We've lost them," Hazel confirmed.

Vine exhaled slowly but didn't ease his grip. "Not taking risks."

He took a longer, winding route home, his electrokinesis subtly pulsing as he ensured no lingering trail led back to the mansion.

Only when the iron gates came into view did Vine allow himself to loosen his grip. The Porsche rolled to a smooth stop, its engine idling once before falling silent. In the hush of the forested driveway, the group exchanged looks—silent but understood.

The team stepped into the mansion, the weight of the night pressing down on them. Their footsteps softened against the hardwood floors as they made their way to Eileen's office, the dim lighting casting long shadows along the walls.

Inside, Eileen looked up, sharp and assessing. The soft glow of her desk lamp flickered across her face, highlighting the focus in her expression. She set her papers aside, giving them her full attention.

"You're back," she said, her tone steady but edged with curiosity. "What did you find?"

Vine stepped forward, exhaustion creeping at the edges of his posture but not his voice. "The ritual is nearly complete," he began. "It's powered by three elemental anchors—water, air, and fire. Each one is heavily protected, but Hazel identified their interconnectedness as a weakness. Disrupting even one could destabilize the entire ritual."

Hazel nodded. "The anchors are a natural spring, an enchanted wind chime, and a brazier. From what I could tell, the ritual has about a week, maybe less, before it reaches full power."

Eileen's expression darkened, but she remained silent, letting them continue.

Alder, still pale but composed, spoke next. "I had a vision," he said, voice measured. "If the ritual succeeds, Seattle will fall. A typhoon will consume the city, and the veil between realms will shatter. Demons will pour through."

His next words landed with weight.

"Kubla Khan sits at the center, unseen but in control. He weaves the storm from the dark, his hand guiding the tide of destruction."

Eileen's jaw tensed. Kubla Khan. The name alone was enough to sharpen her focus.

Alder pressed on, his voice unwavering.

"Gideon commands the Golden Dawn, his followers emboldened with new power, granted by Khan. They will spark the riots, spread the fear, and open the path."

Eileen folded her hands on the desk, her expression unreadable.

Alder drew in a breath. "And Riichi will lead the demons."

Silence stretched, heavy and absolute.

"The army that crosses the veil will bow to him, his wrath binding them. He won't know himself. He won't remember his purpose. Only the call of war."

Eileen's lips pressed together, her fingers tightening slightly. "And if this comes to pass?"

"Destruction," Alder said simply. "Fires, chaos, war in the streets. No one will escape unscathed."

The room remained still, the weight of his words pressing into the space.

Eileen leaned back slightly, her gaze flicking between them, calculating. Inside, her thoughts churned. He's beginning to unravel. Her attention lingered on Vine, taking in the barely perceptible shifts—the faint dullness to his skin, the edges of his presence thinning, like a thread fraying at the seams. Not there yet, but close.

He's fading.

Like the first ones. The ones she had created before she knew how to tether them to the earth. Before she understood what they needed to survive.

Out loud, she said, "You've done well tonight. This gives us something to work with. I'll share the details at tomorrow's meeting." Her voice softened, though the steel beneath it remained. "For now, get some rest. We'll need all our strength for what lies ahead."

The group exchanged brief nods. Vine lingered. His eyes met Eileen's, and for a moment, something flickered behind them—not exhaustion, but awareness. As if, on some level, he could feel it, too.

She said nothing.

But deep down, she knew.

If he unraveled completely, there would be no bringing him back.

As they left her office, the tension didn't lift, but it changed. Alder walked in silence, his mind still heavy with the weight of his prophecy. Hazel's sharp gaze hinted at the strategies already forming. Vine's expression remained unreadable—but calculated.

Their steps faded into the mansion's quiet halls, but outside, the night pressed on, unyielding and full of unseen forces.

★★★

The estate was wrapped in a blanket of silence, the kind that only came in the deepest hours of the night. Faint creaks echoed through its old structure, and the occasional rustle of leaves outside broke the stillness. Most of its inhabitants were lost in sleep. Ariel was not.

She sat cross-legged on her bed, sketchbook balanced on her lap, pencils scattered around her. The muted glow of the TV cast flickering light across the walls, its volume just loud enough to keep the silence at bay. Fuzzy rainbow pajama pants and matching slippers gave her the look of someone cozily defying the late hour, her long-sleeve shirt smudged with pencil marks from earlier bursts of inspiration.

Her stomach growled, breaking her focus. She glanced down at the unfinished sketch, sighed, and set it aside.

"Guess sketching doesn't count as feeding your soul, huh?" she muttered, stretching before swinging her legs off the bed.

As she moved, her gaze landed on the Rubik's cube sitting on her desk. She picked it up, turning it over in her hands. It had been an impulse buy, nothing more.

"Why not?" she mused. "Messing this up might make eating more interesting."

Slipping it into her pocket, she padded out the door. The stairs creaked faintly under her weight, making her wince. She shot a glance down the hall—nothing stirred. Satisfied, she continued toward the kitchen.

The fridge hummed softly as she pulled out leftovers from dinner, Takoda's cooking still fragrant even hours later. Her stomach growled again, this time in eager anticipation.

"I get why Reed can't resist this," she muttered, reheating the meal.

Plate in one hand, cube in the other, she started toward the table—but stopped mid-step. A shadow moved outside on the back patio.

Her breath hitched.

She hesitated, debating whether to ignore it, but curiosity pulled her forward. Pressing her face to the glass, she squinted into the dim moonlight.

Vine.

He was slouched in one of the patio chairs, staring at the sky.

Ariel set her plate down, her hunger momentarily forgotten. She turned the cube over in her hands, mulling it over, then made up her mind.

Stepping onto the patio, she shivered against the crisp air. "So, what's the deal?" she asked, breaking the silence. "You stargazing or planning an escape route?"

Vine glanced at her, his expression unreadable. "Couldn't sleep," he said. "Figured the stars had better answers than my ceiling."

She wrapped her arms around herself. "And you decided freezing was the solution? Solid plan."

Without a word, Vine stood, shrugged off his jacket, and draped it over her shoulders before she could protest. The warmth was immediate, a stark contrast to the cold biting at her skin.

"Better?" he asked.

"Cozy," she admitted, pulling it tighter. "Thanks, but now you're freezing."

"I'll survive."

Ariel pulled the Rubik's cube from her pocket and held it out to him. "Here. Next time you're up late, use this. Keeps your hands busy when your brain won't shut up."

Vine raised an eyebrow as he took the cube, turning it over like it was a puzzle in itself. "A toy?" His tone was dry. "Thought you had rules about gifts."

"It doesn't count," she said. "It's just something to keep you inside at night so I don't catch you brooding out here."

Before he could reply, she snatched it back, twisting the sides until the colors were thoroughly scrambled. With a satisfied nod, she handed it back.

"There. Now it actually works the way it's supposed to."

Her stomach growled again, loud in the quiet. Vine's gaze flicked toward the dining room window, spotting her abandoned plate. He exhaled through his nose, then stood.

"Come on," he said, holding the door open for her. "Since I'm already up, you might as well feed me."

Ariel grinned, grabbing her plate. "Your problem-solving skills need work."

Vine leaned back in the chair opposite her, watching as she took a bite. Their voices dropped to whispers, laughter bubbling up between bites as they tried not to wake anyone.

At one point, Ariel speared a forkful of food and leaned across the table, a mischievous glint in her eyes. "Here," she said. "Try this."

Before Vine could refuse, she shoved the fork into his mouth. He chewed, unimpressed, shaking his head.

"Do you treat everyone like this?"

"Only the lucky ones."

After rinsing her plate in the sink, Ariel motioned for Vine to follow her back upstairs. They moved quietly, careful to avoid creaky floorboards. At the top of the stairs, Vine paused, rolling the Rubik's cube between his fingers.

"Thanks," he said holding the cube up, his voice lighter than before. "For this… whatever this is."

Ariel smirked, giving a mock bow. "You're welcome. Now go solve it before I change my mind."

They exchanged quiet good nights, their paths splitting as they disappeared into their rooms.

In his, Vine sat on the edge of his bed, turning the cube experimentally. Click. Click. Click. The quiet sound filled the space, steady and rhythmic. He didn't think about anything as he twisted the sides, just let the motion take over.

For the first time in days, his thoughts didn't spiral.

For the first time in days, his mind was quiet.

But far from the mansion's calm, the night was anything but still.

At Fort Lawton, the Golden Dawn had not been idle. Beneath the shimmering ward protecting their ritual, figures moved through the shadows. Elemental anchors hummed with power, their energy rippling outward as the typhoon ritual neared completion.

Patrols swept the perimeter, restless. Whispers of retaliation rippled through the ranks.

Kubla Khan's influence had begun to take hold.

The storm was building.

And when it broke, the Fallen wouldn't be ready.

The conference room hushed the moment Eileen entered. She didn't need to command silence—her presence did it effortlessly.

"We've made progress," she began, her tone even but edged with expectation. "But we have less than a week before the ritual reaches full power. The reconnaissance missions gave us critical intel. Now, we decide how to act."

The Fallen listened in focused silence.

"This meeting is about preparation. Every detail matters. Rowan, start with Nihonmachi."

Rowan sat straighter, his expression composed but sharp. "Golden Dawn patrols have increased. They're blending in, posing as tourists, but they aren't just watching—they're adapting. They know we're in the area."

His voice remained level, but a thread of tension wove through it. "We were followed—twice. Holly's illusions threw them off, but they're actively tracking movement. They're watching for patterns, looking for any sign of disruption."

Eileen's face remained unchanged, but the keen gleam in her eyes spoke volumes.

Aislinn took over smoothly. "We found directional symbols woven into the ritual. They're channeling energy toward the site, strengthening the typhoon's foundation. Fumiko confirmed it—she's well-connected and willing to gather more intelligence if needed."

She exchanged a look with Rowan and Holly before adding, "She also confirmed what we suspected—Golden Dawn isn't operating aimlessly. Their leader—Gideon Kross—is furious about our interference. Retaliation is coming."

Takoda folded her hands, her expression thoughtful. "Then we need to act first."

Vine's voice cut in, steady but weighted. "Fort Lawton is anchored to three elements—water, air, and fire. A natural spring, an enchanted wind chime, and a brazier. They aren't just symbolic. They're the ritual's foundation. Break one, and we weaken the whole thing."

Reed's voice was low. "A defensive ward surrounds the site, designed to trap intruders. It's reactive—if we breach it incorrectly, it will reinforce itself."

Hazel nodded. "The anchors are interconnected. If we don't hit them in the right order, we risk backlash—either strengthening the ritual or putting the team in danger. Timing is everything."

Alder's voice carried through the space, soft but absolute. "I had a vision. If the ritual succeeds, Seattle will fall. The typhoon will shatter the veil between realms, and demons will flood the city."

The room stilled, the gravity of his words settling over the Fallen.

Alder continued, his demeanor unwavering. "Kubla Khan is at the center of this. He isn't just a passive force—he's orchestrating it all from the shadows. Gideon Kross leads the Golden Dawn, but Khan is the one weaving the storm."

He glanced toward Riichi and Takoda. "If the ritual reaches completion, Riichi will lead the demons—and Takoda will bind them to him. Her gift will be twisted into the offering Khan needs to anchor himself here. Their Radiant Surge will feed the ritual."

Alder's gaze swept the room. "Gideon spreads the fire. Riichi commands the storm. And Takoda… she's the spark Khan needs to burn the world."

A flicker of tension rippled through the room. Riichi's hands pressing against the arms of his chair, but his voice cut through the quiet, resolute. "That won't happen."

Takoda's voice followed, equally firm. "We'll resist. He won't control us."

The moment stretched before Eileen's unfaltering tone grounded them. "Thank you. All of you. This information is invaluable."

She turned to Ivy, her expression softening just slightly. "Before we continue—tomorrow is your day off. Use it well."

Holly smirked, nudging Ivy with her elbow. "Lucky you. Perfect timing."

A few chuckles rippled through the group, tension easing just enough. Ivy met Eileen's gaze, her confidence unshaken. "I'll make it count."

Eileen placed both hands on the table. "We have the intelligence. Now, we decide how to dismantle this ritual before it reaches full power."

She scanned the room before continuing. "There are five key objectives: enemy reinforcements, the defensive ward, the elemental anchors, disrupting the ritual, and potential retaliation from Khan and Kross. First—reinforcements."

"The Golden Dawn will escalate," she continued. "Kross knows we're interfering. Once we engage, they'll send everything they have."

Reed's expression was impenetrable. "Then we need a way to draw their forces away from the ritual site."

Eileen nodded. "A direct distraction. If we engage them hard enough in one area, they'll be forced to react, leaving the ritual site vulnerable."

Hazel's brow furrowed. "We need to make them believe our main attack is elsewhere—force them to commit before they realize their mistake."

"Exactly," Eileen said. "Timed interference. We pull them away—then strike where it matters."

Eileen's tone remained firm as she continued. "Our next challenge is the defensive ward. It doesn't just block intruders—it retaliates. If we attack it blindly, we risk becoming trapped inside. Neutralizing it is a priority."

Oak's voice carried through the room, calm but certain. "Whoever takes on the ward needs shielding. The Golden Dawn won't sit back and let us dismantle their defenses. We'll need barriers in place—not just for protection, but to disrupt incoming attacks."

Vine leaned forward, considering. "What if we target multiple points at once? Spreading its energy thin could create cracks we can exploit." He glanced at Ivy. "Your reality bending might distort its defenses enough to weaken them."

Surprised glances passed around the table before Holly smirked. "Look at you, Vine. Holding out on us."

Vine shrugged. "First time for everything."

Riichi, ever analytical, nodded. "But if the ward has a self-repair function, an uneven attack could make it stronger instead of weaker. We need to confirm its behavior before we plan a coordinated strike." He glanced toward Eileen. "Rowan, Aislinn, Birch, and Ivy should handle recon. They have the right abilities to assess the ward's structure without triggering it."

Eileen considered his suggestion for only a moment before nodding. "Agreed. Rowan, Aislinn, Birch, and Ivy—you deploy tonight. Identify weaknesses and confirm whether the ward repairs itself."

Rowan inclined his head. "We'll get it done."

Aislinn's voice was stoic. "If it regenerates, we'll figure out how. Ivy's reality bending could test its limits."

Vine tapped his fingers against the table. "Reed's tracking and stealth will be useful for maneuvering. If anything feels off, Ash's shapeshifting can give us a second set of eyes. For signaling, I can handle it—short bursts of electrokinesis. Bright enough to alert our team, brief enough to avoid detection."

A few murmurs passed through the group before Eileen's lips curved slightly. "Creative. You're full of ideas today, Vine."

Holly leaned back with a grin. "Careful. Keep this up, and we might start expecting things from you."

Vine smirked. "Don't hold your breath."

Oak brought the focus back. "Your signal could work, but it has to be subtle enough not to alert the Golden Dawn. We'll need shielding in place when the strike happens—whoever dismantles the ward will be exposed."

Eileen gave a sharp nod. "Shielding and timing will be key. We confirm the ward's weaknesses tonight, then plan the takedown."

The conversation shifted as Eileen steered the discussion toward the elemental anchors sustaining the ritual. "Next, we need a strategy to collapse the spring, wind chime, and brazier anchors permanently."

Oak spoke first, his practical tone carrying years of experience. "Balanced teams are essential—fighters paired with magic users to handle both physical threats and magical defenses. One person focuses on the anchor while the others handle incoming enemies. I also suggest taking out the wind chime first. If it amplifies their ability to monitor the battlefield, removing it weakens their coordination."

Eileen inclined her head. "A sound approach. The wind chime is our first target."

Vine leaned back, considering. "Willow's energy manipulation could be key after we destroy the anchors. If she absorbs the residual magic, it'll stop the Golden Dawn from reactivating them. We also need to test how interconnected they are. If they're feeding off each other, breaking their links might bring all three down faster."

"Excellent insight," Eileen said, noting Willow's role in the evolving plan. "Testing their interconnectivity will also be a priority."

Riichi, as precise as ever, added, "Each anchor carries unique risks. The spring could unleash a backlash of water magic—potentially strong enough to throw the team off balance. Oak and Aislinn should reinforce the area with shielding before anyone approaches. The brazier is another challenge—it could draw power from external fire sources. Vine, your electrokinesis might be able to disrupt its flow."

Eileen's focus moved to Riichi, approval clear in her countenance. "Your insights are invaluable. These contingencies will guide our approach."

A brief silence followed as the strain of the mission settled over them. Then, Eileen straightened, her tone shifting slightly.

"Now, let's address combat strategy and how to permanently destroy the typhoon ritual."

The room remained rigid, everyone's focus locked in as Eileen continued. "Once the anchors are down, we need a way to collapse the ritual core."

Vine, sitting straighter than before, spoke with a growing confidence that caught the room's attention. "I saw Riichi and Takoda training yesterday. There was a moment when their energy surged—he channeled it through his katana and launched it. If they refine that, it might be our best shot at taking out the ritual core."

Silence stretched as the group processed his words. Eileen glanced between Riichi and Takoda before she nodded thoughtfully. "If they can stabilize it, that could work. Elder, Willow—I'll need you both on standby to handle any energy backlash when the ritual collapses. Can you manage that?"

Elder inclined his head, calm as ever. "We'll be ready."

Willow gave a small, knowing smile. "Wouldn't be the first time I've caught something falling apart."

Riichi leaned forward, brow furrowing. "If we go that route, we need to prepare for energy surges. The collapse could send shockwaves across the site, disrupting focus. Birch and Oak should position themselves defensively around the perimeter to guard against sudden attacks."

He hesitated, then added, "Holly should stay close enough to create illusions as decoys if needed. If the Golden Dawn strikes, they'll go for us first. Decoys could keep them off our backs."

Eileen's approving nod was subtle but clear. "Good suggestions. I'll add defensive positioning and decoy support to the plan. Holly, are you comfortable with that?"

Holly leaned back, smirking. "A battlefield full of illusions and confused enemies? Sounds like my kind of party."

Eileen turned her attention to Rowan, her tone crisp and direct. "Your team's objectives for tonight: Confirm changes to enemy defenses. Gather intel on vulnerabilities in the anchors and ward. Assess the energy flow and estimate how close they are to completing the ritual. Be thorough, but above all, stay cautious."

Rowan gave a quick nod. "Understood."

With that, Eileen shifted the discussion. "One last concern—retaliation. As long as we keep them from finding the mansion, Khan and Kross won't launch a full-scale attack. But they are tracking us. Anyone entering Seattle should assume they're being followed."

Takoda folded her arms, her face thoughtful. "They were watching us in Nihonmachi and Fort Lawton. That won't change."

Riichi's voice was firm. "Then we take precautions. Anyone going into the city checks their vehicles for trackers before returning."

Oak nodded. "And if you find one, don't remove it there. Lead them somewhere else first."

Vine leaned back slightly, his tone cautious. "Take the scenic route home. Change paths, double back—don't give them a direct trail to follow."

Holly smirked. "And here I thought you just liked the long way around."

Vine shrugged. "Turns out, it serves a purpose."

Eileen let the brief exchange settle before reinforcing the plan. "Anyone leaving on their day off—avoid Seattle and the surrounding area entirely. No exceptions." Her eyes passed over them, her voice sure. "We stay ahead of them, or we risk losing everything."

She paused, then added, "There's no immediate threat to the estate, but we need to be prepared in case that changes. Take time during training today to analyze the grounds. Look for weak points—places that could use reinforcement. Tomorrow, we'll discuss how to fortify our defenses."

Her tone sharpened slightly as she transitioned. "Now, let's talk about today's training."

Eileen's gaze swept the room, her voice firm. "For today's training, we focus on the anchors. You'll create them, practice dismantling them, and refine your coordination. Once Rowan's team gathers intel tonight, we'll change our focus to the defensive ward."

She let the significance of their preparations rest before adding, "That's it for now. Your input has been insightful." Rising to her feet, she projected the same constant command that had led them through countless battles. "You're dismissed to prepare for training. Every session brings us closer to readiness. Stay sharp, and don't lose sight of what's at stake."

Chairs scraped against the polished floor as the team rose, murmurs passing between them as they dispersed. Eileen's assessing eyes stayed on Vine for a moment, a small nod acknowledging his growing confidence.

As Oak walked past, he clapped Vine lightly on the shoulder, murmuring a few words that earned a faint smile from him.

Sunlight poured into the room, filling it with warmth—a striking contrast to the battle looming ahead.

Outside, the training grounds stretched wide beneath a sky mottled with shifting clouds, the crisp autumn air carrying the scent of damp earth and rustling leaves. The Fallen moved across the field with purpose, magic humming faintly in the atmosphere—a prelude to the day's exercises.

Oak stood at the center, surveying the teams as they formed. "You know the objective," he said, his tone calm yet firm. "Simulate the elemental anchors we'll face at Fort Lawton. Practice creating and dismantling them efficiently. This isn't just about magic—it's about coordination. Let's begin."

Vine, Ash, and Hazel gathered at a scorched section of the grounds where controlled flames could be conjured safely. Vine extended a hand, summoning a plume of fire that curled into shape with measured control. "Focus on the flow," he said, stepping back to let them work. "Fire moves like a current—disrupt the source, and it collapses."

Ash crouched low, keen eyes tracing the base of the flame anchor. His fingers skimmed over the scattered stones and branches feeding its energy. "What if we weaken the support here?" he asked, nudging a stick embedded in the setup.

"A good start," Hazel noted, lifting a hand. Tendrils of water vapor curled from her fingertips, meeting the flames with a quiet hiss. "But without control, the backlash could reignite it before it dies."

Vine nodded, a small smirk tugging at his lips. "Exactly. Try again, but this time, anticipate the reaction."

On their next attempt, Hazel's precision and Ash's speed worked in tandem, the fire sputtering out in a controlled burst, leaving behind nothing but curling wisps of smoke. Vine's guidance created an ease between them, his confidence allowing for experimentation rather than hesitation.

Across the field, Oak and Ivy worked together to weave air and fire into a spiraling vortex of heat and motion. The energy twisted upward in bright arcs as Rowan and Aislinn studied the structure.

"Start with the outer layer," Oak instructed. "Break the air currents first. That'll weaken the fire's hold."

Rowan moved in with controlled speed, his weapon slicing through the shifting streams of air. The vortex trembled, its form loosening. Aislinn followed his lead, her magic channeling in smooth currents, containing the unraveling structure. The synchronized effort began to dismantle the anchor layer by layer.

Ivy, arms folded, observed them critically. "Good, but push harder. A real anchor won't give you this much time."

Rowan adjusted his stance, his next strike more acute. Aislinn met his pace, their rhythm tightening until the structure gave way completely. The air dissipated, fire flickering out moments later as the ritual collapsed in a controlled release of energy.

Near the creek's edge, Willow, Riichi, Takoda, and Reed focused on the interaction between wind and water. A shallow pool shimmered under Willow's influence as she guided the magic, and then she altered the air currents around it. Without magic of their own, Riichi and Reed observed the effects, while Takoda, still inexperienced, concentrated on understanding the flow of energy.

"It's about rhythm," Reed explained, his voice even. "Wind should guide the water, not overwhelm it."

Takoda studied the effect, her fingers twitching as she mimicked the motion. Willow stepped closer, her tone firm but patient. "Try again, but don't overthink it. Feel the movement—let it guide you."

Riichi observed for a moment before offering a quiet suggestion. "One element at a time. Wind first, then water. Keep it simple."

Takoda exhaled, centering herself before making another attempt. The shift in her approach showed immediate improvement—her movements more fluid, the water rising and falling in controlled arcs. Willow gave her a satisfied nod and adjusted the wind, amplifying the effect. Riichi, watching their progress, dismantled the anchor with a precise motion, ending the exercise with practiced efficiency. A faint smile crossed Takoda's face—small but undeniable.

On the opposite side of the field, Holly conjured a ritual combining fire and air, the swirling energy crackling with raw intensity. Birch and Alder studied it, strategizing their approach.

"I'll disrupt the fire," Birch said, his tone pragmatic. "You handle the air."

"Got it," Alder replied, his presence radiating calm as he stabilized the chaotic energy around them.

Holly's grin was unmistakable. "Come on, boys! Don't let me outsmart you."

Birch smirked, but his strike was swift, scattering the flames enough for Alder to unravel the air's hold. Within seconds, the ritual collapsed into harmless embers, leaving Holly with an impressed arch of her brow.

By the session's end, the Fallen regrouped at the center of the field, their expressions reflecting a mix of exertion and satisfaction. Oak stepped forward, his voice carrying over the quiet murmur of voices.

"Good work. You adapted, focused, and worked as a unit. That's exactly what we'll need at Fort Lawton."

Vine stood quietly near the back, watching Ash and Hazel exchange a glance of mutual respect for their progress. A sense of accomplishment settled over him—not pride, but certainty.

The Fallen dispersed, the hum of magic fading as they moved toward the mansion. The crisp autumn air curled around them, a quiet reminder of the battles still ahead.

By the time the group training ended, it was late morning. The hedge maze loomed ahead, its towering walls casting twisting shadows across the frost-laced ground. In the distance, Riichi, Takoda, Rowan, and Aislinn worked on their bonded training, their movements distinct and synchronized. On the patio, Vine sat alone, absorbed in the quiet clicks of a Rubik's cube as he turned it over in his hands.

Nik stood near the back door, just inside the mansion, a quiet observer as the others filtered in after training. His posture was relaxed but distant, his focus turned outward toward the grounds. He had made no move to join the conversations passing him by.

Rain spotted him from the hallway and, without hesitation, closed the distance. She grabbed his hand, tugging him forward before he could react.

"You're coming with me," she announced, her bright smile leaving no room for argument.

Nik blinked, caught off guard but not resisting. "Do I get to know why?" His tone was dry but not unkind.

"Nope," she replied, tossing a grin over her shoulder. "Just trust me."

She pulled him outside, crossing the patio and leading him toward the hedge maze. The frost-dusted ground crunched underfoot as she set a brisk, confident pace. Nik followed without protest, curiosity overtaking hesitation.

"You know, you're kind of an enigma," Rain teased as they entered the maze. "I bet you've got a million interesting thoughts, but you never share any of them."

Nik slid his hands into his jacket pockets. "I don't see much point in talking unless there's something worth saying."

"Good thing I talk enough for both of us, then," Rain quipped, her laugh quick and warm. She glanced back at him, her steps never faltering. "Seriously, though. You're going to have to work with me here. I've decided it's my mission to figure you out."

Nik's lips twitched in a faint, almost imperceptible smile. "That might take more time than you think."

As they rounded another turn, Rain slowed just slightly, letting Nik walk closer. For a moment, their steps were the only sound in the quiet maze. Then Nik spoke, his voice calm but thoughtful. "Everyone's started calling me Nik lately. Instead of Elder."

Rain glanced at him, curiosity flickering in her demeanor. "Yeah? What do you think about that?"

"I'm not sure yet," Nik admitted. "It's... different. But I've been wondering—was it your idea?"

Rain's grin widened, though she tried to feign innocence. "What makes you think that?"

"You tend to notice things," Nik replied, his tone matter-of-fact. "And you're not exactly shy about sharing your opinions."

She laughed, shaking her head. "Okay, fine. You caught me. I might've mentioned it to a few people. Very casually."

"Why?" His question was soft, more curious than accusing.

"Because I believe people should get to decide who they are," she said simply, her tone earnest. "And Elder didn't feel like you. Nik does."

They walked in silence for a moment, her words settling between them. "Thank you," Nik said eventually, his voice quieter now. "It's been a long time since I thought about... what fits."

Rain's usual playful energy softened slightly. "You're welcome," she said, her smile smaller but no less genuine.

As they continued deeper into the maze, their conversation turned lighter. Rain's cheerful persistence worked its magic, and Nik's responses grew longer, his dry humor slipping through in unexpected moments. They talked about the maze, their work with the Fallen, and even shared a few scattered stories from their pasts.

At one point, their hands brushed briefly as they rounded a tight corner, and Nik glanced at Rain with a mix of hesitation and curiosity in his expression. Rain didn't comment, though her laughter softened into a warmer, more intimate note—a subtle change that made the moment feel personal, almost tender.

"You know," Rain said eventually, breaking the moment with a grin. "You're actually pretty good at conversation when you try. Maybe you've been holding out on us."

Nik allowed himself a small smile, understated but real. "Or maybe you just talk enough for the both of us."

Rain let out a mock gasp. "Wow. A full sentence and a joke? Who even are you?"

"Don't get used to it," Nik replied, his voice low but tinged with amusement.

They continued walking through the maze, Rain's laughter echoing softly off the hedge walls. The conversation was light, their steps unhurried, until a distant shout shattered the calm.

"Look out!" Vine's voice rang out from somewhere unseen, sharp and urgent.

Nik's head snapped up, instincts kicking in. Above them, a katana arced through the air, its surface pulsing erratically with wild magic. His mind registered the danger instantly—unstable energy, on the verge of exploding.

Without a word, Nik grabbed Rain and pushed her back against the hedge, his arm braced around her as he shielded her with his body. The katana detonated midair, sending a blast of magical sparks and jagged fragments outward.

The air shimmered suddenly with a protective barrier. The fragments struck the invisible shield and ricocheted harmlessly away, the distinctive hum of Vine's energy rippling through the air.

For a moment, everything stilled. Nik's arm remained braced around Rain, their faces close enough that she could see the tension easing from his features. His breathing was steady, but his expression held a raw intensity that left her speechless.

Rain's heart raced as the silence stretched between them. The proximity, the heat of the moment—it all felt sharper, more real than she expected.

Nik cleared his throat and stepped back abruptly, his hand dropping to his side. "Are you okay?" he asked, his voice awkward but laced with genuine concern.

"Yeah," Rain replied, trying to sound casual. She brushed her red hair back with a quick motion, hoping to hide the blush rising in her cheeks. "The hedge didn't hurt me. I'm fine."

Nik nodded once, his expression inscrutable. "Good."

They started back toward the mansion, the maze suddenly feeling quieter than before. Rain kept her focus ahead, her usual confidence softened by a more reflective, almost cautious demeanor. She couldn't stop replaying the moment in her mind—the way Nik had moved so quickly, the way his presence had felt so grounding.

As they neared the mansion, Nik noticed Vine crouching in the yard, picking up a Rubik's cube from the ground. Their eyes met briefly, and Nik gave him a small, deliberate nod of appreciation. Vine straightened, brushing dirt off the cube, and returned the gesture with a faint, knowing tilt of his head. The exchange passed in silence but carried the importance of acknowledgment.

Rain sneaked a glance at Nik, only to find him looking her way. Their eyes met briefly before Nik looked ahead again, his face calm, though his thoughts seemed far from it.

By the time they reached the mansion, the earlier ease between them had shifted into something quieter. Rain, feeling uncharacteristically flustered, muttered a quick goodbye before heading inside.

Nik lingered for a moment, his attention drifting back toward the maze before he stepped inside, thoughts unsettled in a way he wasn't used to.

★★★

The hedge maze cast long, twisting shadows over the frost-covered lawn in the late morning light, its towering walls a serene backdrop to the bonded training session nearby. The earlier commotion from group drills had faded, leaving only the measured breaths and quiet murmurs of instruction as Rowan and Aislinn stood opposite Riichi and Takoda, their focus entirely on the task ahead.

"Focus on activating your bond," Riichi instructed, his voice calm but firm. "Radiant Surge isn't just light—it's the connection between you. Let it guide you."

Rowan locked eyes with Aislinn, his composure steady despite the pressure. They had been working toward activating their Radiant Surge without touch, but maintaining control without that physical anchor had proven difficult. Aislinn inhaled sharply, her hands clenched at her sides, as their bond flared to life.

The glow around them surged too brightly before stuttering, the erratic energy throwing Aislinn off balance. She winced, stepping back. "It's too much," she muttered, frustration lacing her voice.

"Stop fighting it," Riichi instructed, his voice cutting through the moment. "The light isn't your enemy. It's part of you."

Takoda added, gentler but just as firm, "Picture it blending into you, not pushing against you. You control it."

Rowan, sensing Aislinn's frustration, reached for their telepathic bond. His voice came through, steady and sure. *You're fine. Take a breath. I'm here.*

Aislinn's reply was barely a whisper. *I can hardly hear you.*

Then listen harder, Rowan urged, grounding himself for her.

Aislinn steadied her breathing, her focus sharpening. The wild light smoothed into a controlled glow, wrapping around them in a stable pulse. She looked up at Rowan, a small smile breaking through the tension.

"Good progress," Takoda encouraged, stepping closer. "Your bond is stronger than you think. Trust it."

As Rowan and Aislinn stepped aside, Riichi and Takoda moved into position. Their expressions were honed with concentration. They had only discovered the potential of this technique yesterday, but there was no room for failure.

Their Radiant Surge ignited instantly, orange light streaking between them, sinking into Riichi's katana. The blade glowed, its edges pulsing as Takoda funneled her energy into it.

"Keep it narrow," Rowan advised. "Don't let it flare too wide."

Aislinn added, her tone lighter but focused, "It's like dancing—match his rhythm, Takoda. Follow his lead, but stay in sync."

Takoda exhaled, glancing at Riichi. Their telepathic connection thrummed between them. *You've got this. Stay with me.*

I trust you, she answered, determination hardening her resolve.

The katana pulsed steadily, power flowing in controlled waves. But the strain of maintaining the delicate balance began to show—Takoda hesitated, her energy wavering. The glow around the blade flickered, erratic and volatile.

Riichi's grip tightened as he fought to stabilize it. "Hold it steady," he muttered, though the tension in his voice betrayed his concern.

The sword bucked against their control. Takoda's breaths quickened, her confidence slipping as the unstable energy surged. Riichi caught the warning signs immediately.

"It's going to blow!" he shouted.

With a powerful throw, he hurled the katana high, the blade spinning wildly as the unstable energy reached its peak.

Across the field, Rowan reacted instantly, pulling Aislinn to the ground. Riichi did the same for Takoda, shielding her as the weapon exploded midair, scattering jagged shards of energy.

From the patio, Vine saw the katana arc over the maze, its erratic glow an unmistakable warning. His Rubik's cube hit the ground as he bolted forward. "Look out!" His voice rang out, fierce with urgency.

Without breaking stride, Vine cast a shimmering barrier. The explosion shattered against it, the fragments deflecting harmlessly away. The hedge maze and its surroundings remained untouched.

Vine slowed as the last echoes of the blast faded. His breathing was measured as he walked back to retrieve the fallen cube, brushing off the dirt as if nothing had happened.

Emerging from the maze, Rain and Nik appeared, their steps quick, expressions edged with surprise and relief. Nik's gaze found Vine's, and he gave a small, deliberate nod. Vine returned it without a word, the silent acknowledgment enough.

Minutes later, Riichi, Takoda, Rowan, and Aislinn approached Vine, their energy subdued in the aftermath.

"Nice save," Riichi said. "Didn't know Rain and Nik were in there."

Vine shrugged, his focus dropping to the cube in his hands. "It was nothing."

As they turned toward the mansion, Takoda glanced at Riichi, her voice quiet. "I'm sorry about your katana."

Riichi's lips quirked. "It's just a blade. You're more important. We'll figure it out next time."

Vine lingered behind as the others moved ahead, his fingers idly turning the cube. Watching the bonded pairs work in sync, the ache in his chest deepened. That connection wasn't his anymore—his chapter had closed.

Exhaling, he pushed the thought away and followed the others across the frost-covered lawn.

★★★

The late afternoon stretched over the mansion, the usual hum of activity settling into quieter rhythms. Ariel descended the grand staircase, fingers trailing lazily along the railing. Whatever time she'd spent in her room had clearly done her good—her grin was wide, her eyes glinting with mischief.

Halfway down, she spotted Vine climbing from the opposite direction, his damp hair curling faintly at the edges, droplets of water still clinging to his skin. A towel rested over one shoulder, his shirt slung over the other, leaving his torso bare. The post-workout look softened his usual polished demeanor, but what caught Ariel's attention most was the rare ease in his expression.

He looked good. More than that—he looked happy.

"Looking good, hero," she called, her grin widening. "Heard you saved Rain and Nik earlier. What's next? Saving kittens from trees?"

Vine paused mid-step, a smirk tugging at his lips. "It wasn't that big of a deal."

Ariel arched a brow, leaning casually against the banister. "Not a big deal? A perfectly timed magical barrier, thrown in the nick of time? Sounds pretty heroic to me."

She descended the last few steps, stopping just in front of him, her voice dipping into something softer, edged with flirtation. "Well, I think it's a big deal. Want to tell me about it somewhere quieter?"

His smirk faltered for the briefest moment, caught off guard by her boldness. But the amusement in his eyes didn't waver. "You're relentless," he muttered.

"Absolutely." Ariel flashed him a knowing smile. "Come on."

She turned, leading the way without waiting for him to follow. Vine hesitated for half a breath, glancing back as if debating his original plan. But Ariel's energy was infectious, and with a quiet sigh, he fell into step behind her.

The library greeted them with the scent of old books and the hush of undisturbed quiet. Heavy curtains dimmed the space, the towering bookshelves casting long rows of shadowed aisles. Ariel moved deeper inside, weaving through the shelves with purpose, barely glancing back to check if he followed.

"Where are we going?" Vine asked, bemused.

"You'll see," she murmured, voice dropping to a whisper as they reached the back, secluded from view.

She turned abruptly, pressing him lightly against a shelf. Her hands rested on his chest, the mischievous spark in her expression sharpening a slow, deliberate invitation. "I think you owe me a proper thank you for noticing your heroics."

Vine chuckled, the sound low and warm. "A proper thank you?"

"Exactly." Ariel's fingers traced slow, idle patterns across his skin, her confidence radiant. There was no hesitation in her gaze—only intent.

For a moment, his usual restraint wavered. Then, giving in, he leaned down and kissed her.

It started unhurried, exploratory, but neither of them had much patience for restraint. Ariel's hands skimmed up his chest, pushing his towel and shirt from his shoulder, letting them fall. Vine's grip tightened at her waist, fingers slipping beneath the hem of her shirt, drawing her closer.

Her pulse kicked up as his lips moved against hers, teasing, deepening with each stolen breath. Ariel's fingers tangled in his damp hair, tilting his head just enough to draw him further in, tasting the heat of his mouth against hers. The press of his hands, the firm, deliberate way he pulled her closer, sent heat curling low in her stomach.

Vine exhaled sharply through his nose, his restraint slipping further as she pressed against him, her body fitting against his in ways that tested every line they'd drawn. He let her have control—until he didn't.

With a slow, measured shift, he turned, reversing their positions so she was the one pinned against the bookshelf. Ariel gasped, but he caught the sound with another kiss, swallowing her laughter as his hands traced along her waist.

Then he froze.

The fine hairs at his nape pricked in warning.

A faint creak at the door broke the silence.

His hand lifted, signaling Ariel to stop before he peered around the edge of the bookshelf.

Nik stepped into the room, scanning the space.

Vine exhaled, quickly slipping into nonchalance. "Hey, Nik. Fancy seeing you here."

Nik's brow arched. "I think it's more unlikely to see you in here."

Vine grabbed a random book from the shelf, holding it up as proof. "Just getting a book."

Nik's gaze flicked to the title. "A cookbook?"

Ariel smothered a laugh, shoulders shaking as she tried to stay quiet. Vine shot her a warning look before glancing down at his accidental choice.

"Uh… yeah," he said smoothly. "Thought I'd flip through, see if there's something Takoda might want to make."

Nik's skepticism deepened. "Do you always come to the library without a shirt?"

Vine hesitated a beat before shrugging as if it were the most natural thing in the world. "Yeah… I mean, no. I was hot. Just finished training."

Nik folded his arms. "Right."

Vine shifted tactics. "Actually, since you're here, I was gonna ask for your help. You're the best magic user we've got."

Nik's expression remained guarded. "What's this about?"

"During training earlier, we were working on the elemental anchors—air, wind, fire." Vine kept his tone even, threading enough truth into the lie. "Figured you'd have insight. You can never be too prepared, right?"

Nik studied him for a long moment, clearly weighing the offer. Then, with a sigh, he relented. "Fine. I guess I can spare a few minutes. Let's go."

Vine gave a quick nod and started toward the door, glancing at Ariel one last time as he passed. He leaned in just enough for only her to hear, his voice a low, teasing murmur.

"We'll finish this later, Trouble."

Before she could respond, he straightened, his smirk brief but knowing as he turned to follow Nik out.

Ariel, still breathless from the near-miss, exhaled a quiet laugh and ran a hand through her hair. She pulled her shirt back into place, then bent to pick up Vine's from the floor.

Peeking through the library door, she caught sight of them rounding the corner. Just as she thought she'd gone unnoticed, Vine glanced back, locking eyes with her.

Ever bold, Ariel held up his shirt with a cheeky wave, her grin widening as his smirk deepened. He winked—quick, unspoken—before turning to continue with Nik.

Still smiling, she turned and headed in the opposite direction, Vine's shirt in hand as she made her way to her room.

★★★

The forest surrounding Fort Lawton was dense and still, the towering trees casting jagged shadows in the dim glow of the moonlight filtering through thick clouds. Rowan, Aislinn, Ivy, and Birch moved in silence, their steps soundless against the damp earth as they closed in on the shimmering defensive ward surrounding the ritual site. The distant crash of waves against the cliffs blended with the low, unnatural hum of magic vibrating through the air.

Birch stopped first, his keen eyes narrowing as he scanned the energy pulsing along the ward's edges. "That's not just reinforced—it's been reworked," he muttered. "They're expecting us."

Ivy stepped closer, her perceptive focus locking onto the faint distortions rippling through the barrier. "The layering's complex," she murmured. "Too refined for standard Golden Dawn work." A slow exhale, then a small flicker of her magic as she tested the ward's response. The energy rebounded sharply, pressing back with more force than before. Her lips pressed into a thin line. "Khan's handiwork. He's strengthening their defenses."

Aislinn crouched near the base of the ward, her gaze sweeping between the glowing structure and the ritual anchors flickering in the distance. "No rushing in," she said firmly. "We test everything before we make a move."

Rowan nodded once, his voice measured. "Find weak points. Take note of changes. Then we get out."

They fanned out, keeping low and using the thick underbrush as cover. Ivy moved first, bending reality in the smallest of increments as she studied the ward's responses. A distortion flickered where she applied pressure—then, within seconds, the barrier snapped back, seamless.

"There," she murmured. "That's our opening. But if we hit too soon, it'll recover faster than we can break through."

Birch approached another section, bracing himself as he pressed against the energy field. The ward's pushback was immediate, its force slamming into him with an unnatural strength. His muscles tensed as he absorbed the impact, but even with his endurance magic dulling the worst of it, he pulled back with a quiet hiss. "It's actively resisting," he said through clenched teeth. "Anything too forceful will trigger an alarm."

Aislinn glanced toward the ritual site, her face acute with concentration. "Then we spread it thin before striking," she reasoned. "Force it to divide its energy."

Rowan's eyes remained fixed on the ritual core. "Then that's our approach. Mark the weaknesses and keep moving."

Beyond the ward, the typhoon ritual pulsed steadily, a controlled rhythm tethering its energy to the three elemental anchors—the spring, the windchime, and the brazier. The process was methodical, precise.

Birch scanned the scene, his jaw tightening. "They're reinforcing in stages," he observed. "No erratic power surges, just steady, controlled progress."

Ivy calculated the energy flow, her brows furrowing. "Five or six days," she said confidently. "Hazel was right."

Rowan exhaled. "That gives us time."

They turned their attention to the individual anchors. Ivy reached out first, her reality bending brushing against the air around the windchime. A faint chime resonated in response, its song eerie in the night. A small smirk ghosted across her lips. "This one's fragile," she murmured. "Take it out first, and the rest might collapse with it."

Birch moved to the spring anchor, his magic barely skimming the surface before the energy lashed out violently. He yanked his hand back, grimacing. "This thing is volatile. One wrong move and we're looking at a full-blown explosion."

Aislinn's focus remained on the brazier, her magic skimming over the flames. "This one's stable," she murmured. "Which means it's going to take the most effort to dismantle."

Rowan's stance remained firm. "Windchime first, then the others in tandem."

Aislinn gave a tight nod. "If we miscalculate, though, we trigger a chain reaction."

Rowan's jaw set. "Then we don't miscalculate."

The wind shifted.

The mist hanging low over the ritual site thinned just enough to reveal movement beyond the ward. Shadows peeled away from the treeline—figures emerging from the dark in disciplined formation. At first glance, they were Golden Dawn. But their presence felt wrong.

Rowan's pulse quickened. Too strong. Too precise.

Then he saw them.

Kubla Khan's enhancements clung to the Golden Dawn's forces like an unnatural aura, amplifying their strength, perfecting their movements. They weren't just recruits—they were weapons. And behind them, directing their movements with cold, methodical precision, was Kross. No magic, no supernatural ability—just a strategist who knew how to use every advantage at his disposal.

Rowan barely had time to react.

"We've been made," he muttered. "Aislinn—shields, now."

Aislinn's hands lifted, her magic snapping into place just in time to deflect the first volley of energy. The force of the blast sent a sharp crack through the night air.

Rowan surged forward, closing the distance between him and the first attacker. Enhanced strength met brute force, the impact jarring through his arms as he took the Golden Dawn soldier head-on. The recruit barely flinched.

Aislinn held the shield firm, deflecting another blast as Ivy wove through the chaos with her dual blades. She struck hard, accurate—yet her target absorbed the blow with alarming resilience before retaliating.

"They're stronger," she bit out.

"Khan's enhancements," Birch growled. He stayed close to Rowan, transferring endurance to him mid-strike, reinforcing his strength as he deflected a heavy blow and countered by hurling his chakrams with brutal force.

Then the reinforcements arrived.

More figures emerged, their numbers multiplying too fast. Rowan glanced at Aislinn, their decision instinctive.

Radiant Surge activated.

The glow around them was dim—just enough to enhance their coordination without drawing more attention. Their bond sharpened their movements, turning every strike, every dodge, into a seamless rhythm.

"Take out their leader," Rowan sent through their link. *"That's how we break them."*

"On it." Aislinn moved fast, cutting through the fray with deadly efficiency.

Rowan carved a path through the soldiers, reaching the second-in-command. His first strike sent the man staggering—his second dropped him. The Golden Dawn's formation wavered. Aislinn followed up with a kinetic blast, knocking back the nearest enemies just as Ivy took down the last of the stragglers with her blades—Kross had already vanished into the mist.

Then, silence.

Birch exhaled, wiping a hand over his face. "That was too damn close."

Ivy rolled her shoulders. "They weren't expecting that much resistance."

Aislinn turned to Rowan, her frown deepening as she spotted the blood on his sleeve. "You're hurt."

Rowan wiped it away, unconcerned. "It's nothing. We move now."

No one argued.

Rowan took an indirect route back, doubling back twice to ensure they weren't being followed. The car remained silent, tension thick as Ivy scanned the passing streets, her sharp gaze searching for signs of pursuit.

Once they were well away from Fort Lawton, Rowan took a hard turn onto a side road that led in the opposite direction of the mansion. He killed the engine abruptly. "Check the car."

They moved fast. Ivy crouched near the bumper, Birch ran a hand along the undercarriage, and Aislinn swept her magic over the frame. A faint metallic glint caught the light as Ivy pried a small, sleek device free.

"Tracker," she muttered.

Birch frowned. "Kross's tech."

Rowan took the device and crushed it in his fist before tossing the pieces into the brush. "We'll take a longer route back. Next time, we check before we leave."

No one argued. They climbed back in, and Rowan restarted the car, easing onto the road with even more caution than before.

As they neared the protected grounds of the mansion, Aislinn murmured, "Do you think they know where we came from?"

Rowan's expression darkened. "Not yet. But we need to make sure it stays that way."

Ivy made one last scan of the perimeter, then nodded. "Clear. Let's go."

Without another word, they slipped back into the night, the weight of what they had just witnessed pressing against them like a storm on the horizon.

Chapter Twenty-Nine
What Lies Beneath

The kitchen breathed with the quiet rhythm of a shared morning. Sunlight spilled through the wide windows, painting golden streaks across scattered coffee mugs and a platter of toast and jam. Rain cradled her tea, steam rising in slow, curling tendrils. Ariel perched on a stool, legs swinging. At the counter, Ivy sliced an apple with deliberate care, the blade catching the light.

Takoda leaned back, a smirk playing at her lips. "So, Ivy, what's the plan for your epic day off? Still making a to-do list."

Ivy's mouth quirked as she looked up. "Not exactly. I'm thinking—morning hike, lunch at the café by the lake, and volunteering at the animal shelter."

Ariel's head snapped up, her coffee momentarily forgotten. "Did you say animal shelter? Ivy, you brilliant mastermind. I'm so in."

Rain set down her mug, her smile as soft. "That sounds like a perfect day. A little peace, a little purpose."

"Of course, Ariel zeroed in on the animals." Hazel, chuckled, lounging near the window. She's already picking which ones to snuggle."

At the stove, Holly flipped a pancake with effortless grace. "Just remember, you can't take them all home."

"Who said anything about taking them home?" Ariel gasped, clutching her chest dramatically. "I'm just there to give love. Excessive amounts of love."

Ivy shook her head, barely hiding a smile. "There's a trail I've been meaning to try—Lakeview Loop. It's close, easy, and the views are supposed to be incredible."

Rain nodded, her tone thoughtful. "Afterward, we can stop at the café near the trailhead. They have fresh sandwiches. And pie."

"Pie and puppies?" Ariel's hands flew to her cheeks, eyes wide. "This day just keeps getting better. Think they'll let us stay all afternoon?"

Ivy sliced another piece of apple. "Probably not all afternoon. But enough time to make a difference."

Rain's voice dipped, thoughtful. "They always need help. Animals deserve every bit of care we can give."

Takoda leaned forward, grinning. "I can already see it. Ariel's going to fall in love and walk out with a new best friend."

"Me? No way." Ariel crossed her arms with mock offense. "I'm just there to give cuddles and kisses."

Hazel rolled her eyes, laughing. "That's what everyone says. Until they meet the one."

From the corner, Aislinn raised a brow playfully. "She's probably already picking out names."

Ariel lifted her mug in mock toast. "You can't prove that."

Ivy chuckled as she placed the apple slices on a plate. "Alright, enough teasing. Hike, lunch, then the shelter. Stick to the plan."

Holly turned, offering up the final pancakes. "You better bring back pictures. I expect at least one adorable animal selfie from each of you."

"I'm sure Ariel's got that covered," Ivy said dryly. "As long as she actually helps and doesn't spend the whole time in a cuddle pile."

Rain eased her chair back, getting up. "It's going to be a good day. Let's head out before it gets too warm."

Ariel hopped off the stool, energy radiating from every bounce. "Best. Day. Ever. Did I mention the pie? And the puppies?"

Takoda followed her out, heading towards the meeting, "Don't forget tissues, Ariel. You're going to cry the second you meet your new 'not' best friend."

The room emptied, laughter echoing faintly behind them—an aftertaste of warmth and the promise of a day well spent.

The conference room buzzed with low conversation, chairs scraping softly as the Fallen took their seats. Each brought a distinct energy—the atmosphere charged. Movement stilled as Eileen entered, her presence drawing focus. With a simple gesture, the meeting began.

"Let's start with Fort Lawton," she said. "Rowan?"

Rowan leaned forward. "The outer perimeter has changed. The ward's adapting faster—tighter compression, stronger surges within fifty feet. It's reacting to us."

Aislinn added, "The elemental anchors are charging. The flow's moving faster. They're close but not there yet. The windchime is still the weakest, but the brazier's burning hotter. The spring felt unstable."

Birch nodded, arms crossed. "They've reinforced too. We were ambushed by ten Golden Dawn members. All enhanced by Khan."

Eileen's posture tensed, but she said nothing as Rowan continued.

"We also found a tracker on my car. Magically concealed. We almost missed it." Rowan's voice was clipped.

"They're not just defending the ritual," Aislinn added, her tone calm but edged with certainty. "They're hunting us."

Eileen turned sharply, already assessing. "Willow, Alder, Holly, Nik—you're on recon tonight. Confirm the energy flow, defenses, and how close they are to activation. Focus on vulnerabilities."

"I'll trace the current," Willow said with a faint smirk. "If it's speeding up, I'll find the weak points."

"I'll coordinate movement," Alder said, steady as always. "In and out before they notice."

Eileen gave a tight nod, then shifted her gaze. "Riichi, what's your plan for replacing your katana?"

"I need to retrieve one from my shop in Seattle," he said, straightening. "The blade there—it's my original katana from Japan. It was with me before I became Fallen."

Eileen's brow furrowed. "Wouldn't it be safer to get a blade closer, like Tukwila?"

Riichi's fingers brushed the edge of the table. "This isn't about finding a blade—it's about reclaiming the one I left behind," he said, quieter now. "That katana... it's more than just a weapon. It's the blade I carried the night Khan's army came. The night everything changed. I want it in my hands when this ends—when I finally face him again."

The room stilled, and Takoda rested a hand on his arm in silent support.

Eileen's gaze softened, but her tone remained firm. "Take Reed and Oak. Be quick."

Riichi nodded, resolve steady.

Eileen turned back to the room. "Training today will focus on the defensive ward. You'll work in teams to dismantle a mock perimeter without triggering alarms. Find the weak points. Strike with coordination. We only get one shot."

Her eyes moved to Reed. "You've been pushing hard. Tomorrow's your day off. Use it."

Reed gave a short nod. "Understood."

Eileen scanned the room. "Any questions before we adjourn?"

Birch shifted in his seat, fingers brushing the table's edge. He leaned forward, voice measured. "There's something we need to consider. We've been moving from mission to mission, always on the run. It's time we establish a permanent base—a place to ground ourselves, spiritually and strategically."

The weight of his words drew the group's attention. His expression turned contemplative. "Among my people, land is more than a place. It's identity, connection, and strength. A base would be more than shelter—it would center us. Give us unity. Purpose."

He let that settle before continuing. "I have land we could use. Three options: northern Arizona, the Black Hills in South Dakota, or the San Luis Valley in Colorado. Each one is sacred. And all are far from prying eyes."

Reed nodded. "I've got land too. Picked it up when I was thinking about relocating from Alaska. It's in the Rockies—untouched and completely off-grid."

Nik inclined his head. "I have a property in Texas. Remote and large enough."

Aislinn's gaze swept the room. "It's a good start. But if we're serious, we'll need more than one location. A network of safe houses would make us harder to track and give us more flexibility."

Willow, quiet until now, tapped a finger against the table. "I'd be willing to buy land if it means we can build something lasting. A full network could save lives—not just ours."

The conversation slowed as Vine cleared his throat. He leaned forward, more serious than usual. "If you're building a safe house network, I already have thirty-seven properties. Secluded. Spread out across the country. All move-in ready."

After a collective gasp, Takoda blinked. "You have thirty-seven houses?"

Vine shrugged, a flicker of dry humor passing through. "Real estate investments. Most just sit there. I never got around to renting or selling them."

Rowan leaned back skeptically, arms folded. "And you'd just hand all of them over?"

Vine's mouth curved into a faint smirk. "If they're needed, yes. For the team, right?"

Holly laughed softly, sinking deeper into her seat. "A mansion, an estate in the Rockies, and now thirty-seven hidden properties? We're basically an elite paranormal Airbnb service."

Hazel, more grounded, tapped the table. "We'd need a plan. A network like that won't help if no one knows how to find them when it matters."

Alder spoke next, quiet but resolute. "This could give us an edge. The Golden Dawn moves fast. But with this kind of infrastructure, we'd be harder to pin down."

Willow nodded. "It's not just about safety. A base—or a network—means we stop reacting. We start preparing. That changes everything."

Eileen raised her hand, and the room quieted.

"Birch, Reed, Nik, and Vine have given us a lot to think about," she said. "This is a significant step. One that will take time and coordination. For now, our focus stays on Fort Lawton and the ritual. That comes first."

Her voice sharpened slightly. "We'll revisit this at the first meeting after the typhoon ritual is destroyed. Until then, keep your proposals in mind. Thank you."

Chairs slid back as the group rose, their conversations quiet and measured. Near the doorway, Vine caught Rowan's stare and offered a faint, knowing shrug before moving on.

Eileen remained where she stood, unmoving as the room emptied. Her features revealed nothing—but her thoughts had already moved to the questions waiting just beyond the horizon.

Outside the estate, most of the Fallen had finished training, their laughter and footsteps fading as they returned inside. A crisp October breeze tugged at the hem of Aislinn's jacket as she stepped into the clearing behind the house.

Reed stood near the edge of the trees, sleeves rolled, arms crossed loosely as he watched a hawk trace circles in the sky. He didn't look over when she approached, but his voice met her halfway. "I was wondering when you were going to come find me."

Aislinn stopped a few feet behind him. "You knew I would?"

"You teleported in the middle of a mission," he said, finally glancing her way. "Not exactly subtle. Everyone saw it. Eileen knew you'd figure it out on your own, but she also said you'd probably come to me when it came time to bring someone else along."

A faint smile tugged at her lips. "Guess I'm predictable."

Reed shrugged. "Not predictable. Just smart."

She stepped closer, arms crossing. "I can teleport fine on my own now. But bringing someone with me... that's where I hit a wall."

He nodded. "Shadow-walking's similar. You're not just moving yourself—you're carrying someone else's energy through the slip. If you're not linked properly, you leave them behind. Or worse."

"Comforting," she muttered.

"When I shadow-walk alone, I slip through the space around me like folding paper. But if I'm taking someone, I have to make room for them in the shift. That starts with intention. I don't just reach for myself—I reach for them too. Hold them in the pull."

"So touching them isn't enough?"

"No. Touch helps, especially at first, but the link has to happen up here." He tapped his temple. "It's not about dragging someone through—it's about tethering them like they belong inside the move."

Aislinn studied him. "Alright. Let's try it."

Reed stepped back and motioned her forward. She placed a hand on his arm and summoned the energy. Her body responded immediately, the hum of teleportation sharp under her skin, but when she reached to draw him in, the connection unraveled.

"Didn't hold," she said, stepping back.

"You're still thinking of yourself as the center. You need to think like the two of you are one movement."

She tried again. Her energy stretched, reached toward him, then dropped flat.

"You've got the reach," Reed said. "Now you need the reason."

Her brow rose. "What does that mean?"

"When I bring someone with me, I care what happens to them. I hold on because I want to. That changes the way the power moves."

"So emotion helps?"

"Intent helps. The decision not to leave them behind."

Aislinn took a breath and set her hand back on his arm. She didn't just focus on the energy—she focused on the connection. Not just bringing him, but keeping him. The pull flared again, strong and clean, and the world blinked. They reappeared several feet away.

"You felt that?" she asked.

"Yeah," Reed said. "You pulled clean."

She released his arm, energy still buzzing faintly under her skin. "Thanks."

"Keep practicing. You've got it."

They walked back toward the house, quiet but focused. Aislinn peeled off to find Rowan, while Reed headed inside to meet Riichi, Takoda, and Oak for the trip to Pioneer Square.

The streets of Pioneer Square carried a muted energy, the hum of traffic layered behind brick and shadow. The group moved with purpose, boots quiet on damp pavement. Riichi led, posture rigid, scanning alleys and rooftops as they neared the shop.

"Rooftops," Reed said. "They'll be watching from above."

Oak nodded. "We're not staying long. Get what you came for, and we're out."

Takoda matched Riichi's pace, glancing at him now and then, noting the sharp focus in his features. He gave nothing away.

The antique shop door creaked open, sound swallowed by stillness. Inside, the air carried aged wood, old metal, and faint incense that clung like memory. Faded light touched shelves of relics—blades, scrolls, carved masks—arranged with deliberate care.

Reed gave a quiet whistle. "You didn't mention you were curating a museum."

Oak's voice was low but weighted. "These aren't just objects. They're someone's life."

"The blade's upstairs," Riichi said briskly, "Koda, with me. Oak, Reed—hold the front."

Oak gave a curt nod. "We've got you. Be quick."

The staircase groaned beneath them. The scent of incense thickened with dust and time. Riichi's apartment was sparse, clean, deliberate—everything in its place. He knelt by the bed and slid a long wooden box from beneath it.

Takoda stood nearby, hands loosely clasped. "That's it, isn't it?"

"Yes." His reply was soft as he opened the lid.

The katana lay nestled in velvet, its lacquered sheath catching the light. The blade radiated quiet mastery, centuries of history bound in steel. Riichi reached for it, fingers grazing the hilt with slow precision.

"It's beautiful," Takoda said, stepping closer.

He shook his head. "Not beautiful. It's the blade I carried as a samurai. The one I held when wrath consumed me. When everything fell apart."

Her voice was low, firm. "That doesn't make it less beautiful. It's part of your story. Even the broken pieces matter."

Riichi looked at her then, studying her face as if memorizing it.

"You always find the best in me," he said. "Even when I can't."

Takoda smiled, her hand resting on his arm.

"Do you know how much I love you?"

Her breath caught. She stepped closer. "Show me."

Their kiss was quiet and certain, a meeting of truths that didn't need to be spoken. When they parted, Riichi rose, the katana secure at his waist.

"Let's go."

Downstairs, Oak and Reed stood ready.

Oak's eyes went to the blade. "Looks like you got what you needed."

Riichi nodded. "I did."

Reed smiled faintly. "Good. Let's move. This place feels like it's holding its breath."

Outside, the group moved in silence, the cool air brushing against their skin. They'd barely made it a block before Oak stopped abruptly, his hand twitching toward his weapon. "Wait," he said, voice low, taut with tension. "Something's off."

The air thrummed with unnatural energy, heavy and stifling. Across the street, a figure stood on a windowsill—arms loose at his sides, expression unreadable, save for the slow, deliberate curl of a smile.

"I was wondering when you'd show," Kubla Khan said, voice smooth and unhurried. "I've been curious."

The group froze. The air was thick with anticipation, the weight of his presence alone enough to spark instinct. Khan stayed still, eyeing them as if he had all the time in the world.

"Well," he continued, stepping down from the ledge with effortless grace. "Oak, the barrier-maker. Reed, the shadow walker. Takoda…" His eyes lingered on her, words tasting of something colder. "The empath. I look forward to knowing you better."

Takoda's chin lifted, expression hardening.

Khan's gaze slid to Riichi. "And you… the samurai." A hand tilt sent a pulse through the air. An invisible field crackled into place, muting the city's sounds. "Let's make this private."

He stepped forward, eyes locked on Riichi. "It's been a long time since Hakata Bay. You fought with such fire, even when the tide turned. I remember how your sword trembled—just before we burned your village to the ground."

Riichi didn't move, but his jaw clenched, every muscle pulled tight.

"I wonder," Khan mused, almost to himself, "if that fire still lives in you. Or if guilt snuffed it out."

The pressure built. Wrath pressed in—controlled, suffocating, tailored precisely to Riichi. Rage bloomed beneath his skin, tightening his chest, drowning reason beneath memory. Screams echoed in his ears, the scent of blood rising, the clang of steel as familiar as breath.

"And little Aya," Khan said softly. "Ten years old, wasn't she? We saved her for last. Her final word was your name."

Riichi staggered.

"Riichi!" Takoda's voice cut through the storm, sharp and urgent inside his mind. She stepped closer, her Radiant Surge flaring in a vibrant orange pulse. *"Stay with me. You're stronger than this. Breathe."*

His reply came strained. *"Turn it off. If you keep it active, you'll feel this too. I won't let that happen."*

"I'm not leaving you to face this alone," she shot back. *"We're stronger together."*

Nearby, Oak barked a command. "Reed—get the katana. I'll hold the line."

Reed vanished into shadow without hesitation, reappearing behind Riichi with quiet precision. In one smooth motion, he drew the blade from Riichi's sheath.

Oak raised his hands, casting a barrier between them and Khan. "This should hold—"

Before he could finish, the shield shattered, dissolved by a lazy twist of Khan's fingers.

He turned back to Riichi, pressure surging—thick, blinding, absolute.

Takoda moved on instinct. Her power surged, not through thought but love—pure and protective. Her orange glow flared, but the true shift happened within Riichi. The wrath didn't vanish, but it hit a wall—an invisible seal locking around his inner aura. It wasn't a barrier others could see. It lived inside him, forged from her energy as it wove into his, not repelling the fury but absorbing it, softening the edges before it could break him. Only they could feel it—quiet, unshakable, and theirs alone.

He gasped, breath returning. *"What... is this?"*

Takoda met his eyes. *"This is us."*

The pressure around Riichi steadied—contained by the unseen force Takoda had anchored within him—but before anything more could shift, Reed struck. He emerged from the shadows with Riichi's katana in hand, the blade slicing across Khan's side in one clean arc.

Black ichor welled along the cut. Khan stepped back, more surprised than pained. "You dare strike me?" he asked quietly, voice lacking fury—only intrigue.

A tendril snapped toward Reed, but he vanished into shadow before it could touch him.

Khan didn't pursue. He turned slightly, taking in the scene one last time—Riichi recovering, Takoda glowing, the blade, the teamwork.

"Interesting," he murmured.

Dark tendrils coiled around him, drawing him into the shadows. The barrier vanished. The sound of the city rushed back in.

For a long moment, no one moved.

Oak lowered his hands. "Is everyone alright?"

Reed reappeared, katana still in hand. "We're standing. For now."

Takoda's light dimmed as she turned to Riichi, her voice thoughtful. "Are you okay?"

"I am now," he said. "Thanks to you."

The group stood together, bound by what had passed. They didn't speak of what it meant—not yet. But none of them would forget what they saw in Kubla Khan's eyes.

***

The mansion was quiet in the early evening, the kind of stillness that settled comfortably after a long day. Ariel padded down the hall in her night clothes—an oversized black t-shirt and fuzzy rainbow pajama pants—her bare feet whispering against the wood floors. In her arms, a black-and-white puppy wriggled with excitement, its floppy ears bouncing with every step.

She paused at Vine's door and knocked lightly, hesitant but playful. From inside came the faint click of a remote, followed by the low hum of a TV turning on.

"Come in," Vine called, his voice carrying its usual blend of boredom and disinterest.

Pushing the door open, Ariel stepped inside. Vine was sprawled across his bed, the glow of the TV casting flickers of color across the tangled blankets. An action movie played in the background, but the way he turned to look at her made it clear he hadn't been paying attention.

"I brought someone for you to meet," she announced, lifting the squirming puppy.

Vine arched a brow, his attention shifting from her to the dog. "Please tell me you didn't steal that."

Ariel shot him a mock glare. "For your information, I adopted him. Rain, Ivy, and I volunteered at the shelter today. It was fate."

"Fate," he repeated flatly, leaning into the pillows. "Of course. Too bad I'm allergic."

She narrowed her eyes. "Don't even try it. Ivy already told me Fallen don't get allergies, so that excuse is officially off the table."

Feigning innocence, he placed a hand over his chest. "Who, me? Never. But really—what possessed you to adopt a dog?"

Her tone softened as she looked down at the puppy nestled against her. "I don't know. I just felt… pulled. Like he needed me. I couldn't walk away. Not after what Rowan did for me."

Vine's skepticism faded just slightly, his expression quieting as he studied her. "Sentimental," he said at last. "Even for you."

Ariel ignored the jab and grinned, dropping the puppy into his lap. "You have to love him. Look, he's black. You like black."

The puppy wasted no time, licking Vine's hand with enthusiasm, tail wagging like a propeller. Vine froze, clearly unprepared, before raising his hands in exaggerated surrender.

"See?" she said smugly. "He likes you. That means you're obligated to like him back."

Vine chuckled despite himself, relaxing as the puppy pawed at his arm. "He's persistent. I'll give him that. Kind of like someone else I know."

His gaze drifted to the puppy's new collar. The tag caught the light. He leaned forward and read aloud, "'Spark'? Really?"

Ariel shrugged, avoiding his eyes and glancing toward the TV. "Yeah… cuz… he's spunky. Like me."

Vine's brow arched. His eyes lingered on the tag a second longer. Spark. Too on the nose to be random. His lips tugged into a faint, knowing smile, but he didn't press her.

"Sure," he said dryly. "That's it."

Ariel scooped the puppy off his lap and set him gently on the floor. Spark immediately began sniffing the corners of the room, tail wagging with joyful curiosity. She turned back to Vine, hands on her hips.

"So," she asked, "what did you do today while I was out saving puppies?"

"Fallen stuff," Vine replied, completely nonchalant. "You know, important things."

Her eyes landed on the Rubik's cube resting on his nightstand. She picked it up, turning it in her hands, inspecting the two completed sides. "Does that help?" she asked.

He shrugged, taking it from her and tossing it lazily between his palms. "Surprisingly, yeah. Keeps my mind busy."

"Let me guess," Ariel said, arms crossing as she leaned in. "You were doing that before you gave up and turned on the TV?"

Vine chuckled under his breath. "What can I say? Nothing gets past you."

"Not bad," she mused—then, with a quick flick of her wrist, snatched the cube from his hands and twisted it, deliberately scrambling the work he'd done.

"You did not just do that," Vine said, staring at the now-jumbled cube as if it had betrayed him.

"What?" Ariel grinned, hands lifted in mock innocence. "You said it helps. I'm helping."

He lunged toward her, and they tumbled back onto the bed in a heap of laughter and tangled limbs. Ariel squealed, keeping the cube just out of reach, her pajama pants catching on the blankets as she twisted away.

In the hallway, Rowan slowed at the sound of her laughter. His gaze flicked toward the half-open door just in time to catch a glimpse of Ariel and Vine on the bed—her cheeks flushed, his arm reaching over her, both of them laughing, the tension playful but unmistakably close. His jaw tensed, and he exhaled through his nose. Without a word, he turned away and strode down the hall, his steps just a little more deliberate.

Inside the room, Vine finally reclaimed the cube with a triumphant swipe, holding it overhead like a prize. "Victory," he declared.

Ariel caught her breath, brushing her hair out of her face as her smile lingered. Their eyes met, and the laughter faded—replaced by a charged silence, deeper and warmer than before.

Vine placed the cube back on the nightstand. His fingers drifted toward the hem of her oversized shirt, tugging lightly. "This is mine. Planning to give it back?"

"Nope," she said, swatting his hand away. "It's comfy. Finders keepers."

"You're unbelievable," he murmured with a quiet laugh. His voice dipped lower. "Trouble, as always."

"You like trouble," she shot back, her tone soft but challenging.

He leaned in, closing the space between them, but she tilted her head toward the door. "Your door's open."

Vine looked over his shoulder and grabbed a boot from the floor. With practiced aim, he launched it. The door shut with a quiet click.

"Smooth," Ariel said, one brow raised.

"I have many talents," he replied, the smirk widening.

"Prove it," she whispered.

He didn't wait.

Their lips met—tentative at first, then hungrier, searching. Her fingers found his jaw, brushed the faint stubble along it, then slipped into his hair. His hand slid to her waist, drawing her in, grounding the moment with purpose. They moved together with the kind of urgency that didn't come from lust alone, but from the tension that had been building for days. *I should stop this,* Vine thought, the instinct still clinging to old walls. *But I don't want to.*

Ariel felt it too—the pull, the promise wrapped in every breath they shared. *If this is a mistake, it's one I'm choosing.*

The air between them buzzed with the weight of everything neither of them had said yet—every taunt, every challenge, every glance that lingered too long now finding its answer in the space between their lips.

At their feet, Spark let out a sharp yip, tail wagging like mad. Oblivious to the shift in energy, he padded around the bed, tail thumping happily against the floorboards—his own version of approval, pure and enthusiastic.

★★★

Later at Fort Lawton, the night was cool and still, the faint roar of waves below blending with the distant hum of the city. The Fallen team stood in the shadows atop a rugged cliff overlooking Puget Sound. Across the water, the faint glow of the typhoon ritual pulsed like a heartbeat, its ominous energy brushing the edge of their senses.

Nik's sharp eyes scanned the ritual site below, his voice low and commanding. "Stay sharp. Our job is to analyze, not engage. We get in, find what we need, and get out unseen."

Willow, calm but resolute, nodded. "I'll start with the ward's energy flow. If there's a crack, I'll find it." Closing her eyes, she extended a hand, fingers twitching as she began to probe the unseen barrier.

Alder stood nearby, posture ready, scanning the surroundings. "I'll keep watch," he said.

Crouching slightly, Holly peered down at the ritual site. "If they spot us, I'll throw up an illusion. We'll make them see what we want them to see."

Nik glanced at each of them. "Good. Stick to my signals. If anything goes wrong, I'll raise shields to cover our retreat."

Willow frowned as her focus deepened. The energy around the ward was intricate, almost hypnotic. "The flow here is... strange," she murmured. "It's layered to repel external probes. It feels almost alive—like it's watching."

Nik's focus snapped to her. "Can you push further without triggering it?"

"I'll try," she said cautiously. "But it's going to take accuracy." Her fingers moved as if weaving through invisible threads. After a tense moment, she recoiled. "Wait. This area isn't just part of the ward. It's been magicked to trap someone. The flow is designed to ensnare."

Nik's eyes narrowed. "Who?"

Willow's expression turned grim. "It's tuned for Riichi and Takoda. The magic is keyed to their signatures. If they step into this area, they won't get out."

Alder's jaw flexed. "We need to report this back to Eileen. If this is tailored for them, it's more dangerous than we thought."

Holly rose quickly. "Agreed. Let's move before we overstay our welcome."

Nik signaled, and the team slipped back through the shadows. They reached the car in silence, piling into the black sedan. Nik started the engine.

A few minutes in, Holly glanced out the rear window. "We've got company."

Nik's eyes darted to the mirror, catching headlights two blocks back. "How long have they been behind us?"

Alder looked. "Long enough. They're tailing us."

Willow leaned forward. "Can you shake them?"

Nik's hands tightened on the wheel. "Hold on."

The sedan lunged forward as he slammed the accelerator, tires screeching through a red light. The trailing car surged after them, headlights locked on.

Holly rolled down her window, fingers working fast. "I'll make them see us turn down the next road. Get ready."

A phantom image of the sedan peeled off sharply at the next corner, tires screeching in mimicry. The pursuing vehicle hesitated, veered—then cut back on course.

"They're cloaked against glamours," she snapped. "They saw right through it."

Nik swerved hard down an alley, the sedan clipping a dumpster as sparks burst from the side panel. "If they're tracking us magically, we lose them by force."

Alder turned. "Block their line of sight. Fast."

Nik spun the wheel, careening around a blind turn. The rear car followed but slowed. Up ahead, the alley spit them onto a narrow street.

"There!" Willow pointed. "Side road!"

Nik didn't hesitate. The sedan shot down the street, fishtailing as he cut the wheel. Behind them, the pursuer overshot and slammed into a row of trash bins, metal clanging like a dropped bell.

Holly let out a breath. "They're down. For now."

Nik didn't slow. "We're not going home yet." He wove through side streets, looping through an industrial lot until the glow of taillights vanished. Only then did he ease off the gas and pull into a gravel turnout, engine running low and quiet.

"Check the car," Nik ordered.

They spilled out, each moving with purpose. Alder scanned the undercarriage. Willow swept for enchantments. Holly popped the trunk and checked beneath the wheel wells.

"Clear," Alder said. "Nothing physical."

"No magical traces either," Willow added. "They must've just followed us manually."

Nik nodded. "Good."

They got back in, tension lingering. Only then did he head toward the mansion.

By the time they pulled into the long driveway, the air inside was tight with thought. Nik parked, engine ticking as it cooled.

"We need to report everything," he said quietly. "Especially that trap. If it's targeting Riichi and Takoda, this changes things."

Willow gave a slow nod. "We were lucky tonight. Next time, they might not be."

Alder stepped from the car into the night. "Then we make sure there is no next time."

The others followed—silent, alert. The trap hadn't just been a threat. It was a challenge.

Back at Fort Lawton, the tension was a livewire. The failed pursuit hung heavy in the air, thick with the scent of salt and rust. Kross stormed through the empty hall of the command post, boots pounding against cracked tile. His jaw clenched, fists tight at his sides. The air felt colder than it should've, heavier, like the building itself knew what was waiting for him.

He shoved the door to his makeshift office open—and froze.

Kubla Khan sat in his chair. No fanfare. No theatrics. Just a composed presence in the dark, sharp eyes gleaming like tempered steel in the glow of the single desk lamp. A faint curl tugged at the edge of his mouth, but it wasn't a smile. It was the prelude to judgment.

"You failed again," Khan said, voice smooth, nearly bored.

Kross didn't answer right away. He kicked the door shut behind him and crossed the room, planting both hands on the desk as he leaned in. "They had a geomancer, a reality bender, a master illusionist—and a shield that took a direct hit. We can't track them if they keep changing the rules."

"You had four operatives, armed and waiting," Khan replied. "Yet they slipped through your hands again. That's a pattern."

"I'm doing everything I can," Kross snapped. "You want more results? Show up for more than a lecture."

Khan's gaze sharpened. "You think I chose you to lead because of your compliance?"

Kross straightened, his expression hard. "No. You picked me because I don't scare easy."

That earned a pause. Khan studied him, then nodded faintly. "Correct."

He stood slowly, the movement quiet but heavy. "Then let's correct your limitations."

Kross's brow furrowed as Khan extended a hand. "Your blade."

There was a beat of silence. Kross reached into his coat, pulling out the folding pocket knife he always kept on him. He hesitated—then passed it over, handle first.

Khan didn't even look at it before drawing the edge across his own palm. Black ichor welled up, thick and iridescent under the lamplight. He held out a small, tarnished metal cup from Kross's own desk and let the ichor drip into it, swirling like oil over water.

"Drink," he said.

Kross stepped back. "I'm not drinking that shit."

Khan didn't repeat himself. He didn't need to. The command hung in the air like a blade pressed against the throat—quiet, but absolute.

Kross stared at the cup, then at Khan. His jaw twitched. He picked it up.

It burned before it even hit his lips, but he drank.

The cup hit the desk with a dull clink. Kross's eyes squeezed shut as he sucked in a sharp breath, shaking his head to chase off the bitter taste. Another breath followed—deeper, steadier.

A wicked smile curved his lips.

Slowly, he opened his eyes, revealing a sinister red glow.

<u>Chapter Thirty</u>
Sharpening the Edge

The morning light slanted through the window, casting golden ribbons across the room and brushing warmth over the modest furnishings. Riichi's bedroom blended simplicity with memory—an elegant ceramic tea set, a framed ink painting, and his katana displayed with reverence on its stand. The blade caught the light, a thin ripple gleaming along its edge like a quiet reminder of battles endured—and the ones still ahead.

Riichi lay awake, propped against the pillows, eyes drawn to Takoda beside him. Her breathing remained slow, but tension lingered across her brow, a shadow left behind by yesterday's confrontation with Kubla Khan. With a careful touch, he brushed a loose strand of hair from her cheek. For now, he let the stillness settle around them—not as an escape, but a brief reward for surviving.

Takoda stirred, stretching with a quiet groan before blinking up at him. "You're always awake first," she murmured, her voice still heavy with sleep. "Do you even know how to sleep in?"

A subtle smirk touched Riichi's mouth. "Someone has to make sure you don't steal the blanket."

She sat up with theatrical offense, wrapping the blanket around her shoulders like a cape. "Stealing? Please. It's called strategic borrowing. A necessary survival skill."

Laughter slipped between them, soft and easy, thinning the weight of yesterday's fears. Takoda nudged his arm, the corners of her mouth curling in a smile as she shifted cross-legged on the bed. But that warmth faded almost as quickly as it came. She pulled the blanket tighter, her gaze dipping. "I keep seeing it," she said. "What happened with Kubla Khan... how close he came. Alder's warning—it doesn't feel like a maybe anymore. It's hanging over us, like it's already in motion."

Riichi sat up and drew her into his lap, arms folding around her with quiet assurance. "He didn't win. And he won't. He underestimates us—you, especially."

Her eyes lifted to his, worry etched along their edges. "When he tried to pull you under with that rage... I felt it. I felt it trying to take you." She hesitated, words catching as she tried to make sense of what had happened. "But then something shifted. It wasn't just the Radiant Surge. It came from me. Or us. I could feel his wrath pressing in, but it couldn't reach you. It was like I pushed it back."

His head tilted, curiosity sharpening the look he gave her. "I felt it too. How did you do that?"

"I don't know." She shook her head. "It wasn't planned. It just... happened. I think it came from our bond. And Reed's distraction kept Kubla Khan from noticing."

Riichi's hands moved across her shoulders with slow pressure, thoughtful. "Then we keep it that way. If it's tied to us—and he's blind to it—we use it. Turn it into an advantage."

Takoda looked down at her hands, then back up at him. "It wasn't just a barrier. It felt alive. Like it was protecting both of us—but from within us." Her voice dipped lower, steadier. "We should give it a name."

He nodded slowly, a thoughtful look playing across his features. "It's more than a shield. It stops what would have destroyed us. What about... Protective Aura?"

She tested the name under her breath, then gave a faint nod. "Yeah. That's what it felt like."

For a brief moment, the golden light wrapped around them in silence, soft and warm. But then Takoda's voice pierced the quiet again, hesitant. "Even with this... it still feels like we're stepping into a storm. What if it's not enough? What if he still finds a way to use us?"

Riichi's hands slipped down her arms until his fingers laced with hers. His voice dropped, firm with conviction. "He won't. You and I—we're not what he expects. And we're not in this alone. The Fallen have our backs. And I have yours."

He looked at her fully, unwavering. "Kubla Khan fights for control. For power. That's all he knows. But we fight for each other. That's what makes us stronger. That's what will end him."

Takoda's lips curved, small but certain, her expression softening as she leaned into him. "You make it sound like we've already won."

"I believe in us," he said simply.

She tucked her head against his shoulder, her body melting into his, the tension in her spine giving way to a trembling calm. His heartbeat thrummed against her back—a steady rhythm, grounding and familiar. She tilted her face to meet his gaze, eyes shining with a trust too deep for words.

Their kiss started soft, a tender brush of lips that quickly deepened into a heat-laced urgency—hungry and consuming. Takoda felt warmth surge through her, drawn from the fire building in Riichi's touch. She shifted, straddling his lap, her hands braced against his chest as they moved in sync, each breath between them more desperate than the last.

His hands explored her curves with a hunger that mirrored her own. Every brush of his fingers, every press of their bodies, built the ache higher. Their mouths found each other again and again between shallow breaths, the room growing warmer as pleasure sharpened into need.

I spent a lifetime locked up. If I'd kept that wall up... I never would've known this. Never would've known you, Riichi whispered into her mind, the words pulsing with quiet reverence—unhidden, unshaken.

There was no hesitation.

I saw you behind the wall, Takoda answered, her thoughts wrapping around his like a vow. *And I love every part of you.*

Their eyes met in a glance that said more than words could manage—connection, surrender, trust. When Riichi eased her onto her back, Takoda welcomed him without hesitation, their bodies locking together in a rhythm as natural as breath. The outside world disappeared beneath the crashing waves of sensation, their moans and gasps threading through the stillness like a song only they could hear.

Each movement drew them closer, a slow climb to a place where thought vanished and only feeling remained. And when the edge finally shattered, it left them tangled in each other, breathless and undone, the room hushed in the aftermath.

Takoda traced idle patterns across Riichi's chest with the backs of her fingers, her limbs still wrapped around his. He twirled strands of her hair between his fingers, absentminded and content. In that quiet cocoon, nothing else existed—not the looming threat, not the warnings, not even time.

Across the room, the katana caught the sunlight, a gleam of steel standing silent watch—a reminder that even moments like this came with a cost.

They dressed slowly, neither speaking much, though the atmosphere between them had shifted. Their earlier conversation lingered—not heavy, but grounded. Takoda tugged her sweater into place and glanced toward the hallway, catching the soft sound of voices downstairs.

"The others are up," she said, placing a gentle kiss on his lips.

Riichi sat on the edge of the bed, hands resting loosely on his knees. He looked up at her with a faint smile. "Go ahead. I'll be down soon."

She paused, studying him for a beat before stealing one more kiss. "Don't take too long. If Holly gets there first, she's assigning chores to whoever's late."

His mouth quirked. "I'll take the risk."

Her laugh was quiet as she trailed her fingers along his shoulder, then slipped out the door. The sound of her footsteps faded, leaving Riichi in silence once more. His eyes drifted toward the katana, the sunlight catching along its blade like a promise not yet fulfilled.

The kitchen hummed with life, the smell of coffee and pancakes mingling with easy laughter and conversation. Holly stood at the stove, flipping pancakes with practiced efficiency as Hazel, Takoda, Aislinn, and Willow leaned against the counter, chatting and tossing scraps of food to Spark beneath the table.

Ariel sat at the kitchen table, legs crossed beneath her chair as she buttered a piece of toast. Spark darted around the room, tail wagging furiously as he scampered between the women, his energy boundless and excitement unwavering. Rain and Ivy sipped tea nearby, their quiet presence grounding the buzz of the room.

"Well, well, Ariel," Holly called over her shoulder, a grin spreading across her face. "Didn't we say this would happen? One day at the shelter and you came home with a furry best friend."

Hazel smirked, resting her chin in her hand. "You barely lasted a few hours, let alone the whole day."

Ariel rolled her eyes dramatically, clutching her coffee mug to her chest like she was delivering a heartfelt confession. "First of all, Spark found *me*. Second, I only adopted him because I have an unmatchable capacity for love and compassion."

Willow tilted her head, her tone dry. "Translation: she folded faster than Vine playing poker."

"Poor Spark didn't stand a chance," Aislinn added, laughing.

Ariel huffed in mock offense, reaching down to scoop Spark up as he wriggled beside her chair. Setting him on the floor again, she muttered, "You're all just jealous because Spark likes me best."

As if to prove her point, the puppy bolted away with renewed enthusiasm, yipping as he darted under the table in search of more attention.

Footsteps interrupted the laughter as Vine strolled into the kitchen. His damp hair caught the warm light, his appearance as polished as ever despite the casual setting. Without a word, he moved to the counter and poured himself a mug of coffee with practiced ease.

Spark froze mid-step, ears perking. With a sharp yip, he bounded toward Vine, pawing at his leg.

Holly glanced over her shoulder, smirking. "Look at that—Ariel's new puppy really likes you, Vine."

Vine barely glanced down, one eyebrow raised as he nudged Spark aside with his foot. "He probably thinks I have food."

Undeterred, Spark wagged his tail and jumped back, determined to earn attention.

"Or maybe he senses something we don't," Aislinn teased, her grin mischievous. "Dogs are good judges of character, you know."

"Guess he's still young enough to make mistakes," Vine replied, taking a slow sip of his coffee.

Laughter broke out again, drifting back to Ariel's so-called "capacity for compassion." Vine lingered by the counter, listening with quiet amusement before slipping a hand into his pocket.

"By the way," he said, voice calm and unhurried, "I found this."

He held up a small charm bracelet, its silver charms glinting in the light. The room quieted slightly as curious eyes turned toward him.

Ariel gasped, her hand flying to her wrist. "That's mine! I've been looking everywhere for it. Where did you find it?"

"In the library," Vine replied smoothly, his tone light.

Ariel's eyes narrowed just a fraction, suspicion dancing behind her smile. "Really? I didn't know you were the reading type. What were you doing in the library?"

"Returning a cookbook," Vine said with practiced ease, locking eyes with her. "You know, contributing to the literary world."

Ariel's lips twitched, a faint smile threatening to break through. His smirk deepened, and as she caught the hidden meaning behind his words, his gaze glinted knowingly.

"At any rate," Vine said, setting the bracelet on the table before finishing his coffee, "glad it's back where it belongs. Enjoy your morning, ladies."

As he turned to leave, Spark dashed after him, yipping and pawing at his leg again.

Holly chuckled, flipping another pancake. "Looks like Spark isn't ready to say goodbye."

Vine sighed softly, crouching to pet the determined puppy. His hand moved in smooth strokes along Spark's glossy fur, and for a brief moment, his features softened. "You're going to give us both away if you keep this up, little guy," he murmured.

Spark wagged harder, licking Vine's hand, delighted by the attention.

"Could you grab your dog before he decides I belong to him?" Vine said, glancing at Ariel, his voice edged with amusement.

Ariel crouched beside him, arms reaching for Spark. As she scooped him up, Vine leaned closer, his voice low and meant for her alone.

"You should train him better," he said, mock-serious. "You never know who might notice him following too closely."

Ariel met his gaze, her voice just as quiet. "And you should think twice before playing games you can't win."

Vine grinned, the subtle curve of his mouth carrying the weight of unspoken memories. He knew he'd been caught, and the gleam in his eyes acknowledged it.

Straightening, he gave a casual wave and exited the kitchen, steps smooth and confident.

Spark wriggled in Ariel's arms, eyes fixed on the doorway long after Vine had disappeared.

"He's a troublemaker, isn't he?" she murmured to Spark, a faint smile tugging at her lips.

The women burst into laughter again, their teasing resuming as the kitchen buzzed with warmth and lighthearted chaos.

The comfort lingered as breakfast wound down, laughter giving way to the quiet rhythm of cleanup. Holly flipped the last pancake onto a plate and turned off the stove. Rain bent to scoop up Spark, who had curled beside her feet.

Takoda pushed her chair back, gathering her plate. "Time to head to the meeting," she said, her tone light but purposeful.

Ariel, still cradling her coffee mug, grinned up at her. "Good luck with Eileen. Let me know if she finally cracks a smile."

Rain chuckled, adjusting Spark as he yawned in her arms. "We'll hold the fort here. Someone has to keep an eye on this guy."

Willow smirked as she passed, brushing her hand lightly over Spark's head. "Try not to spoil him too much while we're gone."

The group began filing out, their lively energy shifting to quiet focus as they disappeared down the hallway. A faint murmur of voices trailed behind them, giving way to the low scrape of chairs moving in the conference room.

The conference room carried a quiet weight, the hum of low voices softening as the Fallen took their seats. Sunlight filtered through the tall windows, casting fragmented patterns across the polished wooden table. Despite the warmth of the light, the air was thick with the lingering tension of the prior day's events. Determination burned behind their composure, shaped by the knowledge of what they faced next.

When Eileen entered, the room fell silent. Her gaze swept the team as she moved to the head of the table, her presence commanding focus. She placed her hands on the table's edge before speaking, her voice clear and direct.

"Let's begin with yesterday's events in Pioneer Square. Oak, Riichi, Takoda—report."

Oak leaned forward, calm but alert. "The attack was deliberate. Kubla Khan manipulated the ley lines beneath the square to amplify his reach. He targeted Riichi specifically by pulling on deeply personal triggers—memories, emotions, trauma. His control over wrath was surgical."

Takoda's tone was quiet but steady. "He tried to consume Riichi from the inside out. I could feel the pull of his power—and the shift in Riichi. That's when something changed." She hesitated briefly, then continued. "I created a shield from my own energy. It didn't block the wrath—it absorbed it. Redirected it inward, into us, and softened it before it could break him."

She met Eileen's eyes. "We've named it a Protective Aura. It wasn't conscious. I just focused everything I had on protecting him, and it responded. It's tied to our bond, but it's not Radiant Surge. It's something new."

Riichi nodded. "Khan didn't detect the Aura—Reed's strike distracted him just in time. Without it, I don't think I would've recovered. That moment gave us the chance to retreat."

Oak added, "The barrier I cast was shattered almost instantly. That alone tells us how much control Khan has. He wasn't showing off—he was testing our limits."

Eileen took a breath, processing their words. "This new ability changes our defenses. If this Protective Aura can be accessed again, and controlled, it may be the key to keeping Riichi protected from future attacks."

Her eyes returned to Oak. "Anything further?"

His reply was quiet but pointed. "Now that Khan has seen what Takoda and Riichi are capable of, he'll escalate. This was only the first round."

Eileen nodded gravely before turning her attention to the next matter. "Nik, report on Fort Lawton."

Nik leaned back slightly, composed but focused. "The defensive ward is layered and adaptive. It repels intrusion with a shifting energy structure that reacts to magical interference. It's not static—it adjusts itself based on the type and source of pressure applied. It covers the entire outer edge of the ritual site like a net, and breaching it would trigger a response strong enough to alert anyone nearby."

Willow shifted forward, her expression thoughtful. "While testing the ward, I found something else. There's an area just beyond the outer edge of the defensive layers that didn't match the rest. The energy flow was off—subtle, but deliberate. It was disguised within the ward's movement, but it wasn't part of the ward."

Nik glanced at her, then added, "It's a separate magical structure. Hidden, but potent."

Willow nodded. "It's an entrapment spell, anchored into the ground like a snare. It's keyed specifically to Riichi and Takoda's energy signatures. If either of them steps into that vicinity, the magic activates. But it's not designed to immobilize them. It's emotional—deliberately crafted to provoke wrath in Riichi and pain in Takoda. The kind of pain that clouds focus and forces instinct to take over."

Oak looked up from his notes. "Khan wants them unbalanced. Not restrained—broken."

Willow's tone darkened slightly. "The trap doesn't lash out. It reaches inward."

Holly crossed her arms. "That kind of manipulation in the middle of a strike zone? It's not just a trap—it's psychological warfare."

Eileen's jaw tightened as she processed the information. "This changes the approach. The entrapment area is a direct threat to Riichi and Takoda. We'll need to revise the infiltration path to keep them clear of that zone."

She turned toward the magical map projected across the table. Its glowing symbols marked the edges of the ritual ward, the known anchor points, and now, a pulsing sigil representing the hidden entrapment. Her hand hovered over the area as she began outlining the updated strategy.

"Ward Neutralization Team," Eileen began, her tone crisp, "will consist of Nik, Ivy, Hazel, and Willow. Your priority is to dismantle or bypass the defensive ward and clear viable escape routes without triggering alerts."

Oak continued seamlessly from her side, scanning the map as he spoke. "Surveillance and Distraction: Reed, Holly, Ash, and Nik. Monitor patrols and apply pressure in waves to keep them off the inner yard. Hit fast, move often, and pull focus away from the anchor zones."

"Anchor Destruction Teams," Eileen resumed. "Team A—Windchime anchor: Ivy, Willow, and Birch. Team B—Spring anchor: Hazel, Oak, and Alder. Team C—Brazier anchor: Vine, Rowan, and Aislinn. Each team will move in simultaneously. Timing will be critical. No anchor can fall too far ahead of the others."

She paused, then looked directly at Riichi and Takoda. "Once the anchors are destroyed, the Typhoon Ritual Destruction Team will move in. If you two can perfect the magic Vine observed, we'll use it to strike the core directly. Willow will drain any residual energy to prevent magical rebound, and Oak will hold the perimeter to shield the team during the collapse."

She let that sink in before shifting the map slightly, zooming in on the entrapment zone. "This area is off-limits to Riichi and Takoda. We believe Khan set this trap to provoke an emotional collapse—fury, pain, helplessness. If triggered, it could override even Radiant Surge. Protective Aura will be essential during the final strike, but avoiding the trap entirely is our best option. Nik and Reed will lead a distraction at the far end to keep it inactive."

Her voice dropped into a sharper register. "If Riichi and Takoda are compromised, Rowan and Aislinn will assume combat command. Vine and Willow will target the ritual core with a substitute energy-based attack. Reed, Ivy, Oak, and Holly will lead the extraction. This contingency is not optional."

Silence followed, the finality of her words settling over them.

"Training today will split between two focuses," Oak said. "First, developing shielding techniques and countermeasures to protect Riichi and Takoda from emotional manipulation. Second, refining the strike ability Vine observed—testing its coordination between Riichi, Takoda, Rowan, and Aislinn. Everyone else will reinforce the mansion's defenses. If the Golden Dawn retaliates early, we meet them prepared."

Eileen's expression softened by a fraction, though her command didn't waver. "Yesterday's recon confirmed that time is up. The Day-Off Initiative has worked, but it ends now. Your focus must be absolute."

A subtle shift of warmth crossed her face as she added, "Tomorrow is the full moon. Ariel and Rain's Halloween party will go on as promised. This may be your last chance to relax before we go in. I expect everyone to attend, but as I said before, it is not mandatory."

Holly smirked, leaning back. "Ariel's already planning how to make it the party of the decade."

Willow chuckled. "She doesn't need to plan. It's Ariel. She's already staged the whole thing in her head."

Eileen let the humor breathe, her gaze momentarily soft before it returned to its usual sharp clarity. "Enjoy it. But remember—after tomorrow, we go to war."

She scanned the table one last time. "Any questions before we adjourn?"

None came.

Chairs pushed back quietly as the Fallen rose, their conversations shifting toward preparation. The room emptied not with dread, but with resolve.

They had their orders.

They had each other.

And the time had come to finish this.

★★★

The crisp morning air bit against Reed's bare arms as he sat on the back patio, his worn t-shirt doing little to keep the cold at bay. Frayed jeans and a beanie tugged low over his ears gave the illusion of warmth, but he wasn't out here for comfort. The mansion's grounds stretched quietly before him, wind teasing the trees, the rustle of leaves the only sound cutting through the stillness.

A steaming mug sat untouched on the table beside him, its warmth fading into the air. His gaze rested on the horizon, but his thoughts remained locked on the day before. The memory of Riichi's katana lingered—how it had felt in his hands, the way it responded as if it had always known him.

If I hadn't had that sword, what then?

The question burned. His fists were fast, sure—but not enough. Not for this.

He leaned forward, elbows on his knees, the cold seeping into his skin. A weapon wasn't a backup plan anymore. It was a requirement. But what?

Blades are too heavy. They'd mess with shadow-walking. Guns? Too loud, too flashy. I'm not a trigger guy.

His thoughts drifted to the quiet years in Alaska, when archery had been a way to pass time. He could still feel the draw of the string, the taut pause before release, the soft snap of an arrow finding its mark. That rhythm—silent, efficient, clean—resurfaced now with clarity.

A faint smile tugged at his mouth. *A bow and arrows. I can work with that.*

The back door creaked open behind him. Reed turned slightly as Ariel and Rain stepped onto the patio, bundled in sweaters and scarves, their breaths fogging the air. Spark bounded after them, his paws skittering on frost-slick stone.

"There you are!" Ariel's grin matched the color in her cheeks. "We've been looking everywhere."

Reed shifted in his chair, a smirk tugging at one corner of his mouth. "Didn't think I was hiding."

Rain exaggerated a shiver, pulling her coat tighter. "What are you doing out here? Aren't you freezing?"

Reed reached for his coffee, finally taking a sip. The heat hit his fingers and throat like a grounding current. "I'm from Alaska. Cold clears my head."

Ariel rolled her eyes, laughing. "Probably helps that your beanie's welded to your skull."

He raised a brow but didn't respond, letting the warmth of the coffee do the talking.

Rain's voice muffled behind her scarf. "It's your day off, remember? Can we talk about plans inside, where it's not arctic?"

Reed took one last look toward the tree line before rising. "Fine. Let's go."

Ariel bent down to scoop up Spark, who was still investigating a patch of frost at the edge of the steps. "C'mon, buddy. We're not freezing for fun today."

Spark squirmed in her arms, content and oblivious to the cold as she followed the others back into the house.

Inside, Reed dropped onto the couch and stretched his legs, the cushions sinking beneath him. He let his head fall back, breathing in the warmth. Ariel and Rain remained standing, bundled up like they'd just hiked through snow, their eyes glinting with barely restrained mischief.

Reed tilted his head at them. "Alright. What's the plan?"

Rain grinned. "Wrong question. It's *your* day off—you tell us the plan."

He didn't answer. Instead, he leaned back further, arms crossing loosely. His silence stretched just long enough to press the point. His brow arched as if daring them to keep waiting.

Ariel groaned. "Fine! Since you're basically Grizzly Adams, we figured something outdoors. Maybe paintball, ziplining, or hiking."

"No fishing," Rain added immediately. "Worms are gross."

"And no camping," Ariel said. "You only get one day."

Reed chuckled, low and quiet, then leaned forward. "Did you plan activities or excuses?"

Ariel flashed him a smug grin. "Both."

Reed's tone shifted, more practical. "Alright—one thing I choose, one thing you choose, and one we choose together. Deal?"

Rain looked to Ariel, who nodded.

"Okay," Rain said. "You go first."

"Archery."

Ariel tilted her head. "What's that?"

"Bow and arrows," Reed said, chuckling.

Rain sighed dramatically. "Fine. Our turn."

"Ziplining!" Ariel chimed, practically bouncing.

Rain nodded, clearly on board. Reed gave a slow nod. "Deal. For the last one, how about a fire pit in the backyard? Wood gathering included."

Rain's expression softened, her grin less playful, more sincere. "That actually sounds nice."

Ariel caught the shift in her friend's expression and lit up. "Only if we make s'mores."

Reed stood, stretching out his arms. "Then go grab your coats. Sounds like we need marshmallows and a bow."

They turned for the stairs, but halfway up, Ariel paused and spun around. "Wait—can we zipline first? The arch-thing and fire can be done here."

Reed crossed his arms, pretending to weigh the request. "Fine. As long as you don't bail on the 'arch-thing.'"

Rain raised an eyebrow. "Don't you need a coat?"

He shook his head. "I'm good."

Their laughter followed them upstairs, fading into the hallway.

Reed stayed behind a moment longer, arms folded as he glanced toward the window.

Today was a good day to pick up a bow again.

***

The mid-morning sun cast a golden sheen across the training grounds, its warmth brushing over the Fallen as they gathered in loose formation. Chatter was minimal, the air thick with focus. Muscles stretched, weapons checked, minds already shifting into battle mode. At the center, Oak stood with arms crossed, his sharp gaze sweeping across the group like a silent drillmaster.

"Today's focus is on neutralizing and protecting Riichi and Takoda without causing harm," he said, his voice cutting clean through the morning stillness. "If Khan captures them, we need a way to stop them fast—without doing more damage. You'll need coordination and control. Let's begin."

Riichi and Takoda stepped forward, the faint orange glow of the Radiant Surge pulsing subtly between them. A quiet display of unity. A warning not to underestimate them.

Oak's gaze lingered on them. "Use your abilities—individually and together. Make them work for it."

Riichi smirked and cracked his knuckles, his thoughts brushing against hers through their telepathic bond. *Let's make this interesting.*

Takoda rolled her eyes, her mouth tugging into a smirk. *Just don't overdo it. We don't want anyone unconscious.*

They'll be fine, Riichi replied, his tone dry. *Focus.*

"Takoda," Oak called. "You're first. Let's see how they handle you."

Takoda stepped forward, settling into her stance with practiced ease. Holly, Willow, and Vine stepped into the circle opposite her, their expressions a mix of determination and playful challenge.

Holly cracked a grin. "Come on, Takoda. Don't hold back—we can take it."

Takoda didn't respond. She moved, fast and fluid, dropping into Jujutsu form without a word.

Holly moved first, her form shimmering as illusions split from her figure and scattered across the clearing. They darted in and out like shadows, forcing Takoda to calculate each movement in real time.

She narrowed her eyes, watching for the micro-expressions Holly never could quite hide. In one swift turn, she struck the real one, sending her stumbling and breaking the illusion spell.

Willow advanced next, her hands weaving bursts of pulsing light that formed into narrow walls, boxing Takoda in. The barriers shrank rapidly.

Takoda darted left, then right, before lunging forward through the smallest gap. She caught Willow's wrist mid-cast and redirected the burst into the ground, sending a brief shockwave through the grass as Willow staggered backward.

Vine was already moving. Sparks scattered across the earth near her feet as he used electrokinesis to disrupt her footing. His approach was deliberate, probing, fast enough to force her to react but still holding back.

Takoda pivoted and caught his wrist mid-strike, twisting it into a controlled lock. He shifted his balance quickly, recovering before she could throw him, but her retreat was smooth, her focus unbroken.

Nice moves, Riichi murmured in her mind, watching from the edge. *Keep them guessing.*

Thanks, she replied. *Vine's fast. I'll have to adjust if he changes rhythm.*

Then don't give him the chance.

They pressed again, each round faster than the last. Takoda remained fluid, never allowing them to trap her. Her strikes stayed efficient—controlled enough to disarm, sharp enough to warn. When all three dropped back, breathing heavier but uninjured, Takoda stepped away, calm and composed.

Oak gave a single nod. "Good work. Riichi, you're up."

Riichi stepped forward, the faint glow of the Surge still clinging to his skin. The smirk was gone. In its place—focus.

Birch and Ash stepped into formation while Nik lingered on the edge, watching. Waiting.

Birch made the first move, charging with his usual brute force. Riichi waited until the last second and slipped aside, letting Birch's momentum carry him past.

Ash closed the gap instantly, strikes fast and controlled, but Riichi moved with precision, dodging each blow without losing ground.

Birch grinned as he turned. "Not bad, Riichi. Let's see how long you can keep it up."

"Longer than you," Riichi replied, dry as ever, with just enough bite for Birch to recognize the jab.

Nik joined the fray, sending bursts of contained energy to hem Riichi in. He darted between the strikes with sharp, fluid movements, his focus tightening as he timed each step. With a sudden burst of speed, he flipped over Birch, landing lightly behind him before the trap could close.

Don't get cocky. They're watching your rhythm, Takoda said, her voice slipping through his mind.

They're getting better, Riichi replied, his tone edged with respect—and confidence. *Close, but not close enough.*

The group adjusted quickly. Ash moved to cut off Riichi's path while Nik and Birch boxed him in. Riichi veered left, but Birch anticipated it, forcing him to halt. For a brief second, the trap held.

"That's what I want to see," Oak called, his voice firm. "Work together. Adapt."

He stepped forward, scanning the group. "Now let's see how you handle them together. Riichi, Takoda—synchronize and push back."

The orange pulse of the Radiant Surge intensified as their bond flared to life. They exchanged a single look, their movements syncing before Oak had even finished the command.

We'll split them, Takoda said. *I'll draw Vine and Willow. You take Birch and Rowan.*

Works for me, Riichi replied. *Let's keep them scrambling.*

They launched into motion. Takoda moved like a current through Vine and Willow's defenses, baiting them into overcommitting. She used Vine's own momentum to unbalance him and turned Willow's energy bursts aside with calculated footwork and quick redirection.

Riichi met Birch and Rowan head-on. His movements were deliberate, reading their patterns and cutting between them with effortless precision. He let Rowan's blade skim close just to angle Birch into a misstep, using every inch of space to control the engagement.

Rowan pulled back and moved to the sideline, tracking their movements. "They're talking telepathically," he muttered to Aislinn. "That's how they're staying ahead."

Aislinn's brow furrowed. "We'll need to disrupt their connection. Let's split them up."

Oak heard. "New plan!" he barked. "Break their synchronization. Isolate them."

The team shifted in response. Holly sent a gust slicing through the field, forcing Riichi and Takoda apart. Birch, Ash, and Rowan pressed in on Riichi while Willow and Vine turned their focus to Takoda.

Riichi ducked Rowan's strike, but Birch grabbed his arm mid-motion, locking his footing. Ash followed with a clean hit, and between the three of them, Riichi hit the ground hard enough to stay down.

Across the field, Takoda stumbled as Willow's shadows snagged her just long enough for Vine to unbalance her with a precise sweep. Holly crashed in with a tackle that grounded her completely.

Oak clapped once, his voice rising above the sounds of motion. "That's it. Control the field. Take the advantage."

For the first time during the session, Riichi and Takoda had been subdued. They stood slowly, the Radiant Surge dimming around them as they caught their breath.

Takoda glanced sideways, her voice dry. "Guess we're not unstoppable after all."

Riichi smirked. "Speak for yourself."

Oak stepped closer, his tone even. "This is why we train. If Khan turns either of you, the team has to respond. Now they can."

He motioned for everyone to gather. "Good work. Tomorrow, we build on this. Review where you struggled and adjust. The rest of you—reinforce the mansion. If Golden Dawn moves early, we meet them on our terms. Riichi, Takoda, Rowan, Aislinn—bonded pair training. You've got work to do."

The group began to disperse, some heading toward the mansion, others pausing to swap notes and rehash close calls.

At least they can stop us if it comes to that, Takoda said, her voice quiet in his mind.

Let's make sure it never does, Riichi replied, the edge of his smirk softening.

They exchanged a brief look before turning toward Rowan and Aislinn, ready to dive into the next phase.

★★★

The command post at Fort Lawton was steeped in silence. Not the hollow stillness of abandonment, but the kind that watched—quiet and coiled, waiting to strike. A faint red glow bled in through the windows from the typhoon ritual pulsing on the cliffside, its energy low and relentless, like a war drum miles out but closing in.

Kross lay on the narrow bed against the far wall, shirt clinging to his skin, damp from the fever that hadn't broken since last night. The veins along his arms and neck had darkened to shadow-black, branching like roots beneath his skin. They pulsed in time with the ritual outside, slow and steady—until the door creaked open.

Khan stepped inside.

The woman seated beside the bed—a younger recruit with too much softness in her eyes—stood quickly, her fingers still curled around a cloth she'd been using to wipe the sweat from Kross's brow.

Khan didn't spare her a glance. "Leave."

She hesitated. Kross didn't. "You heard him."

She vanished out the door without a word, and the room felt colder in her absence.

Kross forced himself upright, gritting his teeth against the tight pull of his muscles. "You planning on telling me what you did to me," he asked, "or is this another riddle?"

Khan studied him. "You drank my ichor. I told you it would change you."

"You didn't say it would feel like being rebuilt from the inside out."

"I didn't say it wouldn't." Khan stepped forward, his posture calm, his presence unnerving in its control. "It's already begun. You're adapting faster than expected."

Kross exhaled, but no fog left his lips. "I haven't slept. Haven't eaten. The cold doesn't touch me." His fingers flexed slowly, testing the strength humming just under his skin. "I can hear the recruits three rooms down. I can hear their heartbeats."

Khan gave the faintest nod. "You're stronger. Faster. Sharper in every way. When the time comes, you'll destabilize the bonded ones. The girl will feel the fracture. The boy will burn in it."

Khan studied Kross with cold calculation—measuring him.

"You'll be ready," he said at last, "when you stop clinging to what you were."

Kross met his gaze without flinching. "Then I'll be ready by the end of the day."

That earned him a rare nod of approval.

Kross's brow furrowed, but it didn't last. He leaned forward, bracing his forearms on his knees. "Girl!"

A moment later, the girl from earlier reappeared in the doorway. Kross didn't look at her.

"I just moved up the timeline. Tell the others to have everything completed in three days. Not five."

Khan stepped back toward the door, the faint hum of the ritual pulsing in rhythm with Kross's altered veins.

"Let them prepare," Khan said. "They'll think they're ready. Let them."

Kross sat motionless as the door closed behind him. The fever still burned beneath his skin, but he welcomed it now—like a forge finishing the last of the blade.

By nightfall, he would be sharpened.

And he would be waiting.

The training field had shifted into a quieter rhythm. The earlier bursts of clashing energy and shouted commands had faded, replaced by a purposeful focus. Riichi, Takoda, Rowan, and Aislinn stood in a loose circle near the edge of the field, faint scuffs in the dirt and discarded equipment marking the intensity of the previous drills.

Riichi crossed his arms, tone even. "Taking turns worked last time. Let's keep that up—one pair trains, the other coaches."

"Works for me," Aislinn said, rolling her shoulders and glancing toward Rowan. "We'll start."

Takoda nodded, tucking a loose strand of hair behind her ear. "Good. You've been syncing better, but now we fine-tune the Radiant Surge. Little shifts make a big impact."

With brief nods of agreement, Rowan and Aislinn moved toward the course while Riichi and Takoda stepped aside to observe.

The obstacle setup loomed ahead, a calculated mess of climbing walls, shifting barriers, and glowing magical constructs. Designed to mimic battlefield chaos, it threw everything at them—timed spells, phantom attackers, and sudden terrain changes.

Riichi spoke with the calm of someone who expected results. "Start with Radiant Surge activation—no physical contact. Maintain the blue hue."

Takoda's gaze narrowed as she studied the pair. "Don't rush it. If you lose sync, start over. Precision and consistency come first."

Rowan and Aislinn exchanged a nod before closing their eyes, reaching for the familiar thread that connected them. A soft glow swept across their skin, subtle and cool-toned, a clear signal their Surge was active—and in balance.

Slow and steady. Don't let it spike, Aislinn murmured into his mind.

Got it. Staying level, Rowan answered, his internal voice focused.

They moved in sync, weaving through the opening stretch of the course with seamless coordination. Every barrier was met with calculated responses, their shared thoughts streamlining each move.

Construct ahead. I'll take the right, you go low on the left, Rowan said.

On it.

Aislinn dropped into a slide beneath the construct's rotating base as Rowan vaulted over, landing a clean disabling strike. The shimmer of the magical projection scattered into fragments.

"Perfect timing," Takoda called out, the corner of her mouth lifting. "Keep your rhythm locked in."

Riichi gave a slight nod. "And watch the hue. No darkening."

They pressed on, navigating a series of ascending steps laced with timed bursts of energy. With each movement, their synchronization deepened, telepathic communication becoming second nature. By the time they reached the end of the track, their Surge still held steady—undisturbed and true.

The moment they stepped off the course and their glow faded, Aislinn turned toward the others. "Before we switch, I want to run through my teleportation once or twice. I've only done it with Rowan near me—not with him coming along."

Takoda nodded. "Go for it."

Rowan raised a brow. "You're not going to teleport us into a wall, right?"

Aislinn gave a dry look. "Not the plan."

She stepped in closer and reached for the strange, spiraling pull she was still getting used to. It surged beneath her skin, strange but familiar, and with a tight breath, she latched onto it. The air warped slightly—and with a sharp snap of displacement, both of them vanished.

They reappeared several feet away, slightly off balance. Rowan's foot dragged against the grass, but he caught himself.

"Still standing," he said, brushing a hand down the front of his shirt. "I'll count that as a win."

"Let me try once more," Aislinn said, already shifting her stance. "I want to test further distance."

This time, Rowan didn't even ask—he stepped in beside her and waited. Aislinn focused harder, reached deeper, and the field warped again as they disappeared a second time. When they reappeared farther across the training ground, she stumbled slightly, but Rowan caught her elbow.

"That one pulled more energy," she muttered.

Takoda's brows lifted as she crossed the field to meet them. "It'll get easier. Just make sure you don't try that mid-combat until it's second nature."

"Noted."

Aislinn gave Rowan a quick glance, then turned back toward Riichi and Takoda. "All right. Your turn."

After a brief reset, the pairs switched positions. Riichi and Takoda stepped into the center of the field while Rowan and Aislinn moved to the sidelines, ready to observe and coach.

Aislinn crossed her arms, her voice calm but firm. "Your goal today—perfect the sequence of that final strike. Don't rush it."

"Takoda, channel the right energy," Rowan added, his tone measured. "Riichi, precise control on the launch. It has to hit exactly where you aim."

Riichi unsheathed his katana, the blade catching the light as it gleamed faintly. Takoda stepped beside him, their Radiant Surge flaring softly between them. Without speaking, they exchanged a brief glance, their connection grounded and focused.

We've got this, Takoda said telepathically, her mental tone steady with resolve. *Courage first. Let's start with control.*

Agreed, Riichi replied, his focus unwavering. *Keep it steady.*

Takoda closed her eyes, drawing in a deep breath as she channeled courage into the blade. The katana began to hum, energy glowing along its edge in a stable, controlled pulse.

"Good start, Takoda," Aislinn called out. "Keep it stable."

Riichi adjusted his stance, lifting the katana as he calculated the arc. His grip tightened, ready to launch the energy.

"Eyes on the target, Riichi," Rowan instructed. "Don't let it veer."

With a smooth, deliberate swing, Riichi sent the pulse forward. It wavered slightly before striking, but the impact fizzled, weaker than intended.

"Not enough force," Takoda said, exhaling. "Let's try again."

This time, channel fear, Riichi said telepathically. *I'll tighten the aim.*

Takoda nodded, her expression shifting as she pulled from a different place. The energy surrounding the katana darkened, the hum deepening as fear threaded through it.

It's ready, she said. *Take it.*

Locked in, Riichi replied. *Let's go.*

His next swing was sharper, more refined. The pulse surged forward, slicing through the air with greater speed. It struck the target cleanly, sending out a compressed shockwave that distorted the space around it.

"Better," Rowan said with a nod. "That would destabilize a magical construct for sure."

Aislinn tilted her head, watching the energy fade. "Good disruption. Now focus on destructive force."

For their final attempt, Takoda tapped into anger, channeling it deliberately into the blade. The energy flared hotter, crackling with a charge that radiated heat and pressure.

It's different this time, Riichi said, his focus narrowing. *The katana—it feels like it's responding to it. Like it's been waiting for this.*

Because it has, Takoda replied, her mental voice calm but firm. *That blade was with you the night you died. You were consumed by anger then—but this isn't the same. You're in control now. You're not bound to wrath. You're choosing it—for the right reasons.*

The hum of the blade deepened, the glow steady and fierce.

Don't push the anger down, she added. *Use it. Let it sharpen the strike. Let it mean something.*

Fated, Riichi said after a beat, the word carrying weight between them. *That's what this is.*

Fated Blade, Takoda echoed. *Let's finish it.*

With absolute focus, Riichi moved. His swing cut through the air—measured, precise, and devastating. The energy erupted from the blade, slamming into the target with explosive force. It detonated on contact, the blast shattering the construct into fragments. The residual shockwave rippled outward before dissolving into the open air.

"That's it!" Rowan called, his voice rising with approval. "Perfect form."

"You nailed it," Aislinn said, a faint smile breaking through her usual seriousness. "What are you calling it?"

Riichi and Takoda exchanged a glance, the answer already shared between them.

"Fated Blade," they said in unison.

The four regrouped near the center of the field, their expressions tired but satisfied.

"About time we got it right," Riichi said, sheathing the katana with a faint smirk.

Takoda cast him a sidelong glance. "Let's just make sure we can do it again."

Rowan and Aislinn exchanged a glance, their shared look practical beneath the quiet pride.

"We'll be ready," Rowan said. "Same time tomorrow?"

"Wouldn't miss it," Riichi replied.

The pairs turned and made their way back toward the mansion, their bond strengthened and their technique finally locked into place.

As the bonded pairs headed inside, their momentum still humming from training, Reed, Ariel, and Rain strolled onto the grass, their voices buzzing with lingering excitement from the morning's zip-lining adventure. The air smelled faintly of grass and wood, the breeze carrying a sense of calm that contrasted with their animated energy.

Reed carried his new bow slung over one shoulder, the quiver resting lightly against his back. His grip on the bow was firm yet relaxed as he surveyed the open space. Finding a clear stretch of lawn, he moved to set up a makeshift target on the far side of the property, deliberately keeping their practice separate from the other training areas.

Ariel watched him curiously, arms crossed, a teasing smile tugging at her lips. "You really think you can just pick this up and be amazing right away?"

Reed turned, grin easy. "Not just think. I know."

Rain laughed softly, brushing her red hair back from her face. "No pressure or anything."

Reed chuckled, ignoring Ariel's skepticism as he positioned the target. The setup was simple—a hay bale with a red circle painted in the center—but it would do. After checking the distance, he stepped back and adjusted his stance, notching his first arrow with practiced ease.

He drew the bowstring, the familiar tension sparking an echo of long hours spent honing the skill. It felt distant, but not unfamiliar—like waking muscle memory. He exhaled and released.

The arrow grazed the edge of the hay bale, landing just outside the painted circle.

Ariel's grin widened, her tone smug. "You call that versatility?"

Reed smirked, already reaching for another arrow. "First shot doesn't count. Warming up."

This time, he adjusted his stance slightly, focus sharpening as he drew the string again. The arrow sailed clean and fast, striking the center of the target. His lips twitched in satisfaction as he reached for the next.

When the third arrow hit the bullseye again, Rain let out a quiet, impressed breath. "Wow, you're good at this."

Ariel hesitated before conceding, "Alright, fine. I'll admit it—you're not terrible."

Reed laughed, the sound low and confident. He released another arrow, the thud of its impact echoing as it joined the cluster near the center. "Not terrible? Try flawless."

The rhythm returned easily—draw, aim, release. Each arrow found its mark, forming a tight spread around the center until his quiver was empty.

Reed lowered the bow, surveying the target with a faint smile. "That'll do. I'm ready to take this into the field."

Rain stepped forward, brushing her hands against her sides. "Can I try?"

Reed handed her the bow with a nod. "Sure. Let's see what you've got."

He stepped in beside her, his voice calm but instructive. "Feet shoulder-width apart. Relax your grip. Pull back smoothly, like this."

Rain mirrored his movements with cautious focus. The arrow flew straight, embedding itself in the middle ring of the target.

Ariel groaned in mock irritation. "Oh, come on. Beginner's luck."

Rain lowered the bow, grinning. "Or maybe I'm just that good."

Reed chuckled, giving her shoulder a light pat. "Not bad. With some practice, you could give me a run for my money."

Ariel stepped forward, dramatically squaring her shoulders as she took the bow. "Alright, move over. Let me show you how it's done."

Her first shot missed entirely, the arrow landing in the grass several feet behind the target.

Rain burst into laughter, covering her mouth. "Wow. That's... unique."

Ariel huffed and shook her head. "Hey, the target moved. Totally not my fault."

Reed snorted, stepping in to help. "Sure it did. Here, try again—but this time, don't strangle the bow."

She shot him a playful glare but followed his adjustments. Her second shot hit the outer edge of the target.

Ariel grinned and lifted the bow like a trophy. "See? Progress."

They continued taking turns, with Reed occasionally stepping in to tweak her form. Despite her nonstop teasing, Ariel gradually improved, each arrow inching closer to center. When one finally landed in the middle ring, she threw her arms up.

"Finally! I hit it!"

"Not bad," Reed said, smirking as he took the bow back. "But don't quit your day job."

Ariel laughed, stepping aside as he resumed shooting.

Rain brushed her hands together and took a step back. "I'm going to head inside," she said lightly. "I need to warm up and grab some tea. I'll rejoin you later."

"You sure?" Ariel asked. "You'll miss all my stellar improvements."

Rain chuckled, waving over her shoulder as she walked toward the mansion. "Don't have too much fun without me."

Reed continued practicing after Rain left, his movements sharpening with each shot. Ariel leaned against a nearby tree, her expression more thoughtful than usual.

"You're really serious about this, huh?" she asked, her voice softer now.

Reed nodded, releasing another arrow. It struck dead center with a clean, satisfying thud. "If the encounter with Khan taught me anything, it's that I need to be ready for whatever's coming. Fists aren't always enough. This bow gives me an edge."

Ariel tilted her head slightly, her usual humor giving way to a quiet softness. "Well, you've got the aim to back it up. I think it's a good call."

Reed lowered the bow, a flicker of satisfaction crossing his face. "Thanks. Feels right. I'll take it with me next time."

They exchanged a small smile before he began packing up the gear. Ariel grabbed the quiver and passed it to him as they turned toward the mansion to look for Rain.

★★★

After coming in from archery practice with Ariel and Reed, Rain had stopped in the kitchen to make herself a cup of tea. The warmth of the mug in her hands had been comforting, but it hadn't chased away the lingering thoughts clouding her mind. Tea in hand, she made her way to the sitting room, drawn by the promise of its quiet solitude.

The sitting room was bathed in a warm, glowing light from the fire, its quiet crackle the only sound breaking the hush. Rain sat curled up in an armchair by the window, her knees drawn tightly to her chest, as if bracing against the storm of thought pressing in from all sides. Her gaze lingered on the gray sky beyond the glass—clouds rolled thick above the treetops, mirroring the unrest she couldn't shake.

This morning had been fun. Zip-lining with Ariel and Reed had made her feel, just for a little while, like she belonged—like she could match their pace, keep up with their spark. But now, just knowing they were outside—training, laughing, fitting in so easily—made that fleeting connection feel farther away again.

She'd promised to rejoin them soon, but right now, she couldn't. The sense of inadequacy clung too tightly. Watching everyone throw themselves into relentless training, perfecting techniques, carrying themselves with unshakable confidence—it only reminded her of how far behind she felt.

The soft creak of the door pulled her back to the room. She turned, startled, and found Nik standing in the doorway. One hand rested on the frame, his stance uncertain. His eyes scanned her face, catching the tension she hadn't managed to hide. *Something's wrong.*

"Hey," he said softly. The greeting was quiet, awkward in a way that made it feel unpolished—and oddly sincere.

Rain offered a small smile, brushing her fingers through her hair. "Hi, Nik."

He hesitated. *Should I try to help?* For a moment, it seemed like he might retreat and leave her to the quiet, but instead, he stepped inside, his movements careful. "Uh... mind if I sit?"

He wants to stay? She nodded toward the chair across from her. "Go ahead."

Nik crossed the room and lowered himself into the seat. He sat upright at first, then leaned forward, resting his elbows on his knees. His eyes flicked briefly to the fire before returning to her.

"You, uh, look like you've got a lot on your mind," he said after a moment, his voice gentle, if a bit unsure.

Rain lowered her gaze, her fingers twisting the edge of her sweater. "I'm fine. Just needed a break."

Nik didn't answer right away. He didn't push. He just sat with her, letting the quiet settle between them—not to fill it, but to leave space if she wanted to speak. His presence was unintrusive but grounding, like a door left open without expectation.

Just talk to him, Rain thought. *It might help. Besides, Nik's not the type to say anything to anyone.* Eventually, she exhaled, the sound barely audible but heavy with hesitation. "I've been hanging out with Ariel and Reed today," she said, voice quiet. "We went zip-lining this morning. Now they're outside practicing archery. I told them I'd join them again soon, but..."

She trailed off. Her shrug was subtle, barely more than a breath. Her eyes returned to the window. "I guess I just needed some time. Watching everyone train, seeing how strong and capable they are—it's amazing. But also kind of crushing. It makes me feel like I don't belong. Like I'm just... there."

The last word hovered in the air, her embarrassment prickling as she kept her eyes away from his.

Nik's expression changed, his brow tightening as if the words struck deeper than she realized. "I don't think that's true," he said, quiet but certain.

Rain turned to him, disbelief clear in the line of her shoulders. "Really? Because it feels pretty true to me."

He shifted, his posture loosening slightly as he leaned back. His eyes flicked toward the firelight again before returning to hers. "You're not just there, Rain. You're part of this, even if it doesn't feel like it."

Her tone softened, but the doubt remained. "How? I'm not fighting. I'm not planning missions or leading anything. I don't do anything that matters."

Nik didn't look away. His words came carefully, without hesitation. "You remind us why we're fighting. You keep this place from turning into nothing but battle prep and stress. That matters. A lot."

Rain blinked. Her hands stilled in her lap, the quiet surprise in her expression breaking through the fog she'd wrapped around herself. "You really think that?"

He shrugged, a faint smile ghosting across his lips. "Yeah. You're not on the sidelines, Rain. You're the one holding the threads between everyone when things start pulling apart."

Her body eased slightly, her fingers relaxing where they'd been clenched in the fabric of her sleeve. For the first time since he entered, she met his gaze fully, searching it. There was no teasing, no posturing— ...just a rare calm, unguarded stillness in the way he looked at her.

"I didn't think you noticed things like that," she said, the quiet honesty in her voice edged with surprise.

Nik let out a quiet laugh, low and a little sheepish. "I notice more than people think."

Their eyes held, the space between them tinged with an unspoken pull—quiet tension, warm and undefined. Rain felt her cheeks heat, and she brushed her hair back, breaking the moment.

"Thanks, Nik," she said softly. "I needed that."

He nodded, leaning forward again with his elbows on his knees. "Anytime."

Nik cleared his throat and glanced toward the window, his expression shifting just enough to ease the moment's weight. "You know," he said, voice a little more casual, "Eileen mentioned something today at the meeting. Figured you might want to hear it."

Rain arched a brow, curiosity breaking through her earlier haze. "What is it?"

A faint smirk tugged at one corner of his mouth. "The Halloween party. It's tomorrow night."

Her eyebrows lifted, caught between amusement and surprise. "Seriously? She actually talked about the party?"

Nik nodded, leaning back slightly. "Yeah. And get this—she almost smiled. Tried to hide it, but I saw it."

Rain laughed, light and genuine. "Eileen? Smiling? I wish I could've seen that."

"Me too," Nik said, the warmth in his voice rare but real. "Everyone's looking forward to it. Even her."

Rain shook her head, laughter still slipping through. "Now I'm looking forward to it even more."

She stood and smoothed her sweater, glancing toward the door. "Speaking of relaxing... Ariel, Reed, and I are making a fire out by the pit tonight. Marshmallows and all. You should come."

Nik hesitated, the instinct to decline flashing across his expression. His shoulders tensed for just a second. "I don't know. Big group stuff isn't really my thing."

"It's just the three of us," Rain said, tilting her head with a soft smile. "And you, if you show up. No pressure. I'll even save you a marshmallow."

He let out a quiet huff of a laugh, expression softening. "Alright. I'll think about it."

Rain's smile grew as she turned for the door. "That's basically a yes. See you out there, Nik."

As her footsteps faded down the hall, Nik leaned back in his chair. His gaze lingered on the doorway, his thoughts trailing behind her. Despite himself, a small smile tugged at his lips, the echo of her laughter still warm in the quiet room.

As the day wore on, the sun dipped low in the sky, casting long shadows across the mansion grounds. The hum of activity gradually quieted as the Fallen began retreating to their rooms, faint goodnights echoing through the hallways. Outside, the golden light faded into twilight, and the crisp autumn air deepened into a quiet chill.

Out back, Reed, Ariel, and Rain stepped onto the lawn with supplies in hand. Reed crouched beside the firepit, arranging kindling into a neat stack. With a few firm strikes of a match, he coaxed the flames to life, watching as they caught and climbed steadily upward.

Ariel set a tray of marshmallows, chocolate, and graham crackers on one of the stone benches. "This is a pro-level setup," she said, surveying the display with mock pride.

Rain followed with a tray of steaming mugs, carefully balancing them as she approached the fire. "If we're pro-level, then Reed's about to give us a very amateur marshmallow performance," she teased, setting the tray down next to the other.

Reed straightened and brushed off his hands as the fire crackled higher. "Amateur? Please. You're about to witness marshmallow greatness."

They settled onto the benches as the flames cast a warm glow across the yard, light dancing across their faces. Laughter and easy conversation carried into the evening, mingling with the soft hiss of burning wood.

A short while later, Rain glanced up at the sound of approaching footsteps. Nik emerged from the shadows near the mansion, hands tucked into his jacket pockets as he crossed the lawn toward them.

"You made it!" Rain called, her smile brightening at the sight of him.

Nik slowed, his eyes scanning the fire and those gathered around it. His steps paused for a breath, but when he caught Rain's inviting smile, he moved closer. "Yeah," he said, keeping it casual— though the undercurrent in his voice hinted at more.

Ariel nudged Reed, grinning. "Look who decided to join the fun."

Reed gestured toward the firepit with theatrical flair. "Grab a seat, Nik. The marshmallow artistry is about to begin."

Nik let out a quiet huff of amusement and sat beside Rain. She handed him a mug of cocoa, their fingers brushing as he took it.

"Perfect timing," she said with a grin. "Reed's just getting warmed up."

Reed cast her a dry look but crouched near the fire, marshmallow stick in hand. The warmth wrapped around the group, their laughter drifting with the smoke into the evening air. As the night deepened, the camaraderie grew unspoken but easy, settling among them beneath the glow of the firelight.

Later, the pit burned low but steady, flames casting a soft shimmer across the backyard. Reed leaned forward, holding his marshmallow stick like it was a test of focus and will. Beside him, Ariel's laughter rang out as she offered a steady stream of commentary.

"That's too close to the flame," she said, narrowing her eyes at his handiwork. "You're going to torch it, and then it's just going to be sad."

"I know what I'm doing," Reed muttered with exaggerated patience, carefully rotating the marshmallow as if it were a delicate science experiment.

Across from them, Rain and Nik sat shoulder to shoulder on the opposite bench. Their conversation had slipped into a quieter rhythm, their voices low. Rain cradled her mug, the rising steam softening the air between them. She chimed in now and then with a quiet laugh at Reed and Ariel's antics, while Nik—still reserved—seemed more at ease, the firelight and company gently peeling back his usual guarded edge.

Inside, the mansion's front door opened with a soft creak as Oak stepped through, his boots leaving faint traces of dust from the Fort Lawton mission. Hazel, Vine, and Ash followed behind, their postures shaped by fatigue and quiet accomplishment.

"I'll report to Eileen," Oak said over his shoulder, tone brisk. "You three—go unwind. You've earned it."

He moved down the hallway without waiting for a response. Hazel stretched her arms overhead, her shoulders cracking as she moved toward the glass doors. The glow from outside drew her in, the fire's amber light casting long ribbons across the lawn.

"Looks like they're having fun," Hazel murmured, warmth threading through her voice. "Let's go see if there's room for a few more."

Ash gave a faint nod, the corners of his mouth lifting. "Marshmallows sound pretty good right now."

They turned toward the back patio, but Vine lingered, his steps slowing. His eyes caught on the group outside—more specifically, on Ariel and Reed. Their laughter rose above the fire, bright and unguarded, as Reed lifted his marshmallow stick with a flourish.

"Perfectly toasted," Reed declared, grinning. "Look at that. Absolute marshmallow mastery."

Ariel snorted, leaning in to examine it. "Perfectly toasted? That's your word for this disaster?"

Reed opened his mouth to reply, but before he could, Ariel leaned in and gave a quick puff of air to cool the charred marshmallow. With a mischievous glint, she plucked it off his stick and smashed it onto his face.

"There," she said with a laugh. "Now it's perfect."

The group erupted around them, laughter filling the night as Reed froze, the marshmallow plastered across his nose. With exaggerated calm, he peeled it off and popped it into his mouth.

"Delicious," he said, voice muffled.

Ariel leaned in, still grinning, and wiped a smear from his cheek with her thumb. "Hold still. You're a mess."

Then, without missing a beat, she shoved her marshmallow-covered fingers toward his mouth. "Take it off."

Reed rolled his eyes but obliged, his grin widening as he complied. Laughter rippled again—Rain nearly spilled her tea doubling over, and even Nik gave a quiet chuckle, his reserve softened by the moment.

From just inside the patio, Vine stiffened. His jaw tightened, eyes narrowing as he watched Ariel laugh—unguarded, unbothered—while Reed leaned comfortably into the moment. It was harmless, clearly playful, yet the ease between them struck harder than it should have. That bright, effortless affection lodged beneath his ribs like a splinter he couldn't ignore.

Hazel paused at the patio door and glanced over her shoulder. "You coming?"

Vine didn't answer at first. His eyes lingered on the firepit, then drifted toward Ariel again, her smile still lit by the firelight. He looked away.

"No," he said flatly. "Marshmallows aren't really my thing. I'm heading upstairs."

Hazel frowned, watching him for a second longer. There was an edge to his voice she didn't comment on, but it gave her pause. "Alright," she said. "See you tomorrow."

As Hazel and Ash stepped outside, Vine turned and moved up the stairs, the laughter below trailing behind him—distant, but unmistakable.

The sound of the back door opening turned a few heads. Ariel glanced up, her grin returning as Hazel and Ash stepped into view.

"Look who decided to join the fun!" she called.

Hazel chuckled and dropped into the seat beside her. "It was either this or crash immediately. And honestly? Marshmallows sounded better."

Ash sat near Reed and grabbed a marshmallow stick, lifting the bag with a grin. "Any left, or did Reed burn them all?"

Reed scoffed as he held up his latest creation. "Excuse me. I've mastered the art."

Ariel rolled her eyes. "You mean you've mastered incineration."

Laughter followed as Ash loaded a marshmallow onto his stick. Hazel rotated hers with practiced care, the fire's glow catching in her eyes. After a moment, Ariel glanced toward the mansion, her brow furrowing slightly.

"Wasn't Vine with you?"

Hazel nodded, eyes still on her marshmallow. "Yeah, but he said he was heading to bed. Claimed marshmallows weren't his thing."

Ariel's frown deepened. Her eyes drifted toward the darkened windows of the house. "Huh."

Rain tilted her head, voice quiet. "Maybe he's just tired. Long day."

Ariel nodded slowly, but her expression didn't ease. She stayed quiet, her thoughts lingering longer than they should have. Reed nudged her arm gently, drawing her back.

"Hey, you're up. Let's see if you can manage not to torch this one."

Ariel blinked, then huffed a soft laugh as she reached for another marshmallow. Her smile returned, but it carried an edge of distraction.

The fire crackled, casting long streaks of gold across the group as their laughter picked up again. Across from her, Hazel smiled as Ash yelped—his marshmallow igniting in a flash of flame. Reed groaned, shaking his head.

On the opposite bench, Rain leaned toward Nik, her voice teasing. "You've got a suspiciously perfect technique. I don't trust it."

Nik smirked faintly. "It's not suspicious. It's skill."

Ariel's eyes drifted back to the house. Her smile lingered, soft but distant, as her thoughts returned to Vine. His abrupt retreat didn't sit right, though she couldn't name exactly why.

Still, she let the moment hold. The fire's warmth pressed close, and the comfort of the others gradually pulled her back in. Whatever she sensed from Vine—it could wait.

The firepit was glowing low when Ariel slipped away, leaving the soft hum of laughter and conversation behind her. Spark trotted eagerly at her side, his tail wagging as though he shared her sense of purpose. In her hand, she carried the s'more she had carefully toasted earlier—gooey marshmallow, melted chocolate, and just enough crunch from the graham crackers.

Reaching Vine's door, she knocked softly, the sound tentative in the quiet hallway. "Vine?" she called, her tone light but steady.

There was a pause, followed by faint movement from within. The door opened just enough for Vine to appear, his sharp eyes landing on Spark's bouncing excitement and the s'more in Ariel's hand. Without a word, he stepped back, leaving the door ajar as an unspoken invitation.

Ariel smiled and stepped inside, Spark darting past her to sniff curiously at the unfamiliar space. "I come bearing gifts," she announced, holding up the s'more like a peace offering.

Vine arched a brow, crossing his arms as he leaned against the doorframe. "Gifts?" he echoed.

"S'mores," Ariel said with mock seriousness. "And a chance to prove you wrong. You can't possibly hate marshmallows."

Vine huffed softly, his tone dry. "I can. And I do."

Ariel tilted her head, her grin widening. "You're just saying that because you've never had one made by me." She placed the s'more on his desk, her playful challenge lingering between them.

Vine didn't move, his arms still crossed. "I'll pass."

"Seriously?" Ariel's eyes narrowed. "You won't even try it?"

"No," he said simply, though a faint thread of amusement edged his voice. "They're sticky and overly sweet. Not my thing."

Ariel sighed dramatically and scooped the s'more back up. "Fine. More for me, but I'm still counting this as a win. Spark agrees with me, by the way."

At his name, Spark barked softly and circled Vine's legs. Vine crouched, his features softening as he ran a hand over the pup's fur.

Ariel watched him for a moment, her teasing quieting. "You didn't come out to the firepit," she said gently. "Was it the marshmallows, or something else?"

Vine's hand stilled, his gaze drifting to the window. "It wasn't the marshmallows," he said after a pause, his voice low but certain.

Ariel tilted her head, her curiosity clear but careful. "Then what kept you?"

He didn't answer immediately. The quiet stretched between them, unhurried but heavy with the weight of what he didn't say. At last, he met her eyes. "Sometimes... things hit harder than you expect," he said. "You see something, and it sticks, even when you don't want it to."

Her brows pulled together slightly, her expression softening. "Like what?"

Vine's gaze flicked back to the window. His jaw tightened, but his voice lost its usual edge. "Doesn't matter. It's my problem to sort out."

Ariel nodded slowly, recognizing the line he was drawing but not taking it personally. "Sometimes things stick for a reason," she said quietly. "But if you ever want to talk it through... I'm here."

Vine's posture eased, just slightly. "Thanks," he said, the word quiet but sincere.

They let the silence sit for a moment, not uncomfortable, just full of things left unsaid. Spark let out a soft bark, nosing at Vine's hand, and Ariel brightened again.

"Speaking of distractions," she said, glancing at the puppy, "he's been dying to play. Do you have anything we could turn into a toy?"

Vine stood, scanned the room, and pulled a plain towel from a drawer. He tied two firm knots at either end and handed it to her.

"Perfect," Ariel said, crouching down as she dangled the toy. Spark lunged with a triumphant growl, grabbing it with all the fierceness his little frame could muster.

Ariel laughed as she tugged gently. "He's stronger than he looks!"

Vine crouched beside her, his expression softening again as he gripped the other end. "Let's see how much fight he really has."

Together, they played tug-of-war with Spark, the puppy growling dramatically as his feet skidded along the floor. Ariel's laughter filled the room, and even Vine's lips curved faintly as they let Spark win.

The puppy collapsed onto the rug, panting with pride, tail wagging. Ariel sat back and brushed a lock of hair from her face.

"Told you he'd love it," she said, tossing Vine a playful look.

"You were right," he replied, his tone softer than usual.

Ariel smirked. "Bet you didn't think you'd end your night making dog toys."

"Not exactly." He stood, leaning back against the desk.

She rose, brushing off her jeans. "Next time we build a fire, you should come out," she said casually. "Even if marshmallows aren't your thing, the fire's nice. And so is the company."

He met her eyes, a flicker of conflicted emotion passing just beneath the surface. "Maybe," he said after a pause.

Ariel smiled and stepped closer, pressing a light kiss to his cheek. "Goodnight, Vine," she said, her voice warm.

"Goodnight," he answered, steady but quieter this time.

At the door, she glanced over her shoulder with a soft grin. "And I still think you'd like marshmallows if you gave them a chance."

Vine huffed as the door clicked shut behind her. The room fell quiet. His eyes drifted to the towel toy on the floor... then to the untouched s'more still sitting on his desk.

He crossed the room and picked up the s'more, studying it for a moment before setting it back down. Ariel's laughter still echoed faintly in the air—light and impossible to ignore.

The irritation from earlier tugged at him again, sharper than it should've been.

It shouldn't have mattered. But it did.

And it wasn't just that.

Lately, *everything* hit harder—emotions sharper, harder to shake.

He rubbed his hands together, frowning toward the window.

Whatever this was...

he needed to get a handle on it.

Before it got worse.

The conference room was already full when Riichi and Takoda stepped inside. Maps covered the table, marked with charcoal circles and handwritten notes, while a projection of Fort Lawton hovered above it. A forgotten mug of coffee teetered near the edge. No one spoke—the tension was loud enough.

Eileen stood at the head of the table, composed but unyielding. "This is our final chance to stop the Golden Dawn," she said. "And we all know what happens if we fail."

She turned to the recon team—Vine, Ash, Oak, Hazel—and gave a nod. "Let's hear it."

Vine braced a hand beside the projected map. "The ward's layered. If we break it in the wrong order, we'll either trap ourselves or supercharge their spell. These are the weak points, but it'll take coordination."

Ash pointed to three anchor spots. "They're using terrain—trees, cliffs, chokeholds—to hide ambushes. They know how to funnel us."

Oak added, "Subtle traps. A branch here, moss there—rigged with spells. Step wrong, and you're boxed in."

Hazel crossed her arms. "The ritual's nearly ready. By tomorrow night, their defenses will be sealed. This is our shot."

Silence fell.

Eileen stepped forward. "The mission is tomorrow night. We dismantle the ward, destroy the anchors, and stop the ritual before it completes." She scanned the room. "Teams are split by specialty. We need speed, precision, and control."

She moved through assignments without pause. "If Riichi and Takoda are compromised, Rowan and Aislinn lead the combat team. Vine and Willow, you're on the core. The rest—disruption and retrieval. No improvising. There won't be another chance."

She let that settle. "No recon tonight. Rest. Train. We need everything you've got tomorrow."

Nods followed. Rowan's jaw locked. Aislinn met his tension with quiet resolve. Nik leaned forward, brow drawn—already calculating.

"Training covers three things," Eileen said. "Golden Dawn tactics. Demon defense. And protecting Riichi and Takoda."

That last part made Rowan shift. Across the room, Takoda met his glance.

Eileen's tone dipped. "Use tonight's party. It's your break. Take it."

A few tired smiles broke through—Willow, Holly, even Reed, who muttered something about "parties before apocalypses," drawing a quiet snort from down the table. Riichi glanced at Takoda. She nodded once.

Before anyone could leave, Riichi cleared his throat. "One update."

Eileen looked over.

"Our bonded strike is complete," he said.

Takoda stepped in. "Fully refined. Ready for deployment. We're calling it *Fated Blade*."

Reed raised a brow. Rowan gave a curt nod. Even Eileen's expression shifted—barely—but it did.

"Well done," she said. "That could be what turns the tide."

Chairs scraped back. Some headed toward training, others to breakfast or the courtyard. Rowan and Aislinn stayed behind, voices low. Vine lingered at the door, adjusting his cuff.

Riichi and Takoda stayed at the table a moment longer. No words. Just certainty.

At the front, Eileen remained still, her fingertips brushing the map's edge. For a heartbeat, her mask slipped—uncertainty flickering beneath her resolve.

Then it vanished.

Tomorrow was already coming.

The Fallen gathered on the training grounds, their steps deliberate beneath the overcast sky. The ward shimmered faintly at the property's edge, magic pulsing just beneath the surface. Oak stood at the center of the field, arms crossed, his presence commanding the group's focus.

Holly conjured a figure styled after a Golden Dawn soldier, watching it pace before spawning a small formation. Ivy unsheathed her twin blades, testing their edges with clean, controlled movements. Reed adjusted his bowstring without a word. Spark bolted across the grass until Ariel gave a low whistle—he doubled back immediately, tongue lolling.

Oak stepped forward. "The Golden Dawn rely on formation tactics. Magic, terrain, and coordination. They'll expect us to be reckless. We won't be."

The first drill began without hesitation. Holly's conjured soldiers split into formations. Riichi, Rowan, Aislinn, and Reed moved in unison—Reed vanished and reappeared mid-strike, loosing arrows with sharp precision. Riichi sliced down one target with seamless control. Rowan's strikes landed hard, each one carrying an edge that wasn't just focus.

On the defensive side, Birch, Vine, and Ash held the line. Vine's electrokinesis crackled around his fingers as he shifted their stance with a few clipped commands, tightening their rhythm and closing gaps without wasting movement.

Then came the next wave—Golden Dawn mimicry dissolved, replaced by grotesque demon constructs shaped from raw magic. "Demons don't follow rules," Oak warned. "Instinct. Speed. Think faster."

Ivy moved like water—no flash, no flourish. She manipulated the field itself with clean, unrelenting control. The ground bent subtly beneath her steps, momentum snapping back on her terms as she took down each figure with ruthless precision.

Takoda and Riichi moved nearby, their bond sharpening every motion. When Takoda misjudged a strike and fell out of sync, Riichi caught her eye. One nod. They fell back into rhythm instantly.

Ash and Rowan clashed mid-field. Rowan's technique remained brutal and exacting, but frustration simmered beneath the surface. Reed maneuvered around them with lithe precision, using terrain and movement like weapons.

Oak raised a hand. "If we lose them, we lose everything."

At the center of the field, Holly reshaped her projection into a new scenario—Riichi and Takoda bound inside a ritual ring, constructs forming around them. The others rotated through in tactical teams.

Rowan, Aislinn, and Reed took the front. Rowan surged forward with blistering force, his strikes clean and punishing. Aislinn stayed just behind him, shielding their forward push. Reed flanked left, picking off enemies before they reached the circle.

Birch, Ivy, and Holly dismantled the magical constraints. Ivy's blades sliced through unstable magic fields while Birch broke the ground traps with his spinning chakrams. Holly shifted the tempo again, testing their adaptability.

Behind them, Vine and Willow covered from range—lightning burst from Vine's fingertips, bursting into enemy ranks with pinpoint aim. Willow's own spells amplified the impact. Even Rowan offered a short nod at the coordination.

Sparring rounds followed. Oak split them into pairs to refine their edge.

Rowan squared off against Vine. His strikes hit hard, almost goading. Vine countered with cool efficiency, until one blow clipped his shoulder. He adjusted without comment and continued. *What's his issue?*

Aislinn and Takoda took on Ivy. Her strength forced them into creative footwork, forcing Ivy to shift her own tactics to match their seamless teamwork.

Riichi and Reed's spar was swift and surgical—Reed vanished mid-lunge and reappeared above, firing down. Riichi met him mid-spin, blade arcing into a block so fast it sang in the air.

When the drills ended, Oak addressed them again. "You're getting sharper. Keep pushing. Tomorrow doesn't care how tired we are."

They began to scatter—some to water, others toward gear—exhaustion clear but resolve sharper than ever.

Rowan lingered at the edge, his eyes on Riichi and Takoda, unreadable. Vine passed him briefly, adjusting a cuff with practiced calm, but his glance toward Rowan didn't go unnoticed.

Oak remained behind as the field emptied, watching the tree line like it might strike first.

Takoda clapped her hands, cutting through the lingering stillness. "Alright, enough brooding. We've got cookies to bake, and we're already behind!"

Groans followed, but so did a few reluctant chuckles. Holly brushed flour from her sleeve and grinned. "You heard her! Trade your war faces for cookie cutters—let's move!"

The group filed into the mansion, shaking off the heaviness of the day. The kitchen was warm and sweet with the scent of butter and vanilla. Bowls of dough lined the counter beside trays of cutters and scattered jars of sprinkles. Spark darted between feet, tail wagging like he knew he belonged in the center of the action.

Takoda didn't miss a beat. "Rain, sugar. Willow, Ivy—start rolling the dough. Let's go."

Holly held up a bat-shaped cutter like a relic. "Spooky enough, or should we go full skeleton?"

"Just pick one," Takoda said, smirking. "We're making cookies, not redecorating the underworld."

Rain measured sugar with accuracy. Ivy bumped Willow's shoulder. "As exact as ever."

"Dough-rolling dream team," Willow replied, grinning as they worked side by side.

At the far end, Hazel shaped ghost cookies with quiet focus, pausing only to offer advice. "Chill the dough first—it'll keep the shape better."

Spark sniffed near her boots, nose to the ground. Rain scooped him up. "Nice try, buddy. No cookies for you."

Then Ariel burst through the doorway, Aislinn trailing behind. "Look who we convinced to join us!"

Eileen followed, reluctant but visibly softened by the wave of cheers.

"Eileen in the kitchen?" Holly's grin widened. "Apocalypse confirmed."

Hazel smiled. "We've been saying you need a break. You finally listened."

Eileen waved off the teasing, but the warmth reached her. Ariel handed her a rolling pin with a theatrical bow. "Observe while helping."

Laughter spread as Holly flicked flour at Takoda, earning a mock-glare. Rain and Ariel crouched over a tray, debating decorations.

"This one's genius," Rain declared, showing off a jack-o'-lantern face.

"Or cursed," Ariel countered, adding a crooked mustache.

Eileen hesitated at the counter, then quietly began decorating a pumpkin cookie. Willow watched her with a smirk. "If you're that careful with cookies, no wonder you're a perfectionist during missions."

Eileen laughed—a soft, surprised sound that earned smiles across the room.

When the last tray cooled, they all stepped back to admire their work. The counter was filled with cookies that reflected each person's personality—some whimsical, some perfect, some wonderfully chaotic.

Eileen stood slightly apart, her gaze trailing over the laughter and ease in the room. For the first time in days, the world outside felt far away.

She turned to Ariel and Aislinn, her voice softer than usual. "Thank you—for insisting I join. I didn't realize how much I needed this."

Aislinn placed a hand on her arm. "You never do. That's why you have us."

Ariel grinned. "What are daughters for, right?"

The word lingered between them. Unspoken, but heard.

Aislinn and Ariel exchanged a glance, their bond settling into quiet, unshakable trust. Ariel bumped her shoulder with a smirk. "See? Teamwork. We make a good pair."

"Until you start another flour fight," Aislinn muttered, drawing laughter again.

As it faded, Rain brushed stray sprinkles from her sweater and glanced at the clock. "We're cutting it close."

Ariel, perched on a stool, waved her off. "Relax. The party doesn't start itself—we start the party."

Takoda wiped her hands on a towel and gave the trays one last inspection. "They'll cool in time. Let's finish setting up before the guests arrive."

The group moved with cheerful efficiency, carrying trays of cookies and last-minute decorations to the wide room at the end of the hall. Spark trotted behind them, his orange-and-black bandana bouncing like a tiny banner.

By the time everything was in place, the transformation was complete. Floating candles hovered above, casting shifting glows across the walls. Ghostly projections drifted through the space, murmuring laughter and whispers.

Near the refreshments table, Ariel tapped the talking skeleton on the skull. "Don't embarrass me in front of the guests," she warned, grinning as it fired off one of her preloaded punchlines.

At the enchanted doorway, Rain stood still, her glowing wreath scattering soft prisms across the floor. "It's perfect," she murmured, taking in the candlelight, glowing pumpkins, and the cobwebs strung like gossamer across the chandeliers.

Ariel joined her with a satisfied nudge. "We're perfect. Let's make it official."

The portal flared open, magic coiling at the edges with a welcoming hum.

Spark barked once. Rain crouched to ruffle his ears. "You're right," she said, smiling. "It's time."

Footsteps echoed down the hall. Ariel tossed a glittery jacket over her shoulder. "Places, everyone," she said, mock-commanding. "Let the Halloween extravaganza begin."

The portal shimmered—and Takoda and Riichi stepped through.

Takoda's black kimono shimmered with crimson flowers that shifted as she moved. Riichi's red-and-gold dragon armor caught the candlelight in molten flashes.

"Look at you two!" Ariel called. "Takoda, you're basically on fire. Riichi, I hope you can keep up."

Takoda smiled, casting a look his way. "He picked it."

"It suits her," Riichi said quietly, but without hesitation.

Ariel waved them in. "Cookies left, judgmental skeleton right. He's already gone rogue."

Reed stepped through next, silver embroidery glinting along his rogue's coat. The hilt of his dagger glowed faintly.

Rain beamed. "You look like you just walked out of a quest."

Reed straightened his cuffs. "Only if the quest includes food and no skeleton puns."

Ariel smirked. "Wrong party."

Aislinn and Rowan followed. Her vampire queen costume shimmered like starlight; his hunter ensemble was all shadow and crossbow.

Ariel offered a theatrical bow. "Aislinn, even more intimidating than usual."

Rowan arched a brow. "And me?"

"You're keeping up," Aislinn said smoothly, linking her arm through his.

Next came Vine, his warlock cloak trailing behind him. Blue lightning sparked along the trim, his staff pulsing with restrained power.

"You clean up nice, warlock," Ariel teased.

Vine's expression stayed dry. "Careful, Trouble. You're starting to sound sincere."

Before she could fire back, Alder emerged in silver-etched rune armor, the markings alive with faint movement.

Near the skeleton, Hazel's voice rang out through its speaker. "Nice runes. Think they can conjure a better playlist?"

Alder laughed. "Only if you've got a summoning circle for a DJ."

Nik appeared next, stepping through the portal with quiet ease. His leaf-stitched tunic shimmered in soft golds and greens, the fabric shifting like sunlight through trees.

Rain's voice lowered. "You look… perfect."

Nik's smile was rare but real. "So do you."

Spark barked again. Rain blushed, brushing his fur as Nik stepped farther into the room.

Then the room hushed as the portal shimmered one last time—Eileen stepped through, Oak at her side.

Her white dress caught the magic, transformed into a celestial glow. For a breath, luminous wings unfurled behind her before vanishing like mist. Around her neck hung the delicate key charm Ariel had given her, resting just below her collarbone.

Ariel's breath caught, a quiet smile tugging at her lips. *She's wearing it.*

Oak followed one step behind, grounded and steady. He didn't speak, but the ease between them said everything—at least to each other.

For a beat, the room held its breath.

Ariel broke the silence first, grinning. "Eileen, you outdid us all without even trying."

Eileen's soft smile carried just enough amusement. "I'll leave the theatrics to you."

Conversation resumed, the energy picking back up as guests began to mingle.

Takoda tilted her head to watch a floating candle blink out, then spark back to life. "It's fascinating," she murmured, a faint smile curving her lips.

Across the room, Rowan eyed the ghostly projections. One pretended to sneak up behind him, only to vanish with a cackle. He smirked, unimpressed.

Reed raised his glass toward the skeleton. "Here's to the best heckler in the house."

The bones replied without missing a beat. "I'd say the same, but I've heard your jokes."

Laughter followed. Vine tossed a stick for Spark, who launched after it with unshakable determination.

"Careful, warlock," Ariel teased, breezing past him. "You're losing your spooky edge."

Vine scratched behind Spark's ears, dry as ever. "Spark's the real menace."

The music shifted, drawing attention as Ariel clapped. "Come on! It's not a party if no one's dancing."

She grabbed Rain's hand and pulled her onto the dance floor. Rain laughed and leaned into the music, already moving to the beat.

"Alright, alright," Aislinn said, dragging Rowan with her. "You're up."

Rowan gave a theatrical sigh but followed, syncing with her steps easily.

Reed turned to Hazel with a dramatic bow. "Care for a spin, m'lady?"

Hazel rolled her eyes but joined him, grinning.

The room filled with motion and warmth—dancing, laughter, light. For a little while, the war felt far away.

The music eased into a slower rhythm, and Takoda turned to Riichi, her kimono glowing softly under the floating candles. She tugged gently at his sleeve, coaxing him toward the quieter edge of the dance floor.

"Come on," she said, her voice warm. "Dance with me."

He hesitated for a breath, but the curve of her smile made refusal pointless. He stepped into her space, letting her guide them into motion. The noise around them dulled, softened into a distant hum. Candlelight brushed gold across his armor, and the gentle sway of her sleeves mirrored their rhythm.

Takoda leaned in slightly. "You know, it's rare to see you like this. Out here. Relaxed."

Riichi raised an eyebrow, a hint of dry humor in his voice. "I'm only relaxed because you're here."

Her hand pressed gently against his shoulder. "Then stay that way. Just for now."

Their steps remained slow, natural. And then the air shifted.

A warm orange light pulsed softly from Riichi's skin, spreading outward in smooth waves. Takoda's aura answered instantly, her glow twining with his. The two currents merged, encircling them in a golden cocoon that pulsed in time with their bond.

The others noticed but instinctively kept their distance. The space around them felt sacred—not showy, just intimate.

Within the surge, their thoughts found each other.

You look devastatingly handsome tonight, Takoda murmured, the warmth in her voice unmistakable. *That armor suits you.*

And you, Riichi returned, his hand brushing her waist, *are the most beautiful sorceress I've ever seen. I could watch you for hours and still not have enough.*

Careful, warrior, she teased, her lips near his ear. *Say too many things like that, and I might never let you go.*

Good, he answered without hesitation. *I don't want you to.*

She tilted her head. *You make me feel safe and completely undone, all at once. Not fair.*

That's my secret weapon, he said with a quiet chuckle. *Winning the sorceress's heart is my greatest victory.*

Her laugh was soft and full of delight. His hand tightened just slightly at her waist, anchoring them together.

You've ruined me, she whispered, *How am I supposed to think about anything else when you hold me like this?*

Then don't, he said simply. *Just think about us. Here. Now.*

Her cheeks warmed beneath the glow, but the light surrounding them spared her from showing it. Her thoughts drifted quieter, more certain.

I love you, Riichi.

And I love you. Always.

Their thoughts fell into a calm hush. No more words needed. His hand skimmed along her waist, her fingers finding his cheek. The glow held, steady and full of promise.

Eventually, the light faded, sinking back into their skin as the room's sounds returned. Takoda pulled back just enough to meet his eyes, her hand still resting on his shoulder.

"Thank you," she said softly. "For this. For tonight."

Riichi tucked a loose strand of hair behind her ear, his voice low. "Always."

"I'm not going anywhere," he added, his expression steady. "You know that, right?"

"I do now," she whispered, a faint smile rising to her lips.

They remained like that a moment longer before stepping back from the floor, returning quietly to the room's edge. The Radiant Surge had passed, but the bond between them hadn't dimmed. It wrapped around them like an unspoken vow—quiet, enduring, and unmistakably real.

The party buzzed with music, laughter, and the occasional ghostly snort from an enchanted decoration. Guests wandered freely in magically enhanced costumes while Spark zipped from group to group, tail wagging like he owned the place.

At the heart of the chaos, Ariel and Vine—unofficial agents of mischief—were in their element.

Ariel approached Takoda with a bright grin, eyes glittering. "I still can't get over this kimono," she said, brushing a finger over one of the glowing red blossoms. "Remind me to actually compliment Riichi later—this deserves more than a nod of approval."

Takoda laughed, casting a fond glance at Riichi, who was eyeing a hovering projection as if it were sizing him up. "He did. I think he liked the idea of me in it more than the fabric itself."

As Takoda turned slightly, Vine raised a hand with subtle flair. The embroidery on Riichi's armor stirred—the dragon twisting in place, yawned, then flared its wings with dramatic flair before settling back into position.

Takoda spotted the movement and gave them both a dry look. "I should've known."

Ariel widened her eyes. "We're just encouraging the fashion to express itself."

"We're helping the vibe," Vine added from his casual lean against the table. "Art deserves motion."

They moved on to their next victim: Reed, who stood chatting with Alder near the skeleton, sipping something vaguely orange and fizzy. Ariel raised a brow.

"Watch this," she whispered.

Vine made a subtle motion with two fingers, and one of the jack-o'-lanterns floating near the ceiling slowly rotated toward Reed. A moment later, it projected a tiny illusion above his head—a flickering rogue's mask with devil horns and sparkling red eyes.

Ariel muffled a snort behind her hand.

Reed noticed the glow and turned slowly. The second he saw the illusion, he narrowed his eyes. "Alright, which one of you summoned my evil twin?"

Ariel gave an elaborate shrug. "If the horns fit…"

Vine arched a brow, deadpan. "Looks accurate to me."

Reed laughed, shaking his head. "Remind me never to turn my back on either of you."

The illusion faded as Reed stepped closer, now grinning at Ariel. "Seriously, though—you look amazing tonight. That costume's perfect on you."

Ariel opened her mouth, but before she could reply, Vine stepped in—not rude, not loud, just sharper than he needed to be. "Try not to trip over your compliments, Reed. We wouldn't want the mask to slip."

Reed blinked, then let out a short laugh. "Right. Wouldn't want to ruin the mystery."

He wandered off, still smiling, leaving Ariel staring after him. Slowly, she turned to Vine.

Her brow lifted slightly. "Okay… what was that?"

Vine shrugged, his usual smirk already back in place. "Just a joke."

She didn't press, but her eyes lingered on him a little longer than usual.

It wasn't like him to snap.

Still, she let it go and nudged his elbow instead. "Come on. I see a row of cupcakes just begging for mischief."

Vine gave a half-smile, but his attention flicked briefly in Reed's direction before he followed her into the crowd.

Meanwhile, Spark had found his next audience. He sat politely at Rain's feet while Hazel admired the wreath of moonflowers and ivy woven into her hair.

"That's beautiful, Rain. You make it?"

Rain shook her head, brushing her fingers over a petal. "Nik did. He made it at the pumpkin patch."

Ivy looked up from her drink. "Good with details, huh?" The tease in her voice was light, but it landed.

Rain's blush deepened. Spark picked up on the shift and bounded away.

He darted across the room and made a beeline for Aislinn's dress, batting at the hem with his paws.

Aislinn laughed, lifting the fabric out of reach. Rowan leaned down with a tired sigh. "Go pick on someone else, menace."

Spark wagged once, then disappeared again, ears perked and tail high.

After yet another successful prank, Vine leaned against the refreshment table, the amusement in his expression beginning to fade.

"Alright, Trouble," he muttered, glancing at Ariel. "I need water before you rope me into another disaster."

Ariel folded her arms, pretending to pout. "Fine. But don't vanish. You're my partner in crime, remember?"

Vine gave her a faint smile before turning toward the hallway. He'd barely taken two steps before Rowan appeared from the edge of the room.

"Water sounds good," Rowan said, tone even. "I'll come with you."

Vine raised an eyebrow but didn't argue. With a faint shrug, he continued down the hall.

The party sounds faded behind them, replaced by the low hum of the fridge and the subtle clink of bottles. Vine grabbed a water from the counter and cracked the seal.

Rowan leaned against the far counter, arms crossed. "So," he said, his voice casual in a way that wasn't, "what's going on with you and Ariel?"

Vine took a long sip before replying. "We're friends. That's it."

"I don't believe you."

Vine turned toward him. "That's your problem."

Rowan pushed off the counter, closing the distance between them. "If you hurt her—"

"I would never hurt her," Vine interrupted, his tone unusually calm but edged with quiet sincerity. "Whether you believe me or not doesn't change that."

Rowan's eyes narrowed, his stance still tense. "You think this is a game, but it's not. Ariel's been through hell, and she deserves better than someone playing it cool while keeping her at arm's length."

There was no hesitation—just a shift behind Vine's eyes, quiet and certain. His voice dropped, steady and clear. "I know what she deserves. I see it more clearly than you think."

For a moment, Rowan didn't speak. Then he stepped back, nodding once. "Good. Make sure you remember it."

Vine twisted the cap back onto the bottle, every motion measured. "Let's go."

They walked back into the hallway, Rowan ahead by a few steps. Just before they reached the main room, Alder appeared, heading toward them.

Rowan passed without a word, his posture still stiff. He didn't notice when Alder slowed.

But Vine did.

The moment Alder's eyes locked onto Vine, he froze—like the breath had been pulled from his lungs. His steps faltered.

Vine caught him by the arm, steadying him instinctively. "Alder?"

Alder's fingers dug into Vine's sleeve. His expression went distant, eyes losing focus as if staring through him.

Vine held him firmly. "Hey. Look at me."

Alder's body remained rigid, breath shallow. His voice was barely above a whisper. "She burns so brightly... but you keep walking in the dark."

Vine tensed.

Alder blinked hard and seemed to return to himself. He met Vine's eyes, his grip tightening briefly. "Don't ignore what's right in front of you."

Vine's brow furrowed. "What are you talking about?"

"You already feel it," Alder said, calm now, but not unshaken. "Just stop pretending you don't."

He gave Vine's shoulder one last squeeze before stepping past him into the main room, disappearing into the swirl of music and motion.

Vine remained in the corridor, water bottle in hand, staring after him like he'd just stepped off solid ground.

Right in front of me?

The words echoed louder than he wanted them to.

He didn't want to name it—not yet—but the feeling had been there. Quiet. Persistent.

Was it real? Or just another distraction he'd let get too close?

Either way, Alder saw through him.

And that was the part he couldn't ignore.

Rowan returned to the main room alone, his posture rigid, jaw tight as he crossed to where Aislinn stood. Ariel spotted him immediately.

Where's Vine?

She scanned the doorway, brow dipping slightly—but said nothing.

A few minutes later, Vine appeared, stepping into the room with a bottle of water in hand. His usual energy was muted, his expression harder to read.

Ariel's eyes tracked him as he made his way back to her. The space between his smirk and the quiet tension in his shoulders didn't quite line up.

She didn't press—not with so many eyes around—but a flicker of unease stirred beneath her smile.

Not here. Not now. She tucked the thought away, already planning to corner him later.

He offered a faint smirk when she tossed a comment about their next prank, but the rhythm between them was off.

She felt it. And she didn't like it.

As the night wore on, the party began to quiet, the earlier laughter softening into murmured conversations. The floating candles dipped lower, casting a gentle golden haze across the room as the last of the guests found their way to quieter corners—or disappeared entirely.

Near the back wall, Nik sat alone, leaning against a wooden column with his bow resting beside him. His costume shimmered subtly in the dim light, the leaf-stitched tunic catching soft glints of gold. His expression was calm, but his gaze drifted—not toward the remaining guests, but past them, like his mind had already moved on.

Rain spotted him from across the room. Her fingers brushed the edge of her skirt as she made her way over, her steps unhurried. Spark darted past her in a final burst of energy, chasing a nonexistent threat only he could see.

"You always end up on the sidelines," she said lightly, offering him a smile as she approached.

Nik glanced up at her, a faint trace of amusement in his eyes. "Someone has to make sure the building's still standing."

Rain let out a soft chuckle and took the open spot beside him. "Well, so far so good."

They sat in comfortable silence, the buzz of the party fading behind them. Rain shifted slightly, glancing toward him. "You know... you didn't have to make that wreath."

Nik's eyes moved briefly to the one still nestled in her hair, then back to her. "I wanted to."

She touched it gently, the petals faintly glowing beneath her fingertips. "It's beautiful. And thoughtful. I guess I'm not used to that."

Nik didn't look away. "You should be."

Her breath caught for just a moment—nothing dramatic, just enough to remind her that this was Nik. He wasn't the type to say things unless he meant them.

"I'm glad you're here tonight," she said quietly.

"So am I," he replied.

The quiet between them shifted—not uncomfortable, not charged—just close. Present.

A yawn crept up on her, and she covered her mouth with a quiet laugh. "I think that's my cue to call it."

Nik stood as she did, his movements unhurried. "I'll walk you."

Rain didn't argue. "Thanks."

The hallway outside was quiet, the air cooler. Their footsteps echoed softly against the tile, each one a quiet beat in the stillness.

They spoke in low voices, commenting on Spark's antics and the success of the decorations. It wasn't deep conversation—it didn't need to be. Nik's presence had always calmed her, and tonight was no different.

When they reached her door, Rain turned to face him.

"Thanks again. For walking me. And... for earlier."

Nik gave a faint nod. "You're welcome."

She hesitated, her hand drifting to the edge of the wreath. "You're not what I expected, you know."

He raised a brow, just slightly. "No?"

She smiled, small but real. "No. You're quieter, but not distant. You notice things. You care."

Nik looked at her for a moment, his expression unreadable but not closed off. "I just try to be honest."

"I know," she said. "That's what I like."

She stepped in, meaning only to kiss his cheek, but Nik turned to face her—and the contact shifted. Their lips brushed, quick and unintentional.

Rain pulled back immediately, flustered. "Oh—I didn't mean—"

Before she could stumble further, Nik leaned in again and gave her a gentle kiss. Just a soft press of reassurance. Simple. Deliberate.

"It's alright," he said.

Rain blinked, her heart doing a strange little flutter as her fingers touched her lips. "Goodnight, Nik."

"Goodnight, Rain."

He walked away without fanfare, and she watched him go for a few seconds longer before slipping inside her room, the door clicking shut behind her.

The Halloween party had finally wound down, leaving the room quiet and bathed in the faint glow of the lingering decorations. The soft creak of settling wood echoed faintly through the mansion, and Spark's nails clicked against the floor as he wagged his tail impatiently near Ariel's feet. She crouched to clip his leash, running a hand gently over his head with an affectionate smile.

Near the door, Vine leaned against the frame, his arms crossed as he watched her. There was a faint, contemplative quality to his expression, though the usual smirk still tugged at his lips.

Ariel glanced up at him, a glint of humor in her eyes. "Come on, warlock. Spark needs a bodyguard for his last trip out."

"I'm guessing the pixie can't handle gremlins on her own?" Vine quipped, his voice light but carrying an undertone of warmth.

"Not after the ones I just dealt with tonight," Ariel replied, grinning as she opened the door.

The crisp night air greeted them as they stepped outside, carrying the faint scent of autumn leaves. The floating candles were still visible through the windows behind them, their soft glow a reminder of the lively party now past.

Spark trotted ahead, sniffing the ground with eager curiosity, his tail wagging as he explored the edges of the yard. Ariel followed, leading Vine toward the far end of the patio where the mansion's exterior wall cast deep shadows.

"Let's get out of the spotlight," she said over her shoulder, her tone teasing but tired. "This pixie's had enough for one night."

Vine trailed behind, his smirk fading into a quiet thoughtfulness as the shadows cocooned them, offering a rare sense of privacy from the rest of the world.

Ariel leaned back against the wall, crossing her arms as she studied him. The playful edge in her tone softened slightly as she spoke. "Alright, spill. You've been off since the kitchen. What's going on?"

Vine mirrored her, leaning casually against the wall beside her. His voice was deliberately even. "Nothing. Just tired."

Ariel arched an eyebrow, her skepticism clear. "Warlocks don't get tired. Try again."

Vine chuckled quietly but didn't answer immediately, his gaze drifting toward Spark, who was happily sniffing at a patch of grass nearby. Ariel took a small step closer, tilting her head in an attempt to catch his eye.

"Come on, Vine," she said, her voice softening further. "You can tell me. Did Rowan say something?"

His gaze flicked to her briefly, his tone dropping to a low murmur. "Rowan's just... being Rowan. Forget it."

Ariel narrowed her eyes slightly, her skepticism deepening. "Uh-huh. And you're just being your broody self. Not buying it."

She shifted closer again, her tone growing more serious. "If something's bothering you, I want to know. Don't shut me out, Vine. Not tonight."

Vine hesitated, his hand brushing through his hair as he leaned more heavily against the wall. His expression remained guarded, but there was an edge of vulnerability in the way he spoke.

"It's nothing you need to worry about," he said quietly. "Just... people see what they want to see. Doesn't matter how much you change, they'll still think you're the same arrogant jerk who doesn't care about anyone but himself."

Ariel straightened slightly, her voice soft but firm as she replied, "That's not what I see."

He glanced at her, something searching in his expression.

"I see someone who stayed up all night making sure I didn't prank myself into a coma," Ariel continued, her tone gentler now. "Someone who knows Spark better than I do. Someone who makes me laugh when I'm too stubborn to admit I need it."

Her hand brushed lightly against his arm, the touch brief but deliberate.

"I see you, Vine. The real you. And I like what I see."

Vine studied her for a long moment, his usual smirk giving way to quiet vulnerability, the kind he rarely let surface. "You shouldn't make it so easy for me to believe you," he said quietly.

Ariel's lips curved into a faint grin. "Who said I was making it easy?"

The teasing lilt in her voice faded as the space between them seemed to shrink. Their gazes locked, the air thickening with quiet certainty. Ariel tilted her head slightly, her tone dipping into quiet resolve, more grounded than playful.

"You're not alone, warlock," she murmured. "Not tonight. Not ever."

Vine leaned in slowly, his movements deliberate, giving her every chance to pull away. She didn't.

Their lips met, the kiss starting soft but quickly deepening. The world around them faded as Ariel's hands slid up to rest on his chest, her fingers curling into the fabric of his coat. Vine's hand moved to her waist, pulling her closer, while his other hand brushed lightly against her cheek.

The kiss grew more urgent, their bodies pressing together as the tension of the night melted away, leaving only the moment between them.

Ariel pulled back slightly, her breath coming faster as she grinned up at him. "Not bad for a warlock," she said softly.

Vine's smirk returned, though it carried a flicker of affection that hadn't been there before. "You're not so bad yourself, Trouble."

He leaned in again, his lips finding hers once more. This time, the kiss was more confident, his touch assured as their connection deepened. The cool air seemed to disappear, replaced by the warmth of their closeness.

He didn't need to think it through anymore. Not analyze it. Not bury it beneath dry wit and distance.

Alder was right.

I do feel something. I'm not going to pretend anymore.

Spark barked, the sound sharp enough to break through the haze of the moment. Ariel laughed softly, resting her forehead against Vine's for a brief second before stepping back slightly.

"Guess the guard dog thinks we've had enough fun," she said, her grin playful.

Vine's smirk widened. "Or maybe he's just jealous."

They lingered there, the quiet between them speaking louder than words. Finally, Ariel tugged lightly on Spark's leash, and they headed back inside.

The night sky glowed faintly in the background as they exchanged a look that didn't need defining—just returned.

The mansion had quieted to a hush, the remnants of the party now a faded memory tucked into corners of candle wax and glitter. Ariel and Vine walked side by side, their steps unhurried as the soft glow of the sconces lit their way up the stairs. Shadows stretched across the walls, longer now, heavier—just like the air between them.

Ariel slowed near the top, her fingers brushing the banister. She didn't move forward.

Vine paused a step ahead and turned. "Alright, Trouble," he said quietly, tilting his head. "Your turn. What's wrong?"

Her shoulders lifted in a shallow breath. She didn't look at him at first. "It's just... tomorrow. I keep thinking about who might not come back. Rowan. Takoda." She hesitated, finally glancing at him. "You."

The word hit heavier than she expected. "What if I never get to see you again?"

The smirk that had lingered at the edge of Vine's mouth faded, replaced by a steady calm. He stepped close and reached for her hand, curling his fingers around hers with quiet intent.

"Come on," he murmured, tugging gently.

Ariel blinked. "Where are we going?"

He glanced down at their joined hands, a faint smile tugging at his lips. "We already broke the no-hand-holding rule. Might as well break another."

That earned a soft huff from her. "Warlock," she said, the tease barely masking her weariness, "you're nothing but trouble."

"And you're still following me," he replied, his voice low and warm.

The door clicked softly behind them as they stepped into Vine's room. He didn't let go of her hand until they were inside. Spark trotted in behind them, tail swishing, then stopped in the middle of the floor looking expectantly at them both.

Vine grabbed a blanket from the closet and tossed it into the corner. Spark immediately trotted over and made himself comfortable, circling twice before plopping down with a satisfied grunt.

"You're spending the night," Vine said as he leaned against the dresser. "Non-negotiable."

"Oh, is that right?" Ariel asked, raising a brow.

He shrugged. "Yeah. You're not going to your room to spiral until sunrise."

Her mouth twitched despite herself. "Bossy."

"Only when I care," he said, pulling open a drawer and tossing her one of his soft black shirts. "Here. Wear this. Or sleep in glitter. Your call."

She caught the shirt and gave it a mock glare. "You're lucky I like you."

Vine's response was quieter, more real. "Yeah. I'm starting to think I am."

A few minutes later, Ariel sat on the edge of the bed in his shirt, her bare legs tucked beneath her. Vine sat beside her, close enough that their shoulders brushed. He didn't say anything—he didn't need to. When he slipped his arm around her and pulled her in, it felt natural.

Ariel leaned into him without hesitation, her head resting against his chest.

"Don't start overthinking," Vine said softly. "You're here. That's all that matters right now."

Ariel let out a quiet breath, her fingers absently tracing the hem of his shirt. "Hard not to, with everything coming."

"Don't," Vine murmured, brushing a kiss into her hair. "Just be here with me."

Her fingers moved across the fabric of his shirt in slow, absent circles. Eventually, she tilted her head to meet his eyes. "You're not as bad as you pretend to be."

Vine's smirk returned, but softer. "Don't ruin my image."

She laughed under her breath. "Your secret's safe with me."

Their lips met in a kiss that started slow but deepened with ease, no hesitation between them. Ariel's hands slid up his chest, curling into the fabric near his shoulders as she leaned into him. Vine's arms circled her with quiet certainty, his touch no longer casual—no longer pretending.

So this is what it feels like when I stop pretending.

Like I finally found a reason to keep living.

And I'll be damned if I don't come back to her.

Ariel shifted into his lap without thought, her body curling against his. The kiss intensified, then slowed again, stretching into soft passes of lips and warm hands. Her fingers threaded into his hair. His hand slipped beneath the hem of the borrowed shirt, resting low on her back, grounding her.

They paused only long enough to breathe. Foreheads pressed together. Breath mingling.

"You're annoying," she murmured.

"You love it," he said, brushing her hair back from her face.

"Maybe."

Her voice stayed light, but the way she leaned in again betrayed the rest.

Eventually, they curled beneath the blankets, drawn close by a need neither of them had dared to name. Ariel's head found his chest. Vine's arm stayed around her, the other brushing gently along her spine.

"You're safe here," he whispered. "Just sleep."

Ariel let out a faint sound of agreement, her breathing slowing as her body relaxed against him.

Vine pressed a final kiss to her hair, his words low enough for no one else to hear.

"Goodnight, Trouble."

The meeting room thrummed with quiet intensity, the air sharp with anticipation. At the center, the heavy oak table bore the full weight of their strategy—maps of Fort Lawton layered with glowing diagrams, enchanted objects faintly pulsing with contained energy, and symbols etched in shimmering ink that seemed to breathe with every shift in light. The Fallen sat in a semi-circle around Eileen, a silent current of readiness running through each of them. Some wore grim resolve like armor, others carried a quieter focus, but none looked away.

Eileen didn't need to raise her voice or posture for command—it emanated from her with quiet force. She stood at the head of the table, spine straight, expression composed. As she scanned the room, her gaze brushed over Takoda and Riichi, then moved on to the others.

"Tonight," she said, her cadence deliberate, "we strike Fort Lawton. The Golden Dawn's ritual ends here. No second chances. No errors."

The declaration landed hard, a pulse in the air that settled deep in their bones.

"You've all been briefed. We're reviewing it one final time. Speak now—on the battlefield, there won't be time."

Stillness followed as the team absorbed her words. At the back, Reed leaned into the shadows, arms crossed, eyes tracking the map as if burning it into memory. Rowan shifted in his seat, tension humming beneath his composure. Holly leaned toward Ivy, whispering something that earned a subtle jab from her elbow in return.

Eileen moved one of the diagrams closer, revealing the complex pattern of the ward surrounding the ritual site. "Phase Zero: Ward Neutralization. Nik, Ivy, Hazel, Willow—you're the first team in. The barrier is advanced, but not unbreakable."

She tapped a trio of faded symbols marked near the site's perimeter. "These are the fracture points. Get in fast, dismantle without drawing attention. If this ward holds, none of us step foot inside."

Nik leaned forward, his voice low but firm. "If they reinforce while we're mid-dismantle?"

Without hesitation, Eileen replied, "Willow channels the overflow. Hazel and Ivy destabilize and disrupt. Adjust on the fly. Stay fluid."

Hazel gave a small nod, her posture crisp, eyes steady. "We've tracked its cycle. We'll breach it."

Willow didn't glance up, but her voice carried. "We know what we're doing."

Eileen gave a short nod, then slid the top map aside to reveal the interior layout beneath it. "Phase One: Surveillance and Distraction. Reed, Holly, Ash, Nik—you're the decoy unit. Misdirect, draw attention, and track movement. This phase is about space—give the anchor teams breathing room."

Reed angled his head slightly, jaw tight. "And if they're waiting for us to try just that?"

Holly's grin curved like a blade. "Then I'll show them phantoms worth chasing. They'll burn their resources chasing shadows."

Ash, quiet near the edge of the table, spoke without hesitation. "They won't catch us."

Eileen nodded once and adjusted the map again, her finger settling on the marks denoting the anchors. "Phase Two: Anchor Destruction," she said. "Each team has its target—wind, water, fire. All three must be destroyed at the same time. There's no margin for error."

Rowan leaned forward, forearms braced against the table. "And if one team falls behind?"

Eileen didn't flinch. "Then we fall back and reset. But understand—any delay gives them time to reinforce. That's the worst-case scenario."

Ivy's tone was cool and certain. "We won't be delayed."

Across the table, Vine offered a slow smirk. "The fire anchor won't be standing long."

Eileen moved the top layer aside, revealing the ritual core beneath. Her expression sharpened. "Phase Three: Combat with Kubla Khan." The way she said his name carved a fault line through the room. "Riichi. Takoda. He'll come for you. He has to be drawn from the ritual site—isolated and neutralized."

Her gaze locked briefly on them. "Khan isn't just leading this ritual—he's reshaping it. He knows we're coming. He's already adapted once. Expect him to be ready."

She didn't mention Gideon Kross by name, but they all knew he was acting as Khan's second, commanding the Golden Dawn forces directly.

Takoda straightened in her seat. Her voice didn't rise, but the quiet strength behind it carried. "He won't stop us."

Next to her, Riichi offered a faint smile that didn't quite reach his eyes. "He chose the wrong people to challenge."

At the far end of the table, Rowan turned slightly toward Aislinn. His words were low, meant only for her. "We'll cover them."

Aislinn's eyes met his, a flicker of concern passing through before she nodded. There was no need to say more. Her trust in him held fast.

Eileen gestured to the center of the layout, where glowing runes spiraled inward. "Phase Four: Ritual Destruction. Takoda and Riichi will use Fated Blade to strike the final blow. Willow and Oak—your job is to contain the fallout and keep the collapse from spreading."

Willow's brow drew in as she studied the markings. "And if residual energy lingers after the core's destroyed?"

Eileen met her question head-on. "Your focus will be containment. Shield the team. If that energy flares outward, we lose control of the battlefield."

She paused, fingers brushing the edge of the ritual map. "This isn't just about stopping a storm anymore. Khan is using this ritual to fracture the veil—and what steps through after might be far worse."

Willow exchanged a glance with Oak, who gave a single nod. Their role wouldn't earn spotlight, but both knew the mission couldn't succeed without it.

Eileen stepped back from the table, the maps still glowing faintly beneath her hands. The hum of energy in the room rose, subtle but unmistakable.

"This afternoon's session will mirror tonight's mission exactly," she said. "Every trap, every barrier, every moment of chaos—you'll face them all in training. Treat it like your life depends on it, because it will."

The room shifted—postures straightening, focus sharpening. Reed dropped his arms to the table, his gaze flicking toward Holly, who returned it with a grin.

At the other end, Takoda leaned in close to Riichi, her words too soft to carry, but the calm in her voice grounded them both.

Eileen's attention swept across the group. "Rest. Eat. Use these hours wisely," she said. Her voice dipped—still firm, but threaded with something more personal. "We are ready. We trust each other. And we don't lose tonight."

The room held its breath for a single beat before motion returned.

Reed rose and turned toward Holly. "If your illusions are going to sell this, they need to be chaotic. No patterns."

Holly tapped the side of her head, that glint of mischief returning. "I've got a few tricks even you haven't seen. Try to keep up."

By the doorway, Rowan reached for Aislinn's wrist, halting her gently as the others began to file out. His voice lowered. "Riichi and Takoda can handle themselves—but Khan won't fight fair. If it goes sideways…"

Aislinn didn't let him finish. "It won't." Her tone was quiet steel as she held his gaze.

By the map, Vine lingered, his focus fixed on the ward runes. "If there's anything buried in these lines," he murmured, "it's not going to be obvious."

Willow slid into the seat beside him, her brow furrowed in concentration. "Then let's make sure we see what they don't want us to."

Off to the side, Riichi and Takoda spoke in low voices, their exchange hushed but purposeful. When he placed a hand lightly on her shoulder, she nodded once. The task ahead had already settled between them—not as a burden, but as shared resolve.

One by one, the Fallen filtered from the room, the quiet thrum of magic lingering in their wake, trailing behind them like a charge waiting to ignite.

The morning sun glanced off the warded perimeter surrounding the mansion's training grounds, casting shifting bands of light across the field. What was once a peaceful expanse had been reshaped into a mirror of Fort Lawton's fractured terrain. Magical constructs hovered overhead, pulsing with unstable energy.

Oak stood in the center, arms crossed, a steady command in his posture. The group quieted at once.

"Tonight, we execute this plan," he said, his voice cutting cleanly through the tension. "If we fail here, we fail there. Don't hold back."

The charged silence that followed was immediate.

"This simulation replicates the Fort Lawton site—every defense, every ward, every anchor," Oak continued, motioning toward the glowing dome at the field's edge. "Treat it as real. This is where we find the gaps before they cost lives."

His focus shifted across the team, pausing briefly on Riichi and Takoda. "If they're compromised, we follow the contingency. The priority is stopping them, not hurting them. Keep your control."

A few nods followed, sharp and solemn.

"Phase Zero: Ward Neutralization. Nik, Ivy, Hazel, Willow—take point. Five minutes."

The four moved into formation. The ward shimmered before them, a lattice of glowing sigils interwoven like living circuitry.

Hazel stepped in first, her eyes narrowing. "Multi-layered convergence," she said. "Nik, we need the foundation cleared. Ivy, Willow—break the primary nodes."

Nik dropped to one knee, pressing his palm to the ground. The surface quivered beneath his touch, revealing the ward's buried framework. "Structure's exposed."

Energy lines flared. Ivy moved quickly, unraveling the streams as Willow diverted their flow, dispersing pressure through controlled spirals. The ward flinched in response, throwing off a volatile surge.

"Barrier, now!" Hazel snapped.

Nik reacted instantly, raising a slab of stone to absorb the blast. Sparks scattered across the field. Ivy's jaw tightened as she distorted the energy further, prying at its core.

"Top node's the key," Hazel said. "Collapse that, and the rest follows."

Willow adjusted her stance, fingers slicing through the air as she dragged the upper point downward. A final pulse of resistance rippled outward before the ward fractured, folding in on itself with a hiss of extinguished light.

"Time," Oak called, stepping forward. "You cleared it—barely. That last counterstrike could've taken someone out. Tighten your timing."

The team regrouped with silent resolve, tension still clinging to the edges of the now-cleared field.

"Phase One," Oak said, turning to the next team. "Reed, Holly, Ash, Nik—surveillance and distraction. Your timing sets the tone for everything that follows."

Reed disappeared into the simulated ruins. His voice crackled over the comm link, low and steady. "Two clusters, northwest sector. One group is static. The other's redirecting toward the eastern anchor. Ash, you're clear to move."

Ash shimmered, his form shifting into that of a Golden Dawn operative. He moved confidently into enemy ranks, issuing false commands that splintered their coordination.

From her vantage point, Holly summoned a wave of phantom soldiers—illusions crashing into the enemy like a cavalry charge. "They're taking the bait," she muttered, focused, sweat collecting at her brow.

Nik anchored from higher ground, shaping stone walls to funnel movement into Holly's trap. "Should pin them in."

The field shifted. A new cluster emerged from the southern edge, disrupting their setup.

"New contact—south approach," Reed warned. He reappeared long enough to launch a burst of shadow energy.

Holly staggered, the illusions faltering. "Cover—now!"

Nik responded instantly, stone snapping into place around her. Ash pivoted, feigning a retreat that lured the new reinforcements into Holly's illusions as she regained control.

Oak's voice cut through. "Reed—support Nik. Holly, maintain focus. Ash, drive them west."

The four adjusted in sync, momentum returning. Moments later, the enemies vanished, and the simulation reset.

Oak stepped forward, unreadable. "Better. But the southern breach caught you flat. You hesitated."

He turned to Holly. "Recovery was solid. Keep your output focused. If the illusions destabilize, the whole phase collapses."

Holly nodded, brushing damp hair from her face. "Won't happen again."

Oak's attention shifted to Reed. "Be specific. 'South approach' isn't enough when the terrain shifts beneath you."

"Understood," Reed said evenly.

Oak shifted his stance. "Phase Two: Anchor Destruction. Birch, Hazel, Ivy, Willow—you're on the wind anchor. Bring it down clean."

Ivy moved without hesitation, her focus locked on the swirling construct. The barrier pulsed erratically, its energy snapping like a living storm. She extended her hands, threading magic through the unstable weave. "Willow—stabilize the output."

Willow stepped in, redirecting the currents into smoother channels. Her fingers traced deliberate arcs through the air. "Locked in."

Behind them, Birch murmured an incantation, golden light wrapping around the group just as the anchor retaliated, sending sharp arcs toward Ivy.

Birch stepped into the blast. "Watch it!"

"I've got it," Ivy replied, steady. The barrier cracked under her control, threads unraveling with each pass.

Willow gave a final pull, collapsing the last line of energy. Ivy struck the core—shattering the anchor into harmless fragments.

Oak approached. "Clean. But too slow. You won't get breathing room tonight. Tighten it."

He turned to the next team. "Water anchor. Go."

Hazel stepped forward, already dissecting the vortex of defensive currents. She cut through the outer layer with swift, fluid motion.

"Alder?" she called.

"There's a primary stream feeding the rest," Alder said. "Disrupt that, and the structure collapses."

Hazel adjusted course, slicing into the core. The vortex faltered—then surged. A glyph flared beneath her.

"Trap!" Oak warned.

He dissolved the sigil before it triggered. Hazel didn't miss a beat, dismantling the anchor's core until the construct collapsed.

Oak gave a curt nod. "Better. Expect more traps. They won't be that obvious."

The fire anchor blazed to life across the field, its pulses sharp and volatile. Vine stepped forward, lightning sparking between his fingertips. "Let's see what you've got."

His first strike lit up the brazier, which roared in response, unleashing a wave of wild energy.

Aislinn raised her shield just in time. "Ease up, Vine. I'm not patching you mid-fight."

Rowan surged ahead, cutting through simulated defenders. "Clear the path," he called, his blade driving back the front line.

Vine pushed another surge into the anchor, sweat slipping down his temple. The brazier retaliated with a shockwave that sent him stumbling.

Aislinn's shield expanded, taking the brunt. Rowan moved to intercept a second wave. "Stay sharp!" Oak shouted.

Vine regrouped fast, jaw clenched. With a final surge of lightning, the anchor buckled. Rowan and Aislinn struck together, their Radiant Surge flaring as the brazier collapsed.

"All anchors down," Oak announced. "But you're still too slow. Tonight, you won't have time to recover. Fix it."

Rowan wiped his brow and nodded toward Aislinn. Vine straightened, his expression set.

"Phase Three," Oak called. "Riichi, Takoda, Rowan, Aislinn, Birch—Kubla Khan is waiting. Move."

The terrain shifted once more, the training field darkening as jagged constructs gave way to a battlefield cloaked in shadows. The oppressive atmosphere thickened, a simulated version of Khan emerging at the far edge. His eyes burned with an eerie, intelligent red glow, and dark tendrils coiled around him, moving like smoke with purpose. Simulated Golden Dawn soldiers flanked him, coordinated and deliberate in their movements.

Riichi launched forward, a blur of motion as he intercepted the first wave. His strikes were sharp and exact—no wasted effort, no hesitation. Bodies dropped without lethal force, each takedown clean.

"Takoda, hold the center!" he called, never pausing.

Takoda extended her aura, invisible but potent, thinning the emotional fog radiating from Khan's illusion. The chaos dulled within its reach, allowing the team to regain their focus.

Rowan and Aislinn pressed in from the flank, Radiant Surge glowing faintly around them as they moved as one. Rowan's blade met enemy steel with deadly rhythm, while Aislinn intercepted a surge of dark energy with a sweep of her hand, shielding Riichi before the force could land.

"Left side's collapsing!" Birch shouted, pivoting into position. He deflected a flurry of attacks, then hurled his chakram in a tight arc that struck the lead enemy and ricocheted through the ranks, knocking them off balance.

Across the field, the simulated Khan raised his hand.

Chains of darkness unraveled from his shadow, slithering across the battlefield with a mind of their own. They surged toward Riichi and Takoda—intelligent, seeking, adapting.

Takoda braced herself, barrier flaring again—but the simulation adjusted, tightening its grip. The chains wrapped around her and Riichi, locking them in place as the simulation registered a failed outcome.

"Contingency plan!" Oak barked from the edge of the field, his voice slicing through the rising chaos.

Rowan froze for the briefest moment, his eyes locked on Riichi and Takoda, still bound by the simulation's conjured chains.

"Rowan!" Aislinn's voice cut through the paralysis. She stepped forward, and in an instant, disappeared—reappearing beside him with a rush of displaced air. Her shield expanded around Riichi and Takoda, suppressing the illusion's grip long enough to disrupt its hold.

Willow wove a sigil midair, redirecting the chains' energy just enough for Vine to strike.

"On it," Vine muttered. Electricity arced from his fingers, sharp and precise, shattering the last remnants of the simulated chains without harming either of them.

Freed, Riichi surged to his feet. Radiant Surge ignited around him and Takoda in a sudden flare of light, their bond locking into perfect sync. Takoda's magic surged forward, infusing his katana with raw, focused fury. Riichi didn't hesitate—he pivoted and struck, sending a devastating burst of energy across the field. The arc of power ripped through the illusion of Kubla Khan, splitting it apart in a single, searing impact.

The silence that followed was brittle.

Oak strode into the center, his expression like stone. "You got it done," he said. "But hesitation like that? It'll kill someone tonight. You don't get to freeze. You move, or people die."

His eyes locked on Rowan. The message didn't need repeating.

Rowan's shoulders squared, and he gave a curt nod, tension etched deep into his jaw.

Oak turned to the rest. "Reset. Dismissed. We meet again at sundown."

The Fallen began to disperse, their movements slow, thoughtful. Energy still clung to the air, thick with what the night might bring.

Near the edge of the field, Takoda offered Riichi a faint, reassuring smile. He didn't return it, but his focus stayed on her.

Rowan lingered behind, watching Vine retreat before turning toward Aislinn. She met him halfway and placed a hand on his arm.

"Hey," she said, her voice soft but unwavering. Her eyes searched his. "You good?"

His jaw worked, but no words came at first. Then he exhaled, shoulders still stiff. "I froze. If that happens tonight—"

"It won't." Aislinn didn't let him spiral. "You're not alone in this. You've trained for every possible outcome, and even the ones we didn't expect—you're not the kind of man who folds."

Rowan breathed out slowly, her words anchoring him in a way nothing else had. He gave a small nod. "Thanks."

She stepped back, letting him leave on his own terms. As she watched him walk toward the mansion, her own resolve locked into place. Without another word, she turned and crossed the field to join Ivy and Willow, her focus shifting fully to the night ahead.

***

The sun had dipped lower by the time the Fallen gathered for dinner. Golden light slanted across the polished wood of the long dining table, where steaming plates of food filled the room with the scent of roasted vegetables, seasoned meats, and warm bread. The air was rich with comfort—but the memory of that morning's training clung to the edges of conversation like a shadow that hadn't quite dispersed.

Spark nosed beneath the table, his tail thumping softly as he circled in hope of a dropped scrap. A few quiet chuckles followed him—small, fleeting signs of ease.

Ariel swept into the room with a casserole dish, her usual brightness muted but not gone. "Alright, everyone, eat up. No sense saving anything for leftovers if we're—" She caught herself, her smile faltering. Clearing her throat, she set the dish down and nudged Vine's shoulder. "Are you planning to help, or just sitting there looking smug?"

Vine leaned back, a faint smirk tugging at his mouth. "Sitting here smugly takes more effort than you think."

Ariel rolled her eyes, though the corner of her lip curved. "Maybe try using those effort muscles on the mashed potatoes."

Across from them, Rowan watched the exchange, his brow creased. Aislinn eased into the chair beside him and brushed his arm, drawing his attention back.

Near the center of the table, Rain served herself with deliberate care. Nik, seated beside her, reached over and adjusted the edge of her plate. "Start small," he said gently. "No need to overdo it."

Rain paused, then gave him a small, grateful glance before continuing.

At the far end, Takoda and Riichi sat side by side. They exchanged a brief look—quiet, unspoken—but full of connection.

Holly leaned back with a grin, surveying the table. "So, is this the part where someone makes a big emotional speech, or are we skipping the clichés?"

Reed, beside her, let out a dry chuckle. "This is the warm-up. Real speeches come later—after we've survived."

Ariel nudged Vine's untouched plate. "Don't tell me you're fasting for clarity."

"No," Vine said smoothly, smirking faintly. "I'm saving room for dessert."

Across from them, Aislinn's attention settled on Takoda. Her grip on her fork tightened as conversation ebbed and flowed around the table.

Rain stirred her food absently, her fork chasing vegetables as her eyes flicked toward Riichi and Takoda before quickly shifting away.

Tension thickened.

Eileen set her fork down with a soft clink, drawing the room's attention. Her voice carried easily—calm, clear, and unmistakably firm. "Tonight isn't just another mission. This is about protecting what we've built."

She looked to each person in turn, pausing on Riichi and Takoda. "You'll face the worst of it. But we're with you. All of us."

The silence that followed pressed in around them, broken only by Spark shifting beneath the table.

Aislinn spoke first, her voice trembling but sure. "We'll bring them back. We have to." Her eyes remained on Takoda, unflinching.

Rowan's hand found hers under the table. "We will."

Ariel stared down at her plate, her voice barely above a whisper. "They're too stubborn to let Khan win."

"They are," Vine said quietly. Arms crossed, his focus remained on Riichi and Takoda. "And that's what's going to get us through tonight."

Rain straightened slightly, her voice low but clear. "You're stronger than Khan. Both of you."

The words hung between them—less comfort, more truth.

After a breath, Vine added, "You two... you're the ones who keep us grounded. If anyone can take him down, it's you."

The table stilled. Even Ariel leaned in, caught by the rare seriousness in his voice.

Holly broke the moment with a lopsided grin. "I knew it. He does have a heart under all that brooding."

Takoda's hands rested quietly in her lap before she finally spoke. Her voice was soft but steady. "I'm not letting any of you down." She glanced at Riichi. "We'll get through this. Together."

Riichi's grin eased the tension, his tone light. "No pressure or anything. Just saving the world."

Scattered laughter followed—small, but real.

Birch raised his glass, his voice calm and grounded as it cut through the soft murmur of the dining room. "To Riichi and Takoda—and to all of us. In Hopi, we say Koyaanisqat-si—life out of balance. Tonight, we fight to restore harmony."

The table stilled. His words held in the air, settling with purpose. One by one, the group lifted their glasses, the quiet clink a thread of unity in the tension-laced room.

Hazel leaned back and unwrapped a small cloth bundle in her lap. "I made these," she said, her voice gentle but sure. Nestled inside were intricately carved charms, each etched with delicate runes.

"They'll help us stay connected," she added, her gaze moving from one teammate to the next. "Keep them close tonight."

Hands reached without hesitation. The charms were light, but each carried meaning. Aislinn turned hers over slowly, her thumb brushing the grooves. Rowan took his in silence, holding it with quiet intensity. Rain's hands trembled slightly as she pressed hers to her chest.

Silence returned, deeper this time, threaded with emotion.

Aislinn leaned closer to Rowan, her words low, almost breaking. "They've always been there for us. We owe them everything."

Rowan nodded, his jaw tight. His attention didn't stray from Riichi and Takoda. "And we'll be there for them," he said quietly. "No matter what."

Across the table, Ariel shifted. She leaned toward Vine, her usual spark dimmed. "I hate waiting," she admitted, the cheer gone from her voice. "It's worse than the fight."

Vine glanced her way. The edge in his expression softened, the mask slipping just enough. "Yeah," he murmured. "But when we win, it's worth it."

Rain sat motionless, her charm still clutched in her hands. Her fingers twitched faintly. "What if—"

Nik laid his hand over hers before the question could finish. "No what-ifs," he said, voice calm, unyielding. "We'll bring them back."

She looked at him for a moment, and some of the tightness in her shoulders eased, though the storm behind her eyes didn't clear.

Then Holly leaned toward Ash, her grin tugging the air back into something close to normal. "So," she teased, "are you shifting into something less terrifying tonight? A bunny, maybe? That might boost morale."

Ash exhaled through his nose, a ghost of a grin forming. "A bunny?"

Holly shrugged. "People would remember it."

Reed, nearby, smirked. "If he does, I'm betting Holly tries to keep him."

The soft laughter that followed broke through the heaviness like a crack in thick glass. Riichi leaned toward Takoda, murmuring something under his breath. Her smile was small, but real. The bond between them held fast—solid and unshaken.

As the meal began to taper, chairs shifted and conversations quieted. Rowan rose first, scanning the table with a look that settled briefly on Riichi and Takoda. He gave a subtle nod and turned toward the hallway, his steps controlled but driven.

Eileen remained seated, Hazel's charm turning slowly between her fingers. She closed her eyes—not from weariness, but from focus. The mission loomed, and with it, every burden she carried. She would meet it, as she always had—without hesitation, and without fear.

After the sun dipped below the trees, the Fallen spread throughout the mansion, each lost in their own rituals. Low voices carried through the halls, broken only by the soft clink of charms or the sound of blades sliding into sheaths. Between the preparations, moments surfaced—a quiet glance, a hushed laugh, a few parting words—all steeped in the shadow of what lay ahead.

Nik sat on the back steps, elbows resting on his knees as he watched the horizon fade. The air had cooled, brushing against his skin while the sky deepened into layers of amber and violet. The first stars pierced through. His breathing remained even, practiced—ritualized calm before every mission.

The screen door creaked behind him. He glanced back.

Rain stepped out with a mug in each hand, steam rising in delicate curls. She paused before making her way down the steps, her bare feet thudding softly against the wood.

"I thought you might need this," she said, offering him one of the mugs.

Nik accepted it with a nod. "Thanks." He didn't look away from the sky.

Rain settled beside him, legs folded, her own mug warming her hands. The quiet stretched—not awkward, just full.

"You always come out here before something big," she said softly.

Nik's lips lifted in the faintest smile. "It's easier to think out here. Or not think."

Rain tilted her head. "Which is it tonight?"

He breathed out through his nose, the sound barely audible. "Both. I keep wondering if this is the one. The mission where things don't reset. Where we don't come back the same."

Rain's fingers curled slightly around her mug, but her voice stayed even. "You've come back before. What makes this one different?"

"Kubla Khan." Nik's voice dropped. "He's not just powerful. He knows how to dismantle us. Slowly. That's what makes him dangerous."

Rain's hand touched his arm, light but unwavering. "You're stronger than he is. And you're not doing this alone."

Nik finally looked at her. The guarded edge in his features softened. "It's not just about me. If I fail... everyone pays for it."

"You won't." Her tone was calm, certain. "You've come through worse. You've never let anyone down. Tonight's no different."

Nik didn't answer right away. He set the mug down beside him, exhaling slowly. Then, with a rare glint of humor, "I don't think waiting counts as the easy job."

Rain smiled. "It doesn't. But someone has to make sure there's tea when you get back."

A quiet laugh escaped him, his posture relaxing for the first time.

"Thanks," he said. "For the tea. And everything."

"You'd do the same," Rain said lightly, leaning back on her hands.

They sat there for a while, the hush around them forming a quiet barrier against the night still to come.

★★★

The common room glowed with the low light of a single lamp. Beyond its reach, the mansion buzzed with final preparations, but here, the quiet held. Spark lay curled in Vine's lap, tail thumping lazily against the chair as Vine absently stroked his fur.

Ariel sat cross-legged on the arm of a nearby chair, leaning forward with her elbows on her knees, eyes fixed on him.

"You know," she said, head tilting, "for someone who pretends not to care, you're weirdly good with him."

Vine didn't look up. "I'm full of surprises," he replied dryly, though a trace of amusement warmed his tone.

Ariel smiled faintly, resting her chin in her hand. "You're also really good at dodging questions." She leaned in slightly. "Seriously—how are you doing? And don't say fine."

Vine leaned back a little, still scratching behind Spark's ears. "Fine," he said, smirk slipping into place.

Ariel groaned. "You're impossible."

He stayed quiet for a moment, his attention on Spark, the humor in his expression fading.

"Not everything needs a deep dive," he said. "Sometimes, keeping it together is the goal."

Ariel raised a brow. "So bottling things up is a strength now?"

"Not bottling." His voice stayed calm, but firmer now. "Prioritizing. You think the Golden Dawn cares if I'm processing trauma? Feelings can wait."

Ariel frowned, chin still resting on her hand. "You don't think it's better to let someone in? So you're not carrying all of it alone?"

Vine's hand paused. His gaze dropped to Spark. "Depends," he said quietly. "Opening up can be a distraction. You have to know when it's worth it."

She blinked, her energy subdued. "I never thought of it like that."

Spark nudged Vine's hand with a small huff, demanding attention. Vine scratched behind his ears again, his tone lightening. "He's a good reminder. Focus on what matters. The rest can wait."

Ariel studied him for another beat, her expression softening. "You're not as bad at the 'feelings' thing as you think."

Vine glanced at her, the edge of a smirk returning. "Don't get used to it."

Ariel slid off the chair and crouched beside Spark, ruffling his ears. "Alright, teacher," she said with playful reverence. "I'll try it your way."

Vine's smirk lingered. His voice, unusually warm, followed her as she stood. "Good. Now let me enjoy the quiet while I can."

Ariel stepped toward the door, pausing just once to glance back. Vine remained where she'd left him, stroking Spark's fur, his expression distant—but calm.

★★★

The lawn stretched cool and quiet beneath the fading sun, golden light casting long shadows across the grass. Takoda and Riichi moved in tandem, their steps fluid and controlled as they practiced Aikido. Each breath matched the rhythm of their movements, every shift a meditation in motion.

Takoda eased into a defensive stance, her arms lifting with precision, though a trace of hesitation lingered in her steps. "Do you think it's possible to fight without... fear creeping in?" she asked, voice soft but clear.

Riichi stepped forward, guiding her arm gently into place. "Fear's always there," he said. "But it's a guest. You don't let it take over the house."

She nodded, flowing into a counter-move, her gaze drifting toward the horizon. "What if it's too loud to ignore? What if it throws you off when it matters most?"

Riichi spun with her motion, shifting his weight to stabilize her form. "That's why we train. Breathe, focus, move. Keep your mind clear, your body grounded. The rest follows."

Takoda faltered, her balance slipping. Riichi stepped in without pause, catching the flow of her movement and redirecting it with a slow, fluid circle. "Don't force it," he said, calm and patient. "Let the energy move through you—then guide it."

She mirrored the motion, her shoulders relaxing as she followed his lead. Tension ebbed, and a faint smile touched her lips. "It feels... natural, when you say it like that."

Riichi's mouth curved. "That's the goal. Second nature. No fear, no hesitation—just now."

They paused, holding their final positions in a moment of stillness that felt more grounding than silence.

Takoda glanced at him. "You make it look easy. Like fear doesn't touch you."

His expression softened. "It does," he said. "But it's not stronger than why we fight."

She straightened as the last edge of sunlight dipped behind the trees. Her stance reset, centered. "I'm ready. For whatever comes."

Riichi nodded once. "Good. Stay in the moment."

Without another word, they resumed their rhythm. Motion and breath returned to harmony, the soft rustle of their steps the only sound. As the shadows deepened around them, their movements stayed locked in sync—a quiet promise made before nightfall.

★★★

The central hall was dim, sconces casting soft halos along the stone walls. The Fallen stood in a loose semi-circle, the air between them humming with quiet purpose. Each was dressed for war—charms secured, weapons ready, resolve etched into every line of their posture.

Rowan stood at the front, shoulders squared, the mission already written into his stance. Beside him, Aislinn held her shield charm, her thumb brushing its engraved surface.

Near a pillar, Vine leaned with arms crossed, the usual smirk absent, replaced by cool, quiet focus. He glanced toward Ariel and Rain, who stood near the edge of the room with Spark at their feet. The dog's tail gave a half-hearted wag, subdued by the tension.

Riichi and Takoda stood side by side, their breathing matched, calm and rhythmic—a reflection of the bond that centered them both.

The quiet shifted as Eileen stepped forward. She didn't raise her voice, but the moment she entered the center of the room, everything else faded.

She paused, letting silence anchor the room before she spoke.

"Tonight isn't just another fight. It's the culmination of every step that brought us here."

Her eyes moved across the room, pausing briefly on each face.

"This isn't about Kubla Khan. It's not even just about the Golden Dawn. It's about protecting the people who will never know how close the world came to falling apart. It's about preserving everything we've built—everything we've *become*—through loss, through love, through sacrifice."

She turned to Rowan and Aislinn. "You've both grown into leaders. You've earned every step of that journey."

To Riichi and Takoda, her voice took on a quieter edge. "You carry the most tonight. But you do not carry it alone."

She straightened, voice rising just enough to carry.

"Every one of you brings something vital. *Trust that.* Trust each other."

The room held its breath as her tone deepened, each word struck with intention.

"Remember who we are. We are the Fallen. We fight not because we have to—but because we chose to. We stand between the darkness and the light. And tonight—we do not break."

She looked to each of them again—not with command, but connection.

Rowan's shoulders eased just slightly. Aislinn's grip on her charm loosened.

Riichi met her eyes and gave the faintest nod. Takoda mirrored him.

Vine's mouth pulled into the faintest smirk, more sharp than amused. Nearby, Ivy and Holly exchanged a brief, wordless glance, their tension coiled tight beneath their calm.

Her attention turned to the edge of the room. Ariel's hand brushed Rain's arm, a shared reassurance. Eileen's eyes lingered on both of them before she lifted her hand, forming the sigil of unity.

"Tonight, we don't fight alone. We move as one. One mission. One purpose. And when it's done, we return. *Together.*"

A hush settled around them—not silence, but conviction.

Rowan was the first to break the stillness. "Let's go," he said, his voice clear, unshakable.

The Fallen moved as one. A few exchanged quick glances or quiet words as they passed through the archway.

Riichi leaned toward Takoda, murmuring something that drew a soft smile from her.

Vine nudged Ariel's shoulder as he walked by. She met his look, unspoken humor tempered by everything beneath it.

Nik paused near Rain, his eyes locking with hers. He gave a small nod before following the others out.

As the last footsteps faded, Ariel placed a hand on Rain's arm. Her voice dropped to a whisper. "They'll come back."

Spark let out a low whine and pressed against her leg.

The room held still, full of breath that hadn't yet been released—waiting for the night to fall.

Chapter Thirty-Four
The Raging Storm

The ruins of Fort Lawton loomed on the cliffside, their jagged silhouette clawing into the mist like the bones of a long-dead sentinel. Below, the waters of Puget Sound churned with restless fury, waves crashing against the rocks in a rhythm that mimicked a distant heartbeat. The air pulsed with unease, thick with the coppery tang of blood and ozone, as if the land itself recoiled from the magic gathering ahead. Encircling the ritual site, a defensive ward pulsed with malignant energy—its glow throbbed faintly, like a living thing inhaling in the dark.

Eileen's voice cut through the commlink, clear and exacting. "Remember the plan. Neutralize the ward and reach the anchors. They've reinforced everything. We won't get a second chance."

The Fallen moved into position with sharp, silent precision. Boots crunched over damp stone, their advance cloaked in shadows cast by crumbling ruins and fractured walls. Every step was heavy with purpose, the gravity of what lay ahead pressing down like storm clouds ready to split open.

Rowan's fingers curled around the hilt of his sword, the worn leather grip molded perfectly to his hand. Beside him, Aislinn kept pace, her breath measured, but the faint tremble in her fingertips betrayed the tension beneath her calm. "We've got this," Rowan said under his breath, steady and sure.

Aislinn glanced his way. Her nod was slight but purposeful, the weight in her gaze was enough to anchor him.

Ahead, Hazel stopped short, eyes narrowed at the barrier that crackled just beyond the tree line. Twisting arcs of magic lashed out from the ward in uneven bursts, searing lines into the wet ground and releasing a faint hiss with every strike. "That thing's alive," she murmured. "And it's pissed."

Nik adjusted the strap of his satchel, his posture composed, though the set of his jaw betrayed a flicker of strain. Willow and Ivy exchanged a glance, their synchronization instinctive as they began laying out enchanted tools and sigils, their hands moving with smooth familiarity.

In the distance, figures drifted like phantoms through the fog—Golden Dawn patrols. No longer aimless wanderers. These moved with purpose. Patterned. Synchronized. Empowered. Their bodies glowed faintly beneath their armor, arcane markings pulsing beneath their skin. Whatever Khan had done, it had made them stronger. Smarter. Harder to kill.

"Reed," Eileen's voice came over the line, "keep to the outer line. Do not be seen."

"Copy," Reed replied, already vanishing into the mist, his presence dissolving between shadows as if he'd never been there at all.

"Holly, stay close. If they spot him, we need immediate visual disruption."

"I've got him," she said. Magic shimmered around her fingertips, threads of illusion weaving into the fog with a delicate hum. Her shoulders tensed slightly, but her focus didn't waver.

The ward pulsed again—brighter, angrier. A low hum escalated into a deep, bone-vibrating buzz that rolled through the ground like distant thunder. The stones beneath their feet rattled, dust shaking loose from the fractured ruins around them. The barrier seemed to breathe—its edges warping, tightening, like it was preparing to lash out.

"Ward team," Eileen ordered, her voice slicing clean through the hum of unstable magic. "Hazel, begin analysis. Nik, Ivy, Willow—move now. Oak, shield them from backlash."

Hazel dropped to a crouch beside the pulsating barrier, her fingers hovering just above the damp ground. Water tendrils unfurled around her hands, gliding across the soil in deliberate patterns as she tapped into her Flow of Knowledge. Her eyes moved with fierce calculation, reading the shifting layers of magic embedded in the ward's surface.

"It's triple-layered," she called, voice raised over the buzzing air. "All of it reinforced—Khan's work. Nik, destabilize the structure. Ivy, start unraveling the outer mesh. Willow, be ready to catch the feedback—it's going to hit hard."

The barrier reacted immediately, flaring in defiance. Arcs of lightning cracked through the fog, the strikes wild and laced with kinetic energy. Oak stepped forward, his arms raised. A glowing barrier flared into place just in time to absorb the brunt of the strike. "You're shielded," he said, planting his boots against the shifting earth, the translucent dome pulsing around him.

Nik dropped to one knee, palms pressed flat against the wet ground. The soil rippled beneath his touch, threads of geomantic power surging outward in jagged lines. Cracks tore through the earth, racing toward the ward's core. The barrier flared in response and launched a retaliatory shockwave. Nik flinched, teeth gritting as the tremor knocked him back a step.

"Stabilize and adjust," Eileen snapped through the commlink. "Left—three paces."

Nik shifted, recalibrating his stance. The cracks beneath him deepened, the power flowing more deliberately now, drawn straight toward the heart of the defense.

Ivy stepped into place, her hands carving invisible patterns into the air. Reality bent beneath her fingertips, and the outer threads of the barrier warped under the pressure. The structure resisted, coiling back like a living creature trying to tighten around itself. Sweat slicked her brow, but she held firm. "It's pushing back. Harder than anything we've dealt with."

Willow moved in fluidly, her hands already glowing. When the ward lashed out again, she caught the tendrils mid-air, twisting them sideways and redirecting the magic downward with raw precision. Sparks scattered across her arms, but she didn't flinch, grounding the surge with practiced control.

"Redirect left!" Eileen's voice rang out.

Willow shifted her footing and drove the energy into the fractures Nik had created. "I'm on it!" she called out, voice taut with effort.

From somewhere deeper in the fog, a horn sounded—a low, mournful blast that echoed through the ruins like a warning bell. The Golden Dawn had mobilized.

"Distraction team, move," Eileen said immediately. "Reed, west side. Holly, blanket him."

"Scouts incoming," Reed replied, already moving. His voice remained calm, but his presence vanished between the ruins like smoke on wind.

Holly's magic surged into the mist. Phantom forms shimmered to life, slipping between the ruins in muddled directions. The scouts scattered, drawn toward illusions that danced and twisted out of reach. Reed moved through the confusion like a blade in the dark—fast, clean, and unseen.

Near the barrier, Hazel's water tendrils narrowed into a focused thread of force. She plunged it into the ward's core, channeling raw elemental energy directly into the unstable matrix. "Now!" she called, urgency cutting through the rising hum.

Nik and Ivy moved in tandem. The fissures widened with a groan that echoed through the cliffs, the barrier shuddering under the strain. Willow drew the redirected energy into a tight, focused beam and unleashed it with a snap of her hands.

"Together!" Eileen ordered.

The ward ruptured in a deafening blast. Light shattered outward in jagged shards before dissolving into the mist. The ground where it stood was scorched and smoking, the scent of ozone hanging heavy in the air.

The Fallen stood still, the moment suspended as their eyes traced the destruction.

Then the chanting from the ruins surged—louder now. More voices, more certainty. Whatever lay ahead was already stirring.

Eileen's voice broke the silence, crisp and unyielding. "Ward neutralized. Teams, move into position for Phase 1. The Golden Dawn knows we're here—expect resistance."

Weapons were drawn, stances shifted, and the tension tightened like a bowstring as the Fallen surged forward.

Reed moved like a shadow, slipping between vantage points with quiet precision. His bowstring whispered once before an arrow struck true—one patrol down. "Enemy movement north of the ritual site. Moving to intercept," came his calm report through the commlink.

"Take them out quietly," Eileen responded. "Holly, support with illusions."

He melted into the fog. Holly's magic shimmered nearby, creating false targets that pulled enemy eyes away from Reed's movements.

Ahead, Ivy burst into a skirmish, her dual blades flashing as she intercepted a squad of Golden Dawn soldiers. Her strikes were fluid, brutal, clean. When a mage hurled glowing chains toward her, she distorted the space with a flick of her wrist, stepping harmlessly aside. "Better luck next time," she muttered, dropping him with a slash.

"Ivy, push forward," Eileen instructed. "Don't let them regroup."

To the west, Willow's energy blasts flared with intensity, scattering enemy lines. An elite mage charged her—she caught his spell midair and redirected it into another squad, the explosion rippling through their ranks. "Willow, shift west. Reinforcements incoming."

Holly conjured a final wave of illusions—spectral reinforcements that danced and surged across the battlefield. As strain etched across her face, the phantoms dragged enemy units into traps or dead ends.

"Hold them as long as you can," Eileen's voice grounded her. "Reed's nearly finished his sweep."

On the defensive line, Oak stood immovable, deflecting wave after wave of incoming fire. Nik carved deeper trenches into the battlefield, driving enemy units into Holly's illusions and toward Oak's waiting defenses. "Nik, deeper fissures on the left flank. Oak, reinforce the line."

As the team neared the wind anchor, the air erupted in motion. An enchanted windchime pulsed with magic at the enemy's center, its gusts cutting across the terrain like blades. Each sharp note sent wind lashing against them, slowing their advance.

"Willow, left flank. Birch, cover Ivy. That windchime is the priority," Eileen ordered.

Birch hurled his chakram into the crowd, clearing a path. Willow's blasts countered the elite mages guarding the anchor, each explosion pushing them back.

Ivy advanced fast, her blades catching the light as she twisted through enemy defenses. Reality warped around her, her movements disorienting her attackers. The windchime's melody shrieked louder as she closed in. "Willow, it's vulnerable!" she shouted. "Hit it now!"

Willow gathered her energy and fired a focused blast. The windchime shattered in a shockwave of light and sound. The melody died, replaced by the ringing crack of the anchor's collapse.

The shockwave knocked them off balance. Ivy dropped to one knee, Birch braced and pulled Willow back upright.

"Anchor down," Eileen snapped. "Retaliation incoming. Move out—now."

Golden Dawn forces poured in from all sides.

Rowan was already cutting through the surge, his blade a blur. Aislinn followed, kinetic energy surging from her hands. She struck down two flanking soldiers, then deflected a volley of arrows with a rippling shield. "Rowan, Aislinn—south flank. Hold the line. Buy us time."

Rowan gave a curt nod. Aislinn moved with him, her energy crackling as they pushed forward.

Above the battlefield, Ash soared in falcon form, surveying the new wave of reinforcements. His sharp eyes tracked movement to the northeast—a small group of mages coordinating behind cover. He banked to get a clearer look, but something shifted in the air.

The pressure changed.

A flicker—barely visible—moved from the edge of the cliffside. Then came the strike.

A blast of compressed wind magic, silent and razor-sharp, slammed into him mid-flight.

Ash shrieked once, then tumbled from the sky—wings folding as his body shimmered and shifted back into human form. Blood bloomed along his side, his commlink torn away in the fall.

Aislinn looked up. Her pulse stopped. Ash—

Without a word, she vanished.

She reappeared mid-air, arms open, catching him just before he hit the rocks. His unconscious weight slammed into her, and with a burst of light, they vanished again—landing hard near the edge of Oak's position.

Aislinn dropped to her knees, cradling him. Her palm lit with healing magic as she pressed it to his side, sealing the wound with a determined breath.

Across the field, Rowan paused just long enough to catch it—her teleport, the mid-air rescue, the force in her stance as she knelt to heal. His brows drew together, barely a flicker of expression, but his focus sharpened. *She's not just the girl I love anymore—she's a damn force of nature.*

Ash gasped, coughing once before groaning. "Khan," he rasped. "He's here. Far back, watching. He took me out from a distance. Lost my commlink."

Aislinn tapped hers. "Eileen, Ash is down but stable. Khan hit him. He's not engaging—just watching."

Eileen's response came sharp: "Everyone stay sharp. This isn't over."

Suddenly, the battlefield shifted. A figure emerged from the shadows—cloaked in dark robes etched with crimson runes, his presence radiating arrogance. Gideon Kross.

He moved like a man orchestrating a performance, each gesture precise, each word dripping with superiority. "Let's see what all the fuss is about," he murmured, and flicked his wrist.

A blast of concussive force erupted from his palm. Riichi and Takoda dodged, their instincts sharp—but Kross pressed them hard. Every strike came with supernatural precision, empowered by rituals that warped the very air around them. His magic twisted the ground beneath their feet, disrupting balance and driving them back.

Riichi's katana slashed across Kross's side—but the blade passed through an illusion. Kross reappeared behind them, arms outstretched.

"Time's up."

A glowing barrier snapped into place with a thunderous crack, sealing them inside a shimmering entrapment zone. Its walls pulsed with sickly light, layered in overlapping runes that shimmered like burning oil. Oppressive energy poured inward—crushing, cold, and relentless.

Riichi dropped to one knee, bracing himself with his katana as the pressure intensified. It pressed on his mind, his memories, the sharp edge of grief and rage clawing at the surface.

Takoda staggered, catching herself with effort. Her legs trembled, lungs burning, but she refused to fall.

Outside the trap, Kross tilted his head with mock sympathy. "Don't worry. This part doesn't kill you. It just *feels* like it does." Then, with a smirk, he vanished into the mist.

Inside the trap, Riichi's fists clenched, his thoughts muddled beneath the onslaught of emotional chaos. "It's... too much," he ground out.

"Riichi," Takoda snapped. "Look at me."

Their eyes met, and the fog in his mind thinned just enough to breathe.

Breathe, she urged. *Focus on me. I've got the shield up. It's holding—barely. I don't know how long I can hold this.*

Riichi inhaled slowly, clarity returning. "You've done enough. I'll figure out the rest."

He crouched beside her, his voice low. "We're going to play along. Let them think we're broken."

Takoda frowned. "Pretend to fall apart? Really?"

"It'll buy time. They'll focus elsewhere while we wait for the anchors to fall. Then we end it—Fated Blade cuts the core."

She hesitated. "That's a hell of a bet."

"It's one we'll win," he said simply.

Outside the barrier, Golden Dawn soldiers loomed—watching like vultures circling prey.

Riichi slumped forward, letting his body hang heavy. Takoda knelt beside him, head bowed, her features blank.

But beneath the stillness, their bond pulsed like a live wire.

Riichi shifted slightly, eyes scanning the chaos beyond the barrier until he found Rowan. He tapped the side of his head. *Commlink's dead.* A subtle shake. *We're pretending. She's shielding us.* His hand dropped to his katana, his grip tightening. *We'll destroy it.*

Rowan's expression sharpened. He gave one firm nod.

"Riichi and Takoda are playing dead," Rowan said through the commlink. "Takoda's shielding them. Destroy the remaining anchors and the ritual. They'll drop the barrier with Fated Blade. Aislinn and I will sync Shield of Ages when they do. Move!"

Eileen's voice followed immediately, calm and decisive. "You've got your orders. Hazel, Oak, Alder—water anchor. Vine, Rowan, Aislinn—fire. Willow's team, dismantle the core. Report any shifts."

The battlefield erupted into further chaos.

Rowan and Aislinn led the charge, their movements coordinated and brutal. Strikes landed clean, pushing enemy lines back step by step. Nik and Oak held their defensive position, shielding teammates from incoming waves of Golden Dawn forces.

"Rowan, left flank! Nik, shield the east. Keep the formation tight," Eileen's voice crackled through the commlink.

The Fallen surged forward, focused and relentless, even as exhaustion began to claw at the edges of their stamina. Across the battlefield, within the barrier, Riichi and Takoda maintained the illusion of collapse, their fury coiled tight, waiting.

Then the air changed—abrupt and absolute.

The wind died.

Sound dropped out of the world for a breath.

And then the pressure slammed down like a descending weight.

Fog thickened unnaturally, crawling like smoke across the field. The mist curled away from a figure that hadn't been there a heartbeat ago. Not walking. Not approaching.

Suddenly present.

Kubla Khan stood at the far edge of the battlefield, watching.

His robes moved with the wind though no wind stirred. The storm seemed to condense around him—air pulsing tighter, harder. His presence pushed into every corner of the space like an unseen tide. His eyes, sharp and dark as obsidian, swept the battlefield without urgency. There was no showmanship. No arrogance.

Just certainty.

And then he moved.

The earth cracked beneath him—not from impact, but from resistance. The land rejected him even as he passed.

Ash's warning screamed through the ritual site. "He's here. He's not hiding anymore."

Kross reappeared on the opposite flank, a feral grin splitting his face. "Told you the real fun was just beginning."

Then came the strike.

A pulse of wind magic erupted from Khan's palm—silent and invisible until it landed. The shockwave tore through the central line, sending the Fallen reeling. Weapons clattered. Spells faltered. Oak barely raised a barrier in time to absorb the brunt of the blast.

"Fall back from center!" Eileen's voice snapped. "Maintain anchor positions—don't let him fracture the line!"

Hazel, Oak, and Alder broke toward the water anchor—a crystalline orb suspended over a swirling pool of power. The defenses surrounding it had grown denser since the initial engagement, threads of energy braided into tighter configurations.

Hazel didn't hesitate. She reached for the flow, pulling it toward her hands. Water twisted to her command, wrapping around the anchor like a snare.

"Adjust left," Alder called. "I see a weakness!"

"Hazel, now!" Eileen urged. "Oak, brace for backlash."

Oak raised his arms. His barrier flared just in time to deflect a spear of condensed water launched by a defending mage. The attack ricocheted, narrowly missing Hazel as she pushed more force into the anchor.

Alder stepped in beside her, timing her next strike. "Go!"

A final twist of freezing current snapped through the orb's defenses—Hazel shattered it in a flash of ice and light. Oak shoved his shield outward, catching the resulting shockwave.

"Water anchor down," Eileen confirmed. "Redirect to support if needed."

Across the battlefield, Rowan, Aislinn, and Vine sprinted toward the fire anchor—a blazing brazier flanked by reinforced enemy lines. The heat warped the air, thick and suffocating.

Rowan cut through the front line, sword flashing with brutal elegance. Aislinn followed, her kinetic blasts striking fast and wide, scattering enemy formations to give Vine space.

Vine stayed behind, hands crackling with raw electricity. The brazier fought back, its magical defenses shifting in rhythm with his attacks.

Behind them, Kross raised a hand—and hurled a cursed bolt toward Vine.

Rowan saw it first. He pivoted, blade intercepting the strike. The energy splintered on impact, but a second hit followed from Khan—wind-force magic that slammed Vine backward.

"Vine, up—now!" Eileen's command snapped through the commlink.

Gritting his teeth, Vine pushed to his feet. His shirt was scorched, his breath ragged, but his hands surged with power. He locked onto the anchor again.

Rowan shouted, "Draw their fire!" and stepped directly into Khan's line of sight.

Khan's head tilted, ever so slightly. A calculation made. He lifted his hand once more—

—but Aislinn struck first.

Her kinetic burst slammed into the brazier's shielding, fracturing the outer casing. Energy buckled.

Vine hurled a concentrated bolt of lightning into the crack.

Rowan charged forward and, with a clean, powerful strike, drove his blade into the anchor's core.

The brazier erupted in a roar of flames and falling debris. The fire anchor shattered.

"Fire anchor destroyed," Eileen said through the commlink, her tone clipped. "Ritual core team, go. Now."

Khan didn't flinch.

He simply stepped forward, unhurried.

Takoda knelt inside the barrier, jaw clenched, her breaths short and uneven. The invisible shield she maintained trembled under the strain. "It's… getting through," she admitted, voice tight. "It's not holding like before."

Her hand pressed to her chest, muscles locking against the emotional weight clawing in. Grief. Fear. Doubt. It pushed against the edges of her mind like rising water.

Across from her, Riichi closed his eyes. The Radiant Surge between them pulsed faintly—an anchor point, barely holding. He reached for her through it, not with panic, but with certainty.

I'm here, he projected, calm and grounded. *Just a little longer.*

Takoda exhaled slowly. The shield steadied.

The battlefield pulsed with chaos.

The ritual vortex surged, wind and energy spiraling outward in violent bursts. Willow redirected streams of unstable power as Ivy manipulated reality itself to unravel the vortex's shape. Nik slammed both palms into the earth, fissures racing toward the ritual's base. Birch's chakram spun overhead, slicing through Golden Dawn soldiers who pushed too close.

"Reinforcements incoming!" Eileen warned through the commlink. "Birch, hold them off. Ivy, push harder!"

The vortex pulsed again—harder, sharper, tighter.

Khan raised his hand.

The energy responded immediately, drawn to him like metal to a magnet. The vortex narrowed, intensified, each pulse faster and more erratic. Ivy staggered mid-cast. Willow's containment trembled under the strain, power lashing across her arms.

"He's amplifying it!" Willow shouted. "I can't hold this much longer!"

From the edge of the fray, Kross emerged, cloaked in dark energy, his grin wide and venomous. He hurled a disruption spell at Birch—earth splitting open at his feet, sending the chakram spiraling wide.

"Tsk, tsk," Kross taunted. "You tear down the altar, and you think that buys you salvation? How cute."

No one answered—but tension rippled through the line.

Then Khan spoke—quietly, almost bored, his gaze sweeping across the scattered teams.

"Your coordination fractures under pressure. That is… disappointing."

Another surge blasted outward from the ritual, ripping the containment net wide open. Ivy fell to one knee. Willow cried out as the magic backlash scorched her palms.

Eileen stood abruptly, hands starting to lift—divine power rising like a storm beneath her skin. For an instant, her form flickered—celestial robes shimmering into view before vanishing again.

Across the battlefield, Oak's attention snapped to her, his voice rising like a blade through the commlink.

"Eileen, NO!" His voice cracked like thunder through the commlink. *"Strength in unity! Trust them!"*

She froze, eyes locking on him—furious, fire-bright. Then, slowly, she crouched again, her silence sharper than any retort.

The moment passed, but the line between intervention and restraint had never felt thinner.

Near the core, Nik growled and drove another spike into the ground. "Now or never!" he yelled.

Ivy forced the last distortion into place, folding the anchor's geometry in on itself. "Willow!"

Willow didn't hesitate. She hurled a final burst of energy into the weakened vortex. It shattered.

Nik struck the ritual's heart with a final surge of earth magic.

The ground trembled. The vortex imploded—light swallowing light until only smoke remained. The chanting stopped. The Golden Dawn forces faltered.

"Ritual core destroyed," Eileen confirmed, her voice steady. "Protect Riichi and Takoda at all costs."

Rowan's voice followed, loud and urgent. "That was the hard part—we finish this now. Hold your ground."

Eileen's tone sharpened. "Slow them down. Hold the line."

Khan didn't roar. He didn't have to.

His power surged across the battlefield like a rising tide—unrelenting, invisible, and absolute. The fractured vortex he had amplified now bled unstable magic, twisting the air with every pulse.

Kross darted along the flanks, flinging precision strikes to keep the Fallen from regrouping, his movements fluid and taunting.

Rowan and Aislinn closed in together, their attacks seamless. Aislinn launched kinetic waves to counter Khan's spiraling strikes, while Rowan's swordplay stayed tight and brutal, pressing forward with unrelenting rhythm. Their synchronized assault drew his attention—just long enough.

The Fallen pulled back further from the barrier, drawing the Golden Dawn forces and Khan's storm of magic away from Riichi and Takoda.

Inside the glowing entrapment, they remained motionless.

Through the commlink, Eileen's voice cut through the tension like a blade. "Stay focused. We're not done yet."

Riichi cast a glance at Takoda, his voice steady despite the chaos swirling around them. "You can drop the aura now."

Takoda's brow furrowed deeply as she shook her head. "If I do that, you'll be consumed by this… this rage. You've felt it—it'll tear us apart."

Riichi placed a firm hand on her shoulder, grounding her. "I can hold out. We need it. The anger, the wrath—it's fuel. It worked during training when you filtered it into Fated Blade. This will make it stronger."

She hesitated, her voice soft but laced with worry. "You promise it'll be quick?"

"Quick. On my signal," he said, his determination unwavering as their eyes locked.

At his silent nod, Takoda let the Protective Aura fade.

The tidal wave of negative energy hit instantly, crushing and oppressive, forcing both of them to their knees. For a brief moment, their breaths faltered under its suffocating weight.

Gritting his teeth, Riichi seized the onslaught, channeling the chaos into his katana. Takoda steadied herself and placed her hand on his shoulder, focusing every ounce of her willpower into filtering the emotional storm. The blade flared brilliantly, a wild surge of orange energy spiraling along its length. Its glow grew brighter and more violent with every passing second, forcing them both to strain under the overwhelming pressure.

Aislinn saw the glow from across the battlefield.

She grabbed Rowan's arm without hesitation, and the two vanished in a blink—teleporting directly beside Riichi and Takoda just as the katana reached critical charge.

With a guttural cry, Riichi swung the katana, unleashing Fated Blade. The energy exploded outward in a torrent of light and power, tearing through the barrier in a thunderous crack. The sound reverberated across the battlefield as shards of glowing energy rained down, the oppressive weight lifting instantly.

In perfect sync, Rowan and Aislinn activated Shield of Ages, a shimmering dome of blue energy encasing the four of them just as the explosion's shockwave hit. The ground shook violently, but the shield held firm, absorbing the blast's destructive force.

Static cleared from the commlinks, and Riichi's calm voice broke through the lingering echoes of the blast. "Barrier's down. Thanks for waiting."

Takoda's voice followed, sharp and fierce. "Let's finish this! Khan is ours! Aislinn and Rowan, you can have Kross!"

Aislinn's laugh carried a note of humor. "Ooh. They've pissed her off. They better watch out."

Rowan smirked, a rare flicker of amusement crossing his face. "This is going to be fun."

Through the commlink, a few chuckles rippled, a brief but welcome moment of levity in the chaos.

Orange light flared again as Radiant Surge engulfed Riichi and Takoda. Their movements blurred with speed as they surged toward Khan, their synchronization almost otherworldly. Each step left scorched ground and a trail of light in their wake.

The remaining Golden Dawn forces hesitated, their resolve faltering as the glowing pair cut through their ranks like a storm.

"They're unstoppable!" a mage cried out, panic rising in his voice.

Another called out desperately, "Protect the Reborn Conqueror!"

Khan turned sharply, power radiating from him in a quiet, crushing wave. The air thickened as he moved, not with fury, but with absolute control—like a dam about to break.

"You think you can stand against me?" His voice was calm, almost serene. "Tell me—does Kiki whisper to all of you, or just her favorites?"

Riichi didn't blink. "Quit spouting garbage."

Khan's eyes narrowed—interested, not insulted.

He raised his arm, and the ground beneath them convulsed. Energy surged outward in precise, serpentine lines—not fire, but raw force and gravitational pressure. The tendrils cracked stone and buckled terrain, forcing Takoda to pivot and leap through the chaos.

She twisted in midair and landed in a crouch just beyond Khan's reach, her body low, breathing sharp.

Khan's tone dipped into mockery. "What hope do you have, little one, dancing around ruin?"

He dismissed her as a distraction. That was his first mistake.

Takoda surged forward, movements seamless and unpredictable. Khan's eyes tracked her as she closed the distance, fast and low. She ducked under a second wave of kinetic force, pivoted sharply, and drove her palm into his jaw. His head snapped back.

He didn't stumble. But he did pause.

Then she struck again. As he reached for her, she caught his arm mid-swing and twisted it with a clean jujutsu lock. His shoulder rolled under the pressure, and she used his own weight to slam him into the scorched ground.

Khan exhaled through his nose—calm, but edged.

He struck the earth with his palm, releasing a concussive blast of force that cracked the ground outward. Takoda vaulted over the rippling impact, her boots skimming molten stone.

She landed and faced him again, heat shimmering around her. "Power? All I see is a coward throwing tantrums."

Riichi surged forward, his katana gleaming as he met Khan's next strike. The clash rang out like thunder, the ground trembling beneath their feet. Riichi held firm, his voice cold and certain. "We've already won, Khan. You just don't see it yet."

Khan's hand snapped upward, and the ground beneath Riichi detonated in a column of compressed energy. Riichi pivoted and rolled, evading the blast, but Khan was already in motion—barehanded, fast, brutal.

Riichi parried the next strike with a clean arc of his blade, sparks flying as metal met raw force. A second blow followed—a downward strike, meant to crush—and Riichi deflected it, then twisted away.

Takoda circled to the side, waiting for an opening. When Khan raised his arm again, she dove under his guard and slammed her palm into his ribs. A kinetic pulse blasted from her touch, sending him reeling back a step.

He recovered instantly.

"Insolent," Khan muttered—not angry, but appraising. "Still clinging to purpose. Still pretending it matters."

He turned slightly toward Riichi. "Did your village think the same, when they begged to live?"

Riichi's jaw tightened.

Takoda sprang backward, flipping off a fractured stone ledge to avoid another blast of power. She landed with flawless control and narrowed her eyes. "Trying to rattle him with the past? That's pathetic—even for you."

Khan responded by driving both hands into the ground.

The terrain cracked wide open beneath them. Spikes of earth and kinetic pillars surged upward, reshaping the battlefield around the trio. No chaos—only deliberate manipulation. He was boxing them in.

But it didn't matter.

Riichi and Takoda moved in tandem, unshaken by the shifting ground.

Takoda struck first, a series of sharp, clean blows aimed high and low. Khan blocked with one arm, countering with raw kinetic blasts, but Riichi followed immediately. His katana lashed out, each strike surgically placed, hammering Khan's defenses.

Their Radiant Surge burned brighter. Every movement fed the next. Takoda's strikes opened paths for Riichi's blade, and his counterattacks reset the rhythm for hers.

They drove him back. For the first time, Khan had to give ground—not in panic, but in cold, silent assessment.

His power surged again—but his face remained unreadable.

The ground quaked as Khan summoned a massive column of energy, raw and focused, sending it crashing toward them. Riichi shoved Takoda aside, raising his katana in both hands. The blade pulsed with orange light as he slashed upward, cleaving through the blast and scattering shards of fractured force around them.

Breathing harder, Khan straightened, his aura vibrating with tension. The space around him twisted under the pressure he exerted. "You dare challenge the inevitable?" he said, low and seething. "You'll break beneath me like all the others."

"We've heard that one before," Takoda snapped, darting in and delivering a sharp kick to his knee, forcing him to stagger.

Khan reeled, balance disrupted, and Riichi pressed in with another clean strike, his katana blazing. Their coordination intensified, each blow landing with deadly rhythm as they forced the Reborn Conqueror backward one step at a time.

In the distance, the other Fallen maintained their ground under Eileen's sharp direction. Rowan and Aislinn tore through Golden Dawn reinforcements, their movements perfectly synchronized. Kross met them head-on, hurling razor-edged blasts of wind and force—but they advanced without hesitation.

Aislinn launched a concussive kinetic burst, knocking Kross off balance just as Rowan swept in, his blade slashing upward in a precise, punishing arc. Kross reeled, caught between them. Another kinetic pulse struck him square in the chest, sending him stumbling backward, his stance broken.

For a heartbeat, he looked ready to retaliate—but instead, a cold smirk tugged at his lips.

"You'll regret that," he said, voice low.

And then—he vanished. No portal. No warning. Just gone.

"Target down," Rowan's voice crackled through the commlink.

Eileen's voice followed, focused and clear. "Stay sharp. We finish this together."

Riichi and Takoda delivered a final coordinated strike that sent Khan crashing to one knee. The tension on the battlefield thickened to a breaking point.

A shared thought rose between them—anchored by Rowan and Aislinn's words, sharpened by instinct:

"Together, focus on what matters. Strengthen our allies. Destroy our foes."

They opened their connection fully, and a wave of brilliant orange energy burst from them, radiating across the field. Khan recoiled as the light surged outward, his arms raised to shield his eyes. The wave swept through the battlefield, washing over the Fallen.

The Fallen's wounds vanished as soon as the wave touched them. Torn muscle and broken bones healed in seconds. Fatigue melted beneath the surge of renewal.

Golden Dawn soldiers weren't so lucky. Screams erupted as the wave reached them. One by one, their bodies crumbled to ash, the dark energy that sustained them obliterated in an instant.

Eileen's voice came through the comm—almost reverent. "That... was Veil of Valor."

When the light faded, Khan remained kneeling—glaring.

Riichi and Takoda flinched as a sharp sting surged across their necks. They touched the spot, finding fresh black marks etched into their skin. The symbol glowed faintly, the single Japanese character 力 settling beneath the surface.

Riichi brushed aside a lock of Takoda's hair, his expression unreadable. "It's the character for strength. Chikara. Fitting, don't you think?"

Takoda met his eyes, shoulders still squared, her voice quiet but firm. "Strength. Just what we need to keep pushing forward."

Eileen's voice broke through the commlink. "That mark signifies mastery. You've become the first fully Soulbound couple. Well done, both of you."

Khan didn't speak. He rose slowly, the air tightening as his aura thickened. Space itself seemed to bow beneath the gravity of his fury.

"You think this changes anything?" he said finally, voice low and sharp. "I've broken men far stronger than you."

Riichi glanced at Takoda. "My turn."

She gave a quiet nod, and he stepped forward alone.

Both hands gripped the katana—the same blade that had once belonged to his father. The blade that had witnessed his village's fall. The blade that had carried him through wrath, through redemption.

"This ends now," he said.

Khan met him with devastating speed. The impact cracked the ground beneath their feet. Takoda flanked behind, not to lead, but to amplify—matching Riichi's rhythm with seamless precision.

Their history clashed with every strike.

"You were a child," Khan sneered between blows. "You should've died with the rest." Riichi didn't flinch.

"You showed me what wrath could do," he said, parrying hard and driving forward. "She showed me how to turn it into something useful."

Takoda struck from the side, a pulse of energy slamming into Khan's ribs, breaking his stance. Riichi closed in—faster now—not from rage, but clarity. Every movement was controlled. Every strike had purpose.

"You're not unstoppable," Riichi said. "You're just a relic who doesn't know when to fall."

Khan's composure cracked. Fury surged across his face as he unleashed a brutal wave of raw energy.

Riichi blocked it with an upward sweep of his blade.

Takoda moved in behind him, her hand resting at his back—infusing the katana with filtered anger. The blade lit with Radiant Surge, the orange glow tightening around its edge, refined and deadly.

He felt it—the anger—and he didn't fight it. He shaped it.

Takoda's voice cut through the storm. "Now, Riichi! Finish it!"

He lunged.

Fated Blade ignited, the slash arcing wide—a blazing cut across the battlefield. It struck Khan clean, shattering his defenses. A second pulse from Takoda's palm knocked him back.

Khan dropped to one knee, teeth bared, his aura fraying.

"This isn't over," he growled.

"We know," Riichi answered.

And with a sharp burst of light, Khan vanished—injured, driven back, but still out there.

Silence fell across the battlefield, the Fallen stood frozen, breath held, weapons low.

Riichi lowered his katana, the glow dimming at last. His chest rose and fell—once, sharply—as the silence stretched. Then he turned to Takoda, pulled her into a fierce embrace, and buried his face in the curve of her neck. He didn't speak. He didn't need to. The past was behind him. And for the first time, it felt over.

Takoda held him just as tightly, one hand sliding up his back, steady and sure.

"It's over," she whispered.

"Yeah," he murmured, voice rough against her skin. "It is."

Then Eileen's voice came through the commlink, calm and composed. "Well done. Regroup and assess injuries. Stay vigilant—this may not be the end."

Rowan reached Riichi and Takoda first, his steps measured as he approached. He paused, gazing between them before he gave a short nod. "That was… incredible."

Takoda exhaled, the corner of her mouth lifting. "Just another day saving the world."

Holly's voice crackled through the commlink, bright and tinged with awe. "Whatever that power was, it felt like I could bench-press a truck as soon as it touched me. Can we keep it?"

Laughter rippled through the team—a rare, welcome breath of levity.

The battlefield had fallen still. Only the fading hiss of dissipating magic and the distant calls of seabirds stirred the morning air. One by one, the Fallen gathered, silhouetted against the pale light cresting over the Sound. Their movements were slower now, the adrenaline draining away to reveal the bruises beneath—but their eyes held quiet pride.

Eileen's voice came through the commlink one last time, calm and steady with the weight of conviction. "Well done, everyone. You've accomplished what many would call impossible. Take pride in this victory. Let's go home."

They turned toward the vehicles parked along the edge of the field. The cars rumbled to life, headlights sweeping through the mist as tires carved tracks through damp earth. The scent of ozone and scorched stone remained, mingling with sea air and dawn.

As the team continued to get in their cars and drive off, Vine lingered.

He glanced down at a patch of sand, charred and fractured where the battle's fiercest flames had struck. Lowering one hand, he released a precise arc of electricity into the blackened grit. Heat fused the grains into a jagged, branch-like shard of glass. Vine crouched and turned it over in his fingers, its surface catching the new light.

A piece of it, he thought, slipping it into his pocket. *She'd like this. Something to remember what we fought for.*

The vehicles rolled along the quiet road, mist curling in their wake. As they crested the hill and pulled into the drive, the soft glow of the mansion greeted them like a waiting hearth. The cars came to a stop. The engines clicked and cooled.

On the steps, Ariel stood beside Rain and Spark. The puppy's ears perked at the sound of the doors, and the moment Vine stepped out, Spark bolted forward, tail wagging furiously.

He leapt at Vine's leg with a happy yip, pawing at him with sheer, joyful insistence.

A chuckle passed through the group.

"Looks like you've got a fan, Vine," someone called.

Vine crouched to pat the puppy's head, his tone as dry as ever. "Guess he knows who kept him safe."

Ariel smirked from the doorway, arms crossed. When Vine glanced up, their eyes met and she gave him a shrug and a wry grin that said, *What'd you expect?*

Elder stepped out of the last vehicle.

Rain's shoulders finally dropped, a long breath slipping past her lips as if she'd been holding it from the moment he left. Her fingers brushed over the hem of her shirt before she caught herself and crossed her arms, eyes never leaving him.

Spark bounded after Vine as he straightened, tiny legs moving double-time to keep up as the group headed for the doors.

The weight of the battle still clung to them, but so did something stronger—a sense of resolve, of bonds forged in fire and sealed in survival.

The doors shut behind them with a quiet click, the world outside held at bay.

They'd earned this peace.

The common area off the foyer hummed with quiet activity. The early glow of morning slipped through the windows, casting soft warmth across the room that the Fallen hadn't felt in hours. Chairs creaked as the team sank into them, some rubbing sore muscles, others nursing mugs of coffee or tea. A small table near the center bore an assortment of snacks and drinks—simple offerings, but after the night they'd had, they felt like a luxury.

Ariel, standing beside the table, clapped her hands to draw their attention. "Snacks for champions!" she announced with a grin, gesturing to the spread like a game-show hostess. "We figured this would make everyone's night—or morning—better. You're welcome."

Rain lingered at her side, smiling faintly but letting Ariel take the lead. A few murmured thank-yous passed through the room as chairs scraped against the floor and the group moved toward the table. Takoda smirked from where she perched on the arm of a chair.

"And here I thought you couldn't play and cook in the same night," she teased, her voice dry but fond.

Ariel rolled her eyes, though her smile stayed in place. "Multitasking is my middle name," she quipped, surveying the room to make sure everyone had what they needed. As the others began to settle, she moved through the space, pausing to trade light banter with Hazel and Willow.

Her attention snagged on Vine, posted near the far corner. He leaned against the wall, arms loosely folded, his stance deceptively relaxed. But tension sat in his jaw, and the soft morning wash couldn't mask the fatigue in his features.

Grabbing a drink from the table, Ariel crossed the room and stopped just shy of his space, offering the cup with a raised brow.

"What's this?" she asked, tone light. "The great Vine, hiding in the shadows? Should I be worried you've gone all broody on us?"

Vine's lips curved into a faint smirk, though it didn't touch his eyes. "Just trying to match the ambiance," he said, dry but not unkind.

Ariel laughed under her breath, taking a sip before angling toward him. "Well, you're terrible at blending in. Too quiet for this crowd."

Vine reached into his pocket and pulled out a cloth-wrapped object, holding it out. "Thought you might want a piece of the chaos to remember it by," he said, like he was offering leftovers instead of a keepsake.

Curiosity sparked across her face as she unwrapped it, revealing a jagged piece of glass. Its fractured edges shimmered in the ambient light, catching flashes of gold and amber. Her expression softened as she turned it over in her hand.

"You made this?" she asked, voice low. "It's beautiful—in a 'post-battle, let's-not-die-again' kind of way."

"Don't get used to it," Vine said, voice edged with dry humor. "My artistic phase ends here."

Ariel grinned, cradling the glass in her palm. "Shame. I was hoping for a matching necklace."

For a moment, warmth passed between them—rare, unsaid, unmistakable. Ariel stepped forward and wrapped her arms around him in a spontaneous hug.

Vine stiffened, breath catching with a sharp hiss. Ariel froze and pulled back, brow knitting.

"What was that?" she asked, voice dipping. "Did I hurt you?"

He looked away, keeping his expression unreadable. "It's nothing. Just a bruise. No big deal."

Ariel narrowed her eyes. "Uh-huh," she said, dragging the word out. Without hesitation, she reached forward and lifted his shirt.

"Hey—" Vine started, but she was already looking.

The bruise stretched across his side, a twisted sprawl of green, yellow, and black. Vivid streaks of blue radiated outward like splintered veins. The injury wasn't just severe—it looked wrong. Ariel's breath caught.

"Vine," she said, voice rising. "What the hell? That's not just a bruise—it looks awful."

His jaw clenched as he pushed her hand away and tugged his shirt back down. "It's fine," he said, casual as ever, detachment hardening his edges. "A souvenir from the fight. It'll fade."

Ariel tucked the shard into her palm, her free hand shifting to her hip. "That doesn't look fine. Are you sure you don't want someone to check it out? Maybe Eileen—"

"It's nothing, Ariel," Vine said, cutting in. His voice was softer, but the line was drawn. "I'll be good as new in a couple of hours. Don't worry about it."

The firmness left little room to argue. Ariel hesitated, mouth pressing into a line as she studied him. His shrug of indifference didn't fool her—but the steadiness in his expression said he wouldn't budge. After a moment, she nodded, though her frown lingered.

"Fine," she muttered. "But if you keel over, I'm telling Eileen I told you so."

His smirk returned, faint but genuine. "Duly noted."

He turned toward the showers, walking just slow enough to betray the ache beneath the mask. Ariel watched him go, fingers absently tracing the edge of the glass, its ridges catching the dim glow from overhead. The moment clung to her, heavier than she wanted to admit.

With a quiet sigh, Ariel turned back to the room. Laughter and conversation rolled around her, anchoring her to the present but doing little to ease the gnawing unease beneath her ribs. Her attention swept across the Fallen until it landed on Rowan.

He stood near a chair, one hand resting against the back, his stance rigid. His mouth held a flat line, but it was the fixed focus of his attention—first on the hallway Vine had taken, then back to her—that spoke louder than anything he might've said.

She exhaled, slipping the shard into her pocket like she was tucking away the thought itself. With her usual spark dulled, she crossed the room toward Rowan, bracing for whatever was coming.

The hum of conversation continued in the background, broken by the occasional clink of a mug or scrape of a chair. Rain stood near the edge of the snack table, her drink held loosely in one hand. Light from the windows stretched across the floor in soft patterns, a mosaic of fatigue and calm that blanketed the room.

She set her glass down and drew in a slow breath, her eyes scanning each face. Something was off. No—someone was missing.

Her brow creased as realization struck. Nik wasn't there. He never drew attention, but his absence left a gap, like a thread missing from a tightly woven pattern.

She looked toward the doorway leading to the back patio. Curiosity stirred and sharpened as she headed that way, her pace smooth but purposeful. Without pause, she pushed the door open and stepped outside.

The patio stretched into early morning, stone damp with dew. The garden below shimmered faintly, the leaves glowing as the sun crested the horizon. At the far edge, silhouetted against the golden wash, stood Nik. His hands rested on the railing, his posture composed yet distant, and that stillness pulled tight across Rain's chest.

She paused, letting the cool air graze her skin before crossing the stone toward him.

"You really like your dramatic sunrises, don't you?" she said, tone teasing as she stopped a few feet away.

Nik glanced over his shoulder. His expression was difficult to read at first, then eased with a faint smirk. "And you really like sneaking up on people."

Rain rubbed her arms and stepped closer. "Someone's got to keep you on your toes."

She leaned beside him, forearms braced on the railing. For a moment, silence stretched between them. The sky blushed with soft hues, color catching the treetops and the edges of the stone below. Rain angled slightly toward him, studying his profile.

"I've been thinking... about the other night," she said, voice quieter now.

Nik shifted, guarded but not cold. "Yeah?"

She nodded. "Yeah. And I think it's time we talk about it."

Rain faced him directly, the teasing gone, replaced by a steady quiet. She hesitated just long enough to breathe.

"I like you, Nik. More than a friend should."

The words hung between them, delicate and charged. Nik didn't respond, but his grip on the railing tightened. His focus stayed on the horizon, tension rising in the lines of his shoulders.

Rain didn't flinch. "I don't do subtle well," she said, voice dry but sincere. "So I'm just going to ask—do you feel anything? About me?"

Nik exhaled, the sound barely audible. His focus dropped to the garden, and for a moment, she thought he might deflect. Then he looked at her. Beneath the restraint, his eyes revealed an unfiltered honesty that caught her breath.

"You're different," he said. "Persistent. And... yeah. You're under my skin."

A small smile tugged at her lips, soft and unguarded. "That's not a bad thing, is it?"

He didn't respond immediately. His attention returned to the trees, words forming slowly. "No. It's not bad. But it's... complicated."

Rain shifted her stance, watching him with quiet resolve. "Complicated doesn't scare me, Nik," she said. "I just need to know where we stand."

He went still, jaw tight with thought. When he finally spoke, his voice dropped—reluctant, but honest. "I don't know yet. But you... you matter to me, Rain. More than I realized."

The words struck her, quiet but deep. She didn't trust herself to speak, so instead, she reached out, brushing her fingers lightly against his arm.

"That's a start," she said gently. "And for the record, you matter to me too."

His smile was faint but real, softening the lines of his expression. He nodded, accepting her words without retreating. Together, they turned back toward the view. Warm color spilled across the stone and slipped through the garden below. For a while, neither moved. The silence held a different kind of charge—no longer distant, but open.

Eventually, Rain pushed off the railing and turned to go. Just before slipping through the door, she glanced back, her grin playful.

"Don't stay out here too long," she said. "You might miss the snacks."

Nik smirked, just enough to ease the last bit of tension from his face. "I'll keep that in mind."

Rain lingered for a breath, their eyes meeting, then disappeared inside. The door closed softly behind her. Nik remained, hands resting on the stone, gaze sweeping the garden.

For once, he let the moment remain—not as burden, but as fragile possibility. Uncertainty hovered, but so did Rain's words, quiet and insistent, anchoring him in a truth he wasn't ready to name... but couldn't ignore.

The quiet sounds of chatter and occasional laughter in the common room faded as Riichi leaned against a wall, his attention sweeping the group. The warmth shared between the others hadn't reached his bones; tension held fast in his shoulders, unwilling to loosen its grip. He didn't relax, not fully—not even now.

Eileen's presence broke into his thoughts. She approached with her usual composure, calm but unmistakably deliberate. Her focus locked onto his with a steady weight that spoke for her before she said a word.

"Riichi, may I have a moment?" she asked, voice level but firm. "There's something we need to discuss."

His brows pulled together. Eileen rarely called him aside—and never for anything unimportant. After a beat, he nodded and followed her from the room. The murmur of the common area faded behind them as they moved deeper into the mansion.

She led him to a small, tucked-away room near the back. Pale bands of morning slipped through a tall window, brushing across the bare walls. The room was simple, quiet—and it made the tension between them more pronounced.

Eileen gestured toward a chair but remained standing. "Sit, if you'd like," she offered. She remained standing.

"You've proven yourself again and again, Riichi," she said, her tone threading warmth through authority. "Your strength and resolve have been a guidepost for the others. But now, you're at a crossroads. You have to choose what comes next."

He stayed standing, shifting to lean against the edge of the table, arms dropping loosely at his sides. "You're not one for small talk, are you?" he asked, dry amusement tucked beneath the tension.

A faint smile brushed her lips. "Not when it's this important."

Her voice steadied. "You can remain as you are—a Fallen. That life is familiar. You'd keep fighting, keep serving, without being bound to another."

He gave a slight nod, the line of his jaw tight. The comfort in that path was visible in the pause that followed. But she wasn't finished.

"Or," she continued, her voice dipping low, "you can choose to bond with Takoda as her soulmate. That decision changes everything. It binds your lives in a way few truly understand."

Her words dropped like stone into still water—quiet but rippling with consequence. Riichi's posture shifted, no longer relaxed. His arms tensed at his sides, fingers curling slightly.

"But you need to understand—this bond is absolute." She met his eyes. "If she dies, so do you. If you die, she shares that fate."

The stillness in the room deepened. Riichi's brows furrowed as he took in the weight of what she'd said. He braced a hand on the table, the other pressed flat against his thigh, his stance locked in place.

"And if I stay Fallen?" His voice was quiet, measured. "What happens to her?"

"She stays free," Eileen said. "Free to live a life unbound to ours. Free of the risk. But your connection won't be whole."

A sharp breath escaped him, edged with frustration. He dragged a hand through his hair, fingers tightening in the strands. "I've stared death down more times than I can count. But bringing her into that? Knowing I might be the reason she dies?"

His voice fractured just slightly at the end.

Eileen stepped in, steady but not cold. "Takoda understands what this life is. This decision isn't only yours. She has a voice in it too. Let her choose with you."

The words hit their mark, though his posture remained rigid. He didn't look at her—just stared toward the floor.

She placed a hand on his shoulder, brief but steady. "Love is never without risk," she said quietly. "But it's also where we find our greatest strength. Whatever you decide, it won't diminish who you are or what you've accomplished."

Riichi stayed silent. Eileen withdrew her hand and stepped back, allowing space he clearly needed.

"Take the time," she said, more gently now. "This isn't a decision to make quickly."

She turned and left without waiting for a response. Her footsteps faded, leaving him alone with the quiet.

Only then did he move, lowering into the chair she'd offered earlier. His elbows dropped to his knees, hands clasped as he stared at the floor. Stillness surrounded him, not peaceful, but pressing.

He exhaled through his nose, slow and deliberate, while thoughts swirled beneath the surface. The decision pressed hard against his chest, heavy and inescapable.

He didn't move again for a long while, the light in the room shifting gradually across the walls as the sun continued to rise.

The scent of coffee hung in the air, mingling with the quiet clatter of mugs and muted voices around the common area. Rowan stood near the snack table, hands loosely at his sides, his attention moving across the room while his thoughts drifted elsewhere. Ariel appeared beside him with a casual smile.

"Hey, come with me for a sec," she said lightly. "I need your expert advice."

Rowan arched a brow, suspicion flickering across his face. "This better not be about decorating again."

Ariel grinned and nudged him. "Just come on."

With a quiet sigh, Rowan followed her into a nearby sitting room. The space was calm, the pale warmth of morning spilling across the walls. Ariel shut the door behind them and leaned back against the edge of a desk.

"Alright, Mr. Serious," she said, arms folding. "What's going on?"

Rowan gave a slow blink, his focus narrowing. "What makes you think anything's going on?"

Ariel smirked, unbothered. "Oh, I don't know," she said, her tone thick with sarcasm. "Maybe the fact that you've been wearing your patented 'I disapprove of everything' face since last night. You going to tell me what's on your mind, or should I start guessing?"

He sighed and rubbed the back of his neck before settling into a more closed-off stance. "Why do I feel like this is a trap?"

"Because it is," Ariel chirped, her grin widening. "Now spill."

Rowan's jaw tightened, but after a pause, he gave in. "I don't trust him, Ariel," he said. "Vine's... Vine. Arrogant. Self-centered. Acts like nothing and no one matters."

Ariel raised an eyebrow, smile sharpening. "Wow. Tell me how you really feel."

He ignored the jab, voice flattening. "I've seen how he is. That doesn't just change."

Her grin faded. She stepped forward, arms dropping as her tone shifted. "Really? People don't change? So I'm still that lying, thieving kid you first met?"

Rowan faltered. His mouth opened, then closed again. "That's not what I meant," he said, quieter now.

"But it's what you said," Ariel replied evenly. "Look, I get it. People don't change overnight. But it doesn't mean they can't. I'm standing proof of that."

Rowan looked down, brushing his fingers through his hair before dragging a hand along the back of his neck. Ariel stepped back, giving him space, but her eyes stayed on him.

"I'm not asking you to trust him blindly," she said. "Just... watch. See who he is now—not who he was."

"And what if you're wrong?" His voice dropped, not angry—just tired.

"Then that's my mistake to make," Ariel said without hesitation. "You're the one who made me strong enough to choose. Let me use that."

The tension hung for a beat before slowly loosening. Ariel shifted her weight, her expression softening.

"Besides," she added, teasing again, "I'm a great judge of character. I knew Aislinn was right for you before you did, didn't I?"

Rowan shot her a flat look, though the corner of his mouth twitched. "You're never going to let me forget that, are you?"

"Not a chance," she said, arms folding across her chest like a champion claiming victory.

Rowan exhaled and rubbed the side of his neck as his stance relaxed. "Alright," he said at last, begrudging but sincere. "I'll give him a chance. But if he screws up—"

"You'll be the first to say 'I told you so.' Got it." Ariel bumped his arm with her elbow as she turned toward the door.

"Come on," she said over her shoulder. "Snacks are calling. And you're not off the hook yet."

Rowan shook his head as he followed, a faint chuckle escaping him. "I don't think I ever am."

The door clicked behind them as they returned to the soft energy of the common area. The tension between them had eased, but Rowan's thoughtful expression lingered—Ariel's words still working their way through him.

Elsewhere in the mansion, the atmosphere had shifted. Steam clung to the air as Vine stepped out of the shower, water tracing down his back while he reached for a towel. The quiet pressed in, amplifying each drip from the faucet. He swiped a hand across the mirror, clearing the fog to reveal his reflection. His jaw tightened as his attention dropped to his side.

The bruise was worse than expected. A sprawling mess of black, blue, and greenish-yellow spread across his ribs, the edges jagged and dark from the force that hit him. It pulsed with a dull ache, a steady reminder of the kinetic blast Kubla Khan had sent during the fight.

His fingers hovered over the bruise before applying pressure. Pain shot through him—sharp, immediate, unrelenting. He grimaced, then exhaled through his nose and shook his head.

Veil of Valor should've taken care of this. I saw the others heal. Why not me?

The question gnawed at him. Bracing both hands on the counter, he stared into the mirror, a growing unease coiling behind his ribs.

The memory returned in broken flashes—the jolt of air, the way it struck harder than it should've. *Kubla Khan's blast… Was it laced with dark magic?*

He straightened, tossing the towel aside. Shrugging into a loose shirt, he moved with practiced control, every shift of muscle careful. Whatever this was, it wasn't healing. His fingers tapped once against the counter before curling into a fist. He'd ignored it long enough. It was time to find Eileen.

He found her easily—near the staircase, her presence a constant amid the mansion's fading tension. She stood speaking quietly to one of the Fallen when Vine approached, his steps deliberate.

"Eileen," he said, voice even but edged. "I need to talk to you. Privately."

She turned, reading the tautness in his shoulders. "Of course," she said, motioning toward a nearby hallway. "My office."

They walked in silence, footsteps muffled against the floor. Once inside the narrow, book-lined room, Eileen closed the door and faced him. "What's going on?"

Vine didn't answer right away. He stepped back and lifted his shirt. The bruise stood out against his skin, the sickly colors catching in the low lamplight.

"This," he said flatly.

Eileen's stance shifted as she moved closer. She studied the injury, hand pausing just above it before meeting his eyes. "From the blast?"

"Yeah," he muttered, lowering the fabric. "Kubla Khan hit me. I figured it would've healed by now, but…" His voice trailed off, the rest implied.

Eileen reached out, fingers brushing the edge of the bruise. Vine flinched, the breath he sucked in betraying the sharp pain.

"Still hurts," he muttered, irritation cutting through the words. "A lot."

She pulled her hand back, her brows drawing together. "There's no trace of dark energy," she said after a pause. "It may not be the impact. It could be…" Her voice quieted. "…a side effect of your loss. Your body and spirit might be struggling to adjust."

Vine clenched his jaw. He didn't reply, but the flicker in his eyes had nothing to do with the bruise.

Eileen straightened, tone steady. "I don't have answers yet, but I'll find one. In the meantime, we'll try to heal it."

She stepped back. "I can't help directly. But Aislinn might be able to. Can I call her in?"

Vine hesitated, his eyes dropping. "Do I really have a choice?" he muttered, dry but resigned.

Eileen allowed herself a small smile. "You always do," she said lightly. "But we both know you'll agree."

His lips twitched, a flicker of old humor. He nodded once. Eileen sent a text, and within moments, Aislinn appeared in the doorway, curiosity written across her features.

She looked between them, her steps slow. "What's going on?"

Eileen didn't miss a beat. "Before I explain," she said, tone even, "I need your word. What happens here stays here."

Aislinn blinked. "You're binding me?"

"Yes."

Her eyes slid to Vine, who looked both uncomfortable and resigned. After a pause, she nodded. "Alright," she said seriously. "I promise."

Eileen gave a brief nod and motioned toward Vine. He hesitated, then lifted his shirt again.

Aislinn's breath caught. "That's from Kubla Khan?" she asked, voice hushed.

Vine nodded. "It should've healed. It didn't."

She crouched slightly, examining the bruise. Her hand hovered near it, but didn't touch. "Veil of Valor should've taken care of this. And there's no dark magic?"

"None," Eileen confirmed, tone alert.

Aislinn straightened, pressing her hands gently over the injury. Closing her eyes, she summoned a healing glow that crept along the bruised edges. Her brow furrowed.

"It's resisting," she murmured. "But…"

She drew in a breath, pouring more power into the spell. Her hands trembled. For a long moment, the bruise resisted—but then, slowly, the colors faded. The twisted pattern gave way to healthy skin.

"There," she said quietly, relief in her voice. "How's it feel?"

Vine rolled his shoulder, brushing the spot once. "Better," he admitted. "Thanks."

Eileen stepped forward again, her gaze steady. "I'll let you know as soon as I find anything. For now—go find your friends. Rest."

She shifted her attention more sharply to Vine. "That's an order."

Vine arched a brow, expression tight with annoyance. The pause between them stretched, then he gave a slight nod. "Right," he muttered, heading for the door.

Aislinn glanced between them, confusion flickering across her features. At the threshold, she looked back. Eileen gave a single, knowing nod. With a soft sigh, Aislinn followed Vine out. The door clicked shut behind them.

The foyer was quiet, the early sun casting amber patterns across the marble. Aislinn and Vine stepped out of Eileen's office, their faces drawn with exhaustion. The strain of the day clung to them both, though Aislinn's expression held a quiet determination that contrasted with Vine's guarded demeanor.

By the staircase, Ariel stood beside Rowan, her stance relaxed but alert. A tired smile tugged at her lips, but the circles beneath her eyes betrayed the last twenty-four hours. Rowan stood with his usual composure, his attention shifting between Vine and Aislinn as they approached, protective and calculating.

"Hey! There you are," Ariel said warmly, her voice breaking the stillness.

Vine gave a small nod, stepping deliberately to the side, putting space between himself and Aislinn. Subtle—but Rowan noticed. His brow creased, suspicion flickering across his features. Ariel caught the look and shot him a smug glance, her eyes sparkling with the unspoken: *I told you so.* Rowan's mouth twitched, the beginnings of a reluctant smirk slipping through.

He turned to Aislinn, his voice low. "Want to find Riichi and Takoda? I think I saw Eileen talking to Riichi earlier."

Aislinn nodded, relief softening her features. "Yeah, let's try the kitchen. That's Takoda's comfort spot."

Rowan motioned toward the hall, falling into step beside her. Ariel watched them go, then turned to Vine, her smile fading slightly as concern crept in.

She shifted her stance, leaning one elbow on the banister. Her usual ease was gone, replaced with a more serious note. "So," she said, tipping her chin, "how's the bruise?"

Vine lifted a brow, lips curving faintly as he pulled up the hem of his shirt, revealing healed skin. "Good as new."

Ariel leaned in slightly, examining the spot. "You're sure? No lingering pain or anything?"

Vine's smirk faltered, a shadow brushing his features. *Not yet. I'll tell her when I know more. I promised I wouldn't keep secrets—but I need answers first.*

"I'm fine, Ariel. Promise," he said aloud, tone light but firm.

She didn't look convinced, but let it go, her shoulders lowering with a deep breath. For the first time that night, she looked as tired as she felt.

"You look like you're about to drop," Vine said, the faintest edge of humor in his voice. "Let me walk you to your room."

Ariel blinked, caught off guard by the offer. She hesitated, a faint smile tugging at her lips. "Okay," she said quietly, almost sheepish.

As they turned toward the stairs, soft thuds of paws on carpet followed. Spark, sprawled nearby, had perked up and stretched before padding after them. His eyes gleamed faintly in the low light. Ariel reached down, scratching behind his ears, her smile warming slightly.

The three climbed together, their footsteps soft against the worn wood, the hush of the mansion closing in around them.

The hallway lights cast dim shadows as they reached Ariel's door. She held the piece of glass Vine had given her earlier, its jagged edges catching the glow and scattering delicate patterns on the wall. Turning it in her fingers, she fidgeted, her focus drawn to the shifting reflections.

Ariel looked up, lifting the glass with a small, self-conscious shrug. "It's kind of like a Rubik's cube," she said, turning it again. "Keeps my hands busy."

"What's on your mind?" Vine asked, his voice quiet.

Her attention dropped back to the glass. "Just thinking… this is probably our last night in the mansion before everyone heads home."

Her words hung there, heavy with the shift ahead. Her usual energy dimmed, but she forced a smile, charm flickering back like a light reigniting.

"So," she said, voice lifting into mock casualness, "what do you think? Want to come in for a movie? Or maybe play with Spark? Or…" She hesitated, color rising faintly in her cheeks. "Maybe some cuddles?"

Vine's mouth curved. "Cuddles, huh? That what we're calling it?"

"Oh, shut up," Ariel said, smirking as she nudged his arm. "You know what I mean."

His grin widened, humor sparking in his expression. "And I like it when you squirm."

"Enjoy it while it lasts," she shot back, rolling her eyes as she opened the door and gestured for him to follow.

Vine stepped inside, Spark trailing behind, nails clicking softly on the floor.

Ariel turned toward him, an impish gleam returning. "I could lend you a pair of my shorts if you want," she teased, leaning on the bedpost.

"Lucky for you, I'm already wearing shorts," Vine said with a low chuckle. "Otherwise, I'd be going commando."

Ariel raised a brow, her tone dry. "Not sure I'd call that lucky."

As she scanned the room, Vine spotted one of his old shirts draped over a chair. He picked it up, holding it between two fingers. "Or I could wear this."

Ariel lunged, snatching it from him with a mock glare. "That's mine. Off-limits."

"Whatever you say," Vine replied, laughing as he raised his hands in surrender.

The banter faded into a quiet comfort as Vine stretched out on the bed, his frame relaxed in his shorts. Ariel pulled a set of silky pajamas from a nearby drawer and changed quickly before climbing in beside him. She nestled close, her head resting against his chest as his arm settled around her.

The silence wasn't heavy—just still, the kind of calm that arrived only when the day had taken everything it could.

"Thanks for staying," Ariel murmured, her voice low.

Vine's hand moved lightly along her arm. "I'll always be here for you."

She tilted her head, a small smile curving her lips as she pressed a kiss to his cheek.

The peace didn't last. Spark, dozing near the foot of the bed, suddenly sprang up. With surprising agility, he hopped onto the covers, tail wagging furiously.

Ariel burst into laughter, clutching her sides as Spark sniffed around them. "That's new," she said between giggles.

Vine shook his head. "That might turn into a problem," he muttered, though the flicker at the corner of his mouth betrayed amusement.

Before he could shift away, Spark zeroed in on Ariel, tongue out, licking enthusiastically at her face. She squealed, laughing harder as she tried to fend him off. Spark, undeterred, pivoted toward Vine.

"Oh no, not me," Vine warned, voice dry.

Spark had other plans. One leap later, he landed a wet lick across Vine's cheek before flopping triumphantly at the foot of the bed. He let out a deep sigh, head on his paws like he'd completed a mission.

Ariel wiped her face, still grinning. "I think Spark's trying to steal my thunder."

Vine met her gaze, smirk faint. "That'll never happen."

Her expression softened. She leaned in, brushing another kiss to his cheek. "Good night, Vine."

He ran his fingers through her hair and kissed the top of her head. "Good night."

The room settled again. Spark snored at the end of the bed while Ariel lay tucked against his side. Her breathing evened out. Vine stared at the ceiling, thoughts drifting in the stillness.

His fingers traced gently along her arm, the motion idle, grounding. He'd been doing well—keeping things light, staying in the moment. But Eileen's words from earlier clung to the edges of his thoughts. *Your loss.*

Now all he could think about was soulmates.

The ache returned, sharper than expected. His had been lost before the bond ever truly formed—severed too soon. He'd buried it. Or tried to.

But now... there was Ariel.

She wasn't his soulmate. She couldn't be. And still, here she was, filling the empty spaces he'd stopped trying to mend. She hadn't asked for more—just connection, warmth, simplicity. *Friends with benefits.*

And yet the thought crept in, uninvited and quiet: *What if this could be more?*

His gaze dropped to their hands, fingers loosely intertwined. His thumb brushed across hers.

Not yet, he told himself. *Not now.*

For now, he'd let her rest. Let himself rest. Tomorrow would bring answers—at least, he hoped it would.

The kitchen was hushed, the hum of the refrigerator the only sound. Takoda sat at the island, hands wrapped around a mug of coffee she hadn't touched. Her focus lingered on the dark surface, thoughts circling without shape. The faint crease between her brows spoke of unease—an instinct she couldn't explain, but couldn't shake.

Footsteps pulled her back. Riichi entered, movements deliberate, his expression shadowed by a tension she hadn't seen in him before. He stopped across from her, his eyes locking with hers.

"Takoda, I need to talk to you," he said, voice low.

Her concern deepened, brown eyes dimming. "What is it?"

He drew a slow breath and leaned against the counter, arms folding as his shoulders tensed. "Eileen talked to me earlier. She said... I have a choice."

Takoda's fingers tightened around the mug. "What kind of choice?"

His gaze dropped to the space between them. "I can stay Fallen," he said. "Or... we can become soulmates."

The word hung there—delicate, charged.

Her eyes widened. "Soulmates?" she echoed.

Before he could respond, movement at the entry caught their attention. Aislinn and Rowan stepped in quietly. Aislinn offered Takoda a brief, apologetic glance before turning to Riichi.

"Eileen told you about the ritual, didn't she?" she asked gently.

Riichi nodded, jaw set. "Yeah. She laid it all out—what it means, what it costs."

Rowan leaned beside her, resting a hand on the edge of the counter. "She told you the risk?" he asked. "If one of you dies—"

"The other dies too," Riichi cut in. His voice was clipped, like the words had already been running on repeat. "Yeah. She was clear."

Takoda's breath hitched. Her fingers twitched against the ceramic, eyes flicking between them. "If one of us...?" she whispered.

Riichi stepped forward, his hand covering hers. His grip was warm, grounding. "That's the price. If we choose this, our lives are tied. Fully."

Aislinn stepped in. "It's not an easy decision," she said. "Rowan and I struggled with it too. But... it's the most incredible thing I've experienced."

Takoda's features softened, though hesitation lingered in her gaze.

Rowan's voice followed, calm and practical. "It's about trust. Knowing you're stronger together."

He looked at Riichi, his meaning clear without needing to be said.

Takoda stared into her mug. "But how do you decide something like this? It's not just about us—it affects the team. What if something happens?"

Aislinn stayed close. "It's not about what might happen. It's about what feels right."

The stillness that followed wasn't heavy—it was clarifying.

Riichi's voice dropped. "I don't know if I can risk losing you," he said, eyes on the counter. "If something happened to you because of me, I..."

"Don't," Takoda said, her tone cutting through his doubt. It was firm, steady. "Don't put this on yourself. If we do this, it's our choice. Together."

The tension eased, her strength anchoring him.

Rowan added, "Riichi, you've fought beside her long enough to know what she can handle. She's not someone you protect—she's someone who stands with you."

Takoda glanced at Rowan, a faint smile brushing her lips as she turned back to Riichi.

"He's right. This isn't about protecting me. It's about trust. No matter what."

The quiet that followed carried less weight. Riichi finally met her eyes.

"I need some time to think," he said. "I don't want to rush it."

Takoda nodded. "Take all the time you need. I'm not going anywhere."

Aislinn stepped forward and placed a hand on Riichi's shoulder. Her touch was light, but her words carried warmth. "You'll figure it out. And whatever you decide, we're here."

Rowan nodded once. "You're not alone."

Without another word, they stepped out, their footsteps retreating down the hall.

The silence remained, but it no longer pressed.

Riichi looked at Takoda. His lips lifted faintly. "Thanks for... being patient with me."

Her response was soft, certain. "Always."

Outside the kitchen, the hush of early morning held. The world hadn't stirred yet, but it would soon. And a decision would follow.

The room was bathed in soft morning light, a gentle glow filtering through the heavy curtains. Vine sat on the edge of the bed, elbows resting on his knees, his gaze drifting over Ariel. She lay sprawled across the pillows, her dark hair a tangled cascade, her face softened by sleep. Peaceful. Untouched by the chaos of the night before.

Vine exhaled slowly, rubbing his palms against his shorts. She deserved this—rest, quiet, a moment free from the burden they all carried. For a fleeting second, the thought crept in: *could this become more?* It pressed too sharply against the edges of his chest, and he shoved it back. No. That wasn't for him. Not now. Not ever.

Eileen's words about soulmates had stirred too many raw edges—open wounds he barely knew how to manage. The ache hadn't faded. It lived beneath his skin like splinters, sharp and buried deep. This wasn't about Ariel, not really. It was the echo of a life that had been taken. A bond that had been severed.

Get over yourself, he muttered under his breath, forcing a smirk to cover the sting. Nostalgia was a bitch. Friends with benefits worked. No strings, no mess, no attachments. It was clean. Easy. That's where it had to stay.

The creak of the mattress pulled his attention, but it wasn't Ariel. Spark, her ever-curious puppy, had stretched out from his place at the foot of the bed and padded over. The little dog nudged Vine's hand with a cold, wet nose, his brown eyes wide and questioning.

"What's up, buddy?" Vine murmured, scratching behind the pup's floppy ears. Spark huffed contentedly, leaning into the touch before resting his head on Vine's knee. The small weight grounded him, softened the edge of the ache threading through his thoughts.

The clock on the bedside table caught his eye—9:47 a.m. He grimaced. People would start waking soon, and being caught sneaking out of Ariel's room wasn't on his list of things to deal with. Sighing, he shifted Spark gently aside and stood, careful to keep his movements quiet. The mattress creaked faintly, but Ariel didn't stir.

Sliding his shoes from under the bed, he perched on the edge again, quickly tying the laces. He was just finishing when her voice, thick with sleep, broke the quiet.

"What're you doing?" Ariel's words came as a drowsy mumble, her eyes barely open as she turned toward him.

"Getting ready to go," Vine replied softly, glancing over his shoulder. "Not hiding in the bathroom again if Rain comes knocking."

Ariel frowned, propping herself up on one elbow. Her expression was hazy with exhaustion, but her voice carried a note of vulnerability. "Do you have to?"

His smirk came almost instinctively, breaking the tension. "I could stay, but you'd have some explaining to do when everyone wakes up."

She pouted, her lips pressing together in a way that made him want to stay, if only to tease her more. "You're annoying," she muttered, flopping back onto the pillow.

Vine leaned closer, brushing a kiss across her forehead. "Go back to sleep," he murmured, his voice softer than he intended. "I'll see you later."

"Promise?" Her voice was barely audible, half-lost in her next breath.

"Promise," he said.

Ariel was already drifting back into sleep, her breathing evening out. Vine rose and moved toward the door, slipping out with practiced ease and locking it behind him. The mansion was quiet, the heavy silence amplifying the faint creak of the floorboards beneath his feet. He took the stairs at the end of the hall, the familiar pull of his thoughts curling back around his shoulders as he descended.

At the bottom of the stairs, Vine kept his steps light, his mind already mapping a route through the first floor and up another staircase. Stealth had its perks, especially when avoiding awkward encounters. He turned a corner and stopped short.

Riichi sat in an alcove, barely noticeable in the dim light filtering through a nearby window. The faint glow caught the edge of his katana, which rested across his lap. His head was bowed, his posture rigid. The quiet surrounding him felt thick, almost touchable, like the stillness before a storm.

Vine hesitated. He could turn back, retreat to the safer shadows of solitude, but something rooted him in place. Riichi, the ever-serious samurai, looked like a man carrying the world's burden. And despite his own tendency to keep things simple, Vine wasn't one to walk away when someone might need him—even Riichi.

"Hey, Riichi," Vine said, leaning casually against the wall. "You're up early."

Without lifting his head, Riichi replied, "It's not early. It's after ten."

Vine rolled his eyes, muttering, *Geez, do I really want to talk to him? So serious.* Out loud, he said, "I meant it's early, considering none of us crashed until six or later."

Riichi grunted in response, a sound that was neither agreement nor disagreement.

Crossing his arms, Vine tilted his head. "You look like you've got something on your mind. Care to share?"

Riichi's shoulders tensed, his grip tightening slightly on the hilt of the katana. "No. I'm good. Wouldn't want to bother you."

Vine snorted. "If I was worried about being bothered, I wouldn't have asked. Just saying."

The silence stretched, heavy and uncertain. Just as Vine started to regret his persistence, Riichi spoke.

"You ever have a decision to make where either choice feels like it comes with a heavy price?" His voice was quiet, deliberate, as though each word had been weighed.

Vine didn't answer immediately, sensing there was more.

"One choice means giving something up, knowing it's the safest bet, but you'll be miserable. The other..." Riichi's voice faltered, his hand brushing the blade's edge lightly.

"The other means keeping it. Fighting for it. But it'll take everything you have to protect it. And in the end, it might not even be enough."

The words landed harder than Vine expected. He swallowed, the air around him thickening with the weight of unspoken memories.

Yeah, I've been there, he thought, his mind flickering to a time that defined him. The choice between staying Fallen or fading with his soulmate's passing had left scars that refused to close. And now... a new image surfaced. Ariel.

Her face, framed by a cascade of dark curls, caught him off guard. He stiffened. *I used to picture loss when I thought of soulmates. Now, without meaning to, I picture Ariel. Why?*

Pushing the thought aside, Vine forced himself to focus on Riichi. "Yeah," he said after a long pause. "I've had to make choices like that. Sometimes I think I still do."

Riichi shifted slightly, glancing up, though his gaze remained guarded. Vine continued, his voice measured. "Giving it up—whatever it is—you're admitting defeat before you've even tried. If you keep it, yeah, it's hard. But at least you've got a shot at something better."

Riichi's grip on the katana eased slightly. He watched Vine closely, his brow furrowing in thought.

Vine turned to face him fully, his tone firmer now. "I'd rather take the risk. Put in the effort. Happiness is worth fighting for. Better than choosing misery just because it's easier."

Riichi exhaled, a sound that was almost a sigh, though there was no mistaking the faint smile tugging at his lips. "Yeah," he said slowly. "Right."

Vine clapped him on the shoulder with a grin. "Good talk?"

A quiet chuckle escaped Riichi. "Yeah. Good talk."

Pushing off the wall, Vine resumed his path down the hall, leaving Riichi to his reflections. The pressure on his own shoulders felt a little lighter now, as if sharing the burden had loosened the tight grip of his thoughts.

But his mind circled back to Ariel. Maybe he'd been too quick to shut the door on the idea of something more. Maybe, just maybe, it was worth the effort to see what could be.

The alcove fell silent as Vine's footsteps faded into the distance. Riichi remained still, his grip firm on the hilt of his katana, Vine's parting words echoing in his mind. *Giving it up is admitting defeat. Happiness is worth fighting for.*

He exhaled slowly, the weight of indecision lifting as clarity took its place. Takoda. She wasn't just worth fighting for—she was worth everything. The thought steadied him, filling his chest with a quiet resolve.

Carefully, he slid the katana back into its sheath. The metallic whisper of the blade seemed louder in the stillness, a final punctuation to his internal battle. Rising to his feet, his steps felt lighter as he crossed the hall, making his way to the main staircase. He took the stairs two at a time, his resolve carrying him forward.

When he reached his room, he paused. The door creaked faintly as he eased it open, stepping into the warm, peaceful space. Soft morning light filtered through the curtains, catching the curve of Takoda's shoulder as she lay curled beneath the blankets. Her breathing was steady, her expression relaxed—the chaos of the previous day nowhere in sight.

Riichi set the katana carefully onto its stand, the gesture reverent. He toed off his shoes and shrugged out of his clothes with quiet efficiency before moving toward the bed. Sliding beneath the covers, he shifted into place with practiced ease.

Propped on one elbow, he let his eyes rest on her. She stirred slightly, her lips curving into a small, knowing smile. Without opening her eyes, she teased, "Are you going to just keep staring at me, or are you going to say something?"

A soft chuckle escaped him. "Sorry," he murmured. "I was trying not to wake you."

Her eyelids fluttered open, her dark eyes locking onto his. "I've been awake since you left."

He grimaced, but her light laugh eased the tension. "It's fine," she said, voice soft and playful. "I'm not sleepy. So, where'd you go?"

Riichi hesitated, fingers brushing the blanket. "Just for a walk," he said. "Needed to clear my head."

Takoda tilted her head, hair spilling over her shoulder as she propped herself up. "And? Did it work? Is your head clearer now?"

He paused, gathering his thoughts. "Yeah," he said finally, his voice low. "I think it did."

Her smile widened as she leaned in, her eyes full of quiet curiosity. "And?" she prompted.

Riichi looked at her, heart knocking a little harder against his ribs. *Just say it.* "I think… I want us to become soulmates."

Takoda's smile lit up the space between them as she giggled. "You're cute when you're nervous. I want us to be soulmates, too."

"Glad you're enjoying it," he said dryly, his tension giving way to laughter.

She looped her arms around his neck, pulling him down as she sank back onto the pillow. "Are you sure?" she asked, voice gentler now.

"Positive," he said without hesitation.

She studied him, her expression softening. "What happened that made you decide?"

He considered the question. "Unexpected advice, actually."

Her fingers skimmed his jaw, a grin pulling at her lips. "Well, I will forever be grateful to whoever gave you the advice."

A smile touched his mouth, quieter now. "Yeah, me too. I love you, Takoda."

Her eyes sparkled as she leaned in, her voice a whisper. "I love you, Riichi." She kissed him, the touch of her lips making everything beyond that moment disappear.

A soft knock broke the quiet. Both froze, eyes meeting before Riichi sighed and sat back. "I'll get it," he said, already reaching for his pants and pulling them on.

He opened the door cautiously, but the hallway was empty. No footsteps. No voices. Just the house, creaking gently with age. His gaze dropped to the floor, where a single envelope lay, perfectly aligned with the threshold. He picked it up and closed the door behind him.

"What is it?" Takoda asked, sitting up.

He held it out so she could see the elegant handwriting across the front. "For us."

She took it, her fingers brushing his. Breaking the seal, she pulled out a folded sheet of parchment. The faint scent of herbs and aged paper drifted into the air as she began to read aloud.

Takoda and Riichi,

This is for you once you have made your decision. These rituals are meant to be private, and I will not be there to help you complete them. I've taken the liberty of staging Takoda's room for the ritual. This space will serve either ritual you choose to perform.

Should you choose to stay Fallen, your bond will be broken, and your marks will disappear. Should you choose to become soulmates, your lives will become irrevocably bound. I am confident you will make the best decision for both of you.

With love,

Eileen.

Silence followed, thick with the weight of her words. Takoda lingered on the letter before glancing up. "Should we do the ritual now, or do you want to sleep a little more first?" she asked, light but laced with anticipation.

Riichi smirked, leaning back slightly. "I think we should do it now before you change your mind."

Takoda gasped, placing a hand over her chest. "I would never! You, on the other hand…"

He laughed, cutting her off. "Takoda," he said, reaching for her hand. "I would want nothing more than to share the rest of my life with you." Pressing his forehead to hers, his voice dropped to a murmur. "You mean the world to me."

Her eyes welled as she whispered, "I feel the same way."

Neither of them moved to rise. The ritual could wait. The connection between them had already begun to deepen. Riichi leaned in, kissing her again, slower this time, the moment stretching around them.

Guiding her gently back onto the pillow, his fingers brushed her cheek, his touch lingering. A soft pulse of warmth sparked against her skin as Radiant Surge shimmered to life between them.

He paused. *Do you think you could use your emotional alchemy again?* he asked, the words slipping through their link as he gave a slow, deliberate waggle of his eyebrows.

You're naughty, she teased, her response echoing telepathically.

Riichi chuckled, lips brushing hers. *Only for you.*

Their laughter melted into kisses, the love between them unfolding in each shared breath—wordless, instinctive, and already binding in ways deeper than either could fully grasp.

★★★

The stillness in Nik's room carried a quiet kind of order—the faint scent of worn leather, the crisp edges of aligned books, the subtle chill of undisturbed air. He stirred, blinking as he sat on the edge of the bed, rubbing the lingering fatigue from his eyes. His thoughts drifted, but one surfaced with quiet insistence: Rain.

He remembered their conversation on the patio, her voice tinged with vulnerability as she admitted how she felt. Her boldness in asking if he felt anything in return had caught him off guard, but his reply—*You're under my skin*—had been honest. The memory stirred a conflicted warmth: gratitude for her openness, hesitation from his own walls, and the familiar tension of forming attachments.

Shaking off the thought, he crossed to his desk. A small wooden box rested atop a stack of books. He opened it carefully, revealing a partially finished charm bracelet. Three charms already hung from the delicate chain:

A tree, for stability and growth.

A shield, for protection.

A stone, for endurance and strength.

Nik picked up the bracelet and set it in front of him. Selecting three more charms, he held them in his palm, his brow furrowed in concentration. The first—a feather—shimmered faintly as he imbued it with energy for freedom and resilience. The second, a flame, began to glow softly, representing courage and light. The third, a compass, cool in his hand, pulsed with focus and direction.

For nearly an hour, he worked in silence, attaching each charm with practiced care. When he finished, he held it up, inspecting the chain and symbols. Each piece hummed with quiet power.

Satisfied, he slipped the bracelet into his pocket and returned the box to its place. Grabbing a novel from the stack, he left the room, his steps soundless across the polished floor.

The common area was still. Only the low hum of the refrigerator broke the quiet. Nik settled onto the couch near the patio door, flipping open his book. The house had begun to stir, but no one approached him.

Vine passed down the hall, unhurried. A short while later, Riichi climbed the stairs two at a time. Ivy stepped out the front door in her workout gear, the soft thud of the latch behind her.

Nik turned another page, absorbed in the quiet, until soft footsteps approached. Without looking up, he felt someone settle beside him. Glancing over, he found Rain, smiling as she held out two mugs of tea.

She handed him one, her smile easy and unspoken.

"You could go talk to them, you know," she teased, leaning back against the couch. "It wouldn't kill you."

Nik smirked faintly, setting the mug on the table. "I'm fine. If people want to talk to me, they know where to find me." He paused, glancing at her. "You did."

Rain laughed lightly, her voice relaxed. She tucked her legs beneath her, matching his pace without effort.

After a few minutes of quiet conversation, Nik reached into his pocket and placed the bracelet in her hand. "Thought you might like this," he said.

Rain blinked, brushing her fingers over the intricate charms. Her eyes widened as she took in the detail, each symbol distinct and carefully chosen.

"It's beautiful," she whispered. "What does it do?"

Nik leaned back, his tone calm. "Each charm has a purpose. The tree's for stability and growth. The shield, protection. The stone, endurance and strength. The feather is freedom and resilience. The flame, courage and light. The compass gives focus and direction."

Rain listened, her thumb drifting across the chain. Her thoughts returned to the moment she admitted how small she felt beside the others. This—every charm, every detail—felt like his answer to that. She didn't need to ask if that was why he made it. She already knew.

Instead, she looked up with a soft smile. "Will you show me how it works?"

Nik led her outside to the training grounds. The morning air was cool, tinged with quiet energy. The space still hummed faintly, as if echoes of past spells hadn't fully faded.

"This is where we trained yesterday," he said, gesturing to the clearing. "The energy signatures are still here. You can't see them yet, but with the tree charm, you will."

Rain scanned the space, her brow creased. "So... how do I start?"

He pointed to the charm shaped like a tree. "Hold this one. It'll help you sense what's still around us."

She closed her fingers around it and nodded.

"Think of it as part of you," Nik said. "Close your eyes. Tune everything else out. Let the charm guide you—don't push. Just listen."

Rain drew a breath and followed his instructions. Her face tightened in concentration. Seconds passed. "I don't think it's working," she muttered.

"It's not about forcing it," Nik said. "Just trust yourself. Let it come."

She hesitated, then exhaled slowly, shoulders relaxing. Her grip loosened. The noise in her mind quieted. Gradually, a hum stirred beneath her skin—a subtle vibration threading through the air.

Her eyes snapped open. A quiet gasp escaped.

Lines of light shimmered across the clearing, weaving like rivers through the earth. Blues, reds, greens, and golds moved in intricate patterns, each one pulsing with its own rhythm.

"I see them," she whispered. "I can really see them."

She turned in place, her expression wide with awe. Some trails burned warm and fiery. Others flowed cool and slow like water.

"It's beautiful," she breathed.

Nik watched, silent. His expression unreadable, but his posture relaxed.

"That's what's been here all along," he said. "Now you can see it, too."

Rain looked at him, her smile glowing. "I did it," she said, her voice catching slightly.

Nik nodded, the corner of his mouth lifting. "Told you. You've got this."

She looked down at the bracelet, her voice soft. "This means a lot, Nik. I don't know how to repay you."

He shrugged. "You don't have to. Just use it. Stay safe."

She brushed her fingers across the charms. The meaning behind the gift hit deeper than words, and she glanced up again. "What about the other charms?"

Nik's smirk returned, quiet confidence behind it. "One step at a time. We'll get to those."

On impulse, Rain stepped forward and wrapped her arms around him. "Thank you," she whispered.

He hesitated, then returned the hug—brief but real. As they pulled apart, she leaned in and kissed his cheek.

Her smile was warm and genuine. It threw him off just enough to make him pause.

"Anytime," he said quietly.

They turned toward the house. Rain held the bracelet tightly in her hand, confidence growing with each step. Nik glanced her way and allowed himself to enjoy the moment. His walls stayed up, but he didn't push her away.

★★★

Takoda's room had been transformed. The space felt sacred—quiet, intentional, alive. Symbols of the Fallen glowed faintly on the walls, pulsing with slow, rhythmic light. Candles lined the room in a perfect circle, their flames unwavering in the still air. A woven tapestry bearing the Fallen's mark hung like a sentinel on the far wall. The energy in the room wasn't loud, but it settled in the chest like a vow waiting to be spoken.

Riichi and Takoda stepped inside, their hands brushing but not quite holding. She moved forward first, her breath catching as she took in the space.

"It's beautiful," she whispered, voice catching on a rush of emotion.

Riichi closed the door, his gaze drifting across the room before landing on her. "This isn't just about us," he said. "It's about what we're choosing—and what we're leaving behind."

Takoda turned to face him, eyes shining. "I know," she said, though her voice trembled slightly.

He stepped close and took her hands. His grip was steady, grounding. "Before we begin, you have to understand what this truly means."

She met his eyes. "I do understand," she said, firmer now, though her heart thudded against her ribs.

Riichi shook his head slowly. "It's not just sharing a life. It's sharing everything. Strength. Fear. Pain. If one of us falls, the other does too. Life, death—it's no longer mine or yours. It's both. Always."

The stillness around them deepened. Takoda's fingers tightened on his. "I understand," she said again, voice clearer. "And I'm not afraid. I choose this. I choose you. Whatever comes next, I want us to face it together."

His shoulders eased. His eyes lingered on hers for a moment before he nodded and released her hands. "Then let's begin."

They stepped into the center of the circle. Riichi motioned for her to stand beside him, then raised his hand. He traced a symbol into the air, the lines sharp and deliberate. Light shimmered in their wake. Then came the words—ancient, reverent, spoken like a prayer.

The air shifted. A soft gold light formed beneath their feet, pulsing gently with each syllable. It rose with his voice, circling them in slow motion.

When he fell silent, Takoda stepped forward and placed her hand over his. Their fingers interlaced briefly, and her voice joined his—warm, sure, and full of quiet wonder.

The glow swelled, wrapping around them like a living current. It wasn't just light. It felt like being seen. Known.

Takoda gasped softly as warmth spread through her chest, reaching outward like an unseen thread winding itself into Riichi's presence. She felt him there—calm, strong, and scarred. His protectiveness moved through her like a shield. In return, he felt her openness, the depth of her trust, the way her emotions bloomed without restraint.

Their eyes met. Neither of them spoke.

Takoda placed her hand over his heart. "With this bond, I vow to stand by you. Through danger, joy, and loss. I choose you, Riichi. Not just today—but every day to come. Always."

Tears slipped free before she could stop them, tracing a path down her cheek. She didn't try to wipe them away.

Riichi covered her hand with his. He drew a breath before speaking, his voice low but full. "I vow to protect you, trust you, and share all of who I am. You're not just my partner. You're my strength. My hope. With you, I'm whole."

Together, they spoke the final invocation. The golden light flared—bright, pure—then settled into a low hum that pulsed with life.

The energy between them changed. It didn't feel abstract. It was real. Woven.

Takoda pressed a hand to her chest, her breath hitching softly. "I can feel it," she whispered. "You're part of me now."

Riichi nodded. His voice was barely above a whisper. "You are. Always."

He pulled her into an embrace, arms folding around her like they'd always belonged there. She leaned into him, tears still slipping down her cheeks. Their heartbeats found each other, syncing like steps in a familiar rhythm.

When they finally parted, their hands stayed clasped. Her smile was wet and radiant. "We did it," she breathed.

"Together," Riichi said, his voice quietly pushing past the lump in his throat, his expression soft with pride.

Hand in hand, they walked from the room. The sacred hum had faded, but something deeper remained. They didn't need to speak the change aloud.

They were one.

The low hum of the mansion greeted them as they entered the common area, their bond a silent declaration of all they'd become—and all they were ready to face.

At exactly 1 p.m., the conference room stirred with quiet anticipation. The Fallen filed in one by one, their movements purposeful but unhurried. Eileen stood just outside the doorway, her presence calm and commanding as she offered each member a nod or brief word in passing.

Leaning against the wall nearby, Ariel watched with a bemused smile.

"Do they always march in like it's a board meeting?" she muttered to Rain, her lips twitching.

Rain glanced toward Reed, who tugged at his collar as he entered. "It's like they're trying to out-serious each other."

Ariel nodded toward Nik, who strode past with his usual intense focus. "Bet Nik wins."

Rain smirked. "No contest."

As the last of the Fallen disappeared inside, Eileen turned to them, expression expectant. "Come on, you two. If you don't hurry, you'll be late."

Ariel arched a brow, posture shifting. "Wait. We're in on this now?"

Eileen held the door open, a faint smile touching her lips. "You're part of this team. It's time you joined the table."

Rain and Ariel exchanged a quick glance. Surprise flickered between them before they stepped inside.

The room wasn't what they expected. Instead of pre-mission tension, there was warmth—an undercurrent of ease and shared purpose. Conversations hummed softly, and for once, the space felt inviting.

As they crossed the threshold, movement caught their attention. One by one, the Fallen rose from their seats, a wave of applause filling the room.

Ariel froze mid-step, her hand twitching toward Rain's arm. "What... are they doing?" she whispered.

Rain's smile bloomed, eyes shining. "I think they're clapping for us."

Ariel ducked her head, color rushing to her cheeks. "Okay, this is new," she muttered, somewhere between embarrassment and disbelief.

Rain laughed quietly, her chest tightening. "Guess we're not invisible anymore."

As the applause faded, Eileen leaned in between them, her voice warm. "Take a seat. Officially, welcome to the team."

They slipped into two open chairs near the door. Once they were seated, the rest of the Fallen followed suit, the soft murmur of camaraderie picking up again.

Just before Eileen closed the door, she paused and glanced back. With a small gesture, she beckoned. "Come on, you too."

Spark bounded into the room, tail wagging as he nosed around chairs and boots, his bright energy standing in cheerful contrast to the calm around him. A few of the Fallen chuckled as he sniffed his way around the table.

After a few loops, he circled once and flopped under the table at Vine's feet, his tail thumping contentedly.

Ariel's eyes drifted toward Vine, her lips curving into a knowing smirk. She didn't speak, but her look said enough.

Vine caught it, rolled his eyes, and reached down to scratch behind Spark's ears. His hand lingered.

From across the table, Rowan observed the exchange. Ariel's smirk. Vine's small huff. The way his hand didn't immediately pull away.

Pay attention to who he is now.

Ariel's words came back to him. For the first time, Rowan began to wonder if there was more to Vine than he'd allowed himself to see.

Eileen stepped to the head of the table, her hands resting lightly on its surface. Her expression was calm, but her presence carried quiet authority as she looked across the room.

"Now that our final mission is complete," she began, her tone even but purposeful, "the Golden Dawn defeated and Kubla Khan no longer a threat, our time in Seattle has come to an end."

Her attention shifted to Riichi and Takoda. Their fingers rested lightly intertwined on the table.

"We now have two officially bonded pairs among us: Rowan and Aislinn, and now Riichi and Takoda."

Takoda smiled warmly, her cheeks flushing faintly. Riichi inclined his head in a small, respectful bow.

Applause followed—a quiet, genuine acknowledgment of the bond. Rowan clapped with the others, but as his attention drifted to Vine, he noticed something unexpected. Vine applauded too, but for a brief moment, a shadow crossed his features. A flicker of melancholy.

What's that about? Rowan wondered, the moment planting a deeper curiosity.

As the room quieted, Eileen spoke again.

"Now that our missions here are complete, it's time to discuss what comes next. We've talked before about establishing a permanent base or a network of safe houses. Now, we need to decide."

She began with a recap. "Birch has generously offered land in three locations: northern Arizona, the Black Hills of South Dakota, and the San Luis Valley in Colorado."

She looked toward the others. "Nik and Reed have also offered remote properties—Nik in Texas, Reed in the Rockies. And finally," her attention turned to Vine, "Vine has offered his 37 properties across the U.S. to form a potential safe house network."

Across the table, Ariel made eye contact with Vine, brow arching. She mouthed, *"Thirty-seven?"* Her expression was all disbelief.

Vine gave a quiet shrug, a faint, sheepish smile tugging at his lips. He didn't answer aloud, but his amusement was clear.

From where he sat, Rowan watched the exchange, his attention lingering. Thirty-seven properties, freely offered—that wasn't selfish. And the way Vine shrugged, almost embarrassed by the acknowledgment, felt far from arrogant. Rowan's perception shifted. He began to reassess what he thought he knew.

The discussion moved forward.

"The Black Hills make the most sense," Birch said, leaning in. "It's secluded, central, and there's room for everything we'd need. It's also sacred to my people—a place of grounding."

Reed nodded. "I'm fine using the Black Hills as our main base. My place in the Rockies can serve as backup."

Aislinn added, "A permanent base gives us stability. A place to regroup and train without always looking over our shoulders."

Willow spoke next. "Even with a base, the safe house network is essential. We've seen how important fallback locations are on cross-country missions."

Hazel countered, "But do we need all 37? A smaller network would be easier to manage."

Vine nodded. "I'll narrow it to 14 or 15. That should cover key regions without spreading us too thin."

Nik's voice followed—quiet, but firm. "A network like that makes us harder to track. If one location's compromised, we'll still have options."

After a focused discussion, consensus formed:

The permanent base would be built in the Black Hills of South Dakota, on Birch's land. A safe house network of 14–15 properties would be established using Vine's portfolio.

Eileen turned to him. "Put together a list of your properties—locations, current conditions. We'll decide which to use."

"You'll have it by tomorrow," Vine replied, his usual confidence softened by a touch of humility.

Eileen's attention shifted to Birch. "Since we'll be using your land, I'd like you to oversee construction of the base. Coordinate with the group as needed, and let us know what supplies and resources you require."

Birch inclined his head, his expression calm but resolute. "Consider it done."

Finally, Eileen turned to Ariel and Rain, her tone warm but firm. "Once the base and safe houses are established, you'll have a choice. You can live with us at the base or in one of the safe houses. Either way, you're officially part of this team now."

Rain's eyes widened slightly. "That's... a big step," she said softly.

Ariel grinned, her usual humor kicking in. "Guess we're in for the long haul."

Eileen's attention swept the room one last time. "With that, our work here in Seattle is done. Gather your belongings, rest, and prepare for what comes next. With Kross still out there, we need to be prepared." Her voice remained even, but the warning beneath it was evident. "Meeting adjourned."

Chairs scraped back as the group rose, voices low but animated as they began discussing plans. Ariel bent to scratch Spark's ears, her grin widening as the puppy rolled onto his back for a belly rub.

From across the room, Vine watched. His expression unreadable—until Ariel glanced up and gave him a subtle nod. He answered with the barest hint of a smile.

A sudden vibration broke through the background noise. Aislinn checked her phone, her brow furrowing before she turned to Rowan. "I have to take this," she said quickly, then slipped out, her pace brisk as she exited the room.

On his way out, Rowan paused beside Vine and clapped him lightly on the shoulder. "I believe you now when you say you'd never hurt her," he said quietly. "I'll still come after you if you do, though."

Vine smirked, the corner of his mouth lifting. "Understandable."

Rowan gave a single nod and continued past, a quiet sense of resolution following in his wake.

After the meeting ended, the Fallen returned to their rooms to pack.

Ariel stood in her room, humming softly as she tucked her belongings into a suitcase. The door was open, her back turned to the hallway as she folded and sorted through the last of her things. Her movements slowed when her eyes landed on something familiar at the edge of the bed—Vine's shirt.

She reached for it, holding it close as she took in a deep breath. The scent was unmistakable, and a soft smile touched her lips.

A light knock startled her, and she spun around quickly, hiding the shirt behind her back.

Vine leaned casually against the doorframe, his smirk firmly in place. "Relax," he teased. "I saw nothing."

He stepped inside, closing the door with a quiet click. "I came to see if you needed help carrying your things down."

Ariel slipped the shirt into her suitcase and zipped it closed in one motion. "Sure," she said, recovering fast. "I'm just about done."

She patted the suitcase and quipped, "I think that's everything. Unless you saw my dignity somewhere around here—it seems to have disappeared."

Vine chuckled, his voice rich with amusement. "Not to worry. I've got enough dignity for both of us."

Ariel rolled her eyes. "You've got enough ego for both of us too."

Her sharp gaze narrowed slightly. "So, what did Rowan say to you at the meeting?"

Vine raised a brow, feigning innocence. "Why do you assume he said anything?"

Ariel smirked. "Because nothing gets past me, Vine. Spill."

He shrugged, the smirk softening into something quieter. "He said he believed me. About you."

Ariel tilted her head, the teasing edge fading. "And?"

Vine's voice dropped. "And that he'd come after me if I ever hurt you."

Ariel snickered. "Fair. He's like my big brother, you know."

Vine nodded, the smirk returning. "Yeah, I figured. He's alright, though. For now."

Ariel sat on the edge of the bed, glancing at her packed suitcase. "I guess this is goodbye then. Until the next battle, huh?"

Vine stood still for a beat, considering. "No, I don't think so."

She looked up, her brow furrowing. "No?"

Crossing the room, Vine reached behind her, plucking her phone from her back pocket with practiced ease. "No," he repeated, lighter now. "I don't think I could wait that long."

He tapped something into the screen and handed it back. "That's my private number."

Ariel raised a brow. "Thirty-seven houses and two phones?"

Vine shrugged with mock modesty. "What can I say? I like to keep business and personal separate."

She looked down and laughed. "A trophy emoji? Really?"

He grinned. "Obviously. I am a trophy."

Ariel shook her head. "You're impossible."

She stepped in, wrapping her arms around his waist, leaning into his warmth. "And yet, somehow, I put up with you."

Vine's arms circled her, pulling her close. His voice softened, the smirk never far. "You love it."

Ariel looked up, smile playful, then softened. "Sometimes I wonder why," she teased.

Their lips met in a slow, lingering kiss. The room fell away, the moment stretching as if time had paused for them alone.

When they finally pulled back, Vine rested his forehead against hers. "You'll call?"

Ariel grinned, voice sincere beneath the teasing. "Of course. Someone's got to keep your ego in check."

Vine bent to grab her suitcase, smirk intact. "Come on. Let's go before you start crying over how much you'll miss me."

Ariel laughed, opening the door. "Spark! Let's move!"

The puppy bounded out, tail wagging as he trotted beside them, his bright energy trailing behind them like a ribbon of joy.

The foyer buzzed with the easy flow of conversation as the Fallen gathered for their farewells. Laughter punctuated the chatter, and the atmosphere carried a sense of camaraderie, a rare moment of levity after the weight of their recent battles.

Rowan and Rain stood with Riichi and Takoda, offering congratulations. Rain grinned. "So I guess that means you're staying in Seattle, and I get the apartment all to myself now."

Aislinn bounded over, throwing her arms around both Takoda and Riichi in a quick group hug. "Congratulations! I'm so happy for you two."

She turned to the group, eyes bright. "I have good news, too. I just got off the phone with my brother—Johnny. His military term's over, and he's not re-enlisting. He's coming home for good in a week! He wants to live in San Francisco near me."

Takoda lit up. "Aislinn, that's amazing!"

Rain nodded. "You've talked about him so much—I'm really happy for you."

Rowan didn't speak, but his expression tightened. He had never met Johnny. Fully human, unaware of their world—there was risk.

Aislinn, he doesn't know about us. Should I be concerned? Rowan said telepathically.

Aislinn turned to him, catching the shift in his expression. "Don't worry," she said aloud. "We'll figure everything out when he gets home."

Nearby, Holly stood beside Alder, her arms loosely crossed as she regarded him with a teasing smile. "So, what's the plan when you get back to Boston? Are you going to take it easy, or dive right back into the brooding intellectual thing?"

Alder smirked faintly, his tone dry. "Probably a mix of both. There's a jazz concert I've been meaning to catch downtown, and my favorite bookstore just got a new shipment."

Holly tilted her head, intrigued. "Jazz and books. Sounds very Alder. I guess I shouldn't ask if you'll be keeping up with the Red Sox."

Alder chuckled softly. "They're done for the season, so I'm spared the agony. What about you? Back to Austin—what's the plan?"

Holly leaned casually against the doorframe, her grin widening. "I'm thinking about food trucks, live music on South Congress... oh, and watching your team lose to mine."

Alder blinked. "Excuse me?"

She smirked. "Your Patriots are playing my Cowboys in two weeks. You should come down and watch the game with me. I'm sure it'd be more exciting than jazz and books."

Alder let out a soft laugh, nodding. "Fair enough. You—..." His voice cut off abruptly, his expression shifting mid-response.

His body stiffened, and his knees buckled as he sank to the floor, one hand braced against the tile. His face grew pale, strained, his breathing uneven.

Holly, recognizing the signs instantly, dropped beside him. "Eileen!" she called, calm but urgent.

Eileen was there in a heartbeat, kneeling beside Alder. Her hand settled on his shoulder, grounding him. "Alder, speak. What do you see?"

The room fell silent. Laughter died. All attention shifted to the floor where Alder knelt, eyes unfocused as the vision took hold.

His voice filled the space—deep, distant, heavy with power.

"The air is warm—unnaturally warm. The sun glares from a clear sky, but the heat carries no comfort, only dread."

"A mountain rises in the distance, dark against the horizon, its peak split by fire. Rivers of molten rock spill down its sides, devouring the land as they flow toward the sea."

"Palm trees bend and shatter in the scalding winds. Sand turns to glass beneath the flames."

"The beaches are alight, waves crashing against glowing shores, but the water does not cool—it hisses, steam rising like smoke."

"Shadows claw their way out of the molten depths, their eyes glowing with ember-light. Their steps leave fiery scars on the ground."

"The warmth of joy is a mockery here—colors meant to brighten the season now flicker dimly in the smoke. Wreaths burn; lights fade into the ash-laden air."

"The air is heavy with a stillness that does not belong. A storm brews, but it is not of snow or rain. It is fire, rage, and destruction."

His voice faded, the echo of his prophecy lingering like smoke. His body slumped, and Holly caught him before he hit the ground, her grip firm but careful.

Eileen pressed a hand to his back. "You did well, Alder. Rest now."

Alder exhaled, the tension in his frame easing as his awareness returned.

Eileen rose, her presence regaining its full force. Her attention swept the room. "Nik," she said, sharp and direct, "it seems we'll be visiting for the holidays. Watch for any signs—anything unusual. Notify me immediately."

Nik nodded, expression unreadable but resolute. "Understood."

The room had dimmed. The levity was gone, replaced by the quiet tension of what lay ahead. Ariel knelt to calm Spark, her hand stroking his fur as the puppy whined. Rain drifted closer to Nik, the worry on her face unmistakable.

Holly helped Alder to his feet. He nodded in thanks, still unsteady but alert.

One by one, the Fallen began to leave. Their farewells were softer now, the weight of Alder's vision casting a long shadow.

Eileen lingered near the door, Alder's words still ringing in her mind. As the last of the team stepped outside, she shut it behind them.

Across the room, Oak, who had stayed behind, met her eyes. No words passed—only a shared understanding of what was coming.

The silence that followed landed like a final note—low, certain, and impossible to ignore.

Bridge Chapter
Before the Snow Falls

Ashes and Embers

The house stood in stillness. The others had already gone—off to their homes scattered across the country. Eileen closed the door behind the last of them but left the lock untouched. Her hand fell away from the handle as she turned, scanning the foyer and common area as though expecting the space to shift in their absence.

Oak remained exactly where he'd stood after Alder's prophecy, his position anchored near the center of the room. He hadn't moved when the others departed, offering no farewell or explanation. None was required.

The quiet between them held steady, familiar in its weight. Years of shared history wove through the silence, wrapping it in unspoken understanding.

Eileen crossed the open floor, her gaze catching on the window as dusk unfurled across the horizon. Beyond the glass, the sun lowered behind the trees, casting long shadows across the hardwood floors. Light faded gradually from the room, slipping away like the close of a chapter.

"You held back in the final battle," Oak said, his voice calm and certain. "You chose to let them carry it to the end."

"They had to." Her answer slipped out low but firm. "If I stepped in, I would've exposed myself to the Fallen. To Khan. To Kross. You warned me against it."

"You would have paid the consequence," Oak replied. His tone carried the weight of truth that didn't require explanation between them.

Eileen's focus stayed on the fading daylight. "Riichi and Takoda bonded. Fully. Their marks are sealed."

Oak's attention sharpened, his gaze narrowing with quiet intensity. "They're the first."

"They are," she confirmed, a breath easing from her chest. "Rowan and Aislinn are nearly there. Their bond is close, and I believe they'll soon carry their marks as well."

Though Oak's posture held steady, focus edged through his stillness. "And Vine?"

Her mouth drew tight. "He came to me after the battle with a bruise on his side. Said Khan hit him with a kinetic blast."

Her hand flexed at her side, her memory clear. "I couldn't heal it myself without exposing my nature, so I called for Aislinn. She asked for his permission, and once he gave it, she tried. At first, the bruise resisted her magic." Eileen's eyes lifted to meet Oak's, steady and unwavering. "That's when I understood."

Oak stepped closer, steady as ever, though tension traced beneath his composed exterior. "He's beginning to fade."

"Yes," Eileen confirmed. "But his fading is different. Slower. He carried a soulmate bond for over three hundred years. The others who faded never had a bond at all. It's keeping him here, holding him longer."

Oak waited as she continued.

"After Aislinn healed him, I went to see my boss." Eileen's jaw set, her words clipped by the weight of what she'd learned. "Vine's turning human again. That's why the bruise lingered—he's already shifting away from his Fallen nature."

Oak's brow furrowed slightly. "Can this be stopped?"

"Only if he finds a new soulmate." Her answer held no doubt. "Not someone chosen for him. Not fate's design. Someone he chooses for himself, to love, to share his life with. If that person doesn't love him in return, the bond won't take hold."

She paused for a heartbeat. "My boss gave me no further explanation, but I know there's more beneath the surface."

Oak's gaze deepened. "Do you think he's testing you?"

Eileen shook her head once. "No. If he was, I'd have seen it coming. This is him giving me only what I need for now. He's shown me the path. If I can't see it fully, I'll have to ask again when the time comes. But I need to ask the right questions."

Oak met her eyes without wavering, then reached for her hand. His palm warmed hers as he wrapped his fingers around her, guiding her to the couch. She followed, her breath easing as she sat beside him.

He drew her closer, his arm settling around her shoulders as he pressed a kiss to the top of her head. Eileen let out a heavy sigh, the tension in her chest loosening, as though she'd finally let go of the burden she'd carried since the battle.

Her eyes lifted to meet his, a grateful smile touching her lips. Words felt unnecessary between them, their meaning already shared.

Oak cupped her cheek, his thumb brushing lightly across her skin before he lowered his mouth to hers. She welcomed his kiss without pause, her hand rising to his chest as warmth spread through her.

The distance between them faded entirely. His hand slid to her waist, fingers tracing the curve of her side as he lifted the hem of her shirt to touch her skin. Her fingers worked at the buttons of his shirt, slipping them free one by one as their kisses deepened.

They moved together with purpose, drawn by instinct and history, their connection undeniable.

The Invisible Fortress

Nik stepped through the wide lanai at the rear of the house, the polished koa wood warm beneath his bare feet. The mansion behind him sprawled across the plateau, its thatched roofs and carved wooden pillars blending seamlessly with the wild grandeur of the land.

Curving verandas wrapped the main structure, open to the breeze rolling in from the Pacific beyond the cliffs.

Below, waves collided against the black sand cove, their rhythm distant beneath the hush of the volcanic plateau. To his right, the dense green of the jungle pressed close, and to his left, the stark stretch of ancient lava fields shimmered in the evening light.

He ignored it all.

The perimeter had to be sealed.

Crossing into the first garden, Nik moved past plumeria blossoms and towering ti leaves, their waxy surfaces catching the last rays of the sun. The stone path beneath him, bordered by lava rocks and fragments of coral, guided him to the estate's boundary where the cultivated grounds surrendered to wild terrain.

He lifted his hand, and the tropical air stirred in response. Ancient words slipped from his tongue, weaving into the breeze as the spell took hold. A faint glow bloomed along the earth—pale silver threaded with deep cobalt, etching itself in a curving line beneath the foliage.

The shimmer pulsed once, then sank beneath the surface, vanishing from sight.

He continued, pacing the perimeter with methodical precision. Every few strides, he paused to layer another spell—some cast with hand-drawn sigils traced through the air, others spoken into the weave of natural energy beneath the ground. Each ward intertwined, fusing into the next like a living tapestry.

Illusions alone would not suffice. To cloak this estate, Nik wove layers of deception, shielding, misdirection, and enchantment that bent perception at every level. Sight, sound, memory—each thread manipulated until nothing remained recognizable.

By the time he reached the far edge of the property, near the rise overlooking the cliffs, the outer veil had begun to anchor.

From beyond the boundary, the mansion no longer existed. No winding drive, no gardens, no glint of lamplight through the windows. Only rough, untamed lava fields and dense, unwelcoming jungle. To any outsider, the terrain appeared too wild, too treacherous to cross.

Unless Nik allowed them to see otherwise.

He placed the final ward beside a natural stone outcrop, whispering the locking spell into place. The power sank into the earth like ink into parchment, binding the web of magic tight around the estate.

The illusion snapped into place.

Inside the boundaries, nothing had changed. The breeze shifted, rustling the plumeria and tall ferns. Farther off, wind stirred through the clifftop pavilion, its thatched roof whispering softly.

Nik stood at the threshold of his cloaked domain, every sense tuned to the network of protections thrumming around him. No sound would escape. No tracking spell would hold. No aerial scan would detect movement. It would take more than brute force or casual magic to break through his defenses.

Turning back toward the house, he followed the lava stone path, his gaze skimming across the gardens where twilight settled among the blooms. The estate lay in purposeful silence. He hadn't kept staff in years—no servants, no groundskeepers. No one came here unless summoned, and even then, he preferred they didn't linger.

The great lanais caught the last light of the day, the wooden beams and frosted glass panels glowing amber as the sun slipped lower. From the outside, none of this existed anymore. The mansion had vanished behind illusion and spellwork, shielded from sight, memory, and sound.

Exactly as it needed to be.

Nik crossed through the main hall without pause, his steps silent on the koa wood floors. The carved stone columns rose on either side of him, etched with old designs that caught the light like rivers of shadow.

At the base of the staircase, he hesitated.

Upstairs, beyond the doors of his master suite, the grand piano waited in the sitting room—a familiar sentinel he hadn't touched since returning.

His mind flicked elsewhere, to Seattle. Rain's voice drifted through his memory, quiet but steady, when she told him she liked him more than a friend should.

He remembered his own reply.

You matter more to me than I realized.

He hadn't deciphered what that meant. Not yet.

But standing here, with the wards complete and the estate shielded, he knew at least this much: she would be here. She would walk these halls, cross these gardens. And when she did, every defense he'd woven would stand between her and whatever storm approached.

Nik turned down the west corridor, letting the silence gather around him like a second skin.

Welcome Home

The swirl of airport noise faded into the background the moment Aislinn caught sight of Johnny.

There he was — shoulders squared beneath the weight of his duffel, steps steady but not rushed. His eyes scanned the crowd with a soldier's instinct, always assessing. When he spotted her, his posture eased just enough for his expression to soften.

"Aislinn!" His voice carried above the chatter, warm and familiar.

She met him halfway, wrapping him in a tight hug. "Welcome home," she said, her throat tightening around the words.

He hugged her back just as tightly. "It's good to be back," he replied, his breath rough at her temple.

When they pulled apart, Aislinn motioned toward Rowan, standing a few steps behind her with his usual quiet composure. "Johnny, this is Rowan," she said, her voice steady but carrying an undertone of significance. "My boyfriend."

Johnny's gaze sharpened with a flicker of protective brother energy as he extended his hand to Rowan. "Boyfriend, huh?" His brow lifted, not unfriendly, just assessing. "Is this serious?"

Aislinn didn't flinch. "Yes," she answered simply. "Very."

Rowan met Johnny's handshake with a firm, respectful grip and a nod of quiet acknowledgment. "It is."

Johnny held the shake a beat longer, then gave a faint grin as he released it. "Alright then," he said, an easy acceptance in his tone, though his eyes still lingered on Rowan for a moment longer.

Beside them, Rain stepped forward, her bright red hair catching the sunlight as she offered a friendly smile. "Hi. I'm Rain," she said, her tone light and warm. "Not like the weather — I'm less predictable."

Johnny's grin widened slightly. "I've heard about you," he replied. "Good things, I hope."

"All lies, I'm afraid," Rain teased, giving Aislinn a playful nudge. "She probably left out the part where I set off the fire alarm baking croissants."

Johnny laughed, the tension in his shoulders easing. "I'll need to hear that story later."

As they turned toward the exit, Aislinn looped her arm through Johnny's. "There's something you should know," she began, keeping her voice low but honest. "After the fire, I've been staying with Rowan. I lost the café and my apartment in the same night."

Johnny's expression tightened with concern. "Damn, Aislinn," he said quietly. "Are you okay?"

She gave a small, measured nod. "Getting there."

Rain chimed in, her voice gentle but upbeat. "If you need a place to land, my apartment has a spare room. Takoda just moved out, so it's yours if you want it."

Johnny's eyes widened a fraction, surprised by the generosity. "That's kind of you," he said. "But I'll start looking for a place of my own. I don't want to crowd you."

Rain waved a hand, brushing off the concern. "You won't be. Honestly, it'd be nice to have someone else around."

Aislinn smiled, appreciating Rain's warmth more than she could say.

"Alright," Johnny agreed. "But just until I find my own place."

"Of course," Rain replied. "No rush."

They headed for Rowan's car, and as they approached, Johnny gave the sleek vehicle an approving nod. "Nice wheels," he said with a grin.

Rowan opened the driver's side door and replied with his usual quiet understatement, "Gets us where we need to go."

Johnny chuckled. "Spoken like a man who knows the mission matters more than the ride."

Rowan's glance in the rearview mirror caught Johnny's for a beat, and though he said nothing, there was a flicker of mutual respect between them.

Aislinn's Talk

The apartment welcomed them with a cozy, lived-in feel. Johnny carried his duffel through the door, taking in the warm, comfortable space with a quiet nod of approval.

Rowan turned to Aislinn, his hand brushing her arm lightly. "I'll give you two some time," he said softly. To Johnny, he added, "We'll catch up later."

With that, he stepped out, leaving Aislinn and Johnny standing in the small entryway. Rain offered a friendly wave before retreating to the kitchen, giving them space.

"Come on," Aislinn said, leading Johnny to the spare bedroom. "Let's get you settled."

The room was simple but clean, sunlight pooling across the floorboards. Johnny set his bag down at the foot of the bed and unzipped it.

Aislinn lingered in the doorway, her fingers brushing the frame. She drew a quiet breath, steadying herself.

Johnny, catching the tension in her posture, folded his arms across his chest and met her gaze squarely. "Go ahead, Aislinn," he said. "I want to hear it all."

She exhaled slowly. "Alright," she began, choosing her words with care. "After you deployed, things changed fast. The fire at the café wasn't an accident. There are… forces in this world you weren't trained to face."

Johnny's expression sharpened, but he said nothing, letting her continue.

"I'm part of something bigger now," she went on. "There's a war happening beneath everything you see — demons, supernatural factions, people with powers that defy explanation." She hesitated for a breath. "Rowan is part of it. So am I."

Johnny let out a long breath, not of disbelief but consideration. "Are you safe?"

Aislinn gave a small, honest shake of her head. "Not exactly. But I'm with people I trust."

Johnny processed that, his gaze steady though shadows flickered beneath. "So Rowan's not just your boyfriend. He's part of this fight."

"He is," she confirmed. "And I'm not just a bystander, either. I've… changed. I have abilities now." Her voice softened. "I wanted to tell you sooner, but I didn't want to distract you while you were still active in the military."

She hesitated, then added, "And my mother—Eileen—is alive. She's leading us. She leads the Fallen. People like me and Rowan, fighting for humanity against demons and supernatural forces that threaten us all."

Johnny blinked, as if the weight of it needed an extra beat to land. "Wait—your mom? She's alive? And she's… running all of this?"

Aislinn held his gaze, steady and unapologetic. "She is. She's the one keeping us all together."

Johnny exhaled, his mind clearly working to catch up. "So you're fighting monsters, your boyfriend's in it too, and your mom — who I thought was dead — is leading the charge."

A wry glimmer surfaced in his eyes, a thin attempt at humor beneath the gravity of it. "You couldn't have eased me in with, like… one thing at a time?"

His jaw tightened for a breath, then relaxed. "You're my sister," he said simply. "Whatever you're in, I'm with you."

Her chest pulled tight at his words, emotion sparking beneath her composed surface. She swallowed it down and let a quiet, grateful smile tug at her lips. "That means more than you know," she replied, her voice low but firm.

Johnny held her gaze a beat longer, then opened his arms slightly. "Come on. Bring it in."

A warm rush bloomed in her chest as she stepped into the embrace. His hold was strong, grounding, the kind of sibling hug that said without words: I've got your back.

Her phone vibrated in her pocket, Rowan's name lighting the screen.

She drew back just enough to glance at it, then met Johnny's eyes. "That's my ride."

Johnny released her but didn't step away. "I'll walk you out," he said, already moving toward the door.

They left the bedroom together, crossing into the main living area where light filtered through the windows, casting the space in a soft glow.

As Aislinn stepped out, Rain reappeared, carrying two mugs — coffee for Johnny, tea for herself. She set one down in front of him and settled across the small kitchen table.

"Housewarming coffee," she said with a teasing lilt. "You looked like you could use it."

Johnny took the mug with a thankful nod, wrapping his hands around the warmth. "I definitely won't turn it down."

She took a sip of her tea, watching him with easy curiosity. "So," she began, "welcome to the apartment. We don't have a formal lease agreement, but if you're planning to throw wild parties, I expect an invitation."

A chuckle rumbled from his chest. "You're safe there. Not really my style."

"Good," Rain replied, grinning. "It's a small place, but it's home."

His gaze drifted over the little details — a potted plant on the windowsill, a stack of well-loved books on the side table, the cozy clutter of a life well lived.

"I appreciate it," Johnny said sincerely. "Really. I wasn't expecting to land on my feet this fast."

Rain tipped her mug toward him in a small salute. "You landed just fine."

Their shared smile settled into a comfortable quiet, the kind that only exists between two people who understand what it means to start fresh.

Game On

The knock at the door wasn't expected, but Holly didn't hesitate. She tugged her hoodie sleeves over her hands as she crossed the living room, nudging a stray throw blanket aside with her foot before flipping the lock.

When she opened the door, Alder stood on the porch, a bag of chips in hand like it belonged there.

"You said to come for the game," he said, his tone carrying its usual steady calm. "I brought chips."

Seeing him here, outside the heat of battle, caught her off guard for a heartbeat. He looked so at ease, standing on her doorstep like this was an ordinary visit between old friends.

A grin tugged at her mouth before she could stop it. "Didn't think you'd actually show — all the way from Boston."

"I don't make empty promises," he replied, as straightforward as the words themselves. A small flicker of warmth touched his eyes. "I brought a bag too. It's in the car. Figured I'd get a room, stay a couple days. Maybe take in some of the sights."

She scoffed, waving him in. "Nonsense. You came all this way, the least I can do is offer you my guest room."

Leaning her shoulder against the doorframe, her gaze swept over him with a spark of humor and unmistakable appreciation. "You clean up nicely," she said, lips curving into a faint grin. "Didn't know you owned anything that wasn't tactical gear."

A glimmer of dry amusement touched his eyes. "Figured it was time we all started living a little off the battlefield," he said, then added with a quiet nod, "Rain and Ariel have been good reminders of that."

Her pulse skipped as he crossed the threshold. For just a moment, her gaze caught his a beat too long, her stomach flipping with a flicker of heat she hadn't invited. She brushed it off, motioning toward the cluttered living room. "Welcome to my chaos."

Books were stacked along the end table, a pair of mismatched socks draped over the arm of the couch, and game controllers tangled in a mess of cords across the rug. The clutter had never bothered her before—until now, until his eyes skimmed the space with quiet observation.

But it wasn't the room he lingered on.

His gaze found her again, holding a fraction longer than necessary.

She swallowed the stir that curled in her chest and closed the door behind them, the soft click wrapping the quiet around them like a held breath.

Breaking Ground

Bulldozers idled along the edge of the clearing, their treads dusted with dry soil from the morning's work. Wind curled across the open expanse, lifting traces of earth into the air before scattering them across the flattened ground. The site stretched wide, marked with staked flags and string lines, raw land poised on the edge of becoming something more.

Blueprints spread across the hood of Birch's truck, held in place by a heavy wrench and a stack of survey equipment. Contractors lingered nearby, jackets zipped against the chill, waiting for Birch's signal to continue.

Birch traced a finger along the top page, his focus sharp as he walked Eileen and Oak through the plans. "Central hub will sit here," he said, tapping the marked circle at the center. "Meeting room's designed to hold all of us, with the holographic planning table at the core. Walls will be fitted with maps, monitors, artifacts for mission coordination."

His hand shifted, moving to the right of the layout. "Living quarters in this wing. Fifteen private rooms for the Fallen. Enough space for all of us—or bonded pairs." His mouth tightened slightly before he went on. "Soundproof walls, private baths, enchanted windows. Personal spaces, but not isolated."

He pointed to a smaller section nearby. "Guest rooms here. Close enough for convenience, far enough for privacy."

Birch's attention moved back to the larger blueprint, tapping the communal spaces. "Shared lounge, big fireplace, library. And a dining area that'll actually fit us all for once." His tone held the edge of dry practicality, but there was more beneath it. "Pantry's getting preservation spells. Storage enough to keep us supplied through siege if we have to."

His hand slid to the lower portion of the plans. "Training hall's underground, modular design. We can shift it for combat drills, magic practice, even simulated environments." He glanced at Oak, knowing he'd understand the need for versatility. "Exterior training grounds will wrap the south and east, built into the natural barriers. Stealth and agility exercises, weapons practice, bonded pair training."

Oak's arms were folded across his chest, gaze steady on the construction crews. He wasn't watching them work—he was seeing past it. Seeing the walls rise. The defensive wards locking into place. The observation decks overlooking the Black Hills. Quiet sanctuary tucked inside layers of fortification, the kind they'd needed long before now.

Birch continued, his tone never rising, just anchored in certainty. "War Room's beneath the central hub. Vaulted, encrypted, sealed against any kind of breach. Communication lines, secure storage. Magic lab across from the infirmary—research and crafting space for potions, spells, enchanted weaponry."

Eileen paced the edge of the site as Birch spoke, her boots pressing into the churned soil. Dust clung to the leather, streaking the black with earth and grit. She walked slowly, eyes scanning the boundary as if she could already see the outline of walls rising from the ground.

Her attention held on the far line of the horizon, where the hills dipped and the tree line thickened. "We're going to need more than steel and stone to hold against what's coming," she said aloud, her voice steady and sure. "Cloaking spells — strong enough to shield us from sight, sound, and detection. Escape tunnels beneath the structure. Fortifications built into the cliffs. Layers of defense, hidden and visible."

Oak's gaze followed hers toward the cliffs. "We can blend the fortifications with the natural stone. Conceal them so they're undetectable until it's too late," he said, calm but resolute. "No one will see them coming."

Birch nodded, already thinking ahead. "I'll make sure the escape tunnels run beneath the barracks and storage units. Multiple exits—if one path is compromised, we'll have others." He planted his hand on the blueprints, steadying the corner as the wind tried to lift the page again. "We'll give them nothing easy."

Her gaze swept back to them, settling first on Oak, then Birch. "This place needs to be more than a stronghold. It needs to be a sanctuary."

"We'll build it that way," Birch promised, his voice grounded and certain.

Oak inclined his head once, the gesture carrying quiet weight. "And we'll make sure it lasts."

Her fingers brushed a string line as she passed, the tension vibrating beneath her touch. She let it go, eyes narrowing on the plans laid before them.

When she reached the far edge, she turned, taking in the full spread of the site coming to life. Machinery rested in place. Crews stood ready. Purpose settled into the air around them like a quiet promise.

"Let's make this a home," she said.

Birch didn't hesitate. "We will."

Oak's agreement followed without pause. "And we'll protect everyone inside it."

Eileen's gaze lingered on both of them, her voice low but unwavering. "Then let's build it to outlast the war."

The Call Before the Feast

The quiet hum of prep work filled Donnelly's long before the doors opened for the night. The lights overhead glowed low, casting warmth across the empty bar. Bottles lined the shelves, polished to a fine gleam, waiting for the first pour. But for now, the space belonged to them.

They'd pushed two tables together near the back, plates and glasses scattered between them from an easy dinner. Rain reached for the last slice of flatbread, leaning her elbow on the worn surface.

Rowan looked over at Johnny, his expression steady but open. "If you're looking for something steady while you get your feet under you," he said, "I could use another pair of hands at the bar."

Johnny's brow lifted slightly, caught off guard.

"You'd handle your own sales," Rowan added. "Keep your profits, plus salary and tips. It's not glamorous, but it's a good way to get reacclimated to civilian life."

Johnny's thoughtful look deepened, like he was running numbers in his head already. "Sounds better than sitting around waiting for my next step," he admitted. "I appreciate it."

From across the table, Ariel grinned. "Look at you, turning Johnny into a local legend already." She flicked a glance between them, playful warmth in her eyes. "Speaking of plans, what's everyone doing for Thanksgiving?"

Rain's smile brightened with a note of anticipation. "I already talked to Takoda," she said. "She and Riichi are coming down for Thanksgiving."

Aislinn's smile brightened immediately. "Takoda's cooking?"

Rain nodded. "All of it."

"Get ready," Rowan said, turning to Johnny with a glint in his eyes. "You're about to have the best feast of your life."

Johnny raised his brows, easing back in his chair. "I've never met Takoda or Riichi."

"You'll like them," Rain assured him. "Takoda's an incredible cook. Riichi's quiet, but she's been drawing him out lately."

Aislinn added, "They balance each other really well. And Takoda's as fierce in the kitchen as she is on the battlefield."

Johnny let out a low whistle. "Sounds like I should bring an appetite."

"You'd regret it if you didn't," Rowan said, a faint grin playing at the corners of his mouth.

Rain smiled to herself, glad for the shift in energy. It felt good to have the group relaxed, even if just for a moment.

"I'll bring the stuffing again," Aislinn offered, then gave Rowan a sidelong glance. "Assuming you don't try to sabotage it with those instant potatoes."

Rowan gave a mock scowl. "You say sabotage, I say efficiency."

Before Aislinn could fire back, Ariel rose from her chair, slipping her phone from her pocket. "I need to make a quick call," she said, her voice casual as she headed toward the door.

No one questioned it.

Ariel stepped outside into the cool night air, letting the door swing shut behind her. She leaned against the brick wall, thumbing her phone open to her contacts. There was no name saved for Vine—just a lone trophy emoji staring back at her. Her lips curved as she tapped the screen and lifted the phone to her ear.

"Hey," she said when he answered, keeping her tone easy. "Surprise call. Hope I'm not interrupting anything."

"Not unless you count a very competitive match between me and the punching bag," Vine replied dryly. "Which, given the stakes, you might've just saved me from knocking down the whole room."

A laugh slipped from her, warm and genuine. "Glad to be of service." She paused just long enough for the tease to land, then added with a grin, "And I'm glad you're punching bags and not walls. My medical kit still hasn't forgiven you."

A huff of amusement rumbled through the line, low and rough. "Neither have my knuckles," he said.

She hesitated for a breath, then pushed off the wall with her shoulder. "Rain's hosting Thanksgiving. Takoda and Riichi are coming down. Small thing. Thought you might want to come."

There was a short pause, but his reply carried a teasing lilt. "You sure it's not just my charming company you're after?"

"Maybe a little," she teased back. "I do have a weakness for charming men with exaggerated egos."

Her voice softened, just slightly. "Truth is, I'd like to see you."

His answer came smooth, as always. "It's been too long. I'd probably break a rule."

Her pulse tightened, but she masked it with a smirk he couldn't see. "At least you're honest."

"After Thanksgiving," Vine said, his voice sliding into something more deliberate. "Just the two of us. Somewhere there aren't rules to break."

A slow grin spread across her lips. "Toronto," she offered. "Just me, you, and Spark. I'll head out Saturday after the holiday."

"Toronto," he echoed, considering it. "Sounds like a dangerous idea."

"Good thing I like danger." She kept her tone light, even as a quiet spark flickered beneath the surface. "It's a date," she said, playing it off, and ended the call before anything heavier could settle between them.

★★★

Vine set the phone down on the table beside him, the glow of Las Vegas neon leaking through the hotel window. He dragged a hand over his jaw, leaning back in the chair.

He'd been closer to saying yes than he should've been.

Closer than he wanted to admit.

It wasn't about the rules.

It was about her.

The way she always caught him off guard with that fire in her voice, the way she didn't let him retreat behind careful lines. She'd invited him without hesitation, like she already knew he'd follow. And maybe, deep down, he already had.

His gaze drifted toward the window, to the city lights burning against the dark. Vegas was noise and neon and faceless crowds, but for the first time, it felt empty.

Maybe Toronto wouldn't just be about bending the rules.

Maybe it would be the chance to show her what it could feel like — no rules, no boundaries, just them.

He let out a quiet breath, low and rough.

Toronto.

It wasn't the danger that tempted him.

It was the chance to have her, even if just for a while, without the walls between them.

★★★

Back inside Donnelly's, Ariel slipped back into her seat without fanfare. No one asked about the call, and she didn't offer.

Her gaze flicked toward Rain, catching the quieter set of her expression — a calm surface, but Ariel had known her long enough to see the edges beneath it.

A spark of mischief lit Ariel's eyes. "We should call Nik," she said, aiming it just casually enough, though there was an undercurrent of meaning in her glance at Rain.

Aislinn picked up on it immediately, her lips curving. "Good idea," she agreed, playing along.

Rain shot them both a sidelong look, but the faintest tug of a smile pulled at her mouth.

Ariel's grin widened, but she didn't push. Not yet.

Aislinn, ever the strategist, shifted her attention to Rowan. "Go on, call him."

Rowan, oblivious to the undercurrent, simply pulled out his phone and scrolled through his contacts. "Let's see if he answers."

He put the call on speaker, letting it ring once before Nik picked up.

"Rowan."

"Hey, we're pulling together Thanksgiving dinner," Rowan said, keeping it casual. "San Francisco. You in?"

A brief pause followed, the faint rush of ocean surf carrying through the line.

"There's movement near the islands," Nik replied, his tone even. "Alder's prophecy pointed here. I'm not leaving the estate unguarded."

"Understood," Rowan said, though there was a note of persistence beneath the word. "We'll save you a seat anyway."

Nik didn't dismiss it outright. His answer came measured, quiet. "It's not the right time."

"Stay sharp," Rowan said, ending the call on a familiar sign-off.

The line disconnected smoothly, without finality or abruptness.

Rowan dropped his phone back onto the table, his expression unreadable. "Guess that's a no."

The conversation drifted back to lighter topics, but Rain's thoughts lingered. She doubted it was only about the islands. Nik was withdrawing again, keeping his distance as he always did when things brushed too close to personal. It was just his way.

She left the thought unspoken.

Across the table, Johnny caught the faint shift in her expression. He leaned in with a crooked smile, his voice low and easy. "More pumpkin pie for us, then."

Rain returned the smile, but her mind stayed on Nik.

Feast and Fractures

Rain wiped the counter with a final sweep, even though it gleamed already. She stepped back, adjusting a candle that flickered too close to the edge of the table runner. The apartment smelled of spices and warmth, the oven preheating in preparation for the feast to come. Soft, cozy candlelight illuminated the autumn decorations she had scattered through the space — simple touches of burnt orange, deep gold, and rustic browns, welcoming without feeling forced.

Johnny was finishing up at the far end of the apartment, running a cloth over the bookshelves before moving to straighten the stack of coasters on the coffee table.

"You really think anyone's gonna notice if the coasters are crooked?" he asked, flashing her an easy grin.

Rain chuckled under her breath. "I'll notice," she replied, adjusting them herself once he stepped away.

She took a moment to look around, letting the atmosphere settle in her chest. *This feels right.* Hosting this dinner tonight felt like filling the apartment with new memories, letting it breathe again. No longer a space shared with Takoda, but one she now shared with Johnny. *A fresh chapter,* she thought, *not a reminder of what's changed.*

Before the thought could settle too deep, a knock sounded at the door.

Rain crossed the apartment and opened it to find Takoda and Riichi on the threshold, both carrying a few small dishes and containers for the meal.

"Hey," Rain greeted, her smile warming as she stepped aside to let them in. "Come on in."

They stepped inside, the cozy atmosphere wrapping around them.

As Rain closed the door behind them, she gestured toward Johnny, who had set down the cleaning cloth and was offering a polite wave.

"This is Johnny," she introduced. "He's Aislinn's brother and my new roommate. Also, chief of last-minute cleaning today."

Johnny gave an easy smile. "Happy to be of service."

Riichi nodded in greeting, and Takoda's expression softened with familiarity, offering Johnny a small, appreciative smile.

Rain turned back to Riichi. "How's the new place coming along?"

Riichi set the containers on the counter and shrugged, his tone casual. "Pretty well, actually. Vine sold us one of his properties in Seattle. For a dollar," he added, a note of dry amusement in his voice. "Said it was off the safehouse list."

Rain's brow lifted in surprise. *That's unlike him,* she thought. *But generous. Looks like there's more changes than I thought.*

Takoda, setting her own containers next to his, pulled a small jar from her bag and passed it to Rain. "From our new kitchen," she said softly, her gaze warm.

Rain accepted it, turning the familiar jar of spices in her hands. *Takoda always knows how to make a space feel grounded.* A quiet connection settled between them, one built from easy affection and years of shared moments.

"Thank you," Rain said, her voice carrying more warmth than the flickering candles in the room.

Takoda offered a faint smile, her attention already sliding to the kitchen. Without hesitation, she stepped into the space as though she'd never left it, her movements smooth and practiced. She unpacked her ingredients with quiet assurance, orchestrating the meal like a conductor easing into a familiar rhythm.

Rain watched her for a heartbeat, her chest filling with quiet appreciation. *There she is. Just like always.*

The apartment filled with life as the others arrived, bringing noise and energy with them. Rowan entered carrying bags under each arm, and Aislinn followed close behind, balancing dishes still warm from the oven.

Ariel arrived soon after, bright and bustling with a bottle of spiked cider in one hand, and Spark trotting eagerly beside her. The moment Spark's paws hit the floor, he launched into exploration mode, snuffling around the baseboards before making a beeline for the kitchen.

Ariel held up a small packet of edible glitter with a mischievous grin. "Thinking of adding this to the mashed potatoes," she teased.

"Don't you dare," Aislinn shot back, just as Rowan tried to sneak a roll from the basket.

Her hand snapped out, swatting him sharply. The roll tumbled free, and Spark lunged for it, paws skittering across the tile. But Rowan's reflexes won out — he snatched the roll midair and held it up like a trophy.

"Nice try, Spark," Rowan teased, grinning, while Spark answered with a playful "boof" before flopping down near the oven.

Spark stretched out, basking in the oven's warmth as his tail swept lazily across the floor. His ears twitched at the sound of clinking pans, and when the oven timer dinged, he gave a soft, proud "boof," as if announcing dinner himself.

Johnny, still helping Rain, set the last fork in place on the table. "What next?" he asked, glancing at her with genuine interest.

"Plates and glasses," Rain answered, passing them over.

"Finally, a task I can't mess up," Johnny said with a grin as he arranged the settings.

Rain smiled, amused. "Let's not jinx it."

Their banter flowed easily, a rhythm of familiarity as they worked side by side. Spark trotted between them with a stolen napkin in his mouth, tail wagging like he'd won a prize, until Rain plucked it free and gave him a mock-stern look.

"Spark, really?" she said with fond exasperation, and Spark's tail wagged harder in answer.

Finally, they all settled at the table. Candles flickered between the heaping dishes, casting warm glows over the feast. The conversation bubbled over with teasing and laughter, the soft clinks of cutlery a steady backdrop to their shared joy.

Rowan raised his glass first, a sarcastic grin playing at his mouth. "Here's to surviving another year of magic and mayhem."

Laughter circled the table.

Aislinn followed, her smile gentler but full of warmth. "To chosen family, second chances, and Spark not setting anything on fire today."

At the sound of his name, Spark lifted his head and let out an enthusiastic "woof," drawing even more laughter from the group. He edged closer to Rowan's plate, nose twitching, only for Aislinn to gently push him back with her foot.

During a quiet pause between toasts and bites, Ariel set down her fork and brightened. "Oh—Spark and I are heading up to Toronto on Saturday," she announced with a grin.

Rowan arched a brow. "Aiming for the Canadian Christmas vibe?"

"Exactly." Ariel lifted her cider glass in a playful salute. "Snow, lights, over-the-top decorations—I want to experience it all." *And maybe,* she thought, her heart skipping a little, *I wouldn't mind seeing Vine too.*

Spark thumped his tail approvingly beneath the table, as if fully endorsing the plan.

Rain's lips curved at the image of Ariel and Spark bounding through snowy streets. *It suits them,* she thought fondly.

She clinked her glass with the others, but a quiet drift pulled at her chest beneath the warmth of the moment. *I wonder if Nik's alone right now.*

Not just for the holiday. Not just tonight.

Complicated. That's what he'd called it.

And she believed him — Nik didn't waste words, didn't say things he didn't mean. If he'd said she mattered to him, she did. But still, she couldn't shake the tiny whisper at the back of her mind. *Did I push too hard? Was I too much?*

She caught herself and shook the thought off. *Stop overthinking, Rain. You know better.*

Still, as she traced her finger along the rim of her glass, the question lingered like an unfinished melody. *What did he mean by complicated?*

Spark, as if sensing her drift, nudged her ankle gently with his nose. Rain glanced down at him, a soft smile rising as she brushed her fingers through his fur in quiet thanks.

Johnny caught her distant look and raised his glass a little higher toward her, a quiet gesture of support. Rain returned it with a faint, grateful smile.

Dessert brought another wave of laughter. Takoda's pies vanished quickly, and Aislinn's stuffing sparked playful debate about which dish had stolen the show. Spark circled the table with hopeful eyes and a twitching nose until a dollop of whipped cream landed squarely on his snout.

"Spark, you're a mess," Ariel laughed, wiping it away as Spark licked at the air, trying to catch the cream himself.

The apartment glowed with life, warmth saturating every corner. Rain smiled at one of Rowan's wild stories, but her gaze drifted toward the window, to the quiet world beyond their glowing gathering.

Her friends surrounded her, laughter filled the air, yet her thoughts wandered far beyond the apartment walls — to an island cloaked in wards, to a man who kept his distance not out of indifference, but complication.

What did you mean by that, Nik?

She caught herself, lips pressing into a faint, self-aware curve. *Stop overthinking.*

But as the moment lingered, her heart quietly answered the question she couldn't voice. *I hope I'm not too much for you.*

Her gaze held on the dark horizon a breath longer before she drew it back to the warmth around her, tucking the thought away.

The Unanswered Name

The Seattle sky had deepened into ink-black when Riichi unlocked the door to their new home. The quiet creak of the hinges felt louder than it should have, wrapping the entryway in stillness.

Takoda stepped inside first, arms full with leftover containers from Rain's dinner. Her coat hung over her arm, a soft sigh escaping as she took in the familiar space. "I'll put these away," she said, her voice gentle, warm with the comfort of returning home.

Riichi followed, setting his keys in the dish by the door. His eyes drifted immediately, drawn toward the desk at the far end of the room. The rest of the house faded into the background.

Pinned just beside the desk, a single scrap of paper held his attention. One word, written in his own exacting hand: **Kiki**.

The name pulled at him like gravity, sharper now than it had been hours ago.

He crossed the room and flipped open his laptop, though his focus never shifted from the paper. *Tell me—does Kiki whisper to all of you, or just her favorites?*

Khan's voice lingered in his mind, not like an echo but a deliberate mark burned into memory.

At the time, he'd brushed it off. Garbage, he'd called it, dismissing Khan's words in the heat of battle. But that was the thing about Khan—he never wasted breath. His chaos was a veneer over strategy. Bait laid with precision.

If he said her name, it wasn't random.

Riichi's eyes narrowed as he replayed the possibilities. He'd checked Eileen's reports. Scoured the Fallen archives. Nothing. No trace of "Kiki."

But absence didn't mean nothing. It meant hidden.

Takoda's quiet movements filled the background—containers being unpacked, the fridge door opening and closing.

"Riichi?" she called softly. "Do you want me to keep the pie out?"

He didn't answer. His mind was already three steps ahead, laying out the beginnings of a search pattern.

Patterns of allegiance. Track the ones loyal to Khan, see where they gather, who they speak of in whispers. Not demonology texts—they won't yield anything Khan wants me to see.

His fingers hovered over the keyboard, then moved with purpose as he pulled up encrypted files. He'd dig into old mission logs, interrogations, fragmentary leads no one else would think to revisit.

Someone out there knows this name. Someone has heard it before, even if they don't realize it.

Takoda's voice didn't reach him this time. She didn't push, sensing his focus had tightened into something unshakable.

He studied the word pinned to the wall like it was a cipher waiting to be cracked. His jaw flexed, his mind already constructing avenues of pursuit.

Khan wants me to chase her? Fine.

The glow of the lamp stretched shadows across the paper, darkening the bold lines of the name.

But I'll run the hunt my way.

Northbound Sparks

Toronto Pearson bustled with the rhythm of arrivals and departures, announcements echoing through the terminal. Ariel stepped off the plane, her boots clicking softly against the polished floor as she wheeled her carry-on behind her.

Her phone was already in hand. Without breaking stride, she found Vine's number and hit call, propping the phone between her ear and shoulder as she adjusted her bag.

"Just landed," she said, energy bright in her voice. "Where are you?"

Vine's familiar smooth tone came through, rich with teasing. "You were serious? I'm still in Vegas."

Ariel stopped mid-step, brows lifting in disbelief. "You're kidding me?"

There was a beat of silence, just long enough to let her start questioning. Then, his low chuckle rumbled through the line. "Look behind you."

Ariel pivoted fast, scanning the terminal. Her gaze caught him leaning against a pillar not far away, phone still at his ear, watching her with a glint of amusement in his eyes.

All black, as always. She rolled her eyes — *Vine and his funeral wardrobe* — but couldn't help the flicker of thought that chased it. *Still, he makes it work. Too well, if I'm being honest.*

She lowered her phone, narrowing her gaze. Shaking her head, she strode toward him, her expression unimpressed but her lips twitching.

Vine watched her approach, a quiet pull tightening in his chest. *Even when she's scowling, she's irresistible.* That fire in her eyes, the way she fought a smile — it stirred something far too familiar. Something he wasn't bothering to fight anymore.

"You're lucky you're pretty," she said, her voice dry. "Because your jokes are garbage."

Vine's mouth curled into a slow grin. "Worth it to see the look on your face."

Before she could fire back, he reached out, caught her by the waist, and pulled her into him. His mouth found hers in a kiss that didn't hesitate — heated, thorough, claiming more than permission.

The moment their lips met, something settled in his chest, solid and sure. Like this had been waiting beneath the surface all along, inevitable as breathing. She fit against him too easily, as if the space had always been hers to fill.

Ariel met him with equal fire, matching the energy of the moment. When they parted, a spark lingered between them, as though the kiss hadn't quite finished burning.

She feels too good to let go of. Even as he drew back, his gaze lingered on her lips, the echo of her warmth pulling at him more than he liked to admit.

She arched a brow, catching her breath. "What was that for?"

Vine's gaze lingered on her lips, a faint glimmer of heat in his eyes. "Wanted to see what it's like to kiss you in public without any rules."

A slow, knowing smirk curled her mouth. "And?"

His reply came low, confident, and far too tempting. "I think I'm going to be breaking that rule a lot while we're in Canada."

Then, his expression shifted — still teasing, but with something deeper threading through. "I missed you."

Ariel's brow ticked up. "It's only been a couple of weeks," she shot back, her smirk holding for a beat longer before it softened. Her gaze lingered on his, and her voice dropped a notch, a quiet truth slipping through. "But yeah... I missed you too."

With her pulse still thrumming, she brushed past him with a toss of her hair, and he fell into step beside her.

They made their way to baggage claim, easy in their rhythm.

As they approached the carousel, Spark's crate came into view, already circling. The moment Spark spotted them, he exploded with excitement, clawing frantically at the door, tail slamming against the sides as his paws scrabbled for freedom.

"Easy, Spark," Ariel laughed, hurrying forward. She popped the latch on the crate, but Spark didn't wait for a proper opening. He launched straight past her — directly into Vine's arms.

Vine caught him, more out of reflex than anything, his brows lifting in surprise as Spark's tail wagged furiously and his tongue plastered Vine's face with enthusiastic licks.

"Didn't see that coming," Vine admitted, but there was no irritation in his voice — only a low chuckle as he adjusted his grip to steady the overexcited dog.

"He's growing on you," Ariel teased, fetching her suitcase off the carousel.

"Apparently," Vine replied dryly, still holding Spark as if the dog had declared himself permanent luggage.

They gathered the rest of Ariel's bags, stacking them on a cart. Vine eyed the pile with mild exasperation.

"Did you bring your whole apartment with you?" he asked, deadpan.

"You try packing for winter when you've been living in the tropics," Ariel shot back, unbothered.

Vine's lips twitched in quiet amusement. He grabbed the bulk of her luggage with ease, leaving her only with her carry-on.

"Come on, Trouble," he said, his voice warm beneath the teasing words.

Ariel slung her carry-on over her shoulder, falling into step beside him as they headed for the exit. Spark trotted happily at Vine's side, as though this had always been the plan.

Together, the three of them disappeared into the pulse of the city, the cold winter air waiting just beyond the doors.

The Watcher

Night had settled deep over Nik's estate, the sky an expanse of indigo stretched across the horizon. From his elevated plateau, the Pacific spread out in endless shadow, while the dark silhouettes of jungle and lava fields carved the edges of the world. Within the fortified boundaries of his property, the air felt suspended between breaths — as though even the wind hesitated at the edges of his wards.

Nik moved through the grounds with deliberate purpose, his senses stretched outward, skimming the fine threads of energy woven through the estate. He had built these wards himself, every line of power etched with precision. Now, he inspected and adjusted, refining their strength until they met his exacting standards.

His fingers brushed the final ward line, feeling the pulse of magic beneath his touch. Solid. Flawless.

These wards were not simply meant to obscure his estate. They were a shield. A hidden fortress awaiting the inevitable. Alder's vision had been clear — the confrontation would come here, and soon.

Not if. When.

But Nik's mind, disciplined as it was, found its focus pulled toward her.

Rain.

He held no illusions about her vulnerabilities. Human, without powers, exposed in ways the Fallen were not. And yet, she was part of the team. Not just present — *essential*. In ways he could not, or perhaps would not, fully name.

She will come here, with the rest of them.

The thought struck deeper than simple calculation. Ensuring her safety had weighed heavily in his preparations. He told himself it was strategy. Duty. Necessary. But as his gaze swept across the silent estate, his chest tightened with something less defined.

She matters.

He forced himself not to linger on the thought, but it remained, like the quiet thrum beneath his wards — constant and undeniable. He had turned down her invitation to Thanksgiving, focusing instead on reinforcing every barrier, testing every seal. The choice had been necessary. Tactical.

Still, a shadow of doubt flickered at the edge of his mind.

I hope she didn't misunderstand.

He had not meant to wound her. His priorities had demanded distance, not disinterest. And yet, he wondered if she had seen it that way.

Nik shifted his attention back to the ward in front of him, smoothing a slight imbalance with the sweep of his hand. He forced himself into the present, into action — where answers lived, where control remained his.

Perfect.

The estate would hold. He had made certain of it.

Satisfied, Nik turned toward the house, his steps steady as he crossed the quiet grounds. The hush of the estate wrapped around him, a living breath drawn tight in anticipation.

Inside, cool shadows embraced him as he ascended the wide staircase to the master suite. The space unfolded into an expansive sitting area, elegant and understated, the grand piano positioned against the far wall. Beyond it, the doors to his bedroom and bath stood in silent vigil.

The air felt poised, as if the house itself awaited what he already knew was coming.

Nik crossed to the piano. He drew the bench back and settled onto it, his movements fluid from long-ingrained habit. His fingers lifted the lid, revealing keys that gleamed pale beneath the lamplight.

He let his hands hover above the keyboard, poised but still.

Outside, the wind stirred at the estate's boundaries, brushing against the invisible shell of his wards. He felt it in his chest — not a warning, not a threat, but movement. The subtle shift of tides, the inevitability of change drawing closer.

It begins.

He lowered the piano lid with quiet finality, the soft click sharp in the stillness.

Then, he reached into his pocket and drew out his phone. Before dialing, he paused, his gaze drifting once more to the dark horizon beyond the window, as if to confirm what he already knew.

It's time.

His thumb tapped the screen, and he began making the calls.

The first move had been made.

About the Author

Jayne Anderson is an author and storyteller inspired by books, music, movies, and the timeless tales of world cultures, mythology, and religions. A former social studies and reading teacher, Jayne channels her creativity into crafting meaningful stories that celebrate individuality and imagination. Now a mother, entrepreneur, and writer, she lives in Pennsylvania with her daughter, who inspires her daily with her boundless curiosity.

To learn more, join the Sin & Salvation series community:

Author's Website

The Fallen'
Birch
Arizona
1657-1685
Vine
Massachusetts
1668-1712
Ivy
Peru
1520-1546
Holly
Scotland
1691-1715
Rowan
Ireland
1819-1847
Alde
Germa
1917-19
Reed
France
1766-1794
Ash
Portugal
1729-1755
Oak
Roman Emp
47 C.E.-79 C.
N
S
E
W

Roots

Every Fallen's journey begins long before their transformation. This map traces the origins of the Fallen across the globe, revealing the diverse heritages, cultures, and lives they left behind. Like the roots of a mighty tree, their pasts ground them, shaping their identities and their paths toward redemption.